Davy

Set in the Northeastern United States some centuries after an atomic war ended high-technology civilization, Davy comes of age in a pseudo-medieval society dominated by a Church that actively suppresses technology. In this land turned upside-down and backwards by the results of scientific unwisdom, Davy and his fellow Ramblers are carefree outcasts, in whose bawdy, joyous adventures among the dead ashes of Old-Time culture the careful reader will spot glimpses of the world before the fall.

A Mirror for Observers

The Martians, long exiled from their home planet, have for millennia been observers of the world of men. Forbidden by their laws to interfere with human destiny, they wait for mankind to mature. From the turmoil of mid twentieth-century America, word comes to the Observers that one of their renegades is hoping to encourage humanity in its headlong rush to self-destruction through corruption of a single rare intellect. The struggle between Observer and Abdicator for the continuance of the human species is one the classic conflicts in the annals of science fiction.

Good Neighbors and Other Strangers

From the pen of award-wining author Edgar Pangborn comes this fascinating collection of short fiction: a tearful stray from a herd of alien livestock, which crushes most of Manhattan and causes apologetic herders to make amends; a shivery novelette about the abduction of a country wife by a hairy beast; the story of a pickup truck full of mythical characters asking directions to Olympus; the ten-legged blue bugs from inner – or outer – space that can give you a dream – or a nightmare; the shadow-monkeys who have the absurd habit of following along and changing by what *you* think; the tiny angel that hatches from an egg; and the 'wrens' that hatch from Grandpa's beard the summer he was 106.

Also by Edgar Pangborn

Novels

Davy
The Judgement of Eve
The Company of Glory
West of the Sun
A Mirror for Observers

Collections

Still I Persist In Wondering
Good Neighbors and Other Strangers

Edgar Pangborn
SF GATEWAY OMNIBUS

DAVY
A MIRROR FOR OBSERVERS
GOOD NEIGHBORS AND
OTHER STRANGERS

GOLLANCZ

LONDON

This omnibus copyright © Edgar Pangborn 2015
Davy copyright © Edgar Pangborn 1964
A Mirror for Observers copyright © Edgar Pangborn 1954
Good Neighbors and Other Strangers copyright © Edgar Pangborn 1972
Introduction copyright © SFE Ltd 2015

First published in Great Britain in 2015 by
Gollancz
An imprint of the Orion Publishing Group
Orion House, 5 Upper St Martin's Lane,
London WC2H 9EA

An Hachette UK Company

A CIP catalogue record for this book is
available from the British Library

ISBN 978 0 575 11692 4

1 3 5 7 9 10 8 6 4 2

Typeset by Jouve (UK), Milton Keynes

Printed and bound by CPI Group (UK) Ltd, Croydon, CR0 4YY

The Orion Publishing Group's policy is to use papers
that are natural, renewable and recyclable products and
made from wood grown in sustainable forests. The logging
and manufacturing processes are expected to conform to
the environmental regulations of the country of origin.

www.orionbooks.co.uk
www.gollancz.co.uk

CONTENTS

ENTER THE SF GATEWAY ...

Towards the end of 2011, in conjunction with the celebration of fifty years of coherent, continuous science fiction and fantasy publishing, Gollancz launched the SF Gateway.

Over a decade after launching the landmark SF Masterworks series, we realised that the realities of commercial publishing are such that even the Masterworks could only ever scratch the surface of an author's career. Vast troves of classic SF and fantasy were almost certainly destined never again to see print. Until very recently, this meant that anyone interested in reading any of those books would have been confined to scouring second-hand bookshops. The advent of digital publishing changed that paradigm for ever.

Embracing the future even as we honour the past, Gollancz launched the SF Gateway with a view to utilising the technology that now exists to make available, for the first time, the entire backlists of an incredibly wide range of classic and modern SF and fantasy authors. Our plan, at its simplest, was – and still is! – to use this technology to build on the success of the SF and Fantasy Masterworks series and to go even further.

The SF Gateway was designed to be the new home of classic science fiction and fantasy – the most comprehensive electronic library of classic SFF titles ever assembled. The programme has been extremely well received and we've been very happy with the results. So happy, in fact, that we've decided to complete the circle and return a selection of our titles to print, in these omnibus editions.

We hope you enjoy this selection. And we hope that you'll want to explore more of the classic SF and fantasy we have available. These are wonderful books you're holding in your hand, but you'll find much, much more ... through the SF Gateway.

www.sfgateway.com

INTRODUCTION

from The Encyclopedia of Science Fiction

Edgar Pangborn (1909–1976) was a US composer and author, son of author Georgia Wood Pangborn (1872–1958) and the brother of Mary (1907–2003), also an author, both of whom specialized in supernatural fiction; his own publishing career began with *A-100: A Mystery Story* (1930) as by Bruce Harrison, and other non-genre work under various names in various magazines. Only after many years did he publish his first sf story, the famous 'Angel's Egg'(1951), about a man's touching friendship with a tiny winged 'angel' – one of several such Aliens who have travelled to Earth in hope of understanding and helping us. In his first sf novel, *West of the Sun* (1953), six shipwrecked humans found a Utopian colony on the planet Lucifer in association with two native species. When the rescue ship eventually arrives, they decide to stick with the society they have constructed. The reflective conclusion of this novel was typical of Pangborn's work. In both *West of the Sun* and *A Mirror for Observers* (1954) (see below) – but not always in his career – Pangborn's gracious literacy overcame a tendency towards an emotional intensity some of his stories could not comfortably bear.

After two fine non-genre tales – *Wilderness of Spring* (1958), an historical novel, and *The Trial of Callista Blake* (1961), a moving courtroom drama – Pangborn then created his most successful and sustained work, the Davy sequence. The first of these by a rough internal chronology is *The Company of Glory* (1975), a loosely-constructed tale some of whose contents were reassembled as stories in *Still I Persist in Wondering* (1978), and which sets the scene; the loosely related *The Judgment of Eve* (1966), set early in the shared universe and only loosely related to it, is a fable constructed in mythopoeic terms, as Eve tries to choose a mate among the lifestyles of her disparate male suitors, who include an 'Adam' figure. The trek on which she consequently sends them, in order to find out the meaning of love, probably represents the deepest of Pangborn's descents into tales overburdened with meaning and wisdom, often genuine. The first volume to be published (though the third internally), is the central volume of the sequence, *Davy* (1964) (see below), the weightiest tale of the series, and Pangborn's most famous single title. In most of the stories in the later *Good Neighbors and Other Strangers* (coll 1972) (see below), the inherent decency of his view of life shines through. Throughout his work, Pangborn creates a tone of elegy not normally associated with

American SF in its prime, though in fact he shares with authors like Ray Bradbury and Theodore Sturgeon not only nostalgia but rage, in his case quietly devastating. The America they celebrate is also an America whose citizens did not always behave in a manner worthy of their heritage.

This omnibus begins with the centrepiece of Pangborn's work from the beginning of his career, *Davy* (1964), set in a moderately clement Ruined Earth version of America three centuries after World War Three has ended in nuclear holocaust and the land has broken into small principalities. The novel comprises Davy's own memoir of his picaresque adventures and moral growth – from rambler to statesman – in this charged venue. The America given us, very movingly, in *Davy* is an America capable of rebirth. And indeed, by the end of the tale, it is clear that Davy, and those he inspires, are about to begin to rebuild a more complex world.

But before *Davy* there was *A Mirror for Observers* (1954), which won the 1955 International Fantasy Award, a story whose impact on the SF field, though quiet, has been profound. For thousands of years, Martian observers have been debating over the fate of *Homo sapiens*: whether or not to intervene before Earth is destroyed; or to dignify our species by trusting us to survive unaided. Matters approach crisis in the twentieth century when two Martian observers contest for control over a human boy genius, a potential ethical innovator. Pangborn's language throughout is elegiac, but perfectly under control.

To end this omnibus with *Good Neighbors and Other Strangers* (1972), in which life in America, mostly rural, is celebrated, but with a note of elegiac warning, is effectively to suggest that Pangborn is an author to live with, to visit and revisit. Everything he writes is full of care and love; from 'Angel's Egg' (included here) to his very late stories, we hear his voice. It is a voice that calls upon America, and upon Pangborn's readers, to return.

For a more detailed version of the above, see Edgar Pangborn's author entry in *The Encyclopedia of Science Fiction*: http://sf-encyclopedia.com/entry/pangborn_edgar

Some terms above are capitalised when they would not normally be so rendered; this indicates that the terms represent discrete entries in *The Encyclopedia of Science Fiction*.

DAVY

to
All of Us
including
JUDY

*NOTE: The characters in this novel
are fictitious in a limited sense –
that is, they won't be born for
several hundred years yet.*

1

I'm Davy, who was king for a time. King of the Fools, and that calls for wisdom.

It happened in 323, in Nuin, whose eastern boundary is a coastline on the great sea that in Old Time was called the Atlantic – the sea where now this ship winds her passage through gray or golden days and across the shoreless latitudes of night. It was in my native country Moha, and I no more than a boy, that I acquired my golden horn and began to learn its music. Then followed my years with Rumley's Ramblers into Katskil, Levannon, Bershar, Vairmant, Conicut and the Low Countries – years of growing, with some tasty girls and good friends and enough work. And when, no longer with the Ramblers. I came into Nuin, I must have been nearly a man, or the woman I met there, my brown-eyed Nickie with the elf-pointed ears, would not have desired me.

I learned my letters, or they called it learning them, at the school in Skoar, but actually I knew nothing of reading and writing until my time with the Ramblers, when Mam Laura Shaw lost patience with my ignorance and gave me the beginning of light. Being now twenty-eight and far advanced in heresy, and familiar with the fragments of Old-Time literature, I say to hell with the laws that forbid most Old-Time books or reserve them to the priests!

Somewhere I have picked up the impudence to attempt writing a book for you, conceiving you out of nothing as I must because of the ocean between us and the centuries that you people, if you exist, have known nothing of my part of the round world. I am convinced it is round.

My way of writing must follow an Old-Time style, I think, not the speech or writing of the present day. The few books made nowadays, barbarously printed on miserable paper and deserving no better, are a Church product, dreary beyond belief – sermons, proverb, moral tales. There is some ginger in the common speech, it's true, but it is restricted to a simplicity that renders it, on the whole, hellishly dull – let any man not a priest use a term that cannot be grasped by a drooling chowderhead, and eyes slip sidelong in suspicion, fingers make ready for the flung stone that has always been a fool's favorite means of putting himself on a level with the wise. And finally, English in the pattern of Old Time is the only language I could have in common with you who may exist and one day read this.

We are free men and women aboard this vessel, carrying no burden of cherished ignorance. In the country that drove us out they preen themselves on freedom of religion, which meant in practise, as it evidently did throughout Old Time, merely freedom for a little variety within the majority's religion – no true heretics wanted, although in the last century or so of Old Time they were not persecuted as they are today, because the dominant religion of that time, on that continent, was thinned down to a pallid reminiscence of its one-time hellfire glory. The Holy Murcan Church, and the small quackpot sects that it allows to exist, were certainly latent in Old Time, but so far as one can tell at this distance, Christianity in the America of what they called the 20th Century was hardly capable of scaring even the children. On this schooner there is freedom from religion, and in writing this book for you I shall require that freedom; if the thought offends you, take warning at this point and read some other book.

Our ship, our *Morning Star*, follows a design of Old Time, resembling no other vessel of our day except one experimental predecessor, the *Hawk*, burnt at her moorings four years ago in the war of 327 against the Cod Islands pirates. When the *Hawk* was built, men watched the placing of her timbers, saw the tall pine masts brought from Nuin's northern province of Hampsher, and they said she would sink on launching. She sailed bravely for months, before fire destroyed her off Provintown Island. Something in us remembers her, where her blackened bones must lie in the dark making a home for octopus or the great sea snakes. And we heard the same prophecy about the *Morning Star*. They saw her launched, the masts were stepped, the sails took hold of the sky, she went through her trials in Plimoth Bay like a lady walking on a lawn – they said she'd capsize at the first gale. Well, we have weathered more than one storm since we began our journey toward the sun's rising.

The world is round. I don't think you walk upsydown carrying your heads under your shoulders. If you do I'm wasting my time, for to understand the book I mean to write a man would need to have a head fastened on at the upper end of his neck, and use it now and then.

Our captain Sir Andrew Barr would also be damn surprised to find you walking upsydown, and so would my two best-loved, Nickie my wife and Dion Morgan Morgan-son lately Regent of Nuin – who are partly responsible for this book, by the way: they urged me into writing it and now watch me sweat. Captain Barr suggests further that anyone who seriously entertained that upsydown mahooha would almost certainly piss to windward.

There were enough maps and other items of scientific information at the secret library of the Heretics in Old City of Nuin to give us a fair picture of the world as it was some four hundred years ago and as it must be now. The rise in sea level, which seems to have been catastrophically rapid during the period when Old Time civilization went phut, makes a liar out of any Old-Time map so far as coastlines are concerned. The wrath of the world's waters would have been responsible for many inland changes too – earthquake, landslip, erosion of high ground in the prolonged torrential rains that John Barth describes in his (forbidden) journal.

Well, of course it's the truth, the many kinds of truth in the old books that causes the Church to forbid most of them, and to describe all the Old-Time knowledge as 'primitive legend.' It won't do to have a picture of this earth so jarringly different from the one the Holy Murcan Church provides – not even in a society where hardly one man in two dozen is literate enough to recognize his own name in writing. Too much truth, and too much ginger to suit the timid or the godly or the practical joes who make a good living helping the Church run the governments.

The earth is a sphere within empty space, and while the moon and the Midnight Star circle around it, it circles the sun. The sun also journeys – so the Old-Time learning tells me and I believe it – and the stars are faraway suns resembling our own, and the bright bodies we see to move are planets something like ours – except the Midnight Star, I think that swift-coursing gleam was one of the satellites sent aloft in Old Time, and this I find more wonderful than the Holy Murcan legend which makes it a star that fell from heaven as a reproach to man when Abraham died on the wheel. And I think the earth, moon, planets, sun and all the stars may be journeying, for a while or for eternity, but not, I dare say, with any consideration for our convenience – for we can if we like invent God and then explain his will for the guidance of humanity, but I would rather not.

Until I began it I never dreamed what a labor it is to write a book. ('Just write,' says Dion, for the sake of seeing me sputter – he knows better. Nickie is more helpful: when I'm fed up with rhetoric I can catch her tawny-gold body and wrestle its darling warmth.) I try to keep in mind how much you don't know, how men can't often see beyond the woods and fields of their homelands, nor beyond the lies and true-tales they learned in growing, the moments of pain or delight that may seem to make a true-tale out of a lie, a vision, a fancy, or an error out of a truth as stubborn as a granite hill.

Whenever I get stung by an idea I've got to go on scratching as long as it smarts. My education, as I've already hinted, was delayed. At twenty-eight I believe my ignorance is expanding in a promising sort of way, but forgive me if at times I tell you less than I might or more than you wish. I reached fourteen as empty of learning as a mud-turkle though slightly less homely, being red-haired, small but limber with a natural-born goofy look, and well-hung.

The republic of Moha, where I was born in a whorehouse that was not one of the best, is a nation of small lonely farms and stockaded villages in the lake and forest and grassland country north of the Katskil Mountains and the rugged nation that bears the mountains' name. One day Katskil may conquer all Moha, I suppose. I was born in one of Moha's three cities, Skoar. It lies in a hollow of the hills almost on the line where the Katskil border ran at that time.

In Skoar life goes by the seasons and the Corn Market trade. Wilderness is a green flood washing up to the barrier of the city's rather poor stockade, except where the brush has been cleared to make the West and the Northeast Roads a little safer for their double streams of men, mule-wagons, soldiers, pilgrims, tinkers, wanderers.

There's a raw splendor to those roads, except when wartime makes folk more than ever afraid of travel and open places. In good times the roads reek of horse, ox-team, men, of the passage of chained bears and wolves brought for sale to the city baiting-pits; under sunshine and free winds the stink is nothing to trouble you. You may see anything on the go in the daytime. Maybe a great man, even a Governor, riding alone, or a holy character on a pilgrimage – you know it's that, most likely a journey to the marketplace in Nuber, where Abraham is believed to have died on the wheel, because the man is stark naked except for his crown of briers and the silver wheel hung at his neck. He never looks to left or right when people edge up close shyly touching his head or hands or testicles to share his sanctity and heal themselves of private troubles. Or it may be some crowd of street-singers and tumblers, with whiteface monkeys chittering on their shoulders and caged parrots quarking horny talk.

Once in a while you'll see the gay canvas-covered mule-wagons of a Rambler gang with sexy pictures and odd designs all over the sides, and you know that wherever they stop there'll be music, crazy entertainments, good balltickling sideshows, fortunetelling, fine honest swindling, and news from far places that a man can trust. Rumors come and go, and a Rambler considers it a duty to cheat you in a horsetrade or such-like slicker than a gyppo, but the Ramblers also take pride in bearing nothing but true-tales from the distant lands, and the people know it, and value them for it so highly that few governments dare clamp down on their impudence, randiness, free-living ways. I know; I never forget I was with Rumley's Ramblers for the best years of my life before I found Nickie.

Another thing you might notice would be a fancy litter with drawn curtains, the bearers matched for height, moving in skillful broken step so that the expensive female stuff inside – might even be a Governor's personal whore – needn't stick her head out and blast the bearers for clumsy damned idle sumbitches. Or there might be a batch of slaves chained tandem being marched for sale at the Skoar market, or a drove of cattle for the slaughterhouse distracting the whole road with their loud stupidity and orneriness – those steers don't want to go, not anywhere, but the road pushes them along its gut, a mindless earthworm swallowing, spilling out at the anal end and reaching for more.

The roads are quiet at night. Brown tiger and black wolf may use them then – who's to say, unless it's a night-caught traveler who'll see nothing more afterward?

Farming is heartbreak work in Moha as everywhere. The stock gives birth to as many mues there as anywhere; the toll taken by the wild killers is high, the labor is sweat and disappointment grinding a man to old age in the forties, few farmers ever able to afford a slave. The people get along though, as I've seen human beings do in worse places than Moha. The climate is not as hot and malarial as Penn. There's trade in timber and saddle-horses; manufacture too, though it can't match the industry of Katskil or Nuin. A barrel-factory in Skoar turned out coffins as a sideline and prospered – Yankee ingenuity, they called it. They scrape along, the same poor snotty human race, all of a muddle and on the go, as they've always done and maybe always will until the sun sweats icicles, which won't be next Wednesday.

A maybe. Now that I know the books, I can't forget how this same human race must have survived the Years of Confusion by a narrow squeak, the merest happen-so.

The other two big centers of my homeland are Moha City and Kanhar, walled cities in the northwest on Moha Water, a narrow arm of the sea. Eighteen-foot earthwork walls – that's enough to stop brown tiger's leap, and it makes Skoar with its puny twelve-foot log palisade a very cheap third. The great Kanhar wharves can take outriggers up to thirty tons – the big vessels, mostly from Levannon, that trade at all ports. Moha City is the capital, with the President's palace, and Kanhar the largest – twenty thousand not counting the slaves, who might make it twenty-five. Moha law reasons that if you count them like human beings you may end by treating them the same way, exposing a great democracy to revolution and ruin.

Now I think of it, every nation I know of except Nuber is a great democracy. The exception, Nuber the Holy City, is not really a nation anyway, just a few square miles of sanctified topsoil facing the Hudson Sea, enclosed on its other three sides by some of Katskil's mountains. It is the spiritual capital of the world, in other words the terrestrial site of that heavenly contraption the Holy Murcan Church. Nobody dwells there except important Church officials, most of them with living quarters in the mighty Nuber Cathedral, and about a thousand common folk to take care of their mundane needs, from sandal-thongs and toilet rags to fair wines and run-of-the-mill prosties. Katskil country doesn't produce fine wines nor highly skilled bed-athletes – they have to be imported, often from Penn.

Katskil itself is a kingdom. Nuin is a Commonwealth, with a hereditary

Presidency of absolute powers. Levannon is a kingdom, but governed by a Board of Trade. Lomeda and the other Low Countries are ecclesiastical states, the boss panjandrum being called a Prince Cardinal. Rhode, Vairmant and Penn are republics; Conicut's a kingdom; Bershar is mostly a mess. But they're all great democracies, and I hope this will grow clearer to you one day when the ocean is less wet. Oh, and far south or southwest of Penn is a nation named Misipa which is an empire, but they admit no visitors,[1] living behind an earthwork wall that is said to run hundreds of miles through tropical jungle, and destroying all northern coastal shipping – by the use of gunpowder no less, tossed on the decks by clever catapult devices. Since the manufacture of gunpowder is most strictly forbidden by the Holy Murcan Church as a part of the Original Sin of Man, these Misipans are manifest heathens, so nobody goes there except by accident, nobody knows whether this empire is also a democracy, and to the best of my information nobody cares to the extent of a fart in a hurricane.

Fifty miles south of Kanhar lies Skoar. There I was born, in a house that, while not high-class, was no mere crib either. I saw it later, when old enough to be observant. I remember the red door, red curtains, brass phallus-lamps, the V-mark over the front door that meant it was licensed by the city government in accordance with the Church's famous Doctrine of Necessary Evils. What showed it wasn't high-class was that the girls could lounge on the front steps with thighs spread or a breast bulging out of a blouse, or strip at the windows hollering invitations. A high-class house generally shows only the V-mark, the red door, and an uncommon degree of outward peace and quiet – the well-heeled customers prefer it that way. I'm not over-fussy myself – so far as I'm concerned, sex can be rowdy or brimful of moonlight: so long as it's sex, and nobody's getting hurt, I like it.

In such houses, of whatever class, there's no time for kids. But children are scarce in this world and therefore prized. I was well-formed, nothing about me to suggest a mue, but as a whorehouse product I was a ward of the State, not eligible for private adoption. The policers took me from my mother, whoever she was, and put me in the Skoar orphanage. She would have got the payment usual in such cases, and would then have had to change her name

---

[1] Davy means, no northern visitors. They have some commerce with the region known in Old Time as South America. In 296 a handful of refugees from some Misipan political tempest reached Penn overland, and gave this and other information before they died of malaria, infected wounds and dysentery. They spoke an English so barbarous that there has been argument ever since over much that they tried to say. I learned of this by listening in as a small boy on semi-formal conversations between my grandfather President Dion II and the Penn ambassador Wilam Skoonmaker. My poor uncle, later Morgan III, held me in his lap while he took notes on Skoonmaker's stately talk and I admired his embroidered pants.

– Dion Morgan Morganson of Nuin.

and move to some other city, for the State preferred that wards of my sort should know nothing of their origin – I learned mine only through the accident of overhearing a blabbermouth priest at the orphanage when I was thought to be asleep.

I grew up at the orphanage until I was nine, the usual age for bonding out. As a bond-servant I still belonged to the State, which took three-fourths of my pay until I should be eighteen. Then, if all had gone well, the State would consider itself reimbursed, and I would become a freeman. This was the Welfare System.

At the orphanage nearly everything got done with patient sighs or silence. It was not crowded. The nuns and priests wouldn't stand for noise, but if we kept quiet there were few punishments. We were kept busy at easy tasks like sweeping, dusting, laundry, scrubbing floors, cutting and carrying firewood, washing dishes and pans, digging the vegetable patch, weeding and harvesting it, waiting on table which meant watching scum gather on the soup during Father Milsom's prayers, and emptying the sacerdotal chamberpots.

In spite of considerable care and kindness we grew up familiar with sickness and death. I recall a year when there were only five boys and eight girls, and work got tough – the average population was around twenty children. Our guardians suffered for us, praying extra hours, burning candles of the large economy size that combines worship with fumigation, bleeding us and giving us what's called vitamin soup which is catnip broth with powdered eggshell to stiffen the bones.

There was no schooling to speak of at the orphanage. In Moha schooling belonged to the years between the ninth and twelfth birthdays, except for the nobility and candidates for the priesthood, who had to sweat out a great deal more. Even slave children had to go through a bit of schooling: Moha was progressive that way. I well remember the district school on Cayuga Street, the weariness of effort that never found a real focus, and now and then a sense of something vital out of reach. And yet our school was very progressive. We had Projects. I made a bird-house.

It wasn't much like the ones I'd made for fun, off in the woods on my lone, out of bark and vines and whittled sticks. The birds themselves were uneducated enough to like those. The one I made at the school with real bronze tools was lots prettier. You wouldn't want to hang it in a tree of course – you just don't do such things with a Project.

My bond-servant pay wasn't docked for school hours; a good law saw to that. All the same, compulsory progressive education is no joke, when it takes so much time out of your life that might have been spent at learning something.

The only child friend I remember from the orphanage time is Caron, who was nine when I was seven. She didn't grow up with me but was sent to the orphanage after her parents liquidated each other in a knife brawl. Only a few months and then she was bonded out, but in that time she loved me. She was quarrelsome with everyone else, constantly in trouble. Late at night, when the supervisor dozed off by the one candle, there'd be some flitting back and forth between the boys' and girls' sides of the dormitory, although the penalty for getting caught at sex games was twenty lashes and a day in the cellar. Caron came to me that way, slipping under my blanket bony and warm. We played our fumbling games, not very well; I remember better her talk, in a tiny voice that could not have been heard ten feet away. True-tales of the outer world, and make-believe, and often (this scared me) talk of what she meant to do to everyone in the institution except me – all the way from burning down the building to carving Father Milsom's nuts, if he had any. She must have been bonded out away from Skoar, I think. When I was bonded myself, still lonely for her two years later, I never won a clue to what had happened to her. I learned only that the lost do not often return in life as they do in the kindly little romances we can hear from the storyteller beggars at the street-corners for a coin or two.

Caron would be thirty now, if she's alive. Sometimes, even in bed with my Nickie, I recall our puppy squirming, the wild inconsequences of childhood thought, and imagine that if I saw her now I would know her.

I do remember one other, Sister Carnation, smelling of crude soap and sweat, who mothered me and sang to me when I was very small. She was mountainously fat with deep-sunk humorous eyes, a light true voice. I was four when Father Milsom checked my whines of inquiry by saying Sister Carnation had walked with Abraham. So I was sick-jealous of Abraham till someone explained it was only a holy way of saying she had died.

I was bonded out as a yard-boy at the Bull-and-Iron tavern on Kurin Street, and worked at it till a month after my fourteenth birthday, which is where I mean to begin my story. Board at half price; after that and the State's three-fourths were taken out, I had two dollars a week left, and I supplemented the board unofficially too. Oat bread, stew, and whatever can be 'uplifted' as Pa Rumley of Rumley's Ramblers used to say – a boy can grow on that. And the stew at the Bull-and-Iron was thicker and better than anything at the orphanage – more goat and less religion.

2

On a day of middle March a month after my fourteenth birthday I sneaked away from the Bull-and-Iron at first-light, goofing off. It had been a tough winter – smallpox, flu, everything but the lumpy plague. Snow fell in January an inch deep; I've seldom seen it so heavy. Now, winter being gone, I ached with the spring unrest, the waking dreams. I wanted and feared the night dreams in which some fantastic embrace short of completion would wake me with jetting of the seed. I knew a thousand ambitions that died of laziness; weariness of nothing-to-do while everything was yet to be done – most children call that boredom, and so did I, although childhood was receding then and not slowly. I saw the intolerant hours slip past, each day befooled by a new maybe-tomorrow and no splendid thing coming down the road.

There was a frost in Febry[2] on my birthday; people said it was unusual. I recall seeing from my loft window that birthday morning a shaft of icicle clinging to the sign over the inn doorway – a noble sign, painted for Jon Robson by some journeyman artist who likely got bed and a meal out of it, along with the poverty talk Old Jon burped up on such occasions. (Only Jon Robson's daughter Emmia remembered it was my birthday, by the way; she slipped me a shiny silver dollar, and a sweet look for which I'd have traded all the dollars I owned, but as a bond-servant I could have been slapped in the stocks for having such a thought about a freeman's daughter.) The sign showed a red bull with tremendous horns, ballocks like a pair of church-bells; representing the iron was a bull-ring dart sticking out of his neck and he not minding it a bit. Mam Robson's idea likely. For a harmless old broad she got a surprising bang out of the bear-pit, bull-ring, atheist-burnings, public hangings. She said such entertainments were mor'l because they showed you how virtue triumphed in the end.

The wolves sharpnosed in close that winter. A pack of blacks wiped out a farm family at Wilton Village near Skoar, one of the families that risk dwelling outside the community stockade. Old Jon told every new guest the particulars of the massacre, to make good table-talk and to remind the customers how smart they were to come to a nice inn behind a city-type stockade – reasonable rates too. He might be still telling that yarn, and perhaps mentioning a redheaded yard-boy he once had who turned out to be a

---

[2] Davy has asked Dion and me to ungoof the spelling here and there, but nobody could claim this one isn't an improvement.

– Miranda Nicoletta deMoha.

real snake in his bosom not fit to carry guts to a bear. Old Jon had connections in Wilton Village and knew the family the wolves killed. In any case he never kept his mouth shut more than a few minutes unless aristocracy was present: then, being a Mister himself, the lowest grade of nobility, he'd hold it shut, his blue damp eyes studying their faces in his lifelong search for the best arses to kiss.

He wouldn't keep it shut when he slept. He and the Mam had their bedroom across the wagon-yard from my loft. In mid-winter with their windows closed tight against draft-devils I'd still hear Old Jon sleeping away like an ungreased wagon-wheel. Once in a great while I'd hear the Mam howling briefly during his bedwork. It's a good question how they managed it, a two-hundred-pound lard-bucket and a little dry stick.

In the dark of that March morning I fed the horses and mules, reasoning that someone else could get his character strengthened by shoveling. The tavern did own a pair of slaves for outside work. My only reason for ever cleaning the stable was that I like to see such jobs done right, but that morning I felt they could take the whole shibundle and shove it. It was a Friday anyway, so all work was sinful, unless you care to claim that shoveling is a work of piety, and I want you to think carefully about that.

I crept into the main kitchen, knowing my way around. Although a yard-boy, I practiced the habit of washing whenever I could, and so old Jon let me help at waiting on table, minding the taproom fire, fetching drinks. I was safe that morning: everybody would be fasting before church, comfortably, in bed. The slave Judd, boss of the kitchen, wasn't up yet, so his scullion helpers would also be dead to the world. If Judd had discovered me the worst he'd have done would have been to chase me a step or two on his gimp leg, praising God he hadn't a chance of catching me.

I located a peach pie. I'd skipped fasting and church a long time – not hard, for who notices a yard-boy? – and no lightning had clobbered me yet, though I'd been plainly taught that the humblest creatures are the special concern of God. In the storeroom I uplifted a loaf of oat bread and a chunk of bacon, and started thinking, Why not run away for good? Who would care?

Old Jon Robson would: squaring my bond would hurt in the pocket-book nerve. But then I'd never asked to have my life regarded as a market commodity.

Emmia might care. I worked on that as I stole down the morning emptiness of Kurin Street, true sunrise almost half an hour away. I worked on it hard, being fourteen, maybe more active in the sentimentals than most downyskins of that age. I had myself killed by black wolf, and changed that to bandits because black wolf wouldn't leave enough bones. I felt we should provide bones. Somebody could fetch them back to show Emmia. 'Here's all's left of poor Davy except his Katskil knife. He allowed he wanted you should have it, was anything to happen to him? But I'd never actually got around to saying that to anyone, and anyhow bandits wouldn't leave a good knife, rot them.

Emmia was sixteen, big and soft like her Da, only on her it looked good. She was a blue-eyed cushiony honeypot with a few more pounds than most girls have of everything except good sense. For a year my nights had been heated by undressing her in my fancy, all alone in my stable loft. The real Emmia occasionally had to bed down with important guests to maintain the reputation of the inn, but I wouldn't quite admit the fact to myself. Certainly I'd been hearing the old cunty yarns and jokes about innkeeper's daughters for years, but except for Caron lost in childhood Emmia was my first love. I did somehow avoid understanding that the darling quail was obliged to be a part-time whore.

I was gulping when I passed the town green. Pillory, whipping-post and stocks had become grayly visible, reminders of what could happen to a bond-servant who should get caught putting a hand on Emmia's dress, let alone under it. As I neared the place where I meant to get over the stockade, most of the flapdoodle about bones drained out of my head. I was thinking about running away for real.

Found and brought back, I could be declared a no-brand slave and sold by the State for a ten-year term. But that morning I was telling myself what they could do with such laws. I had the bacon and bread, my flint-and-steel and my luck charm, all in a shoulder-sack that was my rightful property. My knife, also honestly mine by purchase, hung sheathed on a belt under my shirt, and all the money I had saved in the winter, ten dollars, was knotted into my loin-rag – the bright coin that Emmia gave me tied off separately, never to be spent if I could help it. Up in the woods of North Mountain where I'd found a cave in my solitary wanderings of the year before, I had other things stored – an ash bow I had made, brass-tipped arrows, fishline, two genuine steel fish-hooks, and ten more dollars buried. The arrow-tips and fishline were cheap; it had taken a couple of weeks to save enough for those good fish-hooks, seeing how scarce and precious steel is nowadays.

I scrabbled over the palisade logs while the sleepy guard was out of sight on his rounds, and took off up the mountainside. The Emmia who talked in my heart quit whimpering over bones. I thought of the actual soft-lipped girl who would surely want me to turn back and stick it out through my bond-period, although in the flesh I'd done nothing hotter than imagine her beside me on my pallet during those rather sad private games.

Climbing the steep ground away from the city, I decided I'd merely stay lost a day or two as I'd done other times. Then it had usually been my proper day off. Not always: I'd risked trouble before and blarneyed out of it. This time I'd stay until the bacon was gone, and work up some fancy whopmagullion to tell on my return, to soften the action of Old Jon's leather strap on my rump – not that he ever hurt much, for he lacked both muscle and active cruelty. The decision calmed me. When I was well into the cover of the big woods I climbed a maple to watch for sunrise.

From up there the roads out of Skoar were still shut away from sight by the forest. Skoar was insubstantial, a phantom city caught and hung in a veil of early light. I think I knew it was also a prosaic reality, a huddle of ten thousand human beings ready for another day of working, swindling, loafing, stepping on each other's faces or now and then trying not to.

Before reaching my maple I had heard the liquid inquiry of the first bird-calls. Now the sun-fire would soon be at the rim; the singers were wide awake, their music rippling back and forth across the top of the world. I heard a whitethroat sparrow, who would not remain long on his way north. Robin and wood-thrush – could a morning begin without them? A cardinal shot past, ablaze. A pair of white parrots broke out of a sycamore to skim over the trees, and I heard a wood-dove, and a wren exploded his small heart in a shower of rainbow notes.

I watched a pair of whiteface monkeys in a sweet gum nearby; they didn't mind me. The male put down his head so his wife could groom his neck. When she tired of it he grabbed her haunches and helped himself to a bit of love, a thank-you job acted out with his favorite tool. They sat then with their arms around each other, long black tails hanging, and he yawned at me: 'Eee-ooo!' When I looked away from them the east was flaming.

Of a sudden I wanted to know: Where does it come from, the sun? How is it set afire for the day?

Understand, in those days I hadn't a scrap of decent learning. At school I'd toiled through two books, the speller and the Book of Prayers. At a Rambler entertainment when I was thirteen I'd picked up a sex pamphlet because I thought it had pictures, and would have bought a dream book if it hadn't cost a dollar. I knew of the Book of Abraham, called the one source of true religion, and was aware that common men are forbidden to read it lest they misunderstand. Books, say the priests, are all somewhat dangerous and had much to do with the Sin of Man in Old Time; they tempt men to think independently, which in itself implies a rejection of God's loving care. As for other types of learning – well, I considered Old Jon remarkably advanced in wisdom because he could keep accounts with the bead-board in the taproom.

I believed, as I'd been taught, that the world consisted of an area of land three thousand miles square, which was a garden where God and the angels walked freely among men performing miracles until about four hundred years ago when men sinned by lusting after forbidden knowledge and spoiled everything. Now we're working out the penance until Abraham the

Spokesman of God, Advertiser of Salvation whose coming was foretold by the ancient prophet Jesus Christ sometimes called the Sponsor, Abraham born of the Virgin Cara in the wilderness during the Years of Confusion, slain for our sins on the wheel at Nuber in the thirty-seventh year of his life, shall return to earth and judge all souls, saving the few and consigning the many to everlasting fire.

I knew the present year was 317, dating from the birth of Abraham, and that all nations agreed on this date. I believed that on every side of that lump of land three thousand miles square the great sea spread to the rim of the world. But – what about that rim? The Book of Abraham, said the priests, does not say how far out it is – God doesn't wish men to know, that's why. When I heard that in school, naturally I shut up, but it bothered me.

All my doubts were young and tentative: new grass struggling up through the rotted trash of winter. I did think it remarkable how the lightning never roasted me no matter how I sinned. At the close of my last school year a whole week was devoted to Sin, Father Clance the principal giving it personal attention. The Scarlet Woman puzzled us: we knew whores painted their faces, but it did sound as if this one was red all over – I didn't get it. We knew what the good father meant by the Sin of Touching Yourself, though we called it jacking off; a few of the greener boys were upset to learn that if you did it your organs would turn blue and presently drop away; two fainted and one ran outside to vomit. Girls and boys had been separated that week, so I don't know what sacred information got rammed into the quail. I could see that I must be too altogether trifling for God to bother about me, since I'd been taught the technique at least four years earlier at the orphanage, wasn't even slightly blue, and still had everything. Father Clance was large and pale; he looked as if his stomach hurt and someone else was to blame. You felt that before blundering along and creating human beings male and female, God might in common decency have first consulted Father Clance.

The Church made it plain that everything connected with sex was sinful, hateful, dirty – even dreaming of a lay was called 'pollution' – and also deserving of the utmost reverence. There were other inconsistencies, inevitable I suppose. The Church and its captive secular governments naturally wished the population might increase; with so many marriages sterile, mue-births coming nearly one in five, it's an empty world. But the Church is also committed to the belief – I don't understand its origins – that all pleasure is suspect and only the joyless can be virtuous. Therefore the authorities do their best to encourage breeding while solemnly looking the other way. Something like a little show we used to put on when I was with Rumley's Ramblers: four couples munching a nobility-type dinner with slaves bowing in the baked meats, and those aristocrats jawed gravely about the weather, fashion, church affairs never cracking a smile – but the audience could see under the table, where a squirming of fingers and bared thighs and upper-class codpieces was wondrous to behold.

The mind of Father Clance could take that kind of inconsistency with no pain; not mine. Religion requires a specially cultivated deafness to contradiction which I'm too sinful to learn.

Of course at fourteen I understood that you agreed out loud with whatever the Church taught, or else. I watched my first atheist-burning after I started work at the Bull-and-Iron. The attraction was a man who'd been heard to tell his son that nobody was ever born of a virgin. I'm not clear how this made him an atheist, but knew better than to ask. In Moha the burnings were always part of the Spring Festival – children under nine were not required to attend.

From my maple I watched the birth and growing of the day. Unexpectedly I thought: What if someone were to sail as far as the rim?

It was too much. I shied away from the thought. I slid from my tree and climbed on through deep forest, where the heat of day is always moderate. I traveled slowly so as not to raise a sweat, for the smell drifts far and black wolf or brown tiger may get interested. Against black wolf I had my knife – he hates steel. Tiger is indifferent to knives – a flip of his paw will do – but he usually avoids mountain country to follow the grazers. He's said to respect arrows a little, and thrown spears and fire, though I've heard of his leaping a fire-circle to take a man.

I wasn't too concerned about those ancient enemies that morning. My perilous thought was generating others: Suppose *I* went to the rim, and saw the sun catch fire? ...

In heavy woods at any time of day there's an uncertainty of twilight. Objects seem more and less than real, when the light reaches them in a downflowing through the leaves. Part of night lingers. The question what is behind you may hold something more than fear. A good or desired being might walk there instead of danger, who's to know?

My cave on North Mountain was a crack in a cliff broadening inside to make a room four feet wide and twenty deep. The crack ran up into darkness but must have reached the outside, since a draft like the pull of a chimney kept the air fresh. Black wolf could have entered, even tiger though he would have found scant room to maneuver. I'd driven out copperheads when I found the cave, and had to watch against their return; sweeping with a branch for scorpions was another housekeeping routine. The approach was a narrow ledge that widened in front of the cave with enough earth to support some grass and then led on more steeply to the other end of the cliff. The cave was on the east face of the mountain, Skoar in the south shut away. I could build small fires at night, searching the glow for a boy's visions of places unexplored, faraway times and other selves.

That morning I first made sure of my bow and other gear. All there, but I felt a strangeness. I wet my nose to sharpen the scents; nothing wrong. When I found the cause, on the back wall where my glance must have gone at first unseeingly, I was not much wiser. A picture had been drawn by a point of soft red rock. It must have been done since my last visit, in November. It showed two faceless stick figures, with male parts. I'd heard of hunters' sign messages, but this said nothing of that sort. The figures merely stood there. One was in good human proportion, elbows and knees bent, fingers and toes carefully indicated. The other reached the same height but his arms were too long and his legs too short with no knee-crook. I found no tracks, nothing left behind in the cave and nothing stolen.

I gave it up. Someone had passed by since November, and left my gear untouched; no reason to think he meant me any harm. I made sure a horse-shoe hidden under a rock in the front of the cave was still in place, though I'd never heard of pictures being left around by witches or any other supematu-rals. I gathered fresh boughs to sleep on, and a mess of firewood, and lay out in the sun for daydreaming, naked except for my knife-belt. Without such free time now and then, how would we ever find new methods of protecting the moon from the grasshoppers? I didn't forget the picture, but I supposed the visitor was long gone. My thoughts sailed beyond the limits of day.

I thought of journeying.

The Hudson Sea, Moha Water, the Lorenta and Ontara Seas – I knew all those were branches of the great sea that divides the known world into islands. I knew that the Hudson Sea in many places is barely a mile wide, easy for small craft. And I knew that thirty-ton outriggers of Levannon sailed through Moha Water to the Ontara Sea, and then to Seal Harbor, on the Lor-enta Sea, where most of our lamp-oil comes from. Seal Harbor is still Levannon soil, the ultimate tip of that great snaky-long country and the larg-est source of its wealth, the northernmost spot of civilization, if you can call a hell-hole like Seal Harbor civilized. (I was with Rumley's Ramblers, fifteen years old, when I saw it. Shag Donovan's bully-boys tried to grab one of our girls, something that wouldn't be attempted on a Rambler gang anywhere else in the world. We left three of his men dead and the rest thoughtful.) Beyond Seal Harbor those Levannon ships proceed down the Lorenta to the great sea, and south along lonely coasts to trade with the city-states of Main and then with the famous ports of Nuin – Newbury, Old City, Hannis, Land's End. That northern passage is long and bad, travelers said at the Bull-and-Iron. Fog may hide both shores, and they're the shores of red bear and brown tiger country not fit for man. All the same, that route was thought safer than the southern course down the Hudson Sea and along the Conicut coast, and Levannon ships laden with the manufactured goods of Nuin usually returned the northern way too, beating against contrary wind and current rather than risking a clash with the Cod Islands pirates. We've cleaned the pirates out now, but at that time their war canoes and lateen-rigged skimmers had the nations by the balls, and twisted.

Lazing on my ledge that morning, I thought: If the Levannon thirty-tonners make the north passage for trade, why can't they sail much further for curiosity? Sure I was ignorant. I'd never beheld even the Hudson Sea. I didn't know that curiosity is not common but sadly rare, and without experience how could I imagine the loneliness of open sea when land has become a memory and there's no mark to steer by unless someone aboard knows the mystery of guessing position by the stars? So I asked the morning sky: If nobody dares to sail out of sight of land, and if the Book of Abraham won't tell how far is the rim or what's beyond it, how can the priests claim to know?

Why can't there be other lands this side of the rim? How do they know there *is* a rim? Maybe the Book of Abraham did explain that much, if one were allowed to read it, but then what about the far side? There had to be one. And something beyond the far side. So what if *I* were to sail – east—

Nay, I thought – nay, Mudhead! But suppose I did travel to Levannon – that wasn't far – where a young man could sign on aboard a thirty-tonner?

Suppose for instance I started this morning, or at least tomorrow?

3

I thought of Emmia.

Once from the street I had glimpsed her at her window naked for bedtime. A thick old jinny-creeper grew to the second story of the inn where her bedroom was. Behind the leaves I saw her let down her red-brown hair to tumble over her shoulders, and she combed it watching herself in a mirror, then stood gazing out at the night a while. The next building had a blind wall where I stood. No moonlight, or she would have seen me. Some impulse made her cup her left breast in her hand, blue eyes lowered, and I was bewitched to learn of the broad circle around the nipple, of her deep-curved waist, and the dark triangle just visible.

Naked women weren't news to me, though I'd never been close to one. Skoar had the peep-shows called movies, including penny-a-squint ones I could afford.[3] But that rosy marvel in the window was *Emmia,* not a picture

---

[3] They have the Church's grudging permission to exist, and rate a whole paragraph in the Church's celebrated Doctrine of Necessary Evils. This monument of shrewd piety is believed

not a puppet nor a worn-out peep-show actress with an idiot dab of G string
and a face like a spilled laundry bag, but Emmia whom I saw each day at
tasks around the tavern in her smock or slack-pants – mending, dusting,
overseeing the slaves, candle-making, waiting on table, coming out to my
territory to collect eggs or help feed the stock and milk the goats. Emmia was
careful with her skirt, the Emmia I knew – once when the old slave Judd, not
thinking, asked if she'd be so gracious to use the ladder and reach something
down so to spare his gimp leg, she told her mother and had him whipped for
bawdy insolence. This was Emmia, and in me, like stormy music, desire was
awake.

Love? Oh, I called it so. I was a boy.

She drifted out of sight and her candle died. I remember I fell asleep that
night exhausted, after the imaginary Emmia on my pallet had opened her
thighs. It became a canopy bed; I was inheriting the inn and Old John's fortune for saving Emmia from a mad dog or runaway horse or whatever. His
dying speech of blessing on our marriage would have made a skunk get
religion.

I had not seen Emmia naked again, but the picture of her at her window
remained warm in me – (it still is). It was with me on my mountain ledge that
morning as the time glided toward noon …

Ears and nose gave me the first warning. My hand shot to my knife before
my eyes found my outrageous visitor on the upward slant of the cliff side
path.

He smiled, or tried to.

His mouth was miserably small, in a broad flat hairless face. Dirty, grossly
fat, reeking. His vast long arms and stub legs told me he must be the subject
of that drawing. He did have knees: drooping fat-rolls concealed them; his
lower legs were nearly as thick as his ugly short thighs. Almost no hair, and
he wore nothing; a male, but what he had to prove it appeared against his fat
no larger than what you'd see on a small boy. In spite of the short legs he
stood as tall as I, around five feet five. His facial features – button nose, small
mouth, little dark eyes in puffy, fat-pockets – were merely ugly, not inhuman.
He said in a gargling man's voice: 'I go?'

I couldn't speak. Whatever appeared in my face made him no more terrified than he was already. He simply waited there, misery standing in the
sun. A mue.

---

by the public to have been devised by the disciple Simon at the supposed founding of the
Church in 44. Actually the document they call the original is on a type of parchment that was
developed in Nuin, not Katskil, and only about 50 years ago. I examined it myself on a visit to
Nuber. No scholar can say exactly when the Holy Murcan Church began to exist, but it cannot
have been a functioning institution for more than 200 years.

– Dion M. M.

Everywhere the law of church and state says plainly: *A mue born of woman or beast shall not live.*

You hear tales. A woman, or even a father, may bribe a priest to conceal a mue-birth, hoping the mue will outgrow its evil. The penalty is death, but it happens.

Conicut is the only country where the civil law requires that the mother of a mue must also be destroyed. The Church is apt to give her the benefit of the doubt. Tradition says that demons bent on planting mue-seed may enter women in their sleep, or magic them into unnatural drowsiness; thus women may be assumed not guilty unless witnesses prove they copulated with the demon knowingly. A female animal bearing a mue is usually put out of the way mercifully, and the carcass exorcised and burned. The tolerant law also reminds us that demons can take the form of men in broad daylight, with such damnable skill that only priests can discover the fraud ... Stories buzzed at the Bull-and-Iron about mues born in secret – single-eyed, tailed, purple-skinned, legless, two-headed, hermaphrodite, furred – that grow to maturity in hiding and haunt the wilderness.

Everywhere, it is the duty of a citizen to kill a mue on sight if possible, but to proceed with caution, because the monster's demon father may be lurking near.

He asked again: 'I go?' Immense, well-formed on his soggy body, his arms could have torn a bull apart.

'No.' That was my voice. Pure chicken – if I told him to go he might be angry.

'Boy-man-beautiful.'

He meant me, damn it. For politeness I said: 'I like the picture.' He was bewildered. 'Lines,' I said, and pointed into my cave. 'Good.'

He understood – smiled anyway, drooling, wiping away the slop across his chest. 'Come me. Show things.'

I was to go with him and maybe meet his father?

I remembered hearing of a recent witch-scare over at Chengo, a town rather far west of Skoar. Children saw demons, they said. A ten-year-old girl said she had been coaxed into the woods by a bad woman and hidden where she was obliged to watch that woman and others of the town rushing around and playing push-push with man-shaped devils that had animal heads. She was about to be dragged out of hiding and presented to the coven when a cock crew and the revels ended. The girl would not swear the demons had flown off into the clouds, and folk got cross with her about that, since everyone knows it's what demons do, but she did name the women so that they could be burned.

I slipped on my clothes and said: 'Wait!' I entered my cave motioning the mue to remain outside. I was shaking; he was too, out there in the sun. I thought he might run away, but he stayed, scared of his own courage like a human being – and that thought once lodged in my head would not leave it. What after all was wrong with him except his hideous short legs? Fatness – but that didn't make a mue, nor the ugly squinched-up features, nor even the hairlessness. I recalled seeing, at the public bathhouse in Skoar, a dark-skinned man who had almost no pubic hair and only a trace of fuzz under his arms – no one thought anything of it. I thought: What if some of the mue-tales are lies? Did a being as human as this have to live as a monster in the wilderness just because his legs were too short? And hadn't I heard a thousand yarns on other subjects at the Bull-and-Iron that I *knew* to be bushwa, the tellers not expecting belief?

I cut my loaf of oat bread in half. I had some notion of taming him like a beast by feeding him. I wanted my luck-charm. Its cord had broken and I was keeping it in my sack till I could contrive another. I took up the sack – was I for Abraham's sake *going* somewhere? – and the hard lump of the charm through the cloth did comfort me.

They carve such junk for tourists in Penn, as I found out later in my travels. My mother – anyhow someone at the house where I was born – gave me this, for I was told it hung at my neck when I arrived at the orphanage and they let me keep it. I probably cut my first teeth on it. It is a body with two fronts, male and female; the two-faced head has a brass loop embedded so you can wear it on a string. The folded arms and sex parts are sketched in flat and unreal. No legs: the thighs run together in a blob flattened on the bottom so you can set it upright. How the little gods get by without a rump I don't know – maybe that's how you know they are gods. It used to fascinate Caron. She liked to hold it under our blanket, and said it meant we would always be together.

I took the half-loaf of oat bread to the mue. He didn't grab. His flat nostrils flared; like a dog's his gaze followed my fingers as I broke off a piece and ate it myself. Then he accepted the rest, and gnawed, slobbering with eagerness, though with his fat he could hardly have been going hungry, and it was soon finished. He said: 'Come me?' He walked up the path and looked back. Like a smart dog.

I followed him.

Those stub legs pumped along pretty well. On a level he waddled; on rising slopes his hands pressed the ground for a speedy four-legged scramble. Downgrades bothered him; he followed a long slant where he could. He moved quietly as I'd learned to do in the woods, knew the country and must have been getting a living from it. He doubtless had no name.

A state ward, I had no last name. Just Davy.

Don't imagine that thing with the bread came from any grown-up good-ness in me. At fourteen whatever goodness I had was growing in the dark, obscured by shabby and cruel confusions that were inside of me as well as in my world: ignorance and fear; contempt of others for my class, which I was expected to pass on down to the slave class while all concerned made big talk of democratic equality; the cheating and conniving I daily saw people do, and their excuses for it – hi-ho, can't be so wrong because look, even the nobility are bootlickers, pimps, swindlers, thieves, don't you know? That's ancient, I believe, that game of supposing you make yourself clean by pointing at the dirt on somebody else. No, I wasn't good or kind.

Since human beings make and choose their own ends, goodness can be an end in itself without supernatural gimmicks, but that idea never came into words for me until I heard the words in Nickie's voice. Yet I think that I did dimly understand, at fourteen, how if you want to be a good human being you have to work at it.

There was that early protest in my mind, that recognition of the mue's humanity. But as I walked on through the forest with him I was governed mainly by fear and a dirty kind of planning. Schooling and the tavern-tales had told me mues weren't like witches or spooks. Although the offspring of demons they couldn't vanish, float through walls, use spells or the evil eye. God, said the authorities, may not be thought of as allowing such powers to a miserable mue. A mue died when you stuck a knife in him, and it needn't have a silver point.

The law said when, not if. You must if you could; if not you must save yourself and bring word, so the mue can be hunted down by professionals with the aid of a priest.

The leather of my knife-sheath brushed my skin at every step. I began to resent the mue, imagining his hellish father behind every tree, building up the resentment like a fool searching after an excuse for a quarrel.

We reached one of the mountain's flanking ridges, where old trees stood enormous, casting deep shade from their interlacing tops. They were mostly pine, that through the years had built up a carpet of silence. The mue disliked this region – on clear and level ground anything could overtake him. He padded on with worried side-glances, nothing about him to suggest a demon's protection,

They didn't say a demon *always* attended a mue ...

I decided it would be best to kill him on flat ground, and watched a spot below his last rib on the left side. After the stab I could be instantly clear of his long reach while the blood drained out of him. I drew my knife, and lowered it in my sack, afraid he might turn before I was ready. He cleared his throat, and that angered me – what right could he have to do things the human way? Still, I felt there was no hurry. This level area stretched on far ahead; I'd better wait till I was steadier.

At the tavern I wouldn't brag. I'd maintain a noble calm, the Yard-Boy Who Killed A Mue.

They'd send me out with an escort to find the remains and verify my story.
The skeleton would do, considering the leg-bones, and that's all we'd find, for
in the time it took the mission to settle arguments and get going the carrion-
ants, crows, vultures, small wild scavenger dogs would have done their
wilderness housecleaning. Maybe I'd drop something near the body. My
luck-charm – that would fix anyone who set out snickering at me behind his
hand.

It came to me, as I caught the mue's foul smell, that this was no daydream.
I might be questioned by the Mayor, even the Bishop of Skoar. The Kurin
family, tops in the Skoar aristocracy, would hear of it. They could make me
the same as rich, a bond-servant no more. Why, I would ride to Levannon on
a bright roan that none but I dared handle, and with two attendants – well,
three, one to dash ahead and make sure of a room for me at the next inn,
where a maid-servant would undress me and bathe me, wait on me in bed if
I wished. In Levannon I would *buy* a thirty-ton outrigger, and look at that
green hat with a hawk's feather, and that shirt too, a marvel of Penn silk,
green or maybe gold! As an adopted son of the nobility I could wear a loin-
rag of what color I chose, but I'd be modest, I'd settle for freeman's white, so
long as it was silk. I didn't think I wanted britches with a codpiece, a style just
then coming into favor. Those I'd seen looked clumsy, and the codpiece an
unnecessary brag. Moosehide moccasins I'd have, purtied up with ornaments of brass. I might start smoking, with a rich man's fancy for nicely cured
marawan and the best pale tobacco from Conicut or Lomeda.

I fancied Old Jon Robson ashamed of all unkindness and anxious to crowd
in on the glory. I would permit it. Clickety-clackety, he knew all along the
boy had it in him.

Mam Robson might have a go at supplying me with a few ancestors.
Already, when slightly pleased with me, she'd remarked that I sort of resembled a relative of hers who rose through the ranks to be a Captain in the
Second Kanhar Regiment and married a baron's daughter – which showed,
said she, that people with square chins and plenty of earlobe were the ones
that got ahead in the world – this was one for Old Jon, who had several chins
but none of them too clearly connected with his jawbone.

Who can say what man might have visited the house where I was born?

I'm concerned about varieties of time: one reason why I stepped in here a
moment behind the asterisks. You'd best get used to the idea that my brain-
scratching – digression is the word some people would prefer – is not a
suspension of action but a different kind of action, on a rather different time
scale. Your much-abused amiable mind, all of a doodah over women and
children, and taxes and a certain almost needless worry of yours about
whether you exist, may dislike the suggestion that more than one kind of

time is allowable, but give it a go, will you? Meanwhile, on what we might call the asterisk time scale, you can't very well stop me if I choose to claim that Pappy was a grandee, some hightoned panjandrum traveling incognito through Skoar and planting me in an idle moment when he had a hasty hard on and a smidgin of loose change – why not? Well, later in the book I'll tell you why not, or why probably not. Don't rush me.

I used to hate my shadowy father in my early years. I was six when, since I had accidentally overheard talk of my origin, Father Milsom told me what parents are, and said my Da was undoubtedly just a whore's customer, and then added some dismally fit-for-six explanation of the word 'whore' to complete the confusion. Yes, I hated my nameless father's guts; and yet when Caron first slid under my blanket I told her the President of Moha had visited Skoar in disguise, stopping off at the Mill Street house to make a baby – me. After that I felt better about the whole deal. Who wouldn't, with a President in the family? Caron – bless her – was quick to play along and devise generous plans full of arson and bloodshed for establishing my birthright.

A few nights later I learned that her mother, nine months before she was born, had a Passionate Affair with the Archbishop of Moha who also just happened to be passing by, and noticed her extreme beauty and sent litter-bearers after her so she could visit his residence in secret. Kay, so we had plans for Caron too, but were smart enough to keep all such enterprise under the blanket, where sometimes we called each other President and Presi-dentess, with frightful oaths never to speak of the matter in daytime.

If you find that anecdote funny, go to hell.

Walking on behind the mue, my overheated fancy also heard Emmia Rob-son: 'Davy darling, what if *you'd* got hurt?' Maybe not 'darling' but even 'Spice,' the love-name girls in Moha don't use unless they really mean come-try-something. 'Nay, Spice,' s's I, 'it was nothing, and didn't I have to destroy the brute for your sake?'

I decided the conversation had better take place in her bedroom. She had let down her hair to cover the front of her, so my hands – gentle but still the hands that had rid the world of a dread monster – parted the softness to find the pink flower-tips. And here and now, walking behind him in the woods, all I had to do—

The mue stopped and faced me. He may have wanted to reassure me, or transmit some message beyond his powers of speech. I took my hand out of the sack, without the knife. I couldn't do it, I knew, if he was looking at me. He said: 'We go not – not—'

'Not far?'

'Is word.' He was admiring – what a marvel to know all the words I did!

'Bad thing come, I here, I here.' He tapped his ponderous arm. 'You – I – you – I—'

'We're all right,' I said.

'We. We.' He had used the word himself, but it appeared to disturb or puzzle him.

'We means you and I.'

He nodded in his patch of leaf-dappled sunlight. Puzzled and thoughtful. Human. He grunted and smiled dimly and went on ahead.

I sheathed my knife and did not draw it again that day.

4

The region of great trees ended. As if sliding into dark water we entered a place where the master growth was wild grape; here day would always be a kind of evening. The slow violence of the vine had overcome a stand of maple and oak. Many of these were dead, upholding their murderers; others lived, winning sunlight enough to continue an existence of slavery.

Still I found an infinity of color and change. Some of the gleams in the vagueness above me were orchids. I glimpsed a blue and crimson parrot, and a tanager who was first a motionless ember and then a shooting-star. I heard a wood-dove lamenting – so it sounds, though I believe he cries for love.

The mue glanced up at the interlocking tangle and then at my legs and arms. 'You not,' he said, and showed what he meant by catching a grapevine loop and swarming up it until he was thirty feet above ground. He launched his bulk across a gap to grab another loop, and another. Many yards away, he shifted his grip with ease and returned. He was right, it wasn't for me. I'm clever in the trees, and slept in them once or twice before I found my cave, but my arms are merely human. He called: 'You go ground?'

I went ground. The walking became nasty. He traveled ahead above a vile thicket – fallen branches, hardhack, blackberry, poison ivy, rotten logs where fire-ants would be ready with their split-second fury. Snake and scorpion could be here. The puffy-bodied black-and-gold orb-spiders, big as my big toe, had built many homes; their bite won't kill but makes you wish it had.

The mue held down his pace to accommodate me. A quarter-mile of this struggle brought me up to a network of catbrier and there I was stopped: ten-foot elastic stems in a mad basket-weave, tough as moose-tendon and cruel as weasel-teeth. Beyond, I saw what may have been the tallest tree in Moha, a tulip tree at least twelve feet through at the base. The grape had found it long ago and gone rioting up into the sunshine, but might not have killed the giant after another hundred years. My mue was up there, pointing to a vine-stem that dangled on my side of the briers and connected with the loops around the tree. I shinnied up and worked over; he grasped my foot and set it gently on a branch.

As soon as he was sure of my safety he climbed, and I followed for maybe another sixty feet. It was easy as a ladder. The tree's side-branches had become smaller, the vine-leaves thicker in the increase of sunlight, when we came to a mass of crossed wood and interwoven vine. Not an eagle's nest as I foolishly thought at first – no bird ever lifted sticks of that size – but a nest certainly, six feet across, built on a double crotch, woven as shrewdly as any willow basket in the Corn Market and lined with gray moss. The mue let himself into it and made room for me.

He talked to me.

I felt no sense of dreaming. Did you in childhood, as I did now and then with Caron, play the game of imaginary countries? You might decree that if you stepped through the gap in a forked tree-trunk you'd be entering a different world. If then in the flesh you did step through you found you must continue to rely on make-believe, and I know that hurt. Suppose you had been met, in solid truth, on the other side of your tree-trunk, by a dragon, a blue chimera, a Cadillac,[4] an elf-girl all in green—?

'See you before,' the mue said. So he must have watched me on other visits to North Mountain – me with my keen eyes and ears, studied by a monster and never guessing it! He would not have passed the human kind of judgment on the monkey tricks of a boy who thought himself alone; that consoling thought came to me after a while.

He told me of his life. Mere fragments of language to help him, worn down by years of speaking to no one but himself – I won't record much of the actual talk. He waved toward the northeast, where from our height the world was a green sea under the gold of afternooon – he had been born somewhere off that way, if I understood him. He spoke of a journey of 'ten sleeps,' but I don't know what distance he might have covered in a day's travel. His mother, evidently a farm woman, had raised him in the woods. To him birth was a vagueness – 'Began there,' he said, and fumblingly tried to repeat what his mother had told him of birth, giving it up as soon as I showed I understood. Death he grasped, as an ending. 'Mother's man stop live' – before he was born, I think he meant. Describing his mother, all he could say was 'big,

[4] Anyone by paying a candle, a prayer and a dollar may enter the Murcan Museum in the cellar of the Cathedral at Old City and look at ancient fragments of automotive vehicles. In other words Davy knows perfectly well these mechanisms are not legendary, but must have his fun.
– Dion M. M.

good.' I guessed she would have been some stout farm woman who managed to hide her pregnancy in the first months, and perhaps her husband's death made matters simpler.

By law, every pregnancy must be reported immediately to civil and church authorities, no pregnant woman may be left alone after the fifth month, and a priest must be present at every birth to decide whether the child is normal and dispose of it if he considers it a mue. There are occasional breaches in the law – the Ramblers for instance, always on the go, could evade it much more often than they do – but the law is there, carrying a heavy charge of religious as well as secular command.

This mue's mother had no help in raising him to some age between eight and ten except that of a big dog. It would have been one of the tall wolfhounds a farm family needs if it is to risk dwelling outside a stockade. The dog guarded the baby when the mother could not be with him, and grew old as he grew up.

We have two wolfhounds aboard the *Morning Star*, Dion's Roland and Roma. They are friendly enough now, but while Dion's mood was black with misery over what had happened in Nuin – our loss of the war, forced flight, certain destruction of nearly all the reforms begun while he was Regent and Nickie and I his unofficial counselors – no one dared go near them except Dion himself; not even Nickie nor Dion's bedmates Nora Severn and Greta Shawn. The dogs dislike the motion of the ship – Roland was seasick for two days – but keep alive on smoked meat and biscuit that nobody grudges them.

Yesterday evening at sundown Nickie was at the rail, for once looking behind us to that part of the horizon beyond which lie Nuin and the other lands, and Roland came to lean sentimentally against her hip. She touched his head; not with them, I watched the westerly breeze rumple his gray pelt and Nickie's luminous brown hair. It is cut short like a man's, but she's all woman these days, dressing in the few simple garments she has made for herself from the ship's store of cloth – necessity, since most of us came aboard with nothing but what we were wearing, that ugly day. Yesterday in the red-gold light she wore a blouse and skirt of the plainest brown Nuin linsey – all woman but in a mood not to be touched,[5] I thought, and so I did not go to her in spite of a hunger to take hold of her small waist and kiss her brown throat and shoulders. Roland, after winning her hand's casual recognition, stepped away and lay down on the deck not too near, adoring but keeping it to himself, waiting for her to look at him again if she would. He could be

[5] Matter of fact, dear, I was merely wondering if supper would stay down.

           – Miranda Nic etc.

aware, as I am, how in spite of all pressures of male and female vanity, male and female foolishness, women are still people.

The mue's mother had taught him speech, now distorted by the years when he had small chance to make use of it. She taught him to win a living from the wilderness – hunting, snaring, brook-fishing with his hands, finding edible plants; how to stalk and, most important, how to hide. She taught him he must avoid all human beings, who would kill him on sight. I can't guess what sort of existence she imagined for his future; maybe she was able to avoid thinking of it. Nor can I guess what made him risk his life by approaching me, unless it was an overwhelming hunger for any sort of contact with what he knew to be his own breed.

At some time between his eighth and tenth years – 'she come no more.' He waited long. The dog was killed by a woods buffalo – little hellions they are, no more than half the size of tame cattle but frightfully strong and intelligent; we lost a man to one of them when I was with Rumley's Ramblers. The mue gave me most of that story in sign language, crying freely when he spoke of the dog's death and casually urinating through the floor of his nest.

When he felt that his mother must have died too, he made his journey of ten sleeps. I asked about years; he didn't understand. He had no way of telling me how often the world had cooled into the winter rains. He may have been twenty-five years old, when I saw him. During that journey a hunter sighted him and shot an arrow into him. 'Come me sharp-stick man-beautiful.' His fingers squeezed a remembered throat, he cried and belched and made a wet howling noise, his mouth spread open like a little wound. Then he studied me calmly to see if I understood, while a worm of fear stumbled down my back.

'Show now,' he said, and lifted himself abruptly to descend the tree, all the way to the ground.

Inside the catbriers a floor of rocks surrounded the tree, making a circle six feet out from the base. It created a fortress for him; only a snake could penetrate those thorns. The rocks overlapped so neatly the brier did not force its way through; many layers must have been fitted together – yes, and painfully searched out, painfully brought along the grapevine path. He had a stone hammer here, a rock shaped into a chopper, a few other gidgets. He showed me these, not so trustingly, and indicated I should stand where I was while he got something from the other side of the tree-trunk.

I heard rocks cautiously moved. His hands appeared beyond the trunk, setting down a rose-colored slab; I knew it would be the marker-stone of some poor hideaway. He returned to me, carrying a thing whose like I have never seen elsewhere.

I thought at first it might be some oddly shaped trumpet such as hunters and the cavalry use, or a cornet like those I'd heard when Rambler gangs visited Skoar and set up their shows in the green. But this golden horn resembled those things only as a racing stallion resembles a plow-horse – both honorable creatures, but one is a devil-angel with the rainbow on his shoulders.

The large flared end, the two round coils and the straight sections of the pipe between bell and mouthpiece – oh, supposing we could cast such metal nowadays we'd still have no way of working it so perfectly into shape. I knew at once the instrument was of Old Time – it could not have been designed in ours – and I was afraid.

Ancient coins, knives, spoons, kitchenware that won't rust – such objects of the perished world are often turned up in plowing or found at the edge of ruins that wilderness has not quite covered, like those on the Moha shore of the Hudson Sea near the village of Albany that lead down into the water like a stairway abandoned by gods. If the Old-Time thing has a clear harmless function the rule is finders-keepers, if you can pay a priest to exorcise the evil and stamp the object with the holy wheel. Mam Robson owned a skillet of gray metal that never rusted, found by her grandfather in turning over a cornfield, handed on to her at her marriage. She never used it but liked to show it to the inn guests for an oh-ah, telling how her mother did cook with it and took no harm. Then Old Jon would snort in with the tale of its discovery as if he'd been there, while her sad face, unlike Emmia's round pretty one but rather like a Vairmant mule's, would be saying *he* was no jo to ever find *her* such a thing, not him, blessed miracle if he got up off his ass long enough to scratch … If the ancient thing is too weird the priest buries it,[6] where it can do no harm.

In the mue's hands the horn was a golden shining. I've seen true gold since then; it is much heavier, with a different feel. But I call this a golden horn because I did think of it so for a long time, and the name still suggests a kind of truth. If you're sure there's only one kind of truth, go on, shove, read some other book, get out of my hair.

[6] Or if smart he marks it with the wheel-sign and sends it to one of the shops in the large cities that specialize in dudaddery for the sophisticated – that is, the suckers. One in Old City is famous for selling nothing the owner can't guarantee to be totally useless – Carrie's Auntie Shoppy, well I remember it. Because the Regent was expected to encourage commerce, I bought an Old-Time thingamy there, a small cylinder of pale gray metal with a tapered end. That end has a tiny hole, out of which pops a wee metal whichit if you push the other end; push it again and the thing pops back. One of my philosophic advisers suggests it may have been used in the phallic worship that we assume was practised privately along with the public breast-belly-thigh cult of ancient America: I don't find this convincing. I believe you could use the gidget for goosing a donkey, but why wouldn't any Goddamn pointed stick do just as well? There is need for more research.

– Dion M. M.

Uneasily the mue let me take it. 'Mother's man's thing she say.' I felt better when I found the wheel-sign – some priest, some time, had prayed away the spooks. The horn gathered light out of that shady place, itself a sun. 'She bring, say I to keep … You blow?' So at least he knew it was a thing for music.

I puffed my cheeks and tried – breath-noise and a mutter. The mue laughed and took it back hastily. 'I show.' His wretched mouth almost vanished in the cup, his cheeks firmed instead of puffing. I heard it speak.

I wonder if you know that voice in your part of the world? I will not try to describe it – I would not try to describe an icicle breaking sunshine into colored magic, nor to draw a picture of the wind. I know of only one place where words and music belong together, and that is song.

The mue pressed one of the valves and blew a different note, and then another. He blew a single note to each breath with no thought of combining them, no idea of rhythm or melody. Why, at the first sound my mind had overflowed with songs heard at the tavern, on the streets, at Rambler shows, and far back in the time when fat sweet Sister Carnation sang for me. To the poor mue, music was just notes indefinitely prolonged, unrelated. He could have blown that way all day and learned no more.

I tried to ask where it had come from; he shook his head. 'Was it kept hidden?' Another headshake – how should he know? Questions from a world not his, that allowed him no gift but the cruel one of birth. 'Did you use it to call your mother?' He looked empty-faced, as if there might be some such memory, none of my business, and he carried the horn back into hiding without answering.

I again saw his hands on that reddish rock, heard it set back in its former place, and knew I could find that place in ten seconds, and knew the golden horn must be mine.

It must be mine.

He returned smiling, comfortable now that his treasure was safe … I do claim one trace of honor: I did not again plan to kill him, nor even think of it except for one or two random moments. That's my scrap of virtue.

The lantern in our cabin is sputtering and my fingers are cramped. I need a fresh nib in my pen – we have plenty of bronze nibs, but I can't be extravagant. And I'd like a breath of air topside. Maybe I'll bother Captain Barr or Dion, or remind Nickie we haven't yet tried it in the crow's-nest. The night is uneasy; northwest gusts are warm but appear to have a power behind them. The morning came in with an explosion of crimson, and all day long my ears have been tight with a promise of storm. The other colonists – we've lately been calling ourselves that – are edgy with it. At the noon meal Adna-Lee Jason broke out crying from no clear cause, explaining it with a mutter about homesickness and then said she didn't mean that. Maybe I'll just loaf at the bow, taste the weather my own way, and try to decide whether I mean to go on with this book …

I'm going on with it, anyway Nickie says I am. (It was fine in the crows'-nest. She got dizzy and bit my shoulder harder than she meant to, but a few minutes later she was daring me to try it up there again some time with a real wind blowing. Ayah, she can cook too.) I'm going on with my book but I dread the next few pages.

I could lie about what happened with the mue and me. We all lie about ourselves; trying to diddle the world with an image that's had all the warts rubbed off. But wouldn't it be the cruddy trick to begin a true-tale and back off into whitewash lying at the first tough spot? By writing at all I've made the warts your business – of course it's not quite fair, since I'll never know much about you or your Aunt Cassandra and her yellow tomcat with the bent ear. But hi-ho, or as I remember my Nickie saying on another occasion: 'Better spare the mahooha, my love, my carroty monkey, my all, my this and that, my blue-eyed comforting long-handled bedwarmer, spare the mahooha and then we'll never run short of it.'

When the mue and I were climbing up away from that rock floor, seeing the dirt on his back gave me my idea. I asked him: 'Where is water?'

He pointed into the jungle. 'I show drink.'

'Wash too.'

'Whash?' It wasn't his specialty. He might have known the word in child-hood. You see my cleverness – start him really washing and he'd be away from home a long time.

'Water take off dirt,' I said.

'Dirt?'

I rubbed a speck off my wrist, and indicated some of his personal topsoil. 'Water-take-off is wash. Wash is good, make look good.'

The great idea broke like a seal-oil lamp afire – *a* great idea, not quite mine. 'Whash, be like you!'

I swung out along the grapevine, sick, not just from fear he'd kiss me in his delight. He followed, gobbling words I couldn't listen to, believing I could work a magic with water to make him man-beautiful. I never did, I never could have intended he should think that.

We traveled downhill, out of the ugly thicket and into clearer ground. I kept track of landmarks. When we reached the bank of a brook I made him understand we needed a pool; he led me through alders to a lovely stillness of water under sun. I shed my clothes and slipped in. The mue watched in amazement – how could anyone do that?

I was sick with knowing what I was about to do; then with grins and simple words and a show of washing myself to explain how it was done. He ventured in at last, beauty of the pool was wasted on me. But I beckoned him the big baby. It was nowhere deeper than three feet, but I dared not swim, thinking he might imitate me and be drowned. I now hated the thought of his coming to any harm through me except the one loss that, I kept telling myself, couldn't matter – what could he want of a golden horn? I helped him, guiding him to move in the water and keep his balance. I even started the scrubbing job on him myself.

Scared but willing, he went to work, snorting and splashing, getting the feel of it. Presently I let him see me look as if startled at the sun, to tell him I was thinking of time and the approach of evening dark. I said: 'I must go back. You finish wash.' I got out and dressed, waving him back, pointing to the dirt still on him. 'Finish wash. I go but come back.'

'Finish, I be—'

'Finish wash!' I said, and took off. He probably watched me out of sight. When the bushes hid me I was running and my sickness ran with me. Up the easy ground, into grapevine shadows and straight to his tree, up the vine, down behind the briers. I found the red rock at once and lifted it aside. The horn lay in a bed of gray-green moss. I took that too, as a wrapping for the horn inside my sack. I was up over the briers, and gone.

In no danger from the mue if I ever had been, I ran as fast as before, but now like an animal crazed by pursuit. A black wolf could have closed in on me with no effort.

Once or twice since then I have wished one had – before I knew Dion and the other friends I have today, the dearest being the wisest, my wife, my brown-eyed Nickie of the delicate hands.

5

Three nights ago – I was off watch – a hell of a gale swooped out of the northwest, and up went some of these pages like a mob of goosed goblins. Nickie grabbed the ones fluttering near the porthole, and I grabbed Nickie. Then the cabin tilted steep as a barn roof, the lantern smoked viciously and went out, and we were piled up against our bunk hearing the sea beaten to frenzy. But our *Morning Star* bore down against the goaded waters; she righted herself and rushed away with arrogant steadiness into the dark.

Captain Barr had smelled danger and got us reefed down just enough, ready as a racehorse; he didn't bother calling up the off watch.

I remember that square dark block of man at Provintown Island in 327, for I was there when the *Hawk* burned at her moorings. We'd gone ashore to accept the pirates' surrender and take formal possession of all the Cod Islands in Nuin's name. The fire may have been started by a spark from the galley stove. Sir Andrew's face hardly shifted a muscle when the red horror rose out there and roared across her decks. Dying inside, he turned to us and remarked: 'I think, gentlemen, we'd be well advised not to exaggerate our difficulties.' When Sir Andrew Barr dies for the last time it will be with some stately comment like that, pronounced so cleanly you can hear each punctuation mark click into the right place. If the pirate boss, old Bally-John Doon, had nourished any notion of taking advantage of the fire it must have perished at those words; after the *Hawk's* survivors swam ashore and were cared for the ceremony proceeded just as planned.

In 322, the first year of the Regency, Barr was already dreaming of a strong ship rigged entirely fore-and-aft. The dream grew out of a diagram in a magnificent book at the underground library of the secret society of the Heretics – an Old-Time dictionary. We have it on board. The front cover and some of the introductory pages are missing; the borders carry the scars of fire, and on the brittle sheet that now begins the book there's a brown stain. I think someone bled after rescuing it from a holy bonfire, but make up your own story. Sparked by the diagram, Barr searched out more information on Old-Time shipbuilding – all he could get – until through the Heretics he made contact with Dion and his conception was embodied in the building of the *Hawk*, and later the *Morning Star*.

When it was clear, in the last days of General Salter's rebellion, that we would probably lose the final battle for Old City, we divided the books with the brave handful of Heretics who elected to remain. And we did lose the battle, and fled aboard the *Morning Star* – suburbs ablaze, stench of hatred and terror in all the streets – a hard decision, I suppose harder for Dion than for the rest of us. The dictionary was almost necessary for us; I can't think of any one book that would give us more.

Those Heretics who remained were not all of them older people. A good number of the young stayed on, having some love and hope for Nuin in spite of everything. Theirs was the greater risk. We are only venturing on the unexplored; they dared to stay in a country that will again be governed by men who believe themselves possessed of absolute truth.

Captain Barr trusts our spread of eager canvas as no landsman could, and knows the sea in something like the way I knew the wilderness when I was a boy. A relentless perfectionist, he calls the *Morning Star* a beginner's effort. It doesn't conceal his love for her, which I think exceeds any he ever felt for a woman. He never married, and won't bed with a girl who might demand permanence.

That evening when the storm cut loose Nickie and I weren't expecting the universe to turn upsydown, so we got caught bare-ass innocent. I don't think she minded, after prying my elbows loose from her knees.[7] Of course now that she's taken to signing her full name and title of nobility I can see there'll be no dull times ahead. (Dma. stands for 'Domina', which is what you call a lady of the Nuin aristocracy, married or single.) Already I've learned that when I come back to this manuscript after any absence it's best to examine it, the way a dog searches himself after associating with mutts who may have a different entomological environment. I got 'entomological' out of the Old-Time dictionary and I find it beautiful. It means buggy.

That wind blew until the following afternoon, shrill continuous wrath. On my watch I had the wheel. I'm happy then in any weather, overcoming the impulse of the wheel toward chaos, my own strength and its demand for order enough but only just enough, and under me a hundred tons of human creation straining forward against space and time. You may have your horses; I say there's no poem like a two-masted schooner, and I'll hope to ride a ship now and then until I am too old to grip the spokes, too dull of sight to read the impersonal assurance of a star.

That day of wind, Second Mate Ted Marsh had to transmit orders by waving his hands or bringing his mouth next to my ear. Few orders needed, though. We could do no more than run before it under jib and storm-sail, and so we did, taking no harm. Next morning the uproar was spent: we were creeping, and a few hours later becalmed. We still are. The wind had spat us out into a quiet, and fog claimed us. It lies around us now, the ocean hushed as if we had come to a cessation of all endeavor, motion, seeking, a defeat of urgency by silence. The sea level is not what it was when our Old-Time maps were made. The earth has changed, and those who live on it. There's been no man sailing here since before the Years of Confusion.

Tonight our deck lanterns probe a few yards. From our cabin I hear fog-damp dripping off limp canvas. The animals are all quiet – chickens and sheep and cattle aslumber I suppose, and never a bray from Mr Wilbraham penned aft with his two jennies who are expected to love him if anyone can; even the pigs have apparently knit up the ravell'd squeal of care. Nickie too has gone sweetly to sleep – truly asleep: she can't prevent a quiver of the black eyelashes when she's shamming.[8] She said a few hours ago that she doesn't

---

[7] That was easy – all I had to do was give you a bust in the face.
– Dma. Miranda Nicoletta St Clair-Levison de Moha.

[8] Beast! No respect for Shakespeare. Classifies his wife with the rest of the livestock, no special privileges. Rips the veil from her most intimate deceptions. A beast. I'm going to walk home.
– Nick.

feel oppressed by the fog but has a notion it might conceal something pleas
ant, an island for instance.

I intended when I began this book to tell events in the order they happened. But when I woke this morning in the fogbound hush I fell to brooding
over the different varieties of time. My story belongs in four or five of them.

So does any story, but it seems to be a literary custom that one kind
should dominate, the others being suppressed or taken for granted. I could
do that, and you who may exist might be too cloth-headed or stubborn or
too busy keeping the baby out of the molasses to feel anything missing, but
I'd feel it.

There's the stream of happenings I picked up a little after my fourteenth
birthday. Call that the mainstream if you like; and by the way, I shall have to
make it flow a little faster soon, since I haven't the patience for a book seven
or eight million words long. Besides, while it's possible you exist, if I con-
fronted you with a book like that, you might weasel out of it by claiming you
don't.

There's the story I live (pursued by footnotes) as this ship journeys toward
you – unless the journey's already ended: I saw no hint of a wake when I was
on deck, the sails hang spiritless, a chunk of driftwood lies in polished stillness only a trifle nearer the ship than it was an hour ago ... You could hardly
read that mainstream story without knowing something of this other: whatever I write is colored by living aboard the *Morning Star* – glimpse of a whale
a week ago – the gull who followed us until he discovered with comic sud-
denness that he was the only one of his kind, and wheeled, and sped away
westward – why, I wouldn't have begun this chapter here and now, in this
way, if Nickie had not spoken a casual word or two night before last about the
different kinds of tempest. She wasn't thinking of my book, only loafing with
me in the aftermath of a love-storm, when she had been mirthful and sweetly
savage (one of many aspects) – grabbing the skin of my chest with sharp nails
as she rode astride of me, a spark-eyed devil-angel moaning, writhing, laughing, crying, proud of her love and her sex and her dancing brown breasts, all
muscle and spice and tenderness. Quiet in the afterglow, her dark arm idle
across me, she only said that no storm is like any other, no storm of wind and
rain, or of war, or of the open sea, or of love. This book is part of my life, and
so to me it matters that Nickie's drowsy words started a course of thought
leading to Chapter Five in this place, at this time.

A third sort of time – well, I'm obliged to write some history, for if you
exist you have only guesswork to tell you what's happened to my part of the
world since the period we call the Years of Confusion. I think there must
have been a similar period for you – my guesswork. Your nations were
stricken by the same abortive idiotic nuclear war and probably by the same
plagues. Your culture showed the same symptoms of a possible moral

collapse, the same basic weariness of over-stimulation, the same decline of education and rise of illiteracy, above all the same dithering refusal to let ethics catch up with science. After the plagues, your people may not have turned against the very memory of their civilization in a sort of religious frenzy as ours apparently did, determined like spoiled brats to bring down in the wreckage every bit of good along with the bad. They may not have, but I suspect they did. The best aspects of what some of us now call the 'Golden Age' were clearly incomprehensible to the multitudes who lived then: they demanded of the age of reason that it give them more and more gimmicks or be damned to it. And they kept their religions alive as substitutes for thought, ready and eager to take over the moment reason should perish. I can't suppose you did much better on your side of the world, or you would possess ships that would have made contact with us already.

I keep wondering whether, over there, the spooky religion of Communism may not have slugged it out with its older brother Christianity in the ruins. Whichever won, the human individual would be the loser.

Ever notice that only individuals think? ...

After the collapse, human beings evidently existed for some time in frightened dangerous bands while weeds prepared the way for the return of forest. Those bands were interested in nothing but survival, not always in that – so we're told by John Barth who saw the beginning of the Years of Confusion. He gives them that name in his fragment of a journal, which ends with an unfinished sentence in the year the Old-Time calendar called 1993. The Book of John Barth is of course totally forbidden in the nations we have left behind, possession of it meaning death 'by special order' – that is, directly under supervision of the Church. We must make more copies as soon as we can set up our little press somewhere on land with a chance of renewing the paper supply.

Book-voices of Old Time tell me also of the vastly older ages, the millions of centuries extending back of the short flare which is human history to the beginning of the world. When I speak of even a small interval like a thousand years I can hardly grasp what I mean – but for that matter do I know what I mean by a minute? Yes – that is the part of eternity in which Nickie's heart asleep will beat sixty-five times, give or take a few, unless I touch her, and her pulse hastens perhaps because in sleep she remembers me.

By starting after my fourteenth birthday I made myself responsible for yet another time, the deep-hidden years before then, the age no one quite recalls. Once improperly straying I looked up at the underside of a dark long table, myself surrounded by a forest of black-robed legs and big sandaled feet, by the unwashed smell – and there in a corner shadow a gray spider hung and twitched her web, disturbed by me or by the clash of plates, rumble and twitter of empty talk overhead ...

Nickie is my age, twenty-eight, pregnant for the first time in our years of pleasure with each other. (What is time for a being in the womb who lives in time but can't yet know it?) She told me about it last night, when she was sure. Across the cabin from me, staring into the flame of a candle she held, Nickie said: 'Davy, if it's a mue—?'

Touched with anger, I said: 'We didn't bring the priest-written laws of that country with us.' She watched me, Miranda Nicoletta lately a lady of Nuin, and I afraid – I shouldn't have said 'that country' in the unthinking way I did, for Nickie has a natural remembering love of her homeland, and used to share her cousin Dion's visions for it. But then she smiled and set down the candle and came to me, and we were as near as we ever have been – considering the inveterate loneliness of the human self, that is very near. Love is a region where recognition is possible. Her way of moving when she is drowsy makes me think of the motion of full-grown grass under the fondling of wind, the bending with no brittleness, yielding without defeat, rising back to upright grace and selfhood after the passage of the unconquering air.

Captain Barr always calls her 'Domina' because it sounds natural to him even out here where old formalities hold no force. Back in Nuin after he got his knighthood he could have addressed her as 'Miranda,' or 'Nickie' for that matter, but he was born a freeman and recognition came late – not until Dion was Regent and searching for men of brains and character to replace the hordes of seventh cousins, professional brown-nosers and what not who swarmed into the state jobs under Dion's mentally incompetent uncle Morgan III. A respect for the older nobility is ingrained in Captain Barr, and in this instance it's not extravagant, considering the amount of dignity that Funny-puss can pile on at will. Let's clear up that St Clair-Levison thing, by the way. It merely means her pop's name was St Clair and her mama's Levison, both being of the nobility or, as she is inclined to say, 'nobs with knobs on', a peculiar expression. If Senator Jon Amadeus Lawson Marchette St Clair, Tribune of the Commonwealth and Knight of the Order of the Massasoit, had married a commoner, which I can't imagine Buster doing under any circs, Nickie's last name would be just St Clair.

The deMoha is largely imaginary, like a bridegroom's seventh round. I mean, when I became slightly important in Nuin, Dion felt I should possess a more decorative handle, as a social convenience. After kicking my intellect around the bush and coming up with nothing better than Wilberforce, I asked his help and he suggested deMoha. With which I am stuck. You should have seen how relieved and happy the Lower Classes felt about washing my linen and so on after I got thus labeled but not before: for a top-flight snob, give me a poor man every time. And since according to our notions (but not those of Nuin) Nickie and I are most sincerely married, she calls herself deMoha and you can't stop her. She claims I possess a natural nobility that remains in evidence with my clothes off, a rema'kable thing, and she has me so bewitched and bewattled that I naturally agree.

'Even with a light burning?' s's I.

'Or widout,' s's she. Nuin people can pronounce *th* perfectly well, but often they don't bodda.

Now I suppose you want me to explain why Nuin is called a Commonwealth when it's been governed by a monarchy known as a Presidency, and a Senate with two left feet, for going on two hundred years. I don't know.

I had to hug Nickie awake this morning and tell her about varieties of time. She listened briefly, slid her hand over my mouth, and remarked: 'One moment, my faun, my unusual chowderhead, my peculiar sweet-stuff so named because time is far, far too pressing to employ any such dad-gandered and long-syllabled and so deplorably erotic word as beloved, my singular and highly valued long-horned trouble-shooter, before we discuss anything that difficult we ought to wrestle (and don't worry about the baby) to decide who has to go to the galley and fetch us breakfast in b –' I won. Only woman I ever heard of who's just as wonderful at it in the morning. So eventually she had to go fetch breakfast, and returned to our cabin with Dion trailing.

Not that she needed help in carrying the jerk meat and poor-jo biscuits, but I was pleased to see she'd loaded Dion down with a teapot and a jug of cranberry juice – we have to drink it, by his orders and Captain Barr's. We have other antiscorbutics, salt cabbage for instance and sauerkraut; these we face at midday and suppertime with what courage we can summon. I remained respectfully in bed, Nickie slid back under the blanket with me, so the late Regent of Nuin had no place for his highborn rump except the floor, or my built-in desk seat which was obscured by some of Nickie's clothes – anyhow the seat is too low for Dion's long legs. He said: 'Mis'ble lazy crumbs. I've been fishing since dawn, working-type jo.'

'That's nothing,' I said. 'I've been thinking.'

'Catch anything, either of you?'

'Nay, Miranda – tied down the line and went back to sleep. Besides, Mr Wilbraham was watching and it threw me off. Hate to have a donkey look over my shoulder.'

I came out with it, about varieties of time and story.

'Direct narrative's the main thing,' Dion said.

'Why,' said Nickie, 'the story of the voyage is clearly the best, because I'm in it already. Won't be in the mainstream till he's struggled up to his eighteenth year.'

Dion grunted, in one of his lost, abstracted moods. He is forty-three; our tested and satisfying friendship can bridge the gap of totally different birth and upbringing more easily than the gap of age – how could I ever quite know how the world looks to a man who's been in it fifteen years longer than

I? ... The darkness of his skin was a mark of distinction in Nuin. Morgan I, Morgan the Great who stirred up such a king-size gob of history two hundred years ago, is said to have been dark as a walnut. Nickie's deep tan with a rosy flush. I never met any of the Nuin nobility as blond as I am, though some approach it – the Princess of Hannis was a blazing redhead. If I understood the old books a little better or if more of them had survived the holy burnings, I suppose I could find the characteristics of the varied races of Old Time in modern people – an idle occupation, I'd say ...

'You're both spooking up the wrong tree,' I said, 'because all the different kinds of time are important. My problem is how to go from one to another with that utter perfection of grace which my wife finds so characteristic of me.' Captain Barr's cat, Mam Humphrey, walked in just then, tail up, very pregnant, and looking for a soft place to sleep out the morning; she jumped on our bunk, knowing a good thing. 'Historical time for instance. You must admit there's a case to be made for history in moderation.'

'Oh,' Dion said, 'I suppose it's useful material for stuffing textbooks. Lately we've lived rather more than a bellyful of it.'

Nickie was getting maudlin, kissing Mam Humphrey's black and white head and mumbling something Dion didn't catch about two girls in the same fix. As it happened we didn't tell Dion of the pregnancy till later in the day.

'Still are,' I suggested. 'This voyage is history.'

'And the fog still deep,' Nickie said. 'Oh – when I was getting the grub Jim Loman told me he saw a goldfinch skim by just when it was getting light. Do they migrate?'

'Some.' I was remembering Moha. 'Most stay the winter, anyway September's too early for migration.'

'When the fog is gone,' she said, 'and the sun discovers us, let it be an island with none there but the birds and a few furry harmless things, the goldfinches no one could want to kill, the way they dip and rise, dip and rise – isn't that the rhythm of living by the way? A drop and then a lightness and a soaring? Nay, don't speak a word of my fancy unless you be liking it.'

Dion said: 'It could be the mainland of a nation with no kindness for strangers.'

'Damn that prince,' she said. 'I set free a small thing too large for my own head, whang goes the arrow of his common sense and down comes my bird in flight that was all the time na' but an ambitious chicken.'

'Why, I'm liking that goldfinch as much as thou, Miranda, but I'm a thousand years older, the way I used to be the simulacrum of a ruler, and that means to contend with folly – compromise with it – after a while the heart sickens as thou knowest. Nothing strange about my uncle going mad. A good weak man, I think, gone into hiding, into a shell his mind built for him. What we saw – the fat thing on the floor drooling and masturbating with dolls, that was the shell. I suppose the good weak man died inside it after a while, the shell continuing to exist.'

The thing had to be gelded, before the Church would allow it to go on existing in secret and agree to the polite fiction of 'ill health' to spare the presidential family the disgrace of having produced a brain-mue – which could have caused a dangerous public uproar. The priest who castrated him told Dion that after the first shock, Morgan III seemed to recover a moment of clarity and said plainly: 'Happy the man who can no longer beget rulers!'

'Hiding,' Nickie asked, 'from the follies he feared he might himself commit?'

'Something like that. As for me, I suppose I shall be something to frighten good Nuin children for centuries, as the Christians of Old Time used to rattle the bones of the Emperor Julian miscalled the Apostate.'

'Write Nuin's history thyself,' said Nickie, 'outside of Nuin. How else could it be done anyway? – certainly not in the shadow of the Church.'

'Why,' said Dion, thinking it over – 'why, I might do that ...'

'We've thought we wanted to find mainland,' I said, 'but I can go along with Nick – why not an island? Does the Captain still say we're near what the map calls the Azores?'

'Yes. Of course our calculation of longitude is off – the best clocks already three minutes in disagreement. Made by the Timekeepers' Guild of Old City, best in the known world, and by Old-Time standards what are those crafts-men? Moderately fair beginners, gifted clodhoppers.'

I began clacking then, instructing Dion for a while on the political man-agement of an island colony of intelligent Heretics. I have that fault. In a different world – and if I didn't spend so much time more profitably, making music and tumbling my rose-lipped girl, I think I might have become a respectable teacher of snotnoses.

Later this morning we were busy. Captain Barr ordered out the longboat to try towing the *Morning Star* clear of the fog, and we went on a snailpace for some hours. He quit the attempt when the men were tired, though the lead was still finding no bottom. He was sure he smelled land through the fog-damp, and I smelled it too. That land could rise sheer and sudden out of deep water. Tomorrow, if the fog gives us fifty yards or better of visibility, he may try the towing again.

The stillness troubles us. We listen for breakers or the slap of water against stone.

Nickie sleeps; I am suspended in my own mist of memory and reflection and ignorance. How truly is a man the master of his own course?

The unknown drives us. We could not know we were to lose the war in Nuin. How should I have known I would find and covet the golden horn?

But within my small range of knowledge and understanding, driven by chance but still human, still brainy and passionate and stubborn and no more of a coward than my brothers, it's for me to say where I go.

Let others think for you and you throw away your opportunity of possessing your own life even within that limited range. You're then no longer a man but an ox in human shape, who doesn't understand that he might break the fence if he had the will. Early in our years together Nickie said to me: 'Learn to love me by possessing thine own self, Davy, as I try to learn how to possess my own – I think there's no other way.'

As men and not oxen, I suppose we are men with a candle in the dark. Close in the light with walls of certainty or authority, and it may seem brighter – look, friends, that's a reflection from prison walls, your light is no larger. I'll carry mine through the open night in my own hand.

6

I couldn't stop running with my golden horn till I'd rounded the east side of the mountain, passed the approach to my cave without thinking of it, and was looking down on the Skoar church spires. I collapsed on a log gulping for air.

The skin of my belly hurt. I found a patch of red and a puncture mark. I'd blundered through an orb-spider's web and only now would my body admit the pain. I'd been bitten before and knew what to expect. Hot needles were doing a jerky jig over my middle; my head ached, I'd soon have a fever, and then by tomorrow it wouldn't bother me much. I was enough of a child and a savage to marvel at God's letting me off so lightly.

I unwrapped the horn and raised it to my lips. How naturally it rested against me, my right hand at the valves! I imagined the ancient makers putting a guiding magic in it. They simply took thought for the shape of human body and arm, like a knife-maker providing for the human hand. Partly by accident, I must have firmed my lips and cheeks in almost the right way. It spoke for me. I thought of sunlight transformed to sound.

I returned it to the sack, scared. Not of the mue three miles away with the mountain between us, but of his demon father. Fevered already, I said aloud: 'Well, fuck him, he don't exist no-way.' Know what? – nothing happened.

Maybe that was the moment I began to understand what most grown people never learn, and did not even in the Golden Age, namely that words are not magic.

I said (silently this time) that it didn't matter. The horn was *mine*. I'd never see the mue again. I'd run away to Levannon, yes, but not by way of North Mountain.

The spider-bite set me vomiting, and I recalled some wiseacre saying the best treatment for orb-spider's bite was a plaster of mud and boy's urine. Loosening my loin-rag, I muttered: 'A'n't no use account I a'n't a bejasus boy no more.' And laughed some, and piddled on bare earth to make the plaster anyhow. I'm sure it was as good as anything the medicine priests do for the faithful – didn't kill me and made the pain no worse. I went on downhill to the edge of the forest near the stockade, to wait for dark and the change of guards.

A wide avenue, Stockade Street, ran all around the city just inside the palings; after the change the new guard would march a hundred paces down that street, and I would hear him go. That spring they were more alert than usual because of a rising buzz of war talk between Moha and Katskil; border towns take a beating in those affairs. At the end of his section he'd meet the next guard and bat the breeze if the corporal or sergeant wasn't around, and that would leave my favorite spot unwatched. Later on the guards would take longer breaks in safe corners, smoking tobacco or marawan and trading stiffeners,[9] but the first break would suit my needs. Meanwhile I had an hour to wait and spent it unwisely thinking too much about the mue, which made me wonder what sort of creature I was.

I knew of brain-mues, the most dreaded of all, who have a natural human form so that no one can guess their nature till their actions reveal it. Sooner or later they behave in a way folk call the mue-frenzy, or insanity. They may bark, fume, rush about like beasts, see what others do not, lapse (like Morgan III) into the behavior of an idiot child, or sit speechless and motionless for days on end. Or they may with the most reasonable manner speak and obviously believe outrageous nonsense, usually suspecting others of wickedness or conspiracy or supposing themselves to be famous important people – even Abraham, or God himself. When brain-mues reveal themselves this way they are given over to the priests for disposal, like people who develop mysterious discolorations or lumps under the skin, since these are also considered to be the working-out of a mue-evil.

An Old-Time book we have on board describes 'insane' people very differently, as sick people who may be treated and sometimes healed. This book uses the word 'psychopathic' and mentions 'insanity' or 'craziness' as unsuitable popular terms. Ayah, and nowadays if you call a jo 'crazy' you only mean

[9] Moha idiom. Davy means the type of anecdote known in Nuin as a 'tickler' or, for some undecipherable reason, 'smut.'

– Dion M. M.

he's odd, weird, full of mahooha, a long-john-in-summer, a quackpot. Our Old-Time book speaks of these people with no horror but with a kind of compassion that in the modern spook-ridden world human beings seldom show except to those who very closely resemble themselves.

Well, hunkered in the thicket outside the palisade, I knew nothing of books except as a dusty bewilderment of my schooltime, now past. I thought, with none to console me: Do brain-mues act as I've done? *No!* I said. But the idea lurked in shadow, a black wolf waiting.

Behind the palings a man with a fair tenor and a mandolin was singing 'Swallow in the Chimbley,' approaching down a side-street. Skoar folk had been humming that ever since a Rambler gang introduced it a few years before. It made me think of Emmia, less about my troubles.

> *Swallow in the chimbley,*
> *Oop hi derry O!*
> *Swallow in the chimbley,*
> *Sally on my knee.*
> *Swallow flying high,*
> *Sally, don't you cry!*
> *Tumble up and tumble down and lie with me.*

The evening was hot, heavy with the smell of wild hyacinth, so still I could hear that man hawk and spit after goofing the high note the way you expect a tenor to do if he's got more sass than education. I liked that.

You can't live thinking you're a brain-mue.

> *Swallow in the chimbley,*
> *Oop hi derry O!*
> *Swallow in the chimbley,*
> *Sally jump free—*
> *Left her smock behind,*
> *Sally, don't you mind!*
> *Tumble up and tumble down and lie with me.*

The singer was evidently the stockade guard's relief, for now I heard the ceremony of the change of guards. First the old guard hollered at the new to quit making like a Goddamn likkered-up tomcat and get the lead out of his butt. After that, the solemn clash of gear, and a brisk discussion of music, the rightness of the town clock, what the corporal would say, where the corporal could shove it, and a suggestion that the musical new guard do something in the way of sexual self-ministration which I don't think is possible, to which the singer replied that he couldn't account he was built like a bugle. I sneaked over to the base of the stockade, waiting out the ceremony. At last the new guard stomped off down the street on his first round – without his mandolin since he had to carry a javelin.

> *Swallow in the chimbley,*
> *Oop hi derry O!*
> *Swallow in the chimbley,*
> *Sally cry 'Eee!'*
> *Catch her by the tail,*
> *Happy little quail!*
> *Tumble up and tumble down and lie with me.*

The spider-bite hampered me climbing the stockade, but I made it, the burden in my sack unharmed. I sneaked down Kurin Street to the Bull-and-Iron. Emmia's window was lit, though it wasn't yet her bedtime. When I reached the stable, damned if she wasn't there doing my work for me. She had finished watering the mules, and turned with a finger at her lips. 'They think I'm in my room. Said I seen you at work and they took my word for it. I swear, Davy, this is the last time I cover up for you. Shame on you!'

'You didn't have to, Miss Emmia. I—'

'"Didn't have to" – and me trying to save your backside a tanning! Moving away, Mister Independent?'

I squirmed my sack to the floor; my shirt sprung open and she saw the smeary bite. 'Davy darling, whatever?' And here she comes in a warm rush, no more mad at all. 'Oh dear, you got a fever too!'

'Orb-spider.'

'Dumb crazy love, going off where them awful things be, if you was small enough to turn over my lap I'd give you a fever where you'd remember it.' She went on so, sugary scolding that means only kindness and female bossiness.

When she stopped for breath I said: 'I didn't goof off, Miss Emmia – thought it was my free day.' Her soft hands fussing at my shirt and the bitten place were rousing me up so that I wondered if my loin-rag would hide the evidence.

'Now shed up, Davy, you didn't think never no such of a thing, the way you lie to me and everybody it's a caution to the saints, but I won't tell, I said I'd covered for you, only more fool me if I ever do it again, and you're lucky it's a Friday so you wasn't missed, and anyway –' There was this about Emmia: if you wished to say anything yourself you had to wait for the breath-pauses and work fast against the gentle stream that couldn't stop because it must get to the bottom of the hill and there was always more coming. 'Now you go right straight up to your bed and I'll bring you a mint-leaf poultice for that 'ere because Ma says it's the best thing in the world for any kind of bite, bug-bite I mean, a snake is different of course, for that you've got to have a jolt of likker and a beezer-stone[10] but anyway – oh, poo, what did you put on it?' But she didn't wait to hear. 'You take your lantern now, I won't need it, and straight up to bed with you, don't stand there fossicking around.'

'Kay,' I said, and tried to hoist my sack without her noticing it, but she could talky-talk and still be sharp.

'Merciful winds, what have you got there?'

'Nothing.'

'Nothin' he says and it pushing out the sack big as a house – Davy, listen, if you've latched onto something you shouldn't I can't cover *that* for you, it's a sin—'

'It's nothing!' I yelled that. 'You gotta know everything, Miss Emmia, it's a chunk of wood I found so to carve you something for your name-day, 'f you gotta know ever' durn thing, if you gotta.'

'O Davy, little Spice!' She grabbed me again, her face one big rose. I barely swung the sack out of the line of operations before I got kissed.

No one had kissed me since Caron. True, 'little Spice' doesn't mean the same as just 'Spice.' But Emmia was keeping hold of me, her fragrant heat pressing – lordy, I hadn't even known a girl's nipples could grow firm enough to be felt through the clothes! But something was wrong with me; I was growing limp and scared, stomach fluttering, the spiderbite jumping. 'Aw Davy, and I was scolding you so, and you sick with a bite you got account you was doing something for me – O Davy, I feel awful.'

I dropped the sack and tightened my arms, learning her elastic softness. Her eyes opened wide in astonishment as if no such thought had ever touched her so far as I was concerned, and maybe it hadn't till she felt my hands growing a little courageous at her waist and hips.[11] 'Why, Davy!' My hands relaxed too soon and she collected her wits. 'You go up to bed now like I said, and I'll bring the poultice soon as I can sneak back out here.'

I toiled up to the loft, the memory of her flesh printed on mine, reached my pallet without dropping the lantern, and hid my sack in the hay. I flung off my loin-rag but kept my shirt on because of a fever-chill. Under the

---

[10] Any odd-shaped stone supposed to have medicinal powers, more often called vitamin-stone. I made quite a few for sale when I was with Rumley's Ramblers; rubbing with wet sand gives them a nice weathered look. My own footnote, by damn!

– D.

[11] I dunno, Davy. I may form a Sisterly Protective Order of Phemale Women, myself president as well as founder if the salary is right, for the constitutional purpose of taking you out somewhere and drowning you. After the historical event we'd hold commemorative meetings, and drink tea.

– Miranda Nicoletta.

blanket limp and shivering, I watched fantastic nothings ebb and flow in the darkness around the rafters of the loft, so far above my puddle of lantern-light. I smelled the lantern's rancid seal-oil, the dry hay, the sweat and manure of horses and mules below. I wished I dared show the golden horn to someone and tell my story. Who but Emmia? At that time she was my one friend.

The bond-servant caste is a sorry thing in Moha, squeezed from above and below. Slaves hated us for being slightly better off, the lifers not so sharply as the short-term slaves, who probably felt they weren't too different from us, a mere matter of conviction for minor crime instead of our accident of birth or bad fortune. Freemen despised us for the sake of looking down on someone – no real satisfaction in looking down on a slave. Emmia could have got into bad trouble by showing affection for me when any third person was present; I never expected her to, and that she should do so when we were alone was still a puzzle to me that night, in spite of all the lush daydreams I was in the habit of building on the fact – it just hadn't occurred to me yet (outside of daydreams) that there was anything about me a woman would actually love.

I must have heard the whole run of popular sayings: 'All bond-servants steal a little' – 'Give a b.s. an inch and he'll take a yard' – 'A bond-wench may be a good lay but remember your whip!' All the old crud-talk that people seem to need to shore up their vanity and avoid the risk of looking honestly at themselves. In the same way, people said: 'All slaves stink.' They never asked: Who lets them have a basin to wash in or time to use it?

And in Moha you heard that no Katskil man should be trusted alone even with a sow. Conicut people tell you every other man in Lomeda is a fairy and the rest back-scuttlers. In Nuin I have heard: 'It takes three Penn tradesmen to cheat a Levannon man, two Levannese to cheat a Vairmanter, and two Vairmanters have no trouble cheating the Devil.' And so on and on, every-thing your neighbor's fault until some time maybe a million years from now when the human race runs out of dirt.

At school I heard the teacher-priests explain how race prejudice was one of the sins that persuaded God to destroy the world of Old Time and make men pass through the Years of Confusion so there would be only one race with traces of all the old ones in it, and my opinion of God went up several notches. Inside, though, a somehow older boy who wasn't quite ready to show his head went on muttering that it was too nice and simple: if God was going to take that much trouble why couldn't he make modern people decent and kind in other ways?

Today I know it's a mere historical accident that has made us all fairly close to the same physical pattern in that part of the world. We are the descendants of a small handful of survivors, and they happened to include most of the races of Old Time. Anyone who deviates too far is still treated outrageously, if he escapes early destruction as a mue. In Conicut, with Rumley's Ramblers, I would have been uneasy about my red hair, if it hadn't been a strong gang that took care of its own.

Freeman boys, many from poor families living no better than I did, ran in street-gangs and wanted no part of a b.s., unless they could catch one alone, for fun. I could have made friends with a freeman boy, meeting him by himself, but the herd pattern is death on friendship. If the pack must come first – its rituals, cruelties, group make-believes and sham brotherhood – you have no time left for the individual spirit of another; no time, no courage, no recognition.

Against the danger of the street-gangs I had my Katskil knife, but I was so sharp at nipping out of sight whenever I saw more than three boys in a group that I'd never been obliged to use the steel in self-defense. Good thing too, for getting hanged would have interfered seriously with writing this book, and even if you don't exist I'd hate to see you suffer a deprivation like that.[12] But even in fever common sense told me I could not show Emmia my golden horn and tell the story. She would never understand why I hadn't killed the mue. She would be demoralized by the mere thought of a mue existing near the city. Like most women she could scarcely bear the sound of the word 'mue' – she'd sooner have had a rat run up her leg.

Then for a while I think the fever sent my wits wandering out of the world.

While I wrote this morning the fog dissolved. Nickie called me on deck an hour ago – her face was wet – and pointed to the blur of green two or three miles southeast. As I was watching, a white bird circled down to the island. No smoke rises from it; the day is a quiet of blue and gold.

I'll make only this note of it for the present. We have a light westerly, and Captain Barr intends to circumnavigate, tacking as near the island as he safely can. We shall watch for harbors, stream outlets, reefs, beaches, any sign of habitation. Major note: Miranda Nicoletta is happy.

I was pulled awake by feeling another blanket being spread over me. Wool-soft it was and sweet with the girl-scent of Emmia – I mean her own, not the boughten perfume she sometimes used. She must have brought it from her own bed, and I a damned yard-boy not brave enough to kill a mue but low enough to steal from him.

[12] Notice he never pauses to consider how it feels to be married to an Irish bull. However, courage! Am *I* cowed by such a brute? Why, yes, now I think of it.

– Nickie.

Emmia was talking, of what I don't know; in the middle of the pleasant sound I spoke her name. She said: 'Hush, Davy! How you do run on! Be the good jo and let me put on this poultice – don't squirm so!' Her voice was as kind as her hands that eased down the blankets and pressed a minty-smelling pad where my skin still hurt some. The pain was no longer serious; I was pretending to be worse off than I was, to prolong her soft attentions. 'What was you yattering about just now, Davy? Where the sun rises, you said, only it's night, you know it is, so maybe you was fevery the way I heard about a man had the smallpox and he thought he was tumbling off a hoss, so whoa he says, whoa, and falls out of bed for real and dead as anything the next day, the chill you know, come to think, that was Morton Sampson that married a connection of Ma's and used to live on Cayuga Street catacorny from the old schoolhouse ...' I wondered if I could have spoken in my fever about the golden horn. She was coaxing my arms under the blanket. 'Yes, you went running on, about traveling, merciful winds, I guess you must like to talk, I couldn't scarcely get a word in by the thin edge – oh, feel that sweat! Your fever's busted, Davy, and that's what they call a good sweat, you be all right now, only keep warm, boy, and you better get to sleep too.'

I said: 'If a man went far—'

'Ayah, that's just the way you was running on, only now you should get to sleep because like Ma says if a person don't get enough sleep the next day is mint, see?' Resting a hand on the blanket, she was watching me not quite so directly. Her conversational brook went on, but I think already we had some of the special awkwardness a man and woman feel when each knows the other is thinking of the intercourse not yet shared. 'I do marvel – where the sun rises, think of having such fancies when you be fevered, still it must be nice to travel, I always wished I could, like that friend of Pa's, I can't think of his name, anyway he went all the way to Humber Town – oh, who *was* it? – Peckham – I'll think of it in a minute, it wasn't Peckham no-way – why, Hamlet Parsons was who it was, remember? – Ham Parsons of course with the one gone eye account of an ax handle in the one I mean, all the way to Humber Town and come to think, that was just two summers ago because it was the same year we lost old White-Stocking from the bloat – what a nice old thing he was ...'

It was restful, sleepy-making, like a brook, like a tree murmuring the wind, only bless her, Emmia wasn't built like a tree and her bark wasn't scratchy, not anywhere. In my half-sick drowsiness I wondered why I should feel afraid of Emmia when she was being so kind to me, bringing that blanket, sitting now so close that my right arm was cramped because it didn't dare sprawl across her lap. I suppose I knew myself to be two or more people, that common trouble. The Davy who wanted to be a gentle, loving (and safely blameless) friend that's the only one who was afraid. The healthy jo who needed to grab her and lock her loins till he could spend himself was not afraid of Emmia but only, in a practical way, of the world: he didn't want to be slammed into the pillory. What never occurred to me until years later was that all these inconsistent and troubling selves are real as soon as your mind has gone through the pain of giving them birth.

7

'Be you warm enough now?' I made some kind of noise. 'You know, Davy, them fancies you get in a fever a'n't real dreams like, I mean not like the ones that tell your fortune if you go to sleep with a corncob under the pillow. You sure you be warm enough?'

'I wish you was always with me.'

'What?'

'Wish you was with me. In my bed.'

She didn't slap my face. I couldn't look at hers, but of a sudden she was lying on the pallet warm and close, her breath fluttering my hair. The blankets bunched thick between us. She was on my right arm so it couldn't slip around her. She held my left hand away. I had at least three times her strength and couldn't dream of using any of it. 'Davy dear, mustn't – I mean we better not, only –' I kissed her to stop the talk. 'You're being bad now, Davy.' I kissed her ear and the silken hollow of her shoulder. I hadn't known it, but that was blowing on a fire. Her thigh slid over me and she was trembling, pushing against me through the blankets and presently whimpering: 'It's a sin – Mother of Abraham, don't let me be so bad!' She thrust herself free and rolled away. I thought she would get up and leave me, but instead she lay on the bare floor rumpled and careless, her knees drawn up, her skirt fallen, hands pressed at her face.

For just that moment, her eyes not watching me, her secret place uncovered wanton and helpless for me, I was all man responding and could have taken her, never mind whether she was crying. Then my mind went idiot and yelped: If Mam Robson comes looking for her, or Old Jon? I heard her fainting voice. 'Why'n't you do it to me?'

I flung the blankets away. The final cold killing thought arrived, not in words but a picture: a wooden frame on a tall column; holes in the frame for the offending bond-servant's neck, wrists and ankles; a clear space on the earth so that rocks and garbage could be readily cleared away after the thing in the pillory had become a mere lesson in morality too motionless to be entertaining.

Emmia's suffering face was turned to me. She knew I had been ready for her and now was not. She embraced me clumsily, trying to restore me with shaking ineffectual fingers. Maybe that was when she too remembered the law, for she suddenly dragged the blankets over me and stumbled away. I thought: It's all up with me – can I run?

But she was returning. Her wet face was not angry. She sat by me again, not too near, her smock tucked in at her knees. She groped for a handkerchief, found none, mopped her face on the blanket. 'I wouldn't hurt you, Miss Emmia.'

She stared dumbfounded, then laughed breathlessly. '*Oh* you poor sweet cloth-head! It's my fault, and now I suppose you think I'm one of these girls'll do it for anybody, not a mor'l to their name, honest I'm not like that, Davy, and when it's just you and me and us such good friends you don't have to call me *Miss* Emmia heavensake! Aw Davy, things sort of go to my head, I can't explain, you wouldn't know—'

At least she was talking again. My panic faded. The brook ran on, growing more restful by the minute.

Speaking of brooks—

I stopped writing a week ago, and resumed it this afternoon within sound of a tropic brook. The day has been filled with tasks of settlement on our island. We mean to stay at least until those now in the womb are born, maybe longer. Maybe some will stay and others go on – I can't imagine Captain Barr letting the schooner ride too long at anchor … The brook runs by a shelter Nickie and I are sharing with Dion and three others while we work at more permanent buildings for the colony.

The island is small, roughly oval, its greatest length along the north-south axis, about ten miles. It must be within the region where the old map gives us a few dots named the Azores. We sailed around it that first day, then seeing no other land on the horizon we inched into the one harbor, a bay on the eastern shore. We anchored in five fathoms near a clean strand where a band of gray monkeys were picking over shells and finding something to eat – hermit crabs. We waited that day and night on board to learn of the tides – they are moderate – and watch for signs of human or other dangerous life.

No one slept much that night at the anchorage – a deep warm night, rest from the long strain and fears of voyaging, a full moon for lovers – high time for a night of music and drink and cheerful riot. There are forty of us – sixteen women, twenty-four men – and nearly all of us are young. We came ashore in the morning not too hung over, all eager except Mr Wilbraham who never is.

The only wild things we've seen are the monkeys, a few goats, short-eared rabbits, a host of birds. On a walk around the island yesterday Jim Loman and I found tracks of pig, fox and wildcat, and we saw flying squirrels much like the gentle things I used to glimpse in the Moha woods. It must be that human beings haven't lived here since Old Time. We may find ruins in the interior.

On a knoll near the beach we've cleared away vegetation to make room for houses. The brook flowing by the base of the knoll originates a mile inland from the island's highest hill, about a thousand feet above sea level, we guess. Along the brook a tough reed-like grass grows in abundance; it might be good for paper-making as well as thatch. Our houses will be lightly constructed – thatched roofs on tall supports, the thatched walls coming only halfway to the line of the eaves, the kind of airy buildings I saw in Penn when I went there with Rumley's Ramblers in 320. They keep a kind of freshness even on the hottest day, and if hurricane comes – well, you haven't lost too much; you build again.

We wonder of course what snake is in this Eden.

Speaking of brooks—

Look, said Emmia's personal brook, what we almost did was a terrible sin because I was a Mere Boy and an awful sin anyhow, only we hadn't done anything so there *wasn't* any sin and all her fault too, but she'd just take it to God in prayer without having to confess it, and never would tell on me, wild horses wouldn't drag one word out of her, because mostly I was a good dear boy that couldn't help being born without no advantages, except for wildness and goofing off and like that, but when I corrected that I'd be a good man who everybody'd respect, see, only I must prove myself and remember that like her Ma said life wasn't all beer and skittles whatever skittles were, she'd always thought it was a funny word, well, life was hard work and responsibility and minding what wiser folk said, not only the priests but everybody who lived respectable because there was a right way and a wrong way just like her Ma said, and you must *not* be all the time goofing off the way other people had to cover up and so on because they kind of loved you and feed the plague-take-it old *mules*. I said I was sorry.

Well then, I did ought to feel just a *smidgin* of repentance about tonight, not because it was my fault, it wasn't, it wasn't, except maybe I shouldn't ought to've kissed her just *that* way, because boys ought to be kind of careful and try to stay pure and like reverent by not thinking too much about you-know-what, anyhow after my apprentice time I'd prob'ly marry some nice woman and everything would be nice, and by the way I mustn't feel bad about it not you-know standing up like, because she happened to know for a fact the same thing happened to lots of boys if they was just scared or not used to things, see, it didn't necessarily mean they had some enemy doing nasty things with a wax image, although of course if I was a full-growed man it could be that and you had to be careful, anyhow it was all her fault like she'd said before. I said I was sorry.

She said she knew I was and it did me credit, and nobody would ever know, and as for the laws, why, they'd ought to take them mis'ble laws out and drown them, because bond-servant or no I was as good as anybody and she'd say it again, as good as *anybody*, more b' token she wouldn't let anyone hurt one hair of my head, ever, only what she meant about proving myself, well, see, I ought to go and do something difficult, she didn't mean anything wild or goofy, just something hard and well, like noble or something, so as to – so as to—

'Miss Emmia, I mean Emmia, I will, I mean it, cross my heart I will, like what frinstance?'

'Oh, you should choose it yourself, something you don't want to do but know you should, like going to church regular, only it don't have to be that, you ought to want to do that anyway. No, just something good and honest and difficult, the way I'll be proud of you, I'll be your inspiration like – no, you mustn't kiss me again, not ever until you be freeman, mind now I mean it.'

She stood up away from me, smoothing her skirt, her eyes downcast, maybe crying again a little, but in the weak lantern-light I couldn't be sure. 'I'll try, Emmia.'

'I mean I want us to be good, Davy, like – like respectable people, nice people that get ahead and get asked to go places and stuff. That's what they mean, see, by fearing God and living in Abraham and like that, I mean there's a right way and a wrong way, I mean I – well, I a'n't always been too good, Davy, you wouldn't know.' She was at the trap-door, setting down the lantern. She blew it out to leave for me at the head of the ladder. 'You go to sleep now, Davy – little Spice.' She was gone.

I could have run after her then, ready as ever I would be, no more sense than a jack-in-the-box, and no less. But I only went to the window, and saw her vague shape crossing the stable yard, and crawled back under the blankets into a dream-tormented sleep.

I was running – rather, a mush-footed staggering on legs too heavy and too short – through a house dimly like the Bull-and-Iron. It possessed a thousand rooms, each containing something with a hint of memory: a three-legged stool the orphanage kids sat on when they were naughty; a ring Sister Carnation wore; a cloth doll; my luck-charm upright in one of the crimson slippers Caron wore when she first came to the orphanage (they'd been swiftly taken away from her as a sinful vanity). In that house black wolf followed me, in no hurry – he could wait. His throat-noises resembled words:

'Look at me! Look at me!' If I did, even once, he would have me. I went on each room windowless, no sunrise place. The doors would not latch behind me. When I leaned against one, black wolf slobbered at the crack, and I said over my shoulder: 'I'll give Caron my Katskil knife and she will do you something good and difficult.' He shut up then, but I must still find Caron or my threat was empty, and it may be she went on ahead with one brown foot bare and my candle upright in the other crimson slipper, but I don't know, for I tripped and went down, knowing black wolf was about to snuff at my neck, then knowing I was awake on my pallet in the stable loft, but for a while I wasn't certain I was alone.

I was alone. I smelled the dry hay, and Emmia's scent – merely from her blanket. Late moonlight showed me the loft window. The spider-bite was a harmless itch and soreness. I found my sack and felt of the golden horn. It was not mine.

I knew what that action must be, good and honest and difficult. My horn must go back to an ugly creature who could make no use of it. Was that good? Well, it was difficult and honest. I could never tell of it to Emmia – unless maybe I dressed up the story – changed the mue to a hermit perhaps? Nay, when had I ever told the girl anything but the simplest everyday matters? Why, in my daydreams. Then, sure, she never failed to respond wonderfully.

I would run away, scorned, abused, in danger of my life because Emmia had reported me to the authorities for not killing the mue. Then, let's see – would I fall prey to the policer dogs? Facing them, I would say – nope. Well, climb a tree, talk from there? Balls.

However, some far-off day I might revisit Skoar, a scarred and sad-faced man disinclined to mention heroic action in the far-off wars of – Nuin? Conicut? Why wouldn't I captain an expedition that did away with the Cod Islands pirates? So in gratitude a friendly nation made me Governor of them balmy isles—

Kay, in those days how was I to know the Cods are a few lumps scattered through the waters off Nuin as if someone had flung gobs of wet sand out of a bucket?

Emmia, having sorrowfully blamed herself all these years, might recognize me, but alas—

A rat lolloping across an overhead beam scared the bejasus out of me. I slung on my clothes, and felt for the lump of my luck-charm in the sack. I must find another cord and wear it again the right way. I would cut a length of fishline for it when I got to my cave. I tried not to think of the horn. My moccasins went into the sack on top of it, and I settled my knife-belt.

Emmia's blanket mustn't be found here by somebody who'd say it proved we spent the night together under it. I crammed it on top of the moccasins and went down the ladder. Going away for real, I thought.

But Emmia mustn't be harmed, as she might be if the blanket merely turned up missing. All permanent property of the Bull-and-Iron seemed to be attached to Mam Robson by a God-damn mystic cord. Food in moderation you could steal, but let a blanket or candlestick or suchlike walk with Abraham, and something wounded the Mam deep in her soul; she couldn't rest till she'd searched out the cause of the pain, all the better if she could drive Old Jon into a twittering frenzy while she did it.

I stood under Emmia's window studying the big jinny-creeper. The ancient stem was sturdy and should hold me. Old Jon and the Mam slept on the other side of the building. The rooms nearest Emmia's were for guests; below was a storeroom. Only a reckless randy-john would climb up there. I climbed.

The vine gripped the bricks with ten thousand toes, bent and whispered but did not break. I clung with an arm over the sill. I'd carried the blanket up in my teeth and left my sack in deep shadow. I dropped the blanket inside the room that was rich with Emmia's fragrance. I heard a small puppy-moan that must mean sleep, maybe the nudging of a dream. She might wake, see my shadow and scream the house down. This was the shape my fear took that time. I was on the ground and jittering away down Kurin Street before I could stop trembling.

Sick-angry too because I had not gone to her bed, but I could dream up plentiful reasons for not going back *now*. They drove me on – over the stockade, up the mountain. But I would return, I told myself, after I restored the horn. I'd try to please her. Hell, I'd even go to church if there was no way to weasel out of it. And (said another self) I would get it in.

Dion has offered the colonists a name for the island – Neonarcheos. I think I like it. It is from Greek, a language already ancient and unspoken in the Golden Age. Dion is one of the few among the Heretics who studied that, and Latin. (The Church forbids to the public anything at all in a language not English – it could be sorcery.) He introduced me to the Greek and Latin authors in translation; I note that they also looked backward toward a Golden Age preceding what they called the Age of Iron ...

Dion's name for this place says something I wanted said – new-old. It connects us somehow with the age when this island – and the others that must lie close over the horizon, all of different shape and smaller than they were before the ocean rose – was a Portuguese possession, whatever that may have meant to it; yes, and with a time far more remote, when civilization capable of recording itself was a new thing on earth, and this island was a speck of green in the blue inhabited, as when we found it, only by the birds and other shy things who live their entire lifetimes without either wisdom or malice.

*

When I climbed North Mountain again to return the horn I did not see true
sunrise, for by the time it arrived I was in that big-tree region where the day
before I might so easily have killed my monster. I was not hurrying; reluctance made me feel as though the air itself had thickened to a barrier. I did
not feel much afraid of the mue, though when I entered the tangle where his
grapevine pathways ran I was looking upward too much, until certain timor-
ous fancies were flooded out of me by a wrong smell – wolf smell.

I drew my knife, exasperated – must I be halted, distracted by a danger not
connected with my errand? The scent was coming from dead ahead, where
I had to go in order not to lose the marks of my passage of the day before. I
was not far from the tulip tree. Knife ready, I made no effort to be quiet – if
the wolf was lurking anywhere within a hundred yards he knew exactly
where I was.

You can't look quite straight at black wolf even from the rail above the
baiting-pit. Something about him pushes your gaze off true. I spoke of that
once to Dion, who remarked that maybe we glimpse a fraction of our selves
in him. My dear friend Sam Loomis, a gentle heart if ever there was one, used
to claim he was sired by an irritated black wolf onto the cunt of a hurricane;
in such nonsense talk he may have been saying something not entirely
nonsense.

When a man hears black wolf's cold long cry in the dark, his heart does
strain at its human boundaries. You, I, anyone. You know you won't go out
there to hunt with him, quarrel with him over the bleeding meat, run down
the glades of midnight with him and his diamond-eyed female, be a thing
like him. But we are deep enough to contain the desire; it does not altogether
sleep. All nights are resonant with the unspoken. Latent in our brains, our
muscles, our sex, are all the harsh lusts that ever blazed. We are lightning and
the avalanche, fire and the crushing storm.

That morning I found my black wolf quickly. She was below the grapevine
that hung down outside the catbriers, and she was dead. An old bitch wolf –
my knife prodded the huge scrawny carcass, six feet long from her snout to
the base of her mangy tail. Scarred, foul, hair once black gone rusty with
festered spots. When alive, for all her decay she could still have hamstrung a
wild boar. But her neck was broken.

Lifting, poking with my knife – I could not have touched her with my
hand and not puked – I proved to myself that her neck was broken. Doubt it
if you like – you never saw my North Mountain mue and his arms. Her
body was already losing stiffness, and a line of the midget yellow carrion ants
had laid out their mysterious highway to her, so she must have been dead for
several hours. The cover was too dense to admit the wings of crows or vultures, and it is said the small scavenger dogs of the wilderness will not touch
black wolf's body. I rubbed away a bit of the ants' path and watched stupidly

as they fiddled about restoring it. The dry blood on the rocks, the ground, the grape-stem, was not from the dead wolf, who had no wound but a broken neck.

I read the signs. She had ambushed the mue when he was near the vine. Bushes were flattened and torn; a heavy boulder had been jerked out of its earth-pocket. It would have happened the day before, perhaps when he came back from the pool. He could have been careless from distress, wondering why he had not changed to man-beautiful.

Or he might have lifted the rose-colored rock to find his treasure gone, and come storming out ready to attack the first thing that moved.

Either way, I was guilty.

Her mouth was agape, the teeth dry. I noticed one of the great stabbers in the lower jaw had broken off long before, leaving a blackened stump in a pus-pocket that must have caused her agony. I believe it had never occurred to me before that a black wolf like any other sentient thing could suffer. The other long tooth of the lower jaw was brown with dry blood.

I climbed the tulip tree. There were blood-smears all the way. I did not think the mue could have lost so much and still be living, but I called to him: 'I've come back. I'm bringing it back to you. I took it but I'm bringing it back.' I mounted a thick branch above his nest and compelled myself to look down. The yellow ants must have formed their column on the opposite side of the trunk, or surely I would have seen them sooner.

He was human. Knowing that, I was wondering for a while how much of my schooling had been lies on top of lies.

I alone remember him. You may remember what I've written, a book-thing for leisure talk. But as I write this now I am the only one who even knows of him except Nickie and Dion, for I've never told any others, except one person who is dead, how it was that I won my golden horn.

8

I returned to my cliffside cave, and the day passed over me. Right or wrong, for good or evil, the golden horn was mine.

I recall a half-hour blazing with the knowledge that I, myself, redhead Davy, was *alive*. I had to throw off my clothes, pinch, slap, stare at every astonishing part of my hundred and fifteen pounds of sensitive beef. I slapped my palm on a sun-hot rock for the mere joy of being able to. I rolled on the grass, I ran up the ledge into the woods so that I might make love to a tree trunk and cry a little. I flung a stone high, and laughed to hear it tumble far in the leaves.

I would not be going to Levannon on a spirited roan, with three attendants, and serving-maids spreading their knees for me at every inn. But I would go.

With my horn, I dared that day to learn a little. Humility came later: when I play nowadays I know I can only touch the fringes of an Old-Time art beside which the best music of our day is the chirping of sparrows. But before my lips grew sore that first day I did learn by trial and error how to find a melody I'd known since I was a child. I think 'Londonderry Air' was the first music I knew, sung to me by dear fat Sister Carnation. Curiosity drove me on past ordinary fatigue. I found the notes; my ear told me I was playing them true.

Thanks to the great dictionary, I know that my horn is what was known in Old Time as a 'French horn.' The valve mechanism can be kept in repair by modern workmen – I had a little work done on it at Old City; the horn itself we could never duplicate in this age. I have been playing it now for about fourteen years, and I sometimes wonder if a horn-player of Old Time would consider me a promising beginner.

When I quit my studies that day in the woods, the afternoon was nearly spent. I made a belated meal from the leftover bacon and half-loaf of oat bread. Then I scooped a pocket in the earth rather far from my cave, and buried the sack there with my horn wrapped in the gray moss. Only memory marked the spot, for I knew I would be returning very soon. I was going away from Skoar; that, I felt now, was certain as sunrise. But this one night I must return to the city.

I had cut a length of fishline for my luck-charm, but found the cord unpleasantly rough at my neck, so again I put the charm in the sack, along with the horn. And forgot I had done so – you might remember that. Later, when it was important to me, to save me I couldn't recollect if I had put the charm in the sack or continued to wear it a while longer in spite of the chafing. If you exist, your memory has probably goofed you the same way. If you don't exist, why don't you give me a breakdown on that too?

Everything looked simpler to me that evening, when I had buried my horn. I was not daydreaming nor building my fortunes on a chip of the moon. I just wanted Emmia.

I hid again in the brush near the stockade, and after I heard the change of guards – they were late – I crept close to the palings and continued to wait, for I was sure I hadn't heard the new guard march down the street in the usual way. And I must have been more exhausted than I knew, for I fell stupidly asleep.

I'd never done it before in such a dangerous spot, and haven't since. But I did then. When I came to myself it was night, with a pallor of early moon-light in the east.

Now I had no way of guessing about the guard until I heard him, and waited another dreary while. A pig wandered along the avenue inside the stockade, passing private remarks to his gut about the low quality of the street garbage. Nobody shied a rock at him, as a guard would almost certainly have done to keep off dull times. Sick of waiting, I took a chance and climbed.

The guard let me scramble over and down on the city side. Then I heard his quick step behind me and a bang on the head toppled me. As I rolled over his expensive cowhide boot was churning my belly, 'Where you from, bond-servant?' My gray loin-rag told him that about me – we were required to wear them, as slaves wear black ones and freemen white; only the nobility is allowed to wear a loin-rag or britches of interesting color.

'I work at the Bull-and-Iron. Lost my way.'

'Likely tell. They never teach you to say "sir"?' Lamplight from down the street showed me a tight skinny face set in the sour look that means a man won't heed anything you say because his mind was all made up about every-thing long ago when you weren't around. He fingered his club; his boot was hurting me. 'Kay, let's see your pass.'

Anyone entering or leaving Skoar at night had to have a pass with the stamp of the City Council, unless he was a uniformed soldier of the garrison, a priest, or a member of the upper nobility with a shoulder-tattoo to prove it. Of course freemen and the lower nobility – (Misters like Old Jon and such-like) – didn't go off down the roads after dark except in large armed groups with torchlight and foofaraw to keep off wolf and tiger, but there were enough of those traveling groups – caravans they're called – to keep the City Council happy stamping things. However – oh, in the spring after the weather settled to sweet starry nights, and hunting beasts were unlikely to come near human settlements because food was easy elsewhere, boys with their wenches would be slipping over the palisade all the time. Scare-screwing, the kids called it. I never heard of such parties getting killed and eaten, but maybe it does something for a girl if she can imagine that with a boy on top of her. And the guards were expected, almost officially, to look the other way, for as I wrote a while back, even the Church admits that breeding must be encour-aged, especially among the working classes. On June mornings the grass just outside the stockade was apt to be squashed flat as a battlefield, which in a way it was.

'A'n't got a pass, sir. You know how it is.'

'Don't give me that. You know everybody got to have a pass now, with a war on.'

'War?' I'd grown so used to the yak about possible war with Katskil I'd given it no more heed than mosquito-buzz.

'Declared yesterday. Everyone knows about it.'

'Not me, sir. Lost in the woods yesterday.'

'Likely tell,' he said, and we were back where we started. If war had been declared yesterday, wouldn't Emmia have spoken of it to me? Maybe she had, while my wits were wandering. 'Kay, so wha'd you do at this 'ere wha'd you say the God-damn name of the place was?'

'Bull-and-Iron, sir. Yard-boy. You ask Mister Jon Robson. Mister. Member of the City Council too.'

I didn't blame him for not being impressed. Misters are a nickel a pair. Even Esquires don't have the important shoulder-tattoo, and Esquire was the biggest Old Jon would ever get to be. The guard's foot rolled me from side to side, hurting and churning. 'Hear tell they's lots of redheaded scum in Katskil. No pass. Doing a sneak-in. And bearin' down on this crap about Mister like I needed a sumbitch like you to teach me manners, little snotnose fart that a high wind'd blow away. Aw, even if you a'n't lyin' you got to be reamed out some. Take you to the Captain is what I got to do. By him, being Mister Jon Whosit's pansy a'n't helping you.'

I called him a bald-assed son of a whore, and now that I look back on it I believe that was almost the wrong thing to say. 'Give y'self away then, Katskil. You be a Katskil spy. No b.s. is going to talk thataway to a bejasus member of the city gov'ment. Git up!'

He had become an obstacle between me and Emmia, just that, hardly anything more. He'd told me to get up, but his foot was still grinding me. I grabbed it, heaved, and he went flying ass over brisket.

My beef does get underestimated because of my pidlin size and natural-born goofy look. His brass helmet slammed the palings, a bone snapped in his neck, and when he spread out on the ground he was dead as ever a man needs to be.

No pulse at his throat; his head flopped when I shook him. I caught the death smell – the poor jo's bowels had let go. Not a soul near; shadows lay heavy, with only one dull lamp down the street. The noise of the helmet on the logs had been small. I could have climbed back over the stockade and been gone for good, but that's not what I did.

As I knelt staring at him the universe was still full to bursting with the hunger for Emmia that had drawn me back. There seemed to be some connection as I looked at the dead guard, my love-rod stiffening like a fool, as if he'd been a rival. Why, I'm no rutting stag that needs to crash horns into another male to make himself ready for the does. I wasn't heartless either. I recall thinking there'd be others – wife, children, friends – whose lives would be jolted by what I'd done. That pale brown fitfully illuminated thing beside my knee was a human hand, with dirty fingernails, an old scar in the crotch between thumb and forefinger; maybe it could play a mandolin once. But it was dead, dead as the mue, and I was alive and hot for Emmia.

I left him, not hating him at all, nor myself too much. Nor did I think once, as I stole across the city, of the Eye of God beholding every act, the way the church teaching had told me it does, and this seems curious to me, for at that time I was by no means free for any clear thinking.

Nobody was abroad now except the watch, a few idlers and drunks and fifty-cent prosties, all of whom I could avoid. In the more respectable region where the Bull-and-Iron stood there wasn't a cat stirring. The only light at the inn was in the tap room; I caught the drone of Old Jon talking along to some polite guest who likely wanted to go to bed. The moon was fairly high. I saw glints of light from it on the jinny-creeper leaves. I climbed softly, easily, and let myself over the sill.

The moonlight gave me faint shapes: a chair, a bit of angular darkness probably a table, and a pale motion near at hand – why, that was myself, my image in the wall mirror by this window. I watched the image slip off shirt and loin-rag and lay the knife-belt on them, and stand naked as if held fast by its own quietness. Emmia stirred then, murmuring, and I went to her.

My own shadow had been hiding her from the moon. As I moved, the light displayed her; she might have been glowing in the dark, her warmth like a touch as I bent over her and my hand made contact with tender silkiness. She was lying on her side, her back to me. The sheet was at her waist, pushed down because this night was heavy as the rose-season of summer.

My fingers brought the sheet gently further down, barely touching the swell of her hip. Lightly also I touched the dark mass of her hair on the pillow and the dim curves of her neck and shoulder, and I wondered how she could sleep when my ungentle heart was so quickly and heavily drumming. I let myself down on the bed. 'Emmia, it's just me, Davy. I want you.' My hand roved, astonished, for my liveliest imaginings could never have told me how soft is a girl's skin to a lover's fingers. 'Don't be scared, Emmia – don't make no noise – it's Davy.'

I felt no waking start, only a turning of her heat against my thigh, then answering pressure of her hand to tell me she was neither angry nor afraid. Later I wondered if she might not have been awake all the time, pretending sleep for a game or to see what I would do. Now she was staring up at me from the pillow and whispering: 'Davy, you be such a bad boy, ba-ad – why, oh, why did you go away again today? All day? So wild and crazy-like, what'll I do about you at all?' – calm, soft talky-talk as if there was nothing remarkable about the two of us being on her bed naked as eggs in the middle of the night, my hand curling over her left breast and then straying downward bold as you please and she smiling.

Yes, and so much for last night's instructions on virtue and mustn't kiss me-again. Gone like late-staying oak leaves when the spring winds lose patience, for I was kissing her now for sure, tasting the sweet life of her lips and tongue and nibbling her neck and telling her there was a right way and a wrong way and this time we'd bejasus do it the right way because I was going to have it into her come hell or hi-ho. And she whimpered: '*Ah* no!' – in a way that couldn't mean anything except: 'What the devil would be stopping you?' – and twisted her loins away from me, only to remind me I must use a little strength in this game.

I was also driven to say: 'Emmia, I did go off to do something difficult and honest – done it best I could, only it's a thing I can't tell you of, not ever, Spice. And I got to run away.'

'Nay.' I don't know if she heard anything truly except the 'Spice.' I was at her ear again, and kissing the funny tip of her breast, and then her mouth. 'So bad, Davy! – so bad!' Her fingers wandered now and demanded, as mine did, and mine found the little tropic swamp where I'd presently go. 'Spice yourself!' she panted. 'Tiger-tom. I won't let you run away from me, Tiger-tom, won't let you.'

'Not from you.'

'You be all man now, Davy. Oh!'

I did want to say I loved her, or some such message, but speech was lost, for I was over her, clumsy and seeking, understanding for the first time the mimic violence that a loving heart can't allow to go beyond the bounds of tenderness. She who had maybe always understood it, resisted me enough so that I must hold her down, overcome her, until presently the hot sweaty struggle itself was binding us together, as closely as our lips were bound whenever our mouths met and clung in the strife. Then, no longer resisting, her hands helped and guided me toward the blind thrust that took me into her.

I could imagine myself her master then, while she was locked fast to me and groaning: 'Davy, Davy, kill me, I'm dying, my lord, my love, you damn big beautiful Tiger-tom – keep on, oh, keep on!' – but all in a tiny voice, no outcry, mindful of our safety even when my world blew up in rainbow fire. So now I am fairly sure, years later, that in the first embrace I can't have satisfied her completely. Kindness Emmia possessed. I think that to some extent, that first time, she acted a part out of kindness, well enough so that a green boy could feel happy and proud, emperor of her shadowplace, a prince of love.

It's not true to say there's only one first time. My first was Caron who understood what game the grown-ups played, and we played it the witless childhood way, maybe better than most tumbling whelps because in a more-than-childhood way we did honestly cherish each other as people. But you may come to the first time with another as though the past were swept aside and you the same as virgin, entering a garden so new that all flowers taken in the past seem to belong to young years, smaller passions. I don't suppose this could be true for the men who are driven in a mischancy race from one woman to the next, never staying long enough with one to learn anything except that she has – what a surprise! – the same pattern of organs as the last. Nor could it be true of the female collectors of scalps. But it's true for anyone like myself to whom women are people, and is probably true for a woman who can see a bedmate is a friend and a person, not just an enemy or a child substitute or a phallus with legs.

Emmia smoothed my hair. 'Mustn't run away.'

'Not from you,' I said again.

'Hush then.'

I was finding a clarity like what may come with the ending of a fever. The world receded, yet grew sharper in lucid small detail. The dead guard at the stockade, the gleam of my golden horn, the mue become food for the yellow ants – all keenly lit, tiny, perfect, like objects seen in sunlight through the bottom of a drinking glass. In the same vision I could find the fact of Emmia herself, that big-thighed honeypot deep as a well and shallow as a ripple on a brook, whom I now loved unpossessively.

She whispered: 'I know what made you a big lover all-a-sudden. Found you a woods-girl out wilderness-way, one of the you-know, Little Ones, and she must be purtier than I be, and put a spell onto you the way no girl can say no.'

'Why, an elf-girl'd take one look and say poo.'

'Nay – got a thing or two about you, Davy. Some time I'll tell you how I know you been next to an elf-girl.' Emmia was laughing at the fancy, half-believing it too, for elves and suchlike are real to Moha folk, as real as serious matters like witchcraft and astrology and the Church. 'Nay, own up, Tiger-tom, and tell me what she did. Feed my boy one of them big pointy mushrooms that look like you-know-what?'

'Nay. Old witch-woman, terrible humly.'

'Don't say such things, Davy! I was just fooling.'

'Me too. Kay, tell me how you know.'

'So what'll you do for me if I do? I know – scratch my back – ooh, lower – that's it, that's good – more … Kay, here's how I know: what happened to your luck-charm?'

My brain banged into that one head-on. I was sitting bolt upright, scared frantic. I knew I had cut that fishing cord, strung the charm on it, and worn it. And not touched it since – or had I? … That I did not remember, and could not … Had it worked loose when I climbed the jinny-creeper? – impossible: I'd gone up like a slow wisp of smoke. The stockade then? – no.

I'd done that too with great caution; besides, the logs were set so close you couldn't shinny up – had to work your fingers into the cracks and your toes too, climbing with your body curving out; my chest wouldn't have touched the palings. But when the guard clouted me I'd fallen face down and rolled, and his foot came down on my middle. My charm must have been torn loose when he roughed me, and I too mad to notice. Presently I couldn't believe anything else.

'Davy, love, what'd I say? I was just—'

'Not you, Spice. I got to run away.'

'Tell me.' She wanted to pull me back down to her, taking it for granted my trouble was only a boy's fret, something a kiss would fix.

I told her. 'So it must be back there, Emmia, in plain sight. Might as good've stayed to tell 'em I done it.'

'O Davy! But maybe he—'

'Sumbitch is dead as shoe-leather.' I must have been thinking till now that I could run or not as I pleased; now I felt sure it was run or be hanged. Sooner or later the policers would find out whose neck the charm belonged to … 'Emmia, does your Pa know I took off today?'

'O Davy, I couldn't cover for you today – *I* didn't know you was gone. Ayah, Judd wanted you should take the mules out for to turn the vegetable patch – and found you gone – went and told my Da, and he said – my Da said you better have a real fine entertaining pile of – well – I mean, he said—'

'Just tell me.'

'I can't. He didn't mean it, he was just running off at the mouth.'

'Just say it, Emmia.'

'Said he'd turn in your name to the City Council.'

'Ayah. To be slaved.'

'Davy, love, he was just running off at the mouth.'

'He meant it.'

'*No!*' But I knew he'd meant it; I'd tried his patience too far at last. Having a bond-servant declared a slave for misconduct was too serious for even Old Jon to make flap-talk about it. 'Look, Davy – they wouldn't know the charm was yourn, would they?'

'They'll find out.' I was out of bed and hustling on my clothes. She came to me, distracted now and crying. 'Emmia, is it a fact the war's started?'

'Why, I told you that last night!'

'Must have been while I was light-headed.'

'You stupid thing, don't you ever listen to me?'

'Tell me again – no, don't. I got to go.'

'Oh, it was that town off west – Seneca – Katskils went and occupied it and *then* declared war, a'n't that awful? There's a regiment of ourn coming to Skoar to see they don't try no such here – but I *told* you all that.'

Maybe she had. 'Emmia, I got to go.'

'O Davy, all this time we been – don't go!' She clung to me, tears streaming. 'I'll hide you.' She wasn't thinking. 'See, they'd never look for you here.'

'Search the whole inn, every room.'

'Then take me with you. Oh, you got to! I hate it here, Davy. It stinks.'

'Abraham's mercy, keep your voice down!'

'I *hate* it. Home!' She was trembling all over. Her head swung away and she spat on the floor, a furious little girl. 'That for home! Take me with you, Davy!'

'I can't. The wilderness—'

'Davy, look at me!' She stepped into moonlight, her hair wild and breasts heaving. 'Look! A'n't I all yourn? – all this, and *this!* Didn't I give you everything?' Nay, I'll never understand how people can speak of love as if it were a thing, and given – cut, sliced, measured. 'Davy, don't leave me behind! I'll do anything you want – hunt – steal—'

She couldn't even have climbed the stockade.

'Emmia, I'll be sleeping in trees. Bandits – how could I fight off a bunch of them buggers? They'd have you spread-eagled in nothing flat. Tiger. Black wolf. Mues.'

'M-m—'

'In the wilderness, yes, and don't ask me how I know, but those stories are true. I couldn't take care of you out there, Emmia.'

'You mean you don't want me.' I hitched on my knife-belt. 'You wouldn't care if you've give' me a baby – men're all alike – Ma says – don't never want nothin' but put it in and then walk off. I despise you, Davy, I do despise you.'

'Hush!'

'I won't, I hate you – screw *you*, did you think you was first or something? All right, now *call* me a whore!'

'Hush, darling, hush! They'll hear.'

'I hate the whole mis'ble horny lot of you – you dirty lech, you *boy* – so proud of that stupid ugly thing and then all's you do is run off, damn you—'

I closed her mouth with mine, feeling her need of that, and pushed her back against the wall. Her fingers were tight in my hair, my knife annoying where it hung between us, but we were locked in the love-seizure again, I deep in her and not much caring if I hurt her a little. She responded as if she wanted to swallow me alive. By good fortune my mouth still held hers closed when she needed to scream. Exhausted afterward, and desperate to be gone, I said: 'I'll come back for you when I can. I love you, Emmia.'

'Yes, Davy, Spice, yes, when you can, when it's safe for you, dearest.' And what I heard in her voice was mostly relief. In both our voices. 'I'll wait for you,' she said, believing it. 'Always I'll love you,' she said, believing it, which made it true at the time.

'I'll come back.'

I've wondered how soon she understood we'd both been lying, mostly for decent reasons. Maybe she knew it as soon as I was climbing down the vine. Her face, like a faded moon, vanished from the window before I turned away down the street. Nothing in life had ever drawn me with such wondrous power as the unknown road ahead of me in the dark.

9

A thickening fog was turning moonlight to milkiness. As I passed the pillory in the green I said under my breath: 'I had her twice, once in bed and once against the wall.' Wonderful, as if no one had ever laid a woman before. True, the small sound of my own voice scared me, and I continued along the empty street in a more slinky style, like a cat retiring from a creamery under trimmed sail with a cargo in the hold. But I still felt proud, and knew also an unfamiliar charity toward the whole big fat world and everyone in it except maybe Father Clance.

As I passed the baiting-pit I heard the moan of a bear who'd soon be used up in the Spring Festival – odd how human beings often celebrate the good weather by hurting something. I could do the bear no good but I think he did me some, reminding me to taper off a mite on my encompassing love for all mankind, who if they caught me would clobber me as thoroughly as they'd clobbered him. I went on, alert again, to a black alley that would bring me out near the spot where I'd left the dead guard lying.

I felt unseen doorways. A lifeless thing slithered under my feet. Dog, pigling, cat – the Scavengers' Guild would dispose of whatever it was as soon as it annoyed the policers. In later years, when I was living with Nickie in Old City of Nuin where the poorest streets are kept clean, it would have made me angry. But I was Skoar bred and born: in Moha people below the aristocracy took scant pride in their way of living, claiming that dirt and decay held down the taxes – though I don't think the tax collector ever lived who couldn't see through a six-foot pile of rubble to the tender gleam of a hidden dime. When my foot slipped I merely grumbled: 'Ah, call the Mourners!'

In Skoar that remark was so routine it hardly rated as a joke. The Mourners' Guild is a Moha specialty, a gang of professional singers and wailers who close in on a family that's had a mue-birth to create an uproar of the sacred type. The slave woman old Judd was required to live with bore a mue, a blotched eyeless thing – I saw it carried away wrapped in a rag. The cater-wauling demanded by law went on two days. It would have been five for a freeman family, eight to ten for the upper nobility – and no one no matter how blue his blood could break away from the festivities more than just long enough to go to the backhouse and return. The object is to appease the spirit of the mue after the priest has disposed of the body, and to remind the survivors that we are all miserable sinners totally corrupt in the sight of God. It's called planned reverence.

The Guild could be hired for a normal funeral, but charged custom rates for that. At the burial of a mue in Moha, the family was obliged to pay the Guild only a nominal fee, hardly more than a seventh of a year's earnings, plus about the same amount for a casket the neighbors would consider adequate. For slaves like Judd the town itself met the expense of the Guild's fee and a nice basswood box, charging it off to community good will, one of the generous things that made a Moha citizen point with pride.

At the end of the alley I saw a flicker of torchlight by the stockade, distorted in the fog, and heard voices. They'd found him.

Policers, talking softly. I assumed they'd found my luck-charm too – luck, hell. I sneaked off the other way till the curve of Stockade Street blocked out their light; then I crossed to the palings and wriggled over. Unfamiliar with this section of the palisade, I tumbled into crackling brush. Dogs would have caught the noise, but the policers had none with them, yet.

A horned owl in the mountain woods was crying his noises of death and hunger. I heard a bull alligator roar, in a swamp that covered a few acres east of the city – old Thundergut was useful like the bear, reminding me I'd do well to pass through water and confuse the policer dogs. By daylight they'd have them around outside the stockade near where the guard had died, to cast for a scent, and they might follow mine as far as my cave. I must recover my horn and be long gone before then.

One brook ran between Skoar and my cave, a quick trivial stream. It would not kill the scent – on the way down I had merely stepped across it. To confuse the dogs I must find something better beyond the cave, in the morning. But tonight the brook might help me part way. It flowed under the stockade near where I was now, and out again into the alligator's swamp. I might follow it a mile upstream to a willow I knew I could identify in the dark, so I'd be that much further along at first-light.

I inched out of the brush and across a grassy area. The fog enforced a dismal slowness: in ten minutes I walked a thousand years, and heard the wet monotone of water when I had given up hope of it. A big frog ploshed from blackness to blackness unseen.

Struggling upstream, I imagined every danger crowding me. No alligators in shallow upland water, but there could be moccasin snakes. I could lose footing and brain myself. If black wolf caught my smell he could take me before I freed my knife. A swarm of mosquitos did find me.

In time the owl stopped hooting, and the alligator back there in the swamp must have caught up with what he wanted, for I ceased to hear him. When at last I no longer saw any milkiness of moonlight in the fog above me I knew I was under forest cover, where moonlight was always a sometime thing. Fog was still dense; I smelled it and felt the dampness on my flesh. My fingers constantly out exploring touched willow-leaves after another long while. I groped up the twigs to small branches, to larger, finally encountering one whose shape I remembered. Then I could climb, knowing the tree for a friend. High up, I took off my loin-rag, passed it around the trunk and knotted it at my midriff, the hell with comfort. Brown tiger is too heavy to climb.

I have seen him few times in my life, but I can observe the image behind closed eyes at any time, the vast tawny body cloudily striped with darker gold, fifteen feet from nose to tail-tip, paws broad as a chair-seat and eyes that send back firelight not green but red.

A passage in the Book of John Barth mentions a certain wild-eyed crank who, when the last Old-Time war was in the last phases of threatening, visited the zoos in several cities and turned loose some of the beasts at night, choosing only the most dangerous: cobras, African buffalo, Manchurian tigers. He sometimes murdered the night watchman or other attendant to steal the keys, and was finally killed himself, Barth says, by a gorilla he was releasing. He must have felt he was paying back the human race for this and that. Probably no beast ever disliked us as hotly as disgruntled members of our own breed.

Men hate and loathe black wolf, who in spite of his fearsome strength and shrewdness has some taint of the sneak and coward. I never heard anyone mention hating or loathing brown tiger, though when I was with Rumley's Ramblers I heard of a secret cult that worships him. Pa Rumley introduced me to one of them in Conicut, a friendly quack-pot who let me listen in on one of their minor celebrations. They dabble in alchemy but apparently not witchcraft, and cook up a type of love potion for their own orgies that's said to work, though I never saw it proved. Mighty is he – so began their invocation – who walks like the mist at night, mighty indeed is the golden and well-intentioned one, the merciful and all-forgiving Eye of Fire! It was damned impressive, hearing people pray to a creature that actually existed: I enjoyed it, and was willing to overlook a few turns of expression that I felt to be slightly on the inaccurate side.

In my willow tree the mosquitos chewed me all to hell—

Do you mind a little more brain-scratching? The thought of mosquitos just now woke up the memory of a golden hot day in the pine-woods park outside Old City, a few years ago, when Nickie and I had an argument. She said mosquitos are brave, or they wouldn't return under slaps for a mere gulp of gore. I said they're stupid, because when the slap is clearly on the way they linger for one more swallow, and then they're too flat to enjoy it. They linger so's to gamble for glory, s's she. Stupid, s's I, or they'd wear armor over the soft spots like beetles, but they don't wear anything, and to show her what I meant by a soft spot I chewed her here and there. Flinging me down and pounding my head on the pine needles, she asked me did I mean those mosquitos were atchilly lewd and nude? I rolled her over. Look at 'em, s's I. Then she felt I should take her clothes off for the mor'l purpose of showing 'em how dreadful it is to be nude as a bug, and I thought she'd better do the same for me because we didn't want her being dreadful all alone if the going got tough. She also undertook to slap the ones that bit me whenever I was preoccupied with helping her to be dreadful, and I undertook vice versa which is interesting in itself. We agreed further to keep count of slaps, thus determining who the bugs thought had the richest flavor. In order to get undressed we'd been absentmindedly chasing each other around trees and over rocks and rolling about considerably, which takes time, and so had forgotten what the original argument was, but we thought the flavor thing might be it or anyhow just as good. When we were lying face to face engaged in some operation or other, I remembered the first argument, and what happened then *proved* that mosquitos are stupid: they felt that the time was favorable for unpunished biting, and this in itself was lucid thinking, but they never saw we each had a hand free to slap with.

Nickie of course is impossible to beat in any learned discussion on a high plane. She said, the little twirp, that those mosquitos were dying out of heroic generosity and devotion, because they saw how much we enjoyed slapping each other, and so yielded up their lives in altruism. This kind of good will, s's she, is a sign of the vast courage that goes with towering intellect. Look at Charlemagne, s's she, or some of those other Old-Time ninety-day wonders like St George and his everloving cherry tree, or poor Julius Caesar dividing his gall in three parts so as not to offend his friends, Romans, countrymen and other types of etcetera.

Before I fell asleep in that willow my mind was troubled in another way, as it might have been by a glimpse of fire seen as redness on distant cloud. War. It was the knowledge, intruding on me now that I could rest with a trace of safety, that the Katskil war had become a fact, a thing darkly and truly happening.

People said there would always be war; they didn't say why. Of course as a child I could see what a grand thing it would be to perish gloriously, and first to rush about cracking the heads and spilling the guts of wicked joes who happened to be the Enemy. The army as represented by the garrison soldiers of Skoar wasn't exactly glorious, which may have given me some early doubts. The men were let out on pass in small groups; even the orphanage priests with all the power and authority of the Church behind them used to wince and fret when a knot of soldiers went roaring by in the street, skunk-drunk, howling dirt talk, pissing where they pleased, spoiling for rape or a free fight. The policers tried to keep up with them, steering them as quickly as possible into the cheap bars and cat-houses and then herding them back to their barracks ... I had heard of navies too, but never had seen anything to reduce their glory. Outrigger fleets, I heard tell, carrying built-in crossbows, fire-throwers, and captains who had a habit of dying on deck with words of immortal bravery. The fleets had born the brunt of the effort in a war sixty years earlier when, as our Moha teacher-priests put it, Moha reluctantly allowed Levannon her independence. Reluctantly allowed, my celebrated hinder parts! – Moha got the holy godelpus beaten out of her, and hanging on to the Levannon country would have been like a farmer in the west forty trying to keep in touch with an eastbound bull.

It was over my head in those years; now I realize how hard and patiently the Holy Murcan Church worked as an umpire in wartime. Being committed to a policy of loving-kindness (within reason of course) the Church took no part in war except to provide chaplains for the armed forces and facilities for the military type of prayer – which puts a slight strain on monotheism at times. Behind the scenes, however, the top brass of Church and State would be watching for a suitable moment when both sides were wearied out enough to negotiate. When that time came the Church would supervise, examine any treaty proposed, and approve it so long as it wasn't too openly hoggish. For the nations after all are not merely great democracies but Murcan democracies – that is, united in the faith though not in politics. The Church is fond of calling herself Mother Church, enjoying the role of skirted arbiter in the smeary bloody squabbles of her children (whom she didn't beget, but never mind that) and I guess she can truly claim to be the savior and protectress of modern civilization, such as it is.[13] Since those days I have learned so much – from good stern Mam Laura of Rumley's Ramblers who made me solid with reading and writing, from Nickie above all, and from the years when Nickie and I were Dion's aides in his effort as Regent of Nuin to bring

---

[13] According to a famous paragraph in the Doctrine of Necessary Evils, war is a periodic outlet for man's 'natural' violence, unavoidable till the second coming of Abraham; thus it is a duty of the Church to allow a 'limited amount' of violence, under proper control. It is interesting to note that this idea of the inevitability of violence was old in Old Time – not to say moldy – and the proponents of it were as well able then as now to overlook the history of some nations that had passed through many generations without war, to say nothing of the multitude of private lives that reject violence in favor of reason and charity.

– Dion M.M.

some enlightenment into the mental murk of his times – so much more than I ever learned in childhood that it is difficult to sort out what I knew then from later knowledge. It was in my boyhood, at the tavern, that I heard an old man, a traveler, describe the sack of Nassa in Levannon, a city notoriously sinful and a hatcher of heresies, in a war Levannon fought against Bershar soon after winning her independence from Moha. The Bershar hill-men laid siege to the city for fifty days. According to the teller of the tale, this was a case where the Church took sides almost openly, encouraging devout communities in other lands to send Bershar material support. It caused some angry heretical mutterings here and there. When Nassa surrendered at last, the survivors were disarmed, turned loose and hunted down like woodchucks or rats, and then the whole city was set to the torch – 'for the glory of God,' as the Bershar commander put it. His remark was unpopular, especially in the Low Countries, where aid to Bershar had upped the taxes. Church dignitaries were greatly shocked at this 'misinterpretation' of the ecclesiastical position, and the Prince Cardinal of Lomeda was obliged to come out on the steps of the Cathedral and be shocked in public before a grumbling crowd would quit and disperse.

When the war itself ended, the treaty specified that Nassa must never be rebuilt, and Levannon had to agree; it never had been. Our traveler could not recall what year the war was, but he said the pines where Nassa used to stand had grown better than twenty feet tall. And he said that the city of New Nassa, a few miles from the simple war memorial among the pines, was a much stronger town in the military as well as the economic sense – better command of the eastern road ... Joking of course, Old Jon asked him: 'Was you, sir, one of them terr'ble Nassa heretics, sir?' The traveler looked at him too long and unwinking, like an ancient turtle, and then laughed barely enough for politeness, without answering.

A regiment was coming to defend Skoar, Emmia had said. They'd use the Northeast Road – no other available except the West, and that must be busy if there had already been fighting in the Seneca region. It shouldn't matter to me, I thought, since I meant to avoid roads anyway until I was a long way from Skoar. My uneasiness subsided for lack of fuel and I drifted into a sort of sleep.

I woke in slowly lightening darkness, pulled from a warm riot with a girl who was not Caron but only a trifle bigger and older. I can't bring back much of her now except a red flower in the back of her dark hair that tickled my nose. She was singing; I kept whispering to her she better not, we better not do anything until Father Milsom fell back out of sight on the other side of the stockade. I was awake, my thighs gripping nothing but a branch. I ached, and I'll never see her again. They don't come back. Dion remarks it's just as well they don't, for if we hoped to find our unfinished dreams we'd be forever sleeping, and who'd cook breakfast?

Skoar, in fact everything of my fourteen years – (even Caron, even Sister Carnation) – seemed to me in that time of waking to have become like a mixed sound of voices behind me, farther and farther behind me on a road where I could do nothing but go forward.

The fog became swirls of gray replacing the night; I saw the shape of willow branches near my eyes. I wriggled down the tree in the milk-soft confusion and pushed on up the mountain, hungry, not much rested but clear in the head. The policers wouldn't like the fog, so I tried to, though it slowed me down. I arrived at my cave in half an hour, famished. I could spare no time to hunt. The fog was thinning away under the pressure of an invisible sun.

I dug up my money first – fifteen dollars altogether, it ought to help as soon as I came to any place where money mattered. At a moment when sunlight broke through the fog and edged the leaves with wet trembling gold, I had in my palm the shiny dollar Emmia had given me: it seemed not so very bright. After dropping it among my other coins I could hardly tell it from the rest. Then I recovered my sack, with the golden horn – and my luck-charm of course. Could I have known all the time that it was there, but needed some compelling reason for running away? – from Emmia? Skoar? From my boyhood self because I must have done with it?

A slim-witted wild hen came searching her breakfast of bugs barely ten yards off. My arrow lifted her head from her neck – she'd never miss it. I couldn't stop to make a cooking fire, but drank the blood and dressed her off, and ate the heart, liver and gizzard raw, wrapping the rest in burdock leaves for lunchtime. I recall I gave the luck-charm no credit, although in many ways I was still quite religious.

The nearest stream began at a spring on the mountain's northeast slope beyond my cave, a small loud brook with alders and brambles along the banks. I knew it ran two miles or so through the woods and then across the Northeast Road at a little ford. I could follow it almost to the road and then use the road as a guide, glimpsing it now and then to check my position as I traveled east – toward Levannon.

The brook covered the bottom of a scratchy tunnel, a narrow green hell. Thinking of policer dogs, I had to try it. I stuffed my moccasins in the sack again, to save them. My bare feet winced at the thought of snakes, and took a beating on the stones.

Of course when the dogs lost the scent the men would use some brains, following the brook with the dogs searching both banks. At a break where the brambles gave way to common weeds, I stepped out and walked away, to make it look as if I had given up and started back toward Skoar. I passed within grabbing reach of a big oak but went beyond it, to a thicket where I messed around a little and peed on the leaves to keep the dogs amused. Then

I backtracked and swung into the oak with care to leave no damaged twigs. From the oak, by risking one leap far above ground, I passed to another tree, and then from branch to branch all the way back to the brook.

They'd at least lose time beating their gums over it, maybe decide I was a demon and sit down and wait for a priest to come help them louse it up. But I stayed with the stream another half-mile, and when I left it I did so by the way of the trees again, proceeding through the branches to another great oak. There I climbed high, to study the land.

Clouds swarmed eastward playing dark games before the sun. Edgy weather, a petulant wind stirring the oak leaves with sultry insistence. A spring storm might be advancing.

The road was nearer than I thought. I saw a red gash less than half a mile to the east. It could only be red clay, where the road approached and crossed a rise of ground. Though the road was empty I heard an obscure and troubling sound that was no part of the forest noises. Turning my head to puzzle at it, I found I was staring down on what must be another section of the same road, startlingly near my oak, hardly fifty feet away, a spot where branches thinned out to reveal the red clay and some gravel. Confirming it, the unstable breeze brought me a whiff of horse-dung. Not fresh – this near part of the road was empty like the other, but I didn't like it, and clambered to a lower spot where I was better hidden. Whatever the sound might mean it was fairly distant, a dry mutter not resembling either voices or a waterfall.

I cut off an end of my gray loin-rag and tied it around my head. I don't mind being red-haired, but it doesn't help you look like a piece of bark. While I was busied with that, a dot of life appeared on the distant road between me and the uneasy sky.

Even far off, a human being seldom looks like any other animal. In Penn, with the Ramblers, I've seen the flap-eared apes they call chimps, the chimpanzees of Old Time. I could always tell one of those from a man if I wasn't drunk or spiteful. The man I saw on the red clay road was too distant for me to be sure of anything but his humanity – that rather arrogant, rather fine human stance by which even a fool can defy the lightning with a hint of magnificence – and his alertness, his observant stillness under the intermittent sun.

10

That dot of man printed against the sky was studying the road. The noise ceased while he paused, then a tiny arm swung up and forward, and the uncertain sound resumed. Men must have used that signal from ancient days, when there's been good reason not to shout aloud: 'Come ahead!'

He was followed at first by a few like himself in brown loin-rags and red-brown shirts, walking with the long stride of men used to extended journeys with light burdens. Advance scouts. The sound strengthened as the first horsemen appeared over the rise.

Feet of a mass of men and horses – having once heard the surge of it as I did that morning you'd never mistake it for anything else, whether the men are marching in rhythm or coming broken-step like the soldiers who followed that mounted detachment. This was no parade. They were coming to defend the city. I saw presently a group of men without spears surrounding a handsome motion of white, blue and gold – our Moha flag.

The advance scouts would not take much time to reach that near section of the road. I drew back all the way behind the tree-trunk, waiting. They were good – to tell of their passage I heard only a faint crunch of gravel. Then came the plop and shuffle of hoofs. I dared peek around the trunk as the cavalry went by; they'd leave it to the scouts and never think of looking upward. Thirty-six riders – a full-strength unit, I happened to know.

The horses were the breed of western Moha, mostly black or roan, with a few palominos like sunlight become flesh, all bred for grace and glory, maybe the best-looking children of my native land. Bershar is famous for horses too, by the way – mountain type, homely but steady in a crisis as these slimlegged beauties were not.

The horsemen were sleek young aristocrats. Owning their horses and gear, they'd feel they were doing the army a favor. They made a grand military picture. They wouldn't dream of riding any horses except the beautiful breed of western Moha – hell, I'd as soon send a green girl into battle. You can't trust them to stand, and if the rider loses control for an instant they go wild as the wind.

For most of the cavalry – the boys were that young – this would be the first war. Not so for the infantry – old faces there, furrowed by sword-work; hard-case types used to stinking rations and the rule of the bull-whip. Some were clods, others looked repulsively crafty – ex-slaves some of them, and some were petty criminals given a choice between slavery and infantry service.

Any discipline they possessed had been banged into them from outside; they were men for the ugly labors, the uncelebrated dying. Except for the murders and rapes of their profession they had no pleasures but gambling, drink, cheap marawan, stealing, and whatever enjoyment can be wrung out of a fifty-cent prostitute or a complaisant drummer-boy. In their inarticulate heavy way I suppose they welcomed war and thus were good patriots. I'd say that building the infantry out of such trash was another Moha mistake – one that Katskil didn't make. An army of men able to think like human beings may be hard to handle, but it does win wars, so far as any army ever does.

A second mounted detachment appeared on the higher ground. That meant a second battalion – three companies, each of a hundred and fifty foot, plus the mounted unit of thirty-six. A Moha regiment consists of four such battalions. As it turned out, only two battalions were on the road – Emmia had heard it wrong, or some upholstered brass in Moha City decided that since Skoar was only a half-ass city with a twelve-foot stockade, why bother with more than half a regiment?

I watched the foot-sloggers down there. Some were marching with drooping heads – tired, hot, bored. Gnarled masks, two out of three pockmarked. From time to time I saw a dull mouth-gash turn sideways to shoot the juice of a ten-cent chaw. A twist of the wind brought me their reek, more disturbing than the sight of them. An army, however. On them, people said, depended our safety from the Katskil Terror. And, yes, there was a Katskil Terror. So far as any nation can be imagined to possess a personality, that presented by Katskil was iron-gutted, ambitious, stern. A political image of course, which means, largely a fantasy: the Katskil people themselves were and are of every sort, cruel, gentle wise, silly, mixed-up average like the people of any nation.

I suspect the mere fact that their territory encloses Nuber the Holy City on three sides has inclined the nation (as a political fantasy imitating reality) toward a certain pious arrogance which the Church may privately deplore but will not openly condemn. Church decisions have been consistently pro-Katskil (within respectable limits) for so long now that no one expects anything else.

They streamed by below my oak tree, the sodden, witless, beaten faces. On the hill, a trumpet screamed.

Flights of arrows from both sides of the road had cut into our troops like a pair of scissors. Riders were toppling off their mounts, the horses going mad at once and plunging everywhere. No sound reached me yet but the trumpet cry.

The Katskil battalion in ambush had let half our line go by, then stabbed at the center. Moha's flank scouts must have merely skirted the edge of the woods; perhaps some idiot thought the forest too dense for an army to hide in it. Now that the trap was sprung, the Moha men doubling back to help – if they did – would have the hill to climb, and maybe the rush of a storm in their faces, for that fitful growing wind was a northeaster.

The trumpet blast echoed inside me – three short notes and a long. I knew it must be a recall of the first battalion that was passing below my tree. It halted them. I saw grotesque faces empty with shock. Someone started a yelping: 'Skoar! To Skoar!' Noise swelled hideously on the name, and a furious young voice cut through it: 'Get back up there! Move, you God damn pus-gutted slobs! You heard it. Move, move, you whoreson sumbitches, *move!*'

Up here – well, what was in it for them? Why, up there under blackening sky, men in dark green were pouring out of the woods and killing men in brown. I heard for the first time the shattering Katskil yell. And I saw our second battalion still marching over the rise – still in formation, poor yucks, stepping off a cliff in a dignified manner.

Yet there weren't so many of the dark green uniforms. No more had followed the first flood; plenty were already fallen – for make them angry or scared or merely startled like a herd of spooked cattle, and that Moha rabble could fight. Except at the initial surprise blow there can't have been much arrow work. Jammed there in the narrow gut of the road, both sides were forced to infighting, always a deadly business. I don't know how many brown shapes lay mingled with the green-shirted Katskil dead. The brown and red-brown melted at that distance into gory mud.

The flag of Moha reappeared, hurrying up the rise. At least the soldiers of the color guard weren't all of a whimper for the comfort of the city's stockade. To this day I wonder why a b.s. yard-boy on the run, with scant reason to love his native land, should have gulped tears of pride and awe at seeing how the Moha color guard knew where to go. A glory of white and blue and gold, it climbed the rise, that rag with no meaning except the fantasies men had woven into the fabric. A wave of green surged to meet it, a wave of men who just as dearly loved a rag of black and scarlet.

I saw that flag too, wrathful in the wind. Moha cavalry charged it; their horses fell pierced or hamstrung. Black and scarlet are colors of night and fire. That flag was glorious as ours, if there is such a thing as glory.

But down in my neighborhood was disgrace, nastiness of panic. I saw one flash of contrary action – one horseman galloped by toward the battle and in passing whipped the flat of his sword against a mouth that was howling: 'To Skoar!' Only three riders followed him. Maybe the rest were out of my sight trying to stem the disorder of the infantry, the men who had come to defend the city and were now running for shelter inside it – a slow run, like the motion of men caught in momentum who must keep their legs moving or fall on their faces.

I took out my golden horn. Forty feet above them I blew the call that trumpet had sounded, three times.

I looked down. No one had located me. The sound would have seemed to be coming from all around them. They were not running now. I blew the call a fourth time, more quietly, as though the men of their own kind up the road had said in reasonable voices: 'We are in trouble.'

In the silence some cavalry boy dropped the words: 'Kay, let's go take them!' They ran – the other way.

Moha won a dazzling victory that day, if there is such a thing as victory. I'm sure history calls it a victory, for the priests who turn out the little simple books for the schools must have recorded the piffling Moha-Katskil war of 317 – it didn't even last into the following year. Old woman history chewing her mishmash of truth and maybe-so beside the uncertain fire of today.

When I looked again at the distant rise I saw the color guard still cruelly pressed, no more than a dozen Moha men left around the standard-bearer. As the ring of defenders was cut even smaller it held shape in stubborn courage, a shine of steel within a dark green band. At the crest of the rise the demoralized cavalry was winning back some order. They might have been dangerous in a charge. Charging at what? – not at the nimble devils who slid in and out among them like green smoke. Here and there riderless horses broke for the woods leaving man to his own sickening inventions.

But now came the cavalry of the first battalion returning up the hill roaring calamity, crashing first against the green band around the color guard and smashing it like a splintered wheel. The flag danced and moved up the rise. Then Moha's foot-soldiers – recovered, eager, their panic overcome by a simpler lust. My mind could hear their steel cutting through air and crushing flesh – for a minute or two I think I was shivering myself with my own insanity of pride. This was the accomplishment of my golden horn.

I watched a man in dark green flee for the forest cover with three Moha soldiers after him. One pursuer had lost his loin-rag and most of his shirt; distance made the naked man an insect – weedy, prancing high-kneed. A javelin caught the fugitive in the back. The naked jo and his companions slowly shoved steel into him as he lay motionless.

Since that day I have fought without disgracing myself in two wars, against the pirates in 327 and in the rebellion of this year, when we fought to defend Dion's reforms and were compelled to learn that the people will not and cannot benefit from any reforms unless they come gradually; I have never again taken my golden horn near the scene of war ...

All Katskil men were now in retreat, and the flag of Moha already throbbed in beauty at the top of the rise. I saw no banner of black and scarlet; it must have gone with the retreat back into the woods. I saw no more sunlight. The fresh cavalry unit joined the broken one and their captains conferred under a gray sky. Only foot-soldiers were chasing the Katskil men into the woods. One cavalry captain was jerking his arms as if talking in wrath, or self-justification maybe. The other must have managed to strike flint and get a light to his pipe in spite of the dancing uneasiness of his horse, for I saw a tiny spook of gray float above his head.

A trumpet presently recalled the infantry – they could hardly have done much in the woods, where the Katskil men might regroup and make them sorry for it – and the Moha battalions were again in motion. Hardly more than twenty minutes could have passed since I saw that first scout. A skirmish, engaging less than a thousand Moha men, on the Katskil side perhaps four hundred.

The cause of the war was a dreary boundary dispute that had been kept alive one way or another for fifty years. So far as I can see, nations exist because of boundaries and not the other way around; the boundaries are drawn by people more or less like you and me and your Aunt Cassandra, and we like to think that as human beings we know enough not to sit down in wet paint bare-ass, or lift a porcupine by the tail, or hack the baby's head off to cure a teething pain. It's a curious thing; I can probably give you a perfect solution to any contradictions involved, next Wednesday, if I don't oversleep.

Words floated up to me from the road: 'Did y' see the Katty I got, tall sumbitch with a beard? My God 'n' Abraham, don't look like they teach 'em to cover the gut ay-tall.' Another voice was crying and petulant – the wounded were being carried by. A man wanted to see his daughter. They could bring her, he said – it was safe here, no stinking soldiers around – she was nine, she'd be wearing a brown smock her Ma made her – that voice faded out and another said: 'My head hurts.' Over and over, that also growing fainter, obscured by a shuffle of footsteps, clash of gear, other voices: 'My head hurts – my head hurts …' They were gone, leaving the morning peaceful if there is such a thing as peace.

I had heard no noise of dogs behind me; now I was released from that and other fears. Skoar would be soon celebrating the entry of a glorious army, and never mind fugitive yard-boys. There'd be crowds, bonfires with kids dancing naked and shrieking, churches adrone with hymns of thanksgiving, taverns and whorehouses squaring off for a long night's work, policers busy with brawls and drunks and the quackpots who bounce out of their holes at the first whiff of excitement, and public speakers being trotted out of their stables – you know, with a rope at each side of the bit and a third handler in case the speaker should fumble at the happy task of ramming the splendid mahooha into the quivering public mind.

I studied the countryside, wishing the rain would arrive and lighten the air. Black dots were growing large like separated shreds of cloud. The crows were already on the scene; they would have been cynically watching from nearby. Other creatures would join them before long, the rats and wild yellow dogs and carrion ants.

A soldier who should have been dead reached upward and let his arm fall over his eyes. The motion, small to me as the stir of a fly's leg, caused a crow to flap away. I saw a snap of brilliance as light touched something on the moving hand, a ring or bracelet. He was like a sleeper who covers his eyes to preserve a dream. I thought: Man, turn over, why don't you? Turn *away* from the light if it hurts your eyes!

In the talk of the Moha men who passed below me I had heard no one speak of the horn call. Maybe each man supposed the music was for him alone.

It seemed to me I must go to that man whose arm had moved, or I would dream of him. I climbed down from my oak and walked boldly to the road. No danger. A red squirrel was already on a branch beside the road, watching me without scolding. I stepped out from the bushes and turned left, toward the battlefield, and reached it in a few minutes after only a few turnings of the road. The crow sentinels squawked word of me. I saw the lurching run and climb of one of the larger birds, red-necked and hideous, who circled so closely above me that I caught his stench and was almost fouled by a spatter of his muck.

The first man I passed wore dark green. He lay in the roadside ditch, face upturned and no-way angry. His bow was shorter and heavier than mine; it would be hard to bend but easy to carry in thick woods. I might have taken it but for a superstitious feeling that to do so would put me on a level with the vultures. I felt absurdly that all the dead were delaying me, as if they could wish to speak. A wart-nosed Moha veteran, for one, his gashed neck so twisted that although he lay belly-down his spiritless eyes appeared to watch me – why, alive he'd have had nothing to say to me, more than a snarl to get off the sidewalk if he noticed my gray loin-rag.

The man whose arm had moved lay as before, but he was dead. Maybe he had been all the time, the motion only one of those aimless things that occur after death. That sparkle on his hand was a ring, ruby-colored glass. Knowing him dead, I was free to be afraid again. The Katskil soldiers might not have fled far; slave gangs would come from Skoar to carry in the Moha dead. I crossed the rise and started down the other side intending to get back under the forest cover.

There had been some fighting on this side of the ridge; not much. I was halted by the sight of a small sandy-colored beast crouched at the edge of the road. A scavenger dog, large for his breed. They are said to be clever enough to follow an army on the march, as sometimes they follow brown tiger, and for the same reason. The dog, unaware of me, was watching something beyond a patch of bushes at my right. I had come quietly; his nose would have been already charged with the smell of human beings and their blood.

A little stream flowed from the woods into the ditch along the road. Toward this, from the thick bushes, a Katskil soldier was crawling, his bronze helmet slung over his arm. A thin gray-eyed boy, maybe seventeen. He was attempting to pull himself along by his arms, one leg helping. The other leg was gashed from hip to knee, and an arrow-shaft protruded from his left side.

The dog was a poor slinking thing, but it could kill a helpless man. The boy saw the brute suddenly and his face remained blank, curiously patient, shining with sweat. I set an arrow and as the dog whirled at the slight noise to face me I sunk it in his yellow chest. He leaped and tried to bite his flank and died.

The boy watched me, puzzled, when I said: 'I'll get you the water.' He let me take his helmet. It was hard for him to drink, his shaky hands no help. He rolled his head away and said: 'I a'n't nothing to ransom – the old man ha'n't got a pot, never had.' The effort of speech brought a stain of blood to his mouth.

'Will I lift you?'

He looked at the water, wanting it, and nodded. I felt the splash of the first raindrops on my head. At the touch of my arm at his shoulder I saw it was too much for him. I spooned water in my hand, and he got down a little but lost it in a sharp cough. The arrow may have pierced his stomach. He said: 'Shouldn't've tried it.'

I took the rag from my head and tried to close up the long wound in his thigh. The rag was not long nor wide enough; trying to fasten it was a nightmare frustration. A bang and roll of near thunder almost covered what the soldier was saying: 'Let it be. Be you Moha, that red thatch?'

They have an odd speech in Katskil. I had heard it at the inn, though not much in the last two years when the war jitters were building up. They drawl in a pinch-nose way, leave out half their *rs* and any syllable that doesn't happen to suit them.

I told him: 'I got no country.'

'Ayah? You be'n't with us, I know ever' damn fool bum in the b'talion including myself.'

'I'm alone. Running away.'

'I get it.' The rain came then in a sudden and ponderous rush, soaking us, hammering my back. I leaned over him; at least my shirt could keep the downpour from battering his face. 'Ran away once myself – tried to, I mean.' He seemed to want to talk. 'Pa caught me filling a sack, believe me I got no forrader. He wa'n't for me going into the A'my neither, said it was all no consequence. You killed that yalla dog real neat.'

'Damn scavenger.'

'Jackalaws we call 'em down home. Handle a bow real good.'

'I been in the woods a lot.'

'Tell by the way you walk.' His voice was reaching me with difficulty through the roar of water around us. 'Running away. That 'ere gray – your ballock-rag – that mean bond-servant? Does in my country.'

'Uhha.'

'Look, boy, don't let it bug you. I want to tell you, don't let 'em tromp you or tell you where to go. They spit in your eye you spit back, see? ... Nice country hereabouts, might be good corn land. Our outfit laid up all the night in the woods – under stren'th, the damn fool brass, the way they do things, one comp'ny split off yesterday for another job – hell with it. Wanted to say, I was noticing what a pile of oaks you got around here. Means good corn land, ever' time. Last night was a real foggy sumbitch, wa'n't it?'

'I slept in a tree.'

'Do tell. Raining now, a'n't it?' Both of us were drenched, the water bouncing a stream from a crease in his shirt where I couldn't shelter him, and pelting on his legs. But he was really asking, not sure of the world, his eyes losing me, finding me again.

'It's raining some,' I said. 'Listen, I'm going to get you deeper in the woods where won't nobody search, understand? Stay by while you heal up. Then you can come along.'

'Sure enough?' I think he was seeing it, as I was trying to – the journeying, friendship, new places. We'd go together; we'd have women, amusement, something always happening. Above all, the journeying.

I said: 'We'd get along all right'

'Sure. Sure we will.'

I never learned his name. His face smoothed out completely and I had to let him lie back on the earth.

11

I remember the rain. Not long after my friend was dead, it slackened to a dull beating on the earth. I could not hope to scratch a grave in the tree roots and wet clay. In any case I have never liked the thought of burying the dead, unless it might be done as they do in Penn, marking the place with nothing but a grapevine, and taking the wine-harvest in later years with no sense of trespass or disrespect. If that can't be, maybe burning is best. Does it matter? – all the world's a graveyard, a procreants' bed, and a cradle.

I slipped away from the road into the bushes, sure now that there'd be no pursuit by men and dogs. In the dripping woods, however, I still moved softly. I was guessing my northeast direction accurately, for I had been on my way more than an hour when, off to my right where it ought to be, I heard a racket of hoofs galloping on wet road-mud, swelling loud, dying away into little taps like the noise a child can make by flipping a stick along a picket fence. A dispatch rider, probably, bound for Skoar. After that I heard only the diminishing sober discourse of the rain.

I grew hungry, but wanted a fire for my hen – raw chicken is discouraging. The morning was spent by the time I located a good spot. An oak had blown over against a slope years before, its root cluster jutting out aslant and catching a gradual drift of leaves, thus creating a roof of sorts. From the pocket of earth where roots had once grown, rains had dug out a drainage gully. I grubbed under the surface of the forest floor and found tindery stuff to start a blaze in the shelter of that overhang. Soon the fire was comforting me while my hen browned on a green ash spit. I hung my shirt and loin-rag on an oak-root near the warmth, and squatted naked letting the harmless rain sluice off my back. For a while, except to keep track of my cooking hen, I can't have been thinking at all. Rain lulls you out of alertness like someone talking on and on, explaining too much.

The men came quietly. I was aware of them only an instant before the thin one said: 'Don't pull that knife, Jackson. We don't mean you no ha'm.' His voice was firm but weary, like his long face under a bloody dark green rag.

'Don't be scared,' said the other man, a moon-faced giant. 'Matter-fact I been called by the blessed Abraham not to do no hurt to no man, also—'

The thin man said: 'Hold up the mill, will you, whiles I talk to the boy? Jackson, the dang thing of it is, we'd like a snip of that 'ere, bein' stinkin' hungry is all.'

He was about fifty, gray and quiet. The rag on his head gave the hollows under his smoky blue eyes a greenish tinge. Long grooves bracketed his mouth and nose. His dark green shirt lacked a section where his head bandage must have been torn out; a hunting knife at his belt very much like mine appeared to be his only weapon. His belt was broad like a sash, with fold-over parts that would be useful for carrying small things. His lean legs sticking out of a shabby green loin-rag were dark and bunchy as bundles of harness leather.

The other man also wore the wreck of a Katskil army uniform; some kind of belt and rope-soled sandals. He carried a sword in a sheath of brass, a worthless thing in the woods. Both had at their belts long and rather flat canteens made of bronze that would have held about a quart

Stupid as you can get, I said: 'Where you from?' The thin man gave me a good smile, dry and friendly. 'Points south, Jackson. Will you share the meat with a man that fit your country yesterday and got a hole in his head, and a big old jo that looks fit to scare the children but don't want to fight no more?'

'Kay,' I said. They weren't crowding me; I almost wanted to share it. 'Yesterday? Be'n't you from that fight down the road by Skoar?'

'Nay. When was it?'

'Couple-three hours gone. I was up a tree.'

'Couldn't think of a finer place with a fuckin' war goin' on.'

'You Katskils done an ambush and got beat off.'

He slapped his leg, mixed satisfaction and disgust. 'God damn, I prophesied it. Could've told the brass, that's what you get for splitting the b'talion. Comes to me though, the meat-heads never asked me.' He squatted on his heels beside me, giving my hen the gloomiest gaze any chicken ever got and no fault of its own. The moon-face jo stood apart, watching me. 'I feel bad about this, Jackson, If'n it was just me and my large friend standin' over theah in the rain so bungfull of the milk of human kindness a man can't see where he'd squeeze in no more nourishment no-way—'

'Now, Sam,' said the big man. 'Now, Sam—'

But Sam liked to talk, and went on regardless, in his slow-drawly Katskil voice, amusement and sadness exchanging places the way clouds play games with the sun: 'If it was only him and me and you, Jackson, we might make out, but the dad-gandered almighty thing of it is, we got one other mouth to consider which's got itself a bumped knee but still suffers if it don't eat good. You think that 'ere little-ass bird could do a fourway split?'

'Well, sure,' I said – 'two leg-hunks and two half-bosoms and ever'body arise from the God-damn table a mite hungry is good for you as the fella says – where's the fourth?'

'Off into the brush a piece.'

'See like I told you, Sam? Boy's got an open nature full of divine grace and things. What's y' name, Red?'

'Davy.'

'Davy what?'

'Just Davy. Orphanage. Bonded out at nine.' 'Now we got no wish to betrouble you, but maybe you a'n't bound back wheah you come from?'

Sam said: 'That's his business, Jackson.'

'I know,' said the moon-faced man. 'I a'n't pushin' the boy for no answer, but it's a fair question.'

'I don't mind,' I said. 'I'm on the run, ayah.'

'Nor I don't blame you,' says Moon-face. 'Noticed that 'ere gray ballock-rag hangin' there right away, and what I've hearn about the way they'll always do the dirty on a b.s. in Moha, it's a national disgrace. You keep y' chin up, boy, and trust in God. That's the way to live, understand? Just keep y' chin up and y' bowels open, and trust in God.'

'You let him snow you, Jackson, you'll start thinkin' they don't treat bondservants like shit in Katskil too.'

'Sam, Sam Loomis, someway I got to break you of that 'ere cussin' and blasphemin'. A'n't no fitten type talk for a young boy to hear.' Sam just looked at me; I felt he was laughing up a storm inside of him and nobody'd ever know it except himself and me. The big jo went on kindly: 'Now, boy Davy, you mustn't think I'm claimin' I a'n't no sinner no more, that'd be an awful vanity, though I do claim a lot of stuffs been purified out'n me like a refiner's fire and things, but anyway – my name's Jedro Sever, call me Jed if you want, we're all democraticals here I hope, and sinner though I be I fear God and go by his holy laws, and right now I says unto you lo, I says, bond-servant or no, you be just as much a man and citizen in the sight of God as I be, y'hear?'

More casual, Sam asked: 'Things got tough?'

'You could say so.' Then somehow I was blurting it right out: 'An awful accident happened. I killed a man accidental, but nobody'd ever believe it was so, anyhow not the policers.' I suppose I might have held it in if I hadn't taken them for deserters, on the run as I was and not concerned about Moha laws.

Jedro Sever said: 'A'n't no such of a thing as an accident in the sight of God, Davy. You mean, it happened without *you* intending it. God's got his great and glorious reasons that a'n't for such as us to look into. If'n you be truthful about it not being intended, why, no sin theah.'

Sam was looking into me with a cool thoughtfulness I'd never seen in anyone, man or women. I don't know how long it was before he let me off that hook – my hen was well browned, smelling just right, and the rain had slackened to a mere drizzle. 'I'm taking your word,' Sam said at last. 'Don't never make me sorry I done it.'

'I will not,' I said. And I don't think I ever did. The confidence between Sam and me was a part of my life that was never spoiled. In the times that followed I often lost patience with him, and he with me, but – suppose I say it this way: we never gave up on each other. 'Ayah,' I said, 'I run off, and I'd be a sure thing for hanging was I caught and took back to Skoar. Kindly avoid hanging whenever I can see my way to it, that's how I am.'

'Whenever,' said Jed, unhappy. 'Look, boy, if you was ever once—'

'Joke, Jackson. Boy's joking.'

'Oh, I get it.' Jed laughed uncomfortably, the way you might if you accidentally interrupted someone taking a leak. 'You know the country round heah, boy Davy?'

'Never come thisaway this far before. We're near the Northeast Road. Skoar's off west, five-six miles.'

Sam said: 'I was through these pa'ts yeahs ago, in peacetime – Humber Town, Skoar, Seneca, Chengo.'

'Katskil border's a few miles south,' I said.

'Ayah,' said Jed, 'but we be'n't bound thataway. Understand, in the sight of God we be'n't deserters. Me, I labor in the vineyard like on a mission, and old

Sam Loomis theah, why, he a'n't no sinful man ay-tall, spite of his bad talk. One day God's grace is going to bust onto him like a refiner's fire and things. I mean he merely lost his outfit in a scrimmage like anyone might. Same out-fit I was with – I left sooner, bein' called by the good Lord.'

'Ayah,' Sam said. 'I lost track of my comp'ny in the woods after a little trouble yesterday, up the road ten mile. What the A'my does with deserters, Jackson – I mean with people it thinks is deserters – well, what they do, they string 'em to a tree for bow and arrow practise, and then so't of leave 'em. Saves a burial detail. Got my head busted and was knocked out a while, comp'ny gone when I come to, I don't blame 'em for thinking I was a deader, but I don't believe I got the patience to explain it all, was I to see 'em again. One comp'ny was detached from the b'talion, idea was to make a little show up the road, delay you Mohas and make you think it was all we had in the area. Then the main b'talion hiding down thisaway could clobber you. Cute idea.'

'The Mohas a'n't no army of mine. Got no country.'

'Know what you mean,' said Sam, watching me. 'I'm a loner by trade … Well, them no'th Moha apple-knockers, excuse the expression, came along nine hours late, after whoring it up around Humber Town likely, so after they brushed us off they squatted down to camp for the night. I should know, having damn nigh walked into 'em in the dark. Must've been rested and happy by the time the b'talion jumped 'em this mo'ning. We didn't do too good?'

'Not too. Mohas was too many. Two to one or more.'

'Boy's a gentleman,' said Sam, and rested his wounded head on his knees. 'Ayah, the brass gets fanciful and the men get dead.' I'd spotted Sam Loomis for a woodsman; he had my habit of quick side-glances. He wouldn't be caught unready by the unexpected stir of a branch or slither of questing life along the ground. Jed might be; his eyes did not look alert. Baldness had thinned even Jed's eyebrows to pale wisps; it gave him the look of a great startled baby, 'Jackson, that little-ass bird's near done.'

As I took it away from the flame he added: 'Maybe better slip on y' ballock-rag, account that other'n off in the brush – I just damn-all f'got to mention it – well, see, she happens to be a female woman.' Then glancing up at Jed Sever's disapproving mass, he said: 'Moves around real peart for a young boy, don't he?'

When I had my rags on Jed called off thinly into the wet woods: 'Oh, Vilet!'

'Don't fret,' Sam said to me under his breath – 'I wouldn't done it to you only she's broad in the mind as well as in the beam.'

Limping out of a nearby thicket, the woman said: 'I hearn that, Sam.' She gave him the small half of a grin, and the rest of us a challenging stare from under thick brows black as ink. Her dark green linsey smock left her knees bare, and the left one was bruised but not badly. She was anywhere in the thirties, a short slab-sided big-muscled wench with no waist to speak of, but someway you didn't miss it. Even with the slight limp she had a solid animal grace and sureness. She didn't like being wet as a mushrat. 'I did oughta ream y' out, Sam, talking thataway about a tender blossom like me, hunnert and thirty pounds and all of it wildcat.'

'A'n't she the sha'p little thing?' said Jed, and I saw he'd gone all mush-mind and lover-dreamy.

'Ayah,' she sighed – 'sha'p as an old shovel beat out onto the rocks ten-twenty yeahs.' She slipped off a shoulder-sack something like mine, and tried to wring some of the water from her smock and pull it clear of her crotch and meaty thighs. 'You men be lucky, them Goddamn loose shirts and stuff.'

'Vilet!' No longer dreamy, Jed spoke like a stern grandfather. 'None of that cussing! We been into that.'

'Aw, Jed!' Her look at him was cocky, affectionate, submissive too. 'You'd cuss, I bet, if'n you couldn't tell y' clo'es from y' hide.'

'No I wouldn't.' He stared her down, solemn as a church. 'And "hide" – that a'n't a nice word neither.'

'Aw, Jed!' She squeezed water from her black hair. It was short, and shaggy as if she'd hacked it off with a knife, the way soldiers do if there's no barber in the outfit. She dropped into a squat beside me and gave my leg a ringing slap with a square brown paw. 'Your name's Davy, ha? Hiya, Davy, and how they hangin', lover-pup?'

'Vilet dear,' says Jed, mighty patient, 'we been into all that. No more cussing, no more lewd talk.'

'Aw, Jed, I'm sorry, anyhow I didn't mean it like lewd, just friendly.' Her eyes, dark greenish gray with a hint of golden flecks, were uncommonly lovely, set in the frame of her beefy homeliness, violets in rough ground. 'I mean, Jed, things keep slippin' my mind and poppin' out.' She pulled her wet smock out from her big breasts and winked at me, head turned so that Jed wouldn't see it, but she meant her words too; she wasn't fighting him. 'You gotta be patient, Jed, you gotta leave me come unto Abraham kind of a gradual sort of a way, like I gotta creep before I walk, see?'

'I know, Vilet. I know, dear.'

I cut the hen as fairly as I could and passed it around, and was about to start gnawing when Jed dipped his head and mumbled through a grace, mercifully short. Sam and I began eating right afterward, but Jed said: 'Vilet, I was listenin' whiles I prayed, nor I didn't hear you none.'

It's a fact: among the true religioners, if a priest is present, people keep quiet while he says the grace right, but if there's no priest everyone is expected to say it at the same time, leaving it up to God to analyze the uproar and sort out the faithful from the hippy critics. Of course, Jed hadn't heard Sam or me either, but our souls evidently weren't his concern, or else he felt they were too much of a job for him. Vilet's soul was different. She said: 'Aw, Jed, I was just – I mean, I thank thee, O Lord, for this my daily bread and—'

'No, dear. Bread means real bread, so then if it's chicken it's best you say chicken, understand?'

'For this my – Jed, chicken don't *come* daily.'

'Oh – well, kay, you can leave out the daily.'

'For this my chicken and command—'

'Commend.'

'Commend myself to thy service in Abraham's beloved name – kay?'

'Kay,' said Jed.

After the meal Vilet limped off to hunt up more firewood. I wished that while she was busy I could ask who she was and how she came to be with us, but Jed had been observing the luck-charm at my neck, and asked me about it.

I said: 'It's just a puny old luck-charm.'

'Nay, boy Davy, it's a truth-maker. I seen one just like it at Kingstone, belonged to an old wise-woman. This is the spitn-image of it, bound to have the same power. Nobody can look on it and tell a lie – fact. Le' me hold it a minute and show you. Now, look this little man or this little woman right in the face and see if you be able to lie.'

Deadpanning, I said: 'The moon shines black.'

'How about that?' said Vilet, dumping an armload of dead sticks. 'How about that, Jed o' boy o' boy?'

'Why, I got him.' Jed laughed, pleased. 'Other side of the moon's got to be black, or we'd see the shine of it reflected onto the curtain of night, big white patch moving the way the moon does, stands to reason. But all's we see is the holes prepared in the curtain to let through the light of heaven, and a few of them dots that move different, so they must be little chips, sparklers like, that God took off of the moon to brighten things up. See?'

Drowsily admiring, Sam murmured: 'Bugger me blind!'

'Sam, I got to ask you not to use them foul expressions in the presence of a pure-minded boy and a misfortunate woman-soul that's trying to find her way into the kingdom of ev'lasting righteousness, more b' token I won't put up with no more sack-religion, I purely won't.'

Sam told him he was sorry, in a way that suggested he was used to saying it, and more or less meaning it every time. Good people like Jed would find things dull, I guess, if they couldn't arrange to get hurt fairly often. As for the luck-charm – well, Jed was much older than me, forty-plus, and a hell of a lot bigger as well as full of divine grace. I did think if I took another try at making extra work for the shovels I wouldn't be stopped by any dab of clay. But Jed was so proud and happy to have taught me something useful and surprising, I hadn't the heart to spoil it. Maybe I couldn't have anyway. Whatever mahooha I offered, he could have produced some gentle explanation to prove

I hadn't told a lie – working it along easy and patient, pushing and crowding Lady Truth around and around the bush till sooner or later the mis'ble old wench had to come crawling out where he wanted her, whimpering and yattering, legs asprawl and vine-leaves a-twitching in her poor scragged-up hair. 'Well,' I said, 'I never did know it had no such power. It was give' me when I was born, and people have talked me considerable guck since them days, nothing no-way stopping 'em.'

'You just never caught on to the way of usin' it,' he said. He still held the image facing me, and asked me as if casually: 'It was a true-for-sure accident, that thing you told about?'

Sam Loomis stood up tall and said: 'Hellfire and damnation! We take his word and then go doubting it?'

Behind me I could hear Vilet quit breathing. Jed might be forty pounds heavier, but Sam wasn't anyone you'd try to take, head-wound or no. Jed said at last, mighty soft: 'I meant no ha'm, Sam. If my words done ha'm, I'm sorry.'

'Don't ask my pa'don. Ask his'n.'

'It's all right,' I said. 'No harm done.'

'I do ask y' pa'don, boy Davy,' Nobody could have asked it more nicely, either.

'It's all right,' I said. 'It don't matter.'

As Jed smiled and gave me back the clay image, I noticed his hand was unsteady, and I felt, in one of those indescribable flashes which resemble knowledge, that he was not afraid of Sam at all, but of himself. He asked, maybe just for the sake of speaking: 'Was you bound any-wheah special when we come onto you, boy Davy?'

'Levannon's where I want to go.'

'Why – them's no better'n heretics over yonder.'

Sam asked: 'You ever bejasus been theah?'

'Sure I have and wouldn't go again at all.'

'Got to cross Levannon if you and Vilet be goin' to Vairmant like you say.'

'Ayah,' Jed sighed, 'but just to cross it.'

They were still edgy. I said: 'I dunno – all's I ever hearn of Levannon was hear-tell.'

'Some pa'ts may be respectable,' Jed allowed 'But them quackpots! Snatch y' sleeve, bend y' ear. You hear the Church figgers if the quackpot religioners all drift into Levannon that makes it nicer for the rest of us, but I dunno, it don't seem right. Grammites, Franklinites, that's what religious liberty has brung 'em to in Levannon. No better'n a sink-hole of atheism.'

I said: 'Never hearn tell of Franklinites.'

'Nay? Oh, they busted away from the New Romans in Conicut – New Romans are strong theah, you know. The Mother Church tol'ates 'em so long as they don't go building meeting-places and stuff – I mean, you got to have religious liberty within reason, just so it don't lead to heresy and things. Franklinites – well, I dunno …'

Sam said: 'Franklinite a'gument sta'ted up about St Franklin's name not being Benjamin and the dura gold standard not being wropped around him when he was buried but around some other educated saint of the same name. My wife's mother knowed all about it, and she'd testify on the subject till a man dropped dead. One of 'em carried lightning into his umbreller, I disremember which one.'

'The Benjamin one,' said Jed, all friendly again. 'Anyhow them Franklinites did stir up a terrible commotion in Conicut, disgraceful – riots, whatnot, finally made like persecuted and petitioned Mother Church to let 'em do an exodus or like that into Levannon, which she done it, and theah they be to this day. Awful thing.'

'Wife's mother was a Grammite. Good woman according to her lights.'

'Didn't go for to hurt y' feelings, Sam.'

'Didn't. According to *her* lights I said. But when it come to my wife, why, I said to her, "Jackson," I said, "you can be a Grammite like your respected maternal pair'nt and prophesy the end of the world till your own ass flies up," I said, "and bites this 'ere left one," I said, "or you can be my good wife, but you can't do both, Jackson," I said, "account I a'n't about to put up with it." Horned it out'n her too, so't of.'

'Why,' said Vilet, 'you mean old billy ram!'

'Naw, Jackson baby, that a'n't meanness, that's just good sense, that is. All's I mean, she was a lickin' good church-woman ever after, real saint, never had a mite of trouble with her that day fo'th. About religion, I mean. Did have a few other faults such as talky-talking fit to wear the han'le off a solid silver thundermug, which is why I j'ined the A'my so to get a smidgin of peace and quiet, but a real saint, understand, no trouble with her at all, no sir. Not about religion.'

'Amen,' says Vilet, and glanced up quick at Jed to make sure she'd said the right thing.

12

We spent the early afternoon in that place, drying out, getting acquainted. I again said something about Levannon and the great ships, the thirty-ton outriggers that dare to sail to the ports of Nuin by the northern route. And Jed Sever was troubled again, though not this time about religion.

'The sea's a devil's life, boy Davy. I know — I had a taste of it. Signed on with a fishing fleet out of Kingstone, at seventeen. I was big as I am now – too big to listen to my Da, that was the sin of it – but when I got back by the grace of God 'n' Abraham I weighed no more'n a hund'd and twenty pounds. We sailed south beyond the Black Rock Islands, wheah the Hudson Sea opens out into the big water – oh, Mother Cara have pity, that's a lonesome place, the Black Rocks! They say a great city stood theah in Old Time, and that's ha'd to under-stand. As for the big water beyond, oh, it's a hund'd thousand mile of nothing, boy Davy, nothing at all. We was gone seven months, op'rating from a camp wheah we smoked the fish, a mis'ble empty spit of land, sand dunes, dab or two of low hills, no shelter if'n the wind's wrong. Long Island it's called, pa't of Levannon and they's a few small villages at the western end within sight of the Black Rocks; any nation's free to use the eastern end – sand – seldom a living thing except the gulls. Men get to hating each other, such ventures. Twenty-five of us at the beginning, mostly sinners. Five dead, one murdered in a brawl, and mind you, the comp'ny expects to lose that many, expects it. We never saw a new face only when the comp'ny's freight vessel brung firewood and took back the smoked cod and mackle. And on our sailings – ah, some-times we was a couple-three hours full out of sight of land! That's an awful thing. You be in God's hand, amen, still it's a terr'ble test of y' faith. Can't do it ay-tall without a compass, some call it a lodestone. Comp'ny owned one that was made in Old Time, and we had three men in the crew considered fit to han'le it and keep watch lest God should weary of holding the little iron true to the no'th for our sakes out of his ev'lasting mercy.'

Vilet sighed. 'Hoy, I bet them three was the real panjandrums of the outfit, wasn't they?'

'You don't understand these things, woman. Man's han'ling a holy object, y' own life depending on it, stands to reason you treat him respectful. Ayah, boy Davy, that's the blind side of nothing when you're out of sight of land. You work in skiffs, maybe six-seven hours labor with the big nets, and mustn't leave the main outrigger out of sight for that's wheah the compass is – come a sudden fog or a great wide wind, what then? – needn't ask. And when the last net comes in, then it's fight y' way back over the cruel water to make camp, get the fish smoked before they spile. To this day I can't abide the stink of fish, any fish, couldn't if I was sta'ving. It's a judgment onto me for a sinful youth. The sea's not for men, boy Davy. Le' me tell you – when I came home at last, sick and punied-out though I was I had me a woman-hunger fit to drive a man hag-wild, and – well, I won't go into that now, but on my first night back in Kingstone I succumbed to the urging of the evil one, and I got *robbed*, ever' penny of my seven months' pay. A judgment.'

Sam said to the fire: 'You claim God would gut a man just for heavin' it into a chunk of nooky?'

'Language! Nay, why was I robbed, if it wa'n't a judgment? Answer me that! Ah, Sam, I pray for the time when scoffing will pass from you. You harken to me, boy Davy: at sea you be a *slave*, no other word. A devil's life. Work, work, work till you drop, then comes the old chiefs boot in y' ribs, and sea-law says he's got the right. I wish ever' vessel ever built was to the bottom of the deep this moment. I do. You listen to me: it stands to reason, ifn God meant men to float he'd've give us fins.'

We got moving soon after that, to look for a location where we might spend the night in better safety. I learned a few things from Sam as I walked with him, out of hearing of Jed and Vilet. Jed, he told me, was short-sighted, objects twenty feet away from him not much more than a blur, and he was sensitive about it, regarding it as another punishment dealt out to him by the Lord. I couldn't see Jed as any kind of sinner, let alone a big one, but Jed firmly believed the Lord had it in for him – testing him to be sure and maybe friendly at heart, but tough all the same, never giving him a break without taking away something else or reminding him of the Day of Judgment. The poor jo could hardly turn his head to spit or square off by a tree-trunk to take a leak, without the Lord's jolting him up about something he'd done wrong ten days ago, or ten years. Unfair, I thought, and unreasonable – but if that was the way Jed and God wanted it, Sam and I weren't about to butt in with our ten cents worth of suggestions.

In Old Time it was possible to help people with poor vision, by grinding glass into lenses that let them see almost normally. Another lost art, gone down the drain of ignorance in the Years of Confusion; recovered, however, and brought with us to the island.

At Old City, in the underground workshops adjoining the Heretics' secret library, there's been a man at work some thirty years on problems of lens-making; he still is, if he's alive and undiscovered by the victorious legions of God. Am Bronstein was his name originally, but he elected to adopt the first name Baruch after reading the life of an Old-Time philosopher who also inflamed his eyes grinding lenses, and who built a curious bridge of reasoning to carry him a remarkable distance beyond the bumbling Christianity and Judaism of his day. Our Baruch could have sailed with us; it was his own decision not to. When Dion was trying to persuade him to join the group who would sail with the *Morning Star* if we should lose the battle for Old City, he said: 'No, I will stay where there's enough civilization, never mind its quality, so that a man can achieve obscurity.' 'Obscurity's all very well,' said Dion – 'do you want the obscurity of grinding spectacles for people who can't wear them without being burned for witchcraft?' Not answering that, having very likely not listened to it, Baruch asked: 'And what facilities do you provide for contemplation aboard your – hoo, your beautiful *Morning Star*?' He asked that, crouching in the doorway of his musty workshop and blinking pink angry eyes at Dion as if he hated him; crying and swearing, Dion called him a fool, which appeared to gratify him.

Baruch was past fifty when the rebellion began. He said his manuscripts and optical gear made a load too heavy to carry, and he would have no one else burdened with it if you please. I remember him so, in the doorway, stoop-shouldered, shrunken, tortured eyes winking and watering, garments haphazard rags although he had money for good clothes, saying this and plainly meaning instead that he would not trust others, heedless ham-handed blunderers, to carry a load so precious. Then – ready to reject instantly any show of affection – he gave Dion a small book bound by himself, painfully handwritten by himself, a labor of pure love. It contains everything that Baruch knew and could tell of lens-making, so that granted the brains and patience (we have them) we can duplicate the practical part of the work at any time.

Many times since that day of retreat it has disturbed me to think of a lens-maker afflicted with something like blindness; of a man with a love for humanity who can't stand the sight, sound, touch of human beings near him. I can imagine nothing more ridiculous or insulting than 'feeling sorry' for Baruch; I suppose his rejection of communication is the thing that wounds.

We killed a stag that afternoon. I saw him in a clump of birches and let fly my arrow for a neck shot. He went down and Sam was beside him at once, the knife swift and merciful in the throat. Jed was generously admiring. Vilet watched us, me cocky and proud, Sam still-faced with his reddened knife waiting for the carcass to bleed out, and I saw a waking of lust in her, her eyes dilated, lips a little swollen. If Jed had not been there, present but not really sharing the heart of the excitement, I could imagine her inviting Sam to spread her on the ground. There was that in her smoldering gaze at him – and at me, who after all had shot the arrow. But Jed was there, and in a few minutes we were busy cutting what meat we could carry, the heated moment gone.

We camped for that night in a ravine that must have been a good ten miles from Skoar, but still fairly near the Northeast Road – once or twice we heard horsemen. We made a temporary fireplace of rocks for cooking, below the rim of the ravine, where the blaze could not be seen from the road. When Jed and Vilet took their turn at gathering wood, leaving Sam and me alone, he answered a question before I spoke it: 'A camp-follower they call 'em, Jackson. Means she's been whorin' it for a living, puttin' out for any jo in the comp'ny that had a dollar. She's good at it, too – I been in there a few times, never a dull moment. She was doing all right – the men treated her nice, got her food free, no pimp or modom riding her, chance to save up her cash for a rainy day. Every comp'ny's got one – I dunno how 'tis in the Moha army. Our boys always make a real doll out'n the comp'ny whore. It's natural – only female thing they got to love, and so on … Well, old Jed he kindly got religion, or he'd always had it, but I mean it so't of rifted up on him, anyway he decided God didn't wish him to stay in the A'my when there was a war on and a real chance he might be expected to hurt somebody. And it seems God told him to take Vilet along on his way out. He says it was God.'

'So who else would talk thataway?'

Sam gave me one of his long cool stares, checked on the distance of Jed and Vilet off in the brush, and went on with the story: 'It come to a head yesterday after we holed up near the road waiting for the Mohas. I blundered onto Jed and her in the bushes, supposed they was just fixing up for a quick piece, but it wasn't that. Jed he was lit up with the holy spirit or whatever, asked me to stick around and bear witness. He was explaining to Vilet how God wants her to give up the sinful life and love the Lord, along with him who's intending to lead hencefo'th a life of mercy and purity. Damn, he's already so gentle and good-hearted and mush-headed you wouldn't think there was room in him for enough sin to stuff a pisswilly walnut, but he don't think so. Got a conscience like a bull bison, that man, stompin' on him all the time. Well, looked to me like Vilet got a bang-up conversion, and when old Jed cut loose with this 'ere repent-leave-all-and-foller-me, why, bedam if she didn't, she did bedam … Jed he wanted I should come along too. I didn't estimate I was no-way called. He allowed they'd stay close by for a day or two and pray for me, and if'n I changed my mind I could sneak away from the outfit and make screek-owl noises three at a time till they fined up with me. Kay, s's I, and they took off. Dunno how they ever got by our sentries, him that clumsy with his poor eyesight, but Vilet's sharp in the woods, got him by someway. Hadn't no intention of going with 'em, Jackson – I'm a loner by trade – but then I got my head hurt in that skirmish and the comp'ny took off without me. Real lost for a while. Damn nigh blundered into the Mohas like I told you. Bypassed 'em and come on down along the road – wrong way too, didn't realize I was headed for Skoar till daylight. Did the screek-owl thing a few times not expecting anything, but Vilet heard and answered, and we got connected. Know a rema'kable thing? – they got it fixed they'll go all the way to Vairmant and cut a fa'm out'n the wilderness which shall be lo, a temple in the lorn waste land and like that. A'n't bound thataway myself but bless 'em, s's I, hope they do.'

'I notice you be calling 'em Jed and Vilet instead of Jackson.'

'Oh, that. Wa'n't speakin' to 'em direct.'

'I see. Like hell I see.'

Sam put his hand on my head and pushed down – not hard, but I was sitting on the ground the next moment. He rumpled my thatch; all I could do about that was laugh and feel good. 'Jackson,' he said, 'if you wasn't a big serious brain just like me I wouldn't betrouble myself to explain it. You see, in this world a man's got to piss up some kind of a whirlwind or nobody knows he's there. Now, me bein' mean, ugly, common's an old dry bull-turd in an upland medder, if I didn't do something a mite extra-onery – well, tell me, an old dry bull-turd, what does *it* do?'

'Just kindly sets there onto the grass.'

'That's right! That's prezactly what it does. You never knowed a bull-turd, anyway not an old dry one, to get up on its hind legs and call people Jackson as if it didn't know their right names, nor you never will. So now I've answered your question fair and honest, what the hell you got into that sack? Been achin' about it all afternoon.'

I might have told him the full story then about my golden horn – I did months later, when we happened to be alone – but Jed and Vilet were coming back. It wasn't for them somehow – there was all the trouble of explaining why I hadn't killed the mue, other difficulties. Jed heard Sam's question, however, and when he saw me reluctant and unhappy he gave me a little talk about how since the Lord had thrown us together we must try to be all for one and one for all, which meant sharing everything and not having secrets from each other. So it would be *spiritually* good for me to tell about what I had in my sack, not that he supposed for one minute it was anything I didn't ought to have, but – ayah, and meanwhile old Sam is standing off there not doing a thing to get off the hook, just minding the fire and spitting the venison on sticks to grill, and now and then casting me a blank look which might mean: Go ahead, *be* a bull-turd!

'Jed,' I said, 'would you hold this image again, the way I can look at it whiles I talk?'

'Why, sure!' He was startled and mighty pleased. Vilet sat down by me, her chunky hand on my back. Affection was her natural way, going along with the bouncy sex though not the same thing. She liked to touch and nudge and kiss, make known her body's warm presence without any fuss, just as at another time she might say, merely by pouting her mouth or rolling her hip, 'Let's have one!'

'Here's the true-tale,' I said, looking at the clay image, 'about how I come to kill that man accidental.' You know, my pesky clay god-thing did bother me a bit at first. But I had meant to tell this part straight anyhow, about climbing back over the Skoar stockade and tangling with that guard. And when I continued, leaving out all mention of Emmia and saying I'd gone back over the stockade into the woods right away when I knew the guard was dead – oh, Mudface raised no objections.

'Poor Davy,' said Vilet, and tickled me just below my loin-rag where Jed didn't see her hand. 'Right back to the woods, huh? Didn't you have no girl in Skoar, lover-pup?'

'Well, I did so't of, only—'

'What you mean so't of? I wouldn't give the sweat off a hoppergrass's ass for a *so't* of a girl, Davy.'

'Well, I meant *kind* of. But le' me tell you what happened in the woods that afternoon, before I accidental killed that jo. You people ever meet a hermit?'

'Ayah, once,' Jed said. 'Hillside cave outside of Kingstone, done his artful healin' by layin' on of hands.'

'That's just the kind of hermit I mean,' I said – 'woodland type. I'd been goofing off, hadn't no right to quit work that day. Anyway I found this old hermit. All he had was a grass lean-to, no cave. Hadn't been real holy he'd been et up long before, wouldn't you think?'

'The Lord protects his own, alley-loo. That one at Kingstone's cave wa'n't nothing. Kept goats in it.'

Sam asked: 'Didn't it smell some?'

'Little bit,' said Jed. 'You take a hermit, he's got to overlook some things in God's service.'

All right, but the hell with his hermit, I had to get them interested in mine. 'This'n was terrible old and strange. When I first seen him it upsottled me so I almost stepped on a big rattler. But he seen it, told me not to move and made the sign of the wheel, and lo!'

'Lo what?'

'Well, I mean it just lo slid away, no harm done. Old hermit he said it was a manifestation, account the serpent represented cussing, my greatest fault – which he couldn't've knowed except by second sight, because I hadn't done no sort of cussing there, you can believe.'

It got Jed, the way I meant it to. 'Praise the Lord, that's exactly how those things happen! You was led, you was *meant* to meet that holy man. Go on, son!'

'Well ... He wasn't only old, he was a-dying.'

'Oh, think of that!' says Vilet. 'The poor old s – the poor old hermit!'

'Ayah. He looked that peaceful I wouldn't've ever guessed, but he told me. He said: "I'm about to pass on, boy Davy" – nay-nay, there's another thing, he knowed my name like that, without my telling him. I was some flabberjastered and that's a fact. I b'lieve it was another manifestation.'

'I do believe it was. Go on, Davy!'

'Well, he said I was the first to come by in a long time and do him a kindness, only shit – I mean goodness – I hadn't done nothing but set by and listen. He said to dig under his lean-to, showed me where, take what I found there and keep it by me all my life. Said it was an Old-Time relic and he knowed the evil was all prayed out'n it account he'd done it himself.' I remember I was scared at the fine and healthy dimensions of that particular whifferoo – spooked enough to make my voice wobble. Jed and Vilet attributed it to reverence – if there's a difference. 'Old hermit said God had guided me to it, meant the Old-Time thing for me if'n I'd learn to you-know, quit cussing and so on.'

'Praise his name! And you was guided to us too, the way we'll all help you to quit and never cuss no more. So what happened then?'

'Then he – died.'

'You was actu'ly present at the holy passing on?'

'Ayah. He blessed me, told me again where to dig, and then died – uh – in my arms.' I gazed off into the deep woods, sober and brave, and did a gulp. After all, it was the first time I'd ever killed a hermit. 'So – so then I fixed up a hardscrabble grave for him, and –' I stopped, suddenly sick, remembering the rain and a true happening.

But presently – in such a thing the mind sometimes appears to use no time at all – I felt that the soldier (who lived now in me and nowhere else) would be pleased to laugh along with me in there behind my eyes at my damn-fool hermit, and why not? So I was able to go on with hardly a break: 'Took what I found there and came away, was all.'

I showed them my horn then, but dared not blow it so near the road. Jed and Vilet were too much in awe of it to touch it, but Sam held it in his hands, and said after a while: 'A young man could make music with that.'

Later while we were eating, I asked: 'In the battalion – not your company but the men who'd've been in that fight I saw this morning – do you remember a jo, maybe seventeen or so, dark hair, gray eyes, real soft-spoken?'

'Maybe ten-twenty such,' Sam said, and Jed mumbled something to the same effect. 'Don't know his name?'

'No. Found him after the fighting was over, and we talked some. Nothing I could do for him.'

Vilet asked: 'He was hurt bad? Died?'

'Ayah. I never learned his name.'

'Did he die in the Church?' Jed asked.

'We didn't talk about religion.' Jed looked sad and shocked; I didn't understand at once. 'I never did learn his name.'

'Jackson,' Sam said, and tossed me another chunk of venison, not saying anything just then that would make a demand on me. Later, when night had closed down and Sam and I were taking the first watch, I did understand what Jed had meant by his question, and childhood teaching was another burden of darkness.

A member of the Holy Murcan Church must make in his dying moments what the priests call a confession of faith, if he can speak at all, or he goes to hell forever. Should he forget because of pain or sickness, others present must remind him. I had been taught that much, like all children; why had it never entered my head when the soldier was dying? I had doubts, true, including doubts about hell, but – what if there *was* a hell? Everyone else took it for granted …

Sam and I had a small fire going, and the wall of the ravine at our backs. Even with Sam near me, I had hated to see Jed and Vilet disappear in the little brush lean-to we'd flung together, though I knew they were no further off and probably not asleep. I began to see my gray-eyed friend twisting in the tar-pits, the brain boiling in his skull as Father Clance had so lovingly described; and he was crying out to me: 'Why didn't you help?'

In marshy ground somewhere the low thunder of frogs was so continuous it had become a part of silence; the peepers were shrilling, and the big owls sounding off from time to time. When the moon rose at last it was reddened by a haze we had noticed at sundown, perhaps the smoke from distant occasions of war. Then I found myself up to my ears and over my head in the question: *How does anyone know?*

Who ever went down to the seventh level of hell and *saw* them hanging up adulterers by the scrotum, so that Father Clance, rolling his eyes and sweating and sighing, could later explain for us just how it was done? *How did he know?*

In lesser matters, hadn't I seen people win satisfaction and power over others just from knowing or pretending to know what those others didn't? Merciful winds, hadn't I just worked that same kind of swindle with my damned hermit?

Could anyone prove to me that the whole hell-and-heaven thing wasn't one big fraud? I may have started at that or fidgeted. Sam's whisper came: 'What's the matter?'

The moon had shifted to whiteness, and his face was clear. I knew he wouldn't harm me or be angry, but I was still timid with my question: 'Sam, be there people that don't believe in hell?'

'Jackson, you sure that's the question you want to ask? I got no wisdom on such things.'

Of course, a question wasn't the thing; it was only a way of keeping myself off the griddle and putting him on it. 'I mean, Sam, I kindly don't believe in it myself no more.'

'Seen plenty hell on earth,' he said after a while. 'But that wa'n't what you meant.'

'No.'

'Well, the Church kind – I've noticed the only ones that act like they want to believe it are the ones that see 'emselves safe-elected for heaven. Take old

Jed theah, he don't get no hang out'n hell. Believes all right, but kindly arranges with himself not to think about it. Doubts, Jackson?'

'Ayah.'

He was silent long enough to make me a little afraid again. 'Me, I guess I've always had 'em ... You a'n't scared I might talk to a priest?'

'How do you know *I* wouldn't?'

'I b'lieve I just know it, Jackson. Anyhow if I was you, sooner'n eat my heart out thinking that 'ere soldier's frying account of words that didn't get said, why, I'd undertake to wonder if the priests didn't invent the whole damned shibundle.'

So he trusted me that much, and I could no longer have any doubt that Sam and I were both tremendous heretics and no help for it. I remember thinking: *If they was to burn Sam they got to burn me along-with.* And wishing I could say something like that aloud. But then it occurred to me that since he evidently knew so many of my thoughts without even trying, he wouldn't be likely to miss that one.

13

What I've so far written about happened in a few days of mid-March. By mid-June we were only a few miles further on, for we found a place so pleasant that we holed up there for three months. Sam's head-wound finished healing there, after a troublesome infection. We loafed, and I struggled through the first stages of learning to play my golden horn. We talked long, and made a thousand plans, and I was growing up.

The place was a cool deep cliffside cave something like the one I had on North Mountain, but this one was low in the rock wall, fourteen feet above level ground. We had no view of distances from it, but looked into lowland forest as into a vast and quiet room. Shade from the midday sun, and no settlement near enough to trouble us. To study the surrounding country all we needed to do was climb a nearby sentinel pine and look away. From that height I never caught sight of man except wisps of smoke from a little lonesome village six miles east of us. The Northeast Road was two miles the other side of that village, and the name of the village we never learned. It wasn't Wilton Village – we'd slipped by that before we happened on our cave.

The only access to our hideaway was a drooping oak branch – difficult for

Jed – and the only resident we had to disturb was a fat porcupine whom we hit on the head and ate because that was simpler than educating him not to come back and snuggle up to us where we were asleep.

For two weeks Sam was in bad shape from the infection, feverish and tormented by headaches. Jed cared for him wonderfully, better at it than Vilet or me, and even let Sam cuss all he liked. Vilet and I were the food-winners while Sam was sick, and Vilet searched out wild plants to make some healing mixtures for him. Her mother had been a mountain yarb-woman in southern Katskil, Vilet said, and a midwife too. She was full of stories about the old woman, and told them best when Jed wasn't around. Sam was pretty patient with her yarb mixtures, but after a while he did get a look when he saw her coming like a man who thinks that the next tree to go over in the storm will take the roof along with it. Then toward the end of his bad time, when she'd landed him with a potion which she admitted herself would prob'ly hoist the hide off a bear and him running, Sam said: 'Jackson, it a'n't that I mind having my gizzard hit by lightning all twistyways, and I suppose I could get used to the feelin' I'm about to give birth to a three-horned giasticutus – what I can't no-way endure, Jackson, is the trampling.'

'Trompling?' says Vilet.

'Ayah. Ayah. Them microbes and box-terriers that go rushin' along my gut tryin' to get the hell away from your remedies. You can't blame 'em, see, the way they set their feet down, only I can't stand it, Jackson, and so if you please I'll just arrange not to be sick no more.'

We have been living slightly more than a month on the island Neonarcheos. The *Morning Star* sailed two days ago, to search the region east of us where other islands appear on the old map. Captain Barr intends to make no more than a two-day voyage and then return. He took only eight men, enough to handle the schooner.

We are not calling Dion Governor, not yet, because he rather clearly doesn't wish it. Still we all find it natural that important decisions – such as sending or not sending Captain Barr on this voyage – should be made mostly by Dion, and before long I think most of the colonists will want it formalized. We shall require something in the nature of a constitution, small though our group is, and written laws.

Back in Nuin and those other lands, the season will be chilling toward the winter rainy season; here we notice hardly any change. We have erected twelve simple houses; the brookside grass makes good thatch, though we must wait for heavy rains to test it. Seven of the buildings are on the knoll, spaced so that all have a view of the beach and the little bay, and one of the seven is Nickie's and mine. There's another on the beach, three along the creek, and Adna-Lee Jason with Ted Marsh and Dane Gregory have chosen to build their house away up on the hill where our stream originates. That's a love-alliance that began in Old City long before we sailed; they need it as Nickie and I need our more ordinary kind of marriage, and Adna-Lee has been happy lately as I never knew her to be in the old days.

Aboard the *Morning Star* we all learned a little of what it must have been like to dwell in the jammed cities and suburbs of the last days of Old Time. I was just now rereading an ugly passage in the Book of John Barth: 'Our statesmen periodically discover the basic purpose of war. They are, poor little gods, like farmers in a fix: if you have thirty hogs and only one small daily bucket of swill—?

And so the finality, the apocalyptic unreason, the shared suicide of nuclear war is for them the most God-damned *embarrassing* thing. Their one time-tested population control is all spoiled.' A few paragraphs further on he remarks in passing that of course birth control had been a practical solution since the 19th century, except that the godly made rational application of it impossible even late in the 20th when the time was running out. What would he make of our present state, the reverse of the dismal population problem of his day?

I dare say no civilization ever completely dies. There's at least the stream of physical inheritance, and perhaps some word spoken a thousand years ago can exert unrecognizable power over what you do tomorrow morning. So long as one book survives anywhere – any book, any pitiful handful of pages preserved somehow, buried, locked away in vault or cave – Old Time is not dead. But neither can any civilization return with anything of its former quality. Fragments we may reclaim, memory holds more than we know, there's a resonance of ancient times in any talk of father to son. But the world of Old Time cannot live again as it was, nor should we dream of it.

Vilet often came along with me for hunting and fishing while Jed stayed behind to look after Sam. The first day that happened I felt an agreement between us, at first unspoken, created by occasional touches and glances, for instance when she was walking a few yards ahead of me in good forest silence, and turned to look at me over her shoulder, unsmiling. I think Vilet enjoyed being spooked by other people's mysteries now and then, like my hermit whopmagullion, but she wasn't one to make mysteries herself. That moment on the trail she might as well have said in words: 'I could be caught with a little running.'

Work came first, and we had luck with it that day, nailing a couple of fat bunnies and then locating a good fishing pool about a mile from our cave. There was a grassy bank, sunlight, and a quiet as though no man had troubled the place for centuries. We set out fishlines, and when she knelt on the grass to adjust hers, her arm slid around my thighs. 'You've had a girl once or twice, I b'lieve.'

'How d' you know?'

'Way you look at me.' The next moment she was solid on her feet and pulling her ragged smock off over her head. 'Time you *really* learned something,' she said. 'I a'n't young nor I a'n't purty, but I know how.' Naked with not a bit of softness (you would have thought), cocky and smiling a little and moving her hips to bother me, she was a grand piece of woman. 'Off with them rags, Lover-pup,' she said, 'and come take me. You'll have to work for it.'

I worked for it, wrestling her at first with all my strength and getting no breaks at all until the struggle had warmed her up into real enjoyment. Then of a sudden she was kissing and fondling instead of fighting me off, laughing under her breath and using a few horny words I didn't know at that time; presently her hands were gripping her knees, I was in her standing, joyfully stallionizing it with not a thought in my head to interfere. When I was spent she flung me a punch in the shoulder and then hugged me. 'Lover-pup, you're good.' What I'd had with Emmia seemed long ago and far away.

We had other times, not so very many, for there were other sides to Vilet: moods of heavy melancholy, of a kind of self-punishing despair; the religious side, that belonged to Jed and was forever shadowing the rest of her life. Often (she told me once) she dreamed that she was in the act of selling her soul to the Devil, and he in the shape of a great gray rock about to topple over and crush her. She couldn't always be the good randy wrestling-partner when we had privacy and opportunity, but occasionally at such times she did feel like talking to me. It was a time like that, at the fishing pool again and maybe a week after our first romp, that she told me things about her relation with Jed Sever. Whenever Jed was mentioned in his absence by Sam or me, I'd notice a kind of still warning in her kind blocky face, like an animal bracing itself to defend if necessary. She'd hear nothing in criticism of him. At the fishing pool, after we got a few for supper we took a dip in the water to wash off the heat of the day, but she warned me off from playing with her and I wasn't in form for it myself; we just sat by the pool lazing and drying off, and she said: 'I got it figgered out, Davy, the mor'ls of it I mean. Not telling Jed about what we been having, it a'n't a real sin account it might burden him with grief, and anyway I got so much sin in the past to work off, this'n's just a little one. He's so good, Davy, Jed is! He tells me I got to think back through earlier sins and make sure I truly repent 'em, because see, you can't fix 'em all with one big bang-up repentance, you got to take 'em one by one, he says. So, see, I'm kindly working up to the present time but a'n't got there yet. I mean, Sugar-piece, if I don't commit no more'n one sin a day, or say two at the most, and then repent say *three* sins of past time the same day, well, I mean, after-while you get caught up like. Only it's so't of a heartbreak thing, times, remembering 'em all. I'll be all right by the time we get to Vairmant. And Jed he says it's too much to try to give up sin all to once, too rough,[14] the Lord never intended it like.'

I said: 'Jed's awful good, a'n't he?'

'Oh, a saint!' And she went on about how generous he was, and thoughtful, and how he'd explained everything about the way to Abraham; when they got their little place in Vairmant they were going to have sinners in every day to hear the word, just everybody, any freeman that would come. Dear Vilet, she was out of her gloomy mood and all aglow from thinking of it, sitting there by the pool naked as a jaybird and patting my knee now and then but not trying to rouse me up because it wasn't our day for it. 'Jed, see, he's got a great lot of sin-trouble too. 'Most every day he remembers something out'n the past that sets him back because it needs repentance. Like frinstance yesterday he recalled, when he was five, going-on six he'd just learned about fertilizer, see? So here's his Ma's bed of yalla nasturtiums she was so peart about, and he wanted to do something real generous, make 'em twice as big and purty right away, so he pees the hell all over 'em, specially a big old gran'daddy nasturtium that's sticking up kindly impident – well, I mean, by the time he sees it a'n't turning out just right it's too late, he can't stop till he's emptied out.' Vilet was crying a little as well as laughing. 'So the bed's real swamped, petals flat on the ground, and he don't tell, it gets blamed on the dog and he dasn't tell.'

'Oh,' I said, 'that sumbitchin' nasturtium was purely askin' for it.'

'Ai-yah, I laughed too when he told me, and so'd he, just a mite, still it's ser'ous, Davy, because it kindly ties in with a real sin he done when he was nine, poor jo. He done it to the little neighbor girl and his Ma caught 'em into the berry patch. The girl she just larruped on the backside and sent her home bawling, but she didn't whip Jed. He says it's how he knows his Ma was the greatest saint that ever lived, for all she done was weep and tell him he'd broke her heart after all she done givin' him birth in pain and tryin' to raise him up to something. And so ever since he a'n't never put it into a woman, except once.'

'He what? He never?'

'Except once. That God-damn Kingstone whore he talks about, after his God-damn fishing trip ... Well, anyway – anyway he's a saint now, and all's he ever wants me to do is take my smock off and tromple him a little and call him bad names – he says it purifies him and so it's bound to be pleasing in the sight of God, like the whipping, only he a'n't had me do that lately, not

---

[14] I feel that Jed was entirely right about this. My own planned salvation involves getting in as much sin as possible in the next 70 years, so that what I give up at age 98 will *amount* to something.

since we come away from the A'my.' She sighed and stopped crying. 'He's so kind, Davy! And he always knows how 't is for me too, so sometimes he like helps me with his hand or like that, he says that's just a *little* sin, and anyhow we're both getting stronger and stronger in the Lord all the time now. Calls me his little brand from the burning, and I know that's Book of Abraham language but you can see he means it – why, sometimes he can hold me in his arms all night long and never get a hard on, a'n't that ma'velous?'

Those weeks in the cave were also a good time for learning a little about the playing of my horn. I gave it at least an hour of each evening, from deep twilight into full dark. In daylight there was too much danger of a stray hunter hearing and approaching unseen. After twilight not even bandits are likely to stir away from camp, in the Moha woods. I studied my horn, and I took part in our making of plans.

There was my plan about Levannon and the ships, but when I learned that even Sam was unhappy at the notion of my signing on aboard a ship, I shut my mouth about it, and though it didn't perish it remained in silence.

There was Jed's and Vilet's plan about the Vairmant farm. They were sure about the sinners but they kept altering the rest of the livestock. Vilet held out one long rainy day for goats while Jed stood up for chickens, and it began in fun but he wound up bothered and ended the discussion by saying goats were too lascivious, a word Vilet didn't know so it shut her up.

Sam, when he was well again, was more concerned about immediate plans. We wouldn't be able to go anywhere, he pointed out, so long as we had to travel in beat-up Katskil uniforms, a smock of the same dark green, and the gray loin-rag of a Moha bond-servant. He claimed he could see two good ways of acquiring suitable garments, both dishonest, and one honest way that wouldn't work and was fairly sure to get at least one of us jailed or hanged.

'Dishonesty,' said Jed, 'is a sin, Sam, and you don't need me to tell you so. What's the honest way?'

'One of us go to the nearest village and buy some clo'es. Got to walk in naked is all. Be had up for indecent explosion right off. I don't recommend it.'

'I could say I lost 'em some place,' Jed suggested. It was like him to take it for granted he ought to be the one to stick his neck out and get it chopped off. 'I think I could justify that to my Maker as a white lie.'

'But maybe not to the storekeeper,' said Sam. 'Anyhow you don't look like the type jo that would get deprived of his ga'ments casual-like – you be too big and important And me, I look too mean.'

'Maybe I say I lost 'em into a whirlwind.'

'What whirlwind, Jackson?'

'A 'maginary one. I just say it blowed down the road a piece.'

Sam sighed and looked at Vilet and she looked at me and I looked at my navel and nobody said anything.

'Well,' says Jed, 'I could hang leaves around my middle and make like lost in the woods, like.'

Sam said: 'I couldn't no-way justify pickin' innocent leaves for no such purpose.'

'Look,' I said, 'it'd have to be me, account you don't none of you talk like Moha ...'

'Sam, boy,' said Vilet, 'just purely for cur'osity and the sake of argument, which so't of dishonest ways was you in mind of?'

'Might hold up a pa'ty on the road and take what we require, but Jackson theah don't hold with vi'lence, me neither. Somebody'd get hurt or they'd run tell policer. Another way, one or two of us could shadow-foot it into some village or outlyin' fa'm and so't of steal something.'

'Stealing's a sin,' said Jed, and we sat around all quiet and sad, and I blew a few notes on my horn since it was getting dark. 'Anyhow,' said Jed, 'I don't understand how a person could go and steal clothes off of a person without no vi'lence. I mean, you got to think about human nature, specially women and like that.'

Sam said gently: 'So't of general workin' rule, Jackson, the way you steal clo'es, you steal 'em when there a'n't nobody in 'em, like in a shop or onto a clo'esline.'

I said: 'Why'n't we do that and leave a dollar to make it square?'

Well, they all gazed at me in a sandbagged style, the way grown-ups will gaze at something down there that just doesn't seem possible, and then I could see them get happier and happier, more and more mellow, till they looked like three saints bungfull of salvation and pie.

14

We set out next morning for that village six miles away near the Northeast Road – Sam, Vilet and I. We reasoned, and Jed agreed, that temporary sinners on a clothes-stealing expedition would need to be able to move fast and with good eyesight. Besides, we needed to have someone minding the cave and watching our gear. Besideser, he'd been working hard since before sun-up praying good luck into a dollar Vilet provided, because he said that if we left a genuine good-luck dollar to pay for the clothes it would cut the sin down to nearly nothing, and so he'd earned his rest.

I'd scouted the village two or three times on my lone. It was a poor grubby thing with a ramshackle stockade closing in twenty or thirty acres, and so little cleared area outside it that I knew the people must live mostly by hunting and fishing, plus maybe a few handcrafts for trade. A cart-track connected it to the Northeast Road, but there was no road on the back-country side. I'd located three outlying houses with fair-sized gardens, two on the north-east side and one by the back gate which probably belonged to the man such villages call the Guide.

We halted on a tree-covered hillside where we could watch that house by the back gate, for it did have an interesting clothesline, and as we watched, a thin wench in a yellow smock came out and added a basketful of things to what was already hanging there.

In a village like that, the Guide counts for more than anyone except the head priest and the mayor. The Guide bosses any work that has to do with the wilderness, arranges any large hunting and fishing parties, usually leading them himself, keeps track of seasonal and weather signs, distributes whatever the group hunting and fishing brings in, and takes a handsome cut of everything. In a mean small village like this he'd be appointed by the head priest and mayor together; in a baronial village – there aren't many in eastern Moha – he'd be a sales-manager (sometimes called vassal) of the baron himself, and fixed for life. In either case a village Guide is nobody to fool with, and here we were proposing to rob this one's ever-loving clothesline.

We watched from our hillside more than half an hour, watching not only the house but a big dog-kennel at the side. After that girl who hung up the clothes went back inside, we didn't see a soul stirring. Nor a dog. From the nature of a Guide's job, he's away from home a good deal. So are his dogs. And on the line was a huge white smock – it would cut up into three or four loin-rags. Other stuff too, a smallish yellow smock like the one the girl had been wearing, and a whole bunch of lesser items – towels, brown loin-rags. We couldn't pass it up.

Woodland cover ended a hundred yards from the house and a corn patch began; this was June, the young corn tall enough to conceal a man on all fours. That had to be me, for I was small and not wearing Katskil green, and if I got caught I'd at least have a chance to blarney out of it with a Moha accent. We worked down from the hillside through the woods, and I left Sam and Vilet at the forest edge, promising to whistle if I needed help. I crawled down between the corn-rows, sighting on that yellow smock like a target.[15] Late sunny morning was drawing into noon.

I was at the end of the corn-row when I caught a hint of women's voices in the house, faint, not the clack of visiting housewives. The clothesline hung between a post and the corner of the house, which was low and rambling and

[15] That's my Davy. What other shape would get him started?

– Nick

well made, with small windows barred against wolf and tiger and the sneak-bandits who haunt lonely country. I would have to cross a small yard in line with some of the windows. The main door of the house was facing me, and at my right, not more than two hundred feet away, stood the back gate of the village stockade. Beyond the clothesline post I noticed a side door, toward the village, which probably belonged to the kitchen since a neat herb-garden grew just outside. I ducked across the yard, just then realizing that we hadn't contrived a cover for my red thatch. Nobody challenged me, and at the corner of the house where the clothesline was fastened I was nicely hidden from the windows, I was clawing the yellow smock off the line when the stockade gate creaked open.

A gray-haired woman came through, turning with her hand on the gate to instruct someone inside in a manner he'd remember; she'd evidently caught the gate guard snatching forty winks. The pause gave me a chance. I was into that yellow smock and had a towel twisted around my hair so fast I can't tell you how I did it. I'd gathered the remaining laundry into a wopse that hid more of me, by the time the dame ended her lecture and came on.

There'd been a flaw in my thinking: now that I'd become a winsome laundress it wouldn't look right if I just strolled off into the woods with the wash. I was obliged to take the stuff into the house. Beastly damp. If the gray-haired woman was nearsighted and preoccupied she might take me for the proper owner of that yellow smock, so on my way into the kitchen I tried to give my rump a gentle womanly twitch. I can't believe it was very attractive – wrong type rump.

The kitchen was big, cool, blessedly empty. Leaving the village alone, that elderly woman couldn't be coming anywhere but here. Probably visiting – the large white smock couldn't belong to her, designed for someone shaped like a beer-barrel with two full-grown watermelons attached.

Voices came from the next room, where the front door was. One woman, who must have gone to the window right after I'd crossed the yard, said: 'It's her, Ma.'

Ma replied: 'Kay, you know what to do.'

Not much in that, but it chilled me. The young voice was whiny, half-scared; Ma's tone was high, hoarse and breathy, telling me that she owned the big white smock and liked to eat. I remembered hearing it said that country folk like to use the kitchen door, and I smokefooted into a storeroom with my bundle of wash, eased the door shut and got my eye to the keyhole in time to see Yellow-Smock and Ma come in. That storeroom should have had access to the outside, but it didn't – only one high barred window. I was trapped.

Ma was not only ruggedly fat but six feet tall, her dress an ankle-length job of dead black, with expensive cowhide slippers showing at the bottom. Her hair was done up inside a purple turban, and bone ornaments swung at her ears. I still think the man of that house was the village Guide, sober and responsible as they have to be: there was hunter's gear hung in that store-room, and the location of the house was traditional for a Guide's dwelling. Maybe when the man was at home the fat woman was a model housewife, her black gown and turban stashed away where he wouldn't stumble on them. Dressed this way, she had to be a wise woman, and not the legal kind but the kind people sneak to for love philtres, abortions, poisons.

She set a crystal globe on the table, such as I'd heard of gyppos and Ramblers using in their fortune-telling, and plumped down there with her back to my keyhole, but not before I got a look at her face. Small cruel eyes, clever and quick-moving. Her beaky nose had stayed sharp while the rest of her face grew bloated in pale fat.

After that glimpse, her flat-faced daughter slinking by impressed me as a near approach to nothing. Going to the door to meet the gray-haired woman, whose knock I heard, she looked flat all over, as if during her growing up – she was somewhere in the twenties – her mother had sat on her most of the time. Her whispery greeting to the gray-haired woman was rehearsed and phony: 'Peace unto you, Mam Byers! My mother is already in communication with your dear one.'

'Oh. Am I late?' Mam Byers spoke like a lady.

'Nay. Time is illusion.'

'Yes,' said Mam Byers, and added emptily: 'How nice you look, Lurette!'

'Thank you,' said the flat-faced twirp, keeping it on a high plane. 'Be seated.'

The fat woman had not turned her head. She sat motionless, a great bulging buzzard, giving me a view of the back of her fat neck, offering no greeting even when Mam Byers sat down at the table. I saw the lady's face then, lean, haggard, haunted. The fat woman said: 'Look in the deeps!'

Lurette closed the outer door against daylight and drew heavy curtains at the windows. She placed candles beside the crystal, and brought a burning splinter from the hearth in the next room to light them. Then she drifted off behind Mam Byers, watching for signals I think. I've never seen anyone who looked so much like a witless tool, as if she had given up trying to be a person and become a stick that her Ma used to poke things with.

'Look in the deeps! What do you see?'

'I see what I've seen before, Mam Zena, the bird trying to escape from a closed room.'

'Thy mother's spirit.'

'Oh, I believe,' said Mam Byers. 'I believe. I may have told you – when she was dying she wanted me to kiss her. The only thing she asked – have I told you?'

'Peace, Mam Byers!' She sighed, the great hag, and rested her enormous arms on the table, where I saw her fat sharp-pointed fingers curled like the legs of a spider. 'What does the poor bird do today, my dear?'

'Oh, the same – beating at the windows. It was the cancer – the smell – you understand, don't you? I couldn't kiss her. I pretended. She knew I was pretending …' Mam Byers had set down her expensive leather purse. I knew a poor village like this would have no more than one or two aristocratic families, and she would belong to one of them; it did her no good in dealing with these bloodsuckers. 'Is it possible, Mam Zena? Can you truly bring her, so that I could speak to her? – oh, it was so long ago!'

'All things are possible, if one has faith,' said Mam Zena, and Lurette was leaning over Mam Byers, stroking her shoulder and the back of her neck, speaking some words I couldn't catch in her whiny whisper.

'Oh!' said Mam Byers – 'I meant to give you this before.' And she started taking silver coins from her purse, but her hands shook, and presently she shoved the purse into Lurette's hands and seemed relieved to let go of it.

'Take it away, Lurette,' said Mam Zena. 'I cannot touch money.' Lurette carried the purse away to a side-table, and I saw her cringe at what must have been a burny-burn look from Ma. 'Take my hands, my dear, and now we must wait, and pray a little.'

That was evidently a signal for Lurette, who slipped out of the room and was gone a few minutes. She returned silently, coming only as far as the doorway behind Mam Byers to set down a dish of smoking incense which stunk up the place in no time. Lurette on that errand was naked except for a slimpsy pair of underpants, in the middle of a costume change I guessed; as she disappeared again I noticed that she looked flatter than ever in the nude.

It's worth remembering that Magi Zena and her whelp could easily have burned if this sort of thing was proved on them – the Church doesn't put up with that kind of competition. But I dare say there's no undertaking so dangerous, ridiculous, cruel or nasty but what plenty of goons are ready to have a go at it for a few dollars.

I got annoyed, and I suppose a little overcharged with teenage hell; besides, I had to get away with my load of wash. Lurette was obviously going to perform as the spirit of Mam Byers' mother; being the opposition candidate was the only thing I could see that might have a future. I freed my knife from under that yellow smock, and put on the big white one over it. It must have cleared Mam Zena's ankles; on me it swept the floor with considerable dignity, even after I cinched it up with one of the white loin-rags. This left me a pair of bosom-sacks out front which were fine for a lot more laundry. Of course I was a little over-balanced – more a 20th Century style as I look back on it now – and my red hair poking up through and around the towel I'd tied over it probably struck a false note, and there could have been a couple-three other things inconsistent with feminine charm at its best. In spite of being dressed for the part, I didn't *feel* matronly. So almost right away I gave up any idea of being the quiet type, and finding some tomato sauce on the shelves I splashed a gob of it over the front of the white smock, and more on my knife. I wouldn't be Mam Byers' mother after all, but just some well-nourished lady who'd died sudden and still resented it.

Back at my keyhole I saw Lurette about to float in with filmy stuff hung all around her. You could make out a mouth painted large, a pair of eyes, not much more.

Hypnotized in the smoky darkness, wanting to believe, Mam Byers would see anything those frauds wanted her to see. That was proved right away, for Lurette entered before I had my nerve screwed up to act. Mam Byers – poor soul, she couldn't stay at the table as Mam Zena told her to, but jumped up and held out her arms. It somehow gave me the push I needed. I cut loose with 'Murder! Murder!' and sailed in waving my gory blade.

Mam Zena rose like a bull out of a mud wallow, knocking over the table and candles, but it was Lurette who screamed in panic, and I went for her first, snatching hold of the drifting white stuff and tripping her so she hit the floor with a fine solid thud. Then I yanked back the window curtains, and when Mam Zena came for me – she had guts – I nipped behind her and started jabbing her in the rump, just enough to keep her active. 'Run!' I said, and quoted something nice I recalled from Father Clance's teaching: 'Flee from the wrath to come!'

She fled. I don't suppose anyone could stick around for that kind of goosing. She couldn't run for the village, not in a purple turban and black gown. She plunged away into the next room, and I had to let her go – also get out before she returned with some better weapon than mine. But meanwhile Lurette had scrambled up, and she did dart outside for the village, bare-ass, with no more sense than a spooked pullet. She was screeching 'Murder! Rape! Fire!' I never did find out which one she thought it was.

I shoved the purse into Mam Byers' wobbling hands. At least she had seen Lurette unveiled; more than that I couldn't wait to do. I think she was cursing me as I ran out. Anyone is likely to be cursed for smashing a make-believe.

I went down those corn rows to the woods about as fast as I've ever covered the ground, still brandishing my tomato-killer without knowing it. Sam said later that if he hadn't known me real well he'd've been worried about my condition, but as it was he just wondered why so much feminine influence didn't do more to bring out the softer side of my nature. Vilet said she loved me too.

On the way back to the cave, after I'd told them the whole amazing story of my girlhood, I stopped in my tracks. 'Balls of the prophet!' I said – 'I still got that dollar.'

'Oh snummy!' says Vilet, and Sam looked grave. We sat down on a log to reason it out. 'It'd be a sin if you'd meant to keep it, but you just forgot, didn't you, Spice?'

'Ayah. Stracted like.'

'Sure,' she said. 'Still I suppose we got to ask Jed what's the mor'l thing to do.'

Sam said: 'Jackson, I'm halfway wishful we wouldn't do that. I think it'd be mor'lly good for us to solve this 'ere by our lone. Frinstance, could young Jackson, or you, so't of go on keeping it without meaning to? – naw, naw, sorry, I can see that wouldn't be just right. More the kind of thing I'd do myself, being a loner by trade.'

'Of course,' Vilet said, 'them people was frauds and cheats – oh my gah!' She jumped up, spilling part of the loot she'd been carrying and brushing her worn old green smock as if she'd sat down on fire-ants. 'What if that old bag put a witchment onto the clo'es?'

'Nay, Jackson, I b'lieve she couldn't at this distance. Besides, them spirit-maker frauds a'n't real witches. Know what? – they be more so't of quackpot religioners, and you know how Jed feels about such-like. He wouldn't want no dollar going to support heresy, now would he?'

'That's a fact,' said Vilet. She was brushing the dirt off the clothes she'd flung away and folding them back into a nice bundle, her hands knowing and sensitive with the cloth. She had a good deal of faith in Sam's judgment when Jed and God weren't around.

'And look at it thisaway too,' Sam said; 'young Jackson heah has been under a bad strain – nay, I don't mean about was he a boy or a girl, I think we got that clear enough, he's as much a boy as any other jackass with balls, but what I mean, he done good work back theah, savin' a poor lady from sin and folly whiles we was just resting our ass in the brush. I won't say his hair has turned white from the exper'ence, because it ha'n't, but my reasoning is, he's *earned* that 'ere lucky dollar – a'n't that so, Jackson?'

'Ayah,' said Vilet. 'Ayah, that's so.'

'Kay. But now, old Jed, he lives on what we got to call a higher mor'l plane – right, Jackson?'

'That's right,' said Vilet.

'So if we was to tell a bang-up white lie about our boy leavin' the dollar theah, it'd spare Jed sorrow, right?'

'It would do that,' Vilet said. 'Still—'

'It'd keep the wheels of progress greased, *I* think.'

'Ayah,' said Vilet. 'Ayah, that's so.'

'Account of when you live on a higher mor'l plane, Jackson, you got no *time* to figger where ever' God-damn dollar went – if the Lord don't keep you hopping the unrighteous will.'

'Well,' said Vilet – 'well, I guess you're right ...'

We stayed at our cave hideaway a few weeks more, while Vilet fixed up clothes for us. She carried a little sewing-kit, and I never tired of watching her skill with it. Scissors, thimble, a few needles and a spool or two of wool thread; that was it, but Vilet could clutter up the landscape with marvels in a way I've seldom seen surpassed. The huge white smock provided three good freeman's white loin-rags for us and part of a shirt for Jed; then Vilet was able to cobble up the rest of that shirt and two more for Sam and me out of the remainder of poor Miss Davy's wash. That done, she cussed and sweated some, remodeling the yellow smock for herself, asking the woods and sky why in hell Lurette couldn't at least have grown a pair of hips. She dissected it, however, and added whatsits here and there; when she was done, it fit her cute as buttons.

We went on making plans. It seems to be a human necessity, a way of writing your name on a blank wall that may not be there. I can't very well condemn it, for even nowadays I'm always after doing it myself. We planned we'd go a few miles beyond that village and then strike out boldly on the Northeast Road. I with my real Moha accent would do most of the talking, we planned, but we'd all need to be rehearsed in a good story.

Jed and Vilet, we decided, had better be man and wife – they would be truly anyhow when they got to Vairmant. We four were all quite different in looks, but Vilet claimed she could see a kind of resemblance between Sam's face and mine, and was so positive about it I began to see it myself in spite of the obvious differences – Sam stringy and tall with a thin nose, I stocky and short with a puggy one. 'It's mouth and forehead,' Vilet said, 'and the eyes, some. Davy is blue-eyed but it's a darkish blue, and yourn mightn't look too different, Sam, if you was redheaded.'

'Got called Sandy when I was young,' he said. 'It wa'n't never a real red. If I was a real red-top like young Jackson, likely I could've busted my head through stone walls some better'n I have, last thirty-odd yeahs.'

'Now, Sam,' said Jed, 'it don't seem to me, honest it don't, that God'd give a man the power to put his head through a stone wall except in a manner of speaking, like. Unless of course the wall was crumbly, or—'

'It was a manner of speaking,' said Sam.

After kicking it around a good deal, we worked it out that Sam would be my uncle and Vilet's cousin. Jed had a brother in Vairmant who'd just recently died – born in Vairmant himself but moved away when young to Chengo off in western Moha. This brother bequeathed Jed the family farm and we were all going there to work it together. As for me, my parents died of smallpox when I was a baby, and my dear uncle took me in, being a bachelor himself, in fact a loner by trade. When my Pa and Ma died we were living in Katskil, although originally a Moha family, from Kanhar, an important family, damn it.

'I dunno,' said Jed. 'It don't seem just right.'

'A manner of speaking, Jackson. Besides, I didn't mean them hightoned Loomises from Kanhar was aristocrats – just a solid freeman family with a few Misters. Like my own Uncle Jeshurun – Kanhar Town Council give him a Mister, and why? Account the taxes he paid on the old brewery is why, the way it was in the family couple-three generations—'

'Wine is a mocker,' said Jed. 'I don't want you should go imagining things like breweries.'

'Damn-gabble it, man,' Sam said, 'I'm merely telling you what they done, no use telling a story like this'n if it don't sound like facts. I didn't start the durn brewery, more b' token if you ever hear tell of making wine in a brewery I want to know. It was great-gran'ther sta'ted it, understand, and she run along like a beaut till my Uncle Jeshurun, him with the wooden leg, took to drinking up the profits.'

Jed studied away at it, not happy.

'You mean he done that too in a manner of speaking?'

'He sure as hell did.'

'I mean, it just don't seem to me, Sam, that people are going to believe it. About drinking up a whole brewery. He couldn't do it.'

'I can see you didn't know my Uncle Jeshurun. Leg was hollow, Jackson. Old sumbitch'd fill it up at the brewery after a long drunken work-day, take it home and get plastered, carry on like crazy all night long. He didn't just die neither, not my Uncle Jeshurun. He blowed. Leanin' over to blow out a candle, forgot whichaway to blow being drunk at the time, or rather he was never sober. Breathed in 'stead of out, all that alcohol in him went whoom – Jesus and Abraham, Mister, not enough left of the old pot-walloper to swear by. Piece of his old wooden leg come down into a cow pasture a mile away. Killed a calf. My Aunt Clotilda said it was a judgment – onto my uncle, I mean. Still, if it hadn't happened he might've had to leave town.'

15

We started the day after the clothes were finished; we may all have been afraid of coming to like that cave too much. At least Sam and I felt – without ever saying so – that we would always be in some way on the move; and for Jed and Vilet the farm in Vairmant colored the future with the warmth of a lamp.

It's odd how little thought we gave the war, after being out of touch with the world more than three months. We wondered, and made some idle talk of it, but until we were on the move again, and the days were flowing out of June into the golden immensity of midsummer, we felt no urgent need to learn what the armies had done while we were so much at peace. They could have passed and repassed on the Northeast Road, Skoar could have fallen, we'd never have known it.

The border wars of that time and place were a far cry from what I saw and experienced of war later on in Nuin. In the Moha-Katskil war of 317 I don't suppose there were ever more than two thousand men involved in a battle: mostly feinting and maneuvering, armies shoving for position along the few important roads, avoiding the wilderness as much as they could; the forest ambush those Katskil men tried outside Skoar was unusual. As it happened, I saw no more of that particular war. It was settled by negotiation in September. Katskil ceded a trifling port and a few square miles of ground on the Hudson Sea in return for the town of Seneca and a thirty-mile strip of territory that gave them a long-desired access to the Ontara Sea. Brian VI of Katskil had other smart reasons for demanding those treaty terms – I didn't appreciate this until long later, when I was with Dion in Nuin and getting my own inside view of high-level politics. That thirty-mile strip cut off Moha from any land approach to the western wilderness; so if that unknown, probably rich region is ever tapped by land routes it will be a matter between Katskil and Penn – Moha needn't bother.

When we left our cave I was concerned with the more ancient war of human beings against other creatures who desire to hold a place on earth. I felt, superstitiously, that we had been having it too easy. In our hunting and fishing while we stayed at the cave we'd encountered nothing more dangerous than a few snakes. Once a puma started out of the brush ahead of Vilet and me and took off in almost comic terror. One night we smelled a bear, who might have got troublesome if he could have climbed after our supplies. It was only a black of course, as we knew from the prints we found in the morning. The great red bear is so scarce in southern Moha one never really expects to see him. North of Moha Water he is plentiful enough, one of the chief reasons why that great triangle of mountain country bounded by Moha Water and the Lorenta Sea remains mostly unexplored.

I find it strange, in reading Old-Time books, to notice what unconcern the people of that age felt about wild beasts, who were scarce and timid then, overwhelmed by human power and crowding and incredible weapons. Man in that time truly seemed to be master of the earth. In our day, a few hundred years later, I suppose he's still the most intelligent animal at large, even still likely to succeed if he ever learns how to quit cutting his brother's throat, but he is under a slight cloud. We might become masters of the world again, but perhaps we ought to watch out for a certain cleverness I've noticed in the forepaws of rats and mice and squirrels. If they'd develop speech and start using a few easy tools, say knives and clubs, it wouldn't be long before they were explaining the will of God and rigging elections.

Gunpowder is forbidden by law and religion,[16] and this may be just as well, since guns to make use of it are forbidden also by lack of steel, lack of a technology capable of designing and making them, and nowadays by a lack of belief that such instruments ever existed. Since a vast amount of fiction was produced in Old Time, it is wonderful how the Church today can explain away anything unwelcome in the surviving fragments of the old literature by calling it fiction.

We had to remember that some bandit gangs were said to roam the wilderness, though eastern Moha did not have too bad a reputation that way – southern Katskil is lousy with them. Such outlaw gangs care nothing for laws or national boundaries; they live off the wilderness, and now and then take a toll from the villagers. Hardy souls – they kill off their old people, rumor says, and admit new members only after savage ordeals. The gangs are small – in Moha or Nuin you never hear of one attacking a town of any importance, or a large caravan[17] even for hit-and-run raids. The Cod Islands pirates are popularly supposed to have started from a bandit gang that got clever with small war vessels and then almost grew into a nation. In Conicut I heard the tale of a whole army battalion routed by a couple of dozen bandits who decided the soldiers were encroaching. The story was set in the rather distant past; the begging street-corner storytellers preferred a version in which the bandits had trained teams of blade wolves to help them, under the command of a most unusual character named Robin or Robert Hoode.

I knew some unhappy moments when we went away from the cave for good that morning. For one thing I saw few opportunities ahead for playing with Vilet; with the feeling of losing her, I even imagined a little that I was in love with her – her common sense would have taken care of that if I had spoken of it; since I didn't, my own brains were obliged to handle it, and did so moderately well. Leaving the cave was in many other ways a goodbye—

---

[16] The prohibition appears thus in the Book of Universal Law, 19th edition (the latest I believe) published at Nuber in 322: 'It is and shall be utterly and forever forbidden on pain of death by whatever method the Ecclesiastical Court of the district shall decide, to manufacture, describe, discuss, create any written reference to, or in any manner whatsoever make use of the substance vulgarly known as Gunpowder, or any other substance that may by competent authorities of the Church be reasonably suspected of containing atoms.'
– Dion M. M.

[17] Any group of travelers who follow the roads and keep together for safety is called a caravan. The word seems to have been used a little differently in Old Time.
– Dion M. M.

I know: so is any moment. What happened to the jo who was breathing with your lungs five minutes ago? – or don't you care?

We spent most of the day in cautious travel through the woods, until we could be sure we were well beyond the village that had been so good as to furnish us with respectable clothes. I did wish I might have learned what happened there when Lurette crashed in shrieking about rape and fire, but I never shall know, so what the hell, write that story yourself if you're man enough. Then we altered our course, and came out on the Northeast Road at a place where it was climbing a considerable rise, the longer and steeper part still ahead of us. The sun stood behind us in the west; everything lay in a hot bright hush. We saw a few lines of smoke here and there in the south, distant villages. Nothing was moving on the road as we stepped out there in our good clothes – white freeman's loin-rags, decent brown shirts, Vilet in the remodeled yellow smock. And we heard nothing – no voice, no creak of cartwheels, no sound of cattle or horse or man. On the other side of the rise ahead of us there could be anything.

Jed asked: 'What day is it?'

Bedam if we knew. I said Thursday, but Jed wasn't sure, and started fretting that he might have let a Friday morning go by without special prayers. He was for having them then and there by the roadside, but I said: 'Wait, and hush the clack a minute – I want to listen.'

I wanted something more than listening. I motioned them to stay where they were, and stepped a short way up the road to get clear of the human smell and study the breeze. Even then I wasn't sure.

I wished something human might join us, but the hot afternoon was quiet as a sleep. It happens Jed was right – the day was a Friday, the day God is said to have rested from the labors of creation, when all but the most necessary travel is forbidden or at least frowned on. And the war was still a fact, discouraging travel, though nothing in the summer air could make you think of it. Finally, it was late enough in the day so that any sensible traveler would be thinking of supper-time behind stockade walls.

When I rejoined the others Sam asked me carefully: 'Did you catch it?'

'I think so.' I saw Jed didn't understand. 'We best move right on, keep close together till we come to a settlement. I think I smell tiger.'

How steep was that sunny slope, how very long! I wanted us to climb it quietly, and Sam urged that too, but Jed thought best to pray, and when Sam asked him to avoid making noise and save his breath, Jed merely looked forgiving and went on praying, no help for it.

The road approached the illusion of an ending at open sky. You may see that, wherever a road mounts a hill, and you think of a drop into nothing or of sudden dying. If I could return to that strip of road today and travel it without alarm, without the faint ammoniac reek of the thing that was somewhere near us unheard, I suppose it would seem an ordinary climb. It was not so steep that a single ox couldn't have hauled a heavy cart to the summit – I dare say that was the standard of adequate road-building in most parts of Moha. Yet whenever the smell seemed to strengthen, or I imagined some hint of tawny motion among the trees at my left, I felt like a wingless bug climbing a wall.

Nor was that piece of road so very long, really – a quarter-mile perhaps, or less. The sun was not noticeably lower when we reached the crest of the rise – we did reach it, all four of us alive – and looked down, and saw a thing that might save us from the tiger, or might not.

We saw a stockaded village, the walls fairly well made, and it stood boldly at the edge of the road, no hideaway wilderness thing but civilized, respectable, important in its own right. It lay far enough below us in the valley so that we could see all but the north end of it, which was hidden by forest growth coming close to the stockade. We saw behind the palings a graceful church spire, the usual design of an upright bar rising from the wheel, and an orderly array of rooftops, including those of quite a few two-story dwellings. Next to the road, on our side, was a generous area of cleared land, with corn-patches, and black spots that showed where they maintained guard-fires at night to keep the deer, bison, woods buffalo and small creatures from ruining their plantings. Far down, yes, nearly half a mile, and for much of that distance, until we reached the corn planting, there would still be trees and brush creating a mystery at our left.

As we began the descent, Jed Sever would not look to either side of the road, not into the trees nor away into the lovely sunshine and green slopes of the southern side. He trusted instinct to place his feet for him, and looked upward toward his God, asking forgiveness for the sins of all of us. He was asking also that if the beast should strike it might take him first and not one of his friends – for he, though an even more wretched sinner perhaps beyond hope of salvation, was nevertheless more prepared in his mind for judgment and the wrath to come. 'And if it be thy will,' he said, 'let their sins be upon me, Abraham chosen of God, Spokesman, Redeemer, and not upon them, but let 'em be washed clean in my blood[18] forever and ever amen.'

Jed also tried to motion poor Vilet away from him to the other, probably

---

[18] The Holy Murcan Church apparently adopted the fantasy of vicarious atonement from Old-Time Christianity with one curious modification. According to the modern creed, any saintly man, not only Christ or Abraham, can take on himself the sins of others if the Lord agrees to the deal. Like modern believers, the Christians of Old Time seem never to have felt anything repellent or atrocious in the doctrine that a man could get a free ride into heaven on the suffering and death of another. The parallel to primitive god-killing rituals was of course noted only by scholars.

– Dion M. M.

safer side of the road, walking himself nearest to the forest cover, the sweat pouring from his forehead like tears. His big hands swung idle with no look of readiness for sword-work.

I can remember the distress his prayer gave me, in spite of my own fear and alertness. It seemed to me, especially in my new and bewildering acquaintance with heresy, that if there was one thing above all I could let no one else I carry for me, it was my sins. Today I can discover no sin in anything except cruelty and its variations, and this for reasons that have nothing to do with religion, but on that day I was yet a long way from such opinions.

As we continued down the other side of that hill, the tiger scent diminished. I think it was some shift in the barely perceptible currents of the air. He was present but he did not strike. We moved on down the road – passing the forest cover at our left, reaching the corn plantings, passing them, approaching the open region and the village gate, and he did not strike.

From within the village came the sweet jangling of triple bells. Often they are made of the best bronze from Katskil or Penn – the Church can afford it – and the makers try to cast each group so that it will sound a major triad with the fifth in the bass. The third, struck last, floats in the high treble toward a tranquillity resembling peace, and the overtones play with a hundred rainbows. These village bells were announcing five o'clock: '*Time to quit work and pray and have supper.*'

Jed's prayers ended rather flatly. I still glanced behind me as often as I had done when we had the trees at our left, but the tiger did not strike, not then. I did not see him, not then.

The main gate of such a village is usually open during daylight hours so long as a guard is present, but not on Fridays, when it's considered best to keep folk within God's easy reach. So that day the ponderous log gate was shut, but I looked through a chink in the log slabs and saw the guard in his grass-thatched shelter, not asleep but mighty restful, sprawled on his cot with a leg hooked over a raised knee and his policer cap let down over his eyes. He bounced up fast enough when I hollered: 'Hoy!'

Well, there are some things you do and say when approaching a strange village, and some you don't. I'd goofed in my usual rapid way, too rapid for Sam or Vilet to stop me, as I knew when the guard came swaggering with his javelin up and ready. I whispered to Sam: 'Make like a Mister, think you could?'

He nodded, and was in front of me by the time the guard got the gate open and started bawling me out for disturbing the Friday peace – no manners – what ailed me anyhow?

Sam said: 'My man, I apologize for my nephew's hasty speech. I am Mister Samuel Loomis of Kanhar, more recently of Chengo, and the lady is my cousin. This is her husband, Mister Jedro Sever, also late of Chengo but a legal resident of Monster, Vairmant – you may address her as Mam Sever when apologizing for your own bad manners.' Sam had hitched his shirt slightly so that the hilt of his sheathed knife was visible, and he was rubbing a horny old thumb back and forth across the end of the bone knife-hilt, and looking down at that thumb along his thin nose, not as if he gave a damn, just sad and patient and thoughtful.

'Mam, I – Mam Sever, I – Mam, I—'

That could have gone on a long time. Sam cut it short by asking delicately: 'Is the apology satisfactory, Cousin? And Jackson?'

'Oh, quait,' says Vilet, hamming it some but not too much, and I mumbled my own snooty graciousness, and Sam flipped him a two-bit to quiet the pain. Sam had startled me as badly as he had the guard – I'd never guessed he knew how to talk in that hightoned way. Maybe Dion could have found fault with it, but not I. He put me in mind of what I'd imagined about some of the fine old historical characters I'd learned of in school, in what they called a Summary of Old-Time History. Honest, Sam was just as cool and grand and you-be-damned as the best of them – Socrates, Julius Caesar, Charlemagne, or that splendid short-tempered sumbitch, I'll think of his name in a minute, who r'ared up and whipped the Barons and Danes and Romans and things out of merry England and clear across the Delaware before he was satisfied to let them go – Magnum Carter, that's who it was.

'Well, man,' said Sam, 'can we find anything in this village in the nature of decent accommodations?'

'Oh yes, sir, the Black Prince tavern will have nice rooms, I know the people and—'

'How far is Humber Town from here?'

'About ten miles, sir. Oughta be a coach from Skoar going through to Humber Town tomorrow – once a week, Saturdays, and always stops here of course, though with the war and all—'

'Ayah, the rest of our caravan is waiting on that coach at the last village where we stopped, some piddlepot hole in the ground, I didn't trouble to learn its name.'

'Perkunsvil,' said the guard with solemn pleasure. In a jerkwater village you can hardly go wrong by blackening the reputation of neighboring dumps.

'I guess. We got tired waiting for it. What town is this?'

'This is East Perkunsvil.'

'Nice location. There's tiger up yonder, by the way – see many hereabout as a rule?'

'What! No, sir, that can't hardly be.'

Jed spoke for the first time, and reprovingly: 'Why not, man? Brown tiger's like unto the flame of God that burneth where it will.'

The guard bowed, the way you'd better do at hearing anything with a holy sound, but he was stubborn. 'Sir, I can tell you, brown tiger never comes anear this town. We don't ask God's reasons for the special mercy, it's just so.'

I've noticed every village needs a unique source of pride. It may be a claim that nobody in the village ever had smallpox, or all babies are born with dark hair, or the local wise woman's aphrodisiacs are the aphrodizziest within forty miles – no matter what, so long as it provides a mark of distinction. In East Perkunsvil I suppose tiger hadn't come over the stockade within the memory of the oldest inhabitant, so the village was sure God had arranged that he never would. Sam bowed nicely and said: 'You be rema'kably favored, doubtless a manifestation.'

'Yes, sir, it may well be.' He was downright friendly now as well as respectful. 'Yes, sir, lived here all my life, and that's twenty-six years, never even seen the beast'

Vilet said: 'Look up yonder then!'

Now chance never plays into *my* hands that way. If I'd said that, the brute would have been well out of sight before any head turned. And I guess Vilet had never got many breaks of that kind either, for later when we four were settled in our rooms at the Black Prince she had to go over it three or four times, and each time it put her in a warm sweet glow: '"Lookit up yonder then!" I says, right smackdab on the very *second* I says it, and wasn't his o' face just like a fish and you a-squeezin' it to get the hook out? – oh snummy!' And she'd bounce and slap her leg and tell it again.

I must have turned when she spoke as quickly as the others, yet I felt as if my head were moving against a resistance, unready to behold a thing that all my life I had feared and in some way desired to behold. Smelling the beast on the road, I had known him from catching that smell once before in the hill country west of Skoar. It's ranker than puma smell, seems to hang heavier in the air. At that earlier time it had seemed just not quite right for puma, and I had climbed a tree and spent a long night there shivering, smelling him and thinking I did but not once hearing or seeing him. In the morning I'd wobbled down and found his enormous pugs in a bare spot of earth, deep, as if he might have stood there some time observing me through the dark, old Eye-of-Fire, and maybe thinking: *Well, let's wait till Red gets a mite bigger and fatter* ...

Now, I saw him.

A short way down from the crest of the hill we had descended lay a high flat-topped rock, thirty feet from the road on the open side, across from the forest. The top was slightly tilted, away from the road, so that when we walked past, it had looked like a simple edge, nothing to tell of the slanting platform. Had he watched us go by, or only just now arrived there? Maybe he had been not hungry, or restrained by the fact there were four of us. Maybe he knew my bow meant danger. I imagined him amusing himself with false starts, quivering his hindquarters, playing and enjoying the cat-game of delayed decision and finally for his own reasons allowing us to proceed. Now, following his immediate whim, he stood tall, and I saw him in remote dark gold against the deepening midsummer sky.

He gazed down toward us, or more likely beyond us. He must have known or sensed that the distance was too great for the flight of an arrow from my bow, if he was experienced in such things. He turned on his high rock with no haste at all, flowingly, to stare in another direction, off to the south across the valley, perhaps indifferently observing the smoke of other human places.

He sat down and raised a curled paw to his mouth to lick it and rub it comfortably over the top of his head. Then he washed his flank, and up went a hind leg cat-style so he could lean down and nuzzle his privates. He lost balance comically because of the slope of the rock, righted himself with a comedian's ease, and lay down and rolled with his feet in the air. And when he tired of that he yawned, and jumped down, and strolled across the road into the woods, and for a while he was gone.

16

That was the first time I had seen the inside of a village. Since then I've seen more than I can plainly remember, for when I was with Rumley's Ramblers we visited one after another throughout Levannon, Bershar, Conicut, Katskil, more than a year in Penn; the atmosphere and the people may vary a great deal, but the general pattern is much the same in all the nations. Wherever you find them, such villages are designed for one fundamental purpose, to give a small human community a bit of safety in a world where our breed is no longer numerous, not rich and sleek as in Old Time, not wise, and not very brave.

They are usually laid out in a square, in some location where a stream crosses fairly level ground. The drinking water comes from the upstream end, and the rest of the stream is regarded as a sewer – saves digging. Main Street, running down the midline of the village, will be rather wide and ordinarily straight, so that when you enter by the front gate you look all the way to the one in the rear; the other streets will be narrow except for the area, not always called a street, formed by a cleared space just inside the stockade.

Often a green occupies the center of the village facing Main Street, with the usual equipment – bandstand, whipping post, stocks, pillory and maybe a nice wading pool for the children. You'll notice one block of houses better than the rest – bigger yards, maybe flower-beds along with the necessary vegetable patch, even a slave hut out back next the privy demonstrating that the family owns a servant or two instead of renting them out from the slave barracks on the downstream side of town. On that downstream side, beside the barracks, you can find what the people sometimes call the 'factory', really a warehouse, for the village industries – home weaving, baskets, cabinet-work or whatever. The policer station will be on that side, and the jail, the public stable, the legal whorehouse, blacksmith shop, probably the baiting-pit if the village can afford to maintain one; and there will be several blocks on that side where the houses sag together in dejection, the drunks would rather sleep it off in their front yards than indoors, being independent free-men, and if any pigs from the prosperous neighborhood go hunting garbage on that side of town they prefer to travel in pairs.

In between those extremes stand the middle-class blocks, where the ideal is a harking back to Old Time, with all the houses exactly alike, all yards and gardens exactly alike, all the privies exactly alike with small crescent windows of precisely the same size emitting the same flavor of socially significant togetherness.

Now that I'd made Sam a Mister in my hasty way, he couldn't get out of it, and figured he might as well r'ar back and enjoy it. He was still carrying himself like God's favorite adviser when we blew in at the Black Prince. As a result, the weedy ancient in charge of the flea-bag fawned all over us, charging twice the normal rate for two of his best rooms which would have done credit to a hog farm anywhere; Sam wanted to bargain, but was afraid it might damage the picture of ourselves as slightly important nobs. He said later that this was a considerable grief to him, descended as he was from a long line of illustrious chicken-thieves. He caught up on the bargaining later, with Rumley's Ramblers. I've heard Pa Rumley say that Sam could have bargained the beard off a prophet, and he meant Jeremiar himself, which was near-about the finest praise Pa Rumley could give any man. You know how attached prophets get to their beards, and Jeremiar was a vigorous type, who worked up such a thriving trade in woe and lamentations that the opposition finally crowded him into an ark and sent him down-river among the bull-rushes to get rid of him.

A group of pilgrims from up north had already got the very best rooms at the Black Prince, overlooking Main Street; our two were second best, I guess, each with a slit of window looking north; I would have hated to see the worst. Beside the rickety cots they called beds the walls displayed dark smears telling of collisions between the human race and one of its closest, sincerest admirers. And over all things like a saintly benediction lay the smell of cabbage.

In a bedbug, so far as I understand him, there is not a trace of mirth or loving-kindness. Even their admiration for humanity is based on deep-seated greed. They have intellect, to be sure – how else would they know the exact moment when you're about to fall asleep, and select that moment for a stab? Dion says bugs go by instinct. I asked him: 'What's instinct?' He said: 'Oh, you go to hell!' Then Nickie flung in the statement that when you do something p'ison clever without a notion of what it's all about, that's instinct. But I still think they have intellect, and they probably brood too much until it curdles their dispositions, for note this: I never met a bug who showed me a trace of liking or respect, no matter what I'd done for him. Contempt is what they show, contempt. I've known a bug to stare me in the eye with my gore dripping from his jaws, and anyone could tell from his vinegary face that he was comparing me with other meals in the past and finding fault with everything – too salty, too gamy, needing more sass, something. He wouldn't have complimented me if I'd spiced my ass and put butter on it. So I con-temptify 'em right back. I hate bugs. Damn a bug.

The vital philosophic point I'm trying to ram home through the fog of your incomprehension is this: If the human race should perish completely, what would become of the bedbug? I'm sorry I cursed them. We must return good for evil, it says here.

In the evolutionary sense, they must have grown up with us, and now they can't get along without us. Fleas are all right. Fleas don't need us. They'd eat anything, even a tax-collector. But the bedbug is our dependent, our respon-sibility. We made him what he is. He cries to us: 'Strive on, lest we too perish!' Let us therefore[19]—

I was about to digress anyway, before I began to notice how the fermented essence of an attractive grape that grows wild here on the island Neonar-cheos has a curious side-effect, namely intoxication. According to the best information I can get together, that was last night; this is the following morn-ing, somewhat late – any time now I expect to begin thinking that I shall live.

Captain Barr returned yesterday, which made it one of the days we cele-brate, after sailing futher than he had intended. He was driven partly, he says, by a reluctance to believe what he was finding out.

There's no longer any doubt that this island where we have settled is the smallest and most westerly of the archipelago that in Old Times was named the Azores. The islands – smaller and differently shaped of course because of

[19] I put him to bed, Nickie – he'll be all right in the morning.

– Dion.

the rise in sea level – are all accounted for where the old map says they should be. And nowhere in all the group could Captain Barr discover any token of humanity. Goats, wild sheep, monkeys; on one island the men glimpsed a pack of what looked like wild brown dogs chasing a deer. Birds were everywhere, and in a bay where the *Morning Star* anchored, enormous sea snakes were playing in the shallow water, creatures I can't find described in any of the old books. Never a human figure, never any smoke against the sky. In the night hours at anchor, never a light on land, nor any sound but insects and frogs and night birds, and the talk of breakers on the sand. In the best natural harbors, jungle grows to the water's edge, hiding the debris of whatever men might have built there in Old Time.

Our ancient map shows shipping and air lines converging at this obvious way station between Europe and the Americas. We know there had to be developed harbors, airports, towns.

No bomb would have fallen here in what John Barth calls the 'one-day explosion.' Very few fell anywhere, he says, and those were later called 'accidents' by the surviving governments – he adds that the obliteration of twenty-odd million New Yorkers and Muscovites could perhaps be considered a 'fairly major accident.' Perhaps in these islands destruction came from the plagues that followed the war. John Barth wonders in his pages how many of the plagues were directly man-made and how many the result of viral or bacterial mutations, and comes to the reasonable conclusion that nobody can ever know. Or it may have been, here in the islands, the longer, quiet, almost orderly extinction of sterility, natural deaths exceeding the scanty births, in a population so long used to being taken care of by advanced technology that it could no longer look after itself, until eventually, somewhere, an old person died among the weeds with no one to scratch out a grave.

After all, in our own homelands, many non-human species died out from one cause or another. I have never seen a bluebird.

Those pilgrims were a pleasant crowd, in the care of a gentle willowy priest. He had long yellow hair that would be ready for a bath any day, and a homely mild face. His nose appeared to taper in the wrong direction because the tip was small and the space between his milky blue eyes quite wide, so the total effect was mousy. I liked him. When a man's wearing a floor-length shapeless priest's robe it's hard to tell whether he's tiptoeing, but Father Fay did seem to be, anyway there was a tittupy up-and-downness in his walk, and a flowing lift of his pretty white hands at each step, and most of the time a bright mousy deliberating smile. The pilgrims all respected him, even including the ten-year-old boy Jerry, who gave Father Fay a bad time not from any disrespect but just because ten-year-olds are like that.

I noticed Jerry even before we'd entered the Black Prince. The pilgrims were coming away from the church as we approached the inn, an orderly line with Father Fay doodle-diddling along at the head of it, and Jerry had somehow managed to get down at the tail without his Pa or Ma noticing. So what does he do but fall further back and cut monkeyshines in his pretty white Pilgrim's robe, a wavy warplume sticking up at the back of his head that the angels themselves couldn't comb flat. First he sticks out his rear and goes humping along imitating a poor old lady who's one of the pilgrims; then he straightens, and hikes his robe all the way to his navel, and proceeds bare-ass in a fine rendering of Father Fay's tiptoe, with a heavenly smile gleaming among the freckles and his little pecker flipping up at every step like a tiny flag in the wind. Terrible sacrilege, but I remember even Jed couldn't help chuckling.

They were bound for Nuber the Holy City, like almost every pilgrim group you were likely to meet west of the Hudson Sea; their all-white garments along with Father Fay's black would identify them as far off as you could see them, and no soldiers of either side would dare trouble them.

After Sam and I turned in and tried to settle ourselves for sleeping, as Jed and Vilet were doing in their room, I heard Jerry getting a bath. His Ma had evidently insisted on the inn help's bringing up a tin tub and water, just for that purpose. He was enjoying it, and raising all kinds of hell, roaring and splashing and making damn-fool remarks – you'd have thought the poor lady was trying to wash a bandit king. Then Pa came up from downstairs; there was a moment's fearful quiet, a fine solid whack on a wet backside, and from there on Jerry was being an awful good boy.

But as for Sam and me, after the first few attempts at sleep the cots were simply too war-torn and bloody for any use. We gave up and spread well-shaken blankets on the floor, hoping the hostile forces would lose enough time searching to give us a little rest.

The scent of tiger must have been thick in the air that night before we heard him roar. The heavy midsummer dark was trilling and jangling with the noise of insects and frogs, but I heard few other voices – no fox or wildcat was sending any messages abroad. At the inn, with other thick smells around me, I could not pick out the tiger's reek, but I felt his presence. I saw him repeatedly as he had looked on his rock in the late sunlight, and I knew he was out there in the dark, perhaps not far away.

When he did speak at last, even the insect noises briefly hushed, as if each witless clamoring thing had winced in the shell of a tiny body feeling a *What-was-that?*

His roar is blunt, short, harsh. It does not seem very loud, but has intense carrying power. It is never prolonged and he does not soon repeat it. Maybe he roars in order to frighten the game into a betraying shudder. The roar is too all-penetrating, too deep in the bass, too much a pain and quivering in your own marrow, to give you a true knowledge of his location. When I heard him that night he could have been half a mile away, or in the village itself strolling down one of the black streets in massive calm and readiness to destroy. I stole to the window, silently as though even inside this building a noise of my own could endanger me. Sam's voice came out of the dark: 'Sounds like the old sumbitch a'n't too far off.' I heard him shift and brace up on his elbow, listening to the night as I was.

The tiger did not speak again, but in the next room beyond the closed door I heard Vilet suddenly say: 'Oh, Jed! Oh – oh –' and there was the rhythmic squeak of a cot, and a thumping as a wooden frame beat against the wall; for a moment or two I also heard Jed groan like a slave under the lash, and Sam said under his breath: 'I'll be damned.'

It was soon quiet again in there, at least no sound penetrated the doorway. Sam came over to the window and presently murmured: 'Cur'ous – I didn't think he could.'

'Just once, Vilet told me. Just once, with that Kingstone whore he talks about so often.'

'Ayah, told me the same.' I felt him watching me kindly and speculatively through the dark. Then he was leaning out the window, his dimly starlit face gazing down at the lightless village. 'Little cunt been taking care of you, Jackson?'

'Ayah.' I suppose my dull embarrassment was a result of orphanage training, a mixture of sour prudery and piety, that sticky mess with which the human race so often tars and feathers its children.

Sam and I could hear a child crying, away off somewhere in the village, probably frightened by the tiger's roar; it was a persistent helpless whimpering that a woman's tired and kindly voice was trying to soothe. I heard her say – somewhere, bodiless, as if the words hung in the dark – 'Ai-yah, now, he can't get you, baby …'

Getting dressed in the morning, it occurred to me, as I had suspected during dinner the night before – fast-breaking Friday dinner after sundown – that it wasn't all fluff and candy, being advanced from a bond-servant yard-boy, the lowest object above a slave, to the nephew of a long-legged Mister. I'd achieved this wonder myself, sure, but remembering that was small comfort. There are heavy penalties for impersonating an aristocrat, as heavy as the penalties on a bond-servant for wearing a freeman's white loin-rag. I had to burble to Sam about the remarkable powers of a plain white rag, but he was more interested in the practical side than in the dad-gandered almighty philosophy of it. 'It comes to me, Jackson, you got to watch some of the God-damn *little* things, like not picking your nose nor wiping it so loud on the back of your hand, at least not whiles you be eating. Occurred to me last night at supper, but I didn't want to say anything with them pilgrims chomping away right at our elbows.'

'Well,' I said, 'I had a snuffle and besides, I've seen gentlemen do that, at the Bull-and-Iron.'

'There's an old saying, rank got its privileges, but a Mister's nephew an't all that important, Jackson. And another thing – language. Frinstance, when they brang in that God-forgotten smoked codfish last night, which smelt as if a whole pile of moldy ancestors had sudden-like gone illegitimate, why, an aristocrat would've told 'em to take it away, sure, and he'd've said something real brisk that they'd long remember, *but* – with a gang of holy pilgrims at the next table, Jackson, he wouldn't r'ar back and holler: "Who shit all over my plate?" He just wouldn't, Jackson.'

'Sorry,' I said, sulky – I hadn't slept much. 'I didn't know pilgrims didn't have to.'

'It an't that, Jackson. In fact I b'lieve they do, in a manner of speaking. But the dad-gandered almighty thing of it is, you got to consider your influence on the young, the plague-take-it young. You take that 'ere young Jerry. Next time his Ma tells him to eat something he don't fancy, ask yourself what he's going to do and say – if his Da an't within hearing. Just ask yourself.'

'See what you mean. An't he a pisser, though!'

'Ayah.' But I couldn't sidetrack Sam when he was feeling educational. 'And you take farting, Jackson. Common people like what you and me really be, we don't pay it no mind, or we laugh or something, but if you're going to be the nephew of a Mister you got to do a little different. If you let a noisy one go, you don't say: "Hoy, how about that?" No, sir, you're supposed to get a sadful-dreamy look onto y' face, and study the others present as if you'd just never imagined they could *do* such a rude thing.'

Vilet and Jed came into our room then, and Sam let up on me. Jed looked all wrong, dark under the eyes as if he hadn't slept, with a tremor in his big clumsy hands, and so Vilet of course was troubled about him. Sam was inquiring politely about the bugs on their side of the wall when Jed, not listening, crashed into it saying: 'I prayed all night, but the word of God is withheld.'

Vilet said: 'Now, Jed –' fondling his arm while he just stood there, two hundred pounds of gloom, a great harmless bull somehow beat-out, no fight in him.

'I'd ought to leave y' company,' Jed said – 'a hopeless sinner like I be.' He sat on my cot heavily and wearily; I remember seeing him look down and appear dimly surprised to find his hand resting on my sack, on the bulge of the golden horn, and he lifted the hand away as if it weren't right for him to touch a thing that had come from a holy hermit. 'And the Lord said: I will spew thee out of my mouth –'s what he said, it's somewhere in the book. And that an't all—'

'Now, Jed, honey thing—'

'Nay, hesh, woman. I got to call to y' mind what the disciple Simon said: The Lord spoke but I turned aside. Remember? It's what he said after he'd denied Abraham and the Spokesman a-dyin', a-hangin' on the wheel in the Nuber marketplace. "And they brought Simon to the marketplace –" that's how it goes, remember? – "to the marketplace, and Simon said: I do not know this man. And they questioned him again, but he said: I do not know this man." And then you remember, afterward, when Simon was put to the rack in the Nuber prison, he said them other words I mentioned: The Lord spoke but I turned aside. I'm like that, friends. The Lord spoke but I turned aside. The lighning'll find you too if I'm with you when it strikes. I don't wish to leave you, the way you been good to me and us real friends right along, but it's what I ought to do, and—'

'Well, you a'n't *about* to,' said Vilet, crying – 'you a'n't about to account we won't let you, not me or Sam or Davy neither.'

'I a'n't fit,' Jed mourned. 'Wallowing in sin.'

'Well you *didn't* then,' said Vilet. 'All's you done was put it in a couple minutes, and I loved it, I don't care what you say, a holy man like you does it, it *can't* be no sin, it a'n't fair, anyway if it was sin it's me that oughta burn—'

'Oh, hesh, woman! Your sins'll be forgiven unto you account your heart is innocent, but me I got the whole God-given knowledge of good and evil, for me there a'n't no excuse no-way.'

'Well, come on down to breakfast before you make up your mind about things.'

'Oh, I can't eat anything.'

Still crying, Vilet said: 'God damn it, you come on downstairs and eat breakfast!'

17

The pilgrims were already at breakfast, bacon and eggs no less, and thanks to the savings Vilet carried in her shoulder-sack, we were able to afford the same. She insisted on it too, with Jed in mind, for she subscribed to a theory very popular among the female sect, that ninety per cent of male grief originates in an empty stomach.

The dining-room at the Black Prince was so small you could have spat across it, and by the look of the walls many former guests had. There were only five tables. The doddery innkeeper had a couple-three slaves for kitchen

help but evidently didn't trust them to wait on table, and did it himself.
Recalling the good-smelling, orderly, spacious Bull-and-Iron made it easy
for me to despise this tavern, just like an aristocrat.

The Bull-and-Iron, now, was a fine brick building at least a hundred years
old. The story was there'd been a lot more clear land around it when it was
built, and Old Jon's father had sold off most of it for a big profit after the new
stockade went up to accommodate the city's expansion, and land values rose.
The Bull-and-Iron had fifteen guest bedrooms upstairs, no less, not counting
the one for Old Jon and the Mam, nor Emmia's where I'd left my childhood.
Downstairs, there was that grand kitchen with two store-rooms and a fine
cellar, and the taproom, and the big dining-room with oak ceiling-beams
fourteen inches wide and charcoal-black, and tables to seat thirty people
without crowding. Maybe I remember the cool taproom best of all, and the
artwork above the bar, a real hand-painted picture just full of people in weird
clothes, some riding astraddle of railroad trains and others herding automobiles or shooting off bombs, but all sort of gathered around in worship of a
thundering great nude with huge eyes and the most tremendous boobs, like
a shelf under her chin. She sat there with her legs crossed showing all her
immense white teeth and being adored, so you knew it was a representation
of the Old-Time pagan festival of St Bra. The painting carried the Church's
wheel-mark of approval, or Old Jon couldn't have displayed it. The Church
doesn't object to artwork of that type in the proper place, so long as it's decent
and reverent and shows up Old Time as a seething sink of scabrous
iniquity.

But the Black Prince at East Perkunsvil – hell, the only mural was a spot in
the dining-room wall the size of my head where plaster had fallen and
nobody'd ever possessed enough alimentary tubing to replace it. The only
respectable mural, I mean. They had the other kind of course in the privy out
back. One of our Old-Time books mentions some of that kind found in the
excavated ruins of Pompeii: the style hasn't changed a bit.

There were seven of the pilgrims, the usual number because it's thought to
be lucky – Abraham had seven disciples – there are seven days in the week –
and so forth. East of the Hudson Sea, pilgrim bands often head for places less
sacred than Nuber, usually shrines that mark where Abraham is said to have
visited and preached, and those groups, especially in Nuin, are larger, often
lively and full of fun. Itinerant students join them for mischief and company,
and a crowd like that can stir up a really joyous commotion on the roads. The
band at the Black Prince was different – unmistakably a religion-first company, all except Jerry, and from the look of his parents you got the impression
that he would take some holiness aboard when they got to Nuber, or else. The
other pilgrims of the group have become almost faceless for me in memory –
three women and one man. One of the women was young and quite pretty,

but all that comes back is an impression of timidity and a very white face; I think one of the two older women was her mother, or aunt.

'The ruins belonging to the Old-Time city named Albany, which we saw a few days ago, near the modern village of that name,' said Father Fay, 'are the last we shall behold on our way to Nuber.' He was doing all right with the bacon too, for such a gentle man. 'This region we are now traversing is said to have been mostly farmland in ancient pagan times, so no great monuments are to be expected.' Father Fay's baritone was rich, smooth, surprisingly strong; it made me think of warm honey dripping on a muffin, and when I looked again, bugger me blind if they didn't *have* muffins, real corn muffins, and fresh out of the oven, for I saw the vapor rise when Jerry opened one up and slapped the butter to it. 'The truly mountainous territory of Katskil was left in ancient days, as now, more or less in its natural state.'

'I've often wondered, sir,' said Jerry's father, 'what is the source of Katskil's prosperity. One doesn't expect to see wealth in a mountain country.'

Sam murmured to me: 'Levannon – tell by his accent.'

'It's their southern provinces,' said Father Fay, 'Rich farming land south of the mountains, all the way to the mouth of the great Delaware River, which I believe marks the entire boundary between Katskil and Penn … My conscience troubles me. I fear I may have neglected to point out some of the more instructive features of the Albany ruins, for I am always deeply moved by the sad splendor –' Jerry was full of squirm, and watching me in a weird warm pop-eyed way – 'and also the dignity to be sure, of the antique ruined architecture seen at low tide – ah, and by moonlight too!'

'Ma,' said Jerry.

'We were fortunate to have moonlight. One feels often the guidance of a heavenly power, on these pilgrimages.'

'Ma!'

'That door over there – you know perfectly well—'

'Naw, I don't have to. I want—'

'Jerry, the Father was speaking.'

'It's all right, Mam Jonas,' said Father Fay with practiced patience. 'What does the boy want?'

'Ma, I don't want my muffin.' (Why would he? – he'd already had two, one when nobody was looking except me.) 'Can I give it to him over there?'

Damned if he didn't mean me. I felt my face get as red as my hair, but that subsided. I half-understood the little devil wasn't just being a gracious prince favoring a humble subject: he actually liked my looks, and was drawn to me in one of those fantastic surges of childhood feeling.

'Why,' said Father Fay, 'Mam Jonas, this is the beginning I spoke of, blossoming of a truly Murcan spirit.' And Father Fay sent me a wink in a helpless manner, an open request to play along while Jerry got it out of his system.

The introduction of official sanctity embarrassed Jerry and cramped his style, but he brought over the muffin very prettily anyhow, as the whole gathering blinked at us. Ever wake up in a cow pasture and discover that the critters have formed a ring around you and stand there gazing and gazing, chewing and chewing, as if you'd put them in mind of something, they can't think what but it'll come to 'em in a minute? I took the muffin and did my best thank-you, and Jerry retired, face blazing, speechless. The pilgrim lady who I'm certain was somebody's aunt said: 'Aw, isn't that sweet!' Jerry and I could then exchange glances of genuine sympathy because it wasn't practical to murder her.

'In viewing such ruins,' said Father Fay, 'and *especially* by moonlight, one feels always, one says to oneself, ah, had it only been God's will that they should be a little wiser, a little readier to heed the warnings. Such marvelous structures, such godless, evil beings!'

'Father Fay,' said the pretty white-faced young woman, 'is it true they made those great buildings with the flat tops out there in the water for – uh – human sacrifices?'

'Well, Claudia, of course you must understand the buildings were not then submerged.'

'Oh yes, I know, but – uh – did they—'

'One is unhappily forced to that conclusion, my dear Claudia. Often indeed –' I think he sighed there and had another muffin; I'd finished mine under Sam's stern and reverent eye – 'often those buildings are no mere squares or oblongs but have the definite shape of the cross, which we know to have been the symbol for human sacrifice in ancient times. It is saddening, yes, but we can find reassurance in the thought that there is now a Church –' he made the sign of the wheel on his breast, so we all did – 'which can undertake the true study of history in the light of God's word and modern historical science, so that its communicants need not bear the burden of old sins and tragedies and the dreadful follies of the past ...'

Out in the hazy hot morning, perhaps still within the forest shadows but certainly very near our weak man-made stockade, the tiger roared.

Everyone in the dining-room – except Jed, I think – looked first at Sam Loomis when that shattering voice outside struck at our marrow. They were probably not even aware of doing it, and surely had no conscious idea that he could protect them; they simply turned like children to the strongest adult present in the emergency. Even Vilet; even Father Fay.

Sam stood up and finished his breakfast tea. 'If'n it's all right with you,' he said, to a spot of air between Father Fay and the doddery inn-keeper, 'I'll step out for a look-around.' I don't suppose they were asking even that much of him, so far as they knew. He strolled to the door and stepped outside.

I said – to whom I don't know, maybe Vilet – 'My bow's upstairs.' Jed was

standing then, ponderously, and he shook his head at me. I don't think he
had once spoken since we came down to breakfast. I couldn't wait to understand him but darted up to our room. When I returned with my bow and
arrow-quiver, they were all milling around a little. I saw Jed talking to Father
Fay in an undertone, the priest listening in a distracted, unbelieving way,
watching his pilgrim flock also and shaking his head. I couldn't hear what Jed
was saying. Jerry was at the front window, his mother hanging on to him or
he would have been outdoors. Father Fay frowned at my bow as I slipped
past him and Jed, but did not speak nor try to stop me when I ducked out
after Sam.

Sam was just standing out there in the sunny and dusty street with a few
others. I saw occasional wind-devils rise and whirl and die as a sultry breeze
hurried by on no good errand.

The elderly village priest – I heard one of the villagers call him Father
Delune – had come out of the rectory by his little church, and was in the
street craning his neck to look up at the bell-tower. He called – to us, I guess,
since we were nearest – 'Yan Vigo's going up for a look-out. We don't want
too many in the street. It may be illusion.' His voice was good, windy and
amiable and edged with fear under control. 'They should stay within and
pray it be illusion.' Sam nodded, but he was watching me. At that moment a
weedy boy climbed out through a louvered window of the bell-tower and
hauled himself up astraddle of the wheel-symbol, a good ten feet in diameter,
out of which the spire rose. He would have been some thirty feet above
ground, and could probably see over the stockade on all sides of the village. I
remember thinking Yan had it pretty good.

When I reached Sam I knew he wanted to send me back inside. But I had
brought my bow; he would not wound me that way. He just said: 'Hear what
I do, Jackson?'

I did hear it, from near the gate, where the guard who had admitted us the
day before was again posted. He was in light military armor today, helmet,
bronze breastplate, leather guards on thighs and crotch – all no particular
use against tiger except to the extent that it made him feel better. He was
carrying a heavy spear instead of a javelin – that did make sense – and his
honest hands transmitted to the spear-head a tremor as if he were in the
peak hours of a malaria; but he was staying at his post. The sound Sam meant
was a light clicking or chopping noise, combined with blasts of soft snuffling breath like a giant's bellows working on invisible fire. You've probably
noticed some little house-cat quivering her jaws on nothing when she sees a
bird fly overhead out of reach or light on a high branch and scold her;
along with the jaw motion there's a small hoarse cry, a kind of exasperated
explosion not quite spitting or snarling, simple frustration, tension of the
thing she would do if the bird could be grasped. But this noise outside the

stockade gate was more than fifty feet away from Sam and me, and I heard it plainly.

The gate guard called: 'I can see the shadow of him through the cracks!'

Sam said: 'Jackson, you – suppose you go tell them people to stay inside.'

I moved back uncertainly toward the inn doorway as Father Delune walked soberly by us to the gate. I had to stop, look back, learn what the priest meant to do. He stood right against the logs, praying, his arms spread out as if to protect the whole village with his dumpy old body, and his voice rang musically in the hot street. The breeze that clearly brought me the words also brought the smell of tiger. 'If therefore thou art a servant of Satan, whether beast or witch or wizard in beastly form, we conjure thee depart in the name of Abraham, of the Holy Virgin Mother Cara, in the name of Saint Andrew of the West whose village this is, in the name of all the saints and powers that inhabit the daylight, depart, depart, depart! But if a servant of God, if thou art sent to exact a penance and all but one of us unknowing, then grant us a sign, servant of God, that we may know the sinner. Or if it must be, then, come among us, servant of God, and his will be done! Amen!'

Yan Vigo's voice floated down with a break in it: 'He goin' away! – maybe.' His pointing arm followed the motion of the tiger who had evidently come from near the palings into the range of Yan's vision. 'Standing out in the road. Father! It's a male, an old male.'

'Depart! In the name of Abraham, depart!'

'Got a dark spot on the left, Father, like the one come onto Hannaburg last year ... Just standing there.'

Then – so much for my errand – Jed came out of the inn, and Father Fay with him, and though I mumbled something neither seemed aware of me. Vilet was back in the entrance staring after Jed, and the white clothes of the pilgrims made a shifting cloud behind her. Father Fay spoke plainly then: 'No, my son, I cannot consent, cannot bless such a thing, and you must not interfere with the duty of my flock, which is to pray.' Then all the pilgrims – Jerry and his father and mother, and the white-faced girl, and the old people, were coming out in the street, and rather than be stopped by me I think they would have walked through me if I hadn't stepped aside.

'Father,' said Jed, 'if you will not, then I must ask this other man of God.' And he walked up to the gate, to Father Delune, passing Sam as if he didn't know him.

Vilet called to me: 'Davy, he don't hear a thing I say. Don't let him do it, Davy!' Do what? – I didn't know. I felt as if we were all moving about in a fog, no one hearing the others – if little Jerry over there in his white robe quit his vague grinning and said something to me, I'd only see his mouth open, I'd hear nothing except the echo of the tiger's roar and that wet chopping of teeth.

Yan Vigo shouted down again: 'He goin' west side. Can't see – Caton's house cuts me off.' For that boy up there on the church tower it was probably the biggest day in a dull life; you could hear the fun in him like dance music the other side of a door. I was near enough myself to childish thinking to read the envy in Jerry too as he looked up at the tower.

Father Delune came away from the gate, listening to Jed. For a few minutes we made an aimless huddle there in the street – Father Delune, Sam, Jed, myself, and a nameless man from down the street. I saw no one who suggested an active hunter, let alone a Guide. I could look down the entire length of Main Street to its far end, where a smaller gate faced the wilderness. The Guide's house should be outside that.

Jed was suddenly on his knees to Father Delune. 'It must be so, Father! Give me your blessing to go out theah and bring him onto me, so to spare the village, and take away my own burden of sin. I won't be afeared no-way if I can go with your blessing.'

Sam said harshly: 'You be no more a sinner than any other man hereabouts.'

But Father Delune checked him with a crinkled hand, ... raised to ask the rest of us to be still and let him think. 'It's not fitting,' he said. 'I never heard of such an action, it's not in reason. There may be sinful pride in it – my dear son, who art thou?'

'Jed Sever's my name, a grievous sinner all my life, and who's to say I a'n't brung the tiger onto the village account of me? Father, bless my going out to him. I want to die in the hope of forgiveness at the throne of Abraham.'

'Nay, but – why, we all sin, from the moment of birth, but I can't think thou'st been so – so –' and Father Delune looked curiously, anxiously at Sam, even at me, wanting some kind of support from us I think, but hardly knowing what we could give nor how to ask for it. 'Sin, Jed Sever – it writes itself in the face, one may say. You strangers, you be friends of this man?'

'My cousin by marriage,' said Sam, 'and a good heart, the best, Father, but over-zealous. His conscience—'

'You don't understand,' said Jed. 'Don't heed him, Father. He can't see the sin in my heart. The beast won't go till I do. I know that, I feel it.'

'Why,' said Father Delune – 'he may have gone a'-ready, and no need of all this.'

'Where's your Guide, sir?' Sam asked.

'Away. Three-day hunt with our best men.'

The tiger roared, somewhere beyond the jumble of old houses on the west side of the village. I heard a rattling, a dull vibration, a crunch of cracking wood. Sam shouted up to the church tower: 'Is he in, boy?'

'Nah.' Yan Vigo's voice had gone high as a girl's. 'Think he caught a claw in the bindings and something bust, but it a'n't down.' Vigo meant the fastenings that held the stockade logs; they were leather thongs that had been bound there wet and allowed to dry, shrinking to a tight fastening. Only prosperous cities can afford iron bolts or wire. 'He's circling around to the back gate.'

'Father, bless me and let me go!'

I screwed up my own courage to speak: 'Father, I'm a dead shot with this bow. May I try from one of the roofs?'

'No, son, no. Wound him and he'll destroy the village entirely.'

That wasn't true and I knew it. A tiger is only a great cat. A cat suddenly hurt will run and not fight at all unless cornered or unable to use his legs. But I also knew it was useless to instruct a priest. I saw Father Fay's pilgrims kneeling together in the street, in front of the church. In spite of common sense I made one more try: 'Father, I promise you, I could place one of these in his eye, I've practiced on knotholes at fifty yards—'

It only annoyed him. 'Impossible. And what if the tiger is a messenger of God? I'll hear no more of that.' He asked Sam: 'Is this your son?'

'My nephew, and like a son. It's no empty brag, Father. I've seen him nail a—'

'I said I'd hear no more of that! Take the boy's arrows, sir, and keep them till this is over.'

Sam had to take them, I had to yield them, both of us with blank faces. The pilgrims were singing.

The hymn was 'Rock of Ages,' which is from Old Time, a commonplace hymn that has survived the centuries when a limitless literature of better music perished. Jerry's voice amazed me, incredibly clear and sweet – well, I had never heard a trained boy soprano, and never did again until I came to Old City of Nuin, where the Cathedral trains them. At the second verse I heard someone behind me singing too – Vilet, my good warm Vilet still crying but singing through the sick snuffles and more or less on pitch. I couldn't sing, nor did Sam, who stood near me holding the arrows loosely in the hand nearest me.

Down at the far end of the street, above the rear gate which stood as high as the rest of the palisade, about eight feet, down there in the shimmering heat of summer morning we understood there was a face watching our human uncertainties, tawny-pale, terrible and splendid. Across the light gold there were streaks of darker gold, as though between him and ourselves some defensive obstruction still cast the shadow of its bars – and to his eyes, some shadow on our faces too?

We had known it would come; maybe we had all known it would find us, in our various ways, unready. The pilgrims were all aware of that face at the end of the street, I think, but their music did not falter. Vilet stopped singing, however; I saw Jed lift her hand gently away from his arm, and then he was moving a step or two down the long street. At that moment the tiger's face dropped out of view.

'He's gone,' Vilet said. 'See, Jed – he's gone, I tell you.' She must have known as we all did that the tiger had not gone. Jed did not look now like a man crazily determined to rush into danger. He was smiling, with some sort of pleasure. He had gone only a little way beyond the kneeling, singing pilgrims. Father Delune was praying silently, his old hands laced together below his chin; I think he was watching Jed, but did nothing to detain him.

Nor could I, nor Sam. We were all in a way paralyzed, alone, not hearing each other, watching the empty spot at the end of the street, the blind gray-brown of weathered logs and tropic green of forest beyond. Jed's face was pouring sweat as it had done the day before on the road. A tremor shook his hands and legs as if the earth were vibrating under him, yet he was going on, slowly, as one sometimes journeys in the sorrowful or terrifying or seeming-ludicrous adventures of a dream.

The tiger soared in an arc like the flight of an arrow, over the gate and into the village.

The tiger paused for a second, his eyes surveying, calculating lines of attack and retreat, measuring with a cat's wonderful swift cleverness. Jed made no pause but walked on clumsy and brave, disregarding or not hearing the two priests who now called after him in horror to come back. Jed was holding his arms spread wide, as Father Delune had done when praying at the front gate, but Jed seemed more like a man groping for direction in the dark.

The tiger ran flowingly toward us along the hot street, not in a charge at first, but a rapid trotting run with head high, like a kitten advancing in sheer play, mimic attack. I suppose he could not have expected to see a human being walk toward him with those queer forbidding outspread arms. He rose on his hind legs in front of Jed and tapped at him with one paw. The motion seemed light, playful, downright absurd. It sent Jed's massive body twisting and plunging across the street to crash against the gatepost of a house and lie there at the foot of it, disembowelled, in a gush of blood.

The tiger did charge then, a tearing rush so swift that there was time to hear a woman scream only once; then I saw the green fire of his eyes blazing full on us while his teeth fumbled an instant and closed in Jerry's back. Jerry's mother screamed again and lunged at the beast with little helpless hands. A swing of his head evaded her without effort. He was trotting off down the street the way he had come, head high again, Jerry's body in his jaws seeming no bigger than a sparrow's. He was over the gate and into the wilderness, the woman silent but tearing her pilgrim's gown to slash at her breasts and then beat her fists in the dust of the road.

I had snatched one of the arrows from Sam's hand. I remember having it on the string when the tiger was running away down the street, and a black thing crashing against me which was Father Delune snatching my arm so that the arrow flew useless over the rooftops. He may have been right to do it.

Moments later Sam and Father Fay and I were with Vilet, who was fumbling at Jed's body as if there were some way she could make it live. 'Mam Sever,' Father Fay said, and shook her shoulder, and glanced back at the other woman who needed him – but Father Delune and the older pilgrim women were helping Jerry's mother into the church. 'Mam Sever, you must think of yourself.'

She crouched on her heels glaring up at us. 'You could've stopped him, the lot of you. You, Davy, I *told* you to stop him! Oh, what am I saying?'

'Likely we are all to blame,' said Father Fay. 'But come away now. Let me talk to you.'

Sam's hand on my shoulder was taking me away too. We were in some partly enclosed place, the doorway of a shop I think, and Sam was talking to me, bewildering me more than ever, for it was something about Skoar. He shook me to get me out of my daze. 'Davy, will you listen once? I'm saying it was just near-about fifteen years past, and one of them so't of average places—'

'You said "Davy."'

'Ayah, one of them medium places, not fancy but I mean, not so bad neither, can't fetch back the name of the street – Grain – no—'

Part of me must have been understanding him, for I know I said: 'Mill Street?'

'Why, that was it. A redhead, sweet and – nice, someway, nothing like them beat-up—'

'So God damn you, you flang her a little something for your piece and walked out, that what you mean?'

'Davy, a man at such a place – I mean, you don't anyhow get acquainted before you're obliged to go, nor the girl she don't want to know you, come to that. And still and all, maybe you get to know as much as you do in some marriages, I wouldn't wonder.' He would not either let go my shoulders or look at me, only staring over my head, waiting for me. 'I been married – still am, come to that. Wife down Katskil way that damn-nigh talked me to death. But the little redhead at that Skoar place – I mean, half an hour of one night and then it's "On your way, fella!" – and me with never a notion I could've left a package behind. Which maybe I didn't, Davy, we wouldn't ever know for sure. But I was thinking, I'd like for it to be so.'

'I dunno why I spoke to you like that.'

'Still sore?'

'No.' I have never cried since that morning, but I'm inclined to think that, once in a great while, tears are useful to the young. 'No. I a'n't sore.'

'So supposing I am your Da – is it all right?'

'Yes.'

18

The January rains fall more steadily here on the island Neonarcheos than any we remember. For two weeks we have been unable to work at clearing new ground. Nickie is uncomfortable in pregnancy and so is Dion – I mean that like me he is trying to give birth to a book, setting down what he can recall of the history of Nuin before it fades or becomes distorted in his mind. We do have paper now: the brookside reeds yield a coarse product to our primitive methods that takes our lamp-black ink reasonably well.

From lamp-black my mind jumps to lamps and lamp-oil. When the casks of seal oil we brought in the *Morning Star* have been exhausted we'll have no more. We can worry away at native vegetable oils and waxes, and when our sheep have increased there will be tallow to renew the supply of candles. Lambing time in a couple of months will be a major event. Of course, Nickie and I seldom object to going to bed early.

Lamps, candles, animal husbandry – we have enough problems on that level to keep our people busy a hundred years, if there's that much time. There may not be. We needn't suppose that because we were the first in centuries to sail the great sea, our enemies won't follow – soon, perhaps. They have as much courage of the simple kind as we have, or they couldn't have won the war of the rebellion in spite of their superior numbers. True, it called for the imagination of Sir Andrew Barr, the knowledge in old books forbidden, the orders and protection of Dion as Regent of the richest and strongest of the nations, and the labor of many hands, to create the schooner *Hawk* and later the *Morning Star*. Salter's victorious army had no such vessels to send in pursuit of us, no men capable of handling them. However, given the spark, they might build something capable of venturing out, if the Church would relax her prohibitions.

We carried with us all designs and working drawings made by our own people. The lower grade workmen had at first only a dim idea of what sort of ship they were engaged in building, but some of them will remember details, and all of them will talk if Salter wants them to. The Holy Murcan Church, up to now, has hogtied itself in this matter, committed to the doctrine that it is morally wrong, offensive to God, to sail out of sight of the land except by what fishermen call the relay system – one vessel holding in sight another which keeps the land within view. Even Dion could not have safely ordered such a ship as the *Hawk* without explaining to the churchmen that it was needed to overawe the Cod Islands pirates, and would never sail beyond those islands. And the *Morning Star*, he told them, was needed as a replacement – well – hm-ha – an insurance against a possible regrouping by those Satanic men.

It's not merely that it would annoy the Almighty to see a man damn-fool enough to fall off the edge of a flat earth; there's the larger doctrine, that any important kind of curiosity is wrong, a doctrine all religions of the past have been obliged to uphold as the only practical defense against skepticism. Still, theological obstacles are notoriously movable: if the Church knew we were safely ashore out here, a handful of escaped Heretics living in hard work and happiness on islands that could be valuable, I am certain that God's blessing on a punitive expedition could be almost instantly arranged.

Our military intelligence learned beyond a doubt that ex-pirates from the Cod Islands were scattered through Salter's army. They don't know big ships but they know the sea; in the old days before 327, when we had to knock them apart as a nation, their lateen-rigged skimmers may have ventured farther than we suppose. They could handle a large vessel for Salter if he ever managed to build one.

The Cod Islands people – the pirates and their women and slaves and followers – worshiped Satan, the old dark horned god of witchcraft ancient and modern. I'm sure they still do secretly. Likely they considered Old Horny a logical opponent of the existing order of things which they had no reason to love – besides, orgies are fun. The fact that Dion as Regent refused to permit wholesale burning of the Cod Islands people after the pirates' surrender was one of the most serious grievances the hostile section of the Nuin public, as well as the Church, held against him. The islands were taken over by respectable fishermen's guilds and added to the province of Hannis; the rank and file of outlaws and exiles and their women and children were allowed to disperse under a general amnesty. Since we hoped to abolish slavery altogether in Nuin and weren't inclined to set up a mess of new jails, I don't know what else in logic we could have done. I remember warning Dion that most of the pirates were not going to be grateful more than five minutes, and that the Church wasn't about to recognize any kind of mercy except its own. He knew that, but went ahead anyhow – and I suppose Nickie and I would have given him hell if he had changed his mind as a result of our cautions. Four years later, there the jolly pirates were, in Salter's army of the rebellion, ready and eager to fight on the Church's side against the man who had saved them from broiling by that same Church.

Incidentally I think Dion's insistence on amnesty instead of vengeance was the first occasion in modern times when a secular ruler has held out against Church pressure and got away with it for as long as four years. In the days of Morgan the Great the question didn't arise. Morgan was all for the Church, which was new then itself as a definite organization; he was an enthusiast, a warrior for God who could be just as happy converting a human brain as smashing it with a broadax, depending I guess on whether it showed any tendency to talk back.

And after a while, the Church may not find itself altogether happy with the Morgan dynasty ended and Erman Salter President. Salter will cancel the preliminary work we did toward getting rid of slavery; he will destroy our small beginning in the development of secular schools, and there'll be no more sacrilegious talk of relaxing the prohibitions on Old-Time books and learning. But after those matters are dealt with, the honeymoon between Salter and the Church is likely to peter out. Salter is power-hungry, and that is a disease which grows to a climax of disaster as certainly as a cancer. He respects the Church only for the material strength it derives from its power over men's minds, not for religious reasons and assuredly not for any temporal good the Church may do – (I as one of its sincerest enemies will admit that it does quite a lot). Salter is a practical man in the saddest sense of that term: a man to whom all art is nonsense, all beauty irrelevant, all charity weakness, all love, an illusion to be exploited, and all philosophical questions bushwa. I know these things about him, because the fellow tried to get at Dion through me, quite soon after a humorous chance had swept Nickie and me into the presidential orbit and made us important. Salter was quite frank about the quality of his mind while he still believed I had a price. He has no convictions, religious, agnostic, atheist or any other – the religious mask is simply one of many to be worn at convenience. When his kind rules, as it sometimes did in Old Time also – sleep on your knife!

Nay, fair enough – some morning a few years from now we may see on the western ocean the approach of a small clumsy sail ...

Yesterday afternoon Dion wandered in out of the rain with Nora Severn and told us he didn't want to be Governor. We've heard this before, and it makes certain kinds of sense, yet most of us hope he can be talked out of his reluctance. We've been kicking around a number of political ideas since at our last general assembly five were chosen to write a tentative constitution as it was done in Old Time, looking toward a day when these islands may hold a population large enough to need the larger formalities.

'I'm disqualified,' Dion said, 'by the very fact that I did govern in Nuin. Autocrat over maybe a million people – absurd, isn't it, that any man could be in a position like that? I would try, here, and be afraid all the time of old habits rising inside me. Davy, that day eight years ago – when you and Funny-face were sort of swept into office – I think it's eight years, isn't it?—'

'May Day, 323,' said Nickie, and laughed a little.

'Yes. That day, why do you suppose I was so eager to hang on to you after the Festival of Fools was over? Oh, Nickie turning up when I hadn't seen her for two years and I'd even thought she was dead – of course. The little twirp was always my favorite cousin. But there was something else in it. I'd begun to distrust myself already, though I'd been Regent less than a year …'

I remembered the day. I often do; there's a brightness in remembering. Nickie and I were twenty, then. We had been living in Old City for two years – obscurely, because Nickie had run away from her family and couldn't bear the thought of being recognized, knowing the attempts that would be made to draw her back, and how such fuss and uproar would interfere with the work to which she was giving herself body and spirit. Her work was underground, with the Heretics, important and dangerous. Mine, for money-making, was in a furniture factory – Sam Loomis had taught me all he could of joinery when we were with Rumley's Ramblers – and my other work was to learn, to read the forbidden books under the guidance of Nickie and the Heretics who accepted me because of her, to grow up with a wider under-standing of the world I had to live in. She took over, my sweet pepperpot wife, where my substitute mother Mam Laura of the Ramblers had to leave off. Well, but that day, the 29th of April, eve of the Festival of Fools which makes a joyous twenty-four hours of madness for Nuin folk before the gen-tler delights of May Day – that day Nickie and I were careless. It was the gaiety throughout the city, the reckless delicious urgency of a clear evening of spring, when the sky was piled high with violet-tinted clouds, and there were the street singers, and the flower-girls carried everywhere the scent of lilac.

We said we'd only go for a short walk, and keep away from the celebration and foolishness. But straying, pausing at a tavern where the beer was rather too good – oh, before long we were asking each other what harm it could do if we merely went for a few minutes to the Palace Square to hear the singing, and maybe watch from a safe place when the King and Queen of the Fools were chosen. And yet Nickie has told me since then that all along she had a premonition we were going to be much more scatterbrained than that. I remember how as we drifted toward that part of town, Nickie was trying to determine how accurately she could steer my walking by bumping me with her hip, neither of us using hands or arms, and we arrived at Palace Square in that style – honestly not drunk, just happy.

The custom is perhaps a hundred years old, that at some time on the eve of the Festival of Fools - nobody knows the moment exactly, but it comes between sundown and ten o'clock – a boy on a white horse will ride through Palace Square with a jingly cap on his head and carrying a long whip that has a soft silken tassel at the end. He cavorts around the square sassing the crowd and being pelted with flowers; at last he flicks his whip at one man and one woman, choosing them to be King and Queen of the Fools for the next twenty-four hours. They're hustled up to a throne that stands waiting on the steps of the presidential palace, and the President himself comes out to crown them. He kneels to them, with considerable ritual, not all of it comic. The custom of washing the feet of the King and Queen had gone obsolete in Dion's time, but—

It happened to Nickie and me. I ought to have foreseen it. The crowd was large, the light failing, nevertheless my lady's face must have stood out among the other pretty girls in the crowd like a diamond among glass ornaments; I was obviously her companion, and I have red hair. The boy on his white horse bore down on us, making the crowd give way so that his whip could reach us. Then the people were closing in, laughing, kind, noisy-drunk and heavy-handed, carrying us up to the throne on their shoulders. And the Regent, Dion Morgan Morganson of Nuin, appeared in his fancy dress, and seeing Nickie – frightened I know she was, rumpled by the crowd's well-meant horseplay, staring straight in front of her – Dion went pale to the lips. Presently he was ordering one of the attendants to bring the silver basin that had formerly been used in this ceremony – I too ignorant to know this was unexpected – and he washed our feet although it had not been part of the ritual for thirty years.

'And distrusting myself,' said Dion – speaking here in our airy shelter on the island Neonarcheos, his arm around his lovely bedmate Nora Severn, and hearing as I did how a sea wind was wavering through the warm rain – 'distrusting myself, I needed you, Miranda. Later on –' he said this with something more than courtesy – 'I found out I needed Davy too, and the cockeyed useful way the little devil has of looking at things and speaking out.'

I was aware, on that eve of the Festival of Fools, that Dion had loved my woman before ever I knew her. It was years before, actually, for he was fifteen when she was born. Her mother Serena St Clair-Levison was Dion's first cousin. He was often with the family, and used to carry the baby around before she could walk. Her first clear word, spoken when he was swinging her up to the ceiling, was Di-yon ... I could not have avoided knowing it, hearing him speak her name in a helpless, explosive way, there on the steps of the presidential palace when he was holding her little brown foot in his hands. It is not, today, the love of a very young man for a child, since Nickie is not a child. It is the love of friends, and on his side, more than that. We have been able to speak of it a little, the three of us; we do not when Nora Severn is with us, though she knows of it. It is not something that could be solved by a three-marriage, as Adna-Lee Jason and her lovers have done. Dion and I are are both too possessive, and Nickie is certain that for us it would not be the answer. Nay then, how much of our human complexity is our own fault!

'I think,' said Nora Severn, 'that a man who knows the old dangers of autocracy, watches for them in himself – why isn't such a man better as a governor than one who might have less self-knowledge? Not that I'm urging it – you're more fun as a private citizen.'

She was wearing nothing but a little skirt, like most of our girls. Blonde and delicious, you wouldn't think to look at Nora almost naked that she's an expert weaver and spinner, so deft and imaginative that some of the older women have asked her for instruction. At work, she never spends a second of waste motion, though every thin steady finger seems to possess an independent life. She is trying sculpture too, claiming to be no good at it, and has searched the island for usable clay.

'Some of the time back yonder,' Dion said, 'I'm afraid I *liked* being His Excellency by grace of God and the Senate Regent in Our Very Present Emergency – hoo boy! The emergency was good for eight years and would still be perking if we hadn't been kicked out. I think the term "emergency" originally meant "until His Excellency Morgan the Third by grace of God and the Senate President of the Commonwealth shall have the gracious goodness to cork off." But then time spun on and on, and it came to mean 'that period extending from the time your Excellency got away with it until such time as your Excellency can by grace of God and the Senate be safely booted the hell out ..."'

We were obliged to stay in East Perkunsvil until after Jed's funeral. But for Vilet we'd have been forced to do a sneakout, for Sam and I between us hadn't anything like the money needed for the expected religious performances, yet we were thought to be aristocrats and loaded with it – dear Jed, he would have explained it was a punishment on us for lying to the guard that evening. No doubt religion had to be invented for such gentle and simple minds, and perhaps they can't get along without it any more than I can get along with it. Vilet had enough salted away in her sack to meet the expenses, and now – why, now Vilet was a pilgrim and didn't want money.

She rejoined us that frightful morning after a long private session with Father Fay, and gave Sam what Father Delune had told her would be the cost of a good ceremony, our humble way of showing God that we understood and loved Jed for the martyr he was. She told us then how Father Fay had accepted her as a pilgrim, with the prospect that she might some day become sufficiently purified to take the veil. Maybe only Father Fay could have given Vilet that much comfort and saved her, as I hope he did, for the human race.

In the same degree, maybe no one but Father Delune could have helped me so nicely along the path of heresy. I wanted to suggest to him that if God was all-knowing he might be able to catch on without our blowing everything on a church performance, and, if he was *really* all-knowing, how about asking him what the hell good Jed's martyrdom did to anyone, beginning with Jerry? I said nothing at all of course, mindful of Sam's neck as well as my own, but my religious feeling ended just about then. I have never missed it.

I felt Vilet's quiet when she talked to us after that time with Father Fay; quiet and distance, yet she didn't seem a stranger. I had never understood the hidden existence of a nun in her, cool dim sister to the warm lovable wrestling-partner who'd opened her good flesh to me many times. The nun was in charge now, staring somewhat blindly out of the face of a woman who had in the last few hours aged twenty years. I don't think she asked Sam and me what we meant to do. She lost track of her words now and then, as if following some discourse in another room. Father Fay may have given her a penance-shirt to wear – her smock looked ridgy and she moved carefully like one in physical pain. Her left eye was blinking in a tic I'd never seen before. The pilgrims were conducting a private prayer-meeting of initiation for her soon – after which, she told us, she must not so much as speak to any male except Father Fay until the penitential part of her pilgrimage was done. Leaving us, she kissed me on both cheeks and told me to be a good boy.

I saw her once again, dressed in white with the other pilgrims, at the funeral two days later. If she knew where we were sitting she thought best not to look our way … It seems to me now that I loved her a great deal, maybe as much as I loved Caron who is probably dead.

I remember now a decree I pronounced from that throne on the steps of the presidential palace. The evening was wearing on; they'd brought us a musky wine that went to our heads. I decreed that everyone without exception must immediately live happily ever afterward; somehow I could think of no more fitting decree from a King of the Fools.

19

After the funeral – dismal enough it was, and our Jed would have thought it finer than he deserved – Sam and I didn't wait for the coach that might go by on Saturday, but decided to chance it on foot at least as far as Humber Town.

In East Perkunsvil after the disaster I heard virtually no talk about the tiger, and not even a sidelong mention of his possible return. The village Guide brought back his hunting party the next day – sorry, angry men they were when they heard the news – and in the afternoon men went out to cultivate the corn patches with no protection but a couple of bowmen. That night also, men were outside minding watchfires, not against tiger but just to keep the grazing creatures away from the corn. Hunters and old wives and other founts of absolute wisdom agree that unless old or sickly, a tiger will attack a particular village only once in a season, and then move on. It could even be true, though I doubt it.

The senseless, accidental quality of the event was what shook and overwhelmed me, I think. Sam stood by me; we didn't talk much; he was just there, letting me be alone with myself in his presence. Nickie is the only other I've known who can do that.[20] When the funeral was over and we were on the road again, I was beginning to understand how if there is any order, meaning or purpose in the human condition, human beings must make it themselves.

We made an early morning start. On such a summer morning, a west wind running along the hills and the sun not quite risen, a freshness everywhere, a ripple of birds' music, a glimpse of a whitetail deer slipping into the daytime secrecy of the forest, the warmth of the present and the surging life of your own blood make up the whole aspect of truth – how else could it be?

Humber Town is a busy and ambitious place, too small for a city, too large for a village – say about six or seven thousand population and, to use a quaint local expression, growing all the time. On the road Sam and I chewed over a few plans but settled nothing. I still desired Levannon, and the ships. But I had been noticing how often a plan is a scribble on the wind. Sam allowed that, to keep us going, he might look up some journeyman carpentry or mason work – he knew both trades – in Humber Town. He agreed it would be safest to move over into Levannon, if there still was a war going on by the time we reached Albany on the Hudson Sea. At East Perkunsvil the only war news they had was whispery rumors about a battle at Chengo in the west, and another on the Hudson coast a little north of Kingstone, barely outside Katskil territory.

Sam and I had not spoken at all of the relation that might exist between us. But as we were coming up to the gates of Humber Town I said: 'If'n you want to be my Da and I want it thataway, it maybe don't matter if I was or wa'n't out'n the actual seed?'

---

[20] I will praise my love for the honey of his words – honest, Spice, it's simply a matter of keeping one's mouth shut in a pleasant tone of voice.

– Nick.

'Why, that's about the way I had it lined up to myself, Davy,' he said. He'd been calling me Jackson as usual that morning. 'We might leave it at that ...'

The gate guard was happy about something, which made him show uncommonly good manners for a policer. As he let us in I heard the brisk tinkle and thrill of a mandolin somewhere. Then a drum was warming up oom-ta-ta oom-ta-ta, and a flute and a pretty sharp cornet jumped in, not quarreling at all, with the 'Irish Washerwoman.' It was happening out of sight around a curve of the main street, not far away. Wherever the Washerwoman came from, and I believe it was Old Time, she's a grand durable quail and always welcome. 'There they go!' the guard said to us, and I saw his feet were interested, and so were mine. 'Best damn gang ever was here. You be strangers to Humber Town?'

'I was by, yeahs ago. Sam Loomis, and this 'ere's my boy Jackson – Jackson David Loomis. Who be they, sounding off?'

'Rumley's Ramblers.'

'Ayah?' said Sam. 'Well, that cornet's got a power into it, but he don't blow as good as my boy ...'

A small idle crowd was already lounging at the rail fence that bordered the town green, though no special show was going on and it was only mid-morning, when most of the townfolk would be at work. The musicians had drifted together and tuned up to amuse themselves, that was all. But nobody with ears and eyes would just walk by, not with Bonnie Sharpe cross-legged on the grass tickling her mandolin, and Minna Selig with her banjo, and Stud Dabney teasing his drum to funny stuff with his white head stuck out over it and his squabby body in a kind of crouch, like a snowy owl about to fly away. Little Joe Dulin was there too tweedling his flute, and big Tom Blaine stood back of him – far back, following a rule of his own, for Tom always insisted he couldn't make his cornet cough up a decent tone unless there was a plug of *good* tobacco stuffing a hole where a couple of teeth were long gone, which meant spitting at the end of near-about every bar; and he couldn't spit good, he claimed, unless he was free to swing his head real liberal and fair warning to the world. Uhha, Tom was there in all his glory, as Sam and I joined the other loafers to rest our feet on the rails – Long Tom Blaine pointing his crazy cornet at the sky, a man drinking music and turning his head quick as a cat to spit and drink again. Hoy, so I'm running on ahead of myself and don't care. These were people I soon began to know and love; when I touched my pen their names came tumbling out.

The green was large and nicely designed – everything appeared spacious and rather different in Humber Town, or else I'm remembering it better than it was because that was where a good time of my life began, my time with Rumley's Ramblers. The wagons made a neat square within the green; I saw the big randy pictures and strong colors all over the canvas tops and sides, and the well-fed heavy-muscled mules tethered out where they could find shade and space to move about without bothering anyone.

Rumley's was a good-sized gang, with four of the large covered mule-wagons and two of the ordinary kind for hauling gear and supplies. The covered wagons – nothing like the rattletrap vans the gyppos use – are for the gang to dwell in whether they're on the move or in camp. One long covered wagon can provide cubby-hole quarters for more than eight people with their possessions, and you won't be too cramped so long as the clothes and things – dudery, to use the Rambler word – are properly stashed away. It's a thing you learn, and once you do, why, it's rather like living on shipboard and is not a bad way to live at all.

The musicians had polished off the Washerwoman by the time Sam and I got there. The girl with the mandolin was strumming aimlessly; the other had put down her banjo, and when she caught my eye and maybe Sam's her hand went up to her black curls in that feminine hair-fixing motion which goes back to the time when (Old-Time science says) we were living in unsanitary caves and women had to pay attention to the hairdo so that the mammoth-bones they got hit with would bounce gracefully. Minna Selig was a charming bundle, but then so was Bonnie Sharpe. For some time – near six months as I remember – I could hardly focus on one without being suddenly hornswoggled by the other. They planned it that way.

The flute-player and the cornet man strolled a little way off and settled down with a deck of cards. I saw a tall broad-shouldered gray-headed woman, barefoot and dressed in a faded blue smock, come out to sit on the letdown back step of one of the big covered wagons and smoke a clay pipe in solid comfort. The white-haired drummer, the snowy owl, had quit his music too but stayed by the girls, flat on his back with an ancient flopperoo of a farmer's straw hat over his face and his drumsticks weighting it down in case a sudden wind should rise and find him disinclined to move. Stud Dabney was tremendous at that sort of thing: Pa Rumley called him the original God-damned inventor of peace and quiet. He devoted such enormous thought to working out new ways of being restful that it sometimes made him dreadfully tired, but he claimed this was in a good cause, and he'd keep it up b' Jesus 'n' Abraham, no matter if it wore him out into an early grave. He was sixty-eight.

That gray-haired woman on the wagon-steps had caught my attention about as strongly as the girls. It was her calm, I think. She'd done her morning chores and was enjoying the lazy break, but it was more than that. She spread calm around her, as other people may spread atmospheres of uneasiness or lust or whatever. Well, after I had known the lady quite a while – two years later, I think, when I was past sixteen – Mam Laura remarked to me that she thought her even disposition was partly a result of her trade of fortune-telling. 'You can't,' she said, 'predict anything downright awful to the yucks, that's obvious – bad for business even if they could take it, which they can't. But I've got an old yen after truth inside me, Davy, same as your father has. So while I dream up sugartits of prophecy to happify the yucks and send 'em away imagining they amount to something, I'm thinking to myself about the actual happenings likely to come upon 'em – and upon me, merciful winds! – this side of death. It's sobering, calming, Davy. Including the *small* happenings – I mean the ten million little everyday samenesses that leave you weathered after a while like an old rock, like me, like an old rock in sandy winds. Ai-yah, and after such thinking inside of me while I prophesy, I'm beat but sort of cleaned out too, peaceful, feel like acting nice to people for a change and mostly keeping my shirt on. Philosophy's what it is, Davy – nay, and there's another advantage of Rambler life (which I prophesy you'll not be living all your days – you have a complicated future, love, too complicated for an old woman) and that is, a Rambler woman at my age (never mind what that is) can afford a smidgin of philosophy, the way I believe a woman can't if she's running the house and trying to fathom where romance went to and what in thunderuption ails her teener daughters …' She was spreading calm around her that first morning I saw her, smoking her pipe and studying everyone within her view but not seeming to.

I fidgeted against the fence rail and said: 'Sam, for honest – how good do I blow that horn?'

'All I can do about music is like it. Can't even no-way sing. You blow it, to me it sounds good.'

' "Greensleeves", frinstance?'

The mandolin girl had a floppy lock of brown hair that tumbled over her eyes; kay, but the banjo girl had big full lips that started you thinking right away – well, 'thinking' is the word I wrote there and I hate to scratch it out. The mandolin girl was still plinking a little, but mostly they were whisper-giggling together now, and I got the notion I was being analyzed.

'Ayah, "Greensleeves" goes good,' Sam said. 'Ramblers – well, they're touchy people, you hear tell. Might be a wrong tell – never talked to any myself. Prideful, that's for sure, and smart, and full of guts. Folk say they're always ready for a fight but they never start one, and that's good if it's true. They take them big slow wagons into lone places no ordinary caravan woud ever go, and I've hearn tell of bandits tackling a Rambler outfit now and then, but never did hear of the bandits getting the best of it. Every Rambler boss got a silver token that gets him across any national boundary without no fuss, did you know that?'

'No, that a fact? Hoy, that means if we was with these people we could go smack over into Levannon, wouldn't have to steal no boat and dodge the customs and so on?'

He caught my arm and swung me back and forth a little, so I'd keep my mouth shut while he thought. 'Jackson, you been contemplating stealing a vessel for to cross the Hudson Sea and similar suchlikes?'

'Oh,' I said, 'maybe I done some thinking that a'n't so big of a much. But is that a fact, Sam? They could get us across if they was a-mind to?'

'They wouldn't do it smuggling style – lose their token if they did. I've hearn tell they never do that.'

'But they could maybe take us into the gang?'

He looked pretty sober, and let go my arm. 'Wouldn't be a one to say they couldn't – you anyway. You got this music thing, and kind of a way with you.'

'Well hell, I wouldn't go with 'em unless you did.'

He spread out his big clever hands on the fence rail, more than ever quiet and full of reflection, studying all we could see of the Ramblers' layout. One of the plain wagons was parked, blocked up with its open rear toward the fence, near where the girls were loafing, and several large boxes stood in it; that would be the selling wagon, I knew from Rambler shows I'd seen at Skoar – they'd have a pitch going there by afternoon, with cure-all medicines and considerable junk, some of it good: I'd bought my fine Katskil knife from a Rambler trader. Another wagon, a covered one, stood facing a wide roped-off area of ground, and it had an open side; that would be the theater. 'In that case,' said Sam, and I felt he was as nearly happy as either of us could be with East Perkunsvil so short a way in the past – 'in that case I believe you might give it a go, Jackson, for I think I see my way clear to go along.'

'What you got in mind?'

'Terr'ble question, Jackson, always – nay, if I'm a-mind to squeeze, worm or weasel my way into some place where I a'n't expected, I most generally do. Wait a shake.' I'd been about to clamber over the fence before my nerve gave out, but just then a new man came in sight around the wagon where the gray-haired woman was sitting, and leaned against the back step to pass the time of day with her.

He wasn't actualy big – not as tall as Sam – but managed to seem so, partly with the help of a thick black shag of beard that grew halfway down his chest. The black tangle matching it on his head hadn't been cut for two or three months, but I noticed the man had his vanities: his brown shirt and white loin-rag were clean and fresh, and his hairy legs wound up in a pair of moose-hide moccasins as wonderful as any I ever saw, for their gilt ornaments were nudes, and the antics he could make those golden girls perform just by wig-gling his toes would have stirred up the juices of youth in the dustiest Egyptian mummy and I mean a married one.

Sam said: 'I get a feeling that's their boss-man, Jackson. Look him over. Try and imagine him getting mad about something.'

I swung myself over the fence. Once over, I felt everyone watching me – the girls, the card-players, even the white-haired man from under his straw hat, and the black-bearded boss-man whose voice was still going on in a mild rumble like a thunder-roll ten miles away. 'Da,' I said – Sam smiled quickly, wincingly as if all pleasure were partly pain, and I dare say it is – 'Da, I can imagine it, but I can't no-way express it.'

'Uhha. Well, you hearn tell about the hazy old fa'mer that got so near-sighted he set out to milk a bull?'

'And so then?'

'So nothing, Jackson, nothing special except they do say he a'n't come down yet, not to this day.'

I had to go over then, or not at all. My good white loin-rag helped, but crossing the immense twenty yards between me and the musicians, my knees quivered, and my hands too, as I lifted out the golden horn and let the sunlight touch it; however, the way their faces gleamed with interest and excitement at seeing the horn cleared away my jitters and left me free to be another friendly human being myself. I said: 'Can I make some music with you?'

The kitten with the dangerous lock of hair on her forehead and the quail with the bedroom lips were suddenly all business and no mockery. Music was serious. Bonnie asked: 'Wherever was that made? Isn't it Old-Time?'

'Yes. I a'n't had it long. I can only play a few airs.'

'Bass range?'

'Nay, seems best in the middle – I know there's notes on both sides I can't play yet.'

Somebody said: 'Boy 'pears to be honest.' I'd felt all along I was being watched from under that straw hat.

The girls paid Stud no attention. 'What airs do you know?' Minna Selig asked, and I learned she possessed a bedroom voice too, but right now she was all business, like Bonnie.

'Well,' I said – 'well, "Greensleeves" – "Londonderry Air" –' Minna's soft-voiced gut-string banjo immediately sang me a few small chords, and I went wandering into 'Greensleeves' with of course not the dimmest notion of what key I was using, or of harmony, or of how to adapt myself to another performer. All I had was the melody, and a natural feeling for the horn, and some guts and a whole lot of good will, and a keen ear, and a tremendous admiration for the way the neat black-haired girl sat there cross-legged with her banjo and her bedroom thighs. Then right away Bonnie's mandolin arrived, laughing and crying silver-voiced; her big gray eyes played games with me – that didn't distract her from the music, for she could slay a man with those things and never need to give a moment's thought – and her racing fingers gave my playing a translucent trembling background all the way through to what I supposed was the end.

The white-haired drummer had swung his arm to beckon a friend or two. People were coming out of the wagons. The flute-player and the cornet man had given up their card-game and were just standing by, listening, thinking it over. So well was the horn responding to me, for a minute I was in danger of thinking it was my playing that drew them and not the Old-Time magic of the horn itself. When I play nowadays that may be true; it can't have been true that day, though even sweet sharp Bonnie said later on that I did better than any ignoramus had a right to.

When I had (I thought) finished the melody, Minna's hand pressed my arm to check any foolishness, and away went Bonnie's mandolin shimmering and heartbreaking to find the melody on the other side of the clouds trans- figured by a tempo twice as fast and dancing in the sun. Someone behind me had brought a guitar, which now was chuckling agreeably about the fun Bon- nie was having up there. And Minna was intently humming three notes very close to my ear, just audible to me, and whispering: 'Play those on your thing real soft when she goes to singing. Trust your ear how and when to play 'em. We'll goof some but let's try.'

Do you know, we didn't goof, much? I was ready when Bonnie's light sop- rano soared, and Minna unexpectedly came through with a contralto smooth as cream. Well, those girls were good and double good. They'd been making music together since they were Rambler babies, besides having a rare sort of friendship that no man could ever break up. I never knew whether they were bed-lovers. Pa Rumley was a little down on such variations, I suppose a hangover of the usual religious clobbering in childhood, so it was a question you didn't ask. If they were, it didn't turn them against the male half: I had both saying oh-stop-don't stop after a while, and they were both all the more delicious for not taking me too seriously, since we were not, as people call it, in love.

When Bonnie sang a second verse of 'Greensleeves' I heard something more happen along with that guitar. Intent on making my horn do what I hoped they wanted, I felt the addition only as a flowing, sustaining chordal murmur, almost remote although I knew the singers were standing quite close behind me. All our best were there – Nell Grafton and Chet Spender and handsome Billy Truro, the only tenor I ever heard of who could also play Romeo and skin mules. And for the down-in-the-cellar thunder-pumping bass we had Pa Rumley himself.

Bonnie wasn't playing while she sang, but holding her mandolin away, her other hand on my shoulder bedam – never mind, Minna had one on my knee, and some of that was to make a romantic picture for the crowd that was increasing out there in the road, but most of it was real. Bonnie somewhere had learned to sing without too much distorting the charm of her rounded, heart-shaped face – well, with nice teeth, ravishing complexion and brilliant eyes, who'd care if she did have to let the daylight in on her tonsils for some of the big notes? And by the prettiest accident, that day she was wearing a green blouse with long sleeves – you'd have thought the whole show had been planned a month in advance, and I'm sure the yucks believed it was.

When the song was done, and she'd waved and blown a kiss to the crowd, which was stomping and clapping, even a few of them snuffling – why, didn't she grab my shirt to pull me on my feet? 'Cm' on, kid!' she said – 'they love you too.'

There was a dizzying pleasure in it, not spoiled by my knowledge that most of the excitement was for Bonnie and ought to be. Yes, I liked it, and I was growing up, I wasn't too demarbleized—

Nickie and Dion still quarrel occasionally about correcting the places where I goof the spelling. I can't interfere much, because I did ask them to, away back when I started this book. The last time I heard them beating away at it was very recently, in fact only a few minutes ago, I can't think why. I had dozed off in the sunshine or appeared to, and I heard Nickie ask Dion how he could be sure I hadn't meant to write it that way. 'Can't,' he admitted, 'and even if I could, why should I be elected to defend the mother tongue against the assaults of a redheaded songbird, politician, hornplayer and drunken sailor? Hasn't she been raped by experts for centuries past counting, ever since Chaucer made such a bitched-up mess of trying to spell her, and doesn't she still perk?'

'A heartless, mean and lazy brute,' said Nickie. 'I hate you, Di-yon, the way you can't even come to the aid of Euterpe who lieth bleeding in the dust.'

'Euterpe – who she?'

'What! You calling me a twirp?'

'No, but—'

'I 'stinctly heard you say "You twirp!"'

'Miranda – Euterpe was not the God-damn Muse of Spelling.'

'Oh, that's right. That was Melpomene.'

'Sorry-sorry, she was the Muse of Tragedy.'

'So all right! So English spelling always was a tragedy, so what other girl could handle it, so don't give me all that back talk or you'll wake up Davy.'

I'd just perfected a theory of the origins of English spelling, so I woke up officially to share it with them. You see, there was this ancient gandyshank in the dawn of history who had a nagging wife and an acid stomach and chilblains, but English hadn't been invented, which left him in the demarvelizing position of being unable to cuss. However, the people in charge of politics had passed a revelation to make the alphabet and then chopped it into sticky chunks and passed them around so there'd be enough letters for everybody; so when the old jo's wife yakked or his feet hurt or his convictions rifted up on him, he'd snatch the alphabet chunks and heave them at the side of a cliff, the only form of cussing adapted to those early days. Centuries later some scholar with a large punkin head and very small bowels of compassion discovered the cliff and invented English right off whiz-pop just like that. But by then all the combinations a decent man would spell had washed off in the rain or the crows had et them.

Nickie asked: 'How'd old Cliffbottom's wife come to nag and yak so if English hadn't been invented?'

Not a bit demongrelized, I told my wife: 'She was slightly ahead of her time.'

20

While 'Greensleeves' was still being applauded I heard the black-beard rumble at us: 'Put the lid on, kids. They look ripe for Mother.' And as I was wishing I had a clue to what he meant, he said to me carelessly, pleasantly – I might have been underfoot for years and he so used to me he hardly saw me – 'Stick around, Red.'

I gulped and nodded. He slouched over to that wagon that held the boxes. The banjo girl pulled me down to sit beside her again and slid a friendly arm around me. 'That's Pa Rumley,' she said. 'Next time he speaks to you you say "Uhha, Pa." 'S the way he wants to hear it is all. And don't worry, I think he likes you. I'm Minna Selig, so what's your name, dear?'

Hoy! That was demortalizing if you like. I found out soon enough that Rambler people call each other 'dear' all the time, and it doesn't necessarily mean sweethearting, but I didn't know it then, and she knew I didn't. Close to my other ear, the little devil with the mandolin said: 'And don't worry, I think Minna likes you. I'm Bonnie Sharpe, so tell *me* your name too – dear.'

'Davy,' says I.

'Oh, we think that's nice, don't we, Minna?'

Yes, they really worked me over. Well, but for the girls and their mild mischief and warmth and good humor, the end of 'Greensleeves' might have been the end of my courage: I might have gathered the rags of my dignity around my shoulders and fled back over the fence with no more word even to Sam about what I wanted most in the world, which was to be accepted by these people and stay with them on their travels as long as they'd have me.

Pa Rumley standing in the back of that wagon flung up his arms. 'Friends, I hadn't meant for to give you this here message of good tidings till later in the day, but you being drawed by our music – and our kids love you for the nice hand you give 'em – why, I'll take it as a sign to speak a few words, and you pass 'em on to your dear ones. Open up that gate and gether round, for lo, I bring hope to the sick and lorn and suffering – draw nigh!'

It was a pleasant custom in practically all villages and middle-sized towns that had no bigger park, to lend the Ramblers the town green for the duration of their stay, as a camp-site and show area; townfolk wouldn't normally intrude unless specially invited. I'd broken the rule. I think the reason why the girls said nothing about it was my natural-born goofy look, which often does wonders for me. The yucks opened the gate now at Pa Rumley's invitation, and drifted in, shy, and with the yuck's invariable anxiety to watch out against swindling – much good it does him. There were twenty-odd men and half again as many women gathered around the wagon, aggressively dough-faced, wanting to be convinced of something, it didn't much matter what. I saw Sam had strolled in with them. He stayed in the rear; when he caught my eye over a flock of bonnets and broad straw hats he shook his head slightly, which I took to mean that he had something cooking I'd better not disturb.

'There you are, friends, step right close!' A man would give a lot to own a voice like Pa Rumley's, big as a church bell but able to go soft as a little boy whispering in the dark. 'This here is going to be a blessed day you'll long remember. You seem to me like fine intelligent souls, responsible citizens, men and women who've kept the fear of God in their hearts and evermore prayed and done their share. That's what I'll say to myself whenever I think of Humber Town, and good Mayor Bunwick who let us have these fine accommodations, and done so much for us – no sir, folks, Ramblers don't forget, never believe it if you hear they do. My friendship with your Mayor Bunwick, and the Progress Club, and the Ladies' Murcan Temperance Union – this is a memory I'm about to cherish all my days.' As for Bunwick, the old fart certainly wasn't there at that time in the morning, but a number of his ratty cousins undoubtedly were, to say nothing of the ladies – besides, Pa always said that if you set out to kiss an ass you might just as well kiss it good. 'Now, friends, you must have seen how this world is a vale of tears and mis'ry. O Lord, Lord, don't Death on his white charger go day and night raging and stomping up and down amongst our midst? – well, gentlemen hark! Why, it might be there a'n't a one of you except the children, God bless 'em, and maybe even some of them, that a'n't been bereavered already by the grim reaper. And sickness – yes, I'm a-mind to talk to you about the *common* sorrows, them that must come soon or late to one and all. They a'n't fancy things – step in a little closer now, will you? – oh no, nobody makes up stories about 'em, nor sad songs, but I say to you a man laid low by sickness, he's gone, folks, just as sure as a hero done to death in battle for his b'loved fatherland, amen, it's a fact.'

He gave them time to look around at each other wise and serious and agree that it was so. 'Friends, I tell you there do be some sorrows that can't never at all be healed except in the ev'loving hand of God and by the tooth of time that heals the blows of fate and dries up the tears of the wayworn, and gently leads, and allows the grass to grow green over lo, these many wounds. But concerning the grief of common sicknesses – now there, friends, I got a message for you.

'Forty-seven years ago, in a little village in the hills of Vairmant green and far away, there lived a woman, simple, humble, Godfearing, mild, like it might've been any one of the lovely companions and helpmeets I see before me right now in this good town – where I got to admit I a'n't yet beheld a member of the tender sex that a'n't lovely to behold.' (There were just two good-looking women in that whole expanse of landscape and I was sitting between them.) 'That's a fact, no flattery, gentlemen hark! Well, this gentle woman in Vairmant of whom I speak was bereavered of her good man in her middle years, and thereafter she devoted the remainder of a long and blessed life to the healing of the sick. Even her name was humble. Evangeline Amanda Spinkton was her name, and I want you should remember that name, for it's a name you'll come to bless with every breath you drawr. Some do say, and I believe it, that Mother Spinkton – ah yes, so a grateful world calls her now! – had in her veins the mystic Injun blood of Old Time. That's as may be, but there's no doubt at all the dear angels of the Lord guided her in her lifelong endeavor, her search after them essences of healing that the Lord in his infinite wisdom and mercy has placed obscurely in the simple yarbs that do dwell in the whispering woods or the sunkissed fields or along the gently murmuring streams—'

That gives you his style anyway. Pa never let anyone else handle the pitch for Mother Spinkton; even if he was down sick in bed and too mis'ble to live he'd r'ar up out of it to take care of that. He said he reverenced her too much to let any mere God-damn crumb-bum piddlebrained assistant lay a mortal hand on her sacred hide. He claimed also that he could taste and smell a crowd with a special knack nobody else possessed – except his grandfather of course, dead going on forty years – and this knack always told him right off whether to use gently murmuring streams or dark murmuring caverns. Either one might work all right – oh sure, it would *work*, he'd say, and spit over the footboard between the mules if he was driving, which he liked to do – it'd work, but the g.m.s. yucks are the common type, and the dark caverns type is different, that's all, and it's the mark of a real artist to be able to spot that difference and govern yourself accordingly. Long Tom Blaine used to give him an argument about it when the weather was right – Tom said yucks are yucks and that's it.

Pa Rumley blathered on, not exactly *claiming* that God and Abraham and all the angels had worked together showing gentle Mother Spinkton how to construct her Home Remedy, the Only Sovran Cure for All Mortal Complainders of Man or Beast – but you were sort of left of a breathing exercise – he did it because he couldn't bear doing much more than what a musician would call a scale or a breathing exercise – he did it because he couldn't bear to let any crowd get away from him, any time, without selling it something. After five or ten minutes more of Mother Spinkton's character and biography, he squared away for a brisk analysis of a dozen or more diseases, and he was so tender and hopeful and horrible about it – hell, nobody could beat him at that; he'd have you locating so many simpletons[21] throughout your anatomy you simply couldn't spare the time to die from more than half of them. He'd wind up that section with a horde of widows and orphans at the grave, which Mother Spinkton might have prevented same had they but of knowed – come one, come all! Well, it called for an effort – Mother was one whole dollar a bottle. But did she sell?

Yes.

It's a matter of sober fact that she was a bird, and I do know, because Pa believed in her himself or appeared to, and had no more mercy on us than he had on the public. If you got sick and admitted it, you drank Mother Spinkton or faced Pa's displeasure, and we loved him too much for that.

It was Mother's unpredictable nature that made it impossible to get the best of her. Mother Spinkton could tear into anything at all – epizootic, measles, impotence, broken ribs, cold in the head – and if she couldn't cure it she wouldn't try, she'd just start up such a brush fire somewhere else in you that it didn't matter. Dab some of her on a mortal wound and you would, naturally, want to die, but she'd keep you that interested you couldn't manage it, for the sheer excitement of wondering how much she was going to hurt next, and where. Of course it might turn out to be an entirely different kettle of shoes of another color, but I'm trying to analyze the psychology of it.

Pa's own belief in her was a puzzle to me, but I state it for a fact. I've watched him making up a fresh batch according to the secret formula he'd worked out himself, just as careful and hopeful and bright-eyed and bushy-tailed as an Old-Time physicist with a brand new bang. And then by damn he'd drink some. I don't know – sow-bugs, horseradish, hot peppers, raw corn likker, tar, marawan, rattlesnake's urine, chicken's gall-bladder and about a dozen more mysterious yarbs and animal parts, usually including goat's testicles. Those last were hard to get unless we happened to be near the right kind of farm at the right moment, and Pa did allow they weren't absolutely essential, but he said they gave her a distinctive Tone that he was partial

[21] Out to lunch.

– N. & D.

to himself. Tone was important. He'd drunk her with and without that Tone, he said, and it was possible that for the yucks it didn't really matter, because the first swallow was calculated to lift any yuck directly out of the studious frame of mind – still, if you cared, Tone was important. Pa Rumley liked to discuss vintages too. I never became that expert. All I could tell was that in some vintages Mother Spinkton wouldn't much more than stink out a town hall, but in her best years she was well able to clear a ten-acre field of everything movable, including the mules.

That morning in Humber Town, when Pa had wound up his spiel and was about to start passing out bottles with Tom Blaine wrapping up and collecting coin, along comes a hardcase old rip pushing through the crowd snorting and moaning with a hand to his chest and his long scrawny face all puckered up in the wildest sort of misery, so that I had to goggle twice and swallow before convincing myself that this antique calamity was my own Da, Sam Loomis, acting half again as large as life and rarin' to go.

'You theah! You talk of healing'? I'm comin' forward, but there a'n't no hope for me, not the way *my* mis'ry's been ground into me by a life of sin. Ah, Lord, Lord, f'give a mean horr'ble old man and let 'm die, can't you?'

'Why, friend!' Pa Rumley responded – 'the Lord f'gives many a sinner. Come for'd and speak your mind!' He was a little uneasy. He told us later he wasn't sure he'd seen Sam and me talking together, at the fence.

Sam, that old scoundrel – my Da, mind you – said:

'Praise him evermore, but le' me lay my burdens down!'

'Let the poor soul come for'd there, good people – he's a sick man, I can see. Make room, please!' They did, maybe as much from pity as because Sam might have something catching. He did look just about finished – coughing, staggering, fetching up against the backboard of the wagon and letting Tom Blaine support him. If I hadn't seen that head-shake signal I'd have been over there lickety-doodah, and maybe spoiled things. 'Comes on me sudden sometimes,' he said, which took care of any critics who might have noticed him with me before the music, steady and hard as nails. 'Real sudden!' – and with his face turned away from the crowd he sent Pa a wink.

After that you'd have thought they'd practised it for years. I whispered to the nearest ear, which happened to be Minna Selig's: 'That's my Da.'

'Ayah? Did see you together.'

Bonnie said: 'A'n't he a pisser!'

I near-about busted with pride.

Pa Rumley was leaning down to him, a soft angelic smile slathered over what you could see of his face outside the black foam of beard. His voice was globs of maple syrup out of a jug. 'Don't despair, man – nay, and think of the joy in heaven over the one sinner that repenteth. Now then, where at is this pain?'

'Well, it's a chest mis'ry all kind of wropped up with a zig-zag mortifica-tion.'

'Ayah, ayah. It hurts a mite crossways when you breathe?'

'O Lord, I mean!'

'Ayah. Now, sir, I can read a man's heart, and I says to you lo, about this sin, it's already near-about washed away in repentance, and all you need is to fix up the chest mis'ry so to make straight the pathway for the holy spirit and things – only you got to be careful of course.'

Tom Blaine was right there with a bottle of Mother Spinkton, a look of gladness, and the father and mother of a wooden spoon. I have never understood, myself, how ordinary maple wood could hold together under the charring and shriveling effect Mother always had, but there's nothing I can do except tell history the way it happened. Bedam if those two old hellions didn't jaw it back and forth another five minutes, with Tom hold-ing the spoon, before Sam would let himself be talked into swallowing some. They were taking a chance, I think: if the old lady had eaten her way through the spoon while they talked, the crowd might have lynched the pack of us.

Sam took it at last, and for a few seconds things were pretty quiet. Well, often you don't feel anything right away except the knowledge that the world has come to an end. Sam of course had been brought up on raw corn likker and fried food and religion; all the same, I don't believe anything in a person's past could actually prepare him for Mother Spinkton. He got her down, and when his features sort of rejoined each other so that he was recognizable again, I thought I heard him murmur: 'This happened to *me!*' It was all right: any yucks who overheard him probably thought he was looking at the *nice* kind of eternity. Then as soon as he could move, he turned his head so that the yucks might observe the glow of beatitude or whatever spreading over him, and said: 'Ah, praise his name, I can breathe again!'

Well, sure, a man's bound to feel a surrounding glory at finding himself still able to breathe after a shot of Mother Spinkton. But the yucks hadn't tried any of her yet, so I guess they didn't quite understand what he meant. 'I was nigh unto death,' says the old rip, 'but here I be!' And they all pushed in around him then, wanting to touch and fondle the man who'd been snatched from the grave, even tromple him flat in pure friendliness.

Pa Rumley hopped off the wagon. He and Tom pried Sam loose from the public; then Tom went to work selling bottles – for a few minutes he was passing them out about as fast as he could handle them – and Pa Rumley walked the sick man over to that wagon where the gray-haired woman was still sitting smoking her pipe and enjoying everything. I trailed along, and the girls stuck with me.

It's hard to believe how much space you can find in one of those long covered wagons. The inverted-U frames supporting the canvas has cross-bars usually of hornbeam, just above head-height, and a light wickerwork platform rests on the cross-bars, making a sort of attic for storing light stuff. Those cross-bars also carry hanging partitions for the cubbyhole compartments that run along both sides of the wagon with a single-file walkway between. Up in front there's an area without sleeping compartments, just canvas walls with usually a window on each side. For laughs, we always called that area the front room.

That was where Pa Rumley took us now, to the front room of this wagon, which was the one with his own living-quarters. Because it was the head-quarters wagon, the front room was nearly twice the size of those in the others, and had *bookshelves*, a thing I had never seen nor imagined. This wagon had only four sleeping spaces, two double and two single: singles for Mam Laura and old Will Moon who usually drove the mules, a double for Stud Dabney and his wife, and a double for Pa Rumley with whatever woman was sharing his bunk. Pa swept us in there – Bonnie, Minna, Sam and me. Mam Laura came in last with her clay pipe and sat cross-legged as limberly as the girls. I never heard of Ramblers owning a chair – you sat on the floor, or you lay, or sprawled, suit yourself. In that headquarters room, the whole ten-by-twelve floor was covered by a red bear pelt that was the pride of our hearts. Pa didn't say anything until the gray-haired woman had settled herself; then he just looked at her and grunted.

She puffed her pipe till it went out, and rubbed the bowl of it against her thin nose. Studying Sam she was, and he met the stare, and I had the feeling they were exchanging messages that did them good and were none of our business. Though grayer, she was slightly the younger, I believe. At last she said: 'From the no'th of Katskil, be'n't you?'

'Ayah. An't had word of the war lately.'

'Oh, that. It'll be over in a couple-three months. Rambler life attract you, maybe?'

'Might, allowin' for the fact I'm a loner by trade.'

'Did a good job as a volunteer shill out there. Don't know that I ever saw that done before.'

'So't of come over me all-a-sudden like, the way I wouldn't want you to think my boy's the only talented one in the family.'

'You be his Da then?'

'Ai-yah, that's a special story,' Sam said, 'nor I wouldn't be a one to tell it without his leave.'

She looked at me then, and I felt the kindness in her, and I told the story, finding it not hard to do. Bonnie and Minna had quieted down, anyway I guess they wouldn't have carried on the game of dividing me down the mid-dle directly under her eye. I told the story straight, feeling no need to change or soften it. When I was finished Sam said: 'He must be my boy. He don't *lack* my orneriness, you see – just a'n't quite growed up to it yet.'

'Be *you*,' Mam Laura asked me, 'a loner by trade?'

'Likely I must be,' I said, 'the way when my Da makes that remark it rings a bell in me. But I like people.'

'So does your Da,' Mam Laura said – 'did you think he didn't, Davy? Nay, I sometimes wonder if loners aren't the only ones who do.' I was beginning to notice how she spoke rather differently from the rest of us. I couldn't have explained the difference at that time; I did feel that her way of using words was better than any I'd heard before, and wished for the knack of speaking that way myself. 'You truly want to join up with us, Davy, the uncommon way we live that's never a safe thing, often lonely, hard, tiresome, dangerous?'

'Yes,' I told her. 'Yes!'

'Enough to suffer a little schooling in consequence?'

I had no notion what sort of schooling she meant – while I was knocking off my life story I'd already told her I knew all about how to handle mules. But I said: 'Yes, I do – honest, I'd do *anything!*'

Pa Rumley laughed at that, gargling it in his beard, but Mam Laura aimed her smile mostly at the universe and not at me. 'Hoy, Laura,' Pa said, 'didn't I keep telling you I'd raise a big old God-damn scholar for you somewheres, to squeeze the good out'n them books that've been wearing down the mule-power on this wagon all these years? Maybe I've even raised you more'n one. Be *you* a man for the books, Sam Loomis?'

My father looked away through one of the little windows – honest glass they were, sewed cleverly into slots in the canvas so that no wind would dis-lodge them or force the rain through. For a moment or two he looked older and grayer, my father, than ever before; if there was mirth hidden in his craggy face I couldn't find it. 'That wasn't my fortune, Pa Rumley,' he said. 'I tried once to win me a little learning after my young years were long gone – nay, but it don't matter. If the lady will teach my boy, I'll answer for it he'll mind the lessons and get the good of it.' Pa Rumley got up and tapped Sam's shoulder and nodded at me. 'He blows that horn pretty good too,' he said. 'Well – stick around. You're lucky – gentlemen hark! Yes sir, it just so hap-pens you hit me at a lucky time: I got over the shock of being born a good while ago, more b' token I a'n't dead yet. Best time to tackle a man, under-stand? – somewhere in there betwix birth and death. If the sumbitch won't give you a decent answer then he never will.'

21

We did stick around – four years.

Pa Rumley was a sharp-minded observant man, sober; drunk, he was still a good critic of himself, unless he passed a certain point of drinking that he could not always recognize, and tumbled into a black well of despair – then he had no judgment in his darkness, and someone had to stand by and drink with him till he dropped in his tracks. Except during those very rare crises, his sadness always had around it a nimbus of mirth, just as his loudest laughter carried the overtones of grief. True for all of us, but in him it was more obvious, as though the emotional raw stuff that nature, playing safe, doles out to most of us by the teaspoonful, had been sloshed into Pa Rumley with a bucket.

Pa used to claim that he'd fought and toiled and connived to make himself boss-man of the best God-damn gang in the world for the simple reason that he was at heart a benefactor of the God-damn yuman race, which without him would likely drop dead of its own boredom and meanness and hard luck and general shitty stupidity. And it's a fact, when you got down to cases he really didn't seem to have a thing in the world against yumanity except that he never would pronounce the plague-take-it thing with an aitch.

He had a long, thick-bridged nose that spread at the tip into a double knob. The whole organ had been slammed into at some time in the faraway past, so that when I knew him it aimed more or less at his right shoulder. He said it was no battle that bent it, more likely somebody sat on it when he was young. He asserted that in fact he never did fight except now and then with a club, which was why he never got licked. However, when I saw him personally lay out Shag Donovan who thought he was boss of Seal Harbor, Pa used no club except the knobby side of his fist, and all two hundred pounds of Shag went softly to sleep. (I was a bit helpful in that Seal Harbor thing, being fifteen and on the quarrelsome side for a while, a temporary trait, a sort of growing pain.) Another time, I heard Pa say that his nose took that starboard slant from having to keep alert and sniffing for the righteous, who generally come up on a man from behind.

It was a good commanding nose anyway, and useful to the gang because it told of his mood: so long as it stayed red or sunset pink there was nothing much to worry about, but if it went white while Pa was still sober, the wise thing to do was to keep out of sight and hope for the best, supposing you had anything on your conscience. His eyes were important signals too, small and black and restless. Just contrary to his nose, they went bloodshot when he was on the warpath – but of course if you were near enough to notice the swollen veins you wouldn't benefit by running.

I never knew him to clobber anyone who hadn't, according to Pa's lights, earned it. Anyone who did received the quick tranquillizing sensation of a tall building falling on him, and when he dug himself out from under that, always amazingly undamaged, he could do as Pa said, God damn it, or quit. In all my time with Rumley's no one left voluntarily until I did, and when I did it was no fault of Pa or myself: I left with his friendship and good wishes. If I could ever meet him again – idle remark, with all the sea between us and no prospect that any of us will ever turn again toward our native countries – it would be an occasion for affectionate talk and some long drinks. He'd be crowding seventy, now I think of it – and yet, he seemed so durable, it wouldn't surprise me to learn that the gang is still Rumley's Ramblers, still traveling somewhere and himself still the law and all the prophets.

He never got rough with the women, except for the love-roughness he must have provided when he took one as a partner for a night or a week or whatever length of time suited both. Now and then I've heard them wailing musically from the cubby-hole in his wagon – laughing the next instant or shouting wild talk with scant breath the way a woman won't do unless she's truly kindled. And I've seen them come out of there looking mighty rumpled, but never discontented.

Pa Rumley didn't talk about his cot-work – those who do often haven't done it of course – but some of the women did, to me no less, after I'd been with the gang a good while and developed a habit of listening, a thing almost unheard of in the teens. Minna Selig especially, three or four years older than I, was all hell on analyzing her feelings, for some odd time-passing fun she got out of it. I recall one occasion when she couldn't rest until she'd stacked up my performance (her word) against Pa's, detail by detail. I liked that quail, but that was one occasion when I wished she'd shut up – after all, I'd never claimed to be that good! Bonnie Sharpe could let in the daylight on Minna's intellect with a poke or two, but I didn't have the knack. When Bonnie wasn't around, Minna would go after a joke or a light remark as if it were a school problem, and everything else must wait till she'd explained it back to you and sorted out all its unreasonable aspects. I don't mean she was grim, she just got her kicks out of it, some way; I think the sweet kid got as much pleasure out of such operations as a dumb creep like me gets out of laughing. It was Pa Rumley's singleness of purpose, she explained, that made him better in bed than a boy – 'Not meaning for to hurt y' feelings, Davy, it's just something an older man learns, I guess. Pa's like a rock, see, I mean even his *face* gets hard, smooth, cold almost, like he a'n't hearing you no more at all, and you know you can do anything – holler, fight, struggle as much as you want, there's no danger you'll get away. Why, the wagon could catch afire and he wouldn't

stop till he'd have it, right there.' (I said: 'You mean it's like being screwed by
a mountain?' She wasn't listening.) 'Now you, Davy, you be mostly too polite,'
said that nice Rambler quail instructing an ex-yard-boy. 'And this might surprise you but it's a fact, Davy, a woman don't like too much of that.' I says:
'No?' 'No,' she says – 'in fact it might surprise you, but a woman don't always
mean exactly what she says – I know, it's real surprising.' I said: 'Sure enough?'

She said sure enough, and went on explaining it in the very friendliest way,
I remember, while I said uhha and ayah and think-of-that-now – you know,
being polite because it's my nature – while we were hearing also the loud lazy
screak of the wagon-wheels and the country sounds outside. I was seventeen
at the time of that conversation, if my memory hasn't goofed, and the countryside would have been the almost tropic splendor of southern Penn. It
comes back to me with the musky sweetness of scupper-nong grape in the air
along with Minna's fragrance, and I lying politely on her bunk with a leg slid
conveniently under her hot and sweaty little bare brown tail, waiting (politely)
until the never-hurrying wagon should provide just the right amount of jolt
to swing us back into action. I knew Minna was right of course, and what she
said doubtless had some effect, or I'd have heard other complaints about
politeness later on, and I can't recollect that I ever did.

Pa had never married. A Rambler boss seldom does. It's traditional that he
should remain available to soothe the restless, arbitrate quarrels, comfort the
widow, instruct the young, and pacify all concerned by procedures not very
convenient for a married man.

He was wondrous patient with the children, the small ones anyway; until
they were seven or eight years old he scarcely tried to comb them out of his
hair. There were seven when Sam and I arrived, a better showing than most
gangs could make – seven children, twelve women, fifteen men, so Sam and
I brought the gang total up to thirty-six. Three more children were born
during my four years with Rumley's. The oldest child was Nell Grafton's boy
Jack, ten when I first saw him; his father Rex Grafton had gone blind with
cataracts near the time of Jack's birth, and had taught himself harness-
making, basketry, other skills. Jack was a handsome hellion born for trouble.
Nell, that big sweet woman, mothered the whole gang and looked after her
proud sharp husband in a way that sheltered his raw nerves and yet steered
him away from self-pity, but her own wild boy she couldn't control. Once or
twice I tried to beat the cruel streak out of him, and that didn't work either.

The bearing of Rambler children presents a continual problem to the Holy
Murcan Church. How can the authorities be sure that all pregnancies are
reported, no woman left alone after the fifth month, every birth attended by
a priest, with a group that's always on the go, in and out of the wilderness,
over national boundaries without inspection, even excused from the taxes
and other responsibilities that go along with settled residence and national

citizenship? You're right – they can't. A Rambler is called – legally and with the consent of the Church because the Church can't help it – a citizen of the world.

The Church has made sporadic efforts to take over the Ramblers, invariably catching its tail in the crack. Every now and then some enterprising prelate gives birth to an idea he thinks is new. The Archbishop of Conicut had a go at it in 318, not very long before we made a circuit of that country and then headed for southern Katskil and Penn. He decreed that every Rambler gang passing through Conicut must have a priest as one of its members. Simple, s's he – how could they object, and why did nobody think of this before? Word got around before his law went into effect; when it did, every gang had left Conicut. Outside each important border post – in Lomeda, and at Dambury in the south of Bershar, and Norrock which is Levannon's only real southern port, and even away over at Mystic on the border of Rhode – a Rambler gang set up camp within sight of Conicut customs officers, with whom they fraternized agreeably enough, but for three months no Rambler gang set foot on Conicut soil, and no Rambler boss took the trouble to explain why.

They were polite with all visitors, but in those encampments they put on no shows that would be visible from the Conicut side. No music, for music doesn't recognize boundaries. No selling to Conicut customers, and no passing on of news. The gangs just sat there. A three-month block was enough to rouse every town and village in the land to a dither of exasperation and protest – nay, they were still grumbling about the 'Rambler Strike' months later when we passed by, and I wished we'd been in on the fun, but we were away the hell up in northern Levannon at the time. Often during the three months a few hand-picked, soft-spoken priests visited the encampments and offered themselves as members – temporary members, even members with limited privileges, anything to get the gangs back in the country before the public rioted. The hopeful fathers were regretfully told that the boss just hadn't quite made up his mind but would be happy to inform them when he did. I think now, looking on it with the historical background that Nickie and Dion have given me, that if the Church had tried to get tough with the Ramblers the thing could have caught fire in a religious war, with results totally unpredictable; but they were smart, and played it soft. Then at last the gang at Norrock – by prearrangement, and that's a story in itself, the way the Rambler newsrunners went flickering along the back roads and dim trails from gang to gang with few the wiser – did accept a nice wee priest as a temporary member, and set forth across the country.

They'd prepared for it. That was Bill (Lardpot) Shandy's gang. Pa Rumley knew Lardpot; he said the man did everything the way he ate, never by halves. Before they set out with the priest, the big sexy pictures on the wagons were painted over with gray – drab and sad. Wherever they stopped, as if for the usual entertainments, no music was offered, just hymns. No plays, no peep-shows. Instead of the account of news from distant places that a Rambler boss customarily provides at the start of every visit, the priest was invited to deliver a sermon. This really hurt, for as I've said, the Ramblers are the one source of news that the people can trust: nothing else in our timid, poverty-ridden, illiterate world takes the place of the newspapers of Old Time. In much less than three months all Conicut was bubbling with rumors – earthquakes in Katskil, atheist uprisings in Nuin, Vairmant over-run with revolutionaries, prophets and three-headed calves. That priest, poor devil – Lardpot had purposely chosen a born innocent – did actually preach a sermon, twice, the second time to a loyal hard-core group of five elderly ladies; they couldn't hear very well, but were gratified to learn the Ramblers had abandoned their nasty ways in favor of nice family-type instruction.

A law that originates in the Church is, naturally, never going to be repealed.[22] But before Bill Shandy's gang reached the border of Rhode, the Archbishop announced at the Cathedral in New Haven that the wretched clerk who originally transmitted the archiepiscopal message had committed an odious blunder of omission, for which he was now doing a penance that would keep him occupied for a while – here they say the Archbishop smacked his lips and smole a somewhat secular smile. What the Archbishop really said – and if he hadn't been so busy looking after the spiritual welfare of his flock he'd have learned of the error and corrected it much sooner – what he *really* said was that any Rambler gang *which so desires* may accept a priest as a member etc. etc. Observe, please, said the Archbishop, how vast a differ-ence may result from the presence or absence of three little words, and do try to govern yourselves accordingly, and praise the Lord, and be mindful what you say. So there was dancing in the streets. I don't see how the best of Arch-bishops could get much more etcetery than that.

So, in practise, the Rambler citizens of the world live mostly by what the Church, like an uneasy schoolmistress, calls the 'honor system.' This means that a Rambler boss must take over in his own person many of the functions of policer, priest and judge. He is expected to see to it that pregnancies are reported, even if the gang is likely to be a hundred miles away a few months later. He must make sure women are properly attended through the critical time. And if by chance a mue is born when the gang happens to be not within

[22] Correction: the Universal Tithing Law, which took an annual dollar from every individual over sixteen, was repealed in 324. True, the Church replaced it with what they call the More Universal Tithing Law, costing everyone a buck and a half; but the first law was honestly repealed, no crud.

– Dion M. M.

reach of a priest, the Rambler boss himself must take the knife in his own hand and be certain it penetrates the heart, and with his own eyes see the body buried under a sapling that has been bent over on itself to form the symbol of the wheel ...

Rumley's other three wagons, except the theater wagon, each had enough compartments for a maximum of twelve people without obliging anyone to sleep in the 'front room,' which was thought to bring bad luck – Rambler people were full of small superstitions like that, singularly free from the large ones. Including the headquarters wagon, the top limit for the whole gang would have been forty-two. Some gangs have six wagons or even more; that's too big. Thirty-six people, the number after Sam and I joined, was comfort-able, not so big that Pa couldn't keep track of all that went on, but big enough so that the toughest bandit outfit wouldn't attack us – Shag Donovan's boys weren't bandits but town toughs, a far stupider breed.

That first day in Humber Town, after accepting us into membership Pa Rumley took off to look after this and that, and I recall Bonnie Sharpe settled down with the back of her head against Mam Laura's knee making small music with her mandolin, which left no one but Minna to look after Sam and me.

Rambler life followed a rhythm like that, of swift and obvious shifts from tension to calm. Bonnie had clearly relished hearing my story and Mam Laura's questions and my Da's occasional remarks, her humorous girl's eyes huge and gray turning from one to another of us, never missing a thing. Then I was done, and Bonnie knew that Minna would look after us if nobody else got around to it, so for Bonnie I suppose the universe comfortably nar-rowed down to a trifling section of the red bearskin, the shiny mandolin strings, the light sounds of music she was making, the pleasure she took in her own healthy body and the warmth of Mam Laura's knee. A time of ten-sion, a time of uncomplicated quiet with music in it – I learned that rhythm too, after a while. If Nickie had not also learned it I couldn't get along with her as I do – well, without it she'd be someone else, unrecognizable. Spare me from living with worthy souls whose bow of enthusiasm is never allowed to rest unstrung.

Minna Selig, as she took us over to one of the other wagons, was wearing under her black curls a cute frown of thoughtfulness—

It has just this moment occurred to me that some of you who may or may not exist may also actually be women. If so, you would insist on knowing what else Minna was wearing, this preoccupation with what the other quail have on being an ineradicable trait which I have never been able to beat out of a single one of you. Kay – dark cherry-red blouse and sloppy linsey pants, and moccasins like what we all wore – all except Pa, that is, who would have reamed out anyone he caught imitating his gilt nudes.

Minna found places for us, just by chance (she said) in the same wagon where she and Bonnie slept. A happy chance: I kept the same compartment all the four years. Bonnie went over to another wagon when she married Joe Dulin in 319, and Sam later moved in with Mam Laura, a courtship I'll tell about – but only a little, only the surface happenings, for that's all I know: there was a depth to it, naturalness, inevitability, which they would not have wanted to explain if they could, and whatever I wrote about it would be no better than half-educated guesswork.

Yes, I stayed with that place Minna picked for me, making a home for myself out of a hole four feet by eight by seven, learning how to live cramped in small ways but not in large – unless you want to say that we're all bound to be cramped in a moment of time that rarely reaches even a century, on a speck of stardust that's been precariously spinning in nothing for a mere piti-ful three or four billion years. I was also learning how few important material possessions there are that can't be readily stowed in four-by-eight-by-seven, leaving room for yourself, and now and then for Minna.

22

I came to Levannon and the ships, and I did not sail.

What is it, this very certain destiny that overtakes all our visions, our most reasoned plans equally with our fantastic dreams? Maybe whenever we think of the future, as we must if we're to be human at all, the act is bound to include a something-too-much, as if with all due human absurdity we were expecting chance to alter its course at the impact of our noise. A boy imag-ined the great outriggers, the fine thirty-tonners bound east by the northern route; his mind saw their canvas tall, mighty, luminous in a golden haze. A young man in the late summer of 317, the least important member of a Ram-bler gang he'd never heard of a month earlier, came off the flat-bottomed ferry-sailer into the reeking port of Renslar in Levannon, helping old Will Moon wrangle the mules. I suppose he was possibly a quarter-inch taller than when he took hold of Emmia Robson in the way of love. When the two had cussed and coaxed the lead wagon up the ramp and out of the way off the dock – Pa Rumley having pups all over the place, roaring advice to which leathery Will paid no attention – Will called the young man's attention to the vessel in the next slip, with a jerk of his wizened brown chin and a directional squirt of tobacco juice, and shouted in the manner of the partly deaf: 'Can you read, boy?'

'Ayah, I can read.'

'Mam Laura been learnin' you the learnin', I hear tell?'

'I can read, Will.'

'Well, read me the name of that old shitpot yonder.'

'Why, that's the *Daisy Mae*, it says.'

Poor graceless squabby thing, she smelled of spoiled onions as well as dead fish. She was fat amidships with a tubby blunt bow and a square stern, her single outrigger as ungainly as a wooden leg. The oar-benches had been rubbed to a polish by the aching buttocks of the slaves who were likely penned up somewhere in barracks at that moment waiting for the next ordeal. Nothing else about her had any shine; reefing down hid only some of the patches in her sail. Will shouted: 'You any good guessing tonnage?'

'Never saw that kind of boat before.'

He went roaring into laughter. '"Boat" is good – hoy, they'd skin you for that! "Ships" you gotta call 'em when they're that size. Come on, give a guess how big she is.'

She looked ancient as well as puny, a salt-frosted gray, a color of loneliness and neglect. She rode high in the water, empty, sun-smitten; if a watchman was aboard he must have been lurking below, where you'd suppose the hot stench would have been past bearing. I imagined her to be some little cargo tub built for short hauls between ports of the Hudson Sea, likely to be abandoned soon or broken up for firewood. 'She a'n't as far gone as she looks,' Will said – 'they'll be painting her before she goes out again, and you'd be surprised.' A miserable dockside cur had been attracted by the flavor of her garbage but didn't quite dare jump down on her deck. He lifted a scarecrow leg against a dock stanchion, aiming poorly and spattering the ship's rail. With an empty hand Will Moon made a stone-throwing motion; the mutt scrabbled away in terror, tail clamped between his legs. I fancied the dreary old vessel sighing meekly at the indignity, too feeble to resent it. 'Come on, Davy – give us a guess.'

'Couple tons maybe?'

'You got things to learn,' Will said, and cackled with delight – when I'm sixty maybe I'll be all hell on instructing the young too. 'Things to learn, bub – why, old *Daisy Mae*, she won't go a ton under thirty-three ...'

No, I never sailed aboard a Levannon ship, nor ever sped down the road on a bright roan with three attendants, expecting a serving wench at the next inn to bathe me and warm my bed with her willing loins. But I did go with Rumley's Ramblers through all the nations of the known world except Nuin where Pa Rumley had once run afoul of the law, and the Main city states that you can't reach by land without passing over Nuin's province of Hampsher. I lent a hand wrastling those mules on the Renslar dock, and the same evening I was in the entertainment with my horn, never missing one for four years – they loved me. That year we went north along the Lowland Road of Levannon.

It is the greatest road of modern history. Moha's Northeast Road that pointed my way out of Skoar is a fine thing, but a cowpath beside the Lowland Road. There are travelers who would tell you that the greatest of all is the Old Post Road from Old City of Nuin to Renslar: such is the cussedness of the human race when determined to argue passionately about something that can't be any way proved – their whole damn trouble is that always they know I'm right but won't admit it. The Lowland Road of Levannon is not just a road; it's a natural force and a way of living. It runs from Norrock on the great sea, the Atlantic, all the way north to the rich nastiness of Seal Harbor, a distance of three hundred and seventy-some miles. It not only holds the nation of Levannon together like the spinal column of a snake, but in a real sense that road *is* Levannon. You can hardly say whether the towns strung along it like vertebrae are served by it or exist in order to serve it.

Traveling north, you walk in the morning shadow of the beautiful green mountains at your right hand. You see at once why the many small but vigorous towns and villages are needed there. Alert and usually fortified, they are connected to the big Lowland Road by good secondary roads and trails, to protect the artery of trade and travel from bandits and other wild beasts. Levannon is never like Moha, sloppy and shiftless about its roads, the one great road and the many small ones – they mean too much. As for the great Lowland Road, the mountains are sure to be either a shield or a menace depending on who commands the heights; a mountain trail is a nervous sort of boundary. Levannon dreams of possessing both sides of the great range; to Vairmant and Bershar and Conicut the same dream is a nightmare, which they will hold off if they can – those three have had no wars among themselves for at least fifty years, too well aware that they might at any moment need to be allies ...

I have always found it difficult to understand that the whole region of our known world was in Old Time a small part of a very great nation. The idea of a war over possession of what they called the Berkshires and the Green Mountains would have made the men of that time smile indulgently as at a child's nonsense: the wars they were concerned with were, materially, so much bigger! Ethically bigger? – I think not, except that they had it in their power to destroy the world completely and very nearly did so.

Well up in the northern country, the mountains become low hills and finally subside into the flat land along the south coast of the Lorenta Sea. Up there crouches Seal Harbor, a steaming corruption near the mouth of a river that is called the St Francis as it was in Old Time.

Seal Harbor is frankly nothing but a mammoth tryworks. The lamp-oil seal, sometimes called hairseal, breed by the thousands on barren islands far to the north, beyond where the Lorenta Sea spreads out into the Atlantic. Those islands are strung along the wilderness coast of what the old maps call Labrador; modern Levannese call it the Seal Shore. The animals must have taken advantage of man's decline in the Years of Confusion to increase enormously: Seal Harbor people tell of modern voyages of exploration that have been made north of the regular sealing grounds – it's just seal islands and more seal islands, they say, up to the point where you can travel no further because the men won't stand it. They call it Northern Terror and it's a thing beyond argument or reason – partly the cold, and furious wind, but most of all what they describe as the 'madness of the sun.'

But men can manage their business in the southern part of the breeding grounds, and luckily for men, the seal apparently never learn. Greatly daring, the slow outriggers specially built for the task pull out of Seal Harbor late in March and creep down the Lorenta Sea hugging its dangerous northern coast, past the island still named Anticosti and through a strait the sailors nowadays call Belly Wheel. That was once Belle Isle and meant Beautiful Island, but if you tell a modern sealer so, he'll stare you down with the blubber-faced incomprehension of one of the poor beasts who make his living for him; if it annoys him enough, he may charge.

After passing through Belly Wheel they follow the coast northwest. It's tricky work I suppose: they don't dare either to let the cruel land out of sight or to drift too close and risk being caught in the tideways and currents and flung against it. They arrive at the breeding grounds with the winds of the great sea on their necks, and go ashore in small boats to do their butchery in haste, with clubs. They take only the blubber, and the best hides of the baby and yearling seal, leaving all carcasses where they lie to be dealt with by the vultures or swept away in high tide for the swarming sharks. If the voyage were not so tough for those clumsy vessels, and if men were more numerous, less superstitious and a little more brave, the seal would be extinct by now in spite of their massive numbers. The sealers have no least thought of husbandry or mercy, only of the quick dollar. All they can do is kill and kill and go on killing till the fat hulls of the cargo vessels are replete. This they do so that we may have light in the evening.

The untreated blubber is brought back in that state to Seal Harbor. I've heard that the townfolk know when the returning fleet has come within ten miles, from the rancid stink that heralds it even if there's no east wind blowing. It's a cause for rejoicing – after all it happens only once a year. Then comes a few weeks of work, after which the good citizens of Seal Harbor go back to the longer holiday of loafing, hunting, whoring, fishing, brawling – above all brawling – and picking each other's pockets until the next year's 'fat weeks.' During the trying and for days afterward unless a merciful wind arrives, the smoke from the blubber-works lays a black-purple cloud over the shabby city, and even hardened long-time inhabitants are sick. That's one of the main reasons why it is a city of scum, misfits, criminals, failures. No one wants to live there who could earn a living and be welcome somewhere else.

We journeyed north by rather slow stages in the closing days of 317, often spending more than a week in a village if we enjoyed the style of it. Pa Rumley's way was leisurely; I've heard him remark that if a thing wasn't still there by the time you arrived it likely wouldn't have been worth hurrying after. Not many Rambler gangs head north when winter's advancing: as we drifted along the Lowland Road, always with the grave splendor of the mountains at the right hand, the villages were happy to see us and bought well, being somewhat starved for entertainment and news. At a good-sized town named Sanasint we turned east, crossing over the border into the north end of Vairmant. We spent the winter months of December through March in a way most Rambler gangs wouldn't have cared to do, at a lonely camp of our own devising in a pocket of the Vairmant hills. May, Pa explained, was the time to hit Seal Harbor, when the oil buyers had come and gone, and the companies had paid off the workmen but there hadn't been time for all the money to settle into the pockets of a few gamblers and crooks; but that wasn't his main reason for holing up during the winter. He did that for about three months of every year – nay, we did it down in Penn too where there's hardly such a thing as winter – so that the grown-ups could loaf and mend harness while the young stuff, by Jesus and Abraham, would please to settle down and learn something. Two things, Pa said, were capable of taking some of the devil out of the young – birch and learning. Of the two, learning was best, in his opinion, even if it did smart considerably more.

Mam Laura concurred. Gentle and gently philosophic at most other times, capable of sitting in the same position for an hour doing nothing but smoke her pipe and gaze at the landscape, Mam Laura became a demon of energy in the presence of a student who showed some inclination to learn a little. Anything went then – snarling invective, language that would have made my Da blush (sometimes did), sarcasm, intense but thoughtful praise, a slap on the cheek – anything, all the way up to a kiss or one of the honey-and-walnut candies that she kept secretly in her own compartment and that no one else knew how to make. Anything went, so long as she could hope it would help to fix a bit of truth in your mind where with luck you might not lose it.

She was born in Vairmant, south of the tranquil wilderness spot where we made our winter quarters that year. The name of her birth town was Lamoy, a hill town close to the Levannon border. Later, when we were journeying down through that part of the nation, we avoided the turn-off for Lamoy although it was a prosperous place and we might have done well there. Mam Laura had nothing against it, but she had made a complete break with childhood long ago and had no wish to attempt revisiting the past. She was the daughter of a schoolmaster; I could hardly hold my amazement when I learned that in Vairmant, though the Holy Murcan Church controls the schools of course, the teachers are not necessarily all priests. Mam Laura's father was secular, a scholar and visionary, who privately gave her an education far beyond anything he was allowed to impart to the other children of his school: he had a quackpot theory that within her lifetime it might be possible for a woman not a nun to be permitted to teach – a weird thought for which he could have been booted out of the school and into the pillory. In her darker moods Mam Laura sometimes said that he was fortunate because he died rather young. In such moods also, she sometimes felt that his teaching and encouragement had merely unfitted her for any world except the one that existed only in his mind.

I didn't always understand, in the days when I was struggling to win my way into the region of knowledge she opened up for me, how completely a giver Mam Laura was – well, what child ever does grasp the motives behind a teacher's thankless labors, or for that matter the value of the teaching itself? I dare say a child with that much insight would be a sort of monster. But now, when Nickie's twenty-ninth birthday and mine are behind us, it seems to me I do begin to understand Mam Laura and her teaching – now, when we are so much concerned for the child Nickie is carrying, so full of thoughts for the child's future and so uncertain what manner of world that child will be driven to explore.

This is late April on the island Neonarcheos. Lately I have written only sporadically, often unwillingly, angry at a compulsion that can drive an otherwise reasonably intelligent man both toward and away from the pen – ah, who but a fantastic quackpot would ever write a book? Likely you noticed how my method of storytelling altered, a while back. That was partly because my mind is frightened and distracted – Nickie is not well.

She insists her daily and nightly pain and discomfort are entirely natural for the seventh month of pregnancy. The perils of that stately condition are vastly exaggerated, she says – she's never lost a husband from it yet. The child lives and moves, we know; often she wants me to feel 'him' kick.

But there is another genuine reason why I'm writing about my time with the Ramblers in what may appear to you a more hasty style – no detailed story now, merely a touching of what I best remember. I have no inclination to apologize. Your own worst fault, you know, is just the opposite of haste: I mean this dreadful mewling uncertainty, this messing about never quite able to make up your mind whether you exist; you ought to overcome it if it's within your power. No apology, but a moderate effort at explanation.

There was a story I was compelled to write, inwardly compelled, no doubt by an obscure hope that in writing it I would come to understand it better myself. That was the story of a particular part of growing up (as far as an experience so continuous can have any 'parts'), the story of a boy who came out of one condition into another and a wider one, though perhaps even less than a quarter-inch taller in the busy flesh. Now that story, I was surprised to notice a while ago, I have completed. What happened to me with the Ramblers happened to a far older boy; my meeting with Nickie (which I shall tell you about before long, I think) happened to a man. These are other stories, maybe beyond my power to write, maybe not. However – because there was a voyage, because life is continuous as daylight between dawn and dark, because I was concerned with varieties of time, because I heard no objections from your Aunt Cassandra nor yet from her yellow tomcat with the bent ear – that original story of a boy's journey grew inseparably in, out of, over, under, through, around, by, with and for those other stories; which obliges me to complete them too – a little bit. (Ask your Aunt C. how it's possible to complete something 'a little bit' – you would have to exist in order to analyze and enjoy a literary gidget like that one, and you're probably not up to it.) I don't suppose there's any need to explain where that boy's special story ended or partly ended, since it will be obvious almost immediately to a learned, compassionate, profoundly and generously perceptive scholar and gentleman – or quail – like yourself.

Merely notice and remember, if you wish, that for a good many pages now, and on to the end of the book whenever and wherever that may happen, we – I mean myself and you more or less with me, which after all comes fairly close to admitting you might exist – well, we are like people who have finished one day's journey, and find that here at the inn there's still some time for drinks and conversation before we sleep.

'Look at him there!' says Mam Laura – 'only look at him sitting there with a redheaded face hung up perpendicularly forninst his brains, trying to tell me you mustn't split an infinitive! Mustn't, mustn't, mustn't, frig mustn't! Why, Davy? Why?'

'Well, that grammar book says—'

'Bugger the buggerly book!' she'd cry out. 'I want to hear one stunk-up lonely reason *why* you mustn't!'

'To be honest, I can't think of any. It don't explain—'

'Doesn't explain. And being honest is what I'm after,' she said, mollified and sweet and smiling again. 'You see, Sam, the boy has intelligence; he only needs to have the school rubbish beaten out of him like dust out of a rug.

'Well, the grammar book doesn't explain, Davy, because it relies on authority, which is all right and necessary within limits in such a book; if it tried to explain everything along the way it would stop being a grammar and turn into a textbook on etymology – what's etymology?'

'The – science of words?'

'Don't ask me, Brother David! I'm asking you.'

'Uh – well – the science of words.'

'Doesn't tell me enough. Science of what aspect of words? What thing about words?'

'Oh! Word origins.'

'Had to help you on that one. Next time, snap it back at me and no nonsense. All right – that grammar is probably as good as any other on the subject, and it's also the only one I possess – of course nothing written in our day is worth a tinker's poop. Davy – English came partly from the much older language Latin, as I told you a while ago. Kay – in Latin the infinitive is a single word: you don't split it because you can't. And so, some time or other, some grammarian with an iron brain decided that the laws of Latin ought to govern English because he liked it that way – and, I'm afraid, also because that made grammar seem more mysterious and difficult to the layman, which built up the prestige of the clerical class. But language – the English language anyway – always makes mahooha out of arbitrary notions of that sort. Split 'em whenever it sounds right, love – I don't mind – whenever the stuffing is slight enough so that a reader can't forget the little "to" before he gets to the verb. And what's meant by the word "arbitrary"?'

'Decided by will or whim more than by reason.'

'See, Sam? He's a good boy.'

'Blows that horn good too,' said my Da …

At that camp I did my horn practise on an open hillside some distance from the wagons. It was moderately dangerous, I suppose, and Sam generally went along, to loaf nearby and watch the part of the country that wasn't under my eyes while I played. I remember an afternoon late in April; the gang was beginning to get ready for another year's travel, and we knew the first thing would be a serious effort to relieve Seal Harbor of its loose change before we turned back south. Sam had something on his mind that day. My own head was empty except for music and spring fret, and a wish that Bonnie would quit teasing and put out like Minna. She was more interested in pursuit than capture, at that time anyway; later, as I've mentioned, she married Joe Dulin, which showed a lot of good sense. When I got tired that afternoon and was finished with my work, Sam stretched and said: 'Well, Jackson, I done it.'

'Done what, Mister?'

'Impident. Why, yesterday, after Laura was done teaching you, I hung around like I sometimes do, and I asked her flat-out if she figured it was too late for me to pick up a mite of learning myself in my own spare time. "What kind of learning?" she says right away, and when I told her – nay, you know, Jackson, you bein' young as all dammit and horny after the green girls, you'd never believe what a *soft* woman that Laura is, more b' token she's your teacher and such is none of your business, but it's so. "What kind of learning, Sam?" she says, and so to make things plain I told her again about the wife I got behind me in Katskil, for I thought it might be a trouble to her mind. And that's a sad sort of a fool thing, Jackson, about my wife. Always seemed to hold it against me, my wife did, that we could never get kids – hoy, and then unbeknownst to her I went and got you by another and a better woman, anyhow we think that happened. But that wa'n't all. Year by year, seemed she felt it more and more of a duty to whittle me down, nag-nag, tell everyone'd listen the main reason I never got a master carpenter's license was I was too God-damn lazy to rise up off my ass even in a city like Kingstone all bungfull of money and opportunity, only she never said God-damn of course – red saint she was – I mean, why, shit, Jackson, a man couldn't live with it … Ai-yah – "What kind of learning?" says Laura, and I told her – "Look," I says, "I can't follow along with the Goddamn etymogolology or whatever," I says, "account I et too much ignorance when I was young, but I had it in mind to learn about you," I said – nay, Jackson, there's a strange shine to a woman when she's all of a sudden happy, I mean happy for true. I don't suppose a man gets to see it more'n once-twice in a lifetime – the lot of us, men and women, bein' what we are. "About you," I says, "and how I'd share your bed and your nights and days, and so't of stand by, you might say, as long as I last." And here's the thing, Jackson. After I'd said that, and was so't of shifting my feet and wondering where I'd run and hide if she was to get the wrong look onto her face – why – why, Jackson, she said: "Then I'll teach you, Sam." Just like that she said it – said: "I'll teach you that, Sam, if it's all right with the boy." '

'Merciful winds, it's all right with the boy!' I remember I was able to say that quickly, so that Sam would feel sure there were no second thoughts. And if there were any that mattered, they were buried too deep for me to know anything about them myself. I believe I was honestly happy for him and Mam Laura, who was after all the woman I would have picked for a mother if I'd had anything to say about it, and I had no feeling that she was taking him away from me.

That night, I remember, I had to have Bonnie – complaisant Minna wouldn't do, it had to be Bonnie, and never mind her quick and snippy No and her maybe-sometime. And I got her – remembering Emmia, I think. I warmed her up with kissing when I caught her behind our wagon, and followed her to her compartment after she broke away with a friendlier backward look than I was used to from her; when she would have dismissed me there at the curtains I simply went in with her and kept up the good work. When she tried to freeze me, I tickled her under the ribs and she had to laugh. When she informed me she was about to yell and scream and fetch Pa Rumley who'd give me the cowhide but good, I informed her that she probably wasn't, anyway not if she was the sweet, passionate and beautiful Spice I thought she was – in fact prettier than any quail I ever saw – and so I went on with my enterprise, warming her here and there and yonder until there wasn't really one sensible thing she could do, except beg me to wait till she got the rest of her clothes off so they wouldn't be rumpled. And I will be damned if she wasn't a virgin.

Also relieved to be one no longer, and a bit grateful – and a good wife to Joe Dulin when she got around to it – but above all a *hell* of a musician, bless her: I've never known a better, certainly not excepting myself. I was fifteen. You can excuse me (if you like) for going rather cocky and quick-tempered and full of brag the next year or two. However, my half-comic good luck with Bonnie was only a part of the reason for it. I think everything, including the enormous discoveries of the books that Mam Laura was opening up for me, was pushing me just then in the direction of a temporary and fairly harmless toughness. I thought, like most grass-green ignoramuses, that in touching the outer fringes of learning I had swallowed it all. I thought that because a few women had been pleased to play with me, I was likely the grandest stud since Adam – (who had, you must admit, certain God-damned advantages we can't any of us duplicate). I thought that because I could see the absurdity of dreaming about buying a thirty-ton outrigger, heaving an agreeable serving-wench aboard with the rest of the furniture and taking off for the rim of the dadgandered world – why, I was mature, *mature*.

I thought those chunks of whopmagullion, yet it's all right. Humility does arrive. In fact, so fortunate is our human condition, it seems to arrive for many people early enough in life so that we can enjoy it quite a little while before we're dead.

23

We came down on Seal Harbor like a May wind; Shag Donovan and a dozen of his bully boys smacked into us like a wind out of a sewer. As I think I mentioned, three of them got rather dead, but it wasn't much of a brawl. Four of them rushed our little theater while we were putting on our souped-up version of *Romeo and Juliet*. Minna was doing Juliet as usual; the hoodlums' idea was to drag her off into the bushes while the camp was turned upside down. But Pa had smelled trouble, a gift that seldom failed him, and we were ready. There was a personal element in it: Pa had met Shag some years before and got the worst of it; this time he took an artist's pleasure in cooling Shag off before things could get too serious. Two of the three who wound up dead had got as far as grabbing Minna and tearing her clothes – rape was fashionable up there, and I suppose they expected you to get used to it – so Tom Blaine and Sam clubbed them maybe a bit harder than they meant to; luckily Minna wasn't hurt. Third man who perished got caught in a rather unusual way by Mother Spinkton's Home Remedy. He was running fast, myself behind him at the time with my knife out and blood in my eye; he was passing through the shadow of one of our supply wagons just at the moment when four of his friends toppled it over; a full case landed on his back.

In a hazy fashion, the crowd was on our side. They had to live with Donovan's gang, however, and we didn't, so they left the fighting to us, and helped us by stealing less than you'd expect them to while we were busy. Several bottles in that case of Mother Spinkton broke, after which our guests showed a marked disinclination to hang around – you could almost say that Mother won the war. And by the way, we included the full value of those busted bottles in the bill that Pa Rumley presented next day to the Seal Harbor Town Council no less. Don't think they didn't pay it. They whimpered and said they were doing it just to get rid of us before we disturbed the peace. Pa Rumley counted the silver and tied the sack to his belt without asking the obvious question. Life in Seal Harbor had its ups and downs, that was all. A small cheerful crowd followed us to the city gates and cheered us as we departed south.

Speaking of *Romeo and Juliet*, we always did our best by that one, although since our theater was only a curtained opening in the side of a wagon we had to simplify it some. The balcony job for instance – the whole stage opening had to be the balcony, with Br'er Romeo operating from the ground, which was all right – good realism – so long as he remembered not to get himself tangled with a wagon-wheel in a spirited moment and set the whole damned balcony swaying and squeaking. Billy Truro, a romantical tenor type, was usually Romeo, and he sometimes got a little carried away, especially when it came to bellering that line; 'Oh, wilt thou leave me so unsatisfied?' Hung up there on that plague-take-it wagon-wheel with Minna fading out on him, he couldn't help but win the sympathy of the house.

As for the text, Pa used to claim it was a genuine condemned version; Mam Laura allowed he was right. She didn't have it among her books, so I never read the whole thing till I had the freedom of the Heretics' secret library at Old City. It's true there was something slightly drastic about our manner of tearing through the play in two fifteen-minute acts, with an extra sword-fight, but that was the way the yucks liked it: we aimed to please, and what the hell more can an artist do? As Juliet, Minna Selig was an absolute copper-riveted whiz. I can still hear her making with 'Oh, swear not by the moon, the inconstant moon, that monthly changes in her circled orb, lest that thy love prove likewise variable.' Often she'd leave out the line with the orb in it, for she could smell a crowd almost as acutely as Pa Rumley, and tell whether the yucks were the type who'd be so irritated by hearing a word they didn't know that they might start hooting and hell-raising. Frankly I don't know what any yuck could do with an orb.

Hoy, little Minna in her nightgown, with her dark hair a mist around her big eyes! – why, she *was* Juliet, the way she looked innocent as a kitten and not much smarter, and pretty enough to make the dullest yuck want to cry. Bonnie adored watching her perform. I remember we gave *Romeo* another whirl at the very first stop we made after leaving Seal Harbor. That was down in Vairmant, for we'd taken the road on the eastern side of the mountains, where Rumley's hadn't appeared for several years. Bonnie and I watched the show out front – Bonnie was still pretty warm for me after our little excitement in April – and she was in ecstasies whenever Minna-Juliet sounded off, hugging my arm and exclaiming over and over under her breath: 'Listen at them chest notes! Aw, Davy, it's gonna make me cry – ooo-eee – ooh, *a'n't* she a pisser!'

That road east of the mountains was presently leading us down along the west bank of the lovely blue Conicut, and we took our time in that pretty country, which is full of little villages and all of them good for a pitch. Pa never would explain what old trouble it was that obliged him to keep out of Nuin: it was a question you just didn't ask. But he'd been born in Nuin and was bungfull of Nuin history, and disapproved of most of it. I remember a day on the river road when we were approaching the little city state of Holy Oak, north of Lomeda. Old Will Moon was somewhat too drunk to handle the mules – a fault he had – and Pa had taken over for him while he slept it off. Pa enjoyed driving anyway, and carried on a running grudge fight with Old Lightning, the near hind mule on the headquarters wagon. Old Lightning never seemed to pay any attention, but could generally tell from Pa's voice when it was safe to fall asleep walking, or slack off so gradually that his harness-mate never caught on to the swindle. Sam was out on the front seat with me that day, Pa slouching between us with the reins, and the splendid blue of the Conicut making a music of color under a friendly sun.

The mere name of Holy Oak had got Pa started on Nuin history, a subject that always chafed him. 'This little country was part of Nuin,' he told us, 'in the old days of Morgan the First, Morgan the Great they call the old sumbitch. I believe it fit a war of independence after he corked off, and so did Lomeda and the other pisswilly countries this side the river – ecclesi-God-damn-astical states is what they call 'em. Morgan the Great! – gentlemen hark, it's getting so you can't believe nothing you hear no more, more b' token you never could, anyway not with Morgan the Great around. They claim you don't behold his like no more, and I say that's a good thing. Account of he was a bird. This little country, this Holy Oak, is supposed to be named for a tree that was planted by Morgan the Great. Kay, I've seen it – a'n't no great circumstance of a vegetable, it's just an oak tree, and you can say it's a purty little story, but wait a minute. Let's reason it out. Let's look at what history says. You got any idea how many frigging oak trees that old man is supposed to've planted for himself? Why, gentlemen hark, it's pitiful – why, if I had as many hairs growing out of my hide as that old man is supposed to've planted oak trees, I'd be bowed down, gentlemen, I'd walk on all fours like a bear till they skinned me for a rug. You may well ask why he couldn't go and plant a cherry or a pecan or something for a change – *git* up, Old Lightning, you mis'ble petrified three-tenths of an illegitimate hoss's ass, git up, *git* up! – you may well ask, and I'll tell you. The God-durn public wouldn't let him is the reason – had to be oak or nothing and that's the royalty of it.'

'Still and all,' Sam said, 'he called himself a president, not a king, can't get around that.'

'Ayah,' Pa shouted, 'and there's the biggest pile of hoss-shit ever left unshoveled!' Well, Sam had said it merely to keep him perking. 'President my glorious aching butt! He was a king, and that's the only excuse for him. I mean you got to make allowances for a king, the way he's got everybody after him, obliged to king it from dawn to dark – planting oak trees, laying cornerstones and maternal ancestors in sinister bars, why, balls of Abraham and Jesus H. K. Hornblower Christ, they never gave that man any *rest* – git *up*, Lightning, God blast the shiveled-up mouse-turd you got for a soul, I got to speak rough to you? – no rest at all. How'd he ever find time for kinging, 's what I want to know? Look, here's how it was, on just an average day, mind you, when this poor old sumbitch, this Morgan the Great, is trying to address the fucking Senate on a matter of life and death or anyhow a lot of money. You think he's going to get a chance to fit two sentences together end to end? – gentlemen hark! No, God butter it and the Devil futter it, *no* – and why? Because up pops the Minister for Social Contacts or whatever – "Sorry, your Majesty, we got here an urgent message concerning a bed over to Wuster that a'n't been slept in yet by no royalty, only your Majesty will have to sleep into her kind of quick, so to make it up to Lowell in time for to throw a dollar acrost the Merrimac account it says here in the book you done that on the 19th of April – more b' token, your Majesty, we just this minute got in a new shipment of oak trees –" why, goodness, gentlemen, that a'n't no way to live, not for a great man. Takes the heart out of things, don't it? How can you expect a boy to want to be President if he knows it's going to be nag, nag all day long? – you Lightning, God damn your evermore backscuttled immortal spirit, *will* you git up? ...'

It wasn't only Nuin history that bothered Pa Rumley. He didn't actually like any part of history, nor anybody in it except Cleopatra. He used to say he knew he could have made out with her real smooth, if he could have met her in her native California when he was some younger and had more ginger in his pencil. Nothing Mam Laura said could ever convince him that Cleopatra hadn't lived in California. Sometimes he got me to wondering about that myself.

From Holy Oak we went on through the other little Low Countries into Conicut, where they were still feeling the reactions from the Rambler 'strike' I told you about. Business had been very brisk, but we got there late, after too many other gangs had had the same idea. We passed on into Rhode, a dreamy small land hardly bigger than Lomeda, where coastal fishing is the main occupation and trial marriage the main entertainment – only nation where the Holy Murcan Church allows divorce by consent. The Church calls Rhode a 'social testing ground'; they've been testing trial marriage there for fifty-some years now without learning anything except that almost everybody likes it. As I understand it, the Church considers this irrelevant, so they go on testing in the hope of more light. While we were there – most of the summer – I naturally did as much testing as possible: Bonnie was drifting then into her permanent attachment with Joe Dulin, and Minna (I don't like to say it) could now and then be a bore. The testing was fine, and I reached no conclusions that I couldn't duck.

Since it couldn't be Nuin, we doubled back through Conicut, and over the border into the southern tip of Levannon, wintering at Norrock where the sound of the great sea is a quieter voice, most of the time, than the one I heard in later years at Old City – there at Old City, Nickie and I lived our private years within sound of the harbor and the big winds. At Norrock on clear days, we could look south from our hillside camp to a far-off blur of sandy shore, the Long Island that Jed Sever used to tell us about; and that seemed far in the past; and so did his death – and my hot-cool games with Vilet – and shafts of green-gold light remembered, slanting down into the warm stillness of Moha wilderness. Oh, the sound of ocean is the same voice wherever you hear it, and be you old or young – at Old City or Norrock, or along the miles of achingly brilliant white sand in the loneliness of southern Katskil, or speaking of tranquillity on this beach at Neonarcheos.

The spring of 319 saw us traveling north again on the great Lowland Road of Levannon, but that time we stayed with it no further than Beckon, the Levannon harbor town across the Hudson Sea from Nuber the Holy City. Beckon is the first place where there's a reliable ferry-sailer big enough for Rambler wagons. There's another at Ryebeck, opposite Katskil's capital city Kingstone, but that would not have done for us: at Kingstone someone might recognize Sam and pass on word to his wife, who would summon the policers and clobber him with every law in the book. Even the military might get snorty about him, though by this time the pisswilly Moha-Katskil war was in the fading past. At Nuber there wasn't much risk, Sam thought. We put on a mor'l show there, pantaletted up for righteousness' sweet sake, and we cleaned up nicely with undercover selling of horny pictures to brighten the private lives of the brethren; elsewhere, selling them almost openly, we never took in half as much.

We drifted south from Nuber by slow stages. People of the Kingstone district seldom traveled in the south of Katskil. Anywhere in the country, however, there was some slight risk for Sam. He didn't work with the medicine pitch, but just lent a hand at whatever was needed – mule-skinning, scene-shifting, helping Grafton at his harness-making – and kept more or less out of sight of the public.

He particularly enjoyed being what Mam Laura called a 'noise off' during her fortune-telling. She always had a small tent set up for it, with a canvas partition across the middle. In the front there'd be nothing but one little table and two chairs – no crystal or incense or such-like props. But she did love a good noise off. In the back half of the tent she kept a few gidgets – a cowbell, a drum with a crack in it that was no use to Stud Dabney any more but could still make a dismal sort of noise like a bull's intestines rumbling somewhere on a misty night. At cue words, Sam would work these objects for her, or knock something over, or sometimes heave a long horrible sigh that Mam Laura warned him not to use too often because she could hardly stand it herself. He'd build up the racket little by little until Mam Laura would holler 'Hoot-mon-salaam-aleikum!' or 'Peace, troubled spirit!' or something else soothing, and then quit for a while. The yuck could never be *quite* sure that the canvas panel wouldn't suddenly rise up and reveal some fearful apparition such as Asmodeus or a four-horned Giasticutus or his mother-in-law. Sam claimed that his job was good for him because it like kept him in touch with the arts but without any real God-damn responsibility. He also said now and then that he was getting old.

It should not have been true, since he was only in the fifties. But in some ways I suppose it was true.

Southern Katskil is altogether unlike the bustling northern part. A ghostly, evasive land – the big rich farms are in the central part, not the real south. Small sandy roads twist through the pine barrens as if in blind pursuit of a goal you'll never learn. If such a road comes to an apparent end, you feel sure that you must have missed some turn-off that was the road's real continuation. In many places, inland as well as close to the fine white beaches, it is deep wilderness instead of the curious pines, wilderness as profound as the semitropical jungles of Penn, which I have also glimpsed. They say that bands of the flap-eared apes have sometimes been encountered in the jungle regions of southern Katskil – the same kind that are well known in Penn, shy, wild, a little dangerous.

There are no cities in southern Katskil, unless you want to give that name to the dull harbor of Vyland in the extreme south, on the immensity of Delaware Bay; it hardly deserves it, and is hardly worth the effort it takes to reach it on the long road through the barrens and jungle and enormous swamps. Vyland was once a pirate town, headquarters of a fleet that ravaged Penn's coastal commerce with the northern nations. Katskil and Penn for once agreed on something, joining forces to clean out the raiders, as we had to do in Nuin with the Cod Islands lot. The Vyland pirates didn't have the vinegar and cussedness of the Cod Islanders, however, nor any islands for refuge; it was a massacre. Today, Vyland has nothing to show but fisheries and monasteries, which smell alike.

No proper cities there in the south of Katskil, but a good many small villages, widely separated, heavily stockaded, their people often showing a dreary distrust of strangers. We seldom had a really good pitch. I have an impression there was a good deal of hookworm and malaria, possibly other sorry conditions that held the people down through no fault of their own.

One village in that region I am compelled to remember. We came to it in the fall of 319, when we were already moving northwest with the idea of crossing over into Penn near their fine city of Filadelfia. It was late afternoon; the front and rear gates of the village were shut but not locked. We rolled down the road with our customary joyous commotion, playing and singing 'I'll Go No More A-Roving,' a song that usually won us a better welcome than any other. When we were drawn up before the still closed and desolate gates, I blew my golden horn to make it plainer than ever that we came in way of friendship. But no one opened to us. It made Pa angry – well, the whole summer in southern Katskil had done that. 'Why,' he said – 'bugger me blind, we'll be going in anyhow, and ask them nicely why they won't open.'

Poor things, they couldn't – the few who were there in the village were dead, and had been for months. The houses were starting to fall apart, just a little – holes in the thatched roofs where squirrels had gone through, here and there a door fallen off its hinges because the wind had banged it once too often. We went into all the twenty-odd dwellings, finding the skeletons picked clean by the carrion ants and scavenger beetles – only a few, about a dozen in all I guess; all perfectly inoffensive and dry. Most of them lay on the cord or wicker cots that they use for beds in that country; two had remnants of white hair. It was peaceful. Since the dead were all indoors, and the village gates closed against wolves and dogs, the ants and beetles had done nearly all the housekeeping; we were puzzled to notice how little the bones had been disturbed by mice and rats. Pa Rumley said that rats die from the lumpy plague, same as human beings, which I hadn't known at that time. But I had a back-of-the-neck feeling – we all had it, I think – that this could be some other kind of plague.

One man (or woman) had been left behind on the village gallows. The crows and vultures had dealt with that; the bones lay in a meek pile below the still dangling rope. At any rate the criminal was now on a level with the respectable citizens who had been hopelessly sick, or too old to travel perhaps. One body still sat in a rocking chair by a closed window, a woman by the shape of the pelvis, probably an old woman; dry cartilage still held together the spine and legs and one arm. I felt some lessening of the horror as I compelled myself to look on her tranquillity. In the world that the people of Old Time left to us, these things have happened often enough, and will again.

Penn is a land of good artisans, farmers, artists, philosophers, poets, wealth, laziness – and why shouldn't they be lazy, with nature lenient as it is, and all that smell of grape and magnolia? In some parts of the land the climate is over-sweet; the heat after a time seems to come, and mildly, from inside you, although still a gift of the sun. That illusion is strongest in the eastern part of the country, where the sea breeze drives fresh off great Delaware Bay. Filadelfia on the Bay is a fine little city quite near Old-Time ruins that are thought to be harmless – in fact they say some of the modern city is actually built over the site of the old. At Filadelfia all necessary work gets done – the streets are clean, the houses orderly – but you never see anyone, slave or free, seriously exerting himself. The citizens have much more resemblance to each other than the people of the northern countries, on the whole; maybe some of their ancestors in the Years of Confusion were exceptionally prepotent – a dark, tall people with an odd hint of Polynesian as that race appears in Old-Time pictures I have seen. I have no theory to explain that. The girls are big-bodied; deliciously lovely in youth, they stay handsome when in the thirties they begin to look old; and they are kind.

Nearly everyone in Penn seems to be kind, within the limits allowed by religion and politics. Their politics consists of defending the border, which is the Delaware River, and keeping even or ahead of the game in commercial horse-trading. This they manage with a fine fleet of small river craft and a neat army which has never been defeated and has never invaded foreign soil. Trade is assisted by a corps of ambassadors in foreign courts who must be about the most trustworthy and likable liars at large – Dion says so, and my own observation, from the time Nickie and I were with him in Nuin politics up to here, bears it out.

It is a peculiarity of Penn that except for the Delaware River between her and Katskil, and a little jag of territory north of the Delaware's headwaters that used to be a boundary with Moha, her only border is with the wilderness. I believe no one outside the confidence of the republic's government has any notion how far beyond that wilderness border Penn explorers may have penetrated. I can't think of anything more graceful than a cultured Penn citizen changing the subject when the west is mentioned. We were at

Jontown in the summer of 321, as far west as any Rambler gang or other foreign group is ever allowed to go; and yet a small road does lead out of that town westerly, up into the mountains, passing right by a large sign that reads END OF TRAVEL.

As for religion, Penn people appear to take it lightly and calmly, going through the motions, putting up with the flummery in a satisfying tongue-in-cheek manner, as large sections of the population evidently did in Old Time for the sake of keeping peace with the neighbors and avoiding the bitterness of true-believing priests. It is not entirely an honest way, nor a good way in my opinion; I could never take it for my way. But it does make for good manners and a certain peacefulness, and I could blame no one very much for following it, if he has no convictions strong enough to be worth the sacrifice of good nature, or if he feels that a polite conformity with the notions of fools is a necessary protection for his adult labors.

Not that I imagine the Penn people to be a super-race operating in secret of any such fairy-tale crud. There in Penn you encounter a full supply of the old mythologies, ignorance, piety, illiteracy, barbarism. But I did sometimes feel that there might be a good deal of curious thought and ferment behind the smiling indolent surface. And I often felt in the presence of Penn people like an energetic barbarian myself, surely not from any wish of theirs to make me feel so. I think that Penn is, not excepting Nuin, the most nearly civilized of the countries we have left behind us. If one had to live somewhere away from Neonarcheos, one could do worse than dwell in Penn with one or two of the big-lipped, deep-breasted women, and grow old with just enough work and worry to enjoy the other hours of idleness or slow lovemaking in the sun. Penn is not like other lands.

My father died there.

It happened in the autumn of 321 at the town of Betlam, which is forty miles north of Filadelfia – distances are large in Penn – and not far from the Delaware. Sam was fifty-six that year, he told me. Fifty-six, full of piss and vinegar and meanness, he said – but at other times, as I've mentioned, he remarked that he was getting old.

We had gone to Jontown along the southern limits of Penn, which are marked – (so far as we're told) – by a wide twisting river called the Potomac as far as a town named Cumberland. There the only road is one that leads north. From Jontown we came back eastward by a northern route, Pa Rumley having it in mind to winter in western Katskil perhaps, or wherever we might happen to be when November arrived. (Pa didn't enjoy Penn as much as the rest of us – Mother Spinkton sold badly there, the people preferring their own yarb-women and being uncommonly healthy anyhow. Peepshows didn't do very well either, for Penn citizens are remarkably unconcerned at nakedness in spite of all the church can do to distress them about it: I've seen a Penn girl who felt a fleabite flip off her skirt on the street and go to search-ing with no sign of embarrassment, and onlookers didn't regard her with breathless horror – they just laughed and offered bad advice.) There at Bet-lam a number of us fell sick with what seemed at first to be mere heavy colds, with a good deal of coughing and fever. Matters quickly grew worse.

Many of the townfolk had been troubled the same way, we learned, for several weeks. They were disturbed to think we had caught the sickness from them – a generous, decent place, where they understood music also, actually listening as crowds seldom do – and they did everything they could for us.

Pa hadn't even tried a medicine pitch there at Betlam. He snarled – around camp where no Penn ear could hear him – that they were hightoned crum-bums who didn't understand science: Mother'd be wasted on them. But he knew that was foolish talk, and his heart wasn't in it. When the sickness began to alarm us, he took Mother Spinkton himself, and grumbled that it wasn't a good vintage – maybe he'd left out some God-damn essential, getting old and incompetent, somebody'd ought to bury him if he was getting that senile – and he went about miserably among us with a bottle of her, and a lost look. No bullying, no insisting that we swallow her. Some of us missed his natural man-ner so much that we drank her in the hope of curing *him*. It was a bad time.

Nell Grafton's boy Jack, turned fourteen that year, was the first to die.

Sam had been sitting up with him because Rex and Nell were both quite sick. This was in my wagon. I was already nearly recovered from a light attack of whatever it was. I heard Sam call me in sudden alarm, and I got to Jack's compartment in time to see the poor kid with a blazing red face – I'd given him his last licking only two weeks before, for tormenting a stray cat – apparently choke to death on his own sputum. It happened too fast; nothing Sam or I could do. My Da sent me for Pa Rumley, and as I ran off I heard him coughing distressfully; he had been seedy for a couple of days but refused to worry about himself. I found Pa helplessly drunk, no such thing as waking him, and so I fetched Mam Laura instead. I remember how a glance was enough to tell her what had happened to Jack, and then she was staring down at Sam, who sat on a stool by Jack's bunk swaying, his eyes not quite focus-sing. 'You'll go to bed now, Sam.'

'Nay, Laura, I'm not in bad shape. Things to do here.'

'We'll do them. You're to go and rest.'

'Rest. Why, Laura, it's been, like, a mixed-up hardworking time, you could say. You see, being a loner by trade—'

'Sam—'

'Nay, wait. Seems I got the sickness, I want to say something while my head's clear – you seen how it goes, they get off in the head. Now—'

She wouldn't let him talk until we'd got him over to their wagon and into his bunk. I had never before seen her haunted and terrified, unequal to an emergency. Once in bed and yielding to it, Sam did not talk much after all. All I could receive from his difficult and presently rambling speech was that he wanted to thank us – Mam Laura and me – because we had known him without preventing him from being a loner by trade. At least I think that was what he tried to say.

His mind seemed remote after conveying that much to us, but his body was immensely stubborn, unwilling to yield. His battle to breathe lasted three days and part of a fourth night. The medicine priests – there were two in Betlam – came and went, helping us with Sam and three others who were sick, kindly men somewhat less ignorant than those I've met outside of Penn. We made them understand that Sam was unable to speak; he was quite conscious at that moment, sneaking me a grateful look behind their backs and the remnant of a grin when I said my father had made a true confession of faith before speech became impossible.

On the third day we thought he might win through – Nell Grafton had, and Rex, and Joe Dulin. But the decline followed. He regained a slight power of speech for an hour, and talked of his childhood in the hill country and remembered loves. After that, each breath was a separate crisis of a lost war. I am reasonably certain nowadays, from knowing the books, that Old-Time medicine might have healed him. We have no such art.

In the world that Old Time left to us, these things have happened and will again.

During even the last rasping struggles to draw air into his lungs, my father's eyes were often knowing. They would turn to me with brooding and recognition sometimes, or watch a distant thought. They were never angry, peevish, beseeching or apprehensive; once or twice I thought I saw amusement in them, mild and sarcastic, the amusement of a loner by trade. The religion inflicted on him in childhood did not return in his time of weakness, as I had feared it might, to torment him: he was truly free, and died so, a free man looking with courage on the still face of evening.

24

A few weeks later, when we were on the move northward through Katskil, I told Pa Rumley and Mam Laura that I must go away alone. I found explanation was hardly needed. 'Ai-yah,' Pa said – 'I know it a'n't as if you was a Rambler bred and born.' He didn't seem annoyed, although my horn was a valued thing at the entertainments and I had become useful in other ways.

Mam Laura said: 'You're like my Sam – like your father – one of those who go where the heart leads, and they're an often-wounded tribe, no help for it.'

I was thinking again, as I had done hardly at all during the Rambler years, about sailing. Not to the rim of the world: Mam Laura knew as well as Captain Barr that you can't put a rim on a lump of Stardust – but maybe I would sail around the world? Others (she taught me) had done it in ancient days. Thirty-ton outriggers had no share in the fantasy now; they'd been washed away when a poor scrannel pup lifted his leg in Renslar Harbor. I didn't know how it was to be done, but Nuin, one heard, was a nation of brave enterprises. The fancy to sail around the world was certainly there in me at that time, a little while after Sam died, and is in me now, having come this far, this short way to the quiet island Neonarcheos.

'You go where the heart leads,' Mam Laura said. 'And the heart changes in ways you don't expect, and the vision changes, perhaps turning gray. But you go.'

Pa Rumley was stone-cold sober that day. 'Laura, it's a strange time for a man when his father dies.' He knew that, in ways she hardly could for all her wisdom. 'He's not quiet with himself for some time, Laura, no matter was his father a good man or not, no matter was he a good son to his father or a bad one.' Pa Rumley knew human beings; he also knew the God-damn yuman race – yumanity – which isn't the same thing. He was already selling Mother Spinkton again, by the way, in these Katskil towns, and believing in her once more himself – or anyway expecting her to work miraculous cures, which she sometimes did. He may have guessed, out of the foggy backward regions of his own life, how I sometimes dreamed that Sam Loomis was still living. He may have guessed that in the dream I would often be wretched and confused instead of pleased, unable to greet my father in a natural way. I was impotent with Minna once or twice, and she grew bored with me. I doubt if Pa guessed that: whatever troubles he may have passed through in his rambling half-century, I can't imagine him unable to get it up. 'I'm figuring,' Pa said, 'to cross the Hudson Sea from Kingstone, and then winter up somewheres in Bershar. Why'n't you stay with us through the winter? Then if you still be a-mind for Nuin come spring, I'll take you down as far as Lomeda and all you need do is cross the Conicut.'

'Kay.'

'The God-damned of it is, we'll miss you.'

Maybe I said some of the right things then. I was eighteen, beginning to know what they were and why one said them.

Pa also couldn't have known how often I wished I might at least have seen my mother; orphanage childhood was another thing outside his experience. His own mother was warm in his memory. She kept a dressmaking shop in Wuster, a big Nuin town. It was her death when Pa was fifteen that made him take to the roads. He wouldn't have favored that wish of mine, for he was a sensible man. Wishing for the impossible in the future is a good exercise, I think, especially for children; wishing for it in the past is surely the emptiest and saddest of occupations.

The only thing I remember with real clearness about that winter in Bershar, my last with the Ramblers, is the drill that Mam Laura gave me in polite manners. I'd encounter them in Nuin, she said, in fact I ought to do so deliberately, seeking out people who knew how to manage themselves with grace and thoughtfulness. Manners mattered, Mam Laura said, and if I didn't think so I was a damn fool. Which left me brash enough to ask why. She said: 'Would you want to ride a wagon with no grease on the axles? But that isn't all. If you've got an honest heart, the outward show may become something more than that. Be pleasant to someone for any reason and you may easily wind up liking the poor sod, which does no harm.'

They flung a party for me at Lomeda, Rambler style, stalling all work at the wharf and getting the ferry-sailer captain too joyously drunk to object to anything. I remember Minna telling him she'd remember him all her life, because sailors come and sailors go, but ever since she'd been old enough to belay a marlinspike she'd dreamed of seeing a live sailing captain with *balls*. I was well illuminated too when they bundled me aboard, all hollering and crying and giving good advice. I stopped singing when the ropes were cast off and I knew I was actually leaving my people, but I didn't sober up even when the captain brought her in on the Nuin side. He did so with a slam that lifted a timber off the pier, and cussed everyone in sight for building the bald-assed cotton-picking pier so that it couldn't hold up under the impact of a man with *balls*. That was fun.

To my fancy, even the air of Nuin tastes different from the air of other lands. Except for Penn, it is the oldest civilization of modern times, at least on that continent – nay, I can't say that, either, for what do I know of the vague Misipan Empire in the far south, and who could deny the possibility of a great nation, or many of them, in the far western region that I know the continent does possess? Pity me, friends, only if I lose the awareness of my own ignorance.

Penn does not seem to have been much concerned with recording the events of its last two or three centuries – too good-natured, maybe. Nuin is loaded with history, bemused by it, sparkling with it; and shadowed by it. Dion, today still doggedly engaged in setting down whatever he can recall of that history, has never quite come out from under the shadow of it – how could he, and for that matter why should he? It was his world, until we sailed.

Oh, and sometimes I am – not weary of words, but beat-out and a little foolish from the effort, the pleasure and torment of trying to preserve a fraction of my life in the continually moving medium of words. And I think of asking this poor prince – my equal and superior, whipping-boy, cherished friend – to go on with this book if I should give up, stop short of what I set out to do and walk away from it. As I walked away from Rumley's Ramblers when there was no honest need to do so. But he couldn't do that, and with a grain of sense, I hold myself back from asking it.

When I came off the boat at Hamden, the Nuin ferry town across from Lomeda, what I first noticed was the statues. There were some modern ones, clumsy but really not too bad, of Morgan the Great and a few other well-nourished majesties, and these were shown up dreadfully by the fine sculpture of the Old-Time figures – including many bronzes that I'm certain would have been melted down for the metal anywhere except in Nuin. Hamden is proud of them – a fine, healthy, middle-sized town, clean and friendly, open to the river and neatly stockaded on the other three sides; proud of its white-painted houses too, and the pretty green, and the well-conducted market.

All the same, Old City has a flock of statues to make Hamden or any other town look sick. Most of them are of Old Time, which in Nuin is sometimes made to seem almost like yesterday, an illusion I never felt in any other place. I'm thinking at the moment of a fine seated bronze gentleman in Palace Square, who carries clear traces of ancient paint in the cracks and hollows of his patinaed garments. It's Old-Time paint, they say. Some President – Morgan II, I think – had it covered over with thick modern varnish to preserve it. It appears in patches of crimson, green, and purple; no blue. Odd to think that this unknown religious ritual must have been going on in the very last days when the Old-Time world was passing away. The inscribed name of the subject of worship is John Harvard. Nobody seems quite clear about who he was, but he sits there modestly, rather stuffily, with timeless and splendid indifference.

I wore new clothes that day at Hamden, a new shoulder-sack for my horn that Minna had sewed for me, and there was money in my belt, for the Ramblers had taken up a collection and showered me with every sort of kindness. I had still no clear aim, no plan; at eighteen, no true decision what work I would do. I knew a little carpentry, a little music; I knew the wilderness and the ways of the roads. I knew I was a loner by trade.

In the inn at Hamden I found myself in the middle of a bunch of pilgrims who were finishing the last part of what Nuin people call the Loop Journey. It means a trip from Old City up into the wild glorious mountain land of the Province of Hampsher – more people live up there in the cool hills than you'd ever suppose – then south more or less following the great Conicut River as far as Hamden or Shopee Falls, and back to Old City by southern roads. It is a secular pilgrimage. The Church approves it, and stops are made at all the holy shrines and other foci of piety along the way, but there's nothing specifically sacred about the junket itself. Anybody can play, and many do, including respectable sinners and card-sharps and musicians and prosties and all the other folk who keep life from getting dull.

Almost as soon as I entered the taproom after engaging a room for the night, a dark boy made friends with me, and I spotted him for a sinner right away because of his open kindliness and good nature. He was dressed in a Nuin style that was beginning to spread beyond that country but not enough so that I'd grown used to it – baggy knee-length britches and a loose shirt, belted in but allowed to flop out over the belt everywhere except at the knife-hilt, where it might interfere with a quick draw. About half the other pilgrims in the taproom were dressed in that style, but the boy who took it on himself to greet me and make me feel at ease was the only one who carried a rapier at his hip instead of the usual short knife. He had a knife too, I learned later, but wore it under his shirt as I used to wear mine before my Rambler days.

That rapier was a beautiful wicked thing, less than two feet long, light and delicate, scarcely half an inch at the widest point, of Penn steel so fine that it sang to a touch almost like dainty glassware. A rich man's tool, I thought, but I had learned from Mam Laura that one didn't ask about the price of such a thing unless one meant to buy, and often not then. The boy handled it like an extension of his arm. He liked to make it float almost noiselessly from the scabbard, and run his fingers airily up and down the side as if his mind weren't with it at all, which made everyone in the room extremely nervous for some reason and of course anxious not to show it. Nothing indicated how much he enjoyed this except a very light crinkling of the skin at the corners of his brown eyes, and some instinct seemed to tell him when to put it away. Instinct, or a special tone in the throat-clearings of one of the priests in charge of the group.

There were two of these, Father Bland and Father Mordan, one fat and one thin, one greasy and the other a bit dry and scurfy. Father Bland himself remarked that they represented the good bacon of religion, and everyone obligingly laughed except Father Mordan, the lean one who stayed in character, that is to say grumpy. I'd hardly have taken any of the crowd for pilgrims if the landlord hadn't tipped me off, and I learned that some were really just travelers who had joined the group for safety or sociability.

'Compliments of Father Bland and Father Mordan,' said the boy in greeting me, 'and will you drink wid us now or a little sooner?' I hadn't heard much of the Nuin accent at that time. Nuin people don't travel very often outside their own land – Nuin has everything, they say, so what would they gain by it? I guessed the boy to be near my own age, though he acted older. There was a slightness and a delicacy about him that suggested the feminine, but without weakness. I remember in the first half-hour I knew him I wondered if his little games with the rapier might not have a practical side, as a way of discouraging anyone who might misunderstand his nature.

'Honored,' I said – an item of social jazz that I happened to remember from Mam Laura's coaching. 'Honored and delighted to drink anyone under the table or else join him there.'

'Nay, we're a soberish crowd,' he said. 'Everything in moderation. Including, I insist, moderation – but that's a point I can seldom get across to my elders.' He was watching me with uncanny sharpness. 'I'm Michael Summers of Old City. Forgive the impudent curiosity – who are you, sir, and where from?'

'Davy – that is, David – of – well, of Moha – I mean—'

'David de Moha?'

'Oh lordy no!' I said, and noticed that everyone in the taproom had shut up, the better to enjoy our private conversation. 'I just meant I come from Moha, back along. My last name's – uh – Loomis.'

I'm sure he believed, for a while at least, that I was giving a false name, and he wanted to help me with it. He took me over to the others, introduced me as David Loomis with the nicest casualness, pushed me into a comfortable chair, called for fresh drinks – all as if I were somehow important, I couldn't think why.

From scraps I heard before they went quiet, I knew Father Mordan, the thin dry one, had been instructing the company concerning original sin, a regular duty which he'd pretty well wound up for the day – anyway he was ready to acknowledge Michael's presentation of me with a smile. The smile would have quickly hardened the grease on a flaming plum pudding, but he meant it kindly; some people just happen to be born with vinegar for blood and lemons for balls, that's all it is.

'Rest yourself,' Michael said to me, 'and look us over, man, the way you might care to travel wid us a little distance, or all the way to Old City if you're a-mind. We start for there tomorrow, last part of the Loop Journey, back home to our own honest beds and beans and bosoms.'

I couldn't have said no to Michael, and anyway it was what I wished. I loafed there while we talked and sang the day into night. There were two or three fair singers, and a girl with a lively guitar; with my horn, it made an evening of music, and drank enough to help me avoid noticing how far it was from Rambler standards. Nay, it was only the drinks and Michael that kept me from going mad with homesickness – no other word; homesickness for a cubby-hole on wheels with no destination except the next village down the road.

Except for Michael and the two priests and one other, those pilgrims have become dim in my memory, and I've forgotten the name of the one other. He was a fine old gray gandyshank drink of water with droopy four inch whiskers on his upper lip that made you want to ring him like a bell, but he seemed to be a good deal of a scholar, so you let the impulse slide. When Michael introduced us he said on a soft sigh: 'Mmmd.' Michael told me later that this is how you say 'Charmed!' in Oxfoot English, which is what the gandyshank spoke. I don't know why they call it that – there's very little real bull in it, and hardly any English.

Of course I'll always remember Michael's face winking at me, late in the evening, when we had to tear off a Murcan hymn to please Father Bland, for the wink gave me a feverish need to talk to him privately and learn whether I had met another loner of my own kind, even a heretic. Once the thought entered my head, it seemed to me that Michael had been feeling me out along that line, as subtly as a wild creature tasting the breeze, ever since we'd met.

He gave me the opportunity that night, late, slipping into my room with a candle he didn't light until he had closed the door. 'May we talk, David Loomis? Something on my mind, but send me away if you're too beat and want to sleep.' He was still fully dressed, I noticed, including the rapier.

I wasn't sleepy. He pulled a chair near my bed and sat straddling it, relaxed as a little cat. I was afraid of him in several ways along with a powerful affection, thinking also how slight he looked, as if a high wind would blow him away. His voice seemed more like a contralto than a tenor; he had not sung with us, claiming to be tone-deaf, and that wasn't true, but he had his reasons. 'David Loomis, when I turn my face toward you I smell heresy. Nay, don't be alarmed, please. I'm hunting for it, but from the heretics' side, do you understand? – not the other.' Nobody ever watched me as penetratingly as Michael did then, before he rapped out a small sharp question: 'No impulse to run tell Father Mordan?'

'None,' I said – 'what do you take me for?'

'I had to ask,' Michael said. 'I've as good as told you I'm a heretic, the dangerous kind, and I had to watch for any such impulse in you. If I had seen it, I'd have had some decision to make.'

I looked at the rapier. 'With that?'

It seemed to distress him. He shook his head, turning his exploring gaze away. 'Nay, I don't think I could do that to you. If there'd been danger of your betraying me, I suppose I'd have faded – taking you along until we'd made a safe distance. But I see no such danger. I think you're a heretic yourself. Do you believe God made the world for man?'

'For a long time,' I said, 'I haven't believed in God at all.'

'It doesn't scare you?'

'No.'

'I like you, Davy …' We must have talked two hours that night. My life tumbled out in words because he convinced me he wanted to know of it, convinced me it mattered to him – as a personal thing, not solely because we were like-minded and traveling the same road. In the past, only Sam and Mam Laura (and very far in the past, on a different level, little Caron who is probably dead) had made me feel what I said mattered and what I had done was in its own fashion a bit of history. Now the warmth, the reaching out and the recognition, came from one of my own age who clearly had a history of learning and manners equalling or surpassing Mam Laura's; one who was also an adventurer engaged in dangerous work that set my own ambition glowing.

I told Michael what I had dreamed about journeying, thinking long ago that I would see the sun set afire for the day. 'There are other fires to be lit,' Michael said, 'smaller than the sun in certain ways but not others. Fires in human minds and hearts.' Yes, he was concerned with revolution in those days. Here on the island Neonarcheos I am of course never so sure of anything as I suppose we have to be sure at eighteen.

The reaching out and the recognition – why, growing up is partly a succession of recognitions. I have heard that growing old will turn out to be a series of goodbyes. I think it was Captain Barr who made that remark to me, not very long ago.

Michael, that first night while the rest of the inn was snoring, did not tell me as much of his own story in return. Some things he was not ready to tell until he knew me better, others he could not have told without violating his oath to the membership of the Society of Heretics. But he was free to tell me that such a society existed in Nuin and was beginning to have a trifle of following beyond Nuin's borders. He could tell me his conviction that the Church would not rule forever, perhaps not even much longer – optimism of his own youth there, I think. And he said just before he left me that if I wished, he could very soon put me in touch with someone who would admit me to tentative membership. Probation, they called it – was I interested?

Does a fish swim? I wanted to hop out of bed and hug him, but before I could he produced a little flask from inside his shirt and handed it to me. 'Virgin's milk,' he said, 'sometimes called cawn-squeezings – hey, go easy, you sumbitch, it's got to last us all the way to Wuster. Sleep on the talk, Davy, and come along with our gaggle of pilgrims in the morning and we'll talk again. But another time, if a heretic winks at you, don't wink back if there's a priest where he can catch the wind of your eyelashes.'

'Oh!—'

'Nay, no sweat, they didn't notice anything. But be careful, friend. That's how joes like you and me stay alive.'

In the morning, on the road, Father Mordan was still concerned with original sin, and it may have prevented his insides from dealing rightly with a very good breakfast, for his discourse along the first mile or two of a dusty highway was punctuated by the sudden, uncomfortable type of burp. Father Bland endured it as long as he could and then picked on a theological point – I'm sure God alone could have appreciated it – to give Father Mordan the father and mother of an argument. Under cover of this inspiring noise and heat, Michael and I fell behind out of earshot and continued our conversation of the night.

He seemed in a more speculative frame of mind, taking me for granted a little more too. Yet there were also more unspoken things between us, in spite of the agreements and discoveries of a sudden friendship. Most of that morning's talk I remember only in bits and pieces, though all the feeling of it remains with me. 'Davy – you might feel perhaps that Father Mordan is not in possession of absolute truth?'

'Well, after all—'

'Uhha. Father Bland, you know, would honestly like to see everybody safe in a comfortable heaven – no pain, no sin, just glory-glory all day long. It would bore the hell out of you or me, but he truly believes he'd like it, and so would everybody else. And that jo, Davy, gave up a rich man's existence to serve the rest of his life as a small-time priest. And in case you think there's anything trifling about him – well, a month ago he went with me into a small-pox-rotten village up in Hampsher, an escort for a wagonload of food for any poor devils that might be still alive. The wagon-driver wouldn't go without a priest. Not a one of the other pilgrims would go, and Father Mordan felt it his duty to stay behind with them. Just Father Bland and a bond-servant driver and me – and no danger for me because I had the disease in childhood and happen to know it gives immunity, which most people won't believe – but Father Bland never had it. Is Father Bland in possession of absolute truth?'

'No.'

'Why?'

In the night when he went away with his candle he had left me testing my own thoughts a while before I could sleep – testing, and grappling with them to the point of suffering; but then I did sleep, profoundly and restfully. Not that I was in any sense free of confusion or uncertainty – I am not today – but what Michael was doing with me that morning was a very gentle kind of wrestling after all, demanding only that I think for myself, as Mam Laura had done in her different way. I said: 'Why, Michael, I think it's because absolute truth either doesn't exist or can't be reached. A man's being brave and kindly doesn't make him wise.'

We went on a time in silence, I remember, but it wasn't long before Michael took hold of my arm and said without smiling: 'You are now in touch with someone who can admit you to probationary membership in the Society of Heretics. Do you still want it?'

'You yourself? You have that authority?'

He grinned then, more like a boy. 'For six months, but in all that time until now I haven't found anyone who met the requirements. I didn't want to mystify you, but had to sleep on it myself. Probation only – more I can't do, but in Old City I'll guarantee you a welcome, and you'll meet others who can take you further. They'll set you things to do, some of which you won't understand right away.' All I could say was a stumbling thanks, which he brushed aside.

We had halted there in the sunny road, and I noticed I could no longer even hear the pilgrims who had gone on ahead. It was a tranquil open place, where a small stream crossed the road through a culvert and wandered away into a field. The Bland-Mordan argument was less than dust on the breeze, but I said: 'Should we catch up with them?'

'For my part,' Michael said, 'I've no more use for them. I enjoyed traveling with them, if only for the privilege of hearing "Holy, Holy, Holy" sung in Oxfoot English with guitar accompaniment, but now I'd sooner go on to Old City with no company but yourself – if you like the thought. I have money, and a skill with this little pigsticker that makes up for my lack of brawn. I don't know the wilderness in the ways you were telling me about last night, but from here to Old City it's all roads and safe inns. How about it?'

'That's what I'd like.'

He was studying the stream, and its vanishing in taller growth some distance from the road. 'Those willows,' he said – 'away off the other side of that thicket – would they mean a pool, Davy? I'd like a dip, to wash off Mordan's original sin.'

I think that was the first time I'd ever heard a priest mentioned without his title. It gave me a chill that was at first fright, then pleasure, then matter-of-fact amusement. 'It should be a pool,' I said, 'or they wouldn't be clustered like that …'

I suppose there could have been some danger out in the grassland, but it seemed like safe country as we slipped through the grass, the pilgrims becoming long-ago things and then forgotten, and found the pool. I had begun to understand about Michael, but not entirely until I saw the shirt impatiently flung away from a ridiculous bandage that bound his upper chest. Then that was gone, the small woman's breasts set free.

She took off the rapier with care, but not the clumsy trousers – those she dropped and sent flying with a kick. She stood by me then all gravity and abstracted sweetness, proud of her brown slimness, hiding nothing. Seeing I was too dazed and too much in love to move, she touched the bluish tattoo on her upper arm and said: 'This doesn't trouble you, does it, Davy? Aristocracy, caste – it means nothing among the Heretics.'

'It doesn't trouble me. Nothing should trouble me much if I can be with you the rest of my life.'

I remember she put out her golden hand against my chest and pushed me lightly, glancing at the pool, smiling for the first time since she had bared herself. 'Does it look deep enough?' Nickie asked me. 'Deep enough for diving?'

25

Six years ago I wrote that last episode, and laid down my pen to yawn and stretch with pleasure, remembering the pool and the hushed morning and the love we had on the sunny grass. I supposed that in a day or so I would go on writing, probably for several chapters, in spite of my feeling that I had already ended the principal part of the story I set out to tell. I thought I would go on, residing simultaneously here at Neonarcheos and at this imaginary inn of ours on the blind side of eternity or wherever you would prefer it to be – whoever you are – with many events belonging to a later time.

Particularly I had it in mind to tell of the two years that Nickie and I spent in Old City before what happened to us at that Festival of Fools. It is another book. I think I shall try to write it, after the *Morning Star* sails again and I with her, but I may not be able to. I don't know. I am thirty-five, therefore obviously not the same person who wrote you those twenty-four chapters when Nickie was no further away than a footnote and a kiss. I shall leave what I have written behind me, with Dion, when I sail.

The years in Old City after the Festival of Fools, the work with Dion in the heady, exciting, half-repellent atmosphere of high politics, the laws and councils and attempted reforms, the war we won against a pack of thieves and the war we lost against a horde of the self-righteous – all that is certainly another book, and I have a suspicion that Dion himself may be writing it, shielding himself by a dignified reticence from possible footnotes.[23] If I attempt that, it will not be for a long time.

I laid down my pen that evening six years ago, and a few moments later I heard Nickie call me. Her voice brought me out of a hazy brown study: I think I had wandered back to the time of my father's death, and I was reflecting unoriginally how grief is likely to translate itself into philosophy, if you can wait for it, because it must.

---

[23] No, that wasn't the reason for keeping it to myself. The reason is that I have not Davy's open nature. He was able somehow to struggle for truth in autobiography even while 'pursued by footnotes' and with Miranda and me looking over his shoulder most of the time. I could never attempt that. For me the struggle must be in the dark, intensely private, doubtful of outcome. This note is written in May of 339, a full year after Davy's departure with the *Morning Star* – (Barr intended to bring her back in four months). If Davy returns – (we still hope, but don't talk about it any more) – I could perhaps show him what I have written about the years of the Regency, and maybe we could talk more frankly than we ever did in the old days. I would now, of course, give anything I possess for the corniest of his footnotes.

– D.M.M.

As I see it today, my father's death appears to be a true part of the story I was first compelled to write. That story ended, not as I thought at first, when the tiger entered the village and I learned who Sam was, but with the death of Sam Loomis, a loner by trade. For that was surely the occasion when the subject of this book, less homely than a mud-turkle and well-hung, got turned loose on the world (which still turns, I think) – oh, but why now should I bother my head over what did or didn't belong in that story? There were so many stories I could never be certain which I was telling, and it doesn't matter as much as I thought it did when I was bothering you and your Aunt Cassandra about varieties of time. It may be well enough to look at the enigma, the crazy glory and murk of our living-and-dying with a pen in your hand, but try it yourself – you'll find more stories than you knew, and you'll find mirth, tragedy, dirt, splendor, ecstasy, weariness, laughter and rage and tears all so intricately dependent on each other, intertwined like copulating snakes or the busy branches of a jinny-creeper – why, don't be troubling yourself about opposites and balances but never mind, take hold of one branch and you touch them all.

I heard Nickie call me. Her pains had begun. It was the same time of evening that it is now – but this is May 20, 338 – in the same tropic shelter which has held up well for six years, same chair and desk, same view of the quiet beach. But since everything has crept forward six long years in time, nothing at all is the same, not even the flesh of my fingers curved against a different pen. The light appears the same, a luminous red flush receding from the pallor of the sand, and a few high white clouds drifting on the eastward course that the old *Morning Star* will be taking in a few days.

The labor pains were a month premature. That alone did not alarm us too much in the first hours. Ted Marsh and Adna-Lee Jason, who know more Old-Time medicine than the rest of us, did whatever was possible. Old-Time knowledge we have, wretchedly incomplete. Old-Time drugs and equipment we have not – unattainable as the Midnight Star. Therefore diagnosis is mainly guesswork, important surgery unthinkable, and our partial possession of the ancient knowledge often a mockery.

Nickie fought the pain for eighteen hours and was at length delivered of a thing with a swollen head which was able to live an hour or two of shrieking empty existence, but the bleeding would not stop. The mue weighed twelve pounds, and she – why, at our lodgings in Old City I used to carry her up two flights of stairs for the joy of it and be hardly winded at the top of the climb. The bleeding would not stop. She had glimpsed the mue in spite of us and understood, and so could not even die with the consolation of an illusion. In the world that Old Time left to us, these things have happened and will again.

I sail before long in the *Morning Star* with Captain Barr and a small company – five women and nine other men, all of us chosen by Dion because we clearly possess what he calls a 'controlled discontent.' All voluntary, naturally, and me he did not exactly choose, but only asked me: 'Do you want to go, Davy?' I said that I did, and he kissed my forehead in the manner of the old Nuin nobility, a thing I haven't known him to do for years, but we've said nothing more about the sailing and probably won't until the day Barr chooses.

I am thirty-five and Dion is fifty. We fought in two wars together. We tried to draw a great nation a step or two beyond the sodden ignorance of this era. We sailed together into the great sea and found this island Neonarcheos. We loved the same woman. 'Controlled discontent' – well, I think that appraisal was meant for me as much as for the rest. It is a compliment, but with the inevitable dark side too: we fourteen, Captain Barr and myself and the others, fitted by temperament and circumstance for the task of explorers, are to a great degree unfitted for anything else.

The explorer's task has, I'd say, very little of the splendor a boy's imagination gives it. I dreamed a multitude of fancies lying in the sun before my cave on North Mountain; but Captain Barr and I are now much more decently concerned with survival biscuits and pemmican and sauerkraut, and trying to rebuild the head of the *Morning Star* a mite further aft if you'll excuse the expression. But all that doesn't mean that the glory goes out of exploring. It is there, and the inner rewards are real enough. The sea of ignorance is vast beyond measuring, and so I, an animalcule with his dab of phosphorescence, set that light against it and find no reason to be ashamed of my pride.

In the six years we have been able to build another sailing vessel, a neat small thing the Old-Time builders would describe as a yawl. Those who remain behind can make use of the other islands while we are gone.

Our flax seed has grown well on Neonarcheos, so the *Morning Star* has good new canvas. We carry provisions for four months. Our immediate mission is to reach the mainland of what was called Europe, which should take far less time than that, learn what we can of it, and return. Our first landfall should be the coast of what was Portugal, or Spain, we suppose. But currents and winds are not as they were in Old Time.

We who sail are all childless. The women may not be sterile, but none has ever conceived, and the youngest is twenty-five. In the six years at Neonarcheos, twenty-one normal children have been born, to seven of the women. I did not father any of them. I did make Nora Servern pregnant. It was her wish, and Dion's too; they thought, and the same as told me, that they hoped it would draw me out of a black and self-destroying mood that had held me for a long time. What did draw me out of it I'll never know – just time, maybe. Sweet Nora was good to love, and that part of the episode certainly helped bring me back into acceptance of daily living. But though Nora was able to bear Dion two healthy girls, the child she bore me was a mue not unlike the one for whom Nickie's life was thrown away.

Thus I am obliged to understand that the fault was not in Nickie's seed but in mine. I am not illogical enough to say that I killed her; who could live with that? But it is true that she was killed by an evil that Old Time set adrift, that came down through the generations, through Sam's body or my mother's – who could say? – to hide in that part of mine which ought to be the safest, the least corrupted. This happened, to me and to countless others, and will again.

My only children are certain thoughts I may have been able to give you. I can sometimes be tranquil in my heart about this, when I remember how much exploring there is to be done. There seems to be enough undiscovered territory, in the mind and the rest of the world – I think I could have written, in the world and the rest of the mind – so that we shall not have it all mapped before sundown, not this Wednesday.

I went down to the beach last night, because I heard the wind, and the ocean was long-voiced on the sand, and the stars were out. Before long I shall hear that music at the bows, or as a following whisper in the times when I have the wheel in my hands. I sail because I desire it; I have no children except those in your care, but may I not tell you that exploration also is an act of love?

I gave words to the breakers last night, a game I have often played, a harmless way of aiding the mind to speak to itself. You who are the earth can ask, and you who are the sea may answer, and if there is truth spoken you know the source.

I asked whether the generations could some day restore the good of Old Time without the evil, and the ocean that was a voice in my mind suggested: Maybe soon, maybe only another thousand years.

A MIRROR FOR OBSERVERS

To John V. Padovano

... But I observed that even the good artisans tell into the same error as the poets; because they were good workmen they thought that they also knew all sorts of high matters, and this defect in them overshadowed their wisdom; and therefore I asked myself on behalf of the oracle, whether I would like to be as I was, neither having their knowledge nor their ignorance, or like them in both; and I made answer to myself and to the oracle that I was better off as I was.

– PLATO, *Apology*

Note: all characters in this novel are fictitious
except possibly the Martians.

PRELUDE

The office of the Director of North American Missions is a blue-lit room in Northern City, 246 feet below the tundra of the Canadian Northwest Territory. There is still a land entrance, as there has been for several thousand years, but it may have to be abandoned this century if the climate continues to warm up. Behind a confusion of random boulders, the entrance looks and smells like a decent bear den. Unless you are Salvayan – or Martian, to use the accepted human word – you will not find, inside that den, the pivoted rock that conceals an elevator. Nowadays the lock is electronic, responding only to the correct Salvayan words, and we change the formula from time to time.

The Abdicator Namir had not been aware of that innovation. He was obliged to wait shivering a few days in that replica of a bear den, his temper deteriorating, until a legitimate resident, returning from a mission, met him and escorted him with the usual courtesies to the office of the Director, who asked: 'Why are *you* here?'

'Safe conduct, by the law of 27,140,' said Namir the Abdicator.

'Yes,' said Director Drozma, and rang for refreshments. A century ago Drozma would have fetched the fermented mushroom drink himself, but he was painfully old now, painfully fat with age, entitled to certain services. He had lived more than six hundred years, as few Martians do. His birth date was the year 1327 by the Western human calendar, the same year that saw the death of Edward II of England, who went up against Robert Bruce at Bannockburn in 1314 and didn't come off too bloody well. In Drozma's web of wrinkles were scars from the surgery which, about five hundred years ago, had made his face presentably human. His first mission into human society had been in 1471 (30,471), when he achieved the status of qualified Observer during the wars of York and Lancaster, later he made a study of three South American tribes even now unknown to human anthropology; in 30,854 he completed the history of the Tasmanians, which is still the recognized Martian text. His missions were far behind him. He would never again leave this office until it was time to die. He was not only Director of Missions, but also Counselor of Northern City, answerable to its few hundred citizens and, after them, to the Upper Council in Old City in Africa. He carried the honor lightly, yet in all the world there were only three other such Counselors – those of Asian Center, Olympus, and Old City itself. A strangely short while ago there were five Cities. We remember City of Oceans, but it is better to let the mind turn to the present or the deeper past. Soon enough a successor would take over Drozma's burden. Meanwhile, his thought was crystalline-calm as the canals that wind among the Lower Halls of Earth. The Abdicator Namir watched him pet the little ork curled at his feet, the only breed except our own that survived the journey from slow-dying Mars more than thirty thousand years ago. It purred, licked ruddy fur, washed itself, and went back to sleep. 'We had word of you recently, Namir.'

'I know.' Namir sat down with his drink, gracefully in spite of his own advanced age. He waited for the girl who had brought the drinks to pat Drozma's cushion, smile and hover, and go away. 'One of your Observers identified me. So I came, partly, to warn you not to interfere with me.'

'Are you serious? We can't be intimidated by you Abdicators. I value Kajna's reports – she's a keen Observer.'

Namir yawned. 'So? Did she mention Angelo Pontevecchio?'

'Of course.'

'I hope you don't imagine you can do anything with that boy.'

'What we hear of him interests us.'

'Tchah! A human child, therefore potentially corrupt.' Namir pulled a man-made cigarette from his man-made clothes and rubbed his large human face in the smoke. 'He shares that existence which another human animal has accurately described as "nasty, brutish, and short".'

'I think you came merely to complain of humanity.'

Namir laughed. 'On the contrary, I get sorry for the creatures, but the pity itself is a boredom.' He shifted casually into American English. 'No, Drozma, I just stopped by to say hello.'

'After 134 years! I hardly—'

'Is it that long? That's right, I resigned in 30,829.'

'I notice you've picked up human habits of conversation.'

'I did interrupt – beg your pardon. Please go on, sir.'

Not in rebuke but from a private need, Drozma meditated fifteen minutes, hands folded on his belly, which eventually bounced in a chuckle. 'You are bored with the society of other Abdicators?'

'No. They're few. I rarely see them.'

'As one Salvayan to another, how do you put in the time?'

'Going up and down in the world. I've become quite a wizard at disguise. If I hadn't long ago used up my scent-destroyer your Kajna could never have eavesdropped on my talk with the Pontevecchio boy.'

'The law of 27,140 provides that no assistance can be given to Abdicators by Salvayans of the Cities.'

'Why, Drozma, I wasn't hinting that I wanted scent-destroyer. I don't find it hard to avoid horses, they're so scarce nowadays. Odd how no other animal seems to mind the Martian scent – Salvayan: you prefer the antique word even in talking English? Must have been tough in the ancient days before the destroyer was invented. But since human animals can't catch the scent, I don't need the stuff, except to help me avoid your sniffier Observers ... The smart thing, five or six thousand years ago, would have been to develop an equine epidemic, get rid of the damned beasts.'

Drozma winced in disgust. 'I begin to see why you resigned. In all your life I think you never learned that patience is the wellspring.'

'Patience is a narcotic for the weak. I have enough for my needs.'

'If you had enough you'd cure yourself of resentments. Let's not argue it: our minds don't meet. Again, why have you come here?'

Namir flicked ash on the mosaic of the floor. 'I wanted to find out if you still imagine human beings can ever amount to anything.'

'We do.'

'I see. Even after losing City of Oceans – or so I heard.'

'Namir, we do not talk about City of Oceans. Call it a taboo, or just a courtesy to me ... What did you ever hope to achieve by resigning?'

'Achieve? Oh, Drozma! Well, perhaps a spectator's pleasure. The interest of watching the poor things weave a rope for their own hanging.'

'No, I don't think that was it. That wouldn't have turned you against us.'

'I'm not against you particularly,' said Namir, and pursued his original thought: 'I thought they had that rope in 30,945, but there they are, still unhanged.'

'Tired of waiting?'

'Ye-es. But if I don't live to see their finish, my son will.'

'A son ... Who is your Salvayan wife, may I know?'

'Was, Drozma. She died forty-two years ago, giving birth. She was Ajona, who resigned in 30,790 but continued to suffer from idealism until I effected a partial cure. The boy's forty-two now, almost full grown. So you see I even have a father's interest in hoping to witness the end of *Homo quasi-sapiens* ... Might I ask your current population figures?'

'About two thousand, Namir.'

'In all the – er – four Cities?'

'Yes.'

'Hm. Bigger, of course, than our few dozen of the enlightened. But that's deceptive, since you are all dreamers.'

'Men vanish, and you repopulate from a few dozen?'

'I don't suppose they'll vanish completely. Too damn many of 'em.'

'You have plans for the survivors?'

'Well, I don't feel free to give you blueprints, old man.'

'The law of 27,140—'

'Is a routine expression of Salvayan piety. You couldn't use it against us.

207

After all, we have a weapon. Suppose men, with a little help, were to locate the – remaining cities?'

'You couldn't betray your own kind!' Namir did not answer ... 'You consider the Abdicators peculiarly enlightened?'

'Through suffering, boredom, observation, disappointment, realistic contact – yes. What could be more educational than loss and loneliness and hope deferred? Why, ask even Angelo Pontevecchio at twelve. He adored his dead father, there's no one he can talk with, childhood keeps him in a cage with life outside – result, he begins to be quite educated. Of course he's a directionless kitten still, a kitten in a jungle of wolves. And the wolves will give his education another lift.'

'Love, if you'll excuse the expression, is more educational.'

'Now I could never make that mistake. I've watched human beings fool around with love. Love of self mostly, but also love of place, work, ideas; love of friends, of male and female, parent and child. I can't think of any human illusions more comic than those of love.'

'May I know more about what you do, outside?'

Namir looked away. 'Still an Observer, in my fashion.'

'How can you observe through a sickness of hatred?'

'I observe sharply, Drozma.'

'You confuse sharpness with accuracy. As if a microscopist forgot to allow for relative size and saw an amoeba as big as an elephant ... As I remember, after your resignation you were first seen by us in 30,896, in the Philippines.'

'Was I?' Namir chuckled. 'Didn't know that. You get around.'

'They say you made a convincing Spaniard. In Manila, a day or so after the official murder of José Rizal. You had some part in that?'

'Modesty forbids – no, really, his human killers could have managed perfectly well without me. Rizal was an idealist. That made his slaughter almost automatic, a human reflex action.'

'Other idealists have – oh, I think eternity would be too short to argue with you. Not a single kind word for humanity then?' Namir smiled. 'Not even for Angelo Pontevecchio?'

'You're truly concerned over that child? Ridiculous! As I said, he's a kitten now, but I'll make a tiger of him. You'll hear the lambs bleat with blood in the throat even up here among your pretty dreams.'

'Perhaps not.'

'Would you dare to bet on it?'

The Director reached for a primitive telephone. 'If you like. It won't affect the outcome. Nor would any Observer I send, maybe. However ...' He spun the crank. 'Regardless of whom I send, Namir, your real antagonist is not the Observer, not I, but Angelo himself.'

'Of course. Telephones! Getting modern as next week.'

Drozma said pedantically: 'It happens we invented the telephone in 30,834. Naturally when Bell reinvented the wretched thing independently in '876 he made some improvements. We're not gadget-minded. And his successors – oh dear! Fortunately we don't need all those refinements. Anyway we had to wait till men brought their lines north of Winnipeg before it was convenient to talk City-to-City. Now I suppose you might call us – ah – unofficial subscribers. We have a fulltime Communicator in Toronto, sorry I'm not free to give you his name. Hello …? Hello …?' Namir chortled. Drozma said plaintively: 'I suppose the operator is in contemplation. Does it matter? I can always call again. You know, Namir, I had this – ah – gimmick installed simply because I can't easily walk around any more. I don't actually like the things. I – oh, hello …? Why, thank you, my dear, and on you the peace of the laws. When you have time, will you send word that I want to see Elmis? … Yes, the historian. He's probably in the Library, or else the Music Room, if this is his practice time – I can't remember. Thank you, dear.' He put away the receiver with a twiddle of pudgy fingers. 'A gimmick.'

'Can't wait till you grow up to radio.'

'Radio? We've had excellent receiving sets ever since human beings invented it. Obviously we mustn't broadcast, but we hear it. Have you forgotten your history? Radio was known on Salvay, one of the little techniques our ancestors abandoned – from lack of important need, I suppose – during the first miserable centuries in this wilderness. Don't you ever think of ancient times, Namir? The shock, loneliness, no hope of return even if Salvay had not been a dying planet – except to the Amurai, I suppose. They could wall themselves in, accept the underground life that we rejected. And then we had to accept it here after all! Think of the ordeal of adaptation too. History says it was two hundred years before the first successful births, and even then the mothers usually died. What an age of trial!'

'History is a dead language.'

'Can't agree. Well, our mathematicians study the human broadcasts. Over my head, the mathematics, but I'm sure radio's immensely useful.'

'Immensely emetic. While we wait for your big-time operator, would you care for a word of advice?'

'Certainly. Television too – damn it, I love television. You were about to say?'

'On my way here, I passed six settlements in northern Manitoba and Keewatin District, all new since the last time I was near there, in 30,920. The icecap goes faster all the time. You're losing the Arctic shield. No concern of mine but I thought I'd mention it.'

'Thanks. Our Observers watch it. The waterlock will be finished before we need to close the land entrance. And did *you* know that the human plastics industry is almost ready with greenhouse dwellings, size limited only by convenience? In a few decades there'll be garden villages all through the Arctic, independent of climate, and in a century the population of Canada will probably match that of the States – if they're still technically separate countries by that time. Personally I'm pleased about it. Come in, Elmis.'

Elmis was long-legged, slim, powerful, his complexion close to that colorful pallor human beings call white. From his agony of surgery long ago, his face and hands were properly human. The brown-haired scalp and artificial fifth fingers had been almost-normal parts of him for over two hundred years. If he had to show himself barefoot, the four-toed feet would pass for a human anomaly. Drozma explained: 'I'm sorry to call you from the work you prefer, Elmis. I know you'd hoped never to go out as an Observer again. But you're much better qualified than anyone else available, so I can't help myself. This is Namir the Abdicator.'

Elmis' manlike voice said in English: 'I think I remember you.' Namir nodded inattentively. 'You've returned to us?'

'What an idea! No, just passing by, and I must be on my way. A pleasure. By the way, Drozma – care to put up some little consideration to make that bet interesting? Say, a human soul?'

'Why, assuming anyone could dispose of a human soul—'

'Sorry. For a minute there I thought you wanted to play God.' He squirmed into his arctic gear. 'So long, children. Keep your noses clean.'

'?' said Elmis, and entered contemplation, head on his knees.

Presently Drozma sighed. 'A time factor, Elmis, or I wouldn't interrupt your thought. Would the name "Benedict Miles" suit you?'

'"Miles" – yes, a nice anagram. Urgent, sir?'

'Maybe. A human child becomes a man more swiftly than one can write a poem. Is your work in such state that you can leave it?'

'Someone else can always go on with it, Drozma.'

'Tell me more about it.'

'Still tracing ethical concepts as lines of growth. Trying to see through the froth of conflicts, wars, migrations, social cleavages, ideologies. I was restudying Confucius when you called me.'

'Tentative conclusions?'

'A few, confirming your own intuition of a hundred years ago that a genuine ethical revolution – comparable to the discovery of fire, of agriculture, of social awareness – might be in progress about 31,000, and might develop for the necessary centuries. The germs are present. Hard to see, but certainly present, just as the germ of society was latent in pre-language family groups. Of course one can make no allowance for such unpredictables as atomic war, pestilence, a too sudden rise in the water level. Fortunately the dream of security is a human weakness we needn't share. As a very rash prediction, Drozma, I think Union with them might be possible late in my son's lifetime.'

'Truly ...? Seems very soon, but it's a refreshing thought. Well, here's your mission. Observer Kajna came home yesterday. She was overdue, and with the worst of the journey ahead of her, when she had to wait on a train connection in Latimer – that's a small city in Massachusetts. She spent the time in a park. A nice old gentleman was feeding the pigeons and talking to a boy about twelve years old. Kajna caught the Martian scent. She renewed her scent-destroyer, listened in on the conversation from another bench. The old man was Namir. She'd seen him once using a similar disguise in Hamburg, years ago. You know we try to keep track of the Abdicators so long as it doesn't interfere with more important work. Kajna happens to feel rather strongly about them. She wanted to follow Namir, she had to get home to us soon, and as she listened a third necessity developed. In the end, when the old man and the boy went different ways, Kajna followed the boy, not Namir. Followed him to a lodging house where he lives. She inquired about a room, enough to start a conversation, pick up a few facts. The boy is the landlady's only child – Angelo Pontevecchio. The landlady, Rosa Pontevecchio, is – Kajna used the term "sweet-minded". Not much education, and on a very different psychophysical level; a fat woman in poor health. Kajna saw and empathized enough to suggest valvular heart disease, but wasn't sure. Well, then Kajna came home. Used her own judgment. As you will have to do.'

'And Namir?'

'Oh, he identified her after all. Mentioned it when he was here.'

'Whatever brought him? More than a century since he resigned.'

'I think, Elmis, he has some rather dirty little plans for Angelo, and wanted to find out what plans we had, if any. We have none, except as they will develop in your good Observer's mind. The boy may or may not be as potentially important as Kajna felt he was. I hope he is – you know I wouldn't send you out for a trivial cause. You're to go there to Latimer, live in or near that lodging house as Benedict Miles. On your own. I must have your independent judgment. That's why I won't tell you any more about the child, and I'd rather you didn't talk with Kajna about the mission before you go. As for Namir, you know the law of 27,140. The Abdicators aren't to be acted against, so long as they do no positive harm.' Drozma stroked the ork as it rose to stretch squabby legs. His voice shook. 'I can imagine situations in which you might have to review the definitions of that cloudy word "harm". You know also that an Observer must not risk violating human law, unless he is prepared to – to prevent betrayal of Salvayan physiology.'

'Sir, we don't need euphemism, you and I. I'll ask Supply to give me a suicide-grenade recheck. And, I think, a spare grenade, unless you object'

Drozma bit his lip. 'I don't object. I've already told Supply to have everything ready for you ... Elmis, the bitterness I saw just now in Namir – I'd almost forgotten such feelings could exist. Be careful. I suppose he's always in pain. His own thought turns on him and eats him like a cancer. Salvayan pain, remember. No matter how human he acts, don't ever forget he has our lower threshold of suffering along with our greater endurance. I'm sure he still meditates, though he might deny it. And if his angry heart is set on a thing, he'll turn aside for nothing except superior force.' Drozma shifted fretfully on his cushion. 'It's an extended mission, Elmis. If you feel you should stay for the whole of that boy's lifetime, you have my leave. Spare no expense – be sure you draw all the human money you'll need, and I'll authorize the Toronto Communicator to honor any emergency requests. But even if you return quite soon I may not be here, so I think I'll give you this.' From under his cushion he took a wrapped package, heavy but small. 'A mirror, Elmis. Unwrap it and look at it later if you like, not now. An Observer – his name is lost – brought this in 23,965 from the island now called Crete. Bronze – we've kept the patina away from the best reflecting side. I don't suppose it's the first mirror made by human beings, but surely one of the first. You might want the boy Angelo to look at his face in it. You see, we think it possible that he's one of those who can learn how to look in a mirror.'

'Ah …! Am I good enough for such a mission?'

'Try to be. Do your best. The peace of the laws be with you.'

PART ONE

The problem of darkness does not exist for a man
gazing at the stars. No doubt the darkness is there,
fundamental, pervasive and unconquerable except
at the pin-points where the stars twinkle; but the
problem is not why there is such darkness, but
what is the light that breaks through it so remarkably;
and granting this light, why we have eyes to see it
and hearts to be gladdened by it.
                    – GEORGE SANTAYANA, *Obiter Scripta*

PERSONAL NOTE ACCOMPANYING REPORT OF ELMIS OF
NORTHERN CITY FOR THE YEAR 30,963, TRANSMITTED
TO THE DIRECTOR OF NORTH AMERICAN MISSIONS
BY TORONTO COMMUNICATOR AUGUST 10, 30,963.

Accept, Drozma, assurance of my continuing devotion. For reasons of safety I write in Salvayan instead of the English you prefer. This report was begun in greater leisure than I now have, and it follows a humanly fashionable narrative form: I had your entertainment in mind, knowing how you relish the work of human storytellers, and I only wish I had their skill. I have blundered, as you will see. The future is clouded, my judgment also. If you cannot approve what I have done and what I still must do, I beg you will make allowance for one who admires human creatures a little too much.

1

The bars are genial in Latimer in 30,963. A warmer life fills the evening streets than on my last visit to the States seventeen years ago. People stroll about more, spend less time rocketing in cars. It was a June Saturday when I reached Latimer, and found the city enjoying its weekend snugly. There was peace. A pine-elm-and-maple, baked-beans-and-ancestors, Massachusetts sort of peace, to which I am partial. Getting born in the Commonwealth would help, if one had to be a human being.

Latimer is too far from Boston to be much under the influence of what Artemus Ward called the 'Atkins of the West'. Latimer can make its own atmosphere: five large factories, a population over ten thousand, a fairly wealthy hill district, a wrong side of the tracks, two or three parks. The town was more populous a few years ago. As factories become cybernetic they move away from the large centers; the growth is in the suburbs and the countryside. Latimer in this decade is comfortably static – yet not quite comfortably, for there is a desolation in boarded-up houses, a kind of latent grief that few care to examine. In Latimer the twentieth century (human term) rubs elbows with the eighteenth and nineteenth in the New England manner. There is a statue of Governor Bradford half a block from the best movie theater. A restored-colonial mansion peers across Main Street at a rail-bus-and-copter station as modern as tomorrow.

I bought a science-fiction magazine in that station. They still multiply. This one happened to be dominantly grim, so I read it for laughs. Galaxies are too small for humanity. And yet, sometime ...? Was our own ancestors' terrible journey thirty thousand years ago only a hint of things to come? I understand men will have their first satellite station in a very short while, four or five years. They call it 'a device to prevent war'. Sleep in space, Salvay – sleep in peace ...!

No. 21 Calumet Street is an old brick house on a corner, two stories and basement, not far from the inevitable Main Street, which travels from right to wrong side of the tracks. No. 21 is on the wrong side, but its neighborhood is not bad, a residential backwater for factory workers, low-pay white-collars, transients. Five blocks south of No. 21, Calumet Street enters a slum where dregs settle to a small Skid Row, no less pitiable than the massive human swamps in New York, London, Moscow, Chicago, Calcutta.

I found a 'vacancy' card in the basement window. I was admitted by the one whose life I was to meddle with. I knew him at once, this golden-skinned boy with eyes so profoundly dark that iris and pupil blended in one sparkle. Perhaps I knew him then as well as I ever shall, in that mild moment of appraisal before he had even spoken or given me more than a casual friendly glance. When we admit that the simplest mind is a continuing mystery, what height of arrogance it would be to say that I know Angelo!

He was carrying a book, his finger holding a place, and I saw he was lame, with a brace on the left ankle. He led me into a basement living room to talk with his mother, whose body, like a disguise, billowed over a rocking chair. She had been mending the collar of a shirt that sprawled as if alive on the mountain of her lap. I noticed in Rosa Pontevecchio her son's disturbing eyes, broad forehead, sensuous mouth. 'Two rooms free,' she told me. 'First-floor back, running water, bath one flight up. There's a second-floor back, but it's smaller, maybe not so quiet – well, it's that awful copter noise, I swear they try 'n' see how close they can skim the roof.'

'First floor sounds all right.' I indicated a portable typewriter I had bought on impulse in Toronto. 'I'm writing a book, and I do like it quiet.' She was not inquisitive nor obsequiously impressed. The boy spread his book face down. It was a paperback, selections from Plato, opened near the front to the *Apology* or *Crito*. 'My name is Benedict Miles.' I kept my phony autobiography simple, to lessen the nuisance of remembering details. I had been a school-teacher, I said, in an (unspecified) Canadian town. Thanks to a legacy, I had a year of leisure for the (undescribed) book, and wanted to live simply. I tried to establish an academic manner to go with my appearance of scrawny middle age. A shabby, pedantic, decent man.

She was a widow, I learned, managing the house alone. Its income would clearly be inadequate to pay for hired help. She was about forty, half her tiny lifetime gone. The latter half would be burdened by hard work, the gross discomfort of her flesh, many sorts of loneliness; yet she was cheerful in her chatter, outward-looking and kind. 'I don't get around too good.' Her lively hands spoke of her bulk in humorous apology. 'Doing the place mornings is my limit. Angelo, you show Mr Miles the room.'

He limped ahead of me up a narrow, closed-in stairway. This house was built before Americans fell in love with sunlight. The first-floor back was a large room and would be relatively quiet. Two windows overlooked a yard, where a pudgy Boston bulldog snoozed in the last of June daylight. When I opened a window Angelo whistled. The dog stood on her hind legs to waggle clumsy paws at him. 'Bella's a showoff,' Angelo said with unconcealed affection for the pup. 'She doesn't bark much, Mr Miles.'

One never knows how a dog will react to the Martian scent. At least they never object to the overriding scent-destroyer. Namir had no destroyer … 'Like dogs, Angelo?'

'They're honest.' Commonplace, but not a twelve-year-old remark.

I tested the one armchair and found the springs firm. The impress of other bodies was appealing, and gave me a sense of sharing human qualities. I tried to consider Angelo as another human being might. Two things seemed plain: he lacked shyness, and he lacked excess energy.

His father was dead, his mother not strong nor well. Premature responsibility could account for his poise. As for his quiet – I watched him as he moved about softly, drawing away a curtain in a corner to show me the hand basin and two-ring gas stove, and I changed part of my opinion. There was surplus energy, probably intense, but it was a steady burning, not dissipating itself in random muscular commotion or loud talk. 'Like the room, Mr Miles? It's twelve a week. We rent it as a double sometimes.'

'Yes, I like it.' It resembled all furnished rooms. But in place of the customary tooth-and-bosom calendars and prints there was only one picture, an oil in a plain frame, a summer landscape of sunlit fantasy. You would as soon expect a finished emerald in the five-and-dime. 'I'll take it for a week, but tell your mother I hope to be here longer than that.' He took the money, promised to bring keys and a receipt. I tried a wild shot: 'Have you done many paintings like that, Angelo?' A flush spread on his cheek and throat. 'Isn't it yours?'

'It's mine. A year ago. Don't know why I bother.'

'Why shouldn't you?'

'Waste of time.'

'I can't agree.' He was startled, as if he had been braced to hear something else. 'I admit it wouldn't please the modern cults, but so what?'

'Oh, them.' He recovered, and grinned. 'Sissy though. Kid stuff.'

I said: 'Nuts.' And watched him.

He fidgeted, more like a twelve-year-old now. 'Anyway I don't think it's very good. I don't hear that birch tree.'

'I do. And the grass under it. Field mice in the grass.'

'Do you?' Neither flattered nor quite believing it. 'I'll get your receipt.' He hurried, as if afraid of saying or hearing more.

I was unpacking when he returned. I let him see my clutter of commonplace stuff. The hair dye to keep me gray passed for an ink bottle. The scent-destroyer was labeled after-shaving lotion and would smell like it, I understand, to a human nose. The mirror was wrapped. The flat grenades were next to my skin of course. Angelo lingered, curious, willing to get acquainted, possibly hurt because I volunteered nothing more about his painting: bright as he was, he wouldn't have outgrown vanity at twelve. He asked innocently: 'That typewriter case big enough for your manuscript?'

Too smart. When I decided that Mr Miles was puttering at a book I neglected to pick up anything but the typewriter and packages of paper still unopened. 'Yes, it is for the present. My book is mostly here.' I tapped my head. I knew I should dream up some mess of words, and soon. I didn't think he or his mother would poke among my things, but one tries to avoid even minor risks. Fiction? Philosophy? I sought the armchair and lit a cigarette (again I recommend them to Observers deprived of our thirty-hour periods of rest: smoke is no substitute for contemplation but I believe it softens the need). 'School finished for the year, Angelo?'

'Yeah. Last week.'

'What year are you? Shut my mouth if it's none of my business.'

A smile flashed and faded. 'Sophomore.'

The average age in that class would be around sixteen. He would be holding himself back, I knew, in self-defense. 'You like the *Crito?*'

Alarm was obvious in the studied blankness of his face. 'Ye-es.'

Certainty it would be difficult to convince him that I was not talking down, not making secret fun of his precocity. I tried to be idly conversational: 'Poor Crito! He really tried. But I think Socrates wanted to die. In the reasoning to prove he should remain, don't you think he was talking to himself more than to Crito?'

No relaxation. Strained youthful courtesy: 'Maybe.'

'He could have argued he owed Athens nothing; that an unjust law may be violated to serve a greater. But he didn't. He was tired.'

'Why?' said Angelo. 'Why would anyone want to die?'

'Oh, tired. Past seventy.' (What should I have said?) It was enough for the moment, I thought, or too much. At least it was an attempt to let him know I honored his intelligence, and it might help me later. It would have been easier if I had been required to hold a soap bubble in my clumsy hands, since a soap bubble is only a pearl of illusion and if it bursts that's no great matter. More like snuffy Mr Miles, I said: 'Wonder if my typing will bother the other tenants? It's a noisy old machine.'

'Nope.' Angelo was plainly relieved at the prosaic turn. 'Mr Feuermann's bath and closet are between the rooms. Room over you is vacant, and the folks upstairs – the old ladies and Jack McGuire – they won't hear it. We won't downstairs. This is above the kitchen. Don't give it a thought.'

'Not even if I split an infinitive?'

He stuck a finger in his mouth and snapped it to make a pop like a cork out of a bottle. 'Not even if you treat a spondee as an iambus.'

'Ouch! Wait till *I* get educated, can't you?' He grinned sweetly and fled. And that, I thought, is the child whom Namir wants to corrupt. This was the moment, Drozma, when the enigma of Namir himself truly began to torment me, as it still does. I must accept fact: it is possible for a being, human or Martian, to see something beautiful, recognize it as beautiful, and immediately desire to destroy it. I know it's so, but I don't, I never shall, understand it. One would think the mere shortness of life would be a reminder that to destroy beauty is to destroy one's own self too.

I fussed about, as a human creature should in a new nest. I reviewed Observers' Rules. The risk that has always worried me worst is that some trifling injury might reveal the orange tint of our blood. I am prone to bark shins and bruise hands. Our one-to-the-minute heartbeat is not only a risk but a source of regret. It annoys me that I must be cautious in all physical contact, and it's too bad having to avoid doctors – they could be interesting. Observers' work must have been more entertaining as well as safer (except for the horse problem) in the old days when magic and superstition were cruder and more crudely accepted. And I turned the package of the bronze mirror over and over in my hands, wondering at some of your meanings, Drozma. I did not unwrap it. I wish that I had, or that I had examined it in Northern City. Doubtless you supposed I would, but there were many last-minute errands, and I have studied so many human antiquities that my curiosity was dulled. I did not learn its nature until a time when it caught me unprepared. That evening I put the package in the bureau under some clothes, and wandered out to explore the city.

And I met Sharon Brand.

My immediate objective was butter, bread, and sliced ham, though I had it in mind to do any Observer's work that might turn up as a by-product of my mission. A delicatessen on Saturday evening can be a listening post. People lounge, linger, cuss the weather, and talk politics. I found one at once, by drifting toward the grimier end of Calumet Street. It was a tiny corner shop three blocks from No. 21, and the sign said EL CAT SEN.

No one was in it but a girl about ten years old, sitting almost hidden behind the counter with a comic book. Her left foot was on another chair. Her right leg was wrapped around her left in a sort of boneless abandon that might have been experimental or just comfortable. I examined the cases, waiting for signs of life, but she was far away. The wooden shaft of a lollipop protruded from her mouth with a sophistication that went well with a pug nose and dark shoulder-length hair. 'All by yourself?'

Without looking up she nodded and said: 'Uh. Oo i owioffsh oo?'

'Yes, I do rather.' It wasn't baby talk. She just didn't find an immediate need to take out the all-day sucker, but wanted to know if I liked lollipops too.

But then she glanced at me – startling ocean-blue eyes, inescapably appraising – and waved at a box, and gradually got her wide mouth unstuck, and said: 'Well, pick one. Heck, they're only a penny, heck.' She reversed legs, wrapping the left around the right. 'You couldn't do that.'

'Who says I can't?' There was a third chair behind the counter, so I got into it and showed her. With our more elastic bones, I had an unfair advantage, but I was careful not to exceed human possibility. Even so she looked slightly sandbagged.

'You're pretty good,' she admitted. 'Inja-rubber man. You forgot your lolli-pop.' She tossed me one from the box, lemon variety. I got busy on it and we have been friends ever since. 'Look,' she said. 'Heck, could this autothenti-cally happen, I mean for true?' She showed me the comic book. There was a spaceman with a beautiful but unfortunate dame. The dame had been strapped to a meteor – by the Forces of Evil, I shouldn't wonder – and the spaceman was saving her from demolition by other meteors. He did it by blasting them with a ray-gun. It looked like a lot of work.

'I wouldn't want to be quoted.'

'Oh, you. I'm Sharon Brand. Who are you?'

'Benedict Miles. Just rented a room up the street. With the Pontevecchios, maybe you know 'em?'

'Heck.' She took on a solemn glow. She threw away the comic, and unwound and readjusted her skinny smallness. Now she was sitting on both her feet, and had her elbows hung over the back of the chair, and watched me for a time with eyes ten thousand years old. 'Angelo happens to be my best boy friend, but you better not mention it. It would be most unadvisable. I would be furious.'

'I never would.'

'I'd probably cut your leg off and beat you over the head with it. If you detonated.'

'Detonated?'

'Aren't you educated? It means shoot off. Your mouth. Some people call him stuck-up on account he's always reading books. You don't think he's stuck-up, do you?' Her face said urgently: Better not detonate.

'No, I don't think he is at all. He's just very bright.'

'I'd probably turn a ray-gun on you. Tatatata-taah. He happens to've been my boy friend for years and years, but don't forget you promised. Heck, I hate a rat … You know what?'

'No, what?'

'I started piano lessons yesterday. Mrs Wilks showed me the scale. She's blind. Right away she showed me the scale. They've fixed up to let me prac-tice on the school piano for the summer.'

'Scale already, huh? That's terrific.'

'Everything is terrific,' said Sharon Brand. 'Only some things are terrificker than others.'

2

Later (I hoped my friend Sharon was asleep, but somehow I had an image of both those children turning on furtive night lights, Sharon with her space-men, Angelo wandering critically through the intricacy of Plato's dreams) I went out to taste the city's middle evening again, going through the railroad underpass to the 'right' side of the tracks, drifting with other masks past shop-windows, poolrooms, dance halls. I played the watching game with myself: 'One I'd like to know, a gleam of intelligence ... Ah, the Face that Foreclosed the Mortgage! ... A face of bitterness, member of the weasel totem ... A genuine dish ... Gracious with age ... Savage with age ... A schoolmarm (?) – a pick-pocket – a plainclothes cop – a salesman – a possible bank teller ...' In that game you have their voices too, never finished: 'So he gets his gun on this other guy, see, only the Ranger's behind the bush –' 'I told her, I said, if I don't know my own size in girdles by this time –' 'I wouldn't believe him if he had brass knucks—'

I followed a street uphill. Separate houses with lawns, somber men being walked by small dogs. At the crest one looked down at city lights fantastically calm. My night vision, better than human, allowed me to see beyond them to distant fields and woods, delicately secret even in daylight with lovable small life in the grass and bushes. The moon was rising. I strolled in that placid region, admiring some of the houses, reflecting that the owners used the same type of aspirin as their neighbors downtown. I returned to the business district by another route, wondering if it could be true that someone was following me.

A sly footstep never quite heard, a shadow never quite seen against hedge or doorway. Oh, I had been fretting more than I realized, about Namir. That was all, I thought – that and fatigue.

The movie theaters were closed. The crowd had thinned and changed: fewer of the cheerful, more of the predatory. I bought a late newspaper and shoved it in my pocket after a glance at the headlines. The present seems to be an interlude of relative calm, but now human beings are too shrewd to suppose that the volcanoes under the surface are dead. They were fooled that way, I recall, in the '880s and '890s. They have learned a few things since then. The United States of Europe is functioning rather well if creakily, though everyone is afraid of the logical next step of Atlantic Federation, and the One World Government boys and girls are clouding the issue as usual with well-meant enthusiasm. There are three Iron Curtains now: Russia's, China's, and the curious new one, growing higher each year ever since the death of Stalin, between Russia and China themselves. But the seven or eight major civilizations of the world are cohering; except for those two eclipsed by ancient despotism, the civilizations may be feeling their way to an enduring compromise. One doesn't look for the small promises of an ethical revolution in the headlines: the ocean's currents do not derive from the ocean's tempests ... Eisenhower's successor appears to be a reasonable man: I gather that few seriously dislike him, though it's hard to fill such a pair of shoes. The trend is likely to be against him in '964, with the customary jump a little too far left. That doesn't worry me.

Back on the wrong side of the tracks, I entered a park up a side street near Calumet. It was mere leftover space created by an angling cross street. Brick walks too bumpy for roller skates, patches of stubborn grass. Two old men were playing checkers under a park lamp. I rested on a bench in the moonshadow of a maple, wondering if this might be the park where Observer Kajna had overheard a certain conversation.

A hundred yards away were two clusters of benches, deserted except for a gaunt fellow, head bowed in his hands. Drunk, sick, or derelict, I thought. Two soldiers and their girls sat down near him and he got up and lurched away, on a path that would bring him past me. He did not pass me, and I looked again. He was stumbling off in the other direction, crossing grass as if to avoid the checker players' lamp.

My bench was deeply shadowed. He could hardly have made me out with drunken human eyes. I caught no Martian scent, but the breeze was wrong. My own scent-destroyer was fresh, but I had made no change in my face since Namir saw me in Northern City.

Dismissing uneasiness, returning to the now indolent night life of Main Street, I entered a bar (not my first that evening) and listened to the long gush of words, variations on the silly, wise, obscene. That was restful. It spoke well for my manner and appearance that nobody gave the skinny rye drinker a second glance until I invited it, rambling into an argument with a plumber over the future of the world's fuel supply. It has become fashionable to fret about that. We bought three rounds. I said solar energy, wind, water power, and alcohol, but in the end I let him have his atoms, what the hell.

'Thing is,' he said, 'you got to hitch to a star. When I think of the things my kids'll see! You figure there's life on Mars?'

'No atmosphere,' said a fat man the plumber called Joe.

'Now it stands to reason,' said the plumber, and pounded a puddle on the bar and apologized for splashing me. 'They see green in the telescopes, don't they? How about that?'

'Lichens,' said Joe. 'Meant to say not *enough* atmosphere, see?'

'You can take your lichens,' said the plumber, 'and – well, it stands to

reason, and anyway why couldn't they live underground, seal in the atmosphere, what the hell?'

'Not me,' said Joe. 'I'd get this now clusterphobia.'

'All the same you can take your lichens—'

I was back at the lodging house before midnight, happy about moonlight
on square quiet houses, happy about someone plinking a mandolin late and
gently behind drawn curtains, happy about our Salvayan capacity for alcohol. My plumber had gone home under convoy of Joe and another, the three
of them operating rather like a minesweeper with a one-eyed pilot.

There was a night light in the hall, and more light from the open door of
the first-floor front. That would be Mr Feuermann, I remembered, and I saw
him, a white-haired old gentleman in an armchair, his feet up on a stool. He
was cherishing a horsehead meerschaum. Purposely I tripped. He cleared his
throat and came stumping out. 'All right?'

'Yes, thanks – turned my ankle a bit.'

We examined each other with the furtive measuring of human strangers.
He was obviously lonely. 'Too bad,' he said, and studied the carpet with some
hostility, plainly worried about trouble for Mrs Pontevecchio. 'It looks all
right.'

'It wasn't the carpet. Fact is I had one too many.'

'Oh.' A solid old man, though tall and not stout. 'Sometimes,' he said, 'if
you make the hair on a long-haired dog a mite longer ...?'

So I went into his room and he broke out a pint of bourbon and we discussed it for an hour. He claimed he'd left the door open to clear away stale
smoke, but then admitted he was always hoping someone would drop in. He
had been a railroad engineer until twelve years ago, when he retired, because
of age, because Diesels were hooting the end of steam and he was too old for
new techniques. He had been a widower for six years; his only child, a daughter, was married and living in Colorado. Once his work had taken him all
over the States. He spoke warmly and poetically of that wandering on steel
pathways, but Latimer was home and he would not leave it again.

I did not try to steer the talk to the landlady's son: the old man did so
himself. Jacob Feuermann had lived in that house since his wife died. I
understood, without words, that the Pontevecchios had become an adopted
family for him. Their troubles were his, and perhaps he knew that there was
on him a reflected glow of Angelo's strangeness.

He remembered Angelo as a huge-eyed six-year-old, not talkative but
intensely observant, given to fierce fits of temper – caused, Feuermann
believed, by frustrations that would not have badly troubled ordinary children. In retrospect, Feuermann took a sort of proprietary pride in those
tantrums. Angelo had never been a naughty child, he said. Angelo took

punishments with good grace and rarely repeated an offense; but a toy out of reach, a tumbling block house, a missing jigsaw fragment could turn him blue in the face. 'Even now, when he's got over that, you couldn't call him a happy kid, and I don't think,' Feuermann said, 'the bad leg has much to do with it ...' When Feuermann first came to the house, Rosa had been bearing a private crucifixion of despair over those temper fits, her mind approaching and skittering away from the word 'insanity' (that fog-word, Drozma, still terrorizes any human being who has learned no discipline of definition). She had confided much in Feuermann. He also remembered her husband in the flesh.

Silvio Pontevecchio seems to have been a baffled alcoholic marshmallow. Intelligent, Feuermann considered him, but unable to profit by it. Silvio had tried a dozen or more ventures, taking his dozen or more failures with the same meek surprise and a few quick ones. Even before Angelo's birth, Feuermann deduced, it was Rosa's work with the lodging house that supported them. Silvio did manage the furnace, but carrying ashes bothered his back. And so on. In the end (just as humbly and mildly, maybe) Silvio fell on the ice in front of a skidding truck, after drinking up money intended for a life insurance premium. 'Poor bastard,' said Feuermann with genuine pity – 'couldn't even die right.' That happened when Angelo was seven. Angelo had loved his father, who told good stories and was kind in small matters. A year after Silvio's death Rosa told her friend Feuermann how Angelo had said to her: 'I will not, repeat not, lose my temper again.' And kept his word. She quit worrying about his mind and worried instead about his small size and his impatience with the tedium of school. ('Enforced play' – but that was a term Angelo himself used, to me, and much later.)

'He skipped three grades in secondary school,' Feuermann told me. 'They didn't like it. The kid drove 'em, Miles – talked 'em into a position where they had to let him take the examinations, which were nothing to him. Made 'em look silly, so they went to fussing about his "manner" and "attitude" and – what's the word? – "social adjustment", some damn thing. Brrah! Boy's bright, that's all, but wasn't bright enough then to hide how bright he was.'

'Genius?'

'You tell *me* what that is – I dunno.'

'Supernormal ability generalized, let's say.'

'That he has.'

'I sometimes wonder what the schools aim at nowadays.'

He made a business of refilling the meerschaum, sensing that I honestly wanted his opinion. 'My Clara – it's almost twenty years since she was in high school. I remember beating my brains about *her* schooling. They never seemed to want to teach her anything except how to be like everybody else. When she finished – bright, you know, nothing stupid about Clara – she could add a column of figures after a fashion, read a little if she had to. Hated books, still does. Always been a heavy reader myself, be lost nowadays if I wasn't. Damned if I know what she did learn. Self-expression before she could have anything to express. Social consciousness, whatever that is, when even now she hasn't enough command of language to tell you what she thinks society is. Scraps of this and that, no logic to hold 'em together. Everything made easy – and how are you going to make education easy? You might as well try to build an athlete by keeping him in a hammock with cream puffs and beer. Why, Miles, I've put in seventy years trying to get an education, and only done a half-baked job of it. I guess Angelo's school is about the same. Only, bless your heart, he's learned by now to treat it as a joke, and damn well keep the joke to himself.'

'Maybe the schools have come to regard education as a sort of by-product, something it would be nice to have if it isn't too much trouble.'

'Oh,' said the gentle old man, 'I wouldn't say that, Miles. I believe they try.' He added, with I think no trace of humorous intent: 'Maybe if they started by educating teachers it would help. And there still are a few with high standards – I found that out when it was too late to do Clara any good ... Anyway Angelo's a good boy, Miles – nice' – he was fumbling for words himself – 'clean, goodhearted. Mean to say he's no damn freak. If it wasn't for his peewee size and that poor little game leg ...'

'Polio?'

'Yes, at four. Happened before I came here. Gets better as he grows. Doctor told Rosa he might be able to drop the brace after his teens. It shuts him out of a lot. But he never seems to mind that much.'

'Might've helped him develop his brains.'

'Might.' We left it there, for my friend was suppressing yawns. I sought my own room, went to bed lethargically like a tired human being.

I woke in a fog to a sound of snoring. My wrist watch said four-thirty. It was never my way, nor the way of any Salvayan, I should think, to wake with a thick head. The snoring was on the first floor, had to be Feuermann, but was unreasonably loud. I was aware of a nasty sweetish stench and my forehead was a block of dull pain. Something tumbled from my pillow to the floor, and another smell fetched me furiously wide awake: the Martian scent, individualized as it always is and certainly not my own.

I snapped the light on. The thing fallen from my pillow was a wad of cotton, still foul with common chloroform.

I thought at first that nothing was missing. Then I snatched up my bottle of scent-destroyer. Two thirds gone.

My door was ajar. Out in the hall, I learned the snoring was loud because Feuermann's door was open too. A street lamp showed me his bed. No chloroform here. I made sure the old man was unharmed, his sleep natural though noisy. Back in my room, I saw that my clothing, hung on a chair, was disarranged. The bronze mirror in the bureau was safe. My wallet was too, the money intact, but a note had been shoved in among the bills. A note in our tiny Salvayan script, which looks to human eyes like random dots. It was unsigned and casual:

Please observe that I play fair. Your S-D bottle is not quite empty.

Nothing so artless as a human-style burglary had occurred to me. But Namir was only following the oldest Observers' Rule: *Act human.* I stopped laughing when I considered one non-human element: I could not drive Namir into the grip of the police without betraying our people. He would exploit that fact and never lose sight of it. It was like yielding a handicap of two rooks to a chess player no weaker than myself.

One window was more widely open than I had left it. Namir had come in there from the backyard. A ladder rested against the wall short of my window sill, an easy climb. I had noticed it on its side yesterday by the fence, likely left over from a recent paint job on the window casings. And what about that bulldog? Sunrise was not far away. The wooden backyard fence had a blank door to the side street – Martin Street. A pile of rags near it troubled me because I couldn't recall seeing it before.

I returned sniffing to the hall, a bathrobe over my pajamas. I heard a fuzzy murmur of another snore upstairs. No scent. Namir would surely be gone. He would not waste the scent-destroyer, but would wait till he could strip and dab it on the scent-gland areas. I tried the second floor. The bathroom was empty, and the vacant room over mine. The two tenants' doors were open a crack. From the room in the middle came that cozy snoring and a whiff of sachet. No chloroform. Angelo had mentioned old ladies. They were probably safe. I looked in the front room.

Here I did smell chloroform. I flipped on the light, snatched the pad away from the young man's pillow, and shook him. He struggled up and grabbed his head. 'Who in hell are you?' Jack McGuire was built to ask such questions, a fine mountain of man, mostly shoulders. Redheaded, blue-eyed, and sudden.

'Moved in yesterday, first floor. Prowler broke in, but nobody –' Mac was into his pants and barking about the old ladies before I finished, and then out in the hall shouting: 'Hey, Mrs Mapp! Mrs Keith!' Nice boy. Plain-spoken. He'd have the house steaming in three minutes. Meanwhile I gave his room a photographic glance. Decent poverty, self-respecting. A work shirt with oil stains – mechanic? Glamor photograph on the bureau, a cute wench with a heart-shaped face; another beside it of a muscular lady, unquestionably Mom. Razor, toothbrush, comb, and towel laid out as if for Saturday inspection by a second lieutenant. I shoved the toothbrush into a comfortable diagonal to please myself, and withdrew to a sound of screaming.

They were nice old ladies in a hugely cluttered nest. A double window overlooked Martin Street. That would be their headquarters in normal times, but now the thin one was standing up in bed and screaming while the fat one asked her if everything was all right. Mac said it was. Having touched off the eruption, he was shoving the lava back, barehanded. I liked Mac.

Agnes Mapp was stout, Doris Keith lean. I learned later that they were from New London, and had a low opinion of Massachusetts, where they had been living on widows' pensions for twenty-six years; this burglary was the first occasion when the Commonwealth had snapped back at them. Mrs Keith subsided to the horizontal, and Mrs Mapp took over the screaming, waving at the bureau. 'It's all unsettled!' In that mass of furniture, corsets, work-baskets, china ornaments, and, yes, antimacassars, I wondered how she knew. 'We never let the red vahz set next the pink hairbrushes, *never!* Oh, Dorrie!' she wept. 'Look! He's stolen our *album!*'

I mumbled I'd call the cops. Mrs Keith was recovering, and demanding in a severe baritone that Mac explain. He and I contemplated each other in a sympathy bridging the Salvayan-human gap. I went downstairs.

I met Angelo limping up from the basement in yellow pajamas. Feuermann, roused by the screaming, padded after me. I asked him to call the police and he ducked back to the hall telephone without fuss. Angelo was muttering.

'Save Mama climbing the stairs.'

'Sure. She needn't. Come back down with me. Just a prowler, maybe got away with a few dollars. Ladder under my window. Chloroform.'

'Oops!' said Angelo, catching some normal pleasure of excitement. 'But Bella –' He forgot Bella, hurrying to his mother as we entered the basement living room. She was in her rocker, gray-faced, clutching a blue wrapper. I wasn't sure she could get up. I tried to be stuffily humorous and soothing in the account I gave her.

'Never had *nothing* like this happen, Mr Miles – never—'

'Mama,' Angelo urged, 'don't fret. It isn't anything.'

She pulled his head against her. He drew free gently, and rubbed her aimless-wandering hands. Her color improved. Her breathing was almost right by the time Feuermann joined us. Reassuringly important, he said the police would be along shortly, meanwhile we'd better see what was missing. His common sense was golden, his Jovian fussing over Rosa more useful than my efforts. Angelo mumbled about Bella and slipped out. I spoke of the old ladies' missing album.

'Funny,' said Feuermann. 'If they say it's missing it is – couldn't misplace a pin in that room. They won't even let Rosa dust. Got a notion my own is missing. Remember, Miles, I showed you a snap of old 509 when she was new out of the yards, and one of me and Susan and Clara when she was twelve. Where'd I put that album when we were done with it?'

'Top of your bookcase.'

'Right. Always do. Seems to me it was gone when I put on the light. Now what would a burglar want of pictures? Huh?'

I wondered if I knew ...

The others missed the small cry outside. My Martian hyperacusis is sometimes a burden: I hear too much I'd rather not. But it can be useful. I don't recall running. I was just there, in the backyard, in light from the kitchen window, with Angelo. He was kneeling by that pile of rags. It partly covered Bella, whose neck was broken. 'Why?' said Angelo. 'Why?'

I helped him to stand, frail in his rumpled pajamas. 'Come on back in the house. Your mother might need you again.'

He didn't cry or curse. I wished he would. He squinted at the ladder and the ground between it and the fence. Earth and paving stones were dry, unmarked. Angelo said: 'I'm going to kill whoever did that.'

'No.'

He wasn't listening. 'Billy Kell might know. If it was the Diggers—'

'Angelo—'

'I'm going to find him. I'm going to break his own neck for him.'

3

'Angelo,' I said, 'stop that.' And I searched my fair memory of the *Crito*. '"And will life be worth having, if that higher part of man be destroyed, which is improved by justice and depraved by injustice?"'

He recognized it, and remembered. His stare turned up to me, foggy and sorrowful but at least becoming young. He tried to curse them, and it changed to crying, which was better. 'The damn – oh, the damn—'

'All right,' I said. 'Sure.' I held his forehead while he tried to vomit and couldn't. I steered him back into the kitchen, made him splash cold water on his face and comb his wild hair with his fingers.

There was a new bumbling voice in the living room, a broad-beamed cop getting the story from Feuermann and being nice to Rosa. His prowl-car partner was upstairs conferring with Mac. I took him outside to look at the ladder, and showed him Bella. 'Why, the damn dirty—'

The difference was that Angelo had spoken from inner flame. Patrolman Dunn merely resented violence and disorder. He didn't talk about breaking necks. Nor read the *Crito*. I learned from his comments that the job had the trademarks of someone named Teashop Willie – the backyard approach, carefully non-lethal use of chloroform. Teashop would have an alibi, Dunn said, and it would be a pleasure to bust it over his think-box.

'Does he specialize in lodging houses?'

'Nup,' said Dunn, not liking me much. 'And this ain't a money neighborhood, Lord knows. But it's got the marks. You missing anything?'

'Haven't really looked,' I lied. 'My wallet was under my pillow.'

Dunn went back in the house, murmuring: 'Known the missus here ten years. People're mighty fond of Mrs Pontevecchio, mister.' There was warning in it, but only because I was what New England calls a foreigner.

They used up an hour or so, and sent for a fingerprint team. Teashop Willie rated that, as a favorite old offender; I suppose Dunn would have been startled if they'd found anything. I could have told him the burglar was wearing gloves. We were not grafting fingertips when Namir resigned in 30,829. The stolen photograph albums tormented Dunn. I think he decided Willie had gone whacky under the stress of a demanding profession. Feuermann and Mac had both lost a little money. The old ladies kept their cash in what Mrs Keith referred to as a safe place, and she invited no deeper inquiry, implying indirectly that all policemen were grafters, Cossacks, and enemies of the poor. I thought: 'Hoy!' Dunn and his pal left us at six-thirty with kind wishes. My only recollection of Dunn's partner is that he was a modest man with a modest wart, who told me personally that no stone would be left unturned. We never heard any more from them about it, so I picture him as still somewhere in the broad uncertainties of the world, turning stones. With all deference to Mrs Keith, I think policemen are a very decent lot, and I only wish human beings wouldn't make things so tough for 'em.

The evening before, after an enjoyable half hour of space travel, Sharon Brand had keyed herself up to selling me such items as coffee and bread. Her mother had been in the back room with a headache, Sharon said, and Pop had gone to a lodge meeting. Sharon enjoyed minding the store. She had dealt competently with the two or three other customers who had interrupted our interstellar activities. Now opening my packages for breakfast reminded me of her, if I had needed any reminder.

I called it a justifiable preoccupation. If she was Angelo's (self-appointed?) Girl Friend, she ought to be studied for the sake of my mission. Then I stopped fooling myself. I admitted she had made me lonely for my own daughter in Northern City. I suppose Elmaja and my son will be living four or five hundred years from now, when nobody at all remembers little Sharon Brand. The one year's flower and the oak – it isn't fair of course.

Still the seed lives, and the flowering of individual selves can be glorious even in the niggardly threescore and ten.

I admitted more. Sharon as a person had reached me somehow, touched me in almost the way that Angelo had done. She lacks his precocity, she may lack his blazing intellectual curiosity. But you put me on my own, Drozma. Observer Kajna did not learn of Sharon. If she had …?

From my window I saw Angelo and his mother go down Martin Street before nine o'clock, nicely dressed, to Mass. Rosa was walking with weariness, Angelo too spindling-small to help her much. I went out too, and strolled down Calumet Street the other way. The morning was muggy, sun pressing through windless haze, a tropical day, a day for the lazy, a day to make me remember the palms of Rio or a warm ocean dreaming against the beaches of Luzon, where I lived once – but that was a long time ago.

I heard trouble before I reached EL CAT SEN: Sharon's voice, cold, tight, and terrified, from the recessed entrance of a boarded-up house next door to the shop. 'Don't, Billy! I'll never say it – *don't!*'

I hurried, but my steps must have made noise. Nothing seemed to be happening when I arrived. Sharon was leaning stiffly against the nailed-up door, almost hidden from me by a big-shouldered boy who drew away from her as I appeared. Her right hand was behind her. I had an impression the boy had just released it, and he turned a blond head to stare at me. Much taller than Sharon, thirteen or fourteen and blocky, handsome but blankly so as if he were already expert at wearing a mask. Well, human beings are sometimes good at that. Sharon grinned feebly at me. 'Hello, Mr Miles!' The boy shrugged and moved away.

I said: 'Come back here!' He only turned to stare again, hands in his pockets. 'Were you bothering this girl?'

'Nope.' He was unalarmed, unashamed. His voice was adult, no adolescent croak. He might have been older than he seemed.

'Was he, Sharon?'

Barely audible, Sharon said: 'Nuh-nuh-no.' She had a red rubber ball on an elastic string, and bounced it thoughtfully. I noticed she used her left hand for that. 'Sharon, may I see your other hand?'

Reluctantly she held it out. I saw nothing wrong with it. When I looked up the boy was gone, around the corner. Sharon poked at a wet eyelid with annoyance. She said in a manner too ornate for the Court of St James's: 'Mr Miles, how can I ever abdiquately thank you?'

'Think nothing of it. Who's the yellow-haired phenomenon?'

That helped. She nodded in acknowledgment of a valuable word. 'Just Billy Kell. He is, heck, indeed a phenomenon.'

''Fraid I don't like him. What did he want?"

Her mouth went tight. 'Nothing.' She bounced the ball with desperate concentration. 'He's a mere phenomenon, think nothing of it.' In need of small talk, she added politely: 'I hear you had a burglary.'

'Yeah. News does get around.'

'Heck, I stopped by your house this morning before Angelo had to dress up for church. He says Dogberry will never abdiquately get to the bottom of it, and so phoo on Dogberry, don't you think so? By the way, do you swear never to tell if I happen to show you something?'

I said swearing was a serious matter, but she knew that. She studied me a nerve-twisting while, and made up her mind. She peered up and down the street, and darted down to the basement areaway. The lower entrance was half hidden under the front steps, only one board nailed to its wooden door. 'You have to swear, Mr Miles.'

I examined conscience. 'I swear never to tell.'

'You have to cross your heart if it's going to be legal.'

I did that, and she lifted away the loose board with slight effort, using her left hand. But she was not left-handed: I notice such things. I followed, closing the door behind us as she ordered, and we were in a hot dingy gloom, musty and vague, with a smell of rats and old damp plaster. I assured her I could see my way, but she gripped my thumb to guide me through a wilderness of empty crates and nameless litter, to a back room that had been a kitchen before the house was abandoned. There are too many such houses in Latimer, and the drift of population to the countryside may not be quite enough to explain it. I wonder sometimes if human beings have begun, a little, to hate the cities to which they have given such effort.

A large flimsy structure loomed in this kitchen, something knocked together from old crates, a house within a house. Sharon said: 'Wait.' She ducked into the contraption and struck a match. Two candles glowed. 'You can come in now.' As I squeezed in, she was hushed and solemn, the sea-blue of her eyes lost in enormous black. 'Nobody ever did before, except me ... This is Amagoya.' With obvious second thoughts and fear that I might not deserve the trust, she said: 'Of course it's unequibblical make-believe.'

It was and it wasn't. There was an altar here, the upturned bottom of a box. On a makeshift shelf above it was what some might have taken for a rag doll. 'Amag,' Sharon said, nodding to him. 'Just merely a representation, used to be a doll. Dolls are so childish, don't you think so?'

'Maybe, but make-believe is real. The inside of your head is real. Things outside are a different kind of real, that's all.' The objects on the box-altar were flanked by the candles. A boy's cap, frayed at the brim, a penknife, a silver dollar. 'Am I really the only one to see this, Sharon? Not even Angelo?'

'Oh no!' She was shocked. 'Amagoya is me when I'm alone. And now you, is why I had to make you swear. Well, because you don't laugh only at the right times.' A pity, Drozma, that I had to live 346 years before receiving a compliment of such magnitude. 'The dollar, He got that for a school prize and gave it to me for a luck piece. The penknife because I wanted one and He said keep it.' You could hear her capitalize the pronoun. 'The cap He just threw away.' There was no room for polite comment even from a Martian, and Sharon wanted no comment. I looked respectful and that was sufficient. She changed the subject with relief, saying apropos of nothing and with a gusty sigh: 'Pop came home drunk from lodge meeting. I veritably couldn't sleep, with them fighting. He hit the lid lifter against the stove just to make a noise, busted it to hell square off, frankly you wouldn't believe the things I put up with, frankly ...'

'Look, Sharon – that Billy Kell. I think he did hurt your hand. You could tell me about it.'

'I couldn't permit you to beat him up. Frankly I couldn't take the responsibility.'

'I don't beat people up, but I might scare him a little.'

'He don't scare, anyway I'm not afraid of him. He didn't really push my finger back, just pretended he would.' She had no real resources of deception; I took advantage of that, by simply waiting. 'Well, he was trying to make me say – something I wouldn't, was all. About me and Angelo. Billy can go drown. He is a mere phenomenon, Mr Miles ...'

'And the finger?'

'Honest, it's all right. Look, this is how you play a scale.' She demonstrated, on the floor. I saw not only that her hand was unharmed, but that her thumb already knew how to pass under the fingers in clean precision. After only one lesson. Slow, of course, but right. You yourself, Drozma, have spoken kindly of my ability as a pianist. But I know that we can never equal the best human players, and not merely because our artificial fifth fingers are dull. Do you think it might be because human beings live only a little time, and remember this in their music?

'I'm puzzled, Sharon. This morning Angelo said something about Billy Kell. As if they were friends, or so I thought.'

She said with adult bitterness: 'He does think Billy's his friend. I tried to tell him different, once. He wouldn't believe me. It's because he thinks everybody is good.'

'I don't know, Sharon. I don't think anybody who wasn't would fool Angelo very long.'

Well, that was good doctrine, and seemed to make her feel better. She again changed the subject delicately: 'If you want to, we could make Amagoya a space ship. I do that sometimes.'

'Sound idea.'

There was nasty furtive scampering somewhere in that dead kitchen. 'Think nothing of it,' said Sharon. 'You see, when I leave here I cover up everything with that other box, to keep off the phenomenons ...'

Handsomely dressed, Angelo met me on the front steps when I returned from the space ship, and transmitted an invitation to stop downstairs for a little coffee. Feuermann was already there. Rosa's idea of a little coffee included pizza and half a dozen other items, all tempting. Rosa herself, in Sunday clothes, looked wilted from something more than the heat of the morning. She reminded me ruefully: 'You wanted peace and quiet, Mr Miles.'

'Oh, call me Ben.' I tried to relax without losing the primness of Mr Miles – which had never had a chance to get established with Sharon. We kicked around the question of photograph albums, Feuermann returning obsessively to the main point: what could a burglar want of them?

'We aren't missing any down here,' Angelo said. 'I looked.'

Later Feuermann said hesitantly: 'Angelo, Mac told me he'd – well, dig a place. In the yard. If you want him to.'

Angelo choked on a mouthful. 'If it'd make *him* feel better.'

'Dear,' Rosa muttered. *'Angelo mio* – please—'

'Sorry, but can't somebody tell Mac I don't wear diapers nowadays?'

'Why, son,' Feuermann said, 'Mac just thought—'

'Mac just didn't think.'

In the raw silence I suggested: 'Look, Angelo – have patience with the human race. They try.'

He glared across the pretty kitchen table, hating me. The hatred softened and vanished. He seemed only puzzled, perhaps wondering who and what I was, what place I had in his secret widening world. He apologized with not much difficulty: 'I'm sorry, Uncle Jacob. Glad to have Mac do that. I was mad because I can't manage a spade with my damned leg.'

'Angelo, don't use those words – I've asked you—'

He turned beet-red. Feuermann intervened: 'Let him, this time, Rosa. I would too if Bella'd been mine. A damn never hurt anybody.'

'Sunday morning,' Rosa whimpered, 'only an hour after Mass ... It's all right, Angelo, I'm not cross. But don't do it. You don't want to sound like those tough kids down the street.'

'They aren't so tough, Mama.' He fooled with his food. 'Billy Kell puts on a show but it doesn't mean anything.'

'Tough talk makes tough thinking,' said Feuermann, and Angelo seemed not to resent that.

When I made my manners Angelo followed me to the basement stairs and asked without warning: 'Who are you, Mr Miles?'

His way, to fetch up the hardest questions – and I don't mean I was worried about the Martian angle: I wasn't. I disliked having to fence with him. 'A not very exciting ex-teacher, as I told your mother. Why, friend?'

'Oh, you sort of understand things, maybe.'

'Don't lots of people?'

His Latin shrug dismissing that was desperately mature. 'I dunno ... I met an old man in the park, month or so ago. Maybe he did. He said he'd lend me some books, but then I never saw him again.'

'What were the books, remember?'

'Somebody named Hegel. And Marx. Well, I tried to get Marx out of the public library, but they threw a whing-ding.'

'Said mere children don't read Marx?' He looked up quickly, with some incredulity. 'I could get those for you if you like.'

'Would you?'

'Those and others, sure. You can't study out a thing for good or bad if you don't go to the source. But look, Angelo: you scare people. You know why, don't you?'

He flushed and scraped his shoe tip on the floor like any small boy. 'I don't know, Mr Miles.'

'People think in fairly rigid patterns, Angelo. They think a twelve-year-old boy is just thus and so, no argument. When one comes along who thinks ahead of his age, well, they feel as if the ground shook a little. It scares 'em.' I put my hand on his shoulder, wanting to say what words could not; he didn't draw away. 'It doesn't scare me, Angelo.'

'No?'

I tried to imitate his very fine shrug. 'After all, Norbert Wiener entered college at eleven.'

'Yeah, and had his troubles too. I read his book.'

'Then you know some of what I was trying to say. Well, other books. What do you *like* to read?'

He abandoned caution and said passionately: 'Anything! Anything at all …'

'Roger!' I said, and squeezed his shoulder and started upstairs. I am not sure, but I think he whispered: 'Thanks!'

4

Early that afternoon I had my feet up in my own room, frustratedly trying to guess what Namir's next move might be. Feuermann wandered in, spruced up but not solemn. He said he had a date with his wife. At his age I suppose one needn't be portentous about a Sunday afternoon visit to the cemetery. He was taking Angelo along for the drive and invited me to join them.

His 'jalopy' was a '58 model. I marveled at the swooping lines of some '62s and '63s that Angelo pointed out as we purred down Calumet Street. He and the old man talked automobiles, somewhat over my head. I was the only one who noticed a gray coupé sticking behind us as we worked through town and out on a splendid country highway. 'The cemetery isn't in Latimer?'

'No, Susan's people were Byfield folks. She wanted to be buried out there. About ten miles. Susan Grainger she was – been Graingers in Byfield since 1650, they say. My papa, he came over on the steerage.'

'So'd my grandfather,' said Angelo. 'Anybody care nowadays?'

Feuermann glanced at me over the small brown head and drooped an eyelid and smiled. I said: 'One world, Angelo?'

'Sure. Isn't it?'

'One world and a good many civilizations.' He looked bothered.

'Well now,' said Jacob Feuermann, 'I kind of like the idea of one world government.'

'I'm afraid of it,' I said, watching Angelo. 'Too easy for it to turn monolithic, for individualists to kill individualism without knowing it. Why not seven or eight federations corresponding to the major civilizations, under a world law recognizing their right to be unaggressively different?'

'Think we could ever get such a world law? And where's your guarantee against war in that, Miles?'

'There can't be any except in human ethical maturity. A sensible political structure would help enormously, but there's going to be risk of war so long as men think they can justify hating strangers and grabbing for power. Human hearts and minds are basic – the rest is mechanics.'

'Pessimist, huh?'

'Not a bit, Feuermann. But scared of the wishful thinking I sometimes do myself. In politics, wishful thinking just gives the wolves a license to howl.'

'Mm.' The old man squeezed Angelo's bony knee. 'Angelo, you figure Miles and me are old enough to sweat out these things?' Angelo might have disliked that gentle sarcasm from anyone but Feuermann. He chuckled and flung a make-believe punch at Feuermann's shoulder, and we pushed it around on that more comfortable level all the way to Byfield. That gray coupé stayed behind us and I didn't mention it. This was a well-traveled road. My imagination could be overheated. Still, Feuermann drove with slow caution and many other cars whooshed by us impatiently. When we pulled into a parking lot near the cemetery the gray car speeded up to hurry past, the driver bending down with averted face.

Angelo had been here with Feuermann before. I would have gone all the way with Jacob to the grave, but Angelo shook his head and led me to a green bank overlooking the most ancient part of the graveyard – quite ancient in the American-human sense, for some of the crumbling stones dated from three hundred years ago when I was a boy. Angelo pointed those out to me, not snickering as most youngsters would have done at the labors of a long-dead stonemason who symbolized angels by eyed circles with a few gouges for hair. 'Guess all they had was that sandstone or whatever it is.'

'Yes, marble would have done better by a few centuries.'

'Sure.' He did laugh then. 'Sure, what's a few centuries?' He sat on the bank, chewing a grass blade, swinging his feet. Jacob Feuermann was fifty paces away, seeming on his island of contemplation more distant than he was, full of stillness, with sunlight on his white head. He looked down at whatever truth he saw in that modest swell of earth, and then away toward summer clouds and eternity. In a younger man it might have appeared morbidly sentimental, at least to human beings, always swift with labels for the quirks of others. But Feuermann was too solid, too tranquil inwardly, to worry over labels. Later he sat on the ground, chin in hand, unconcerned about dampness or creaky aging joints, and Angelo murmured to me: 'Every Sunday rain or shine. Sure, even if it's raining, though maybe he doesn't sit on the grass then. Winter too.'

'I suppose he loved her, Angelo. Likes to be here where nothing much comes between him and the thought of her.' But I was losing myself in shadow. My mind smelled chloroform, saw that blank-faced young Hercules looming over Sharon in the doorway, glimpsed a gray coupé that should not have hung behind us. Small things. Nothing ugly had happened except Bella's death; the warm sweetness of this day made it seem absurd that any more ugliness could happen. But even in a sunlit hush of jungle you may see some distant fluid motion of black and orange stripes in the grass, or hear the whisper of a leaf no wind disturbs. I produced a yawn and hoped it sounded comfortable, lending a phony casualness to my question: 'You go to church, Angelo?'

'Sure.' Though mild, his face became too watchful. Probably he knew the question was not casual, knew I was groping for his thoughts and wondered whether to grant me the right to any such exploration … 'I even sang in the choir last year. Kid in front of me had ears like an aardvark. Threw me off pitch.' He hummed, a clear contralto with a curious effect of distance: 'Ad Deum qui laetificat juventutem meant –' he spat out the grass blade and smiled off at nothing.

'And has he made your youth joyful?'

Angelo chuckled. 'Now you sound like that man I talked with in the park. He said religion was a fraud.'

'I don't consider it a fraud, though I happen to be agnostic myself. Matter of individual belief. You should go anyway, if only on your mother's account – at least I suppose she's devout, isn't she?'

He sobered quickly. 'Yes …'

'Tell me something about Latimer.' I watched his feet swinging, the finely shaped one, the twisted one with the brace. 'Keep thinking I might decide to settle here.'

He spoke doubtfully: 'Well, there isn't much. People say it's kind of gone to seed. I dunno. Lot of empty houses. Nothing much ever happens. The country's nice, like here, when you get out in it – Cheepus, I wish I could! You know: just walk all day, climb hills. I go a mile and then it's pain up the back of the leg, have to quit.'

'Think I'll get a car. Then we could go out in the country a bit.'

'Cheepus!' He lit up from inside. 'Spend a whole day in the woods maybe? I could go for that … You know, that painting, the one in your room, it wasn't any place I ever really saw. I've seen places like it – birches – Uncle Jacob takes me for drives sometimes. But when I want to get out and walk he has to come along and worry about my leg instead of letting me worry about it and quit when I'm ready to … I like animals. You know? The little things that – I've read, if you sit still in the woods a while they'll come around and not be afraid.'

'That's true. I've often done it. Most of the birds don't mind if you do move a little, in fact they prefer it, looks less suspicious. I've had orioles come pretty close. Redwing blackbirds. Fox almost blundered into me once. I was sitting in one of his favorite paths. He just looked embarrassed and made a detour … Met a friend of yours, by the way. At the delicatessen. Sharon Brand.'

His mind was still in the woods. He said absently: 'Yes, she's a nice kid.'

'You sort of grew up with her?'

'Sort of. Four-five years anyway. Mama – doesn't like her too much.'

'Oh, why? I think she's swell.'

He picked a fresh grass blade. He said carefully: 'Sharon's people aren't Catholics—'

'Is Billy Kell Catholic?'

'No.' He looked puzzled. 'Billy? When did I—'

'This morning, Angelo. When we found Bella. You said: "Billy Kell might know …"'

'Oh. Did I?' He sighed uncomfortably. 'Cheepus …!'

'You said something about the Diggers too. What are they? A gang?'

'Yeah.'

'Round about your age?'

'Yeah. Some older.'

'Tough?'

He grinned in a way I hadn't seen, as if he were trying out toughness to see how it felt. 'They think so, Mr Miles, to hear 'em bat the wind.'

'Sounds as if you didn't like 'em.'

'They're a bunch of –' He stopped, weighing me, I think, and wondering if I'd tolerate an obscenity from a twelve-year-old, and deciding against it. He said mildly: 'Nobody likes those bastards.'

'What all do they do?'

'Oh, they fight dirty. Some stealing, I guess, fruit-stand jobs or stuff off the back of a truck. Billy says some of the older ones are muggers, and some of 'em carry shivs – knives, I mean.' I didn't like his smile: it was a dissonance in the character I thought I was beginning to know. 'Most of 'em come from the sh – the crumby end of Calumet Street, the south end … Got a cigarette?'

I gave him one, and lit it for him. Feuermann wasn't looking, and I suppose I could have argued it with Feuermann anyway. 'Don't the Diggers have any competition, Angelo?'

He hesitated, only a little. 'Sure. The Mudhawks. That's Billy Kell's gang.' He was smoking casually, inhaling without coughing. 'You know, I saw Billy crack a walnut once, just putting it against his biceps and closing his arm. Nobody tangles with Billy Kell.' He said as if trying to convince himself of something that mattered: 'The Mudhawks are all right.'

'Can you talk with him? With Billy Kell?'

He knew what I meant, but said uneasily: 'How do you mean?'

'When I first saw you, yesterday, you were reading the *Crito*. I just meant, things like that.'

He said evasively: 'Books aren't everything … He's good in school, straight A's all the time.'

'How is the school? Pretty fair?'

'It's all right.'

'But you have to put on an act, is that right?'

He rubbed out the cigarette against a stone. He said presently: 'They play around an awful lot. Maybe I do. Some of the time. I'm no good in mathematics. Or manual training – honest, you should see a birdhouse I tried to make, looks like a haystack in a blizzard.'

'What are you good at?'

He made a face at me, enjoying it. 'The things they don't teach. All right – like the *Crito*, Mr Miles. Philosophy.'

'Ethics?'

'Well, I got a college text on that, out of the library. I didn't think it got down to cases very much. They've got Spinoza there. I didn't try it.'

'Don't.' I took hold of his good ankle and hung onto it a moment 'You're way ahead of your class, my friend, but you're not ready for Spinoza. Not sure I ever was myself. If you can take him all in at one gulp, I suppose it's good, but let it wait … History was my subject when I used to teach school. How about that?'

'They just don't teach it, not to say teach. Formula stuff. They tell you one thing, and you get something out of the library that says just the opposite, so who's right? I mean, the teacher dishes it out the way he sees it, and then you're supposed to wrap it up and give it back to him the same way. Or you're wrong: E for effort. Schoolbook says we broke away from England in 1776

because British imperialism was spangling the colonies economically. Dec-
laration of Independence says we did it for political reasons. Really both,
wasn't it?'

'Those were two of many reasons, yes.' I can never be reconciled to our
deception, Drozma. How I should have loved to tell him that afternoon of
the way I saw the French fleet come into the Chesapeake before Yorktown! I
remember the early autumn storm too, that came up when the poor devils of
redcoats were trying to get across the river – I suppose I might not have
wanted to describe that to him completely. Or I might, I don't know. 'History
frustrates all teachers,' I said, 'simply because it's too endlessly big. There has
to be selection, and the best of teachers can't escape his own bias in making
that selection. But of course they ought to keep reminding you of that difficulty, and I suppose they don't.'

'No, they don't. The Federalist Papers don't explain everything with eco-
nomics either. I said I'd read 'em. Wasn't supposed to. I don't mean she gave
me hell or anything. She said it was fine that I should make such an effort,
only she was afraid they were a little over my head. And besides, although the
Federalist Papers were "quaint and interesting", they weren't part of the
course, and wouldn't I try to be a little more attentive in class and show a better all-round attitude?'

'You mean, Angelo, some days it just don't pay to get up?'

He liked that, and blew out a grass blade in a puff of laughter and pulled
another one to chew. 'Level bevel, Mr Miles.' In the teenage argot of 30,963,
that means you're all right. Angelo uses that cant very seldom, being far more
at home in the precision and beauty of normal English than any adults I have
met on this mission.

'Are you a member of that gang you told me about? Billy Kell's? Not that
it's any of my business.'

He looked away, all pleasure gone. 'No, I'm not. I guess they want me to
join. I don't know …' I waited, which was not easy.

'I couldn't let Mama know about it if I did.'

'Joining would mean agreeing to a lot of things, wouldn't it? It usually
does.'

'Maybe so.' He got down off the bank, lounging with his hands in his pockets. I didn't see again that flash of phony, half-experimental toughness. But I
did realize presently that I had intruded on a matter in which he would
accept no counsel, and that he wasn't going to answer the unspoken question. He had taken on a look not distant but almost sleepy; he was hidden in
the thousand-colored privacy of a mind I'd never know, yet not far away. At
that moment and at others I remember, he reminded me of that slumbrous
creature of heaven who leans on the shoulder of another in Michelangelo's
'Madonna, Child, St John and Angels'. (I bought a fair print of that painting

and still have it; sometimes it seems more like him than a snapshot, which is supposed to tell the truth.)

'Any car I get,' I said, 'will have to be a jalopy. How were the '56 Fords?'

'Good, I guess.' He smiled brilliantly, thinking of my promise, and held up circled thumb and forefinger in that American gesture which appears to mean that everything's jake. 'Any old wheeze-on-wheels, you won't be able to get rid of me.' He limped to the nearest of the graves and rubbed a finger on the eroded carving. 'Here's a guy who "sought his reward 10 August 1671, a servant of Christ". Name of Mordecai Paxton. Must've figured he was pretty sure what reward.' He started to brush a cobweb from the slanted, half-submerged stone, but his hand fell. 'Nah, she'd only build it up again, and besides ...'

'She and Mordecai get along. Might even be descended from a spider who knew Mordecai personally.'

'Might be. Other people are neglecting Mordecai though.' Angelo picked a few saucy dandelions and tucked them around the stone. 'Him and his whiskers.' He glanced up with shyness. 'Kind of thing Sharon's always doing. Looks better, huh?'

'Much.'

'Gaudy whiskers, I'll bet.'

'A caution to the heathen.' We pushed Mordecai around. I said ginger whiskers, but Angelo claimed Mordecai was roly-poly, with black cooky-brushes, and had been tempted by Satan in the form of a pork chop. We quit when Feuermann returned, not that the old man would have minded laughter.

I thought I saw that gray coupé behind us on the way home. It shot by, again too quickly, when we stopped at a roadstand, where Angelo consumed a forbidding quantity of pistachio ice cream. Back in the car, he burped once, said: 'Ah, hydrogen chloride!' and fell asleep.

I was in danger, since he drooped against me. But his head was not directly on my chest; he was too sound asleep to notice that my heart beat only once in sixty seconds. What are we, Drozma? More than human, when we observe them; less, when we batter our wings against the glass.

5

The following week is, in my mind, a kaleidoscope of small events:

Waking late, when Sharon and Angelo were installing a bit of paving stone to mark Bella's grave in the backyard. If I had not witnessed Angelo's earlier resentment I should have thought he was enjoying it, until he happened to step behind Sharon and his face abandoned pretense, becoming patient, puzzled, tender like that of any adult watching make-believe, himself remembering the forests and plains and deserts of maturity. Later they strolled down Martin Street into the city's jungle ... Sitting empty-brained before my typewriter, deciding at length that Mr Ben Miles would be convincing enough as a guy always on the point of writing a book but never doing it ... Visiting EL CAT SEN with Angelo (Tuesday that was) and finding not Sharon but a harassed little chap, Sharon's father, who became determinedly hearty talking baseball with Angelo; he didn't look like a smasher of cast iron ... Meeting Jack McGuire in a bar after his day's work at a garage. We started with the burglary but wound up with Angelo. 'Ain't healthy,' Mac said. 'Nose all the time in a book. Couldn't ever be an athalete with that bum leg, but all the same it ain't healthy, irregardless. He'll grow up lopsided or queer. Soon put a stop to it if he was my kid, but what can you do?' I didn't know ...

Nothing that week made me suspect the presence of Namir.

I saw Billy Kell again, from my window, playing catch with Angelo in Martin Street, and I wondered if my bad first impression of him could have been distorted. Had Sharon been at fault too? He had been tormenting her, but maybe she had goaded him to it. In that ball game Billy was a different person. He was throwing so that Angelo would not have to run much, yet he contrived to make Angelo work for it. There was no air of condescension or pulling punches, nothing patronizing in Billy's shouted comments. He was taking a lot of unboyish trouble to give Angelo a good time. When they tired of it they sat on the curb, blond head and dark in some amiable conference. It was all casual: Billy did not seem to be urging or arguing anything. When Rosa called him in for supper, Angelo exchanged some parting gesture with his friend – turn of the wrist and upraised palm. I remembered that Billy Kell led the Mudhawks. But Angelo had also said that he hadn't yet joined the gang ...

I had Thursday evening dinner with the Pontevecchios, the old ladies present. Rosa's cooking was from the heart. She was light on her feet in front of the stove, or bringing a dish to us. I wondered how much of her tiny income was lavished on that sort of thing. It was not waste: Rosa was a giver, hospitality as necessary to her as oxygen. When she could break out a fresh handsome tablecloth and stuff her guests with kindness, Rosa came glowingly alive, and then I saw not a tired worried fat woman but the mother of Angelo.

Mrs Doris Keith, majestic with white hair, gray silk, amethyst brooch, tended to glare – daring me to remember that when I first met her she was in several yards of cotton nightgown and screeching. She stood six feet and must have been rugged when she was on the warmer side of seventy. Mrs Mapp would always have been soft and poky, in youth a charming valentine.

Yet it was Mrs Mapp who had once taught school – she 'gave' art and music at a girls' finishing school – while Mrs Keith had now attempted any career but housewifery and rather defensively told you so. When their husbands quit the struggle years ago these two had worked out a symbiosis plainly good for the rest of their lives. I hoped they'd be lucky enough to die at the same time. 'Angelo;' said Mrs Keith, 'do show Agnes your latest work.'

'Oh, I'm not doing much of anything.'

She labored graciously to treat him as an adult. 'One can't advance without expert criticism. One must avoid getting in a rut.'

'I just horse around.' But he was petted and hectored into bringing two paintings. On his way to get them the little devil winked at me.

Three mares in a high meadow, heads lifted to the approach of a vast red stallion. Colors roared. No mountain wind. A meeting of wind and sunlight, savage and joyful, shoutingly and gorgeously sexual. Angelo should have been spanked. The other painting was a mild dreamy landscape.

I had to admit to myself that the ladies were desperately funny as well as pathetic, in their painstaking comments at everything but the obvious. 'The color,' said Mrs Mapp daringly, 'is – uh – quite extravagant.'

'Yes,' said Angelo.

'This leg is a trifle long. You lacked a model, I presume.'

'Yes,' said Angelo.

'Masses. Learn to balance your masses, Angelo.'

'Yes,' said Angelo.

'Now *this* –' Mrs Mapp took up the landscape with enormous relief. 'This is – uh – not bad. This is lovely, Angelo. Very lovely.'

'Yes,' said Angelo.

Rosa laughed. Totally unaware of embarrassment because there was none in herself, full of nothing but warmth and admiration, she couldn't keep her hands out of his curls as he took the paintings away. Nor was she much aware of them as paintings: just as Angelo's books were unknown country, so Rosa could not imagine that a twelve-year-old's work might have meaning for the world outside, or that his almost contemptuous virtuosity had achieved what most adult painters only struggle for. The shield of her kindly ignorance could have its uses.

While those two helped Rosa with the dishes, Angelo showed me his room. I did not try to stay angry with him, or to explain that dazzling and shocking little Mrs Mapp was a shabby victory. He knew it, and was already sick about it.

The room was a tiny oblong, one grudging window at the level of Martin Street, hardly space for more than his cot bed, a bookcase, an easel. It was also the studio which had produced certain triumphs that were undervalued even by himself. He selected another painting from a stack against the wall.

It was simple, technically unfinished, but he was right in not wanting to do any more with it. A hand curved to shelter what it held, and what it held was a tiger, fallen, mouth curled in a snarl of uncomprehending despair at the javelin in its side. 'Evidently you do believe in God, Angelo.'

He looked annoyed. 'Hand could symbolize human pity, couldn't it?' But it seemed to me that his mind abandoned the picture in the moment when I offered my half-baked interpretation. He slumped on the cot, chin in hands, woebegone. 'I better apologize?'

'Not necessarily.'

'How d'you mean?'

'Might just embarrass her worse. Why not let it go? And remember for the future that nice old ladies and randy stallions don't mix too well. Matter of empirical ethics.' I watched: old man 'empirical' didn't worry him. He knew the word without even finding it unusual.

He thought it over and sighed: 'Okay.' Relieved but not satisfied. It went on bothering him. I suppose that was why soon afterward he gave the soft land-scape to Mrs Mapp with sentimental flourishes, and took it like a gentleman when she kissed him and thanked him too much.

The next Sunday came in with warm persisting rain. I spent the morning reading the Sunday paper. It was difficult to evaluate the news when I so badly needed more light myself. After a week I had no plan worth the name. I knew something of the environment; something of Rosa and Feuermann and Sharon, scarcely anything of Billy Kell. I had shopped around for a cheap used car the day after our talk in the cemetery, but found nothing safe, so I put through a call to Toronto. A justifiable expense, Drozma, if only to let Angelo discover the woods – at any rate I have been in most of the temples and cathedrals of the world, and the peace I sometimes found in them was never more than a small substitute for what there is under the arches of the leaves. I had no clue to Namir's whereabouts and intentions. With the stolen photographs, scent-destroyer, and Martian skill in disguise, he might be planning a masquerade. Or did he only want to make me afraid of that, so that I would distrust Feuermann and others, wasting my strength in point-less suspicions? To make me turn my own ignorance and weaknesses against myself, to make me stumble from my own blindness, to make Angelo do the same – that would be Namir's way, and his pleasure. In intelligent life, human or Martian, maybe there has always been a genuine division between those who honor the individuality of others and those who are driven to control and pervert it. A shifting division, I admit, since some of us, confused, may have a foot in both camps at times, and some spirit-killers may reform, and some of the generous may be corrupted.

From the front page I deduced that the new government of Spain would join the United States of Europe before long. That could be of profound human importance contemplating Angelo's birch tree and the other paint-ing, the wounded tiger, which he had blandly given me. I read, too, about the projected satellite station. In 1952, said the article, it had been thought that ten years would do the job – ten years and some small change amounting to four billion dollars. It seems it will take a mite longer than that, and a billion or so more. Exhaustive tests simulating conditions of outer space had hinted at possible long-term damage to the human system, which early briefer experiments could not reveal. Nothing too serious. Candidates would have to be even more critically screened, that was all. Nineteen hundred and sixty-seven, maybe, or '68. We could have told them a little, from our ancient history, but I recognize the wisdom of our law: we must let them alone with their technological problems. It was all right to help some of the early tribes find the bow and arrow the way we did, but times have changed.

In the afternoon Feuermann came in to see me. He was visiting the ceme-tery again. Rain was still gray and whispering, and I spoke of it. He smiled at wet window glass. 'Sun's up beyond it somewhere.'

'Jacob' – we were on first-name basis now – 'do you know anything about this Digger-Mudhawk business? Hate to see Angelo mix into that.'

'Kid stuff, I guess. Hard to get him to talk about it.'

'Seems the Diggers include older boys, some of 'em tough.'

'So?' He was concerned, but not seriously. 'I figure a boy's pretty much a wild animal. They work it out of their systems. Not that I'd favor it for Angelo. But that Kell kid seems to be all right.'

I still wondered. 'Where does he live, do you know?'

'South Calumet Street neighborhood somewhere, the crumby section. I believe his parents are dead. Lives with a relative, guess it's an aunt.' Jacob had found my discarded newspaper, and was forgetting Billy Kell. 'Or some woman who adopted him, I don't know. They get sort of casual in the south end. He's in Angelo's class in school, supposed to be a good student, so I hear ... Hey, did you see this? Max is in jail again.'

'Max?' I recalled a front-page item. It was a New York City paper, with the usual random mass of political maneuvering, speeches, oddities, personali-ties, disasters. One Joseph Max had been arrested for causing a near riot with a handful of followers at a meeting addressed by some senator. There was a write-up on Max himself, but I had not followed its continuation on an inner page.

'An heir of Huey Long.' Feuermann was reading intently. 'Missed my paper this morning. Long, and Goat-gland Brinkley, and the Ku Klux, with a dash of communazi to flavor the brew ... Ach, they never die!'

'One of those? Don't think I've heard of Max before.'

'Maybe the Canada papers didn't bother with him. All he needs is a special-colored shirt. He turned up first in 1960, I think, with – now wha'd he call it? Crystal Christian League, some damn thing, made capital of the word "Christian". Christian like a snapping turtle. You know how the freak parties always emerge in a presidential year. Froth on the pond.'

'Yes, they thought Hitler and Lenin were froth, for a while.'

'Well, I tell you, it's the damn human way, not to look at what scares us. Max dropped out of sight for a couple years, started making headlines again a year ago. "Purity of the American race" it says here. We never learn.'

'That's Max's line?'

'Yeah, but it looks as though he'd chucked some of the fantastic stuff. He's formed something he calls the Unity Party. Claims a million of the faithful, nice round number. "Right will prevail!" says he on his way to the clink after busting a few heads. Hope they don't make a martyr of him – what he wants, naturally.'

(I believe it might be worth a fulltime Observer, Drozma, if one has not already been assigned.) 'You think he might become big-time?'

Feuermann sighed. His good engineer's hands knotted and relaxed in his lap. 'I sit around too much, Ben, and think too much. I'd give an awful lot to be out on the rails again; 509 and me, we were sort of friends' – he was shy about that – 'you understand? Active all my life, hard to get it through your head you're old. Maybe I imagine things. Sitting around … No, likely Max is just froth. Ought to be enough common sense in the country to sort of disinfect him before he gets a-going. Wouldn't you think, all the time we've had, troubles we've seen, we could do a little better, Ben? Use more love and less pride? Hang onto your own self but treat the other guy like he had one too? Do unto others … Care for a drive to Byfield?'

He was lonely, but I declined, blaming the rain. He left me, with a characteristic, openhearted smile on his face that I never saw again …

The rain ended in late afternoon. I found Angelo and Billy Kell on the front steps, lazy in the moist warmth. Probably the quality of their talk altered when I appeared and fussily spread a newspaper on the top step to sit on. It was my second face-to-face meeting with Billy. Angelo introduced us formally, and Billy gave no open sign of remembering me. He was polite, as a fourteen-year-old can readily learn to be. Ironically, I thought. He offered a skillful imitation of grown-up small talk – Canada, baseball, this and that. He had an unlimited fund of it, and I couldn't isolate any one part of it to call it mockery.

Sharon appeared on the other side of the street in what I believe was a new pink dress. She looked small and lonesome as well as starchy in the waning sunlight, studiously tossing her red rubber ball on its elastic string. Angelo called: 'Hey, kid! C'mon over!' She turned her back. Angelo poked Billy's ribs. 'One of her moods.'

'Deep bleep,' said Billy Kell. A teenage formula, I guess.

Having made her point, Sharon did approach. She marched up the steps with no recognition for the boys, and addressed me in brittle dignity: 'Good evening, Mr Miles. I wondered if I'd find you here.'

I gave her some of my newspaper to sit on. 'The steps are still damp, and that looks to me like a new dress.'

'Thank you, Mr Miles.' She accepted the paper with absent-minded queenliness. 'I am glad to know one's efforts are not wholly unappreciated.'

Angelo's ears turned flame color. I was in the cross fire and saw no way to get out of it. Billy Kell was enjoying it. Angelo mumbled: 'Time for some catch before supper – huh?'

'I oughta be on my way,' said Billy Kell.

'Mr Miles, have you ever noticed how some people are always persistently changing the subject?'

I attempted sternness: 'I might change it myself. How have the lessons been going this week, Sharon?'

That reached through her thin-drawn politeness. She talked of the lessons with pleasure and relief, not forgetting, of course, to use the conversation as a saw-toothed weapon, but nevertheless enjoying it. The lessons were terrific and getting terrificker all the time. Mrs Wilks was going to give her a real piece to memorize Monday. She could almost stretch an octave, Sharon said – anyhow by rolling it a little; it was true that her fine fingers were long in proportion to her size. Angelo suffered in silence, and in spite of his remark Billy Kell was lingering. At length Sharon ran down and began to repeat herself. Angelo turned, not smiling at all. 'Sharon, I'm sorry.' He put his hand on her shoe tip. 'Now tell me, what should I be sorry for, huh?'

She ignored her own foot, allowing it to remain where it was. She addressed an imaginary Mr Miles somewhere on the rooftops across the street: 'Mr Miles, have you any idea what this child is talking about?'

'Oh, bloop,' said Angelo, and Billy Kell guffawed. I sought myself for a change of subject, asking whether Mr Feuermann usually stayed in Byfield as late as this.

Angelo pulled his mind from the exasperations of the eternal feminine. I'm not entirely sure what Sharon was mad about that evening, besides his failure to notice the dress. I think it was Billy's mere presence when she wanted Angelo to herself: a grown-up jealousy in a ten-year-old frame that could hardly bear it. Angelo began to be puzzled about Feuermann too, and worried 'No, Ben – no, he doesn't.'

Billy murmured: 'Isn't that his car now?'

It was. The white-haired man waved as he drove around the corner, headed for a garage down Martin Street. Angelo was still having woman trouble when Feuermann returned on foot, swinging his door keys, smiling at the children, noticing me and nodding stiffly. Something was wrong with Jacob

Feuermann. He halted on the bottom step and said, apparently to Angelo: 'Nice out there in spite of the rain.' His voice was tense.

I needed to hear that voice again. I said as if idly: 'Doesn't seem to've cooled things off much.'

He would not look at me, and he spoke with a note of sober slyness not natural to the Feuermann I thought I knew: 'Doesn't ever get this hot in Canada, I guess?'

I thought then: Namir has met him. Namir has dropped a whisper, to make him think I am not what I seem. Of course. Namir would know all the uses of scandal and innuendo and half-truth. Strange weapons, so easy to take up, the stain indelible on user and victim. I had tried to foresee other methods of attack, and stupidly overlooked this one, so natural to any creature who believes that the end can justify the means. Now I would have to find out somehow what the whisper had made of me – Asiatic spy, anarchist, escaped criminal. It could be anything: the whole field was open, and when I traced down one lie to kill it, another would replace it. I said: 'Why, yes, sometimes it does. Not apt to be as damp as this, inland.'

'That so? You remember it pretty well?'

Angelo looked merely puzzled, Billy Kell blank. And Feuermann had parted with me in such a friendly way only a few hours before! 'Not very long since I was in Canada.'

'No? Your mother in, Angelo?' Not waiting for an answer, he went around to the basement entrance. To avoid passing near me.

6

The money came from Toronto the following day.

I acquired a pretty fair one-lunged '55 job with a cauliflower fender, and during the next two outwardly quiet weeks Angelo learned a little about the woods. Or perhaps a great deal, because there was no need to teach him how to listen. He met the living quiet of the woods with a wonderful receptive quiet of his own, and we didn't trouble much with words. Under the trees his normal boy's restlessness disappears: he can sit still, and wait, and watch, so rather than make any stuffy effort to teach him about what he saw, I kept quiet and let the earth speak for itself. We had four such expeditions, about thirty miles out of town into the piny foothills of the Berkshires – two full days and two afternoons. Since talk would have been intrusive, I can't say that it advanced my knowledge of him, but that doesn't matter: he was happy, and learning things with all five senses that Latimer could not show him. Rosa trusted me, and seemed glad to have him with me.

Not so Feuermann. On the evening of that rainy Sunday I visited his room. He was unwilling to face me, brusque to my small talk; he dreamed up an outside errand for himself to get rid of me. I didn't comment on the change – humanly speaking, I didn't know him well enough. But there was a false note in it. Reading this far unbiased, Drozma, you have probably seen the truth. I didn't, then. I only thought that if he suspected something ugly about me the Feuermann I had known would have investigated, or put his suspicion in open words. Sulky withdrawal wasn't properly in character.

It was nearly two weeks after that day when Rosa bared some of her worries to me. She was cleaning my room, on another muggy morning. Her color was poor, her breathing labored; when I urged her to rest, she took the armchair gratefully. 'Aie! – if I can ever get up again … Ben, when you were a boy, did you ever get into one of those, you know, kid gangs?'

I bypassed my own youth. 'I don't think Angelo will do that.'

'No? … You've been good for him. I appreciate it.' I remember thinking it strange that she was still friendly, if Namir was using the poison knives of whispers. 'Well, I almost married again, just on account he needs a father so bad. Wouldn't've worked, I can see now.' She mopped her kind face, round, sad, shining under the towel she used to guard her hair. 'He sure enough told you he wouldn't join up with Billy Kell's gang?'

'Well, no. But maybe the gang isn't so bad, Rosa.'

'It's bad. They get into fights, I don't know what all. And I *never* can figure out what's best for him. All I can do to add up a grocery bill. How'd I ever come to have such a boy? Here I'm common as mud—'

'Far from it.'

'You know I am,' she said, and not coquettishly. 'Well, Father Judd (he's dead now) he christened him Francis, that was Silvio's idea. For, you know, the blessed Francisco di Assisi, so that's really his name, Francis Angelo, the Francis never stuck. When he wasn't a year old yet he looked so – so – anyway I had to use the name *I* picked … Ben, would you sort of talk to him, about not joining that gang? You could say things that I – that I—'

'Don't worry. Sure, I'll talk to him about it.'

'If he joins maybe I won't even *know*.'

'He'd tell you.' Her face said bleakly that there was much he never told her. 'By the way, Rosa, is Mr Feuermann sore at me?'

'Sore?' She was astonished, then adding two and two in some private hurried way. 'Oh, it's the hot weather, Ben. He feels it bad. Hardly seen him myself all week.' She pushed herself upright and finished her work …

That afternoon I took out my car – Angelo and I had named it Andy after Andrew Jackson because it's always quarrelsome with body squeaks – and drove past EL CAT SEN when I knew Sharon would be on her way to a practice hour at the empty school. She accepted the lift with gracious calm. 'Seems to me you ought to have your own piano at home, Sharon.'

'Mom has headaches,' she said politely. 'And besides … It's a good piano at the school. Mrs Wilks told 'em they hadta. Mrs Wilks is terrific. I love her beyond comprehemption.'

'Like to meet her sometime.'

'She's blind. Looks at your face with her fingers, all kind of feathery. I memorized the first piece in two tries, no mistakes.'

'That is terrific.'

'I get terrific sometimes,' said Sharon, preoccupied.

At the school we were admitted by the janitor, a dim-eyed ancient who took my word for it that I was a friend and shuffled off into his forest of cold steampipes: no protection there. The piano was in the assembly hall – too big a place, too empty, but in a yard under the windows teenage basketball practice was going on, and I noticed two young women working in an office we passed. I shoved aside the worried parent in me, and paid attention to a half-expected miracle.

Not music, naturally: beginner's stuff, the five-finger, the scale of C major, a kindergarten melody with plimp-plump of tonic and dominant in the left. That didn't matter. Touch was there, and a hunger for discipline and self-discipline. Left hand and right were already partners, after a scant fortnight of lessons. Yes, touch. Call it impossible: I heard it.

I tiptoed down into the auditorium and slumped in a seat with my mouth open. A shaft of sunlight was making her brown hair luminous in a haze of gold. Certainly she was the Sharon of Amagoya, of the red rubber ball on a string, but I could see the woman too. I saw her as beautiful, even if she retained the pug nose – likely she wouldn't. The gown for her debut ought to be white, I thought, and she would not be really tall, but would seem so, alone under the lights, a massive black Steinway obedient to her. It was real to me. For her, there should be that transitory dazzling of crowds they call fame; there should be the greater achievement to which contemporary fame is a thin echo. But even if the end was in black frustration, Sharon was a musician and could never escape it. I would have to meet blind Mrs Wilks: we could talk.

I ought to have heard the soft opening of the door at the back of the hall, but I was intent on Sharon, and on shutting out the basketball squeals, until I caught faint motion at the edge of my field of vision. I was slouching in shadow; he must have been unaware of me until I jerked up to look around. Then he was retreating quickly, face averted, head low. Even with a glimpse of yellow hair I could not be certain it was Billy Kell. The door clipped shut gently. He was gone.

I could try to dismiss it. Some boy wandering in, not knowing the assembly hall was in use. Some harmless playmate of Sharon's who became shy at seeing an adult. But the hurried retreat had been furtive, ratlike. I felt that coldness in the throat – the human equivalent is what they call goose flesh.

From one of the windows I studied the basketball crowd. I didn't see Billy, and he didn't rejoin the handful of spectators down there. But that meant nothing.

A glance at my wrist watch amazed me. Sharon had been working a full hour. Perhaps I was partly in Martian contemplation but I don't think so. I think it had been a one-way communication, her toiling fingers holding me, compelling my mind to share the effort, the promise, the small but mighty victories. She had stopped now, and was observing me out of her sunshine. 'Heck, do you play?'

'Some, honey. Want to rest?' She gave me her seat, and I did as well as I could. For a school piano it wasn't bad, though it hardly reminded me of the three Steinways we so painfully brought and reassembled for Northern City a few decades ago. It was more like an elderly Bechstein I once played in Old City. They like things mellow in Old City, and the voicing of this school piano was over-mellow, the bass tubby and disagreeable. But it would serve. I played as much as I could cleanly remember of the Schumann 'Carnaval'. Sharon had no objections, but asked for Beethoven. I suggested 'Für Elise'.

'No. Mrs Wilks' played me that. Something bigger.'

Heaven forgive my stupid fifth fingers, I played the 'Waldstein'. I may have hoped (in vain) that by associating the sonata with Sharon I could displace a deep memory. Drozma, perhaps you recall my tour of the Five Cities in 30,894? For me the 'Waldstein' must always create again the auditorium in City of Oceans, its windows dreaming into the heart of the sea, windows fashioned with such effort, so long ago – they told me there that some of the builders' names were lost. It is hardly strange that our people in City of Oceans were always a little different from the rest of us. When I played there that year, honestly I believe I approached the level of the modern human masters, and if so, the reason was in City of Oceans itself, not in any new virtue of my hands or heart. The long motion of the seaweed beyond those windows, always and never the same, the flicker and change and passing and returning of the fishes in scarlet and blue and green and gold – I see that now, and cannot help it. And of course everyone there was more than kind to me. They listened from within the music, and treated me as though they had wanted my visit for a century. It was later, as you know, that the study of human history became my necessity. The necessity is genuine and enduring; but the reason why I shall never make another tour is that I would remember City of Oceans too much. Drozma, what hideous blindness of chance, that our far-off ancestors should have chosen an island so near Bikini! Well, at least it was ours for twenty thousand years, and we must be glad there was warning enough so that some of our people could escape. And there may be another City of Oceans in some century after Union is achieved ...

Sharon was a nearby buzz, suggesting: 'Now some Chopin?'

'Oh, darling, I'm tired. And out of practice. Some other time.'

'By the way, I love you beyond comprehemption.'

And that really broke up the meeting so far as I was concerned, though I was able to bumble something or other from behind the facade of Mr Miles. She was tired too and we adjourned.

The door had been opened again, harmlessly, by those office workers who wanted to hear my thunderings. I was suitably flattered. Sharon went on out to the car while I had a word with them. I spoke of someone sneaking in while Sharon practiced and hurrying out at seeing me. I suggested the hall was too lonely. Probably just another kid, but – etc. One of the girls wanted to practice sweet eyes on a real live pianist, but the other caught on, and promised me that henceforth the janitor would find a way to keep busy in the corridor during the practice hour. The bothered parent in me was soothed.

Partly. Until, after letting Sharon off at EL CAT SEN, I saw a familiar blond head down the street, not hurrying exactly. I crawled a block in the car, and parked when I was out of Sharon's sight. Then I followed Billy Kell on foot. Mainly, I told myself, to find out how much I remembered of the difficult art of shadowing. Oh sure.

Small streets branch off from the southern end of Calumet, twisting like cowpaths. The houses are mostly detached, old frame buildings stooping from neglect. The district may have been better before so many families moved to the country, abandoning what had never been much loved. There were still children, cats, dogs, pushcarts, a few drunks, but these scarcely lightened the burden of desertion and loneliness. In spite of the still clustering life there was the smell of desolation. Boarded windows, or unboarded windows broken and gaping like missing teeth in an abused face. Litter. Broken glass and grayness. A rat watched me with pert lack of fear before oozing through a crack in a foundation wall. Human beings have never been very adult about cleaning up after themselves. A panhandler put the bite on me for a dime and got it. That was on the side street that Billy Kell had taken, turning off Calumet, and when I was rid of the beggar I saw Billy cross that street rather abruptly, a block ahead of me.

Half a block beyond Billy there was a junk-wagon horse hitched at the curb – ribby, scabby, drooping in the heat. Automatically I crossed the street myself to avoid walking near him, although my scent-destroyer was fairly fresh. It ought to have occurred to me then, to wonder why Billy Kell had done the same thing; perhaps I may be excused, for without scent-destroyer no Martian could have passed in that narrow street without scaring the poor old plug into a tantrum. Even as it was, with my scent suppressed, the horse tossed his head when I passed and cleared his velvet nostrils in discomfort.

Farther on Billy Kell stopped to chat with a group of ten or twelve young-sters who were lounging against the fence of a discouraged-looking churchyard, perhaps waiting for him: he had the air of a leader or counselor. I found a handy empty doorway. They were giving Billy the flattery of shrewd attention, admiring stares, laughter at his jokes. Boys and girls both wore that cocky tam-o'-shanter which seems to have replaced the zoot suit as a teenage badge. The voices were squeaky and vague and loud, using a gabbling argot of transposed syllables and made-up words – I could not follow much of it. When Billy left them I saw again that motion of turned wrist and raised palm …

He took several turnings in those patternless streets and at length entered a frowzy two-story shack, but just before that I learned what I should have understood earlier. I was half a block behind him, strolling, my hatbrim lowered. As he mounted the shabby steps a breeze lifted and dropped a scrap of wastepaper near me. I barely noticed the slight sound; but Billy, half a block away, heard it. His head snapped about with the speed of an owl's. A swift stare identified the source of the noise and swept over me, whether with recognition or not I couldn't tell. He passed indoors, unconcerned.

I have seen human beings with muscular responses as rapid as ours – Angelo's are extremely rapid at times. I never knew one whose hearing approached our Martian acuteness. I had to remember then: Namir has a son. As I write this, I still have no definitive proof. He could have turned his head for some other reason; his avoidance of the horse could have been acci-dental, or caused by a human aversion for the animals. But I think I am right: other Observers ought to be warned.

There was no good place for me to hide and linger, nor any reason why Mr Ben Miles shouldn't wander in this sorry region if he chose. I walked past the house, as a storm of squalling abuse broke out in there. A woman's mono-logue, so blurry with drink that I caught only a few words: 'No-good jerk' – a gust of whining profanity – 'try 'n' be a mother to you, what's the use – get out! Don't *bother* me! I ain't well …'

I glanced back in time to see Billy come back out, after the smash of a bot-tle splintering on wood. He ambled around a corner without haste. On impulse I returned. I pounded on the door until I heard dreary cursing and a shuffle of slippers. I said: 'Fire Department survey.'

'Yah?' She blocked the doorway with beefy arms. She was blinking, red-eyed, vague, not really old – fifties perhaps – and not badly dressed. Hostility in her face dissolved in a silly simper, and her breath was fearsome. Over her shoulder I saw a dingy front room filled with dressmaker's gear. She was cer-tainly human – after all, a Salvayan practically can't get drunk. I think that sober she might have been quite different, perhaps grimly respectable and hard-working – the dressmaking equipment looked professional. The drink would be an addiction, an escape from smothering hardship and frustrations, and the years of it had beaten her down like a disease, leaving her frightened, peevish, isolated, old: so much was written on her face in coarse print. The bottle (empty) had crashed against the doorframe, scattering shards everywhere; I guessed that Billy would have been safely clear of it before she let it go. 'Had lil accident,' she chuckled. 'It's the hot weather, I ain't well exactly.' She struggled with a wandering strand of gray-brown hair. 'And what have I the honor do f'you, mister?'

'Routine survey, ma'am. How many live here?'

She lurched away from the door. 'Me and the boy is all.'

'Oh – just you and your son, ma'am?'

' 'Dopted – that be any damn business yours? I pay taxes, no offense of course, 'm sure.'

'Just routine. May I look over the wiring?'

She waved and patted her lips. 'Anybody stopping you?'

I left her making futile passes at the broken glass, and took a swift trip through the house, unopposed. There were only two rooms upstairs, the neat one obviously Billy's; sorry and rather ashamed, I did not linger in the other bedroom. Billy's room told me nothing, unless the very absence of boy's trinkets meant something. A military-looking cot, a pile of schoolbooks noticeably unmarked, though Feuermann and Angelo had said he was supposed to be a good student. If there was any Martian scent it was so faint I could not separate it from my own; but the absence of it would not be negative proof, for Namir had stolen enough destroyer to take care of two users for a long time. At any rate Billy could not be Namir himself, since even the Abdicator's skill in disguise could not make him convincingly square-bodied and a foot shorter.

The woman was painfully apologizing as I left. Hot weather, she said. She'd offer me a lil drink only there wasn't a thing in the house, though ordinarily she liked to keep some on hand for her digestion, so's the food wouldn't all the time rift up on her. We parted friends.

If I am right about Billy Kell, I suppose he talked and charmed his way into some makeshift unofficial relation with this woman, playing on her loneliness and thwarted maternity, to give himself a temporary name and a screen of human association. In calling him 'adopted' her manner had displayed truculent fear of authority. Legal adoption, I believe, is hedged about with formalities that neither he nor she could have satisfied. When her usefulness to him is ended, no doubt Billy Kell will vanish – without conscience or pity or any debt of loyalty if he is the son of Namir.

7

Back at the lodging house, I wanted to make good on my promise to talk with Angelo. More reason than ever now, after seeing the human background of Billy Kell. But there were difficulties in any direct approach.

Angelo was fond of me, I felt sure. He listened if I spoke. The interludes in the woods were a delight for him: he wanted to say so, and managed to do it, with an adult's command of words and a boy's shyness. I had bought books for him, and drawn others from the library. He was very handsome with his thanks for that too. (One was *Huck Finn*, which he had disgracefully never read.) Somehow we got into no really satisfying discussion of those books. He wallowed in Mark Twain and Melville; I knew he was startled by Dostoevski, and amused by the thin wind of fallacy that blew through the unsanitary beard of Marx. But there were reservations: whole regions of his thought and feeling blocked off by invisible signs: NO TRESPASSING. He didn't seek me out in unhappy moments, though I knew he had many. So – grandfatherly advice against joining the gang, such as Feuermann might already have given him? The gentle barrier of Angelo's humor made that absurd. Stern advice then? When actually I go in fear of his sleepy smile? If he were Martian I might have known what to do. I notice men themselves have never invented a god capable of understanding them.

I slouched tired in the warm hallway, still seeing the bloated, vulnerable face of Billy Kell's 'adopted mother', presently hearing Feuermann's voice behind the closed door of his room. Its meaning reached me slowly. 'Any experience is useful. Maybe the Mudhawks are tough – can you get anywhere in this world without toughness? You have to fight back. Can't afford not to, with your intelligence. People hate intelligence, didn't you know?'

'Depends on what it does to 'em, doesn't it?'

'Not so much, Angelo. Dream up a new gadget, they'll be grateful for a while,' said Feuermann's voice. 'It'll be only the gadget they love, not the brain that made it – that they fear. They may have enough superstitious dread to worship it – devil-worship – but never will they respect it except superstitiously. I haven't talked to you this way before because I wasn't sure you could take it. But I guess you can.' I heard a thing like Feuermann's kindly, wheezy laugh. 'Of course, the superstitious awe of your brains that people will have – that can be used.'

'How d'you mean?'

'Oh, that'll take care of itself.' I heard an old man's sigh. 'Anyway, remember it's gadgets they want. Gadgets, simple ideas that seem to explain but leave basic prejudices untouched. They'll pay a price if the gadget or idea is shiny enough. I know 'em, Angelo.' It just wasn't Feuermann. Feuermann wouldn't have spoken disparagingly of gadgets. In his sober way he was as much a gadget-lover as any other American of the '960s. Hadn't most of his life been spent in service of a mighty gadget that altered the face of the earth? 'No, you have to fight all the way, all the time, with any weapon you can grab. I'm old, son. I know.'

'Oh,' said Angelo lightly, 'I can battle my way out of a damp paper bag. But if you don't go for fighting for the sake of fighting—'

'Then you lose. Sometimes you must even do evil – oh, so that good may come of it, but it's all tooth and claw, devil take the hindmost.'

So I began to know, Drozma, that Jacob Feuermann was dead.

I knocked and entered. Hardly prepared at all, driven to intervene as some human beings are, when they sense danger to those they love. I recaptured Mr Miles in time to close the door peacefully and light a cigarette. It was only Mr Miles whom Angelo saw from his lazy perch on the window seat. I did not care what was seen by that other in the room.

He was in the armchair with his feet on the hassock which Feuermann had worn threadbare. He was even smoking the horsehead meerschaum. That added illogically to my wrath: I may have made one of those human identifications with the inanimate which we are warned to avoid. 'Hope I'm not intruding,' I said as I intruded. 'Had a hankering for the consolations of philosophy.' I couldn't have cared less about philosophy. 'Throw me out if the spirit moves.' I straddled a chair near the window. He would have had to throw chair and all, and he couldn't have done it. It was at least some comfort to have no physical fear. 'That's a beautiful meerschaum, by the way. You must be a fancier of horseflesh, is that a fact?'

I saw his eyes. When a human being is startled, the pupils may dilate, never the whole iris; I believe the entire structure of the eyeball is subtly different. My last doubt was gone. He said careless-carefully: 'Oh yes, in a way ... Philosophy, huh?'

'Ah, philosophy!' Angelo chirped. 'Here's where we dish it out, Ben. Step right up, ladies and gentlemen, and state your problems in words of less than one syllable. Feuermann and Pontevecchio, brought here at enormous expense, will solve it in the merest flick of a hysteron proteron: they walk, they talk, they crawl upon their bellies like a rep-tyle. For a nominal fee, they look into the past, the future, even the present, your money back if not satisfied. Why, ladies and gentlemen, it was these seers, these incomparable counselors of the unseen world' – he was warming to it, and as friendly as a puppy chewing my shoe – 'who recently unscrewed one of the most inscrutable riddles of suffering humanity, namely, who put the overalls in Mrs Murphy's chowder.'

I asked him who did.

'Divil a soul,' said Angelo. 'They fell in when she lost her temper, and Mr Murphy entirely in them at the time.'

The image of Feuermann didn't speak or smile. I said: 'Try the future, Prophet. Andy's got valve trouble, or maybe it's the carburetor. So, how long before petroleum gets so scarce we go back to – horses?' Under my breath I added the Salvayan word for 'horses,' so seldom used among us and always with the jar of indecency. It is onomatopoetic enough so that to Angelo it must have sounded like throat clearing. Namir's Feuermann-face remained frozen in calm.

I cannot evade blame for that stupid error, Drozma. I might well have hidden the fact that I recognized him. I tossed away that clear advantage because of an anger for which no Observer can be excused.

'Now that's a very good question,' said Angelo, and fingered an imaginary beard at his round chin. 'I would say, sir, that the extrapolated eventuality will eventuate in the due course of events, not before.' I tried to listen to his nonsense, knowing that somewhere a warmhearted, harmless old man must be lying dead – hidden; buried, I supposed – solely because his death was useful to one who hated his breed. I wondered if Namir still possessed the dissolution-grenade he must have had when he resigned so long ago. Even the old style is quiet enough, and I know of no reason why it wouldn't disintegrate a human body as easily as one of ours. If Namir had used that, human law would never catch up with him. And it must not, as I knew. What had seemed almost funny at the time of the burglary was so no longer. Americans are not casual with prisoners, who must submit to physical examinations and are autopsied after execution, I believe. Human criminals occasionally obliterate their fingerprints by surgery. From where I sat I could see that Namir had not done so: his fingers were, Martianly speaking, normal; that alone would start a blaze of curiosity, the moment our unlooped angular ridges appeared on a police record. And if he were cornered – Drozma, I cannot share your feeling that he would be deeply inhibited against betraying us.

He has become like a creature of no race, a law to himself, past reach of reason, loyalty, or compassion. What other sort of being could have gone through with the murder of Feuermann? (At the time I write this I have proof. I had none that afternoon, but a sickening certainty took the place of it, and proof, when I did find it, was only a bloody period to a sentence already written.)

I tried again to listen to Angelo, who was bubbling merrily along like a little fountain in the sun: '– and this invention, this crowning triumph of the Feuermann-Pontevecchio genius, is a simple, simple thing. Allow me to sketch the reasoning which led to the blinding consummation. Earthworms love onions. They are alliotropic, a term derived (as every schoolboy knows) from *Allium*, the botanical genus embracing the common or garden onion. Alliotropic – five dollars, please. We propose therefore to design light carts – ain't flat-out done it yet on account we ain't got the capital – for hitching to the rears of a calculated sufficiency of earthworms *(Lumbricus terrestris)*. An onion will be supported on a pole in advance of the worms, which crawl in pursuit of it, applying traction to the car. In the event of a halt one need only jump from the cart (assuming it is not moving at excessive speed), dig a hole in the ground, lower the onion into it. The worms will then go underground after it, but their harness will be so contrived that they can never reach it, thus obviating any replacement of the onion – but of course a good team of worms must be properly fed and cared for at all times. And whereas their strength will be insufficient to pull the cart underground, their efforts to do so will provide a gentle braking action and the cart will eventually come to rest. Why be old-fashioned? Why wear yourself out with uneconomical, unreliable, dangerous horses? Why suffer from horsemaid's knee, when a trip to your nearest dealer will put you in possession of the streamlined, fur-lined, underlined, air-conditioned, trouble-free Feuermann-Pontevecchio wormobile?'

'Have you incorporated?'

'Not yet, Ben. We could let you in on the ground floor with a very nice proposition – and where've you been all day?'

'Listened in on Sharon's piano practice. She has talent, Angelo.'

'So?' Sharon had been nowhere in his thoughts. 'Can you tell?'

'The way she goes at it. The touch. She seems – dedicated. There aren't so many things that call for that. The arts, the sciences. Politics, though not by the man in the street's definition. Religion – again only if you have an intelligible definition of it.' Namir-Feuermann was deep in abstraction, the pipe gone out. 'The study of ethics.'

'Dedication to the study of ethics,' said the old man's voice. 'Sounds like a formula for the care and feeding of prigs.'

'Why?' said the boy.

Namir faked a cough, and in the breathy noise I heard a whispered Salvayan word, the one best translated by the more polite English 'Get out!' Then the image of Feuermann was smiling in kindly deprecation. 'You're not far enough along, Angelo. Wouldn't beat my brains too much if I were you. Likely to make yourself introverted.' Namir was making a mistake there, and I could rejoice at it, seeing Angelo's face veil itself in the resigned quiet that said: *'Okay, sonny, I'm twelve.'* 'Get around more, Angelo. Enlarge experience. As I was saying a while ago, everything is struggle. You'll need to be out there in the middle of it more and more, not locked up in an ivory tower.' Well, the old railroad engineer had probably been familiar with that phrase. I decided that Angelo was not bothered by the change in him because conversation with the real Feuermann had probably never been very penetrating. The real Feuermann had offered undemanding affection and tolerance, but could hardly have treated Angelo as a mental adult. Now the old man's attitude would seem to Angelo to be only a grown-up shift of mood. The physical disguise was perfect of course: trust Namir for that. He had even reproduced a tiny white scar at the hairline which few human eyes would ever have noticed.

I asked Angelo: 'Would you say Beethoven was fighting anybody when he wrote the "Waldstein"?'

'Not prezactly.' Angelo was off his perch. 'Grocery errand – the mighty brain just remembered.' I got up too, nodding politely to the one I intended to kill.

I justify this intention by the law of 27,140 – 'harm to our people or to humanity'. I needed only proof of Feuermann's death, then I could act. I would find a means to draw Namir away from human surroundings, and would use the extra grenade Supply gave me. Afterward I would sleep well. So I thought I allowed myself no backward look as I closed the door and caught up with Angelo, expecting to find him still full of fun and unworried.

He wasn't. He had started downstairs but came back before I spoke, and glanced at my door uneasily. 'Could I stop in a minute?'

'Sure. What's cooking, friend?'

'Oh, just ham and eggs.' But there wasn't any laughter in him. He fidgeted around my room. In a comic way he had, he pulled down his upper lip with thumb and finger and pushed it from side to side. 'I dunno ... Maybe everybody feels like two people, sometimes.'

'Sure. Two or more. Many selves in all of us.'

'But' – he looked up, and I saw he was genuinely frightened – 'but it shouldn't be – sharp. Should it, Ben? I mean – well, there in Uncle Jacob's room, it was like –' He fussed with trifles on my bureau, to hide his face maybe; added miserably: 'Wasn't any errand at the store. I just wanted out ... I mean, Ben, there's a me that likes it here – everything: living here, Sharon, Bill, the other kids, even school. And – well, especially the woods, and – oh, talking with you, and stuff ...'

'And the other one would like ...?'

'Chuck everything,' he whispered. 'Just every damn thing and start fresh. In there, in that room, I was like – like cut down the middle. But that's whacky, isn't it? It doesn't make any sense. I don't really want to go anywhere else. If I could ...'

'I think it'll pass,' I said, finding no better words than these weak ones that could hardly help him.

'Oh, I guess.' He started to go.

'Wait a minute.' I took the wrapped mirror from the back of a bureau drawer. 'Something you might like to look at. I brought it from Canada. When I taught history, Angelo, it was ancient history mostly. This thing was given me by a friend who knows his archaeology, who –' Drozma, I think I had been afraid of that mirror. That may be why I had never unwrapped it until this poorly chosen moment. Is it a product of accident or a lost art? Some subtle distortion in the bronze that compels many truths to cry aloud? I saw the young Elmis, the almost-good musician, the scatterbrained youth whom you taught so patiently, the persistent student of history, the absent-minded lover and husband, the clumsy Observer, the inadequate father. How can this be, in a poor frail artifact of the long-dead Minoan world? At other shifts of the mirror – oh, let that escape words. It is one thing to know, with the mind only, that one will be old, that one has different faces for victory, shame, death, hope, defeat; another thing to watch it brilliant in the bronze. I was lost there, seeking for what I was once at City of Oceans, when I heard Angelo say: 'What's the matter?'

'No, nothing.' I did not want to show it to him now, but it was passing from my silly fumbling fingers into his innocent brown ones, and I went on talking somehow: 'It's Minoan – anyway, came from Crete, likely made before Homer lived. You see, the patina's been kept away – I mean, taken away, polished off, so it's still a mirror as it was—'

He wasn't hearing me. I saw him shaking, his face crumpled and twisted as if in nightmare. 'Here, let me take the damn thing – I hadn't looked in it before, myself. I didn't know, Angelo. But it's nothing to be afraid of—'

He twitched it away when I would have taken it, forced to stare in spite of himself. 'Cheepus, what a –' He started laughing, and that was worse. I took it out of his hands then and flung it on the bureau.

'I ought to be kicked. But, Angelo, I didn't know—'

He pulled away from my hand. 'Look out – I'll prob'ly erp.' He ran for the stairs. When I followed, he glanced back up out of the well of darkness and said: 'It's all right, Ben. I get whacky, that's all. Forget it, will you?'

Forget it?

8

That night I could neither sleep nor enter contemplation. I heard humanlike sounds from my enemy next door. If Namir had gone out I would have followed him. If the grenade's disintegration were complete, I might have destroyed him that night, in his room. But there would have been some noise, even if I caught him asleep. There would have been the stains, the purple glare, the reek of gases, handfuls of rubbish to clear away.

I did not go to bed but sat dressed near my window, and was rewarded by a moonrise I could not enjoy. At midnight a copter-bus thundered, the last until six in the morning. Smaller human sounds persisted: late footsteps, a girl laughing behind a curtained window, a few cars whispering by on Calumet Street but none on Martin, which ends blindly at a lumberyard three blocks east. A baby fretted till someone hushed him. Past one o'clock I heard the Chicago-Vienna jet liner, far and high and lonely.

The opening of the door in the backyard fence was a ghost of noise. The moon had climbed; no light touched my face. It was near two in the morning. I watched him slip in, fog-footed, pale-haired, dangerous. He had to pass through moonlight, then scratched on the kitchen screen delicately as an insect's wing. He was aware of my open windows, but I was in darkness.

Angelo came out. They did not talk. They faded across the yard, Angelo moving in spite of his lameness as softly as Billy Kell.

I let them gain some distance down Martin Street, then eased the screen out of a window and jumped. Only fifteen feet, but I had to be cautious of sound. They did not look back. I found moon shadow, and they were stealthy in that shadow too, gliding toward the lumberyard like embodiments of a mist that was making dampness on the walks, aureoles around the street lamps. From my window I had hardly noticed the mist. Now I breathed it. It was all around me, wandering, melancholy, less bewildering than the cloud in my mind. Earth can weep too, my planet Earth.

As I sneaked into the lumberyard after them I heard the suppressed muttering of a dozen voices, most of them treble, a few mature like Billy Kell's. A tall stack of two-by-eights loomed black in front of me, and I knew the gang was on the other side of it. With luck I could climb that stack in silence and look down. The voices became individual. I heard Billy Kell's: 'You passed all the other tests, you won't fluff this one.' And some small excited whiny voice encouraged: 'He's nothing but a damn dirty Digger, Angelo.' A shuffling of feet lent me a covering noise. I mounted the stack and wormed across it to peep over.

A thin lad was tied by the waist to a timber of the next stack. His hands were bound behind him, his shirt hung in rags over the cord at his middle, his face and chest were begrimed. He was the only one facing me. His head drooped forward; even if he looked up he might not see the blot of my head against the greater dark. He was cursing mechanically, sounding rugged, contemptuous, and not in pain. I supposed I could jump down if I had to and break it up in time to prevent major disaster. Meanwhile I had to try to understand.

Billy Kell was embracing Angelo's shoulder, urgent and coaxing. He drew

Angelo away from the others and near to my hiding place. The cricket-voices of the other boys ceased to exist for me. 'Angelo, 'tisn't as if we were going to do him any real harm, see?' Billy Kell's whisper was smooth and soft. I could watch him smile. 'Look –' and he was showing Angelo a knife, turning it to catch the wan light, which gave me Angelo's face too, a dim battlefield of terror and excitement, fascination and revulsion. 'Just a five-and-dime gimmick,' said Billy Kell. 'It's plastic. Look.' He jabbed the knife at his own palm, so realistically that I winced before I saw the blade curl harmlessly at the tip.

'Just scare the pants off him, that it?'

'Sure, Angelo, you get it. Poke it to him without touching, see, and then a jab – oh, at the shoulder or somewheres. But listen: the other guys think you think it's a real knife, see? I'm giving you a break because, hell, you're my friend, I know how you feel. You couldn't use a shiv. I understand, see, but they don't. So put on an act for us, huh?'

'I get it. And that other thing you told me about him—'

'Oh, that was real. He did the burglary all right. We been giving him the works. He squealed. He sang, fella. He did it on a dare from the Diggers, had to take something from each room, only he went chicken about the money, just took a little and then grabbed the pictures and stuff instead – chicken. He was supposed to keep away from your apartment too. Know why? To make it look like you'd stolen from the tenants.'

'Oh hell, *no!*'

'Fact, kid. And he killed the pup. We made him sing, I'm telling you. He chunked her a bit of hamburg and busted her neck ...'

'Mr Miles didn't lose anything, and that was the room—'

'May say he didn't. Listen, Angelo: one of these days I'll tell you a couple-three things about your Mr Miles.'

'What d'you mean? Miles is a good guy.'

For this relief much thanks ...

'Think so? Never mind – later sometime, kid. Here, take this.' And Angelo reached for the knife. There was fumbling. Billy dropped it, and stooped, searching in the dark. Then they were moving away from me, and Angelo had the knife in his hand, and the others crowded close to watch, a rabble of goblins in a confusion of troubled night. So I blundered again, Drozma. I ought to have guessed.

Angelo's voice was thin now, thin to the cracking point: 'You killed my dog? You killed my dog, you dirty Digger?'

The thin boy spat at Angelo's foot without answering. But his nerve was crumpling, and he whimpered, watching the blade. He cringed as Angelo's little hand lashed out with it. But he was not the one who screamed when that knife bit flesh – I saw it – and blood jumped from the bony shoulder to splash Angelo's fingers. It was Angelo who screamed. Screamed and flung the knife away; ripped a handkerchief from his hip pocket and tried to stop the blood before the others had done more than gasp and giggle. 'Damn you, Billy – damn you—'

'Shut up, kid – what's a little blood?' Billy shoved Angelo away. Swiftly and competently, Billy untied the thin boy, motioned two others to hold him, and wiped the wound to examine it. 'A scratch,' said Billy, and that was true, in a way. The wounded one was Angelo.

I saw Angelo nauseated and shivering. His stained hand made abortive motions toward his mouth, and dropped. Dreamily he groped for the handkerchief Billy had discarded, and made feeble efforts to clean his fingers with it, and threw it down, and retched.

Billy twitched the captive around and kicked him. 'You ain't hurt. Now run, Digger, run! Run and tell your drips we've burned the wax.'

The thin boy reeled away from him, clutching a fragment of his shirt against the cut 'You wha-at?'

Billy chuckled. 'We burned the wax. We'll meet your guys any time.'

The thin boy ran. The goblins snickered. Billy Kell grabbed Angelo's wrist and held it up. 'A full member of the Mudhawks! And is *he* all right?'

'He's all right,' they said. A spooks' chorus.

'Listen, studs, you know what? He switched knives when he guessed the other was a phony. He didn't wanta, but he did, because he knew it was right. Now there's a *real* Mudhawk. *I* knew it, when he put his blood on the stone for the first test.'

They swarmed around then, with hugging and jittery laughter and naive obscenities and praise for Angelo, who took it all with a sick smile, with submerging shame and hidden contempt and swelling pride, with unwilling acceptance, as if now he were making himself believe Billy's lie. Because the lie was good politics? I couldn't know. 'Well,' said Angelo, 'well, he killed my dog, didn't he? Cheepus …'

Fog was swallowing Billy Kell's covine one by one, with turned wrist and raised palm. Too deep a fog: I can't pretend to understand these children. I wish I were old enough to remember four or five hundred years ago.

There is a lost quality, a vagueness in them, which I did not find in the gangs that I studied a little when I was in the States seventeen years back. The gangs of that day were, on the surface, much more vicious and noisy and difficult, motivated more by wordless resentment of the grown-up world and by obvious material hungers – sex and money and thrills. These waifs (in a sense, they are all orphans) have reverted to more primitive fantasies. Their witchcraft – in some modern dress and slanguage but still witchcraft – suggests that the mental and moral desertion by their elders has progressed to the stage of genuine indifference. It may or may not be due to the decay of the cities. South Calumet Street is a backward eddy in the stream, and I might find matters very different in the suburbs or the countryside – I don't know. But it is hardly strange that this desertion, this adult delinquency, should occur, in a culture which has not yet learned to replace the antique religious imperatives with something better.

It is transition – I think. The force of the ancient piety was lost in what they call the nineteenth century, and millions of them, in the hasty human fashion, tossed out the baby with the bath. Such concepts as discipline, responsibility, and honor were discarded along with the discredited dogmas. With the prop of Jehovah removed, they still don't want to learn how to stand on their own feet; but I believe they will, I see twentieth-century man as a rather nice fellow with weak legs, and a head in bad condition from banging against a stone wall. Perhaps fairly soon he will cut that out, get sense, and go on about his human business, relying on the godlike in himself and in his brother.

Billy and Angelo were the last to leave. I followed them back to No. 21. Before Angelo went in I saw him bend his wrist and raise his palm, a full member of the Mudhawks. I dreaded for him the pain that would assume shapes of unclean horror in his dreams, if he could sleep. I shadowed Billy Kell down Calumet Street. When he was a block beyond EL CAT SEN I overtook him and swung him around. I spoke in Salvayan: 'Son of a murderer, are you proud?'

He watched me with a baby-face human stare, undismayed, then permitting a human fear to show. Naturally or by calculation? He stammered in English: 'Mr Miles, what the hell, you sick or drunk or something?'

I said wearily in English: 'You understood me.'

'Understood? Thought you was choking. You taking H on the main line or something? Get your hands offa me!'

I had grabbed his shirt. I knew my intention. I intended to rip his shirt away, and though that fog-blind moonlight would not have been strong enough to show me the tiny scent glands on his lower chest (if they were there) I could have ground my hand across them and smelled my hand. He knew it. Or else he was human, terrified in a human way. 'Where did your father find surgery for you? The Abdicator Ronsa had the art – is *he* still living, for his sins? Answer me!'

He wrenched his shirt free – he was strong – and stumbled back from me. 'You cut that out! Let me alone!'

But I went on, in Salvayan, quite slowly and plainly: 'By tomorrow night I shall have proof of what your father did. Finished, child. He'll have to die, I think, and I know that you will be taken – by other Observers if not by me – for judgment and help to the hospital in Old City—'

'Goda'mighty, you're *really* high! Want me to call copper? I will if I got to. I'll yell, mister.'

And he would have. (But would a human hoodlum have made that particular threat? To a menacing adult, yes, maybe.) He could have roused the neighborhood and brought police on the double. Then I would have been an ugly, outsize, not very well dressed man, accused of roughing up a defenseless boy. Rather, before that could happen, before the prowl car was abreast of me, I would have had to pull the key on my grenade. There would have been the brief purple flare, the heap of trash on the sidewalk, the nine days' wonder in Latimer – my mission over, Angelo deserted, undefended against those who seemed to be his friends. I snarled in English: 'Oh, go to hell!' I walked back up the street as swiftly as I decently could.

When I was passing EL CAT SEN, and heard a whispered 'Hey!' above me, I had to glance back and make sure that Billy Kell had gone, before I dared look up to the pale flower that was Sharon's face in a second-floor window. 'Hello, honey – too hot to sleep?'

'Yeah, heck.' I could see her arms on the sill, and darker flowers that would be her eyes. 'The moon was all smoky round the rim, Ben. Well, I might come on down the rainspout, but frankly I haven't got anything on, frankly.'

'Some other time.'

'Were you chasing Billy?'

'Was that Billy? I didn't notice. No, just out for a breath of air. Maybe you'd better go back to sleep in time to wake up.'

'Think I better? By the way, I drew a keyboard on my bed table, only I couldn't fix anything to make the black keys stand higher.'

'I'm going to figure out something better than that.'

'Huh?' It was the blank puzzlement of a child not accustomed to expecting much unqualified good from anyone. Having met her peevish little father, I wondered how even the money for the lessons had been forthcoming. Some probably transitory pressure from the mother with Headaches, I guessed: it wouldn't see Sharon through on the steep road I knew she had to travel. I made up my mind, and found comfort in doing so.

'I'm going to talk with Mrs Wilks. I think I can arrange better practice time than you can get at the school … Ter?'

'Rif,' Sharon sighed. 'Can you? Oh, rif!'

I did not see Angelo that morning or afternoon. I went downstairs in the late morning, but Rosa told me he was under the weather; she was keeping him in bed and thought he was asleep. A cold, she guessed. She was not worried: he had them rather often. That alone informed me that he had said nothing to her about the gang. A *cold!*

In the afternoon I did accomplish one thing. I have committed us, Drozma, to an obligation which I think our little department of finance in the Toronto enclave will be pleased to honor. The money required is not much, and I can think of it as something good achieved even if my mission should end in failure. I went to see Mrs Wilks, who used to be Sophia Wilkanowska, and as I had anticipated, it was not difficult to establish a meeting of minds. She is a genuine teacher – that is to say, a lover of her own kind, uncorrupted by the pressures of every day: they beat upon her as they do upon everyone, but without destroying her spirit.

She is tiny, porcelain-pale, with a deceptive look of fragility. She lives on a quiet street just barely on the right side of the tracks (I have sent the address to the Toronto Communicator) with a sister who has scant English but is not blind. They manage. Sophia's English is adequate. When I spoke Polish she was happier, and friendship was easy from that moment on. These two escaped from blighted captive Poland in 30,948, when Sophia was already fifty, her sister forty-eight; I thought it better not to ask how Sophia's husband died. They both dye their hair brilliant black, and they have a few other gentle vanities, and music is in Sophia like the fire in a diamond, indestructible.

We talked about Latimer, which is not indifferent to music in this fairly leisured decade. Prematurely, because there were many other pressures on my mind, I suggested expanding their studio into a small school. They said: 'But – but—'

'I'm an old man. I have money – Canadian securities, other resources which I can't take with me. What better monument?' I pointed out that the house next door to them was vacant. There could be a partnership, perhaps, with one or two other Latimer teachers – and free practice rooms for promising students like Sharon Brand. Sophia Wilkanowska was not displeased to notice that cat coming out of the bag. She knew what Sharon was: if she had not, she would not have been the teacher I wanted for the child. I would buy and equip the house, I said, my part in it strictly anonymous. I would deed it over, guarantee upkeep for ten years; the rest was up to them. For an hour or so I let the idea develop in their disturbed, not quite believing, but essentially practical minds, as we sat about and talked Polish and drank wonderful coffee from tiny transparent cups which had somehow made that dark journey with them fifteen years before. Sophia was pleased to call me a good pianist after I played a Polonaise to her restrained satisfaction. I was an expansive, eccentric, aging gentleman, vaguely Polish-American with money in the background, who wanted a little unlabeled monument for himself. It made sense gradually. More to me than to them, but at length I 'confessed' – told them I had happened to get acquainted with Sharon and hear her practice. I had learned that she could not have a piano at home and I was angry. I loved her, I had no children of my own, and anyway I still wanted that monument.

They took it from there. 'It is dangerous,' said Sophia, 'to have that little one's hunger. Before her first lesson I had thought my own hunger was – do you know? – hammered away under the fingers of little brats who – never mind. But what is there for her, Mr Miles? School or no school? In this world or any other?'

'Trial. Victories, defeats, maturity. The worst cruelty would be to protect her from the pain of struggling.'

'Oh, dear God, true enough. And we accept your offer, Mr Miles.'

This much is done.

9

I finished that chapter a week ago, in my stuffy room, the evening after meeting Sharon's teacher. I was waiting there for the gradual coming of summer darkness. Tomorrow I shall not be dead, but Benedict Miles will be. I am writing now in haste, Drozma, to complete my report, to convey to you a resolution from which not even you, my second father, can swerve me.

When darkness came that evening I took Andy out of the garage on Martin Street – seeing there the neat car that had been Feuermann's – and drove to Byfield. I parked off the highway, cut through a small patch of woods, clambered over the cemetery fence. Moonrise had not yet come.

I could always find peace among the human dead. They are surely our kindred here at least: our five or six hundred years make no more ripple in eternity than the comic hurry of a second hand. I found the bank where Angelo and I had waited on Jacob's ritual, and fumbled at Mordecai Paxton's headstone for traces of the dandelions. They were still somewhat more than dust. I went to the grave of Susan Feuermann.

It was ten days since Feuermann had gone to Byfield and only an image of him returned. That had been a day of rain; none had fallen since. They are tender of their memorials here. The grass is trimmed; I saw fresh decorations on many stones. There are other places, away from this modern part, where nature has been allowed to shelter the fallen in her own fashion, and grass is tall, with here and there a few of the unimperious flowers that men call weeds.

I searched for signs of a tragedy darker than any of the deaths commemorated here: Jacob Feuermann had died not from age, or chance, or in the witless attack of illness, or through any fault or quality of his own, but, like a child in a bombed city, had been arrogantly shoved out of life in a conflict not of his making.

In ten days the grass had fairly righted itself, patiently following its own privilege of life, but still leaned enough for me to discover where something had been dragged to an area of lower ground behind a screen of willows. In that hollow Namir had covered his traces casually: it might cheat the uncritical eye of whatever attendant cared for the graveyard. On this ever-shaded ground the turf was thin and mossy. Namir had rolled some of it back, scattering surplus earth with scant effort at concealment. Replacing the turf, he had joined the edges: I could find them.

Kneeling in the unremembering dark, I could look across ten days and see that rain-drenched afternoon as it must have been. Feuermann had said: 'Sun's up there somewhere.' Few would have thought of that. No human being at all would have visited this small cemetery on such a weeping day, except the old man. He did. He stood in the rain for whatever harmless consolation it gave him, and the thing came on him out of the grass.

I ran my thumb through earth where there should have been a network of grass roots and was not. Behind me – oh, moonrise was still far off – behind me, Namir said: 'He's there. You needn't undo my grubby work.'

He watched from the higher ground, a killing animal with the face of Feuermann and glints of our blue night-fire in his eyes. You reminded me, Drozma, that he is a creature always in pain. He seemed so, tight-mouthed, head thrust forward on wide shoulders. But I think the pain of those who live with evil becomes something other than pain. I think they come to love it, as a victim of heroin bitterly loves his affliction. How else to explain the desperate recidivism of so many criminals, the persistent fury of a fanatic with the black dog of one idea on his back, the mountain of corpses around a Hitler? It was no simple hysteria when the witches of other recent centuries boasted of coupling with the devil.

His very pose was tigerish. But a tiger is innocent, merely hungry or curious at the wriggling of smaller life. I said: 'Do you care to tell me how you justify it to yourself?'

'Justify? No.'

'Explain, then?'

'Not to an Observer. Some will honor what I am, in the future.'

'You have no future. But you still have a choice.'

'I make my own choices.' I saw the simple long-bladed knife come into his hand. 'Sometimes with this.' He did not see the round stone I took from Feuermann's burial place before I stood.

'Is that how Feuermann died?'

'Yes, Elmis, if you want to speak of anything so definite as death after the mean half-life of his tribe.'

'He had no chance to defend himself?'

'Should he have had? Why, Elmis, he even smiled. He said: "Here, you

269

don't want to do that, I haven't done you any harm." You see? His small mind simply couldn't imagine that anyone could regard his life as of no importance. He said: "What's the gag?" And held out his hand for the knife as if I were a naughty boy – *I!* Then he saw that his face was already mine, and it confused him. He said: "Does every man have another self? I'm dreaming this." So I ended the dream for him, and now for you.'

'Nothing to you, that my blood on the grass would be orange blood?'

'Nothing. Why let it worry you? If they find you in time for autopsy, you'll be back on page three as soon as there's a livelier murder with a sex angle.'

'You're only a small devil, Namir. Back of me there are thirty thousand years on Earth, my planet Earth.'

'Then defend yourself with your thirty thousand.' And he came down the slope, stumbling in haste, panting as if he suffered. The stone caught him on the cheek, jarring the true skullbone under his artificial flesh, half stunning and toppling him. The knife leaped away into the dark. He rose immediately and closed with me, hands at my throat and mine at his, his face straining toward me as if he loved me but loved the thought of my death a little more. I broke his clutch on my windpipe and gripped his shoulders over the subclavicular nerve clusters where a Martian should feel pain, but he was hard to down.

We swayed and struggled so for a longer time than I can measure. It may have been only seconds, since the moon had still not risen when it was over. Once I heard him gasp: 'Do you yield, Elmis? Do you *now?*' Later, when I had forced him back to the broken turf of Feuermann's grave, he choked on other words, sensing the shadow of his own death as a weasel might know the shadow of sudden wings: 'I am old – but I have a son …' He felt uneven ground under him, and raised his knee to foul me with it, but I had been waiting for that. My foot wrenched his other leg and he went down at last on the soft ground; his arms were straws and with his body he ceased fighting. He groaned: 'I am one of many. We live forever.'

I found his knife and slipped it under my belt. 'There's still a choice. The hospital in Old City, or this.' I showed him the grenade. 'I have another. Perhaps you still have one of your own you'd rather use?'

'Little snot-nose cousin of the angels – no, I have none.'

'When was yours used?'

'In Kashmir.' He fumbled aimlessly at the grass, his eyes a blue blaze of memory and some laughter. 'Maybe a century ago – want to hear?'

'I must.'

'Oh yes, your precious duty. What a milky vanity! Well, there was a little chap with something of the Buddha in him. Rather like Angelo. I taught him a while, but he abandoned me. He might well have been another Buddha. I had to dispose of him. He'd already begun preaching, you see. I didn't want his body turned into holy relics, so I used the grenade in such a manner that he is still a vaguely remembered *devil*, Elmis, in two or three illiterate villages. Peace, he was saying; magnify the inner light by honoring the light of others – dreadful stuff, you know the style, and he only a beginner. He liked to quote the last words of Gautama, and other fools had started to listen. "Whosoever now, Ananda, or after my departure, shall be to himself his own light, his own refuge, and seek no other refuge, will henceforth be my true disciple and walk in the right path –" and so on and so on, with little additions of his own.'

'And for that you found it necessary to destroy—'

'Yes, give me credit for nipping at least one tiresome religion in the bud. I was fond of him, too. He was quite like Angelo, who was sneaking down toward South Calumet Street, by the way, when I left the house to follow you—'

'How's that?'

'South end. War, you know.' He smiled up at me, not looking at the grenade. 'The Diggers are meeting the Mudhawks tonight. Angelo and Billy Kell – that's quite a boy, Billy.' He could not quite control the slyness with which he glanced away, and that may be one more grain of proof for what I suspect about Billy Kell. 'Well, they had a council of strategy, on which I eavesdropped. Angelo had some very sound ideas. One in particular, making use of rooftops, appealed to me. The Mudhawks will occupy the roofs on Lowell Street, where the Diggers have to pass on their way to the prearranged engagement, which is to be in Quire Lane. I believe both armies use what they call gleep-guns. Instead of bullets they shoot twenty-penny nails, variation of the arbalest. You might get the best view from the corner of Lowell and Quire Lane, if it isn't all over when you get there – *don't* let me detain you!' Some of his laughter may have been genuine. 'Ah yes, the choice! Elmis, I wish you could know how funny you look. You imagine *you* can destroy me?'

'An instrument of my people and others. Hospital or grenade?'

'Grenade, of course.' And he ceased laughing.

'Only twelve Salvayans in all history have died by execution. They took the grenade with unbound hands. I'd like to respect that tradition, if I thought I could trust you ... Do you respect it?'

'Of course. A signal honor: No. 13.' He stretched his arms above his head and spoke with real sorrow, although I heard no overtone of regret. 'I am Salvayan too, Elmis. Also old and tired.'

I set the grenade at his waist and stood back.

He taught my foolish mind, then, what 346 years had never quite taught me: there is no such thing as hearing truth from those who despise it. He snatched the grenade and flung it in a great arc. It missed me, struck a willow, filled the graveyard with a second's purple brilliance as sap and new wood of the lower trunk dissolved. The treetop plunged toward me in a long whispering and rushing. I had to jump like a fool to save myself. Namir's high laughter snarled back from among the graves: 'Explain *that* to your adopted people!'

I could not assume that what he had told me of the gang war was a lie. I cleared the fence behind him, though not pursuing him now. Seeing his knife in my hand, he swerved into the woods, his one backward look a mad smile. I shall see him again, if I don't die first of my own hesitating stupidity. His car – Feuermann's car – was parked behind mine. I slashed its front tires, and drove in my own car back to Latimer.

I parked Andy well beyond No. 21. After killing the motor I could hear something, a distant squealing, more like steam in a kettle than anything else. The dark clutter of houses muffled and shut it away. The moon had risen at last while I was driving back from Byfield, but gave poor help as yet in these blind-faced streets. Lowell Street branched from Calumet two blocks beyond EL CAT SEN; I did not quite know Quire Lane. The houses on Lowell Street were not detached but all one mass, making the narrow street resemble a New York City canyon. When I turned the corner the vicious clamor was no longer far off, but doubled in volume. A breathless running man bumped into me. 'Hey, mister, don't go that way! The gangs –' He caught my arm to steady himself. 'Sent for cops, ain't come, damn it, always the way when you *want* 'em – thought I'd try 'n' find the beat cop on Calumet—'

'Anybody hurt?'

'Kids with busted heads – there'll be worse. Mister, you better—'

'I'm all right. I live down that way.'

'Well, stay inside, I'm telling you. Little bastards chunking rocks off the roofs, right here on Lowell. Hit a little girl – she wasn't with 'em, just running after 'em—'

'Where? Where is she?'

'Huh? Oh, some woman grabbed her, took her into a house—'

'My daughter—'

'My God! Don't borrow trouble, bud, could be any kid. Anyway, she wasn't bad hurt, wasn't even knocked out, see, and this woman—'

'Which house?'

'Other side, second from the next corner.'

I squeezed his arm for thanks and ran.

A stone hit the pavement behind me. Just one (Angelo's idea?) and the bang of its fall was nearly drowned by the yelling from what must be Quire Lane ahead. My mind declared it could not be Angelo who threw it – not now, not at a single grownup, after the Diggers had already passed by that block. Part of me still insisted on that as I burst into the house.

It was Sharon. They had her on a bed in the front room, two women, one cleaning the gash on her head, the other fluttering. Sharon stopped whimpering when she saw me. I abandoned all Observers' Rules, kissing and scolding her. 'What were you trying to *do?*' I suppose my irises were gray soup plates, but she wouldn't have noticed. It was all right, as people say: the bleeding had nearly ceased, and Sharon's rescuer had the wound properly cleaned. 'Sharon, Sharon, what—'

'I wanted to make them stop it. Will you make them stop it?'

'Sure, I'm on my way. It's all right, Sharon.'

She relaxed partly, and sighed, and wiped her nose with an angrily competent sweep of her whole arm. 'Frankly, Ben, you always turn up when I want you, frankly.'

'It's all right, Sharon. I'll make 'em stop it.' The women crowded me away then, one of them wanting to know what I meant by letting my little girl run around in the streets. I escaped by saying she wasn't mine, damn it, I just knew where she lived, and would come back presently and take her home. I ran out in search of a war, and found it.

Quire Lane was a foul alley, a dead end, bordered by two warehouses, ending at the blank rear wall of a third. Later, from the police, I learned what the Mudhawks' strategy had achieved. The Diggers had stormed up Lowell Street, expecting a prearranged fracas in the relative seclusion of Quire Lane. The idea was simply to see how much mayhem could be dealt and received before the sirens sounded off. Probably the Diggers didn't exactly understand when the rocks fell in Lowell Street. They themselves had gone to the trouble of smashing the street lamp at Lowell and Calumet. One boy was killed outright. Police found another afterward, in an areaway, with a broken shoulder. The dead child must have been somewhere in shadow when I was running down that block ... After passing the shower of stones, the Diggers sighted a small detachment of Mudhawks who staged a phony retreat into Quire Lane. Then the main force of Mudhawks closed the trap, swarming out of their hiding places in doorways and up the street, reinforced by the stone throwers from the roofs – by all but one of them, that is. Billy Kell has not been seen since, by myself or by the police, and he was not in the brawl in Quire Lane. Careful of his orange blood?

It seems to be necessary for me to believe that Billy Kell was alone on the roofs after the Diggers had gone by.

The Mudhawks forced the Diggers back to the blind end of the alley, with fists, stones, knives, gleep-guns. By the time I reached that smeared corner of Quire Lane and Lowell, the Diggers understood matters very well and were fighting back with total fury. A certain loathsome moonlight had reached the alley then. I could see plainly.

I could not find Angelo.

Some of the boys had flashlights that shot a writhing illumination when they were not being used as clubs. While I was yelling futile things that nobody heard, a Mudhawk – I knew him by his black tam-o'-shanter – dashed by me with a thing that looked like a wooden gun. I glimpsed the elastic bands, the nail in the slot, and tore it out of his hand. He glared foolishly, covered his face with his arm, and ran.

I could not find Angelo.

But now at last there was the thin imperative wrath of a siren, somewhere off on Calumet Street. The boys heard it too, and their stampede began, a stampede of those who could move at all. At least three were lying still at the rear of the alley.

I saw him now. He jumped up from nowhere. He jumped on a box near the clogged mouth of the alley, his shirt ripped away from flailing pipestem arms, blood and dirt all over him, his face beautiful, defiled, insane, and he was screaming: 'Get 'em *now!* Don't let 'em break away! What are you – chicken? It's for *Bella*—'

Few heard him. The sirens were louder and spoke in clearer terms. The boys were all trying to get free of the alley, Diggers and Mudhawks in common panic, blundering into the warehouse walls, into me as I tried to plow my way through to Angelo. Then two patrol cars squealed into place, shutting off retreat, the sirens' question ending in the affirmative of a growl. Angelo heard that. He leaped off his box before I could catch him – I don't think he knew me then – and ran unseeingly straight into the grabbing arms of Patrolman Dunn. 'One anyway!' said Dunn, and struck him on the ear.

In the next few howling moments they rounded up six or seven besides Angelo. Three of the four policemen were trying for arms or shirt collars instead of using their clubs, but some of it had to be frantic and dirty work. There was an ambulance beyond the patrol cars. I was cursing Dunn root and branch, but I stopped that, and don't know if he heard it. While he still gripped Angelo's arm I yelled in his ear: 'Dunn! You can't take him to the station, it's going to kill his mother if you do.'

'His mo –' It might have been only then that he recognized Angelo. Gore, mud, gravel marks on a mask of anguish – it wasn't strange.

I pressed my small advantage: 'Her heart, man – you can't. The kid's only twelve anyhow. He was sucked into it, I happen to know – tell you later. Take him home, Dunn. Don't book him.'

'Who're you?'

'I live there. Saw you when we had that burglary.'

'Ah, yah …' He shook the boy, not roughly but slowly. Angelo swayed at the end of his arm, and spat blood from a cut lip. 'Jesus, kid! But you was always a *good* boy – never in no trouble before, what the hell?'

Angelo asked quietly: 'Is that true? I don't exactly know.'

274

'Huh? You never done nothing like this before.'

'I have,' said Angelo drowsily, and his head drooped and I could scarcely hear him. 'Yes, I have, in my dreams. They come like clouds. Which is the sky: the clouds or the blue?'

'Now, boy, now. What kind of an answer is that? You're high-sterical is what it is. Pull yourself together. You see that ambulance? You see what's going into it, huh, Angelo?'

'Take him home, Dunn. Take him home.'

'They all go to the station, mister. But you could be right. I won't book him, maybe. I'll get him home. Understand, Angelo? A break. On your mother's account, not on yours, believe you me. And if there's ever a second time, no break, no break at all. Now come on—'

'Ben! Ben – ask them to clean me up before they—'

'In with you. In with you now …'

Those women had given Sharon a sleeping pill. (It is increasingly a sleeping-pill culture, Drozma. Seventeen years ago I don't think a respectable woman in a poor district would have had a supply of barbiturates, much less given one casually to a child without even a doctor's word. It could be a small symptom of the many forces that may make fools of us and our hope of Union within five hundred years or so. Yet I don't blame them too much. Life in its growing complexity nags and bedevils them: rather than learn the uses of simplicity, they reach for sleep.) I carried Sharon to my car, and home, cutting short the startled mooings of her parents with some ill-tempered noise of my own. It wasn't their fault, in a way – to make her frantic effort, Sharon had slid down the rainspout when they supposed she was in bed. It was another playmate, a seceding Mudhawk, who had let slip word to Sharon of what was planned. So Sharon told me a day or two later. I must finish this report quickly, Drozma.

Namir as Feuermann had not returned to No. 21. I did not think he would. (As I write this, the body of Feuermann has not been found. There was an item about 'mysterious summer lightning' destroying a tree in Byfield; the damage done by the falling top may have canceled out the marks of the shallow grave. If the old man is ever found, I suppose his motiveless murder will become a popular mystery to addle the experts.)

No. 21 was gently quiet. I found Rosa sewing in her basement living room, unconcerned, mild, too far from the war in Quire Lane to have heard its crying, comfortable in the belief that Angelo was asleep in his room with a bit of a cold. It was too much for me. I don't understand either the strength or the fragility of human beings, as I see them sometimes bending viably before enormous pressures, sometimes snapping at a touch.

Rosa knew from my face that something was wrong. She put her sewing away and came to me. 'What is it, Ben? You sick?' Still unhurt, still safe behind her unreal shield of love and security – the house quiet, Angelo surely in his room – she could be sorry for me, and anxious to help. 'What *is* the matter, Ben? You look awful.'

So I gabbled. 'Nothing serious, but—'

I might have succeeded somehow in preparing her for it. I don't know. I was hopelessly human in my stammering hunt for words that might warn without wounding. While I stammered, Dunn came in. Through the basement door, without ringing, holding Angelo by the arm. Yes, they'd tried to clean him up a little, but couldn't hide the cut lip or the gash over his eye. They'd washed his face, but couldn't wash away the shame, the glaze of withdrawal, the agony.

I saw Rosa's hand leave her wobbling lips and clutch at her left arm. I could not reach her, nor could Dunn, in time to check her fall.

There was no rising. Only the choking, the brief struggle, and the relinquishment. Even after her face turned cyanotic I think she was still trying to see where Angelo was, or perhaps say something to him – that it was all right, not his fault, something like that …

'May I go and get Father Ryan?'

That blank whisper made Dunn remember him and turn to him. 'Why – she's gone, boy. She's gone.'

'Yes, I see, I know. I did that. May I go and get Father Ryan?'

'Of course.'

He never returned, Drozma. The priest came quickly, but Angelo was not with him. Father Ryan said Angelo had run on ahead of him.

In the week since then, the Latimer and state police have done everything possible. There is an eight-state alarm, everything else that human intelligence can devise. They are looking for Feuermann too, the worthless rumors like the haze that hangs on after forest fire. Since it seems that he ran into night, and night took him, I will go into night myself, and look for him there.

A word about Sharon. I saw her last in Amagoya, but she knew its magic had perished, as well as I knew it, and it was unavoidable that we should talk like grownups. I told her that of course Angelo would be found, or more likely come back by himself when he could. I told her that I was going away alone to look for him. It was hard for her to accept the obvious fact that she could not come with me. She did accept it. I have never been so dangerously close to revealing what we must not, as I was there in Amagoya when she said: 'You know everything, Ben. You *will* find him.' So I know everything! She was a woman, Drozma. Even her mangled big words weren't funny, they weren't funny at all. I made her promise to do what she already knew she must – stay, stay with her music, grow up, 'be a good girl' – we found we could laugh some at that last, nevertheless knowing what it meant.

If I end this here, I have time to make myself a passable new face before dawn. As soon as there has been time for this report to have reached you I will call through the Toronto Communicator and learn your orders.

Whatever they are, I cannot return to Northern City if it means abandoning this mission. I will yield no such victory to Namir and his kind. We are a little less than human, Drozma, and a little more.

PART TWO

In our barbarous society the influence of character is in its infancy.
– RALPH WALDO EMERSON, *Politics*

1

Drozma, tonight I am racked by an old malady, a love for the human race.

I have searched more than nine years. As you know from my reports, I have not found him. If living, Angelo is twenty-one. You have been kind, to support me with money and counsel. With the Russo-Chinese War reeling into a third dreary year and the rest of the world in a frenzy of indecision, I know you cannot spare other personnel to aid me, but I must go on searching. I will send this journal later in place of a formal report. A few hours ago something happened which will be a pleasure to record, but otherwise I have little to tell: frustrations, false clues, dead-end journeys. I have come here to New York and taken an apartment, because of a newspaper photograph that made me think of Billy Kell.

It was a picture of that fellow Joseph Max being interviewed by some journalist. Behind Max was a face alertly blank like a bodyguard's, enough like Kell to excite my wondering. Namir (and his son?) may have been searching for Angelo as persistently as I. In the nine years I have had no more hint of their whereabouts than of his. I was in Cincinnati when I saw the picture a week ago. I had gone there because one of my hobo friends slipped word to me that someone resembling my 'grandson' was hanging around the river docks. Nothing in it. One more dark-haired bum with a limp; a face like a woodchuck. The world's full of dark young men with lame left legs. The tramps and prostitutes and petty criminals who try to help me are not people who know how to describe a face. When I make contact with them I am a crazy old coot hunting a grandson who might have died long ago or (they think) never lived. They try to be kind, supplying rumors to keep the old man going, partly for laughs. I have no good reason to suppose that Angelo sank into the shadows of the underworld: it's only that those shadows are easier to explore than the endless multitudes of the respectable. Quite possibly some decent family gave him shelter and another name. I go on. I can't mingle in any crowd without sooner or later seeing some dark youth with a limp. Once I saw one who not only resembled Angelo but had a scar over the right eye, as Angelo must have. That was on the copter-bus from Sacramento to Oakland. I trailed him home, watched him a few more times, made inquiries in the neighborhood. Nice kid, not even Italian, lived in Oakland all his life. Some hopes won't die.

No doubt you have Observers keeping track of Joseph Max and the antics of his Unity Party. I shall be another, at least until I satisfy myself about Billy Kell. Maybe I can turn up something interesting as a by-product. Hell's a-brewing around Joe Max. And by the way, what is there about his party to attract a man of the stature of Dr Hodding? At risk of repeating what other Observers may have told you, this is the Hodding story as I saw it in the papers two years ago: Jason Hodding was director of the Wales Foundation (biochemical research and very good), and startled the world out of its pants with a propaganda blast for Max's party in the congressional elections of '70; supposed to have helped elect that freak Senator Galt of Alaska. Then Hodding quit the Foundation (or was fired?) and dropped out of sight of the public. Lives prosperously on Long Island, 'retired'; said to know more about virus mutations than anyone else at large …

Max calls it the Organic Unity Party now. He no longer yelps in public about racial purity, though some of the whispers against the Federalists' Negro-Indian candidate must originate with Max. In public he approves of human brotherhood: there are votes in it. He'll make a try in the fall election, shouting for America to rule the world. 'Clean up Asia!' – a banner with that legend decorates his headquarters on Lexington Upper Level, and nobody laughs. We must go in and reform Asia (for its own good of course) while the Russian and Chinese giants are (apparently) gasping their last. Maybe they are: everything Max says carries the virus of half-truth. The techs say, and Satellite observations are supposed to confirm, that no atomic explosions have taken place in Asia since last summer. I give the Satellite Authority credit for resisting the pressure a year ago to solve everything with a few hydrogen jobs. That took courage, up there on the Midnight Star, since the humanitarian opposition was, as so often, tiptoeing by on the other side. As of March, 30,972, we don't know – frantically, elaborately, diplomatically don't know. If you believe Satellite Authority communiqués (I do, more or less) there must be idiotic trench-and-outpost warfare all along the north-and-south backbone of Asia, Siberia remaining the darkness it always was. Now and then the Authority says plaintively that it really can't collect social and economic data from 1075 miles up. Drozma, tell me when you write whether Asian Center is still safe. I had friends there.

Here, only the Organic Unity Party appears to have no doubts.

Nobody laughs at Max. That frightens me. The public is hardened to seeing his fanatic puss on the front page, telescreens, newsreels, always a bit sallow and sweat-shiny when they catch him without make-up, a bad animated caricature of John C. Calhoun with nothing of Calhoun's honesty or personal gentleness. When, last year, Max developed a flopping cowlick – damn the thing, nobody laughed. He saves his juiciest venom for the newly formed Federalist Party. I haven't made up my mind about them. Seems to be nothing disingenuous in the movement and much sense, if they'd tone down the doctrinaire certainty of their one-world members. They sometimes lose sight of their own good premise, that difference-within-union is the essence of federalism. Toward the Democrats and Republicans Max has only contempt – he says they are on the way out and that's that. They make the mistake of paying him back in his own coin or trying to ignore him out of sight. The Republicans have been fresh out of ideas since '968, when the Democrat Clifford got in (and how wrong I was about '64! Would've lost my shirt, only I'm not the type.) Rooseveltian splash followed by Wilsonian bubbles. Nice chap, Clifford. Progressive, they tell me. I sometimes wonder if he knows his aspirations from his elbow.

A word about the Philippines, Drozma. Watch that Institute of Human Studies. Founded in '968. I have a hunch the personnel is earthquake-proof, same as the buildings, which I hope I'll live to see someday. Not just another inflated foundation. It has the quiet sort of courage behind it. I like their prospectus: 'To collect and make accessible to all the sum of available human knowledge' – large order, but they mean business. 'To continue research in those studies most directly related to the nature and function of human beings'. And they explain that the use of the term 'human beings' instead of 'Man' is deliberate – that would naturally appeal to my cantankerous bias. Point is they're thinking in terms of centuries and not scared by next week. You remember how Manila ought to have been one of the world's greatest centers of trade and culture, if European rule-and-grab hadn't smothered it in what they call the eighteenth century and later. I don't know why it shouldn't be the Athens of the twenty-first. When my mission is ended one way or another, I want to go there before returning to Northern City.

Tomorrow morning I shall visit Organic Unity Party headquarters and pose as a snarky old man with money. My new face suits me, I may have used a bit too much heat when I raised the cheekbones, but that merely makes me apple-cheeked, cute as hell, six feet two of short-tempered Santy Claus, talking slightly daown-East, and I've practiced a deadpan stare that comes in handy. I mean to be a potential angel for the campaign fund, not quite convinced but open to indoctrination. They'll lay down some kind of carpet. If Billy Kell is in there I'll smell him out.

Now I can turn to something that has lightened my 355 years.

After I left Latimer, to follow up a rumor that someone had seen a kid hitchhiker twenty miles out of town, I knew that the police were not uninterested in Benedict Miles. I had my new face, and it seemed best to inform Mrs Wilks, through Toronto, that Miles had died, leaving the school provided for in his will. Less harassed and hurried judgment might have produced something better than that, but once it was done I couldn't undo it. Mrs Wilks wrote faithfully to the Toronto 'trustees' until two years ago, and the Communicator sent her letters on to me when possible – often I had no address. Two years ago Sophia's sister died. Sophia turned the school over to a successor, and took Sharon to London, feeling that her own teaching could carry the girl no further. Sharon's family wasn't mentioned in that last letter. I have not been too severely distressed by my separation from the child I loved, because I have known that, chance permitting, I would hear of her again. When I came to New York last week, Sharon's debut was in the announcements. This evening she played, in Pro Arte Hall.

It is a new auditorium, part of a splendid development along the Hudson. You wouldn't recognize New York, Drozma. I almost didn't, for the last good view I had of it was back in 30,946. I have passed through a few times in the nine years, but with scarcely a chance to pause.

In the '960s New York decided to make its waterfront beautiful instead of hideous. A great Esplanade runs from George Washington Bridge to Twenty-third Street, with tall buildings at intervals, some set back among the lower structures on the inner side of the Esplanade, others rising sheer from the river. They tell me the railroad still rumbles down below. Dock facilities have actually been expanded, but it doesn't look so: to come in on a ship or ferry is to enter an archway in a gleaming cliff. When I have time, think I'll go over to Jersey in order to come back on one of the chubby Diesel ferries and see for myself. The heavy automotive traffic on the second level is not felt up on the Esplanade, as you don't feel it when you walk on the upper levels of the north-and-south avenues. On the Esplanade you have only the sky, the graceful buildings, human beings, and the Hudson River wind that now seems not hostile, gritty, and snarling but a refreshing part of the city's majesty. It was difficult to have any patience with New York in the old days. Times change. Hell's Kitchen was wiped away long ago; blest if I know what they did with Grant's Tomb but I'm sure it's tucked in down there somewhere. This waterfront was planned soon after they snatched the city from the politicians and tried the manager system. They have kept out catchpenny concessions. On the wide Esplanade itself not even bicycles are allowed, though children are everywhere.

The city's resident population has gone down by about a million, with corresponding increase in the huge area of the metropolitan district. There's revival of the old proposal to make the district a separate state. Civic groups kick the idea around. One in particular is gathering petition signatures and doing spadework in Congress. They want the new state to be named Adelphi. I've got no objections.

Pro Arte Hall is high up in one of the buildings rising directly from the river – clean-shining steel and stone and glass. Conditioned as we have been,

Drozma, to the hidden life, we'll never quite know how they do it. These buildings are wholly human, artifacts of their complex science, yet married to nature also, to wind and sky, stars and sun.

The auditorium itself is severe. Cold white and self-effacing gray. Nothing irrelevant to tickle or distract the eye, only an uncomplicated stage and stern classical dignity of the piano. (But it was good, during intermission, to go into a lounge and find, beyond its glass west wall, an open space from which one looked down to the river. How far down I don't know. A bright liner passing downstream was a playroom toy. In spite of the March chill I was happy to watch it until the bell rang for the second half of Sharon's miracle.)

Few in the audience knew anything about her, I think. Just one more New York debut. I had a case of nerves, my heartbeat shaking me each minute. I read the program a dozen times, and knew nothing of what it said except that the first number was the Bach G Minor Fugue.

Then she was there. Slim, slight, seeming tall – oh, I'd known that! In white. I'd known that too. Her corsage was a tiny cluster of blue scillas and snowdrops, absurdly modest. She still wore her brown hair shoulder-length, misty with strange lights. She didn't find it necessary to smile. Her bow was almost perfunctory. (She has told me she was totally petrified, couldn't bow deeper for fear of going over flat on her face.) I remembered Amagoya.

She seated herself, touched her palms with a handkerchief, adjusted the long skirt to clear her ankles. Dimly I knew she was still sort of snub-nosed. Somewhere there must have been a red rubber ball on a string ...

Then I had to pay her the best compliment: forgetting her. The fugue took hold with clear-cut authority. What unreal and therefore eternal cities did Bach know, to create his architecture out of the marble of dreams? Was the G Minor written after his blindness? I don't remember. Not that it matters: his visions need no common eyesight. It was as if Sharon had said (to all of us): 'Come here with me. I can show you what I saw.' No other way to play Bach, but who at nineteen is supposed to know that?

In spite of the fugue's enormous ending there was not the usual burst of excitement killing the last chord. Instead they gave her some seconds of that enchanted silence all human performers pray to receive (an experience I can't quite share, since Martian audiences grant the silence as a matter of course, for music's sake). When the crash came it was not prolonged, for Sharon did smile then, and the shy grimace touched off sympathetic laughter, a way of saying they loved her, and the applause broke off short at the merest half turn of her head back to the piano.

The rest of the first half was all Chopin. The sonata; three nocturnes; two mazurkas; the F Sharp Minor Impromptu, which I think is the extremest distillation of Chopin, a union of ecstasy and despair nearly unbearable. Sharon thinks so, played it so. Even with that still burning inside us, we demanded an encore at the end of the first half, a thing unheard of nowadays. When the shouts were unmistakable, she gave us the little first Prelude, as she might have tossed a flower to a lover who deserved it but wasn't too bright. Pianissimo all the way through, disregarding the conventional dynamic marks: like opening a window on a waterfall and closing it before you can guess what the river is saying. I never played it like that. Frederic Chopin didn't, when I heard him in 30,848, but I don't believe he'd have minded. I can't fathom the phonograph-intellects who insist on 'definitive interpretation'. You, might as well insist, when a friend gives you a jewel, that only one facet may be looked at, world without end. You might as well ask for a definitive moonrise. Sharon grinned after that tour de force – not a definitive grin either, a big human one. She ran off. The lights went up.

It was an uncommonly long program, especially for a debut. A newcomer is still expected to be humble before tradition. A chunk of Bach for the critics, a chunk of Beethoven, maybe some Schumann to fill in the cracks, Chopin to prove you're a pianist, finally a scintillant gob of Liszt for bravura and schmaltz. Sharon had paid her respects with Bach all right – what Bach! – but only because she wanted to. My mangled scrap of program told me the second half began with a suite by Andrew Carr, an Australian composer not known till a year ago. And it ended with Beethoven, Sonata in C, Opus 53.

Realization came slowly. I'm not in the habit of thinking in opus numbers, but it came through then to my dazed intelligence that 53 is the 'Waldstein.' I think that was what made me reach one of those impulsive, wholly emotional decisions which I don't expect to regret. I scratched on the rumpled program: *Not dead, had to change face and name to help me hunt for A. No, dear, I haven't found him. May I see you? Alone, please, and don't tell anyone about me yet. You're a musician. I love you beyond comprehemption.*

I found an usher, a girl who promised to get my note to Miss Brand. I wandered outside. I watched that ship going downstream in the open night. After a while, as I've told you, I was quite happy. When I went back the popeyed usher located me, pushed a slip of paper in my hand, and whispered: 'Hey, know what she did when she read your note? Kissed *me!* Well, I *mean* …'

I bumbled like Santy Claus. The lights had already dimmed, but I could read the huge scrawl: *Blue River Café 2 blox down Esplan riverside wait for me lounge escape earliest poss O Ben Ben* BEN!!!

She may have tried to see me in the audience, though I had mentioned a changed face. There was a blind look about her. I knew terror, fearing I might have upset her and hurt the second half of the concert. But then she was resting her fingers silently on the keys, as if the towering Steinway had its own will and could communicate, soothe, clear away confusion and leave her free. I needn't have worried.

The Andrew Carr suite is excellent. Complex, serious, young; perhaps too heavy, too immense, but with a cumulative passion that justifies it. Likely a greater maturity will teach Carr the value of the light touch. In the program notes, I remember, he acknowledges a major debt to Brahms. All to the good, especially if it means that composers of the '970s have finally buried the I-don't-really-mean-it school of the '930s and '940s. Carr has learned more from the young Stravinsky than from the old; Beethoven glances over his shoulder, he needs more Mozart in his system …

I won't play the 'Waldstein' again. Anything else, yes – I don't despise my own talent. Not the 'Waldstein'. For anyone else it would have been bad programming to let the sonata follow the shattering climaxes and nearly impossible athletic demands of the Carr suite. Not for Sharon. She wasn't tired. She made it a summing up, a final statement to throw the colors of a thousand flames on all the rest.

Maybe I've heard the opening Allegro done with more technical finish; never with more sincerity. In the melancholy of the brief Adagio I was lost. I don't know all that Sharon meant; Beethoven's meditations are not altogether ours at any time. She took the gentle opening of the Rondo more slowly than I would have done, but she was right, and the acceleration of the A Minor passage became all the more a terrifying flash, a blaze of longing abruptly revealed.

… The sonata's conclusion was blinding. No one looks at that much light.

I don't recall much about the ovation they gave her: we were all hysterical. I don't even remember what all her encores were. There were seven. We let her go at last only because she put on a small comic pantomime of exhaustion.

You could not imagine, Drozma, the first thing she said when she slipped into the Blue River Cafe, astonishingly small, shy, a mousy gray wrap over her gown – slipped in and knew me somehow through all my changes, caught up the clumsy skirt to run like a child and throw herself at me and bury her snub nose in my shirt. She said: 'Ben, I fluffed the Prestissimo, I *fluffed* it, I went too fast, I scrabbled it – where, where have you *been?*'

'You never fluffed anything.' I must have muttered more such stuff while we struggled for calm.

We found a booth, with a window overlooking the river and the night. Tranquil and civilized, that restaurant, mild lighting, no fuss, hurry, or noise. It was past eleven o'clock, but they produced a hero-size dinner for Sharon, who admitted to fasting before the concert and now looked with pathetic astonishment at the lobster, saying: 'Could I bodaciously have ordered *that* in my madness?' She ate it though, with all the fixings, and we grinned and mumbled and made groping reaches for the unsayable. Then the lobster was gone, coffee and cognac were with us; Sharon squared her little shoulders and sighed and said: 'Now …!'

If there was anything in the nine years I failed to tell her it was either an unavoidable part of our Martian deception or too small to remember. I am 'Will Meisel' at present. She found it difficult not to call me Ben. My departure from Latimer had been, in a way, cruel – I knew it at the time. She did not reproach me for it, or for the false message of my death – not directly. But once she took my fingers and pressed them against her cheek and said: 'When Mrs Wilks told me – you see, until Angelo went away I'd never lost anybody – and then you –' But rather than let me flounder and beg forgiveness she went on quickly: 'Your hands are the same, just the same. How was it possible to change your face so much? I saw you recognize me, or maybe I'd've known you anyway, but—'

With careful vagueness and wholly genuine embarrassment, I lied about having suffered a serious face injury, years before my time in Latimer. I hinted that part of my facial structure was prosthetic, under a successful skin graft, and that I could play tricks with it. I conveyed too that I was sensitive and didn't like talking of it. 'Nine years' aging too, Sharon, and the white hair is natural.'

'Ben – Will – why was it necessary? But, darling, don't tell me unless you want to. You're here. I'll get used to it sometime ...' I told her that my going away had made the police suspect me in connection with the disappearances of Angelo and Feuermann. She confirmed that Feuermann had never been found. My search had to be unhampered, I said, so I juggled personalities and faces, burying an old identity. It was all too far from the human norm and I don't think it satisfied her, but it was the best I could do. She too remembered Amagoya. She hasn't a suspicious heart. Sharon at ten had been somewhat sheltered from grown-up speculations and rumors, missing the real and unreal implications of that disaster in Latimer. Music and Mrs Wilks had held her steady when the loss of Angelo and myself had shaken her world. Soon there had been time, and adolescence. I had foolishly not quite grasped the vast difference between nine of my years and Sharon's nine between ten and nineteen ... I told her too how I thought Angelo might have been swallowed by the underworld – joined the hobos, something like that – or even suffered amnesia because he felt lost and condemned himself for his mother's death.

'Why did he mean so much to you?'

'I felt responsible, perhaps. I ought to have kept him out of trouble because I knew he was supernormal and vulnerable, and I didn't do it.' She wasn't satisfied. 'And I came to think of him as like a son.' There was too much truth in that. 'I should have been a better guardian, because I don't think anyone else saw the dangers.' Not for the first time, she started to ask another question, but held it back, frowning into her cigarette smoke, cherishing my hand. 'How well do you remember him, Sharon?'

'I don't know.' She has developed a number of vivid little mannerisms, none of them posed. A trick of leaning forward suddenly, shoving both hands up into her hair and keeping them there, while a tiny frown-crease comes and goes in her smooth forehead; pouting her big sweet mouth without knowing it; smiling so fleetingly you can't be sure afterward that she smiled at all. 'I don't know. I know that I loved him pretty terribly. Ten years old is such a *long* time ago, Ben ... Afraid I don't even know much about the famous male sex. It's been – you know: technique, not parties – Czerny, not boy friends. And worth it, too – I haven't minded that.'

'Plenty of time.'

'Oh – time ... I suppose I began to feel he was dead, after Mother Sophia – I'm sort of in the habit of calling her that, she likes it – after she told me that you were. I never forgot him, Ben, I just had to let it go into the past, like a station on a train. I didn't finish high school, by the way. My mother died when I was thirteen, and Pop remarried – oh well, make way for Cinderella, I couldn't stand the stepmother and she sure-to-God couldn't stand me, so Mother Sophia took me to live with her – all I could've prayed for. I – hear from Pop now and then. Stiff little letters. Exceedingly grammatical.'

'He wasn't there tonight?'

'Ah no, he' – her wonderful fingers were gripping my hand hard again – 'he doesn't get around much, as the jellyfish said to the sea serpent. Means, translated, that while the heller he married runs the store, he goes down to the corner. Got it in all its beauty, darling? He's Brand Anonymous. And little daughter can no more reach him than – oh, the devil with it. He writes only when he's sober, about once in two months, Ben—'

'Will.'

'I'm sorry – Will, Will. I've thought so much about *Ben* ... Well, he wrote that he would like to come to the recital but was very busy and not well. Could be the lady dictated it. She knows he still loves me, in his fashion, that's her cross. People are so ... so ...' She gave it up.

We were both silent too long. I said: 'Oo ill owioffsh?'

For some reason that made her cry, but even while she groped impatiently for a handkerchief, and snatched mine, she was saying: 'O. Ah ery ush. But I could go another cognac ...'

'And Mother Sophia?'

'Splendid.' She was still annoyed at her eyes, wiping them, and repairing make-up. 'Immortal – my God, if only she were! I didn't know what to say, about coming away tonight. Lousy liar. Said I had a whim to be completely alone an hour or so, guess she didn't mind. She'll sit up for the press notices and not sleep, so can't I take you home to see her?'

'Not this time, dear. Later.' I had saved that newspaper photograph, and presently showed it to her. 'The man just behind Max, on his left. Remind you of anything?'

'Heck, it almost does.' She held it at different angles, then leaned back, closing the veils on the ocean-blue, opening them widely. 'Billy Kell!'

'Just could be. Old Will Meisel has to find out.'

She stared awhile, darkly perplexed, not distrusting me but perhaps hurt by her certainty that I was withholding too much. 'Will – what *for?* Do I sit quiet and play the piano while you butt your head on a stone wall? I have you back just in time to see you get hurt.'

'Angelo is alive, somewhere.'

'Faith,' she said gently. 'But, Will darling, I just never have seen any of the mountains they say it moved. Well, you think if Angelo's alive he might be in touch with – that fellow?'

'It's possible.'

'I do remember Billy Kell, and a nasty piece of work he was, not that he ever actually did anything to me. He *would* grow up to be a Unity Party job, wouldn't he! I've got to say it: what if you're just breaking your heart over something that – I mean, it was *so long ago!* And *none* of it your fault anyway. Why, Ben – Will – the police must have looked, good and hard, it's what they're for and they have the means, they wouldn't've let it drop. But you – look, if he's – if he died, you probably wouldn't ever even know it. Would you? Or maybe by this time he's a bank teller or a physics professor *or* some ghastly thing, and you – I could shake you.'

'I'm old,' I said. 'I have money. I could help him. Now that I know you're a big girl, there's nothing I want to do more.'

'Then I'll eat my words. If it's what you have to do ...'

'It could mean a lot to you, if I find him. Couldn't it?'

'Darling, to be filthily honest: how do I know?'

2

New York
Thursday, March 9

Today and yesterday make an ending and a beginning. *Drozma, I am nearly certain Angelo is alive.* I'll fill in some background.

Damn the Organic Unity Party, at least it doesn't hide itself. It occupies the first floor of an office building that went up when Lexington was remodeled as one of the two-level avenues – the others are Second and Eighth, a triumph of the Gadget. Lower levels are only for cars equipped with electronic

controls; no wheeled traffic on the upper levels except busses in narrow center lanes; overpasses for crosstown traffic.

My apartment is in a plush downtown development near the ghost of the
Bowery. I started early this morning and walked above Second Avenue Upper
Level for the fun of it. There is a game for the young on those airy overpasses:
you can't climb the guard fences, but through the mesh you can register an
occasional hit on a bus top with wet chewing gum. I don't know what scoring
system is used.

I took a bus on Lexington Upper Level. Organic Unity Party headquarters
is uptown near 125th. And Harlem is not as you remember, Drozma. Negroes
live anywhere in town, or almost anywhere: still some plague spots of white
supremacy, but these are dwindling and unimportant. Harlem is merely
another part of town, with as many pale faces as dark. I didn't find any dark
faces at the Organic Unity offices … Prosperous place. Saving the world for
the pure in heart is profitable. Always was, I reckon.

The receptionist blonde had glassy perfection like a rhinestone. She
assessed my good clothes, turned on welcome – Smile, Standard B-l; semiau-
tomatic; Sugar Daddies, for the control of – and waved me through a frosted
glass door labeled DANIEL WALKER. He's a synthetically jolly endomor-
phic mesomorph softening with fat in his thirties. Just a greeter, one step up
from the blonde. I took my time and got a cigar out of it. Nothing too blatant
about Walker. His gaze is carefully candid; he speaks with the odd hollow
noise of a man whose every word is a quotation. 'I'm interested,' I said. 'You
don't seem to be getting a good press.'

'You're from a newspaper, Mr Meisel?'

'No.' I looked shocked. 'Retired. Used to be in real estate.'

'Never worry about the press,' he quoted. 'Joe doesn't. It's all reactionary.
Doesn't Express the Organic Unity of the People.' He talked in capitals while
I nodded and looked grim and wise. 'In the Larger Sense, we do get a good
press. They hate us, that makes talk, and talk brings us Intelligent Inquiries
like your own.' I bridled: a durned old goat. 'What interests you most about
The Party, Mr Meisel?'

'Your Sense of Purpose,' I said. 'You're not afraid of Stating an Aim.' I lit the
cigar with a lighter that cost me forty-eight bucks – lingeringly, so that Mr
Walker's candid eyes could price-tag it. (I'll bring it home, Drozma. It has a pop-
up white-gold nude half an inch high who whangs the flint with a hammer and
kicks up behind. Aesthetic value about a nickel – the kids might enjoy it.)

'When you're Alone in the World –' I sighed. 'Frankly, Mr Walker, I feel
the Party might give me a Sense of Purpose of my own.' I told him the world
was dangerously drifting. Internationalist delusions. Losing touch with the
Eternal Verities. Skepticism rampant. Speaking as a skeptic myself, wonder if
it *could* ramp? Think maybe it could.

'Yes indeed,' said Mr Walker kindly, and pumped me for autobiography. I let it be dragged out that I was from Maine, widower, no children. Used to be a Republican of course. Not now, by God. They were Reactionary: didn't understand the inevitability of taking steps in Asia. No Sense of Purpose. I was good and cross about the Republicans.

'They're on the way out,' Walker quoted. 'Don't give 'em a thought. Have you wondered why we call it the Organic Unity Party?' He didn't wait to hear. 'Here's something confidential, Mr Meisel. You notice the word "unity" has one inconvenience. Can't call ourselves Unionists or Unitarians – heh-heh. Nor Organists for that matter. The word, Mr Meisel, is *Organite*. Something the Leader gave us only a few days ago, so it isn't in the literature yet, but I'm sure you get the point. Soon it will be on everyone's tongue. On the tongues of our enemies too, who will make fun of it.' He pointed ten manicured fingers at me. 'Let them! We profit by that too.' That was the only moment when true masochistic fanaticism peeked from behind the mask of this soft athlete. 'Now! Why Organic? Because it's the *only* word that expresses the Nature of Society and the Basic Needs of Man! Society is a Unitary Organism. Now! What must any unitary organism have? Simple, isn't it? Means of locomotion. Means of satisfying hunger, of reproducing. Sense organs. Certainly a unitary nervous system. Now! What, for instance, is Society's means of satisfying hunger?' Under his busy hands, his desk leaked pamphlets and throwaways till my pockets were full.

'Agriculture and its workers,' I said, having seen some of the pamphlets and memorized the patter for these ideas, ideas so old and stale that human beings had begun to be hypnotized or repelled by them at least five thousand years ago.

'And what is the nervous system of Society?'

'Well naow, that right there, that bothers me some, frankly. Everybody wants to be part of the nervous system, seems as though.'

'No, friend, there you're wrong – you don't mind my saying it? Not everybody. The man in the street, Mr Meisel, *wants to be ruled*. Don't forget, Democracy must be defined as the greatest *good* for the greatest number. Ask yourself, sir, how many people know what's good for 'em? The man in the street, Mr Meisel, is in need of Enlightened Reeducation. He must find, understand, and accept his appropriate place in the Organism. Or accept without understanding, sometimes. Now! Who's to tell him? Who *can*, except an elite body of the well informed, the natural rulers, in other words the nervous system of Society?'

I attempted to look as if I'd just thought of something bright and shiny. 'Seems as though that's where the Organic Unity Party might come in.' I had let the cigar go out, so that the forty-eight-dollar nude could flip her lid again. I puffed, looking so pleased with myself that I am still queasy at the memory. Walker was pleased too. Nor was I mistaken about the glimmer of contempt I saw in him, swiftly hidden as a weasel peeping over a rock pile.

'You put it very well, Mr Meisel.'

'Doesn't the Forward Labor Party have kind of a similar idear?'

That may have been a slip, a question slightly too intelligent for Old Man Meisel. Walker grew more watchful. He said quietly: 'They have several good ideas. Better understanding of Society than the old parties. They see, same as we do, where the greatest danger is.'

I tightened my tough old Martian neck, to make a flush appear in my well-made cheeks. 'I guess you mean those damn Federalists?'

It was the right noise. I think he was reassured. He said, still softly: 'Worst traitors to America since the Civil War. Yes, of course ... Have you had any connection with Forward Labor, Mr Meisel?'

'Oh no.' So far as I can tell, Drozma, he was reassured.

He made up his mind. 'Like you to have a talk with Keller. Wonderful guy, you'll like him. If you have any doubts about what we're doing, what we stand for, he can clear them up better than me.' Studying me sidelong as if I were a work of art, he boomed into the telephone: 'Bill? How's it?' My throat was cold. This was what I came for. Bill Keller. Billy Kell ... I strained my wicked Martian hearing, but the voice at the other end was only a wiry squeak. 'Uh-huh, Bill ... Like you to meet him when you get a bit of time.' Code, I guessed, for 'allow time to check on the sucker'. Presently Walker covered the mouthpiece to ask me affectionately: 'Going to be free this afternoon, latish?' I was free.

He was easing me to the door. He didn't put an arm over my shoulder because I am three inches taller; he did everything else to make me feel like the Grand Old Man of the Kennebec. 'Confidentially, Bill Keller is *very* high up. Don't misunderstand – just as democratic as you and me. But you see, a Leader like Joe Max, all his responsibilities, worries, he can't give as much time to everyone as he'd like. Has to rely on a chosen few.' Walker showed me crossed fingers. 'Bill Keller is right *up* There!' He patted my back. Old Man Meisel marched out, squaring his shoulders with a Sense of Purpose.

I didn't think they had anyone tailing me; didn't care much. They had my address and could smell around if they chose. I wandered all morning. Had lunch I forget where and wound up at Central Park Zoo. That March day was like a little girl fresh out of her bath, cool, sweet, ready for mischief. I could respond to it now. We're almost human, Drozma: if you can't find the one you love maybe an enemy is the next best.

The bears were restless with spring. An old cinnamon patrolled the front of his enclosure in neurotic pacing, ten steps left, swing of the head, ten right, talking dolorously to himself. The only other watcher at the moment was a brown-faced boy who acknowledged my presence after a while with a bothered inquiry: 'What he moaning about?'

'Doesn't like being in a cage, specially this time of year.'

'Would you turn him loose, mister? If you could?'

'No – too fond of my own skin.'

'Bet he'd chaw us plenty. Wouldn't he?'

'Uh-huh. Couldn't blame him.'

'Naw?'

'It was people like us who put him in there.'

'Yeah. Gee!' He strolled off, frowning at it.

It was past four when I returned to the Organic Unity offices. The lounge was crowded. Walker was busy. I sat for a quarter hour watching the coming and going of Organites. Sad, strained, introverted faces, many of them; others had the power-hungry look. Several were shabby, several prosperous. Only one clear common denominator: they all wanted something. And between a little chap with a placating smirk who probably sought a job sealing envelopes, and a lean paranoid with some brand-new design for the universe, I couldn't find a great deal to choose.

Walker at last escorted me down complex lanes between desks to an office in the rear. Big. They measure rank as Mussolini did, by the amount of carpet between door and desk. When that door opened ...

Drozma, the Martian scent was thick enough to slice.

Yet I would have known him without it, that heavy figure looming like Il Duce. He had altered his face only in the direction of maturity. Thicker cheeks; a practiced, half-genial scowl. He waited impressively before rising to greet us. An underling certainly – there's no doubt in my mind that the grimly human Joseph Max is the fount of authority – nevertheless William Keller was bloated with power and loving it.

I had renewed scent-destroyer in a pay toilet, and my new face is good. True, Sharon had known me. But Sharon loved the memory of me, and saw my look of recognition before she ran to me. In Billy Kell (I must learn to call him William Keller) there was no recognition. He came solidly around the desk, shook hands, grandiosely tolerated Walker's backslapping introduction, dismissed Walker with an eyebrow.

Keller didn't spout ideology. He made me stiffly comfortable, and expected me to talk. I did. I used the lighter, I gabbled autobiography interlarded with Party catchwords. I couldn't afford to be as crass as I had been with Walker. At length, contriving to be severe and yet respectful of my white hairs, he said: 'I'm interested to know what brought you to us, Mr Meisel. The Party's greatest strength is among young people. We wake their crusading spirit, give them something to believe in – that's why nothing can stop us. People with your background are more apt to be hostile. Or tired or discouraged. I'm happy you're here, but tell me more about what made you come.'

I wondered: 'What if I go around that desk and strangle you into telling all you know?' It was a moment of grueling loneliness, the full weight of nine bad years settling on me. I managed to say: 'I think your Leader's personality was a deciding factor, Mr Keller. I've followed Joseph Max's career – radio, television – and then, well, one morning I woke up wanting to *do* something … I've studied his book …'

He nodded after stern reflection. 'The bible of the movement. Can't go wrong if you go by *The Social Organism* – it's all there. And you do seem to have a grasp of the theory – actually not theory: plain social fact. What I want to be sure you understand: this is serious business. We don't play at it, got no patience with dabblers, no time for 'em … There are two types of Party membership: associate and sustaining. Associate membership is for anybody who cares to pay the dues and sign a card. Sustaining is something else again, given only after a period of study. And examination.'

'Seems reasonable. Don't know if I could qualify for anything like that. But I do feel I belong at least among the rank and file of the' – I smiled most humbly – 'of the Organites.'

He asked too softly: 'Now where did you hear that word?'

'Why, Mr Walker said it was to be used in the literature soon.'

'Oh …' His mask was cold as a funeral. 'It happens he shouldn't have said that.' Keller's fingers drummed on the desk. 'Since he did, I'm obliged to tell you – that word is *not* going to be used. Some of the Leader's minor advisers considered it at one time. Inappropriate, too open to ridicule. Naturally Max saw the objections at once. I suggest, Mr Meisel, that you never heard it.'

Damn all calibrated jokes. These people are as humorless as the communazis. I stammered pathetically: 'Well, of course – I didn't realize—'

'Quite all right. You couldn't know.'

'Mr Keller, would it be possible for me to meet – Him?'

He watched secret meditations, shrugged, and nodded. He looked tired now, in almost a human, sympathy-stirring way. 'Sure. Could be arranged. This evening if you're free. Max – by the way, he avoids the Mister: just Max when you meet him the first time – Max has Thursday evening open house for friends of the Party. Take you up myself if you like.' He waved away thanks. 'Glad to. Another thing – among other members of the Party he does like a certain formality. I think of it as a quirk of greatness. Don't care a damn myself, but when we go there we call him Max and use the Mister for each other, you see?' I nodded reverently. 'Drop by at my apartment about eight-thirty if you will. Green Tower Colony, last apartment building up the Esplanade short of the bridge. If you're going back downtown now, a taxi on Eighth Lower Level is the best way to get back uptown to my place. Tell the driver to set the rob for Washington turnoff.' He reached for his telephone. 'See you then.' As I left I heard him ask for Walker's office.

I took wrong lanes among the clattering desks and ran into a snafu of dead ends from which I was rescued by a stenographer. It used up a few minutes. When I reached the lounge Walker was outside at the water cooler. His hyperthyroid gray eyes peered at me blindly, perhaps without recognition. Would a trifling error in the routine of Party termihology have made his big hand quiver so badly he couldn't hold a paper cup?

I wanted to telephone Sharon. But after that interview with the cold and secret thing that used to be Billy Kell I was in a bad reaction, a foul temper. I would have snarled, and scared her, or said too much. I promised myself a talk with her after meeting Max, if it wasn't too late in the evening. I ate a dull dinner alone, then trusted my fortunes and my sacred honor to a taxi driver who whisked me across town and into Eighth Lower Level. In a single-lane entrance radiant with white tile, the motor died of itself; the driver pressed a coin into a wall slot. A panel on his dashboard bloomed in orange light; he touched a tab on it marked W. The motor woke without his guidance and the taxi rolled into a mystery of humming and radiance. My driver lit a smoke with both hands off the wheel. 'What the hell?'

'First time, bud? Never get used to it myself.' He slid to the right, to rest both arms on the back of the seat and face me companionably. By the speed-ometer, we were doing 120. 'Uptown traffic ain't heavy this time of evening. All done with this here Seeing Eye. It ain't human. But you know, bud, it ain't that I'm used to it, but I'm getting so all I think is, hell, here's a chance to stretch. Got a little shocker on the wheel, don't hurt, just reminds you to keep your hands off of it.' He yawned.

I watched a blur of lights and pillars. 'Ever have any accidents?'

'Not a one, they say. It's the scanner. Gives a once-over, the second you drop in your four bits. I got snagged that way once – points was bad, I hadn't known it. Robbie shunted me over into the repair yard just inside the entrance. Repair man's *plenty* human – cost me three bucks and you know what? My fare wouldn't pay it. Sulked. Well, it was a dame with a date to meet. Funny thing, they still get a few folks that think the lower level will take any old car. Got a cop at each entrance to weed 'em out. Damn fool out-of-towners mostly ... Here comes the turnoff.'

'Already?'

He chortled. We hummed through a subterranean clover leaf and up to an exit, where he sighed and took over the wheel. 'Thing of it is,' he said, 'it ain't human ...'

Green Tower Colony is in soaring modern design. Whatever the surfacing material may be, the effect is of green jade with a muted shining. The tower dwarfs the uprights of the bridge, without diminishing the airy pride of a structure now thought of as very old. Keller's apartment is on the fourteenth floor immediately above the twelfth.

Keller admitted me, absently friendly, tired but not relaxed. At his doorbell two other names were listed: Carl Nicholas and Abraham Brown.

As I entered the elaborate foyer I heard piano practice softened by closed doors. Someone was trying to make sense of the eighth Two-Part Invention of Bach, with fingers and brain by no means ready for it. The same left-hand blunder was repeated twice as Keller took my coat and steered me into a solemnly expensive living room. The player knew the error but hadn't learned that only slow practice could correct it. Though muffled, it created a maddening background of frustration, impatience goaded to futility. 'Scotch?' said Keller. 'Still a bit too early to go up there.'

'Thanks.' He busied himself at a fantastic little bar. Something nagged me, besides the stumbling music. Not the lavish evidence of money: I already knew that Max's type of messianic enterprise is a gold mine. The legions of the lonely, the mentally and emotionally starved, the bewildered and resentful, the angry daydreamers – who of them wouldn't chip in five or ten dollars to buy a substitute for God, or Mom, or Big Brother, or the New Jerusalem? It wasn't that: it was something the corner of my eye had noticed as I entered the room and then lost. I rediscovered it while Keller fussed with the drinks. Simply a painting near the arched entrance from the foyer. I had to drift toward it, and stare.

There was a background of melancholy darkness deepening to black. A mirror, and perhaps some light was felt as coming impossibly out of the mirror itself. A young man looked into it. Of him you saw only a bare arm and shoulder, part of an averted cheek; these alone were enough to speak, and poignantly, of extreme youth, whereas the face in the mirror was bitterly knowing with many years. There was in it no grotesque, no exaggeration of age. Taken alone, that sorrowing outward-gazing face might have belonged to a man with thirty or forty difficult and disappointing years behind him. I suppose any imaginative artist might have hit on such a conception, and while the technical skill was great, so is that of a thousand painters. But …

'Like it?' said Keller idly, coming behind me with my drink. 'Abe gets the damnedest ideas sometimes. Not everybody cares for it.'

I put my face in order. 'Rather startling work.'

'I guess so. He doesn't really work at it, just tosses 'em off.'

'Abe – oh, Abraham Brown? I saw the name on your doorbell.'

'Uh-huh.' He was without suspicion: Will Meisel is quite functional. 'Friend of mine, shares this apartment with my uncle and me. He's practicing now, don't like to bust in or I'd introduce you.'

I thought: 'Your uncle?' 'Some other time,' I said. 'Is he – uh – interested in the Party too?'

'More or less.' Keller sat down with his drink, sighed, waved smoke away from his face in a human gesture. 'Not really politically conscious. Just a kid, Mr Meisel. Hasn't found himself. Only twenty-one.'

297

I had to change the subject or betray myself. 'Max live near here?'

Keller smiled tolerantly; his eyes said I was a little slow with the drink. 'Right upstairs. Penthouse ...'

Angelo is alive. I finished my drink, not obsequiously but fast.

A gorilla searched me politely in the penthouse foyer, and Keller apologized for not warning me about it. It's fortunate the grenade fits flat to the skin. Joseph Max was already in a chattering crowd. Keller ran interference for me through a forest of arms, bosoms, cocktail glasses. My mind was downstairs with 'Abraham Brown.' I believe my foggy abstraction was mistaken for the tongue-tied veneration I was supposed to feel in the presence of a Great Man.

At close range the resemblance to Calhoun ends with the jaw. The rest of the big sallow face is blurred and puttyish under a graying mane. Hyperthyroid eyes like Walker's and with the same weak look, almost of blindness. He probably avoids glasses out of vanity, but of course Max is anything but blind: he had Will Meisel weighed, taped, card-indexed in one smiling glance. I saw in him, Drozma, something of the paranoid intensity of Hitler, not very much of the peevish intellectual fury of Lenin and his mirthless bearded schoolboys; plenty of naked power hunger, but very little of the genuine ruggedness we associate with Stalin or Attila or Huey Long. Max is in the tyrant tradition, but there's a weak core. His first major defeat may be his last – he'll shoot himself or get religion. But the machine he's built won't necessarily crack when he does.

'Mr Meisel! Mr Keller spoke of you today. Fine to meet you, sir. Hope you'll want to work right along with us.' He has charm.

I said: 'This is a great year for America.'

Thought that one up all by myself. The large eyes thanked me. I watched him testing the words for a campaign banner. A bright platinum girl blazed a smile at me. Glasses went up in a toast to something or other. At a directive glance from Max, Platinum took me in tow, provided me with a drink, and clung. Miriam Dane, and a smoldering bundle she is.

Vividly, self-consciously female. Her mouth is unhappily petulant when she forgets to smile. She has an air of listening for something that might call her any moment. She was practicing little-girl awe at anything that fell from my lips. I guess I'm into the Party, Drozma, if I choose to play it that way. But now that I know *Angelo is alive*, all bets are off. I have no plan beyond tomorrow morning, when I shall go to that apartment after Keller should have left for his office.

Miriam was watching for someone, and presently asked: 'Abe Brown didn't come up with you and Bill, did he?' Her hand wandered toward a solitaire diamond on her finger as she spoke.

'No, he was practicing. I didn't even meet him ... Honey, I'm a horribly observant old man.' I beamed a Santa Claus look on the diamond. 'Abe Brown?'

There was something wrong with her little act of cute annoyance. It was acting twice removed: meant to look like pretty irritation hiding pleasure, what it hid was not pleasure but some sort of confusion. 'You don't miss much, Mr Meisel – can I call you Will? Yes, that's how it is.' And then she was introducing me here and there. I shook something moist and unappetizing that belonged to Senator Galt of Alaska, and he brayed. Has a hirsute fringe like William Jennings Bryan.

And Carl Nicholas. Yes, Drozma. Max's big room was so full of smoke and women's perfumes that I did not distinguish the scent from Keller's until Miriam took me over to meet him. Gross, ancient, pathetic. His Salvayan eyes are far down in morbid flesh. The nine years have brought him into our change of old age, Drozma. And whereas you, my second father, accepted the change graciously as you accept all inevitable things, and spoke of it once in my presence as your 'assurance of mortality', this Abdicator, this Namir – why, he's a bottle imp, irreconcilable, locked up in fat and weakness and still aching to overturn an uninterested universe. He wheezed and touched my hand but hardly looked at me, intent on Max's performance. Nevertheless I was worried and escaped quickly. Miriam said under her breath: 'Poor guy, he can't help it, gives me the creeps though. Know I shouldn't feel that way. He's done a lot for the Party, Max thinks everything of him.' She patted my arm. 'You're nice. Silly, aren't I?'

'No,' I said. 'You ain't. Just young and slim.' She liked that. 'You're – full time in Party work, Miriam?'

'Oops!' She round-eyed her lovely face at me. 'Didn't you know? Little me, I'm secretary to – Him.' The eyes indicated Max's gaunt grandeur and misted over. 'It's wonderful. I just never get used to it.' After a pause resembling silent prayer (no, I don't dislike Miriam: she's funny and pretty and I think she's going to get hurt) she took me to see Max's famous collection of toy soldiers.

They have a room apart: broad tables, glass-covered cases. Red Indians, Persians, Hindus on elephants, Redcoats, Dutchmen of the Armada. Some are old; one set resembled some I saw at the Museum in Old City – French medieval. They say Max plays with them when he can't sleep. A quirk of greatness? That room was dim when we entered. Miriam turned on overhead lights, disturbing a muttered conversation of two men in shadow at the far end. Miriam ignored them, leading me from case to case. One of them was Daniel Walker, and his smooth round face was ravaged, desolate. The other – old, white-haired, taller than I, absurdly cadaverous – was far gone in drink, glassy-eyed, holding himself upright with silly dignity. As we left, Miriam whispered: 'The old man, that's Dr Hodding …'

Same Hodding, Drozma. Late of the Wales Foundation, and evidently still with this crowd. I don't get it. May have a chance to dig up something.

Max was showing fatigue, darkness under the eyes, when I shook hands for good night. Interesting, being near enough to a Great Man to notice the bad breath. But what I saw at that leave-taking was not a Great Man but a scared child, the kind who's just put an iron pipe on a railroad track. For that matter I met a really great man once. It makes a difference, a greater ease in meeting malign pygmies such as Joseph Max. I visited the White House in 30,864. One doesn't forget.

3

New York
Friday afternoon, March 10

Through the thick apartment door I heard limping footsteps, and turned my changed face away, though I knew I would never be any readier to look at what nine years had done. The door was opening. It was after ten-thirty; I assumed Keller would have gone to work. Namir? To hell with him.

The boy's no taller than Sharon. I realized I was staring at his shoes. No brace; the left sole is thickened. 'Mr Keller home?'

'Why, no. He's at his office.' He has a good voice, mature and musical. I had to meet his eyes, which haven't changed. A V-shaped scar over the right one. No recognition. 'He left about an hour ago.'

'I should've phoned. You must be – Mr Brown?'

'That's right. Phone him from here if you like.'

'Well, I …' I blundered in past him, a confused and silly old man. 'Think I left something here last night. Stopped in for a drink before he took me upstairs to meet Max. You were practicing, I think.'

'Left something?'

'Think so. Can't even recollect what – lighter, notebook, some damn thing. Ever have your memory go back on you? Guess not, at your age. Only had a couple of drinks at that. Name's Meisel.'

'Oh yes. Bill spoke of you. Look around if you want to.'

'Hate to bother you. If I did leave something, guess Mr Keller's uncle wouldn't've noticed – no, he'd already gone upstairs.'

'Mr Nicholas? Hate to wake him. He's not well, sleeps late—'

'Heavens no, don't bother him … Smoke?'

'Thanks.' I used the fancy lighter. While he was intent on the flame I managed for the first time to look directly at his face. The angel of Michelangelo has hurt himself, Drozma. 'I'm always forgetting things too,' he said. Yes, even at twelve he had that sort of tact.

'Just my eighty-year-old memory playing tricks.'

'You don't look eighty, sir.' Sir? Because I'm old, I guess. It's an almost obsolete courtesy.

'Eighty just the same,' I said, and dropped in an armchair with a grunt. 'You have another sixty to go before they call you well preserved.'

His beginning smile vanished as he cocked his young head at me. 'Haven't we met somewhere?' I couldn't answer, before my eyes found the painting near the foyer entrance, I glimpsed fear in him. 'It's your voice,' he said. Fear, and defiance too. 'I can't place it though.'

'Maybe you heard me when I stopped in last night with Keller.'

He shook his head. 'I don't hear anything when I'm practicing.'

Yes, that dreadful Bach … 'Going to music school?'

'No. I may be next fall. I don't know.'

But why was he afraid? 'I heard a fine recital Wednesday. Newcomer. Sharon Brand. Audience went nuts and no wonder.'

'Yes,' he said with too much control. 'I was there.'

So much for our celebrated Martian sixth sense! He was there, remembering Sharon. Perhaps even near me on that balcony, seeing the gleaming downstream passage of that ship as I saw it. Near enough to touch. And because his mind must have been full of Sharon, perhaps, he even remembered me too, now and then – a ghost, a moving shadow. 'Splendid talent,' I said. 'She must've given up everything else for it, to get so far at nineteen. Well, I happen to know she did. Known her since she was a little girl.'

I still peered stupidly at the painting, knowing the hand with his cigarette had stopped halfway to his mouth. He said with desperate politeness: 'Oh …? What sort of person is she, off the stage?'

'Very lovely.' I wanted to yell at him. He should have been bursting with a need to say: *So have I! So have I!* 'Mr Keller told me you painted that.'

'He shouldn't've hung it there. Most people don't care for it.'

'I suppose … Still, why not?'

'Too gloomy maybe. I was trying to find out how Rembrandt made a heavy background mean so much. Unfortunately I'm not an artist, Mr Meisel. I just …' *Not an artist, Angelo?* 'Look, I could swear I've heard you speak somewhere, sometime.'

I gave it up, Drozma. A revulsion against all pretense. I know: that's the medium in which we Observers must live. Yet if I didn't have that vision of Union within a few centuries I don't think I could stand this swimming in lies. The superimposing of a human lie on our inevitable Martian lie was too much for me, that's all. I slumped back in my chair and watched him helplessly. I said: 'Yes, Angelo.'

'No …' He started toward me. He gazed foolishly at his cigarette fallen on the carpet, and did not bend to retrieve it until a feather of smoke was curling upward. 'No,' he said.

'Nine years.'

'I can't believe it. I don't believe it.'

'My face?'

'Well?'

I shut my eyes and talked into reeling darkness: 'Angelo, when I was middle-aged, years before I met you in Latimer, my face was badly injured. A gasoline explosion. I'd been a lot of things before then – actor, teacher (as I told your mother), even a sort of hobo for a while. Shortly before that injury I'd struck it rich – invention, happened to catch on. So I had money, took a chance on a surgeon who was working out a new technique. Prosthetic material I don't begin to understand myself. Unfortunately he had success in only about a third of his attempts, and it raised hell with the failures. Never publicized. He had to give it up. Died a few years ago, knocked himself out trying to develop a test that would eliminate the sixty-odd per cent who couldn't use it. But I was one of his successes, Angelo. What it amounts to: the stuff is malleable under heat; I can alter the cheekbones if I like, and that changes the whole face.' A smaller lie anyway: one that needn't cloud our relation – if we were to have any relation. 'I did that, when I left Latimer. Took on a new personality, as most people can't readily do. There was a pos-sibility the police would think I had something to do with your disappearance, and Feuermann's. Do you remember Jacob Feuermann?'

'Of course,' he whispered, and I could look at him. 'What – what became of Uncle Jacob?'

I wobbled on the edge of forbidden truth. 'Disappeared, same night you did. All we ever knew. Tried to find you maybe. As I have.'

'Find me … Why?'

I didn't even try to answer that. 'Do you believe I'm Ben Miles?'

'I – don't know.'

'Remember the headstone of Mordecai Paxton?'

'Mordecai … Why, yes.'

'Ever tell anyone, who might have passed word to me (whoever I am), that you put dandelions around that headstone?'

'No, I – never did.' And Namir was somewhere close by – sleeping? The doors were closed, our voices very low.

'Did you ever tell anyone about that mirror?'

'Oh! No, never.' He sat on the floor by my chair, his head on his knees. 'You must have had better things to do than look for me.'

'No. I still have that mirror, Angelo.'

'Abraham. Abraham Brown, please.'

'All right, it's a good name.'

'I had – reasons, for taking it in place of my own.'

302

'Well,' I mumbled, 'what's a self? I've lived a long time and don't know ... Glad to see me?' A stumbling human question.

He looked up and tried to smile along with his muttered 'Yes.' A smile of confusion.

'What do you want to do, Abraham? Music?'

'I don't know.' He stood clumsily and walked to the painting, his back to me; lit another smoke as if cruelly hungry for it. 'Bill got me a piano a year ago. I – oh, I work at it.'

'Mm. Billy Kell.'

He didn't look around. 'So you recognized him too.'

'Newspaper photograph. Looked him up on the chance he'd be in touch with you. I'm pretending to be interested in the Organic Unity Party.'

'Only pretending, huh? You never liked Bill, did you?'

'No ... Look at me, Abraham.'

He wouldn't. 'Bill Keller and his uncle have done everything for me. They saved my life, really. A chance to start over, when –' He stopped.

'I met your fiancée last night, at Max's.' He just grunted. 'Keller and his crowd didn't buy your brain, Abraham. You know that gang of power-hunters isn't your dish. You can't look at me and say it is.'

'Don't!' He choked on it, but wouldn't turn around, and somehow there was little force in his protest. 'My brain! If you knew – if I had a good one, would I be –' Again he couldn't go on.

'How long have you been Abraham Brown?'

'Ever since I was picked up in K.C. for breaking a window.'

'What did they do with you?'

'Home for the homeless. Reform school – we weren't supposed to call it that. The court was my legal guardian. Unfortunately it was a jeweler's window, though I hadn't noticed it.'

'Kansas City – that was soon after you left Latimer?'

'Soon? I guess.' He spoke as though suddenly indifferent whether he relived this dream of the past or not. 'Latimer – I simply walked away. Junk yard, patch of woods, think I slept there. Didn't eat anything for two or three days. Later I happened on a rail siding, couple of hobos gave me a hand up. Kansas City. They wanted me to stick with them, but I didn't belong – not with them or anywhere—'

'Wait a minute—'

'You wait a minute. I've never belonged anywhere. I wasn't even a good hobo, so I walked out on 'em.' He faced me at last, quickly as if to catch me off guard. 'I didn't want anything. Can you understand that? Can you? Twelve years old, hungry, not a cent, but I did – not – *want* anything! Oh, Christ, there's not a worse Goddamn thing in the world – well, all right, I saw that plate-glass window – late at night – nice half brick in the gutter, so I thought: "*Here!* Suppose I do that, maybe it'll make me interested in something" – like a nightmare – you try to wake yourself up by hurting yourself ...'

'Was it interesting?'

'Made a hell of a fine smash ... I graduated six years later.'

'Never told about the real past?'

'I did not.' He grinned savagely. 'History's a process of selection, remember, Mr Miles?'

'I met some of your mother's relatives after her death. Nice people.'

'They were nice people,' said Abraham Brown. 'At the school I told three or four different stories. Safer than faking amnesia. They followed up the first two or three, you see, and then decided I was a pathological liar. K.C.'s a long way from Massachusetts. Homeless kids a dime a dozen.'

'Are they, Abraham?'

'That was the impression I received for six years.'

'And it was important not to go back to Latimer?'

'Do you understand *your* mind?'

'No. But you're still the boy who was interested in ethics—'

'Oh, Ben!'

'And you're still blaming yourself for your mother's death: I want you to stop that.'

He stared blindly, but not without understanding. 'Who else—'

'Why blame anyone? Dunn maybe, for hauling you in there without warning and looking like the wrath of God, but he was merely doing his job as he saw it. Why blame anyone? Is blame so important?'

'Yes, if it reminds me that I'm capable of spoiling anything I touch – reminds me never to love anyone too much, or care too much—'

I scrambled up and caught hold of his wrists. 'That's one of the worst damn-fool monkey traps in the world. And there you are, with the biggest mind and heart I'll ever know, running circles inside the trap with your tail in your teeth. You think nobody ever got hurt before? You've got life, and you're saying: "Oh no, there're flies on it, take it away!" '

'I'll live,' he said, and tugged at his wrists a little. 'Miriam, for instance, she's just my size, a nice brassbound decorator's job with her heart in the right place and I don't mean her chest.' I guess he was trying to hurt me with words thrown back in my face. 'Just bitchy enough so I don't have to care whether I'm in love with her or not—'

'Nuts! She's a harmless little woman who could be hurt like anybody else. I think you got engaged to her because Keller and Nicholas and maybe Max planned it that way.'

'What!'

'Yes ... What happened after you graduated?'

He stopped pulling at his frail wrists. 'Oh, I – saw Bill on a telecast. Hitch-
hiked to New York. That's all. What did you—'

'Three years ago?'

'Two.'

'After a year of what, Abraham?'

'What did you mean about – Keller and Nicholas—'

'Skip it – I could be wrong, if I am I'm sorry. Tell me about that year after
you graduated, Abraham.'

'I – oh, I'd never make a good criminal, I'm simply one of the school's failures. Matter of fact I was a good boy. Grease monkey in a filling station for a
month, till they missed something out of the cash register. Hadn't taken it,
but there was the record. Couple of dishwashing jobs. Not good at that either.
Often wondered if I'd make a good flagpole sitter—'

'Why not stop whipping yourself?'

'Ever sleep in a barrel, Mr Meisel?'

The doorbell rang. 'Abraham, you must promise me never to tell Keller or
Nicholas or anyone about knowing me in Latimer.'

He looked up with his wounded, half-cruel smile. 'I *must* promise?'

'If anything connected me with that ancient history, it could mean my life.'
His anger vanished. 'Like you, Abraham, I'm vulnerable.'

He asked softly with no wrath at all: 'Outside the law?'

The bell rang again, long, urgently. 'Yes, in a way, and I can't explain it. If
you ever spoke of that it could be a death sentence.'

He said with immediate sincerity: 'Then I won't speak of it.' I let go his
wrists. He limped into the foyer, where I heard him exclaim: 'Hey, take it
easy! Are you ill, Dr Hodding?'

He looked ill, that old man, so ill and changed that without hearing his
name I might have failed to recognize him from the evening before. He had
been drunk then, fish-eyed drunk. Now there were fires in his cheeks; his
necktie was under one ear, his silvery hair wild. He lurched past Abraham as
if the boy were intrusive furniture. 'Walker – let me see Walker—'

'Dan Walker? He isn't here. Haven't seen him for days.'

'Well, damn the thing, boy, you know where he is.'

'But I don't.'

I stepped forward. Hodding looked frantic enough for physical violence.
But then he shuddered and collapsed in the chair I had abandoned. 'Not at
the office,' he said, and fumbled at his wrinkled lips. 'I called.' He noticed me
and croaked weakly: 'Brown, who the devil is that?'

'Friend of mine. Look, I don't know, haven't heard anything—'

'You will. You will if you don't find him. You'll see—'

One whose voice I remembered said: 'Hodding, cut that out!'

He stood in the silently opened doorway, massive and sodden. His bulk was wrapped in a huge black and orange dressing gown almost hiding the wobbling columns of his ankles. His artificial hair is appropriately white; it was rumpled from the pillow, not much whiter than bloated slabs of cheek.

He still has power. He glanced unconcernedly at Abraham and me. He walked – not a waddle but relentless rolling motion – to stand over Hodding with a mountain's calm. Hodding was choking. 'Ten years. Ten stupid years ago, that's when I should've died—'

'You're hysterical,' said Nicholas-Namir.

'That strange?' Hodding groaned. 'You people bought me – I didn't bargain much, did I? Damn the thing, I was sincere, too. I thought—'

Nicholas slapped him. 'Get up, man!'

Hodding stood, weaving like a dry weed in the wind. 'You've got to find Walker. He's crazy. I am too, or I wouldn't – listen, Nicholas, I was drunk. I let him get in there – yes, sure, into the laboratory. Last night. I was drunk. I must've told him. And now—'

'Be quiet. Come in the back room.'

'Never mind me, damn the thing. You've got to find Walker—'

Nicholas raised his puffy hand again. Hodding cringed. 'Back room. You need a drink. Quit worrying. I'll take care of everything.'

'But Walker—'

'I can find Walker.' While Abraham and I stood bewildered and silly, they were gone. The door closed without a slam.

'Abraham, what was that all about? – if you know.'

He said shortly: 'I don't.'

'They worked on virus mutations at the Wales Foundation. Before Dr Hodding left the place ... Got a laboratory of his own now?'

'How would I – hell, yes, you heard him speak of it.'

'Money and incentive supplied by the Organic Unity Party?'

'Ben, I don't have anything to *do* with all that, with – with the Party. And why should you?'

'I shan't, from now on. It was just a device for getting in touch with Keller, in the hope of finding you.'

'Well,' he said emptily, 'you found me. But why question me about the Party?' He was frightened. In some limited, unwilling way, he was lying to me. 'I'm not even a member, and nobody's urged me to join. I just live here.'

There was an answer to that, but he knew it as well as I. 'Abraham, come and have lunch with me. We need to talk about a lot of things.'

He moved away. 'I ought to be practicing ...'

'I saw Sharon Wednesday evening, after the recital. I think I'll see her again this evening. Will you come along?'

He was far away across the room, pressing his forehead against the coolness of window glass. Presently he said: 'No … She wouldn't remember me. That was childhood. Can't you understand?'

'She does remember you of course. We talked of you.'

'Then let her remember the kid she used to play with, and leave me out of it. Ben, please understand. All right – I've got a brain. I was a damned prodigy, and ran away from it. Because I couldn't stand what my brain showed me. So I'm a coward. Born one.'

'You use an imaginary cowardice as a shield.'

He winced at that, but went on as if I had not spoken: 'And the only way I can keep from going nuts is *not to think at all*. You mean well. But you're trying to stir me up into being something important. I don't think I could. I don't think I want to be anything.'

'Except maybe a musician?'

'Different sort of thinking. You never meet anything mean or cruel in music. I'd like to be able to play Bach before they blow up the world. I'd like to be at the keyboard when they do it.'

'Quite sure they're going to?'

'Aren't they?'

'I wouldn't even dare predict whether the baby will have a harelip. Will you come and have lunch with me?'

'I'm sorry.'

'Tomorrow? Meet me tomorrow noon, Blue River Cafe?'

'I'm – going away for the weekend.'

I wrote my address on a notebook leaf and tore it out. 'Keep this somewhere, Abraham.' He reached for it, red-faced, miserable at his refusal but not changing it. The voices of Namir and Hodding were blurred noise beyond the door. I think Abraham watched me as I went out. I don't know …

4

New York
Friday midnight, March 10

I wrote that last entry here in my apartment only a few hours ago. I feel so changed tonight that the day seems a long time past. When I finished writing this afternoon I telephoned Sharon Brand. I told her nothing of Abraham: she didn't ask, unless some of her silences were questions. I invited myself to call on her and Sophia Wilks in the evening. They live in Brooklyn. Yes, I remember you did too for a few months, Drozma; 30,883, wasn't it – the year the bridge was opened to traffic? It's still in use, parts of it a hundred years old. (Don't know yet how the Dodgers are shaping up this spring.) I needed Sharon, if only to remind me that I don't always blunder ... Now it is midnight, and I imagine new sounds put there, underneath the city's murmurous quiet. They are not there: my mind is creating them because I am frightened.

Drozma, you must have often reviewed the logic of our Observers' laws. By what right do we intrude on Abraham's or any other life?

No right at all, I should say, since 'right' in this case would imply the existence of a superworldly authority dispensing privileges and prohibitions. We Salvayans are agnostics born. Having neither belief nor dogmatic disbelief in any such authority, we interfere in human affairs simply because we can; because, conceitedly or humbly, we hope to promote human good and diminish human evil, so far as we ourselves can know good and evil. How far is that?

After three and a half centuries I have found, for an empirical ethics, no better starting axiom than this: cruelty and evil are virtually synonyms. Human ethical teachers have insisted over the ages that a cruel act is an evil act, and men on the whole endorse the doctrine no matter how repeatedly they violate it. There is inevitable revulsion against any blatant attempt to make cruelty a law of behavior. Unrecognized cruelties, cruelties generated by primitive fears or sanctified by institutional habit – these may continue for centuries; but when human nature sees Caligula in his plainest shapes it will vomit him up and sicken at the memory. Conversely, I recognize nothing as evil unless cruelty is its dominant element. Here, manifestly, human nature isn't quite so willing to follow the logic through. To satisfy semantic order, one must distinguish between mindless cruelty and the malevolent sort. It's a humanly evil thing if a tiger chews a man, but the tiger is impersonal as lightning or avalanche, merely getting his dinner with no malevolence involved. A butcher killing a lamb is similarly impersonal, and I think he drives a rather decent bargain, though an articulate lamb might bleat reproach at me for saying so: the lamb's juicy little carcass in return for a sheltered, well-fed life and a death more merciful than nature is at all likely to provide. If the term 'cruelty' allowed to include the non-malevolent causes of suffering I think the axiom will stand. I notice that a massive amount of human cruelty is non-malevolent, a result of ignorance or inertia or simple bad judgment and misinterpretation of fact.

It doesn't follow that any such mild and limited conception as kindness is synonymous with good. Men trick themselves with the illusion that good and evil are neat opposites: one of the mental short-cuts that turn out to be dead-end traps. Good is a far wider and more inclusive aspect of life. I see its relation to evil as little more than the relation of coexistence. But evil nags us, obsesses us like a headache, while we take good for granted as we take health for granted until it is lost. Yet good is the drink, evil only a poison that is sometimes in the dregs: in the course of living we are likely to shake the glass – no fault of the wine. It is good to sit quiet in the sun: there is no nicely balanced opposing evil to that. Where is there any matching evil to a hearing of the G Minor Fugue? As absurd as asking, what is the opposite of a tree? Recognizing many partial ambivalences between birth and death, we overlook their partial quality and are fooled into supposing that ambivalence is exact and omnipresent. It seems to me that men and Martians will never be very wise until they carry their thinking much further beyond the sign language of deceptive and tempting pictures. I would defy anyone to measure, as in a scale, even the homely equipoise of night and day.

If I must justify my actions on the impersonal level (and I think I should), I concern myself with the life of Abraham Brown because I believe him to have potentially great insight. If I am right, he is bound to train that insight (he cannot help himself) on the more dangerous and urgent of human troubles. If he can reach maturity without disaster, with that growing insight fully grown, I don't know why he shouldn't aid others of his breed to hold the glass steady and throw away the dregs. His means might be any of several – artistic creation, ethical teaching, even political action; that question is secondary, I think. It is certainly not his intelligence alone that made me search nine years for him. Intelligence alone is nothing, or worse: Joseph Max is damned intelligent. Nor is it his heart, which is wounded and confused, nor is it his present self. His present self can be foolish, timid, and disagreeable, as I found out this afternoon. No: in Angelo (and in Abraham) there was and there remains a blend of intelligence, curiosity, courage, and good will. The intelligence is perplexed and tormented by the enormous complexity of life outside him and within. His curiosity and courage, reinforced by blind chance and the inevitable loneliness of the intelligent, have brought him face to face at twenty-one with more ugliness than his heart is ready to endure – he will see greater ugliness in the future, if he lives, and find that his heart is stronger than he thought. His good will is a river blocked with rubbish, but it cannot remain so: it will flow.

I suppose that, like anyone else, Abraham Brown would like to be happy now and then before he dies. I have had much happiness, and expect more. I never won it by seeking it. Long ago, when I loved and married Maja, I thought (just like a human being!) that I was engaged in the pursuit of happiness. Neither she nor I ever found it until we stopped searching; until we learned that love is no more to be possessed than sunshine and that the sun shines when it will. When she survived the difficult birth of Elmaja, we were richly happy, I remember. If one must hunt a reason for happiness, I say it was because we were living to the full extent of our natures: we had our work, our child, our companionship; the sun was high. After I lost her at the birth of our son, my next happiness came a year later, when I was playing the 'Emperor' Concerto with the Old City orchestra, and found that for the first time I knew what to do with that incredible octave passage – you remember it: the rolling storm diminishes and dies away without a climax, where anyone but Beethoven would have written *crescendo*. I understood then (I think I understood) why he did not. My hands conveyed my understanding, and I was happy, no longer enslaved by a backward-looking grief but living as best I could – not a bad best. And so I think that if his maturing mind can guide him through the complex into the simple, if his curiosity and courage can show him the relative smallness of a reform school in Kansas City, if the river of his good will can find its channel, Abraham Brown will be happy enough, more than most. And I think, with all respect to one of the most vital of human documents, that the pursuit of happiness is an occupation of fools.

Drozma, if you're as clever as I know you are, you may deduce from the tone of these reflections that I have already seen Abraham again. That is true. He is in the next room, a room of his own if he cares to use it so. I don't think Max's people have followed him here, but I don't intend to sleep anyway, and I dare say I could handle any of them. There may be a worse thing abroad in the city, or perhaps beyond the city by now, a thing before which the human or Martian mind winces and draws back, refusing belief. Abraham thinks it's there. I am still able to doubt, to cherish a hope that he could be wrong. Being helpless in any case to act against it tonight, I stay awake in partial contemplation, and have written these subjective matters for you, Drozma, with a sense that there may be no opportunity for such things in the days and nights coming toward us. Abraham is sleeping off a pill I prescribed. It should hold him in peace until morning. He snores occasionally, rather like a puppy who's run himself ragged during the day. Now about Sharon:

It's still tough to find your way around Brooklyn: good thing for humanity, to hang onto a few problems it just never can solve. Nowadays you can go over in a new tunnel equipped with an electronic road – Robbie-roads they call 'em – which is actually a continuation of Second Avenue Lower Level. Sharon had claimed that if I took the Greene Avenue turnoff I couldn't miss it – sure, she's human. Maybe I couldn't, but my taxi could. We got lightly involved in something that was called Greenpoint, it didn't say why, and then we tried a handsome avenue which gradually became more or less Flatbush. In the course of time we located Sharon's quiet street, away the other side of Prospect Park. She was right about the turnoff, I'm sure, only we were supposed to turn right after leaving it and then do some other rights and lefts and then – the hell with it. Next time I'll use the subway.

The apartment house is a sort of colony of musicians, refugees from exasperated neighbors. A feminine living room, but Sharon's studio is severe as a laboratory — nothing but the piano, a bookcase, a few chairs. No decoration at all, not even the conventional bust of Chopin or Beethoven. When she took me in there I said: 'Not even one flower vase?' And she said: 'Nup.'

But that was later. When I arrived she was maturely concerned with getting a drink in my hand and surrounding me with cushions. Almost a snowstorm of cushions. I could have done without them, but it made Sharon happy to work away at it, inserting a cushion here and a damn cushion there, wherever I had or might have a bone. Some of them spilled when I stood up to shake hands with Mrs Wilks, but Sharon got them back. Laughing at herself, but quite determined. Inexorable. And pretty enough to make you want to cry out loud.

To Mrs Wilks I was an ancient ex-teacher and musicologist, old enough to remember hearing Rachmaninoff in Boston almost fifty years ago. I had taught 'out West' until my health began to fail. I was fascinated by Sharon's talent, and had introduced myself when I 'happened to recognize' her at the Blue River Café. The lies come so easily, Drozma! I didn't mind that one too much. Sharon was quite willing to collaborate on it. It would have been impractically difficult to explain a resurrected Ben Miles to Sophia Wilks, for she has aged greatly in the human way. In every part of life except music and Sharon's welfare, Sophia has grown dim and forgetful. Faraway memories have taken on a present life, confusing her. She met me graciously, but did not even ask to 'see' my face with her fingers. She settled in what was evidently her accustomed corner of the living room with some complex knitting, aware of us but not quite with us, tranquil among images not ours. When she joined the conversation, as she did only two or three times, her remarks were not completely apropos, and once she spoke in Polish, which Sharon has never learned. However, by unspoken consent, Sharon and I did not talk then about Angelo …

I had bought a late-edition newspaper on my way over, and stuffed it in my overcoat without a glance. Coming back from the kitchen with a second martini for me, Sharon pulled out the paper for a look at the headlines and said: 'Huh!' I got up, spilling cushions but holding fast to the drink, and looked over her shoulder. Because it was an ugly and tragic thing which might have disturbed Sophia to no purpose, Sharon made no more comment except for a silent finger on the black front-page type:

UNITY PARTY WORKER PLUNGES TO DEATH
Leaps Thirty Stories from Max's Penthouse

'Let me show you the studio,' said Sharon. She hovered briefly by Sophia's chair. 'Comfortable, darling?'

'Yes, Sharon.' Sharon inserted a cushion or two to be on the safe side. She hooked a finger in my shirt so that I could walk, drink, and read the paper at the same time.

March 10. Daniel Walker, 34, a worker at the offices of the Organic Unity Party, jumped to his death late this afternoon from the thirtieth-story penthouse of party leader Joseph Max. Mr Max told police that Walker had apparently suffered a nervous breakdown from overwork. Walker had called at the penthouse earlier in the day, in what Mr Max described as a 'distressed and incoherent' state. He was alone in a room of the penthouse while Mr Max spoke on the roof garden with other visitors, among whom were Senator Galt of Alaska and video actor Peter Fry. Walker ran outside and climbed the parapet before the others sensed his intention. He stood there some moments; witnesses agree that his speech was incoherent. Then he either lost his balance or jumped, falling thirty stories to the Esplanade.

Mr Walker was unmarried, a native of Ohio. He is survived by his mother, Mrs Eldon Snow, and a brother, Stephen Walker, both of Cincinnati.

That was when I looked around the good sober studio and made my maundering contribution about a flower vase. 'Nup,' said Sharon. 'Ben, you're acting different, as if something had happened. Come clean.'

'I found him.'

'Ah?' She whispered it, and caught hold of my coat lapels and stared up a long time, trying, I think, to learn without words what finding him had done to me. 'He – is he mixed up the way you thought he might be, with those' – she nodded in distaste at the paper – 'those people?'

'Yes, indirectly.' I told her everything – everything in the way of fact, that is. In trying to describe what Abraham Brown was like in this year 1972, I probably made a mess of it. 'He heard your debut. He thinks you wouldn't remember him ...'

'Reform school – poor kid!' But I hadn't made him real to her as a person: words can't do that. She was still concerned with what might be happening to me, and though it was sweet and flattering, I wished she would abandon that preoccupation.

'I met Walker yesterday. A sort of greeter for high-class suckers, and rather good at it. He pulled a very small boner on Party slanguage, and I believe Billy Kell alias William Keller reamed him out for it.'

'So for that he jumps off the roof?'

'I had a glimpse of him when I was leaving the office. Keller'd had him on the phone. Walker looked as if he'd had it – between the eyes.'

'And this – Hodding?'

'I don't know, sugar. And I'm sure Abraham didn't. It's like seeing only the tail of a beast vanishing behind a tree.'

She shivered, thrust her hands into her hair, looked for comfort to her other friend in the room, the piano. 'Not that I know beans about politics, seems like a terrible lot of noise for small returns, but I did join the Federalist Party a while back. Infant school branch, seeing the lady's under twenty-one. Card and everything, heck. Was that sense, Ben – I do mean Will, Will – or was I swope off my feet by good dialectic?'

'I like their views.'

'You're going to try to get Angelo away from those neo-nazis?'

'He must get away under his own power.'

'And if he doesn't?' She studied me with worried tenderness. 'What if he's sold on their stuff and spits in your eye?' Somehow I must make her stop thinking about me.

'He isn't and wouldn't. He hasn't changed that much, not down, inside. He's tied by gratitude to Keller for practical kindnesses – as I don't doubt Keller meant he should be. Trapped into loyalty toward something that's foreign to him, a loyalty with roots dangerously deep in childhood. He's still the boy who admired Billy Kell. Funny: I just remembered watching you and Angelo bury that little pup of his in the backyard. You probably didn't know I was in my window. You were wrassling a chunk of paving stone – I remember the way your skinny little behind stuck up in the air—'

'Mister! My present dignity!'

'Well, previously you'd been sitting on something dusty, you and your white drawers. Yes, the old things come back.'

'Ah, they come back!' she said. 'Or they've never gone away.'

'The cloud-capped towers – look at them again, Sharon.'

'Why, we had a country, Ben, one of our own. A year or so before you came to Latimer. It began at a special crack on the side-walk of Calumet Street, a twisty crack that looked like S and A together ...'

'Go on, Sharon.'

'We'd known for a long time that the country was there. And speculated about it. The population was primitive, or say quasi-medieval – mighty high percentage of kings and villainous viziers, afreets all the time monkeying around, heck, you couldn't hold 'em ... Angelo drew a gorgeous map of the place, so I had to draw one too, only his was better. I had a river going right over a mountain range, he wouldn't stand for that. It was *my* river, and I got mad, so' – she pressed light finger tips over her eyelids – 'so he said, "Well, then it's a river that goes underground, under the mountains." And redrew his own map to accommodate it, worked swell – caverns and subterranean lakes and stuff ...'

'There might have been a blue-white light that came from nowhere, and your voices came back to you from the wet rocks.'

'Oh – *you'd* know! Well, one day we decreed that we'd step over that crack

313

at last in a certain way, and remain in – the name of the country was Goyalantis – remain there as long as we chose. Of course to others it looked as if we were still in this world. A necessary convention. We felt quietly sorry for the poor souls because they'd look at us (and oh! even make us wash and comb our hair and eat oatmeal and not say damn) and they'd think we were with them when heaven knows we weren't at all. We stayed – in fact I don't remember any ceremony of coming back. I think we never did bother to come back.' She opened her eyes, and they were swimming. 'Your hands haven't changed. Play for me.'

Small stuff. One of Field's sentimental nocturnes I happened to remember, because there was a warming night of March beyond the windows. And then the First Prelude of Chopin, as Sharon had taught me it might be played. She was looking down at me, but seeing Goyalantis too, never having left it, and though there were colored mists in Goyalantis, its air could be crystal, a crystal lens for observation of this other world which is not alone in possession of a special seeing we like to call truth. She said: 'I wasn't mistaken.'

'About what, dear?'

'About you. You see, I never believed you were dead. I remember flatly denying it when I was told. I think I went on denying it, though I learned I couldn't talk about you even to Mother Sophia. I knew all along that the "Waldstein", at the recital – that it was for you. You know, they didn't want me to program it – even Mother Sophia didn't like having it follow the Carr suite. But it had to be there. As I knew three years ago when I started serious toiling over it ...' She added, so softly that I barely heard it above an idle chord I had touched: 'You want me to see him?'

'Only if *you* want to.'

'I'm afraid to, Ben.'

'Then let it wait. But he hasn't left Goyalantis.'

'Do you *know* that?'

'Almost.'

'But maybe he ought to leave it. It's good country for me. I live with dream stuff, and now they're beginning to pay me for it, bless 'em. But for Angelo? You said he was trying for music.'

'Miserably. Fighting it. Like this.' I spoiled a few measures of the Two-Part Invention as Abraham had done. Sharon winced. 'Then goes back and plays it again – same way, *du lieber Gott!*'

'That won't help,' said Sharon Brand. 'Think he's reaching for what he can't ever have?'

'Kid with both hands full of cake reaches for a plum and drops the cake. But you could judge of that better than I.'

She laughed, not happily. 'You get sort of wicked now and then. Oh, you know I'll see him – sometime soon. Feminine curiosity.'

'I'll settle for feminine curiosity.'

I left early, for I learned that Sharon had been working hard that day. An appearance with the Philharmonic, in response to popular demand, had been arranged for April, a first fruit of her triumph. Time to prepare for it was short. She was to give the Franck Symphonic Variations, and told me she still had the thing only three-quarters memorized. Wasn't worried about it either – brr!

The door of my apartment was locked. But I had left it off the latch, on the chance that Abraham might come while I was away – sneering at myself for such a hope but compelled to act on it. Now I had trouble with the key.

The light was off when I opened the door and glimpsed the coal of his cigarette. He knocked a lamp over by groping, laughed helplessly as I found the wall switch. 'Graceful,' he said, and lost his cigarette trying to retrieve the lamp. We got straightened around. He was glad to see me, ashamed, scared. He said: 'The c-cat came back. Kind of singed.'

'Did you think I was sore?'

'You had a right to be.'

'Nah. Hold everything.' I mixed him my Double Grenade: three fingers brandy to one of applejack. Nobody can like it, but if you already feel ghastly, it likes you. Abraham gasped and commented: 'Why'd they bother to split the atom?'

'Go another?'

'Soon as I get the burnt meat out of my throat, not right away …'

'I read about Walker in the paper.'

He shuddered, not at the drink. 'What're they saying?'

'They quote Max: nervous breakdown from overwork.'

'And that's all?'

'His speech was incoherent, it says here.'

'It wasn't, Ben. I was there.'

'Will – Will Meisel. Get used to it. Could be important.'

'I'm sorry. I'll try. I've thought of you the other way.'

I built a milder drink. 'Take this one slow. It's supposed to glaze over the charred spots.' He was looking at horror, and words wouldn't come. But his young face was not, as it had been this morning, a battleground. It was the face of a sleeper beginning to wake – to a most ugly day, but at least waking. 'Abe, suppose I run through what I know or guess. You catch me up if I have any facts wrong.' He nodded gratefully. 'Daniel Walker is – was – a man for big emotional conversions. He couldn't just step out of the Organic Unity Party. If he fell out of love with it he'd have to hate it, probably with a phase of hating the whole world and everyone in it. Call him manic-depressive, for a label. No middle ground: all black and white for Daniel Walker. I was at the Party office twice yesterday. Walker slipped up, told me something that was out of favor, already obsolete when I went back in the afternoon. Keller jumped on him for it. Walker's mind flopped over on its other side. Much faithful service and then a kick in the teeth—'

'Bill? Bill jumped on him?'

'Yes. Had him on the phone, and I happened to see Walker afterward on my way out. Looked sandbagged. So – Walker, in his tailspin, and Dr Hodding, pie-eyed drunk, conferred last night. I saw 'em at Max's, among the pretty toy soldiers. Then Walker got into Hodding's laboratory and took – something.' Abraham whitened under his tan; I was afraid the glass would jump from his hand. 'Just guessing: a new virus?'

He managed to set his glass on the floor. 'New. Can be airborne. Indefinitely viable, and no defenses in the human – no, no! – *mammalian* organism, that's what Dr Hodding was mumbling when – well, Mr Nicholas gave him sleeping powders, after you left, but, poor devil, he wasn't quite out, he started mumbling and tossing on the bed after Mr Nicholas went upstairs and left me with him. Mammalian – it isn't just us, Ben – Will – it's everything. Medium of distribution too – some stuff like pollen – green—'

'Slow down, boy. Walker did get it, then?'

'Yes.'

'Contagious-plus, of course.'

'Respiratory system. He kept muttering about his monkeys and hamsters. Kept saying: "Macacus rhesus eighty-five per cent." I don't know if that meant mortality. I think it did. Neurotoxin. Reaches the nervous system through the respiratory. Spinal paralysis …'

'And Walker?'

'Had it with him this afternoon. I stayed with Hodding – hours, I guess – chewing my damn nails, not knowing anything to do. Bill came home early, at three. Hodding was sound asleep then. Bill went up to Max's. I tagged along, don't think he wanted me to. They were out on the roof garden: Senator Galt sounding off about nothing much, Max pretending to listen. Miriam was there. That drip Peter Fry. Mr Nicholas' – Abraham was shaking all over, reaching toward the drink but not taking – it up – 'Nicholas, taking it easy in a lounge chair built to hold him. God, what a beautiful afternoon! Warm … I don't think Galt and Fry knew Walker was there in the penthouse. I saw Miriam was worried about something, got her alone a second and asked. She started to tell me something about Walker in there building up a jag, but right then he came tearing out, ran to the parapet. Nobody could've stopped him, but nobody tried. He was balancing there with that – that damned peewee test tube, looked like green powder. Waved it at us. He was yelling: "Airborne! Airborne!" He wasn't incoherent. Laughing like crazy, but wasn't incoherent. He flung it out over the Esplanade – must've shattered into dust, you wouldn't even find the cork. Then he went after it. Not like jumping. Like floating out, as if he thought he could fly ... Max – Max had some kind of fit. Heart maybe. Turned white and started to fold. I think Miriam took care of him. Mr Nicholas said: "Get the kid out of here!" And Bill hustled me downstairs. I didn't see the police. The others must have agreed to say nothing about me, I don't know why they bothered. Police didn't hear about Bill's being there either, I think. He stayed with me, couple of hours, I guess, until somebody phoned down from Max's and he went back up there. Then I – then I—'

'Then you came to me. Do they know you're here?'

'I don't think so. Just walked out, didn't meet anybody.' He could finish the drink now, the glass rattling against his teeth.

'Are you through with them, Abraham?'

He cried out: 'Christ, I had every chance to ask myself, "What's a political party doing, paying a man to invent – to discover" – I *knew!* I must have known, and wouldn't look. Just some important abstract research, Bill said – yes, that's something *Bill* said to me, when I was curious—'

'Quiet down, friend. Probably what Hodding thought himself, at least when it started. He used to be a good scientist. Emotional flaw somewhere, maybe just an overdeveloped ability to kid himself about anything not related to his field—'

'But why didn't I – why didn't I—'

'Why don't you get some sleep?'

He raved then about how he'd only bring trouble to me too. I won't record that. There were questions I could have asked. Nicholas, 'taking it easy in a lounge chair', must certainly have known what Walker had with him. Max perhaps didn't know until too late. Max and Nicholas together could surely have overpowered Walker and taken the thing away. I asked none of those questions. I fetched a sleeping pill and made the boy swallow it.

So it's out there, Drozma – probably. I cling to frail scraps of possibility. Walker stole the wrong test tube – no, because Hodding discovered the loss in a horribly sober morning and knew what it meant.

Maybe it's not as 'successful' as Hodding thought. He couldn't be positive that the human organism has no defenses. Maybe wind will sweep it away, and factors not discoverable in the laboratory will make it not so viable. Maybe the tube fell unbroken in the river. Oh sure, Drozma, maybe there are 'canals' on Mars.

5

New York
Saturday night, March 11

Sunrise was gradual and deep this morning. I sat by one of my living-room windows and saw the grayness above the East River take on a slow flush and then a hint of gold. Spires and rooftops on the Brooklyn side were catching hold of light like cobwebs on the grass after a rain. I watched a tug slip across the river on some errand clothed in magic by the latter end of night. It drew a soft line of smoke on the water, for there was a small breeze out of the east. The line broadened to a pathway, white and gold at my end, total mystery beyond.

Abraham stirred and sighed. Without turning my head, I knew it when he crept into the room with his shoes in his hand. I said: 'Don't go.'

He set the shoes on the floor and limped toward me in stockinged feet. In that dimness I could see that his face was calm, without anger and perhaps without fear. An empty calm, spent, like despair. 'Lordy, didn't you even go to bed?'

'I never need much sleep. You don't need to go, Abraham.'

'But I do.'

'Well, where?'

'I don't know – haven't thought.'

'Not back to Keller and Nicholas.'

'No … I can't bring on you the trouble I bring to everyone who knows me.'

'That's nothing but vanity upside down. Something made you come here, so why go away?'

'I had to talk to someone who could listen. Selfish need. So I – did talk. But—'

'You never brought any trouble on Keller and Nicholas. They brought it on you. You could see that if you'd look at it straight.'

'I don't know …' He knelt at the windowsill, staring out with his chin on his arms. 'Good, isn't it? And doesn't need the human to be good. Except for eyes to see it. Ears for the boat whistles – that won't be there if – oh well, who's to say a chipmunk couldn't enjoy a sunrise? But then, maybe there won't even be –' He was silent a long time. 'Have you thought about it that way? Will? What if all those buildings over there were empty? Heaps of steel and stone. How long would they stand, with nobody to care about 'em? Maybe not even any rats to gnaw away at the wooden parts. Birds might use the roofs, don't you think? Gulls – where do seagulls build?'

'Dead trees.'

'Other birds might use 'em, though. They ought to make good small mountains, cliffs. A world of birds and bugs and reptiles. Orioles, ephemerids, little snakes with nobody to tread and kill 'em. Trees everywhere, or grass. First just a funny little green finger between two paving stones, and then before too long – you know, I read somewhere that the water level is rising much faster than in the last century. Maybe that'll take care of everything. The big waves would make short work of the best of towers, I'm sure of that. Nice old Hudson an inland sea. And the Mohawk Valley. New England would be a big island, New York State a bunch of little mountainous islands, and just nobody to bother the garter snakes.'

'Kind of rough on Gimbel's Basement. Abe, the Black Death of the fourteenth century probably knocked over only about half of Europe, and that was in a time when everybody and his brother had fleas, to make things easy for *Bacillus pestis*. The flu of 1918 killed more than the First World War, but statistically it hardly made a dent in the human race.'

He rolled his forehead on his arms. 'Yes, they might find it necessary to use a few hydrogen bombs to help things along. That'll do it, that and a rising water level.'

'Abe, I really do believe there's time for coffee before the end of the world.'

He sighed sharply and stood up, smiling faintly, perhaps making up his mind, or yielding to my insistence only because he no longer cared much about anything. 'All right. Let me get it. I won't run away.'

'You mean you won't ever run away from anything again?'

He glanced back at me from the doorway, stooping to push his shoes on. 'Why, I wouldn't even predict, and I quote, whether the baby will have a harelip. You like it strong and black?'

'Strong enough to grow *short* hair on a billiard ball.'

We were still lingering over breakfast in the kitchen – a good breakfast at that, and Abraham didn't refuse to enjoy it – when Sharon came.

I write that baldly, because I don't know any words that tell what it is that happens when someone enters a room. The air changes. The whole orientation is something that never happened before. If the person is Sharon, the changed air has spice and sparkle, the orientation is toward warmth, toward what we call hope: merely another name for a desire to go on living. A lot of talk, maybe, for the process of hearing the doorbell, telling Abraham to sit still, walking through to the door, seeing a bright bit of human stuff in a wrapping of bunny fur – and of course, being Sharon, no hat.

'I'm coming in anyway, so may I? How can anyone *be* so early? How do I know it's early? Because you've still got egg on your chin.' She kicked the door shut behind her. 'Nup, on this side.' She rubbed the place with a peewee handkerchief and pulled me down to kiss it. 'Just to make it well, poor egg.'

She flung the coat somewhere or other. She was wearing leaf-brown trousers – they don't call 'em slacks any more – and a crisp yellow blouse that made music with ocean-blue eyes. It's always trousers nowadays except for evening dress-up, unfortunate for fat girls but fine for Sharon. 'Smoke me a light, Will – I mean light me – I mean I couldn't stay away. You won.'

'Things happened when you couldn't sleep?'

She watched me with a rather helpless smile above the match flame. 'Do you telepath or something? Not that I'd mind awfully … Oh, I began remembering more and more, couldn't stop – please, Will, without prejudice to my right of being nine years older, huh? But – take me to him.'

'Sure?'

'Why, you sevenfold so-and-so, I can't rest till I see him. Once anyway. And you knew I couldn't. Green Tower, you said – I sort of wouldn't care to go alone. Well, look –' She unfastened a button of my shirt, puffed a lungful of smoke through the opening, and stood back to study the effect. 'Like that, you – you character. Make people start smoldering with silly ideas, you've got to take the consequences.'

I slipped an arm around her and walked her into the kitchen. I felt the shock in her like an electric charge, and took my arm away.

Abraham was standing on the other side of the cluttered table. I saw his small brown hands spread out, fingertips supporting him, and heard him say raggedly: 'Don't look now, Will, but you're still smoking.'

I ignored that, as Sharon did. I don't know how long they stood quietly, staring at each other. Long enough for a universe to spin a while. I remember picking up a spoon and setting it down with great care lest I hurt the silence. Neither had spoken when Sharon walked around the table. She raised her hands to his forehead and moved them down slowly, over his eyes and cheeks and mouth, until they were resting on his shoulders. He said nothing, but she spoke as if answering something, with gravity and a little surprise: 'Why, did you think you could love any woman but me?'

I said: 'For your information, Abraham, the world won't blow up.' He might have heard it; I don't know. I stepped into the living room and shrugged on my overcoat. At the door I glanced down and muttered: 'Nah, Elmis, not slippers.' My shoes were by the armchair where I had kicked them off, so I studiously shoved my old four-toed feet into them. I didn't hear any conversation from the kitchen. I went out to the elevator and rode down and walked a mile or so into the city's morning. The wind was chilly but very fresh and sweet.

After a time I was aware that someone was following me. I put on an act of window-shopping in one or two places, but couldn't get a fair look at him. A small man in nondescript gray-brown, busily peering into windows himself, his face averted. I tried a few aimless turnings, enough to make certain that I was his quarry: there was no doubt of it; he clung. I climbed to Second Avenue Upper Level, and walked a few blocks before pausing at a bus stop to look back. He was no longer with me. That I found strange – if a bus came now he'd lose me – unless he had turned over the task to some other shadow. I strolled away from the bus stop and entered a drugstore on the Upper Level, finding a seat at the soda counter from which I could study the sidewalk over my coffee. No one else came in while I lounged there. No one even looked in, except a harmless-seeming woman who halted to glance at the menu in the window and moved on.

I couldn't detect anyone tailing me as I gradually retraced my course to the apartment house. I had used up about an hour and a half. It was past ten o'clock and the sky had grown dingy, preparing a spring storm.

Someone with a familiar back was hurrying for the self-service elevator when I came into the lobby. Bright platinum hair, a fine hip-swing. Not good. I grabbed the elevator door as she was going to close it. 'Oh, *hello*, Will! But how lucky! I was on my way to see you.'

'Fine.' I searched a bumbling and semiparalyzed brain for something that might work. 'Things are kind of upset – can't I take you out somewhere? Had breakfast? Coffee anyhow—'

'Oh my, no!' She batted cute eyelashes at me. 'Too much trouble, and anyway I had breakfast.' She poked the button and the cage started up. I could have asked how she happened to know my floor. I didn't. 'I don't mind a bit, Will – I've seen how you helpless men keep house, everything just everywhere—'

'But—'

'Now, that's all right, don't give it a *thought!*' She captured my arm and hugged it to her side. 'Simply had to talk to you about something, awfully important, that is to me –' Miriam Dane chattered on, managing to say actually nothing at all, until we were in front of my door. I tried again. 'Got a friend staying with me, he's been ill and – well, sleeping late. Small apartment. Really be better if we—'

'Now you stop fretting. I'll be *so* quiet, and it's only for a minute.' She wasn't exactly the woman I had met at Max's. In some subtle fashion she looked older. I had not sensed any steel of determination in her then. She had it now, and there was coldness in the steel. She quit smiling and chattering, because I had quit being Santa Claus. She watched me as if she intended to hypnotize the key ring out of my pocket. It wouldn't do. I stared back at her, not wanting to get rough or disagreeable, not reaching for my keys either. The smile was all gone. A tiny shoe with a rhinestone buckle began to tap on the floor. She said without any pretense, evenly and clearly: 'It's necessary that I see Abe Brown.' So they had followed him last night. Followed, but hadn't done anything. Until now. Too busy maybe: Max and his boys might not be having an easy time over the death of Daniel Walker, with a New York police force which they say has been incredibly honest for the last thirteen or fourteen years. 'Why, Miriam?'

'Why!' Her neat shoulders rose and fell. 'After all! We're engaged. As you know. I could ask, why's it any of your business?'

'He came to me. That made it my business.'

'Really! He's of age. And this happens to be Party business.'

It was already open war. I said: 'I still want to know why.'

'You're not a member. What right've you got to know?'

'He's not a member either.' I was making my voice reasonably strong, hoping it might carry through the thick door.

'Needn't shout.' She was showing the whites of her eyes. 'That's got nothing to do with it, Mr Meisel. Don't be so difficult.'

'All right. Come in. But do you mind if I look in your handbag?'

'My – handbag?' I saw then that she used a trace of rouge: her cheeks displayed unhealthy little roses as the blood drained out of them. Her right hand darted to the blue bag, and my hand closed over hers before she could open the catch. It could be tough for me, if she screamed. I didn't think she would, and I was right. She let the bag go, stood away with fingers pressed to her bright mouth.

It was there, in the bag. A .22, like a toy but big enough. I hate the things anyway. I made sure of the safety, dropped the gun in my hip pocket, and returned the bag. 'I carry it for protection,' she said, pathetic now. 'Have to go around queer places sometimes.' The pathos became precariously held dignity. 'I've got a license for it. I can show you. It's here – somewhere.' As she groped in the bag a tear spilled and rolled to her mouth corner. Uncalculated. So was the sniff, the flirt of her little tongue to her mouth corner while her hands were flutteringly busy. 'You don't have to be so damn *mean*—'

'Keep the license,' I said, 'and I'll give you back the ordnance, when you leave.' I punched the bell a couple of times and thrust my key noisily in the lock. 'Coming in?' Impolitely I marched in ahead of her.

Sharon was in the armchair by the window with her feet tucked under her. Abraham at least had not noticed our voices out there. He sat on the floor beside her, full of quiet, drowsily conscious of her hand in his hair, not of much else maybe. Sharon smiled and murmured: 'Knew it was you so I didn't get up. We've talked ourselves into a coma, and—'

Then Miriam stepped in behind me and said: 'Oh.'

I waved my hand, a foggy human gesture that tried to say this wasn't my doing. At the sound of Miriam's exclamation Abraham looked around but didn't rise at once, only stared in shock. When he did stand up Sharon laced her fingers in his, and I could see he wanted that. Sharon was intent, outwardly cool. So is a good artilleryman getting ready for a big one.

Miriam had probably never looked prettier herself. She had won her small brush with tears: they only swam in her eyes without falling. Trim and exquisite in her blue trousers, white fur jacket, a little sparkling something-or-other of a hat on the white shining of her hair, she was a gentle pin-up deeply wronged. Sharon said neutrally: 'Miss Dane, I think?'

Miriam tried to dismiss her with one contemptuous flickering glance. 'Abe, don't on any account let me *disturb* anything, but Bill Keller wants to see you, I do mean right away.'

'I'm sorry.' Abraham spoke evenly; painfully conscious of his own words, but there was quiet in him; I knew it. 'I don't want to see him.'

'What!'

'I'm sorry, Miriam. That's how it is.' I leaned back feebly against the wall, an old man obscurely minding his own business. That would do, what Abraham had said. The next few minutes were not going to be nice, but the boy needed no help. 'If you see Bill, you might as well tell him that. I'm not going back there, Miriam, not seeing any of them again.'

I don't believe Miriam had been braced for anything like that. She had come looking for a confused, easily managed boy. She stared into her hands, flushed and paled, unable to conceal her growing sense of defeat and a growing panic which, I sensed, had little to do with her relation to Abraham. After a few false starts she said softly: 'Abe, there's such a thing as loyalty. Or wouldn't you know?'

Abraham nodded. 'They'll have to think of me as a heel, Bill and Mr Nicholas and the rest. That's all right. I do myself, but for a different reason: I gave my loyalty where I should've known it couldn't remain. I'm not going back, Miriam.'

Sharon said: 'There are other loyalties, Miss Dane. Your leader Joseph Max is what I'd have to call disloyal to his fellow men.'

I didn't think Miriam's policy of ignoring Sharon would work much longer. But she went on trying it. Staring at Abraham and then at the ring on her left hand, she whispered: 'None even to me, apparently …'

Sharon said: 'People change.'

Even that did not make Miriam look at her. It was like another answer to the same thing when Abraham said: 'Dr Hodding was already broken when the Party bought him – wasn't he, Miriam? Sick, turning to alcohol dreams for escape because even the good work he did at the Wales Foundation had alarmed him, alarmed part of him anyway. Miriam, tell me this: why did a thing supposed to be an openly registered political party want to subsidize a man to invent a new disease—'

'That's a lie! It wasn't *like* that, Abe!'

'It's what happened.' Abraham shook his head. I could see pain growing in the deep shadow of his eyes, pain and perhaps a hint of uncertainty. 'You were there on the roof garden, Miriam. Once you told me yourself that nothing happens in the Party without your knowing all about it.'

'But you don't understand. We didn't know what Hodding was—'

'Didn't *know!*'

'No, we did not. He – I could tell you – all right, I will tell you, though I wasn't supposed to …'

Sharon noticed her free hand had become a fist. She relaxed it carefully. She said: 'Yes, do.' And still Miriam managed to ignore her.

'Abe, Max has only just found out what Hodding really was, only just this morning. That's why you've got to come back. Nicholas says you were alone with Hodding, heard some of his talk. Max has got to see you, hear about it directly from you – you owe us that much, seems to me. And Bill, Bill Keller is *sick*, Abe. He broke down. We didn't have any sleep, any of us, and Bill is sick, can't get hold of himself, keeps asking for you …'

She could see as well as I did that it made him waver. Perhaps she didn't see Sharon's hand, which was saying more than I could have said with any verbal interference. 'Why, Bill's never sick—'

'But he is! I just came from him. Oh, Abe, he's done so much for you – and nobody's asking you to do any Party work, just to come and see him, talk to him. Did he ever ask you for any help before—'

'Miriam, if he's sick it's not going to help him to see me, when I've rejected the things he believes in. And you haven't told me what you started to. What is Dr Hodding, as of this morning?'

'That's a nasty thing to say.' Miriam had dignity when she wanted to use it. 'I don't think your present company's improved you, Abe, do you mind my mentioning it? Hodding's what he always was, only we didn't know it. All right – and you'd better listen. You won't like it, maybe you'll refuse to believe what we finally got out of that poor crazy old man—'

Sharon said to no one in particular: 'Methods?'

Miriam swung toward her at last. 'I *beg* your pardon?'

'Interested in the methods used, for getting information from a poor crazy old man.'

It was war of course, and Sharon had chosen a moment when a little goading might sweep Miriam toward revealing hysteria. It didn't quite work. Miriam stared, and sputtered, and turned back to Abraham. 'Abe, if you can get your mind off your imaginative friends long enough to listen: we haven't done a single thing that wasn't justified by the emergency. A man like Hodding can't be handled with gloves. I'm trying to tell you what he is. We found out.' Her voice was rising. 'Never mind how – you've got that weak, soft streak – it doesn't matter anyway. Abe, Hodding has been in the pay of China for the last three years.' I believe I laughed; Abraham didn't. 'He's been using our American facilities to work up something to use in Asia. And fooling us with talk of abstract research, research that might have a humanitarian purpose – Max went for that, naturally – Max thought Hodding was working on a – a—'

Abraham had gone very white. He understood her hesitation too, I think. He said: 'Is that going to be given to the press? Like that?'

'Certainly!' Miriam cried, and the high edge of hysteria was there. 'Certainly, when we're ready.'

Sharon cocked her head at her little stockinged feet and dropped them softly. She started to speak, but Abraham checked her. He said: 'All you need now is a written confession from Hodding? Something like that?'

'We have it already,' she snapped.

'Then you don't need me. Miriam, it stinks.'

She pressed her hand to her forehead with the pathos of weariness. 'So you can't see. Like a spoiled child. With a new toy too.' She studied Sharon with the same show of weariness, dazed indifference: 'Just who are you, or aren't I supposed to ask?'

'A junior member of the Federalist Party.'

'Oh. One of those. I might've known. And this cheap clumsy spy' – she looked me up and down; I let it ride – 'what do you pay him, may one ask? Not that it matters. Well, Miss – Miss—'

'Brand. Sharon Brand.'

'Oh yes. Thought I'd seen your picture somewhere. You write children's books or something, don't you?'

Sharon chuckled. 'Uh-huh. Nice big ones.'

'Well, you might tell your nigger boss in the Federalist Party that, as a spy, friend Meisel is a flop—'

'Oh, that tail you had on me this morning,' I said. 'Wondered why he quit so easy. It was to phone you, wasn't it? Let you know I was away from the apartment house or something?'

But she was ignoring me now. 'Your own methods seem to have worked better, Miss Brand? Must be hard on the heels, starting so young. My fault really, only I never would have thought Abe had a yen for children. Oh, here, you might want this when you're of age.' She twisted off the ring and flung it clumsily. Except to twitch her feet aside so that the ring rolled under the armchair, Sharon didn't look at it or move.

Even after yielding to that need for a gesture, Miriam must have held some frail hope of success, slow in dying. She approached Abraham with outstretched appealing hands. Though I had almost no doubt of the outcome, I found I was holding my breath. Miriam had talent.

It was not his *distant* quiet that broke her control. Something else; something I saw in him, and though I know he tried to hide it, Miriam must have seen it too. Pity. I heard her gasp, saw her make a savage unthinking motion toward her handbag. I saw Sharon jump up; if Miriam had completed the motion, I believe Sharon would have thrown herself in front of Abraham before he could stop her. But Miriam's mind remembered where the gun was, more quickly than her hand. She choked and turned away harmless and pitiful. 'I'll take – what you said, to Joe Max.' It was interesting to me that she said 'Joe Max' just then. 'Abe, you're making a terrible mistake.'

I was glad that Abraham answered nothing. She went by me slowly, not looking at me, perhaps not even thinking about the gun which I would not have returned to her. She didn't slam the door.

Sharon's arms were around Abraham, tight and close. 'Will,' she said over her shoulder, 'Will, is the sun by any chance over the yardarm, and I don't mean on my account?'

6

New York
Sunday night, March 12

Sharon went into the country with us today. A holiday, a half-impromptu picnic. Not an escape, unless Sharon may have thought of it that way, a little. Spring has come earlier than ever this year. There was some small rain last night, and today the earth was washed and sweet and ready; we found bright winter aconite in the woods, and the first of the tiny white violets that hide in corners of the rocks.

We rented a car, Abe and I, and rather than oblige us to grope through Brooklyn, Sharon met us at a subway exit uptown. We didn't venture on a Robbie-road, but went over the old bridge and followed one of the fine North Jersey highways until we came on a modest road that promised to lead into the Ramapos. Just the three of us, and by unspoken consent we said not a word during the drive about what had happened or might have happened at the Green Tower Colony Friday afternoon.

It seems that in order to contemplate a major calamity to the human species you need distance. More than the Martian distance. When the black wings swoop too close your eyes blur; Martian or human, you must look away, not so much for the sake of hoping or pretending, but because your heart says: 'I am not ready.' Or it says, perhaps: 'There was no need of this.

There could have been another way …' The pilot over Hiroshima – could he look down?

Certainly there was nothing in the spring woods to remind us of grief.

There had been no more approaches from Max's people since Miriam's visit. Abraham and I were not followed when we hunted up that rental garage. Nothing was prowling behind us when we took that little road off the highway. Sharon had brought a basket with lunch, and we had wine – good Catawba wine from somewhere in the smiling lake country.

I could turn my face away from the homely ugliness of our rented car; I could forget our stuffy American clothes and imagine that we were – no matter where. Perhaps a mountainous island in that country where once upon a time human life was a pleasant thing to explore – or so said Theocritus, Anacreon, other voices. Pan never died. He watches and breathes across the pipes, wherever earth and forest, field and sky can come together and make their harmony for the Arcadian son of Hermes.

Often enough, Drozma, I think of your great-grandfather, how he labored to collect and recopy the writings of his own great-grandfather, who knew Hellas as it truly was, when the sun was high. Those writings could be published, if Union is ever possible. I tried to imagine Union, this afternoon. The dream was blotted away by another image – the image of a neat little tube full of green powder.

I saw Abraham stretch comfortably with his head in Sharon's lap. He said: 'Will, I begin to tell myself it couldn't happen. Anyway there's a good chance. Isn't there?'

'A chance.'

'What Hodding developed wasn't as powerful as he thought. Or maybe not as easy to spread, not as viable outside the laboratory. Or the tube fell into the river and was carried unbroken out to sea.'

'In Hodding's ramblings, did he say anything about the incubation period?' I asked that, not wanting to know.

'Not that I heard … Out to sea – but the cork would come loose sometime, and Lord, what then? The sea's mammalian life – transmission sooner or later back to—'

'Don't,' said Sharon, and slid her hand over his eyes.

'Well, it didn't happen,' said Abraham, for her sake. 'So far as today is concerned, it didn't happen.' She bent down until her tumbling hair hid his face, to whisper something that they thought was none of my business; no doubt something to do with the hour when they left me in a contemplation that looked like human sleepiness, and strolled away into the woods. They are very sweet and natural children, when civilization relaxes its grip on them. Capable of unspoken understanding, too – that should help, if it turns out that they have years together and not just a few bright moments snatched before the climax of a world disaster. It seemed to me that he was following a train of thought parallel to mine, for presently he said: 'Will, assuming nothing happened when Walker threw that thing – assuming any of us can have such a thing as another slice of, say, forty or fifty years – what about my forty or fifty? I'm thinking about work. This blue-eyed lady's got no such problem: she already knows what she can do. And it looks to me as if most people had no such problem: a few have a very plain call to one kind of achievement or another, and the big majority just think of work as an unavoidable unpleasantness, something to be got out of the way so that they can play at nothing in particular, if they can't find some means of dodging it altogether – which is no good for me, but if I have a call to anything, damn it, it usually sounds like a hundred voices calling all at once. Locomotive with no rails … You told me a while ago that you'd bummed around a lot, tried several different things. Ever hit on the one kind of work you really wanted to do? Something that made all the rest a prologue?'

Yes, but I couldn't say so. Forcing myself back into the human frame of reference, and hastily, I said: 'Nothing to offer but a moth-eaten bromide: find out what you can do best and stay with it. Finding out might take a while. I'm merely passing it back to you.'

He smiled. 'Yes, but that might be one of the hard bromides the moths can't chew. And one finds out by trial and error? Mostly error?'

'Maybe. At twelve you were rather preoccupied by the plague-take-it mysteries we like to wrap up in a bundle named ethics.'

'Yes.' He watched me a long while, his dark eyes hazy. 'Yes, I was, Will …'

'And?'

'Yes, I still am. Learning more and knowing less all the time.'

'Oh, after a while you work out a synthesis that holds up to your satisfaction. In your thirties perhaps, if you're lucky.'

'And to translate preoccupation with ethics into terms of life work?'

'Teach. Write. Preach. Act, though action is always dangerous.'

'Always?' said Sharon.

'Always, unless you can trace out the possible consequences to a pretty large distance. Sometimes you can, with a moderate degree of certainty, enough for practical purposes. If you can't, then the time-tested actions are – well, safer anyway, as the man in the street has always recognized: not necessarily better of course.'

'I wonder,' said Abraham, 'if I'd ever think I knew enough to act.'

'If you don't, then study all your life and talk a little when you believe you have something to say.'

He chuckled and threw a handful of pine needles at me. Sharon framed his head in her hands and moved it from side to side, not very playfully. 'I'd like to take you home with me this evening. You haven't met Mother Sophia yet.'

I could see her face as he did not. She was thinking not only of Mother Sophia but of the piano. 'How long, Abe, since you've done any painting?'

He hesitated; there was a frown that she rubbed away with a finger. 'Quite a while, Sharon.'

'Maybe,' I suggested, 'it doesn't hitch up closely enough to a preoccupation with ethics?'

'Maybe.' He was startled and interested. 'You can preach in oils, but—'

'Not really,' said Sharon. 'Propaganda is bad art.'

'Aren't you thinking in terms of music, though?'

'No. In music the problem just doesn't exist. You don't even start looking for propaganda in music unless your head's already addled.'

'Yes. But in art – well, Daumier, Goya, Hogarth—'

'They live,' said Sharon, 'because they were good artists. If their social ideas had been the kind we don't happen to like in the twentieth century, their work would last just the same. Cellini was a louse. The piety of Blake and El Greco almost doesn't exist nowadays. Their work does.'

'I think you're right,' said Abraham after a while. 'I think Will is right too. Painting isn't enough for a frustrated moralist late of reform school.'

Sharon winced and tightened her fingers, but Abraham was still smiling. I thought I had heard something she missed. I said: 'Abe, that's the first time I've heard you speak of the past without bitterness.'

He twisted his head to look up at his sweetheart almost with merriment, reminding her, I think, to share the memory of some words they must have spoken earlier. 'I don't think I have any, Will. Not any more.'

'Not even for Dr Hodding and the men who bought him?'

Abraham murmured: 'Bound on the wheel.' He sat up then and pulled Sharon into the hollow of his arm, kissing her hair, sensing that for the moment she wanted to be the sheltered one.

'So now the boy is a Buddhist,' said Sharon.

'Of course. Buddhist, Taoist, Confucian, Mohammedan—'

'One moment. One wife will be quite enough—'

'Hoy! Mohammedan, Christian, Socratic, Hindu—'

'Okay, only kind of hard for a girl to keep up with on a Sunday afternoon, and I still say—'

'You get used to it,' said Abraham. 'We dispense with the veil. It merely means you have to take your shoes off when you go through the house in order to reach the bo tree in the backyard.'

I said: 'You forgot Mithra.'

'Tradesmen's entrance,' said Abraham. 'Plenty room. Not forgetting the Greek Pantheon, which can use the front door any time.' He stuck out his tongue at me, not much more than twelve years old. 'Syncretism in North Jersey yet! Will, this bottle still has life in it.'

We killed it without help from Sharon, who didn't want to move. But it seemed to make Abraham more sober, not less. He watched me over her drowsy head, and at length he asked: 'Do you still have that mirror?'

Dubiously I said: 'I've always carried it with me, Abraham.'

'So ...?'

'And never exactly forgiven myself for letting you see it when you were twelve.' Sharon looked up at him, with questions unspoken. 'Since then I've looked in it many times.'

'And found ...?'

'Oh, if you can stand it, if you turn it often enough this way and that, you can usually find something like the truth you look for. Most people would say it's only a distortion in the bronze, imagination supplying the rest. I wouldn't say yes or no to that.'

'Mirror?' said Sharon sleepily.

'Just something I carry around with me. Call it a talisman. It was given me years ago by an archaeologist. A little Cretan hand mirror, Sharon, said to be about seven thousand years old.'

'You see, honey? Just modern stuff after all.'

'Uh-huh,' I said. 'Yes, if you're interested in ethics, you could do worse than think in terms of geological time. Well, Sharon, you can't find any wave or imperfection in the reflecting surface, but there must be one, for the plague-take-it thing never looks the same twice, I wouldn't care to have you peep into it unprepared. Usually it doesn't show your face as other people see it. It might show you very old, or very young. Different. Things you might never have guessed yourself – and who's to claim there's any truth in it? A trick. A toy ...'

When I said nothing more and made no move to take out the mirror, Sharon spoke with her head drowsy again on Abraham's shoulder: 'Will, don't be so damn gentle.'

'Really I'm not. But I learned some years back that human nature is volatile stuff in a world full of lighted matches.'

Meeting my eyes tranquilly, Abraham said: 'We wouldn't be scared to look, Will.'

I unfastened the mirror from the strap hidden under my shirt, the same strap that holds my old grenade and the new one Supply sent me, and put it in Abraham's hand. They gazed into it, two young and uncorrupted faces side by side. Not so very young. Twenty-one and nineteen. But out of certain black places even I could never explore, Twenty-one had groped his way, undefiled; and Nineteen was a grown-up, proud, and humble priestess in what may be the greatest of the arts.

Drozma, I felt the beginning of that peace which we Observers know when the end of a mission is not far away. What Abraham had predicted was not quite true; they were frightened. That was almost unimportant. What mattered was that nothing they felt – fright, shock, amazement, disappointment – made them turn away from what they saw. I can't know what that was. They are both articulate with words. They also knew as I did that this was beyond the narrow territory of words. I could guess, from the passage of emotional lights and shadows in their faces – puzzled, rapt, startled, hurt, sometimes amused and often tender. I could guess as much as I had any right to know. I asked nothing when Abraham handed the mirror back to me. Showing that sleepy smile which I remembered from long ago, from a summer afternoon in the cemetery at Byfield, from a few other nearly silent summer afternoons in the pine woods, Abraham said: 'Well, it would seem we're human. I did have a suspicion of it all along.'

'Yes. You, and the maker of the mirror, and Mordecai Paxton.'

He grinned and remarked softly: 'Hi-ho, Mordecai! Whad'ya know – is she asleep?'

'Not entirely,' said Sharon. I think that's what she murmured. I had glanced into the mirror before putting it away, and I saw nothing of myself.

I saw nothing of myself, Drozma.

Did you know, my second father, that there might be a time when I would look there and see only the motion behind me of friendly trees and open sky? A bush of viburnum, a rank of heavy undergrowth dividing the clearing from the forest and full of the innocent secret hurry of birds. This and the maples with leaf buds newly stirring, and the pines, and far and high the passage of a white cloud … Did you also foresee that there might be no pain in that moment at all – or at least only such daylong, nightlong pain as we and humanity must live with because of our mortality, finding it a sort of background music not very different from the love song of tree frogs at night or the imagined music of Mayflies in the late sun? Did you know that I might be able to smile, and put the mirror carelessly away, stretch like a human being, and remind Sharon that we ought to be starting home?

'He's right,' she said. 'I don't want Mother Sophia trying to get supper for herself …'

This time we ventured with the car into the maze of Brooklyn, Sharon acting as guide and pretending there was nothing to it. I observed a different Abraham there at Sharon's apartment, one I had known about but never truly seen. It was manifest in his behavior toward Sophia Wilks, a tenderness and consideration without any of the condescension of extreme youth. He liked her, and found easy ways of making it plain. She looked at his face with her fingers, prolonging that inquiry probably because of the singing note in Sharon's voice, and she smiled at whatever she found there – she who seldom smiled even when she was amused. After supper, when Sharon and Abraham went into the studio, I sat and talked with Sophia about Abraham. Most of her questions had unspoken ones behind them: she was more interested in his temperament than in any practical circumstances, and I told her only those things Sharon might have told me of the boy who used to live in Latimer. In Latimer Sophia had never known him, except after his disappearance, and then only through the halting and grief-confused words of a ten-year-old girl. I was careful with my voice, but there was scant danger that Sophia could ever connect Meisel with the funny old quasi-Polish gentleman who had wanted a monument: her mind was elsewhere, and her own quiet memory of Benedict Miles another monument. 'Should an artist marry, Mr Meisel? I did, but only after I had learned that the heights were not for me – in any case my husband was also a teacher. Sharon is all fire and devotion. Do you know that for seven years now she has never practiced less than six hours a day, often ten or twelve?'

I said something comfortably useless, about how it had to be a separate problem for every artist, one that only the artist could answer. Unfortunately that was true as well as useless, but Sophia already knew it as well as I. 'We never drove her, my sister and I. There was a year, Mr Meisel, when she was fifteen, after she had come to live with us – she would get up from the piano not knowing where she was. Once my sister saw her blunder into the door-frame on the way to her bedroom because, you understand, she was not in the room at all, she was in some place – I think you understand – some place where nobody else could be with her. We were so frightened that year, my sister and I. It was too much, we thought – we never drove her, and sometimes tried to hold her back, but that we couldn't do either. The fears were foolish, you see. Such a flame does not ever burn out. It is only the little flames that – ah there!' The piano in the studio had spoken. 'No – no, that isn't Sharon. Why, does he—'

I said quickly: 'He's a beginner. Something pulled him toward music, I don't know what. He'll probably find out his talent is elsewhere, before too long.'

'I see.' I am not sure she did, and she was not pleased. Abraham was playing the somber Fourth Prelude of Chopin almost correctly, with a fair touch and some insight. I muttered to Sophia that I would be back in a moment, and I strolled into the studio as Abraham was finishing it. I saw his upward glance of inquiry – why, there was amusement in it too, how genuine I don't know, defensive perhaps. I also saw Sharon shake her head a little, involuntarily, I believe.

She softened it at once by saying: 'Not yet.' And stepped behind the piano chair to put her arms around him, bring her mouth close to his ear. 'Do you really *want* it, Abe?'

'I don't quite know.'

'It's rougher'n hell – well, you know that. Point is I don't think you'd want it just for your own pleasure – if you did it would be good, but if I know you, Abe, you'd want to give with it. That takes eight hours a day, for years, and it might not be there.' She glanced up at me over his head, and she was very frightened. 'And it might take away from – oh, other things, things worth more, things you could do better.' Yes, she was horribly frightened, and I couldn't help.

But Abraham said: 'I think it was a fever, Sharon. I think I notice some nice cool sweat on the brow.' His mouth was unsteady, but he was smiling with it. 'Do something for me?'

'Anything,' she said, nearly crying. 'Anything, now or any time.'

'Just play it the way it ought to be.'

'Well, there's no one way it ought to be,' said Sharon Brand. 'But I'll play it as well as I can.' She did of course. It would have been a cruelty to play at anything less than her best, since he would have known it; but I wonder how many others would have sensed that at such a moment? I've known a lot of pianists, human and Martian. They fall readily into two classes: Sharon and then all the rest of 'em. I never could quite bear that prelude anyhow. She blinked at me rather desperately, and followed the prelude immediately with the tiny, half-humorous one in A Major, the Seventh, simply because something had to follow it, it couldn't hang in the air.

'I have a special corner in the temple,' said Abraham, and put a cigarette between her lips and lit it for her and kissed her forehead. 'The corner where you can hear best. Remind me to tell you sometime that you're slightly snub-nosed.'

'Are you p-partial to pug noses?'

I went back to Sophia …

Abraham needed to talk to me, a little, as we started home. Fortunately the automobile is one human gimmick that doesn't overawe me. I feel almost at home with it so long as it stays on the ground. Don't think I'll ever try the plane-car they're experimenting with nowadays. The damn thing has wings folded over its back like a beetle's; it's supposed to snap them out at a comfortable seventy miles per hour and take off. Retractile propeller. Slow stuff, not intended to do anything over three hundred when it's airborne, but all the same I think they can keep that one. Nice, of course, for kids anxious to find some new way of breaking their necks. Poking through those quiet and sober streets that had grown empty toward midnight, I was able to listen to Abraham without thinking much about my driving. He wanted to talk about the reform school. Not, I think, on his own account, but to satisfy possible questions that I had not spoken.

He had grown a shell in that environment, except for a few friendships. And those, he said, were all shadowed by the sense that nothing could ever last very long. I said something commonplace to suggest that human growth had much in common with the growth of insects: old chrysalids tossed on the rubbish heap and new ones grown. 'Still,' he said, 'as a larger bug I probably have a better memory of earlier states of bugginess than, say, a weevil.' He went on to make a rather horrible and intricate pun deriving *pupil* from *pupa* which, out of respect for our Martian community, I decline to record. He told me more about how the lost boys came and went. It had been a large school with, I guess, a fairly sensitive conscience somewhere at the top. The boys were of all sorts – the sickly, the morons, the majority called normal, the few bright ones; making a fenced-in, neurotic community, it seemed to Abraham that they had had little in common except bewilderment. Even bitterness was curiously absent in some of them. They were abused more by each other than by authority. Such violence as he saw was mostly furtive. Discipline was rigid enough, and the school had made a serious effort to weed out bullies or clip their claws. 'I carried a knife,' Abraham told me. 'Never could have used it, but it was the thing to do. Like a fraternity pin, I guess. A new boy would get beat up a few times, then someone would befriend him, see that he learned to carry a knife, talk the accepted language, and he'd be let alone. I was able to get some books. Last two years I had a sort of trusty job, in the so-called library. Except for the physical thrills, even beating up a new candidate was a sort of – oh, dutiful routine ... Well, they did have one thing in common besides bewilderment. The nobody-loves-me feeling. Those who had parents coming to see them had it worst. But we all felt or imagined or tried to imagine that no one had ever cared much about us. I knew better, Will, so did a lot of the others, but you couldn't say so. Saying so would have been admitting that you might be partly to blame yourself, but it was more than that. You *had* to believe you were unwanted, or you'd be a social outcast. The school of paradox. Maybe not such a bad preparation for what's outside. You know, Will – the old school tie. Alumnus Brown recalls the golden age.' But there was no overtone of bitterness. 'Will, I wonder – can anything turn around and kick itself in the teeth like the human mind?'

'I dunno. Did you ever help beat up a new one?'

He said with remarkable gentleness: 'You could almost guess the answer to that one.'

'Uh-huh – you never did.'

'Almost right. I never helped beat up anyone, but to offset that, I never had the guts to try to stop it either. Except once.'

'And that time?'

He rolled up his left sleeve and showed me his arm in the dashboard light. The scar was nearly white, running from elbow to wrist. 'I'm proud of that hash mark,' he said. 'It tells that on one occasion I did have a little guts, and it taught me something.' Still I heard nothing in his voice except a reflective serenity neither sad nor happy. 'It taught me: unless you're a gorilla, don't interfere with the pleasures of chimps.' And somewhat later he said: 'Punishment – that's the idea that taints the whole system, reform schools, prisons, four fifths of the criminal law. Cure the curable, keep the incurable where they can't hurt others – anything else is just humanity picking at a sore and half enjoying the pain.' He was talking to himself as much as to me. 'From all I've read, Will, it seems that enlightened people with experience have been hammering that idea for at least a hundred years. Reckon the law will catch up with them in another hundred?'

'First you need a science of human nature, that doesn't exist. I don't blame the law for being not much impressed by the battle of terms we call psychology. The various Freudianities can't stop to hear the various behaviorisms, and vice versa. We have the beginnings of a knowledge of human nature, but it's a study that has to creep slowly because it scares people to death. It was all right for the Greek to say, "Know thyself" – but how many would dare to do it even if they had the means?'

I spoke mainly because I hoped he would go on talking to me, in any way he chose. He would have, I think, but the world stood still.

Is it my biased sense of history, Drozma, that makes me use those curious eroded human phrases for such a thing as this?

I saw the man step off the sidewalk half a block away. It was a well-lit street near the bridge approach, and quiet. There were no headlights behind me, only one red taillight a block or two away. Endless time. No urgency. My foot found the brake, without panic, for we were not moving fast, and there was no possible danger of hitting the man, who had dropped to his knees in front of us, under my lights, under the orange glow of a sodium street lamp. All in control. I came to an easy, soundless stop five or six feet away from him. He was in profile to us but never turned his head, only knelt there, first with his hands raised toward his chin in the ancient attitude of prayer. The arms dropped, limp; I saw the fingers of the left hand go into a lively dance as if he were scratching the air at his thigh. His mouth hung open and he began to sway from the knees as I forced myself to clamber out of the car and go to him.

He was toppling over when I reached him. I was able to ease him down on his back and keep his head from striking the asphalt. A small, elderly man, well dressed, clean. He made me think of a sparrow, with his little jutting nose and brilliant eyes that would not shut. His cheek was flame-hot. I never felt such fever but once before, long ago, in a human friend who died of blackwater malaria. I think this man was trying to say something; nothing came out but 'Uh – ah –' sounds without control of throat or tongue. There was no choking. For several moments the glitter of his eyes was firmly, intelligently focused on me. I am sure he would have liked to speak.

I stared across him at Abraham, who had also touched his burning flesh. There was no speech for us either, then.

7

New York
Thursday night, March 16

Only today comes the first newspaper announcement of the disaster. Last night at ten o'clock – Wednesday night, just one little week after I heard Sharon's miracle – there was confusing mention of trouble on the radio. We heard it, Abraham and I, heard the repressed hysteria in the broadcaster's voice as if someone were plucking a taut deep wire behind his rapid gabble. He said only that there were 'several' cases of what might be a new disease in Cleveland, Washington, New York, and the West Coast. Medical circles were interested, although there was 'obviously' no occasion for alarm. 'West Coast?' said Abraham. The broadcaster lurched on hastily to the most recent vital information on a divorce case involving a video star and a wrestler.

'Plane travel,' I said. 'Paris and London are only a few hours away ...' Abraham brought me a drink. We couldn't talk much, or read. He sat near me most of the evening in my dull little living room, which seemed to me more than ever like a well-upholstered cave in a jungle of the unknown; both of us haunted, understanding the panic in each other's minds. Now and then we tried the radio again, but there was nothing except the usual loud confusion of trivialities. Toward bedtime Abraham telephoned Sharon. It was just a lovers' conversation – 'What've you been up to all evening?' – and since he didn't mention the broadcast to her I assumed she hadn't heard it. After hanging up he simply said: 'I couldn't ...'

The three days since Sunday had allowed us to crawl back on a flimsy raft of hope. That man we found in the street – oh, it could have been pneumonia, a dozen other things. So we told each other then and for three days. Abraham had called an ambulance, which came quickly and whisked the fallen man away, after a few inquiries from an intern who seemed to have a worry in the back of his mind that wouldn't come into words. Other similar cases? I almost asked the young doctor that, but held my tongue. As we drove home Abraham and I began passing each other counterfeit words. We knew they were counterfeit, but they bought us a little phony peace.

This morning the *Times* as usual had the best soberly factual account, offering statistics with a rather terrible restraint. There have been 50 hospitalized cases in the New York metropolitan area, and 16 deaths. In Chicago, 21 reported cases, 6 deaths. New Orleans, 13 and 3. Los Angeles, 10 and 3. This is the fourth day since Sunday, the sixth since Friday. The first reported case, according to the *Times*, was a Bronx housewife – Sunday morning. She died Monday afternoon.

The *Times* prints a statement from the A.M.A.: the disease 'resembles an unusually virulent type of flu, with several atypical features. Nationwide medical resources are being mobilized to meet the unlikely event of an emergency, and there is no cause for alarm.' Close quote.

The *Times* goes on to describe the thing without quotation marks and apparently without pulling any punches. The first symptoms are merely those of the common cold – sniffles, moderate fever, general malaise. After a few hours of this, fever rises abruptly, there is deafness with violent head noises, perversion of the senses of smell and taste. Numbness of hands and feet, legs and forearms, followed quickly by more general motor paralysis, which in all cases so far has included paralysis of throat and tongue; patients cannot speak or swallow. Fever remains at a very high point for several hours – twelve in one case; it follows no pattern of fluctuation. Evidence of delirium in most cases, and the behavior of the speechless patients suggests vivid visual hallucinations before unconsciousness intervenes – as it does at the third or fourth hour after onset of major symptoms. Death, when it has occurred, has come during deep coma, after a gradual subsidence of fever, and may be due to paralysis of cardiac muscle. Cheyne-Stokes breathing very marked in all fatal cases so far. In 'some' other patients the temperature, instead of dropping to deep subnormal, has leveled off at about 101°, the patients remaining unconscious but with some improvement of involuntary reflexes: prognosis obviously unknown. Except for the quote from the A.M.A. the *Times* isn't telling us there's nothing to worry about. Nor do they speculate about origin and cause. Nor do they say directly that the arsenal of drugs and antibiotics has proved ineffective, but there is one small sentence difficult to forget: 'Patients have responded to supportive treatment in some cases.' So it's that bad. I suppose a newspaper reader would have to be somewhat familiar with medical argot to grasp the implications. You couldn't expect the *Times* to say: 'They try to keep them comfortable, knowing nothing else to do.'

I have seen no follow-up account on the death of Daniel Walker. No mention anywhere, these three days, of Max or the Organic Unity Party. I commented on that this morning, wondering out loud if Max had gotten away with it. Abraham said: 'No. He won't.'

It is terrifying to see controlled and quiet anger in a face designed for gentleness. It was all the worse because of his physical slightness and soft voice. I waited for the look to go away. It did not. He had spread the paper on the table and stood looking down at it, but as if the black and white square were a window, as if there were immeasurable distances beyond. 'What's going on in your mind, Abraham?'

He only said: 'They won't get away with it.'

'You're thinking of what Miriam said? Hodding in the pay of China and all that?'

'Hell, they won't use that pipe dream, Will. I think that was spur-of-the-moment, and a poor effort. No, I think they'll hope for silence, hope that nobody can make the connection. And nobody could, unless one of us talks – I mean one of those who were up there on the roof garden. I don't think Fry or Senator Galt understood anything of it – they're freaks, nobodies. Nicholas, Max, Miriam – and Bill, and me – those five may be the only ones who know.'

'Should you speak, Abraham?'

He was all grownup when he said, with no tension in his voice, without even looking at me: 'I haven't quite decided ...'

We went for a walk that afternoon. No objective, simply here and there in the streets, a bus uptown, west on 125th, back down – town through the West Side, walking. We saw no one collapsing in the street. Perhaps things were rather too quiet for a weekday afternoon. There wasn't quite the normal amount of talk and laughter in those who passed us. We heard the bell and siren of ambulances five or six times in our aimless journey – but one does anyhow: illness and accident have always claimed their victims through the nights and days of any city ...

Hodding is dead. We got that from the evening paper.

His house and laboratory in a Long Island suburb caught fire from 'an explosion of unknown origin.' His body and those of his wife, daughter-in-law, and grandson, aged nine, have been identified. The four were in the laboratory when the explosion occurred. The laboratory, says the paper, was a private enterprise which Dr Hodding had carried on after his retirement from the Wales Foundation. Dr Hodding's son had been away from the house; the paper quotes him as saying that the laboratory was designed for some limited type of biological research, hardly more than a retired man's hobby. Young Hodding is an architect, and claims he knew nothing about his father's line of work; but he is certain that nothing was ever kept in the laboratory that could have caused an explosion. Police, says the paper, are investigating the possibility that a bomb may have been set by a crank. 'One,' said Abraham. 'One who can't talk any more. If Fry and Galt are insured, the companies ought to be worrying a bit.' And then, pursuing another line of thought: 'Will, such a thing could be no use to anyone as a weapon, unless there were a means of immunizing the users. I keep coming back to that. I think Max wanted to dictate terms to the world, including Asia. I think he hates the Federalists worse than others because he sees himself as – oh, the first President of a world government, something like that. He'd feel it was quite all right to kill off a few million commonplace human animals if that would make him Leader – for the world's good of course, always for the world's good. But first he would have to have a means of immunizing the faithful.'

'Perhaps Hodding was working on that, and got only halfway. He developed the disease but not the protection.'

'I think so,' said Abraham, with the same dangerous quiet that had been in him all day. 'So now, in order to hide the truth and escape the consequences, they've killed the one man who knew most about it, who must have already done a lot of work toward finding an immunization or a cure. Killed his family too, but they wouldn't consider that – another product of the doctrine that the end justifies the means. I met the little boy once. He was a bright kid …'

'Promise me something, Abraham?'

'If I can.'

'Don't start anything unless I'm with you.'

He came and stood over my chair, smiling down with more straightforward unconsidered affection than he had ever shown me. 'I can't promise that, Will.'

Presently I said: 'I know you can't.' Nor could I have made the same promise to him, so I had to tell myself that it was fair enough. I have learned a little since that night in the cemetery when Namir escaped me. Namir will not escape again, and I think Keller will have to die with him: Keller is a well-trained son of his father, and I don't think the Old City hospital could do anything with him. The only problem now is to isolate them from human contact long enough to do what I must. And I must do it before this flame in Abraham explodes into some action he may not have the strength to carry through.

That evening paper added nothing to our knowledge of the spread of the disease. More demoralized than the *Times*. No statistics. The radio has been silent about it all evening. Abraham is sleeping, I think. Fortunately I do not need to.

New York
Friday, March 17

From this morning's paper: New York area, 436 reported cases, 170 deaths.

I think they were right to hold the St Patrick's Day parade. It would have been against the public interest to cancel such an expected and time-honored thing, in spite of the clear danger that large gatherings might help to spread the contagion. We didn't go to see it. Abraham has been in a faraway abstraction all day, his mind talking to his mind, demanding answers. The evening paper says the crowds were small, and there was 'some disturbance' when one of the paraders fell from his horse in a 'sudden heart attack.' A heart attack?

There was also a broadcast statement from the White House at six o'clock, urging the nation to keep calm. Panic, said President Clifford, was more dangerous than epidemic. The country's medical resources are adequate to deal with the emergency. He had some slight trouble with that word, his voice not quite in control, his deep-lined, still handsome face tightening itself to force out the syllables smoothly. His television make-up wasn't too good. I think they had tried to soften the furrows in his forehead, but they couldn't make him anything except a frightened, essentially brave and decent little man carrying a burden too heavy for anyone. Civil Defense organizations, he said, have been placed under the direction of the Surgeon General of the Army – who followed Clifford on the video with a fair display of jaw and stop-this-nonsense eyebrows. Avoid crowds, said Surgeon General Craig, stay home from everything but essential work, obey all, repeat all, orders of local medical authorities and Civil Defense personnel. All theaters, stadia, bars, other public meeting places will be closed for the duration of the emergency. Use your radio to keep in touch with the efforts of your government. The pandemic – Craig stopped there for a second, shaking his big head as if at a buzzing fly; he had meant to say 'epidemic' but the other slipped out. The pandemic, Craig said, is caused by a new virus, possibly a mutation from the virus of poliomyelitis. Promising efforts are under way to isolate it and to develop a serum. This will take time. Repeat, avoid crowds, stay home except—

From a ten o'clock broadcast: the disease is reported from Oslo, Paris, London, Berlin, Rome, Cairo, Buenos Aires, Honolulu, Kyoto.

Friday midnight

I have got up from a sleepless bed to write down something Abraham said before he went to his room. I force myself to admit that the disease could strike him too; that he could die tomorrow; my need to write what he said derives from that admission.

After I turned off the radio we talked a little of what men call the Second World War, meaning that phase of the twentieth-century war which came to a partial end in 30,945, six years before Abraham was born. In giving him some (humanly censored) memories, I referred to the 'expendable millions.'

Abraham said; 'No one is expendable.'

8

New York
Saturday, March 18

From the *Times*: in the nation at large, 14,623 reported cases, 3561 deaths, as of Friday, 8 P.M. More than twenty-five per cent mortality: the proportion is rising. Those patients whose fevers level off above normal merely take longer in dying. But several of those stricken earliest are showing 'probable' signs of recovery – temperature normal or nearly so, consciousness recovered although usually with sense impairment and varying degrees of localized paralysis apparently due to damaged or destroyed neural tissue. They are calling it paralytic polyneuritis. The headlines have already shortened that to para.

Abraham went over to Brooklyn early this morning to see Sharon. I went to the Green Tower Colony.

Para ...

The streets are not as they were Thursday afternoon. Human beings still pass you, in groups of two or three, not more. They glance at you quickly, and away quickly, huddling together, clinging to the selves and the faces they know, afraid of strangers. You hear their voices, not always like individual voices. The city is whispering *para*. Over and over, the one word, a faraway drum-beat, or a giant muttering in tormented sleep. *Para*. One word, which means ...

A man staggers on the sidewalk, reaches out for the wall of a building to steady himself with one hand; the other hand joins it, as if he wanted to embrace what was never there. Both hands begin to dance at the finger ends. No one hurries to help him as his knees give way and his forehead touches the wall. The couple who had been walking behind him swerve and run scramblingly across the street, the woman pressing a handkerchief over her mouth, the man glaring back as he runs with a meaningless square-mouthed smile. They would like to help, but ...

Para means a little dog trotting down the center of Third Avenue dragging a leash. Traffic has thinned to nearly nothing. The golden spaniel isn't quite right in the legs: a hind leg gives way now and then, but he hurries on, hunting for something – help, I suppose. The small head jerks repeatedly to the left; he tries to bark, with only a strangled wheeze. Then both hind legs fail him, and he struggles to keep moving, pulling with his forepaws, a dog's patient determination in unaccusing eyes. A car approaches slowly, turns out to avoid him. A woman screams at the driver, pointing: 'He's got it! Finish him!' Obediently the car backs and shoots forward, then crazily off uptown as if the mechanism itself had sickened at a thing which at the moment seemed necessary. The woman snatches up a wire waste receptacle and hurls it at the little smear of blood and golden hair. Ordinarily she could hardly have lifted it. She takes out her lipstick, carefully paints a new mouth, fumbles at a place where the wire snagged her dress, but walks away without looking for the compact that fell from her fingers and rolled into the street.

Para means a man throwing open a front door to stare up and down the street. He is crying, and shouts (not to me or anyone else): 'Those bastards won't *ever* get here!'

Para means a mob looting a liquor store. I saw that on Third Avenue from the corner of Twenty-third Street. There were a dozen or so, including a few women. The store must have been locked, for there were plate-glass fragments on the pavement. The looters seemed comically serious about it, until a woman broke away from them and plunged toward me, clasping three bottles like a baby to her breasts. She called back: 'You can't live forever!' and squalled with laughter when two men started after her. I don't know what happened when they caught her; I turned into Twenty-third Street to get out of the way. By evening they will be shooting down looters, most likely. Vigilantes will organize to do it if the police can't.

Para means a man lying in the gutter, his gray hair moving curiously in a brown stream from a leaky hydrant. He has a four-day beard and his clothes are frayed, with buttons sprung open on innocent meaningless nakedness. He is elderly. He isn't drunk. His stiffly upright shoes are cracked, with holes in the bottom, and he isn't drunk: the wagon will come when it can.

Para means a rat running out of an empty restaurant. There weren't supposed to be any rats left in New York. This one stops in front of me, not frightened, not aware of me, just dying. No resistance when my foot pushes him into the street.

The busses weren't running on Lexington Upper Level. As I went back down the stairway I noticed eight or ten crows flying northwest. Odd – you never see crows over the city. Northwest toward Central Park. I think the Robbie-road was functioning, but I didn't see a taxi anywhere. I went on down to the subway level, and there the robot change-maker was in operation. I passed through a turnstile to a deserted platform and waited a dreary while. One other man came through, saw me, and walked to the other end of the platform to wait.

The train came in at low speed. I noticed two men in the motor-man's cab, another outside – in case one should collapse? The car I entered had only two other passengers in it, a thin woman whose lips moved silently, a frozen-faced Negro studying his shoe tips. They sat at opposite ends of the car;

something in the way they both glanced at me suggested that I ought to sit in the middle or go to the next car. I sat in the middle ... Only a few pedestrians were on Lexington Upper Level when I climbed back to it at 125th Street. They hurried as if on desperate secret missions, giving each other wide clearance. I saw no one stirring when I looked through the big windows of the Organic Unity Party office. A policeman stopped me at the entrance. 'Staff?'

'No. Place closed?'

He spoke with the harassed patience of a man forced to repeat the same thing to the point of nausea: 'No public gatherings allowed. Only the office staff goes in.'

'Do you happen to know Mr Keller by sight?'

He looked me up and down coldly. My Santa Claus appearance may have restrained things he would have liked to say. 'I don't know any of 'em, mister. I just work here. On the sidewalk. Only staff goes in.'

'Okay, I don't want in. But – uh – it's just the rule about public gatherings, isn't it? What I mean, there isn't anything to the rumor that's going around about these Organic Unity people?'

He was large and quiet and Irish and most unhappy. 'Now what rumor would that be?'

Drozma, I shall never know if what I did was right. It was an action deriving more from emotion than from reason. It had the human thread of vengeance in it: I have been away from Northern City too long. I said: 'Talk I overheard in the subway. Other places too – everyone's whispering it. I've got nothing to do with this damn Party, but I'm slightly acquainted with Keller, man who works here, thought I'd like to ask him about it, about that rumor.'

He was monumentally patient. 'What rumor?'

'Hell, you must've heard it.' I tried to look more than ever distressed and stupid and ancient. 'About that fella Walker who jumped off Max's roof garden, week ago Friday, I think it was.' He stiffened with alertness, and some woman, half seen, was passing on the sidewalk as I spoke. I can't be certain that her steps paused for a listening second. I think they did. 'The rumor was that Walker had a test tube with some kind of bugs in it, virus or something, and chucked it over before he jumped.'

It went home, I know. A moment of dark intentness, perhaps horror, before he rumbled: 'I wouldn't be repeating stuff like that.'

'Why, I won't. But other people are. On the subway was where I just now heard it, one guy yakking at another.' I shrugged and moved away. 'Well, hell, Keller wouldn't tell me the truth anyway.' I walked on slowly, terrified that he might call me back for questioning. He didn't. My impersonation of a half-witless antique must have been convincing. With the tail of my eye I saw him step inside the building – to a telephone, I imagine. I don't know, Drozma.

343

Maybe it was the old bum in the gutter. Or that little golden spaniel. It was not what an Observer should have done, yet under the same pressures I would very likely do it again.

I walked on, west, on 125th Street.

I cannot see the thing as a whole, Drozma. Not yet and maybe never. I know (with my mind only) that, because of the blind madness of a few and the almost unknowing acquiescence of the many, human beings have once again stumbled into calamity with no assurance of survival. I know (in theory) that a wiser society might be able to detect and isolate such creatures as Joseph Max before they have done their work. Yet who can shape the realities of any such society in his mind, or tell how to arrive at it? With the study of human nature in its half-sickly infancy, we come back (in theory at least) to the unwillingness of men to look at themselves: but that is too simple. Even self-knowledge, if it should ever be achieved by more than a handful in each generation, is simply a means to some end that neither man nor Martian is wise enough to guess. I know these things with some clarity, but at this moment I can truly see only certain disconnected pictures from today's bleak journey.

Para means a little Negro girl, about the age Sharon was when I first knew her, walking directly into me on 125th Street, wide-eyed and tearless. She said mechanically: 'I'm sorry, mister. I didn't see you. My pop's dead.' I kept her from stumbling; maybe she knew it, but she moved on, stiff-legged, while I fought back the need to follow and tell her – well, what? What? I couldn't make him live.

I climbed from 125th Street to the Esplanade. Not many blocks north of here, a small tube of glass …

The express elevators in the Green Tower Colony were not running. There was a bank of self-service elevators, and there has been no power failure – yet. I used one of those, and stood for a time outside Keller's door, not thinking much. It was like waiting for some signal which of course never came. I noticed that the card with Abraham's name was still above the bell; I took it out and dropped it in my pocket, a touch of cold metal reminding me, quite casually, that I was still carrying Miriam's automatic. Then it was also a casual thing to punch the bell. One and perhaps both of my grenades would have to be used. Both, if Keller and Nicholas were both here, or if I should be wounded and unable to escape.

Nicholas opened the door.

I reminded myself further that I had not used scent-destroyer for several days. It hadn't seemed to matter. And although as soon as Abraham decided to go over to Brooklyn I knew where I would go, it still hadn't mattered. Nicholas opened the door. He recognized Will Meisel and stood back with a human stare of resentment, dislike, anger, sternness – all quite irrelevant, as he understood himself when I had shut the door behind me and my Martian scent reached him. He said with sober quiet: 'I should have known.'

'Is your son here, who goes by the name of William Keller?' I spoke in English; it has become almost more natural than my native tongue.

He waddled away to close the door on the back rooms, and held his voice to a neutral dead level: 'My son is in Oregon, or maybe Idaho, with a new face. You'd only waste your time trying to find him – I couldn't myself, probably.' It had a flat sound of truth; I think it was truth. If it was, then I must leave Keller to be dealt with by other Observers in the course of the years. Such a being cannot hide himself long, and we have always had patience on our side.

I indicated the closed door. 'What's there?'

He leaned against it, perhaps to block me away with his mass. 'One of my students, who should have lived to do his work.'

'Joseph Max? He took refuge here?'

'Refuge? No one was looking for him. He came to consult me, and he was stricken while he was here. The hospitals are already crowded, and have nothing to offer. It shouldn't matter to you, Elmis. He's dead.'

'Para—'

'Yes.'

'It's fitting, I think … The Organic Unity Party is dead too, Namir. Or will be soon. There may be some trouble down there at your office. A mob perhaps. At any rate the party will receive due credit for what's happened. Did you think it could be any other way?'

'Why, I hadn't thought.' He lifted and dropped his fat hands. I think he laughed a little. 'It doesn't matter where the credit goes, if the thing works, does it? The Party doesn't matter – a tool useful once, thrown aside. Like myself – as you see, I have only a year or two to live.'

'Well, less than that. A year or so could be too long.'

'Vengeful, Elmis?'

'No. A matter of sanitation. I shouldn't have fumbled, nine years ago.' He didn't look interested. 'If there's anything you want to say to me, I'll hear it. The laws require that much.' I showed him the automatic. 'Sit down over there.'

He obeyed me, smiling dimly. With my left hand behind me I locked the door on the back rooms. He asked: 'May I have a cigarette? I've become quite fond of them.'

'Of course. Just keep your hands in sight.' I tossed him a pack, and matches. 'In the future as you saw it, you'd have had to keep a lot of human beings alive – you know, to cultivate food and tobacco, run a few machines, sweep the streets if you intended to have streets.'

Namir laughed in the smoke. 'I never racked my head over blueprints. I only wanted to help get the creatures out of the way. The building of a sensible culture would have been for others – but as you say, they might have wanted to make human beings good for something.'

'I think you came to enjoy destruction as an end in itself, didn't you? Any other ends you might have had at the beginning were swallowed up in the pleasures of smashing windows, tying a can to the tail of the poor human dog, chalking up words on blank walls. Is there any way I could show you that the pursuit of evil is a triviality?'

'You see it that way.' He shut his eyes. 'I see, as I always have, that it was best to help men destroy themselves, because they aren't fit to live.'

'Not fit, by whose decision? Whose scale of values?'

'Mine, of course.' He was tranquil behind closed eyes. 'Mine, because I see them as they are. There's no truth in them. They project the wishes of a little greedy ape against the blank of eternity, and call it truth – there's triviality if you like. They invent a larger ape somewhat beyond the clouds – or some-what beyond the Galaxy, which is the same thing – and call it God; they use this invention as an authority, to justify every vice of cruelty or greed or van-ity or lust that their small minds can imagine. They talk of justice, and say that their laws derive from a sense of justice (which they have never defined); but no human law ever derived from anything except fear – fear of the unknown, the different, the difficult, fear of man's own self. They make war, not for any of the noisy noble reasons they produce, but simply because they hate themselves almost as much as they hate their neighbors. They gibber of love, love, but human love is merely one more projection of the ape-self, superimposed on the invented image of another person. They invent reli-gions of charity such as Christianity – if you want to know how they practice them, look at the prisons, the slums, the armies, the concentration camps and execution chambers; better still, look into the not very well hidden hearts of the respectable, and watch the maggots squirm, the maggots of jeal-ousy and hate and fear and greed. They are stupid, Elmis. They have always done their best to smother and destroy the few abnormal ones who have a little vision, a little ability beyond the ordinary, and they always will. Do you think Christ could live any longer in the twentieth century than he did two thousand years ago? Galileo recants again, Socrates drinks the hemlock again, every day of every year – but now there are three billion units in the swarm, in a smaller world, and they have learned simpler methods of cruci-fixion, without embarrassing publicity. The three billion crawl about, all over the helpless earth, destroying and defiling, killing the forests, polluting the air with smoke and radioactive dust and the torturing noises of the machine. In place of meadows, filling stations. The lakes are puddles of human filth. Two years ago the whole area of San Francisco Harbor was covered with dead fish: even the ocean is sick from the human taint, and this they call pro-gress. I have done what I can, Elmis, and I hope you will make my death reasonably tidy. The floor of this room is some new kind of glass – the gren ade won't affect it. I always hated disorder.'

'You make a reasoned indictment,' I said. 'I notice you put it all on abstract grounds. You must have had a more personal reason, to hate them as you do.'

'No.' His half-hidden Salvayan eyes watched me curiously, honestly, I think, temporarily interested in what I said. 'No, I don't believe so. As an Observer, I suddenly realized the blindness of Salvayan hopes, the futility of any effort depending on human nature. I abdicated because I saw that the only cure for the human situation was annihilation. Of course, once you declare war on the human race' – he shrugged amiably – 'it tends to become a personal matter. Possibly my own vanity and ambition entered into it, after a while. Unimportant. Oh, I worked hard over Joe Max.' He yawned heavily. 'I didn't overlook the pitiful instability of creatures like Walker and Hodding – that was the material I had to work with, the chance I took … As a favor to me, Elmis, would you spare me listening to the counsel for the defense, and use that gun now? I'm tired.'

'No defense. I admit almost every charge of the indictment. The only thing wrong with it is that it's too partial, too trivial. You've spent your life hunting for counterfeit money in a pile of treasure. You looked for evil all your life, to prove your case – naturally you found it, and where it was absent you created it. Any fool can do that. I've looked for good in human nature and elsewhere, and found it, heaped up and flowing over. Anyone can do that too, though good may be a little harder to see, because it's all around you, no further away than the nearest leaf, the nearest smile or pleasant word, no further away than every breath of air. You say there's no truth in men. Do you know what truth is, any more than Pilate did? Human beings are in the early stages of trying to accept and understand empirical truth. It's difficult. It's like going into a jungle without weapons or foreknowledge. No other terrestrial animal ever tried it, or even guessed the jungle was there. Well, Namir, our views of man are not altogether different. We both see him as someone stumbling through that jungle. You want to slip a knife in his back because you don't like him. I'd rather take his hand, knowing that he, and I, and you are all in the same jungle, and the jungle is only a small part of the universe. Justice? That's an ideal, a light they see ahead of themselves, and try to reach. Certainly they stumble: because they try. If that weren't so, they couldn't even have invented the word. The same is true of their visions of love and peace. Fear goads them from behind, because they're flesh and blood. If you blame them for being afraid, you're only blaming them for being alive and capable of suffering. The products of fear – war, hate, jealousy, even greed develops from fear – those will diminish as fear diminishes, if they have a few more centuries to learn. Centuries are short for us, rather long for them, Namir. On the whole, I don't think they're much more stupid than Martians. As for the ugly aspects of their twentieth-century progress – another temporary sickness, I think, like the different sickness of, say, the ninth century, probably no more important. The earth will heal – my planet Earth, Namir, that might have been your planet too if you hadn't blinded yourself with the very human sickness of hate – it will heal, when they learn how to live with it. Perhaps another century of learning how to control the machine—'

'Oh yes, yes.' He spat out his cigarette on the floor. 'They want the stars. Kill me, Elmis. It turns my stomach, to think of men reaching the stars. Regard it as an act of mercy, if it troubles you.'

'It is,' I said, for I could regard it in no other way. I suppose the little gun finding the center of his forehead – because even now I had to remember the cemetery in Byfield – I suppose that was as merciful as death ever is. I rolled back the rug. The floor was inorganic, as he had said. I spread his pathetic bulk there, and stood well away until the purple flaring and sputtering had ended, and nothing remained but some coins from his pocket and the distorted bullet. The rest was dust; the rug could cover it. A lump of lead, a half dollar, two quarters, a dime, and a handful of dust – Namir is dead.

But not his son.

I went through the back rooms, having a certain need to know with my own senses that Joseph Max was dead.

I found him in a bedroom at the back. He was quite dead, lying in pallid dignity; someone had had the courtesy to close his mouth and eyes – Miriam, I think, for she was not dead, not yet. She sat beside him on the bed, her hand moving aimlessly through his hair and over his cheek. Her nose was reddened, but not from tears: her eyes were dry and somewhat feverish. *The first symptoms are those of the common cold ...*

It was of interest (to state it in the coldest way) to note that as a woman she had loved Joseph Max, perhaps a great deal; that her engagement to Abraham had been on her side a matter of politics, a device of Keller and Nicholas to bind Abraham into the Party in the hope of using his abilities. I had guessed that, much earlier; now it was hardly even of academic importance. When history moves swiftly it leaves us all behind, men and Martians. She said something to me, hoarsely and with difficulty. I think it was: 'Go away ...' I could not speak to her, as one cannot speak to an insect forced to live a while after its body is crushed. In this room, para was and would be merciful.

Abraham had not returned. It was early afternoon when I got back to the apartment. The subway was still functioning and there were more passengers, though nothing like the normal crowds. In the walk from the subway to my apartment I saw nothing more that I want to record. Other Observers, Drozma, will be telling you of these things. I knew, as I came home, that I had seen only the small beginnings of the disaster. Before long – a day, a week – there will be not one old man dead in the gutter and waiting for a wagon that can't come quickly, but many more. There will not be a wall in the city that doesn't hide a human loss. There will be breakdown of communication, transport – for New York and most other modern cities, that means starvation. There will be riots; some will die even while throwing stones at what they believe to be some enemy. There will be lime pits. If even the rats die of it …

Abraham did not come home all afternoon. At three I telephoned Sharon, and she answered quickly, asking at once whether I was well. Abraham had been there in the morning, she said, and had left a little before noon. She took it for granted that he would be going home, though he hadn't said so. She was well, Sharon told me; she and Sophia were well …

Never mind the next six hours. I lived through them. Abraham came home at nine, and limped to the sofa, taking off the prosthetic shoe and nursing his left foot on his knee. 'Just standing on the damn thing too much,' he said. 'I wanted to call you from the hospital, but every line was jammed all day.'

'Hospital—'

'Working there. Cornell Center. Impulse – one I should've had sooner, only that brain you say I have wasn't operating. Sure, just walked in, volunteered. Maybe it takes a pestilence to slice the red tape. They'll use anybody who can still crawl, run errands, carry a bedpan. I'm to go back at 3 A.M. – bit of sleep and something to eat.' He gulped the drink I brought him, half blind with an exhaustion more than physical. 'Will, I didn't know – you couldn't imagine – the babies, the old, the great husky men who look as if nothing could hurt 'em – down like the corn in a hailstorm. There aren't any beds left, you know. We'll use the floor while the extra mattresses last, and then – go on using the floor. We try to be sure they're really dead before we—'

'I'll go along with you at three.'

This was not the first time that human nature has put me to shame, but it is the time I shall always remember best.

9

New York
Monday, March 20

Sophia Wilkanowska died this morning. So did President Clifford, but I think of Sophia, and one other.

Yes, the President of the United States died this morning. According to the newspaper, he went out like a gentleman, after some seventy-two hours without sleep, upholding the massive burden of duties and decisions even after the cold symptoms began and he knew the virus was in him. Disaster, as human beings would say, always does separate the men from the boys. He was still quite young – fifty-nine. Rest in peace. Vice-President Borden is the usual political unknown; time enough to worry about him if he survives the siege. I am thinking of Sophia and one other.

Abraham and I came home at one o'clock Sunday, after ten hours at the hospital. We were to return at eight in the evening. Sharon's telephone did not answer. I think that for Abraham the hours had become a black tunnel with a light at the end, the light of the moment when he could talk to Sharon. Now the telephone did not answer, and I had to watch the light go out. I heard the dead impersonal rings. He broke the connection. 'Maybe I dialed wrong.' He tried again. He hadn't dialed wrong. 'I'll go over,' he said. 'You'd better get some sleep.'

'What about that leg?' His left leg had swollen at the ankle. He had not stumbled at the hospital; now he did, a little, as he crossed the room to retrieve a wet raincoat. There was a sorry drizzle on the streets, and March chill had returned.

'That? Oh, the hell with it, it works. You're going back at eight, Will?'

'I think I'd better. But you should stay with Sharon. You'll find she's just stepped out somewhere, but – stay with her anyhow.'

'Sophia – almost never goes out, Sharon said: her blindness.'

'I know. You stay with them. It's more important.'

'Yes – "importance" is a word' – he was reeling with fatigue – 'and you taught me not to be used by words.'

'Besides, another ten hours on that leg and you couldn't walk, Abraham – better admit it.'

He found second wind – or third, or fourth. It was not to steady himself that he turned in the doorway and caught hold of my coat lapel. 'Will – thanks for everything.'

I tried to look irritated. 'Cut that out – this isn't goodbye. I'm coming over to Brooklyn myself tomorrow, soon as I'm through at the hospital. You stay with them, and keep off that leg as much as you can.'

'All the same, thanks.' His dark eyes were upturned, inescapable, blazing with the unsayable. 'Sharon told me how it happened that Mrs Wilks started her school. I was thinking about the woods too – the woods in Latimer.' He grinned suddenly, and shook my coat lapel, and limped hurriedly for the elevator, leaving me – not exactly alone.

He called back in the late afternoon, but found it difficult to talk. I asked: 'Sharon—'

'She's all right. She's all right, Will, but—'

'Sophia?'

'Has it ... Sharon had gone out, when I was trying to call, out to find a doctor. There aren't any available. Not one.'

'Yes, it would have come to that by now. Better to keep her there, I think. Better than a hospital.'

'Yes, we've seen that.' Sophia would die. We both knew it; both remembered a statement in a newspaper we read on the way home from the hospital: *So far, all patients showing signs of recovery are under thirty-five years of age.* 'They say, Will, they say two Brooklyn hospitals are turning them away – simply no place to put them.'

'I'll come tomorrow, soon as I'm through. You stay there.'

'Yes,' he said.

'You're certain that Sharon—'

'I'm certain,' said Abraham, and his voice cracked all to pieces as if someone had struck him in the chest. 'I'm certain.' He hung up.

Abraham had not stumbled there at the hospital. I did, a few times, that night, not so much from fatigue as from a sense of helplessness that became physical, as if I were trying to swim in molasses. They came in so fast! There was no such thing as separating the light cases from the severe – there were no light cases, not there at the Center. My duties were to fetch and carry on three wards, lend a hand wherever I was at anything the nurses or doctors thought I could do. I did my best, but it was not like Abraham's best, and now and then I stumbled.

They were strangely silent wards. Full of the sound of tortured breath, the feeble scraping and shuffling of bodies that could move a little, but no groaning, no speech except among us who tried to care for them. When one died there was scant struggle; no convulsions or violent contractions of the muscle: you might not be sure until you stooped to feel the coldness. The smell of the wards was foul of course – two or three worn attendants can't keep paralyzed patients clean, when there are sixty or seventy of them in a room meant to hold not more than twenty. Ten million are said to have died in the flu of 1918; that was nothing, Drozma, compared to this. There has been nothing like this since the fourteenth century. Statistical charts have gone into a fever like that of para. By this time, I suppose, technicians will have fed the nightmare figures into some of the electronic brains that have become so important in the last twenty years; but I don't think the papers will publish what the machines have to say.

As night crawled into morning I found I was leaning more and more on the memory of how Abraham had done this same work with me the day before, and yet his way would be difficult for me to describe to you, Drozma. In actual work, perhaps he did no more than the other devoted attendants, although he seemed to: he was everywhere. There was what I must call some kind of communication between him and the conscious patients, even when the deafness of the disease prevented them from hearing anything he said. Sometimes I saw him shaping words carefully for them; sometimes he would scribble a note, or it might be only a smile or pressure of the hand or an almost telepathic understanding of an unspoken need. They knew it when he was there; those who could moved their heads to watch for him ...

Most dreadful of all were those patients in the stage before unconsciousness, when their eyes glared at unknown images and their hands twitched frantically in a struggle to rise and push away some monster of the mind. Three times I saw Abraham achieve communication with such patients, making them aware of him so that his real and human face became a shield between them and the hallucinations. For one of these, a giant Negro who could have strangled a bull a few days earlier, Abraham lifted the straining hand and brought its fingers against his cheek to prove the reality; the wildness passed, and there was a kind of peace, a third victory. That man, and one of the other two, were still living when I went back Sunday night; their fevers were not very high, and the nurse had tagged their mattresses with a blue X, which was emergency shorthand for *Good resistance, possible recovery*. If Abraham lives, I can return soon to Northern City.

Mission accomplished. If Abraham lives ...

I worked a twelve-hour shift that night, and it was ten o'clock in a rainy morning when I reached Sharon's apartment in Brooklyn. She let me in, and cried in my arms. I could see Abraham sitting across the room frowning at the floor, and through an open door beyond him I saw Sophia's room, and Sophia herself, already composed, her eyes shut, hands quiet. Abraham nodded, though it wasn't necessary to tell me. Two men were coming up the stairs behind me. I had not closed the door because Sharon still clung to me, and one of the men tapped my shoulder gently. 'You sent for us, sir?' They had gauze masks over mouth and nose, a singular futility. Sharon smothered a scream.

Abraham took charge, motioning Sharon and me to the studio. She was explaining to me: 'You see, there can't be any regular funerals—'

'I know, Sharon. Let Abraham—'

'Because the dead outnumber the living, do you see? Why, they always did, didn't they? Oh yes.' She coughed and blew her nose and shivered. 'And so they just come and take them, do you see?' She pulled the chair away from the piano and sat down facing me, lacing her hands together, wanting to explain. 'Ben, she always liked a little ceremony. Oh, she was a very formal lady, I always tried to live up to it. I think she'd've liked me to play a Polonaise – not the *Marche funébre* – no, *not*. But a Polonaise, only I don't think I could, anyway she's not here, is she? We have to think of it that way, don't we?'

'Of course. Let yourself go, Sharon. You're all wound up—'

'Oh no, because the dead outnumber us, and some of them like a little for-mality, I'm sure of it. It's a matter of keeping up appearances.' I heard the front door softly close. 'Would you get me a wrap, Ben? It's miserably chilly in here, isn't it?' It was somewhat chilly, but she was warmly dressed. 'The jani-tor is sick, I heard. I suppose the furnace is out. I think I'd like to sit here awhile. Look at the keyboard, but I don't think I could play anything. Would you like to, Ben?'

'No, I – I'll get you a coat.'

Abraham came in then, and I went to look for a coat or blanket. I found her bunny fur in a closet, and as I was taking it down I heard the piano for a moment. Not playing, just an upward ripple of notes. She would be standing by it, moving the back of her finger up the keyboard, a kind of caress to a friend, as if she were saying goodbye. I hurried back with the coat, but Abraham was bringing her out of the studio then, and she smiled brilliantly. 'Thanks, Ben. That's what I wanted.' Putting out her arms for it, she stumbled. Abraham kept her from falling. I picked her up and carried her to her bedroom – cool it was, orderly and virginal, with white walls, a blue bed-spread. Simplicity and innocence. She said carefully: 'I've had a bit of a cold all morning, but I don't think it's anything. Feel my hand, Abe. See? I'm not feverish.' I had carried her; she was hot as a coal, and the hand that Abraham was not holding was restless at the finger ends.

'Of course you're all right, Sharon,' he said. 'Shoes off. I want you to get under the covers—'

'What did you say, Abe?'

'Shoes—'

'I can't hear you.' She must have known it, must have been living with the thought for hours, but this was the first time that the shield of brave pretense had been torn away from her, and now she cried out: 'Abe, I love you so! I wanted to *live*—'

After that she could not speak ...

It must be near midnight. Abraham has never left her, of course. I spent some of the morning and afternoon trying to find a doctor who could come. A desperate waste of time: they are all red-eyed wrecks, working twenty-four hours a day at the hospitals and elsewhere. Not only with para: people still run their cars into lampposts, carve each other with knives, die of other dis-eases. There can be no home visits, and to send a victim to the hospital at this stage is merely to give him a more crowded place to die. I do not feel able to think of Union, Drozma. The end justifies the means, Joseph Max believed, following certain earlier theorists who should have died in infancy. I doubt if I ever knew before what it is to hate. Loving their best and hating their worst as I do, I can never go out again as an Observer. I am disqualified. I shall be old before I can look at this under the aspect of eternity.

I was right that what I saw Saturday was only a beginning. These streets are full of the dead; crews work with panel and half-ton trucks, taking them – I don't know where. Such a crew is usually followed by a protecting patrol car. Other police cars cruise slowly, watching, I think, for any knot of citizens that might become a mob. I bought a paper. It was a *Times*, down to an eight-page skeleton with no advertising. Some foreign news, almost all of the spread of para. Nothing about Asia. The death of President Clifford – that, of course, is the long banner headline, and at any other time the front page would have held almost nothing else; but the story of his death reads as though the writer had done it with his left hand, or as though his own head were aching with the symptoms of the common cold … The front page carries public notices, giving the telephone numbers of what they call Civil Defense Relief Crews – those are the men with the panel trucks. Statistics too – I've already forgotten most of them: over a million cases in the New York metropolitan area alone. In boldface type, standing instructions for treating victims who cannot be hospitalized. Supportive measures: keep the patient warm and quiet; don't try to make him swallow, too likely that he will strangle; keep the head level with the body to avoid constriction of the windpipe; the room should be darkened, since the eyes are hypersensitive during the conscious phase …

Sharon passed through the delirium in the middle afternoon. We were both with her. I could only be quiet while Abraham fought with devils, and the gentleness of his hands and face were the only weapons he could use. As I knew from our service in the hospital, there have been many deaths during the delirium, from a spasmodic closing off of breath, perhaps due to pure fright at the nightmare hallucinations. Sharon did not die.

I think she knew even at the height of her distress that Abraham was there, touching her, watching for every shadow that might cross her face, demanding that she stay with him and be afraid of nothing. It was natural to see my friend as the young St George – it would have been so much easier, so much simpler, if he could have opposed his frail body to a tangible dragon spouting flames! But the real dragons are always quiet, without form, and the profoundest courage a man can have is the kind that will uphold him against the attack of shadows.

We knew it when Sharon passed into unconsciousness, and shut her eyes in the stupor of the high fever. Abraham lost his grip then, briefly; probably because she had gone beyond communication, and there was nothing he could do. He was shaken with a kind of convulsive crying that had no tears in it. I forced him to swallow some black coffee. I found a cot in the spare bedroom, and brought it into Sharon's room, and made Abraham lie down, though I knew he would not sleep. He came out of the collapse quickly, and sat up again to watch her. At the hospital, a few patients have been kept alive with artificial respiration. He could not take his eyes away from her, for fear of missing the moment when she might need it. There had been something on an inner page of the newspaper: no more oxygen cylinders; a transportation breakdown was blamed. Since I knew there was no way to get any for Sharon, I couldn't care …

It must be nearly midnight. I am in the living room with this notebook, where I can hear if Abraham calls me. The fever is 105°. But average for this phase of the sickness is nearer 107°, and she is breathing well. She is strong; she wants to live; she is very young.

These hours stretching ahead of us must be moving toward some sunrise. It is quiet here, everywhere. I can hear her breathing, evenly, not too weakly. The city is strangely silent. This journal will be miserably unimportant, if she dies. I'll go in now, see if there is anything I can do.

Tuesday afternoon, March 21

Sharon's fever broke this morning at four o'clock, after fourteen hours of the burning. There was no ominous leveling off at a high point. She is unconscious still, but it could almost be taken for natural sleep. 99.1° – you can't call that a fever. In the early afternoon I went out to buy a paper – the radio broadcasts are maddening gabbles, and two of the best stations have gone silent – and found a newsstand with a few of the four-and eight-page sheets they are putting out. The dealer wore one of the useless gauze masks, and tossed change to me, careful not to touch my fingers …

Monday afternoon, it seems, a mob destroyed the offices of the Organic Unity Party. The policeman guarding the entrance – I shall always wonder if it was the same big decent Irishman – fired into the crowd as a last resort, but they trampled him to death in spite of that. They set fire to the interior, and slaughtered another man who was probably an innocent caretaker. Partly my doing. I can never go out again as an Observer. I threw away the paper, and told Abraham I couldn't find one.

He was at last willing to sleep. I have promised to wake him if there is any change, and I will. Incredible that in spite of all Martian and human science of the last thirty thousand years I can do nothing but sit here, sponge her lips, watch, wait.

Tuesday night, March 21

She is still unconscious, but her temperature is 98.7°; her breathing is excellent, not entirely mouth breathing now; there have been some apparently voluntary swallowing motions. I thought I saw her hand move slightly, but may have imagined it. That was early this evening; Abraham did not see it, and I did not mention it for fear I was wrong. I thought too that there was some dim responding motion when I felt her pulse just a few minutes ago, but again I could have been wrong. Anyway the pulse was good: regular, strong, fairly slow, none of the fluttering, pounding, hesitation that were so marked during the fever.

They recommend stimulants as well as liquid nourishment as soon as the patient can swallow. She must be conscious first. That will come. The wasting, the terrible hollows under her cheekbones that have appeared in the last forty-eight hours – those will pass. We have coffee and warm milk ready. It may be difficult to buy food outside now, but they had a well-stocked freezer, and so far the power has not failed. Canned stuff too, enough for four or five days. In the few exhausted words that Abraham and I have for each other, we take it for granted that very soon she will open her eyes and be able to see us. He speaks to her often; there has been no response to that, but I thought or imagined that the unknowing mask did change faintly once, when he kissed her.

We talked of other matters too, this evening. I wanted to draw Abraham away from the inner violence of his personal ordeal, and I said something vague, to the effect that human society as we knew it could never be quite the same again after the pandemic had run its course.

'It must be known,' said Abraham, 'that this thing was man-made. They must have that fact driven into them, driven into their guts, driven into the germ plasm. And I think their great-grandchildren had better remember it.'

'It is known,' I told him. I told him what I had done, and what the mob had done.

'I think you were right—'

'That I'll never know, Abraham. It's done, and I shall be judging myself the rest of my life – likely with a hung verdict.'

'For what my opinion's worth, you did right. But it's not enough. After this is all over, Will, I ought to write down everything I know – after all, Hodding and Max are dead: who else is there to talk? Somehow I ought to see to it that there isn't a corner of the planet where that truth hasn't reached.'

'Are men going to listen any better when it's over, Abraham? If you approach authority, for instance, and they say, "Where's your proof?"'

'Why, I'd even lie and say I had a hand in it myself, if that was the only way to get the fact across.'

'Wrong, for several reasons—'

'Oh, Will, the individual isn't so much as all that—'

'He is, but that's not the greatest reason. I'll ask you to look at this one in particular: if you did that, you'd be a scapegoat, nothing more, and haven't you stopped to wonder why men want a scapegoat? What is it, what was it ever, but a device to help them avoid looking at themselves? This is the kind of world where it's possible for a Joseph Max to run wild. If there must be blame, then all citizens – you, I, everyone – are responsible for letting it be that kind of world, for not placing ethical development ahead of every other kind. We understand ethical necessities quite well; we've been capable of understanding them for several thousand years; but we haven't been willing to let them rule our actions – it's that simple. Spend yourself in the long labor, Abraham, not in the passionate gesture or the unheeded sacrifice. On the personal level – because I've always seen a special flame in you that burns more dimly in others, and because I've always loved you – I forbid you to give yourself to crucifixion for no purpose.'

After a while he said, to me, to himself, to the girl who was so silent but not dying: 'Is maturity the acceptance of conflict?'

And I said, silently, to myself only: *Mission accomplished.*

Wednesday, March 22

Early this morning, before dawn, she moved her hands up to her face, and her eyes opened – wide, knowing, full of recognition. 'Sharon—'

'I'm all right,' she whispered. 'I'm all right, Abe.'

'Yes, you're out of it. You—'

'Darling, don't whisper. I want to hear everything you say.'

'Sharon! Sharon—'

'I can't hear you,' said Sharon Brand. 'I can't hear you.'

10

Aboard the S.S. *Jensen* out of Honolulu for Manila
July 24, 30,972

The ocean, forever changing and the same, was awake with deep music tonight; I was alone and not alone at all. Not alone, looking down some hours from the moving bow, seeing the flash and lingering subsidence of the noctilucae, those living diamonds of the sea, their light as transient as the sea foam and eternal as life, if life is eternal. Everything goes with me, the cherished faces, the words that endure although no embodied voice is near my body but only the great continuing voice of the sea and of a westerly wind out of the open regions of the world. I am not alone.

As we measure time it is not long, my second father, since I was in Northern City with you: nine years, a moment – it will seem nothing indeed when I am there with you again, in a few weeks or months.

You have my journal. Now that more time has passed, letting some pain recede, some anger die away, I must ask you to destroy that letter which I wrote to accompany the journal. I wrote it only one day after I knew that Sharon was deaf; I should have known better than to write anything at such a time. It was several weeks before I dared entrust the journal to the crippled human transportation system with any hope that it would reach Toronto and be forwarded to you, but in those weeks the anger and despair did not release me, and perhaps I could have written nothing better at the end of them. Now, however, I ask you to destroy that letter. From pride and vanity, and from the thought that my children are almost old enough to study my work, I do not want such a mood to be preserved. Put with the journal this message I am writing you now, and throw away what was written at a time when I was too heartsick to know what I said.

I cannot truly hate human beings for anything they do. If I said I did, that was an aberration of weakness, because I love Sharon more than any Observer should allow himself to love, and because I knew, as well as anyone can, what effort, sacrifice, and devotion it had cost her to make herself so fine an artist, only to have it torn away. 'I live with dream stuff,' she said. Yes, she did; and to all who could hear she gave those dreams with a most free sharing. And the world responded – with para, with permanent deafness, not curable, not to be remedied with any device, for the beautiful magic nerves themselves are destroyed: she must live all the rest of her life in total silence. And for a while, as I admit now, I was not myself and I could not endure it.

It was Abraham who saved my reason, and probably Sharon's. He upheld all three of us, forcing us to understand what richness of life remained in spite of everything. Well, let me tell in a couple of dozen words what Abraham has done since I wrote that wretched letter. He married her in April, as soon as she could be up and about, and took her to a small village in Vermont. Now he's a clerk there, in a general store: dry goods and fish-hooks and a pound of this and a pound of that. Laugh at it, Drozma – he does – and you'll see that it makes sense. I'll come back to that presently.

This freighter is an old tramp in no hurry. The air liners are flying again. There are fast boats. The whole huge complex of human transport and commerce and communication has staggered back to maybe forty per cent of normal; by the end of a year I suppose things will seem very much as they did a year ago. Superficially. I chose this old tub because I wanted a month with the ocean, and near it, where I could feel the voice of it, not slipping across it in a vast fission-driven city or soaring above it more swiftly than sound, but down here in the swells, the salt smell, the long whispering, the blue and green and gray. I wanted to watch the humorous pace-setting of the fulmars, whose flying is a kind of singing; the hasty brilliance of the flying fish; the large unhurried fins of danger that sometimes follow; the distant spouting of leviathan. I wanted to see the Pacific sunshine on the water through the hot days, the uncaring splendor of its setting in the evening – and with the sense that I was in that sunset, not overtaking it, not challenging it with my tiny conceptions of duration and motion. I wonder whether, some day, human beings will settle down, relax a little, discover that eternity is a long time.

I'll talk with you directly from Manila, Drozma, if I can. If there should be difficulty about that, I suppose this may reach you first. I want to arrange matters so that Sharon and Abraham will learn of my 'death' in a way that will distress them as little as possible and yet leave no doubt. They know I am going to Manila – 'for a sort of vacation and to see some old friends'. I told Abraham once, casually, how I had always hoped that when I died it would be in the ocean, a relinquishment, a slipping downward into calm without a grave. That was not true, to be sure – I want to die in Northern City, after many more years of interesting work. But it was a humanlike notion that Abraham would not find strange in me, and I said it to prepare the way. I want about two months in Manila. Then I'll take another slow ship for the States. If one of our little exploration subs could meet the ship, say about thirty miles out of Cavite? I could be a 'man overboard' with not too much fuss, and Abraham would think that the old man died the way he wanted to. But if this would be too expensive and troublesome to arrange, Drozma, we can work out some other gentle fraud when I get in touch with you.

The worst was over at the end of April. Gradually, grudgingly, the curve on the graph sagged downward. By the end of May the fire was out: no new cases were reported, and the survivors found that there was still civilization, of a sort. How much it may have set back the 'progress' that Namir hated so badly, I don't know; and about ten years from now, I think we might begin to assess what it has done to men's thinking.

It is known everywhere, as Abraham desired, that the tragedy was man-made. Known from a rather unexpected source: Jason Hodding's son, who found a tormented diary the old man had kept during the final weeks of his work, and gave it to the authorities – and then shot himself. He must have felt, as Abraham did, that it was a thing men had to know; he was also the son of a man who was neither good nor bad, but human.

These are some of the figures I remember. The United States, with a population of more than two hundred million, lost forty-two million dead. This was from para alone: it does not include those who died in riots, and in the famines that gripped many communities, causing panic evacuations into a countryside that had no means of caring for the refugees. It does not include the millions who survived with major disablements – usually deafness like Sharon's, but there were some who came out of it with limbs crippled as if by poliomyelitis, and some whose throats never recovered speech; and there were a few – I am speaking in terms of thousands – whose brain tissue was so damaged that they are not actually among the living. The United States of Europe, and South America, suffered in about the same proportion; Africa and India rather more. Interesting to note, however, that the death rate was only slightly higher in those countries where sanitation and public health work had never advanced to anything like the American level. It is supposed to have been somewhat higher in those countries merely because convalescents could not receive the care they did in more prosperous places, and therefore many died from inevitable neglect who might have lived.

The disease certainly reached Asia. That much we know. It must have done its slaughter there, after two years of major war, more horribly than anywhere else. But we also know, from the Satellite Authority, that some kind of war still goes on there, a slow fire of death, perhaps dying down, perhaps not. There is talk of sending in medical rescue expeditions – with armies in front of them for protection. I don't know. It couldn't be done sooh; not until the rest of the world has had a little time to recover. It should be easy enough to bypass Canton, Murmansk, Vladivostok, where they combined demolition with radioactive cobalt, but all effort at communication since the war began has been met with the sullen fury of silence; so far as I know all the land approaches to the sick continent are still viciously guarded in depth; their radar is good, and somehow they still have the means – aircraft, anti-aircraft, guided missiles – to destroy all foreign planes without inquiry, as they have done for the last three years. To break through would require a major military operation. The Western world has no heart for that at present; quite probably the slave populations would consider it an invasion, and hate the foreign devils as thoroughly as their masters do. It may be the logical finish for a national paranoia – all the same, you can't throw away a third of a planet. Sooner or later sanity will have to tear down the barrier, if only for its own sake.

What has been the quality of the years for you, Drozma? In your letters you say little of yourself. I know you stand apart, watching both worlds with a clarity I have never achieved. I hope (though you do not say so) that the administrative burdens have been lightened, to give you better hours of contemplation. In spite of the plague, in spite of the continuing division of the world and the great weariness that will linger everywhere for a long time, I still believe that Union may be possible toward the close of my son's lifetime. We must discuss that when I see you, that and many other slow-maturing fruits of the centuries. I gave the Minoan mirror to Sharon and Abraham, thinking you would approve the gift.

They have the essentials of maturity. Now I wish you could see Abraham waiting on the customers in that little store, or sometimes presiding over the rambling talk of old men and young on the rickety porch! He has even picked up a trace of the accent, though nobody could take him for a Vermonter. The small village was ravaged by para, like all the rest of the world – about a hundred dead from a population of less than four hundred – but it coheres and goes on about its decent business in the stubborn Vermont way. The owner of the store is an old man who lost all his family to para; he is worn down to a gray shred of humanity, but he is not confused. He thinks of Sharon and Abraham as his 'new children', and for himself he chiefly wants just to sit in the sun and wait a while.

They live over the store. One room has become a library, and Sharon reads a great deal ... 'We shan't be here always,' Abraham said to me. It is a pleasant and probably necessary temporary retirement from the livelier world. They need some years of quiet and study – Sharon to build a wholly new life on the ruins of what she lost, Abraham to digest and understand the past and the present and go on to new discoveries, new efforts that I would never dare to predict. He learned the deaf-mute sign language before Sharon did; learning it from him was one of the first steps she took out of her private maze of despair. He has other methods too of bringing the world to her. Sharon had never read a great deal before; the piano took the place of it. Now she is following his mind wherever it goes, and they are never lonely.

There is no undercurrent of guilt in his devotion to her, only love and a receptive interest in the endless mystery of another personality. He has no tendency now to blame himself for the world's troubles. He sees himself very simply, I think – as a human being with possibilities that are not to be thrown away or lost or stultified. He has learned, Drozma, how to look in a mirror.

He is painting, too, for his pleasure, and Sharon's, and for whatever others may choose to see in his work. I have two new canvases he gave me, in a waterproof cylinder, and am bringing them home to you. I wish you could see a certain fantasy of the underground river of Goyalantis – but I couldn't accept that one, because I knew that Sharon wanted it even more. And tentatively, not too humbly, Sharon is approaching that art herself, partly under his guidance, more under the guidance of her own warm imagination – something may come of that; it's too soon to tell. They are never lonely.

All that I have told you has the pathetic incompleteness of words. I remember my report of 30,963, and my journal of this year, and I am constantly amazed to think how intricate was the reality, how partial my story of it, like those telescopic photographs of Mars that tickle and excite the human imagination with a sense of truth just beyond reach. I remember Latimer, New England's queer blend of history and tomorrow: I can smell it, and hear again the street sounds, yet my words were feebler than a photograph, and a photograph would have told you very little.

I remember my first meeting with Angelo Pontevecchio. How can I describe the certainty of recognition in myself when he limped into the house, set down the *Crito*, studied me with twelve-year-old curiosity behind his mother's friendliness – the certainty that I was in the presence of what I must always love without ever understanding it?

Did I make you see Feuermann? Or any of those other bewildering complexes of contradiction we call human? Mac – I'll never know if I wounded him by shoving that damn toothbrush out of alignment. Mrs Keith and her amethyst brooch ...

I shall always remember Rosa, the pretty eyebrows in her round face always slightly lifted in wonder at her son and at the world beyond him.

I remember Amagoya.

I remember too the first time I saw the Satellite. In the Americas they call it the Midnight Star, and I saw it rising from the north and passing, not swift like a meteor but far more hurried to the eye than any star. The most dramatic achievement of human science, I think, and something more than science too – a bright finger groping at the heavens. It moves in daytime, invisible, over the Pacific, but I shall see it again when I am coming home.

I remember the sea, from centuries past and from tonight, the sea that changes forever only to be the same.

Never, beautiful Earth, never even at the height of the human storms have I forgotten you, my planet Earth, your forests and your fields, your oceans, the serenity of your mountains; the meadows, the continuing rivers, the incorruptible promise of returning spring.

GOOD NEIGHBORS AND OTHER STRANGERS

This one is for
BOB MILLS

GOOD NEIGHBORS

The ship was sighted a few times, briefly and without a good fix. It was spherical, the estimated diameter about twenty-seven miles, and was in orbit approximately 3,400 miles from the surface of the earth. No one observed the escape from it.

The ship itself occasioned some comment, but back there at the tattered end of the twentieth century, what was one visiting spaceship more or less? Others had appeared before, and gone away, discouraged or just not bothering. Three-dimensional T.V. was coming out of the experimental stage. Soon anyone could have 'Dora the Doll' or the 'Grandson of Tarzan' smack in his own living room. Besides, it was a hot summer.

The first knowledge of the escape came when the region of Seattle suffered an eclipse of the sun, which was not an eclipse but a near shadow, which was not a shadow but a thing. The darkness drifted out of the northern Pacific. It generated thunder without lightning and without rain. When it had moved eastward and the hot sun reappeared, wind followed, a moderate gale. The coast was battered by sudden high waves, then hushed in a bewilderment of fog.

Before that appearance, radar had gone crazy for an hour.

The atmosphere buzzed with aircraft. They went up in readiness to shoot, but after the first sighting reports a few miles offshore, that order was vehemently canceled – someone in charge must have had a grain of sense. The thing was not a plane, rocket or missile. It was an animal.

If you shoot an animal that resembles an inflated gasbag with wings, and the wingspread happens to be something over four miles tip to tip, and the carcass drops on a city, that is not nice.

The Office of Continental Defense deplored the lack of precedent. But actually none was needed. You just don't drop four miles of dead or dying alien flesh on Seattle or any other part of a swarming homeland. You wait till it flies out over the ocean, if it will, or at least over somebody else's country.

It, or rather she, didn't go back over the Pacific, perhaps because of the prevailing westerlies. After the Seattle incident she climbed to a great altitude above the Rockies, apparently using an updraft with very little wing motion. There was no means of calculating her weight, mass, or buoyancy. Dead or injured, drift might have carried her anywhere within one or two hundred miles. Then she seemed to be following the line of the Platte and the Missouri. By the end of the day she was circling interminably over the huge complex of St Louis, hopelessly crying.

She had a head, drawn back most of the time into the bloated mass of the body but thrusting forward now and then on a short neck, not more than three hundred feet in length. When she did that the blunt turtle-like head could be observed, the gaping, toothless, suffering mouth from which the thunder came, and the soft-shining purple eyes that searched the ground but found nothing answering her need. The skin color was mud-brown with some dull iridescence and many peculiar marks resembling weals or blisters. Along the belly some observers saw half a mile of paired protuberances that looked like teats.

She was unquestionably the equivalent of a vertebrate. Two web-footed legs were drawn up close against the cigar-shaped body. The vast, rather narrow, inflated wings could not have been held or moved in flight without a strong internal skeleton and musculature. Theorists later argued she must have come from a planet with a high proportion of water surface, a planet possibly larger than Earth though of about the same mass and with a similar atmosphere. She could rise in Earth's air. And before each lament she was seen to breathe.

It was assumed that air sacs within her body had been inflated or partly inflated when she left the ship, perhaps with some gas lighter than nitrogen. Since it was inconceivable that a vertebrate organism could have survived entry into atmosphere from an orbit 3,400 miles up, it was necessary to believe that the ship had descended, unobserved and by unknown means, probably on Earth's night side. Later on the ship did descend as far as atmosphere, for a moment ...

St Louis was partly evacuated. There is no reliable estimate of the loss of life and property from panic and accident on the jammed roads and rail lines. Fifteen hundred dead, 7,400 injured is the conservative figure.

After a night and a day she abandoned that area, flying heavily eastward. The droning and swooping gnats of aircraft plainly distressed her. At first she had only tried to avoid them, but now and then during her eastward flight from St Louis she made short, desperate rushes against them, without skill or much sign of intelligence, screaming from a wide-open mouth that could have swallowed a four-engine bomber. Two aircraft were lost over Cincinnati, by collision with each other in trying to get out of her way. Pilots were then ordered to keep a distance of not less than ten miles until such time as she reached the Atlantic – if she did – when she could be safely shot down.

She studied Chicago for a day.

By that time Civil Defense was better prepared. About a million residents had already fled to open country before she came, and the loss of life was proportionately smaller. She moved on. We have no clue to the reason why great cities should have attracted her, though apparently they did. She was hungry perhaps, or seeking help, or merely drawn in animal curiosity by the endless motion in the cities and the strangeness. It has even been suggested that the life forms of her homeland – her masters – resembled humanity. She moved eastward, and religious organizations united to pray that she would come down on one of the Lakes where she could be safely destroyed. She didn't. They may have looked too dirty.

She approached Pittsburgh, choked and screamed and flew high, and soared in weary circles over Buffalo for a day and a night. Some pilots who had followed the flight from the West Coast claimed that the lamentation of her voice was growing fainter and hoarser while she was drifting along the line of the Mohawk Valley. She turned south, following the Hudson at no great height. Sometimes she appeared to be gasping, the labored inhalations harsh and prolonged, a cloud in agony.

When she flew over Westchester, headquarters tripled the swarm of interceptors and observation planes. Squadrons from Connecticut and southern New Jersey deployed to form a monstrous funnel, the small end before her, the large end pointing out to open sea. Heavy bombers closed in above, laying a smoke screen at 10,000 feet to discourage her from rising. The ground shivered to the drone of jets and her crying.

Multitudes had abandoned the metropolitan area. Other multitudes trusted to the subways, to the narrow street canyons and to the strength of concrete and steel. Others climbed to high places and watched, trusting the laws of chance.

She passed over Manhattan in the evening, between 8:14 and 8:27 P.M., 16 July 1976, at an altitude of about 2,000 feet. She swerved away from the aircraft that blanketed Long Island and the Sound, swerved again as the southern group buzzed her instead of giving way. She made no attempt to rise into the sun-crimsoned terror of smoke.

The plan was intelligent. It should have worked, but for one fighter-pilot who jumped the gun. He said later that he himself couldn't understand what happened. It was court-martial testimony, but his reputation had been good. He was Bill Green – William Hammond Green – of New London, Connecticut, flying a one-man jet fighter, well aware of the strict orders not to attack until the target had moved at least ten miles east of Sandy Hook. He said he certainly had no previous intention to violate orders. It was something that just happened in his mind, a sort of mental sneeze.

His squadron was approaching Rockaway, the flying creature about three miles ahead of him and half a mile down. He was aware of saying out loud to nobody: 'Well, she's too goddamn big.' Then he was darting out of formation, diving on her, giving her one rocket-burst and reeling off to the south at 840 MPH.

He never did locate and rejoin his squadron, but he made it somehow back to his home field. He climbed out of the plane, they say, and fell flat on his face.

It seems likely that his shot missed the animal's head and tore through some part of her left wing. She spun to the left, rose perhaps a thousand feet, facing the city in her turn, side-slipped, recovered herself, and fought for altitude. She could not gain it. In the effort she collided with two of the following planes. One of them smashed into her right side behind the wing, the other flipped end over end across her back like a swatted dragonfly. It dropped clear and made a mess on Bedloe's Island.

She too was falling in a long slant, silent now but still living. After the impact her body thrashed desolately on the wreckage between Lexington and Seventh Avenues, her right wing churning, then only trailing, in the East River, her left wing a crumpled slowly deflating mass concealing Times Square, Herald Square and the garment district. At the close of the struggle her neck extended, her turtle beak grasping the top of Radio City. She was still trying to pull herself up, as the buoyant gases hissed and bubbled away through her wounds. Radio City collapsed with her.

For a long while after the roar of descending rubble and her own roaring had ceased, there was no human noise except a melancholy thunder of the planes.

The apology came early next morning.

The spaceship was observed to descend to the outer limits of atmosphere, very briefly. A capsule was released, with a parachute timed to open at 40,000 feet and come down neatly in Scarsdale. Parachute, capsule, and timing device were of good workmanship.

The communication engraved on a plaque of metal (which still defies analysis) was a hasty job, the English slightly odd, with some evidence of an incomplete understanding of the situation. That the visitors themselves were aware of these deficiencies is indicated by the text of the message itself:

Most sadly regret inexcusable escape of livestock. While petting same, one of our children monkied (sp?) with airlock. Will not happen again. Regret also imperfect grasp of language learned through what you term Television etc. Animal not dangerous, but observe some accidental damage caused, therefore hasten to enclose reimbursement, having taken liberty of studying your highly ingenious methods of exchange. Hope same will be adequate, having estimated deplorable inconvenience to best of ability. Regret exceedingly impossibility of communicating further, as pressure of time and prior obligations forbids. Please accept heartfelt apologies and assurances of continuing esteem.

The reimbursement was in fact properly enclosed with the plaque, and may be seen by the public in the rotunda of the restoration of Radio City. Though technically counterfeit, it looks like perfectly good money, except that Mr Lincoln is missing one of his wrinkles, and the words *five dollars* are upside down.

A BETTER MOUSEHOLE

So now Irma will be at me to do something about them blue bugs. I got to do something about Irma.

Dr West is wise too, as good as said so when him and Judge Van Anda was in today for a couple beers. Pity Dr West is not the doctoring type doctor but just has letters and stuff. Sort of explorer people say, account of his Independent Income, gone for months till the town's forgot him and then he turns up full of what the bull was done with.

I don't think the Judge knows about the blue bugs. If they bit him like they done me he'd never go to dreaming, not him up there, six feet five, looking back at what he figures the world used to be. Still if you was old like him, you might want big dreams more than ever, about being young.

If you could *tell* them bugs, if you could name your own dream! No way, I guess. I take the dreams I can get.

Dr West certainly knows something. I'd no sooner drawed them beers when he starts mentioning mice. I told him Look, I said, you do not see the Health Department climbing all over my back the way they would if I had mice. He asks me, so what is that hole in the floor below the liquor shelves? I had to make like hunting for it, and act surprised. Knothole, I says. Oh, knothole, he says, knothole the regal twin-cushioned back of my lap, how come a knothole in linoleum? So I had to say it could be mice. Judge Van Anda says Ha.

I went down the bar to pass the time with Lulu who doesn't get much business in the afternoon because the light is too strong. Lulu is like blonde this week. If only I could tell the bugs to put Lulu into a dream with me! The only time they done that she turned into Irma. I can't figure it.

What if Lulu got bit and had some dreams herself?

I suppose Irma thinks because I married her I can't do nothing without she comes clomping into it? If her ass is solid gold why don't she move to Fort Knox, get laid amongst the goldbricks?

I had not hardly started talking to Lulu when Dr West goes to booming. Desolation, he says, do you think you know what desolation is? It's the sub-Arctic tundra, he says, and me alone in that borrowed Cessna that might've got its engine tuned three or four months earlier, and no reason to be there except my itch to see more of the poor wonderful planet before they poison it or blow it up. Lulu, he says, what do you think? What do you say desolation is?

Oh, she says, maybe the Stadium, game over, crowd gone and you know, empty popcorn bags and match cards and spit.

You, Al? he says to me. What's desolation?

I said, oh, say, a dark night and nobody shows you where to go.

I believe Dr West is sad in his heart in spite of that education which is over my head. It would be like him to take off in a borrowed plane for the flat side of nowhere. I like to watch him standing by Judge Van Anda who he is always telling siddown siddown and the Judge merely says Ha. I can feel sad too, without no Independent Income. I am forty-two and I have this ulcer.

The tundra, says Dr West – a nothing of dun colors, rotting snow, and you wonder when the whole earth will look like that.

No! says Lulu, about to cry. Don't talk thataway!

Never mind, chicken, he says, I was just bleating.

Suppose you took Irma to this here tundra and told her to walk home. Flies, she says last night, flies all over you and you drunk as a pig. God, I pretty near shut her up for good. But she just don't know no better. She don't have too much of a life with a busted-down hack like me that couldn't even last five rounds with Willie Donohue and him not in his best years.

Dr West went on about borrowing that plane from a friend has got this lodge in the north woods, and flying over the tundra till he saw like a blue spark down there. Landed and picked up the object, size and shape of a basketball he said, not really blue, more like daylight split and turned a million ways. It hummed when he held it in his ear. That's when he broke off to ask me is there a basement under this part of the bar.

He knows damn well it's got no basement. He was in town when I got this addition added on. Already a cellar under the main part, I didn't need another, got this part done with merely the footing and concrete under the lino. I mean if there is any excavation in forty miles Dr West will be there watching. It's the people with an Independent Income or them with not any that get the excavations watched. Guys like me that work for a living, we are up that creek with a little bitty plastic spoon and no breeze. All's I said was Hell no, this here is an addition was added on, it's got no basement.

Unless somebody walled it off on you, says Judge Van Anda. You won't find a better way to dispose of a body, the Judge says, that's if you have time and materials and don't mind the labor. Well, the Judge is retired after forty years on what they call the Bench, and keeps saying with his experience he ought to write detective stories. Yes, sir, he says, if the walling off has been done right, proper pains taken, you can give the whole thing a very attractive finish. I guess he meant the wall. You never know, with the Judge. I must of said to him a hundred times Look, I've said, the surprising type things that have happened to me, you ought to put them into a book if you're going to write one. He just goes hrrm hrrm and Ha.

I hated him sounding off about bodies that way, account of Lulu's nerves. Before Dr West begun his story Lulu was talking to me about that murder over to Lincolnsville, the one that done in his whole family with a kitchen knife, and the shooting down in Jonesburg a couple weeks ago. She was real nerved up. His whole family, and with a plain kitchen knife. When the cops come for him – Jesus, he was like asleep, it said. Lulu takes the news real personal, it's the woman of it.

Dr West's little blue eyes – why, damn, they're near the same color as my bugs, like sky with the sun caught in it.

Maybe the bugs are something new to science that Dr West has to keep top secret? Then this tundra story would be the educated crappola he's obliged to shovel over it? His eyes are bloodshot like mine have been getting the last few weeks. I been losing weight too and it ain't my ulcer. The blood the bugs take out couldn't make no such difference, and them so gentle I float off into the dreams almost as soon as they come settle on me.

I'd give anything to have another dream where Irma is like when we got married, not bony and mean but soft, brown hair with all them goldy lights, voice like country cream.

When Dr West quit talking Lulu was crying. She says she feels sometimes like everything was on top of her, usually goes to the Ladies and comes back with a rebuilt mouth and a fresh bounce to her ass. Lulu could put her shoes in my trunk any time. She ain't had a real happy life.

Aw, who does? For young people it's always a maybe-tomorrow, for the rest it's where-did-everything-go? The Judge he should be happy looking acrost all them years of playing God and sticking people in jail? Dr West never married, chases moonblink all over the world with his Independent Income, but once he told me what he honestly craved was hearth and home, nice woman to warm his slippers and his bed, only a devil in him couldn't ever let him rest. And I have this ulcer.

The Bible or somebody says if you build a better mousetrap they'll like put you on teevy. All's I got is a better mousehole. What do they give you for that?

Dr West waited till Lulu come back from the Ladies to go on with his story. He wasn't telling it for her, though, spite of her coming to sit on the stool by him and give him a feel or two for friendship's sake. Not for the Judge neither. It was for me and that hole in the floor. I could of told him they never come out till I close the bar and dim the lights.

He said he smuggled the blue ball home, not a word to anyone. As a story it wasn't nothing, which is one reason I can't believe he was shitting us. He kept calling the thing a sphere. I always thought a sphere was some type musical instrument.

When he says home he means the ram-and-shackle mansion at the edge of town with backland running up Ragged Rock Hill and Johnny Blood rattling around in the mansion being a caretaker with one eye that used to be an actor and still lets go with some of this Shakespeare if anything startles him. He said he sent Johnny away for two months vacation to this sister in Maine who has been trying to make Johnny come to Jesus anyhow thirty-four years, only when Johnny hears that special tone of voice he shuts the good eye and lets go with something from this Shakespeare. I wish I had the education to make with Shakespeare when Irma is at me about talking to Lulu or drinking up the profits as if I could do that with this ulcer unless I would drop dead, she never thinks of that, or why don't I at least try to earn enough we would spend winters in Florida if I had any zing.

Sent Johnny away, he says, and kept the sphere at room temperature. Dr West is always talking thataway. A room don't run a temperature, or if he means hot like some special room what's so scientific if somebody monkeys with the thermostack or leaves the goddamn door open?

Winter in Florida for Christ's sake.

The blue thing hatched one night after he'd gone to bed – except he says it was not an egg but a figure of speech. He found the two halves in the morning not chipped like a hatched egg, just separated, like they'd been fitted originally so slick you couldn't find the joint. Nothing else disturbed, but a hole in the window screen that looked like it was melted through, the ends of copper wire fused so the hole looked like a grommet.

Judge Van Anda asked him did he keep the busted eggshell. Dr West says, Now I did try to make it plain it was not an egg, nor do I know why I waste my experiences on you, like when I showed you that comb my mermaid gave me it could of been a paperclip all the impression it made. So it could, says the Judge kind of brisk, seeing they make such combs in Bridgeport you can buy them in any drugstore upwards of nineteen cents plus tax. All right, says Dr West, so if she did happen on it in the billows off Bridgeport, God damn it, she *gave* it to me, didn't she? Oh, don't get red-eyed about it, says Judge Van Anda.

I'm not, says Dr West. Al's the one with bloodshot eyes, late hours likely. He was watching me real sharp. No sir, you too, says the Judge, you look in the mirror you'll see you're red-eyed like a weasel, I snow you not. Now if you could have brought home just one mermaid scale. And Dr West says Do I have to tell you again they do not have scales? No more reason to have scales than a seal or a whale or any ocean-dwelling mammal. Ocean-dwelling mahooha, says Judge Van Anda.

And I suppose, says Dr West, back there ninety-six years ago in the little red schoolhouse the only biology you ever learned was out in the bushes during recess. Which was a friendly type remark because the Judge could go hrrm hrrm reminding hisself how horny he wants you to think he used to be. All the same I quick took them another round of beers.

Lulu says You got out of that too easy, Doc. I remember she pushed her shoulders back showing she has got a pair. She could put her shoes in my trunk any time. She says Do you still have the eggshell or do you don't?

I do not, says Dr West. I do not still possess the two halves of that vehicle.

Well, excuse me for living, says Lulu, but she wasn't mad. She likes everybody, you could call it a weakness.

And why don't you still have it, says the Judge, as if I didn't know?

Because, says Dr West, I carried the halves outdoors to see them in the sun, was disturbed by the telephone, set them down in a thicket, answered the phone at which you bent my ear for half an hour about a detective story you plan to write any day now. When I got back the two halves were gone.

Naturally, says the Judge. Naturally.

Gone, says Dr West, from a patch of soft earth in the thicket that showed no footprints but my own.

Naturally.

They left it at that. Ever since, I been thinking about it. Only fifteen minutes now till closing time or I would flip my lid.

Dr West was not lying or he would have done like a mermaid story. That don't mean he told the whole truth. How could anybody ever tell that like they say in the law courts? Maybe the bugs bit him before they went off through the hole in the screen? One bite would be enough to show him what it does to you. Could we sort of share the bugs?

I would like that. Something's gentled me down lately. I got no jealousy about him and Lulu going off together like they done this afternoon after that naturally thing. I don't seem to have no angry feelings of no kind except about drowning Irma into the bathtub if it was practical. Aw, I guess I mean I might make that type *joke*, a man couldn't *do* no such thing. Besides it could be some way my fault Irma is like she is. How about that, Al, how about that?

Anyhow I'd sooner Lulu went off with Dr West than with say this salesman type looks like a shaved pig and wants a beer.

Beer. Why can't they ask for something unusual just once so I would have to think about it and stop thinking so much?

Five minutes to closing.

It was last night Irma found me with my bugs and called them flies. I bet she believes that. It was the finest part of my dream – gone, clobbered, and here's Irma in her nightgown come down and turned on the light standing there all bones and temper saying Drunk as a pig, now I see where the profits go, all down your gut. Her that used to talk like a lady and had them goldy lights in her hair. Flies, she says, flies everywhere.

She don't know about the hole, my better mousehole, or she would of poured cleaning fluid down it and they would of come out and fixed her little red wagon. I would not like that to happen. It's funny how gentle I feel now-adays. I used to be what they call a ruffed diamond.

I guess Irma will have took her twenty-year grouch to bed by now. Oh no, it wasn't like that *all* of them years, not by no means – but my Jesus, I'm sup-posed to be some godalmighty Valentino Rockefeller or I'm no good? I'm good in them dreams. I been seven feet tall and bronzy, had this thing was ready whenever I said so.

There they go again talking about that thing in Jonesburg where this lady shot up a radio-teevy store account she claimed them noises spoiled her dreams. Look – things like that – it can't mean my bugs are—

I won't have a dream tonight, not till I can get a real talk alone with Dr West. Well, speak of the—

It has come to be morning, hot and quiet outside in that golden street. I bet-ter try to think through what happened and what Dr West said. That about inner space for instance.

When he come at closing time I seen he wanted talk, same as me. I told him stick around, I closed up, doused the lights in front and we carried a Jameson into the back room. He flung down a shot and said, I took Lulu up to my place, the Judge too. Johnny Blood'll be gone another couple weeks, but I suppose maybe the Judge'll be missed.

Missed? I says.

He says, Don't be like that, Al. The Judge is asleep and dreaming. Lulu is asleep and dreaming, and don't you go acting surprised on me, because I come back to talk to you. Beat-up crocks like you and me, Al, he says, we're into middle age, we can wait a mite longer for our dreams, seeing we've spent more'n half a lifetime doing not much else.

While I poured him another he said It was Lulu brought them back to me. I asked him how come.

She didn't do anything, he says, she's just overweight with a big blood pressure. They like that. They must need the blood, maybe to help them breed. Only a couple dozen came out of that sphere, but now they might have several colonies. I wasn't quite truthful, he says – I saw them come out, and a few of them flew around me with things in the fifth pair of limbs that looked like weapons. While I was holding still because of that, one of them bit me and I dreamed a wonderful journey to Alpha Centauri.

He's got eyes, that Dr West. All the time my blue bugs been around me I never noticed they was ten-legged.

Maybe, he says, they always give us the dreams merely to hold us quiet so they can drink. Maybe it's from loving kindness. Maybe they don't even know they're giving us dreams.

I asked if it was true what he told us about the halves of the shell

377

disappearing. He said yes, and he said that afterward he went searching and grieving all over, till one night he caught a bluish gleam up on Ragged Rock Hill. He went to it, working his way through the trees with a flashlight to where he thought it had showed, and settled down to wait. Sure enough they came and gave him a dream. That's when he told me it breaks his heart too the way a man can't name his own.

They come for Lulu. All we did, he says, we turned off the lights and set by the open window. Coming for Lulu because she's right for them, I guess, they took care of the Judge and me. My dream was a short one, Al. I don't have much blood in me.

He put down another Jameson while I told him what I been going through, and that's when he stepped over to one of the other back room booths to pick something off the floor. He's a noticing restless man. Just a buckle like a gold rosebud off a girl's shoe. The back room gets lively Saturday nights, and I ain't been sweeping up too good, last couple-three weeks. Only light I turned on for us was the 25-watt in our booth with the pink shade. Irma chose them shades. They're real nice. You won't find no goddamn interior desecrator that's got taste like that. Dr West he set there playing with that gold rosebud and going slow on his Jameson while I talked. And I asked him Where do they come from?

Oh, he says, outer space, where else? He was turning the buckle in and out of the light, reflecting a glow into the drink itself, a kind of glory. And he says, Or else inner space.

I asked him did he think the bugs had anything to do with them killings. He just wiggled his shoulders.

That's when I said Look, couldn't my Irma have a dream? He give me no answer. I says Maybe it would change how she acts and feels about some things? That's all I said.

And he says maybe. We don't know, he says, we don't know much of anything. More we know, better we get at asking questions we can't answer. Then he poured himself another Jameson and afterwhile I went upstairs.

Irma wasn't asleep. When I touched her shoulder she says God give me patience and flounces clear acrost the bed. I says Irma honey, I ain't after you thataway, I just want you should come down talk something over with I and Doc West. Ain't that all I said? And she says West, that dirty old man, what for?

I says, Irma, this is special, you give me lip I'm big enough to make you. You get up and fling some clothes on and take that goddamn cold cream off of your face and come down. All's we want is have a couple drinks and talk about something.

Well, she says, aren't we the lord and master all of a sudden! You fuckin' right, I says, and get going. Only I didn't say that mean, did I? No, and then she just wipes the guck off her face meek as anything, slippers on, bathrobe over her pjs and comes along. In the light of the upstairs hall I seen some of them goldy lights. I know I did.

Dr West had dropped his head on his arms. Small he was, and always clean as a dry stick, I don't know why she would call him a dirty old man, got no bad habits except needs to get his ashes hauled like any man. He hadn't finished his Jameson. I thought he was having a dream but he looked up and said, I brought it on us, I brought it on the world. I and some other few billion, he said. I don't know what he meant.

Irma seen the bugs and she screamed. Only five-six of them, nothing scary. I put my arms around her to gentle her. Irma, I says, all they do is give you beautiful dreams. I want you should have some like I've had. Let 'em bite a little, they don't hurt.

But you screamed and tried to fight me off. You said I don't want to, I just want – I just want—

I didn't listen. So hellbent you should have dreams like mine, I didn't listen. You did jerk around so, and them pjs got twisted away from your little boobs, and I must of just hung on, too lamebrain dumb for anything else. Them things is like when you was a girl. Used to kid about what would the babies eat, didn't we? Only we couldn't have any, but that was all right, I never minded about that. So one bug lit there and I must of just held you – why, them bites don't hurt, I got a hundred onto me, they don't even itch.

And so you didn't scream again but that shock went through you and you said Oh, oh, oh, a kind of crying like what I used to hear in bed and you with a voice like country cream. And I saw the bug fly away and I found your mouth and kissed you but you sagged away from me and you was dead.

I think Dr West said Your little lady, she's asleep?

I carried you over to this lounge chair, I guess I been just sitting here. I don't know what to do. I remember Dr West he come over and stood by though I wanted him to go away. I know I said something about maybe some people just couldn't have such dreams.

He says Maybe it's that or maybe she dreamed *more* than us, Al. Maybe this thing gave her too big a dream for her to stand. Dreaming's dangerous, he said, it's got a dark side. If the bugs shoot in something that makes the dreaming part of us blaze up, the way the rest of us can't take it—

And I told him I wasn't going to try to understand it no more. I said I ought to knowed you can't make another person to have a dream. It's not right, it's not right someway.

Dr West said more, didn't he? I can't just bring it back. I think he said dreaming's not a sickness but it's like one partly. It made the world what it is, different from ancient days, it could unmake it.

I asked him not to notify no one, just go away and leave me be. People will figure the bar is closed, give us a bit of time before they start crowding in.

And there was something he said about how things might even get better with the bugs taking over, if that's what they meant to do. I told him I didn't care so much about the world, all's I ever wanted was to have a decent life with work I knowed how to do and a nice woman and maybe some kids. I guess that's when Dr West went away. He's just a lonesome little guy trying to figure it out. I oughtn't to said nothing that sounded mean.

See, it wasn't like I was trying to make you have *my* dream exactly.

You look like you was dreaming now. You look real sweet, I meant to tell you. I don't know why I couldn't ever tell you.

LONGTOOTH

My word is good. How can I prove it? Born in Darkfield, wasn't I? Stayed away thirty more years after college, but when I returned I was still Ben Dane, one of the Darkfield Danes, Judge Marcus Dane's eldest. And they knew my word was good. My wife died and I sickened of all cities; then my bachelor brother Sam died too, who'd lived all his life here in Darkfield, running his one-man law office over in Lohman – our nearest metropolis, population 6,437. A fast coronary at fifty; I had loved him. Helen gone, then Sam – I wound up my unimportances and came home, inheriting Sam's housekeeper Adelaide Simmons, her grim stability and celestial cooking. Nostalgia for Maine is a serious matter, late in life: I had to yield. I expected a gradual drift into my childless old age playing correspondence chess, translating a few of the classics. I thought I could take for granted the continued respect of my neighbors. I say my word is good.

I will remember again the middle of March a few years ago, the snow skimming out of an afternoon sky as dry as the bottom of an old aluminum pot. Harp Ryder's back road had been plowed since the last snowfall; I supposed Bolt-Bucket could make the mile and a half in to his farm and out again before we got caught. Harp had asked me to get him a book if I was making a trip to Boston, any goddamn book that told about Eskimos, and I had one for him, De Poncins' *Kabloona*. I saw the midget devils of white running crazy down a huge slope of wind, and recalled hearing at the Darkfield News Bureau, otherwise Cleve's General Store, somebody mentioning a forecast of the worst blizzard in forty years. Joe Cleve, who won't permit a radio in the store because it pesters his ulcers, inquired of his Grand Inquisitor who dwells ten yards behind your right shoulder: 'Why's it always got to be the worst in so-and-so many years, that going to help anybody?' The Bureau was still analyzing this difficult inquiry when I left, with my cigarettes and as much as I could remember of Adelaide's grocery list after leaving it on the dining table. It wasn't yet three when I turned in on Harp's back road, and a gust slammed at Bolt-Bucket like death with a shovel.

I tried to win momentum for the rise to the high ground, swerved to avoid an idiot rabbit and hit instead a patch of snow-hidden melt-and-freeze, skidding to a full stop from which nothing would extract us but a tow.

I was fifty-seven that year, my wind bad from too much smoking and my heart (I now know) no stronger than Sam's. I quit cursing – gradually, to avoid sudden actions – and tucked *Kabloona* under my parka. I would walk the remaining mile to Ryder's, stay just long enough to leave the book, say hello, and phone for a tow; then, since Harp never owned a car and never would, I could walk back and meet the truck.

If Leda Ryder knew how to drive, it didn't matter much after she married Harp. They farmed it, back in there, in almost the manner of Harp's ancestors in Jefferson's time. Harp did keep his two hundred laying hens by methods that were considered modern before the poor wretches got condemned to batteries, but his other enterprises came closer to antiquity. In his big kitchen garden he let one small patch of weeds fool themselves for an inch or two, so he'd have it to work at: they survived nowhere else. A few cows, a team, four acres for market crops, and a small dog Droopy, whose grandmother had made it somehow with a dachshund. Droopy's only menace in obese old age was a wheezing bark. The Ryders must have grown nearly all vital necessities except chewing tobacco and once in a while a new dress for Leda. Harp could snub the twentieth century, and I doubt if Leda was consulted about it in spite of his obsessive devotion for her. She was almost thirty years younger and yes, he should not have married her. Other side up just as scratchy: she should not have married him, but she did.

Harp was a dinosaur perhaps, but I grew up with him, he a year the younger. We swam, fished, helled around together. And when I returned to Darkfield growing old, he was one of the few who acted glad to see me, so far as you can trust what you read in a face like a granite promontory. Maybe twice a week Harp Ryder smiled.

I pushed on up the ridge, and noticed a going-and-coming set of wide tire tracks already blurred with snow. That would be the egg truck I had passed a quarter-hour since on the main road. Whenever the west wind at my back lulled, I could swing around and enjoy one of my favorite prospects of birch and hemlock lowland. From Ryder's Ridge there's no sign of Darkfield two miles southwest except one church spire. On clear days you glimpse Bald Mountain and his two big brothers, more than twenty miles west of us.

The snow was thickening. It brought relief and pleasure to see the black shingles of Harp's barn and the roof of his Cape Codder. Foreshortened, so that it looked snug against the barn; actually house and barn were connected by a two-story shed fifteen feet wide and forty feet long – woodshed below, hen loft above. The Ryders' sunrise-facing bedroom window was set only three feet above the eaves of that shed roof. They truly went to bed with the chickens. I shouted, for Harp was about to close the big shed door. He held it for me. I ran, and the storm ran after me. The west wind was bouncing off the barn; eddies howled at us. The temperature had tumbled ten degrees since I left Darkfield. The thermometer by the shed door read fifteen degrees, and I knew I'd been a damn fool. As I helped Harp fight the shed door closed, I thought I heard Leda, crying.

A swift confused impression. The wind was exploring new ranges of passion, the big door squawked, and Harp was asking: 'Ca' break down?' I do still think I heard Leda wail. If so, it ended as we got the door latched and Harp drew a newly fitted two-by-four bar across it. I couldn't understand that: the old latch was surely proof against any wind short of a hurricane.

'Bolt-Bucket never breaks down. Ought to get one, Harp – lots of company. All she did was go in the ditch.'

'You might see her again come spring.' His hens were scratching overhead, not yet scared by the storm. Harp's eyes were small gray glitters of trouble. 'Ben, you figure a man's getting old at fifty-six?'

'No.' My bones (getting old) ached for the warmth of his kitchen-dining-living-everything room, not for sad philosophy. 'Use your phone, okay?'

'If the wires ain't down,' he said, not moving, a man beaten on by other storms. 'Them loafers didn't cut none of the overhand branches all summer. I told 'em of course, I told 'em how it would be ... I meant, Ben, old enough to get dumb fancies?' My face may have told him I thought he was brooding about himself with a young wife. He frowned, annoyed that I hadn't taken his meaning. 'I meant, *seeing* things. Things that can't be so, but—'

'We can all do some of that at any age, Harp.'

That remark was a stupid brush-off, a stone for bread, because I was cold, impatient, wanted in. Harp had always a tense one-way sensitivity. His face chilled. 'Well, come in, warm up. Leda ain't feeling too good. Getting a cold or something.'

When she came downstairs and made me welcome, her eyes were reddened. I don't think the wind made that noise. Droopy waddled from her basket behind the stove to snuff my feet and give me my usual low passing mark.

Leda never had it easy there, young and passionate with scant mental resources. She was twenty-eight that year, looking tall because she carried her firm body handsomely. Some of the sullenness in her big mouth and lucid gray eyes was sexual challenge, some pure discontent. I liked Leda; her nature was not one for animosity or meanness. Before her marriage the Darkfield News Bureau used to declare with its customary scrupulous fairness that Leda had been covered by every goddamn thing in pants within thirty miles. For once the Bureau may have spoken a grain of truth in the malice, for Leda did have the smoldering power that draws men without word or gesture. After her abrupt marriage to Harp – Sam told me all this: I wasn't living in Darkfield then and hadn't met her – the garbage-gossip went hastily underground: enraging Harp Ryder was never healthy.

The phone wires weren't down, yet. While I waited for the garage to answer, Harp said, 'Ben, I can't let you walk back in that. Stay over, huh?'

I didn't want to. It meant extra 'work and inconvenience for Leda, and I was ancient enough to crave my known safe burrow. But I felt Harp wanted me to stay for his own sake. I asked Jim Short at the garage to go ahead with Bolt-Bucket if I wasn't there to meet him. Jim roared: 'Know what it's doing right now?'

'Little spit of snow, looks like.'

'Jesus!' He covered the mouthpiece imperfectly. I heard his enthusiastic voice ring through cold-iron echoes: 'Hey, old Ben's got that thing into the ditch again! Ain't that something …? Listen, Ben, I can't make no promises. Got both tow trucks out already. You better stop over and praise the Lord you got that far.'

'Okay,' I said. 'It wasn't much of a ditch.'

Leda fed us coffee. She kept glancing toward the landing at the foot of the stairs where a night-darkness already prevailed. A closed-in stairway slanted down at a never-used front door; beyond that landing was the other ground floor room – parlor, spare, guest room – where I would sleep. I don't know what Leda expected to encounter in that shadow. Once when a chunk of firewood made an odd noise in the range, her lips clamped shut on a scream.

The coffee warmed me. By that time the weather left no loophole for argument. Not yet 3:30, but west and north were lost in furious black. Through the hissing white flood I could just see the front of the barn forty feet away. 'Nobody's going no place into that,' Harp said. His little house shuddered, enforcing the words. 'Led', you don't look too brisk. Get you some rest.'

'I better see to the spare room for Ben.'

Neither spoke with much tenderness, but it glowed openly in him when she turned her back. Then some other need bent his granite face out of its normal seams. His whole gaunt body leaning forward tried to help him talk. 'You wouldn't figure me for a man'd go off his rocker?' he asked.

'Of course not. What's biting, Harp?'

'There's something in the woods, got no right to be there.' To me that came as a letdown of relief: I would not have to listen to another's marriage problems. 'I wish, b' Jesus Christ, it would hit somebody else once, so I could say what I know and not be laughed at all to hell. I *ain't* one for dumb fancies.'

You walked on eggs with Harp. He might decide any minute that *I* was laughing. 'Tell me,' I said. 'If anything's out there now it must feel a mite chilly.'

'Ayah.' He went to the north window, looking out where we knew the road lay under the white confusion. Harp's land sloped down on the other side of the road to the edge of mighty evergreen forest. Mount Katahdin stands more than fifty miles north and a little east of us. We live in a withering, shrinking world, but you could still set out from Harp's farm and, except for the occasional country road and the rivers – not many large ones – you could stay in deep forest all the way to the tundra, or Alaska. Harp said, 'This kind of weather is when it comes.'

He sank into his beat-up kitchen armchair and reached for *Kabloona*. He had barely glanced at the book while Leda was with us. 'Funny name.'

'Kabloona's an Eskimo word for white man.'

'He done these pictures ...? Be they good, Ben?'

'I like 'em. Photographs in the back.'

'Oh.' He turned the pages hastily for those, but studied only the ones that showed the strong Eskimo faces, and his interest faded. Whatever he wanted was not here. 'These people, be they – civilized?'

'In their own way, sure.'

'Ayah, this guy looks like he could find his way in the woods.'

'Likely the one thing he couldn't do, Harp. They never see a tree unless they come south, and they hate to do that. Anything below the Arctic is too warm.'

'That a fact ...? Well, it's a nice book. How much was it?' I'd found it second-hand; he paid me to the exact penny. 'I'll be glad to read it.' He never would. It would end up on the shelf in the parlor with the Bible, an old almanac, a Longfellow, until someday this place went up for auction and nobody remembered Harp's way of living.

'What's this all about, Harp?'

'Oh ... I was hearing things in the woods, back last summer. I'd think, fox, then I'd know it wasn't. Make your hair stand right on end. Lost a cow, last August, from the north pasture acrost the rud. Section of board fence tore out. I mean, Ben, the two top boards was *pulled out from the nail holes*. No hammer marks.'

'Bear?'

'Only track I found looked like bear except too small. You know a bear wouldn't *pull* it out, Ben.'

'Cow slamming into it, panicked by something?'

He remained patient with me. 'Ben, would I build a cow pasture fence nailing the crosspieces from the outside? Cow hit it with all her weight she might bust it, sure. And kill herself doing it, be blood and hair all over the split boards, and she'd be there, not a mile and a half away into the woods. Happened during a big thunderstorm. I figured it had to be somebody with a spite against me, maybe some son of a bitch wanting the prop'ty, trying to scare me off that's lived here all my life and my family before me. But that don't make sense. I found the cow a week later, what was left. Way into the woods. The head and the bones. Hide tore up and flang around. Any *person* dressing off a beef, he'll cut whatever he wants and take off with it. He don't sit down and chaw the meat off the *bones*, b' Jesus Christ. He don't tear the thighbone out of the joint ... All right, maybe bear. But no bear did that job on that fence and then driv old Nell a mile and a half into the woods to kill her. Nice little Jersey, clever's a kitten. Leda used to make over her, like she don't usually do with the stock ... I've looked plenty in the woods since then, never turned up anything. Once and again I did smell something. Fishy, like bear-smell but – *different.*'

'But Harp, with snow on the ground—'

'Now you'll really call me crazy. When the weather is clear, I ain't once found his prints. I hear him then, at night, but I go out by daylight where I think the sound was, there's no trail. Just the usual snow tracks. I know. He lives in the trees and don't come down except when it's storming, I got to believe that? Because then he does come, Ben, when the weather's like now, like right now. And old Ned and Jerry out in the stable go wild, and some-times we hear his noise under the window. I shine my flashlight through the glass – never catch sight of him. I go out with the ten-gauge if there's any light to see by, and there's prints around the house – holes filling up with snow. By morning there'll be maybe some marks left, and they'll lead off to the north woods, but under the trees you won't find it. So he gets up in the branches and travels thataway? ... Just once I have seen him Ben. Last October. I better tell you one other thing fast. A day or so after I found what was left of old Nell, I lost six roaster chickens. I made over a couple box stalls, maybe you remember, so the birds could be out on range and roost in the barn at night. Good doors, and I always locked 'em. Two in the morning, Ned and Jerry go crazy, I got out through the barn into the stable, and they was spooked, Ned trying to kick his way out. I got 'em quiet, looked all over the stable – loft, harness room, everywhere. Not a thing. Dead quiet night, no moon. It had to be something the horses smelled. I come back into the barn, and found one of the chicken-pen doors open – *tore* out from the lock. Chicken thief would bring along something to pry with – wouldn't he be a Christly idjut if he didn't ...? Took six birds, six nice eight-pound roasters, and left the heads on the floor – bitten off.'

'Harp – some lunatic. People *can* go insane that way. There are old stories—'

'Been trying to believe that. Would a man live the winter out there? Twenty below zero?'

'Maybe a cave – animal skins.'

'I've boarded up the whole back of the barn. Done the same with the hen-loft windows – two-by-fours with four-inch spikes driv slantwise. They be twelve feet off the ground, and he ain't come for 'em, not yet ... So after that happened I sent for Sheriff Robart. Son of a bitch happens to live in Dark-field, you'd think he might've took an interest.'

'Do any good?'

Harp laughed. He did that by holding my stare, making no sound, moving no muscle except for a disturbance at the eye corners. A New England art;

386

maybe it came over on the *Mayflower*. 'Robart he come by, after a while. I showed him that door. I showed him them chicken heads. Told him how I'd been spending my nights out there on my ass, with the ten-gauge.' Harp rose to unload tobacco juice into the range fire; he has a theory it purifies the air. 'Ben, I might've showed him them chicken heads a shade close to his nose. By the time he got here, see, they wasn't all that fresh. He made out he'd look around and let me know. Mid-September. Ain't seen him since.'

'Might've figured he wouldn't be welcome?'

'Why, he'd be welcome as shit on a tablecloth.'

'You spoke of – seeing it, Harp?'

'Could call it seeing … All right. It was during them Indian summer days – remember? Like June except them pretty colors, smell of windfalls – God, I like that, I like October. I'd gone down to the slope acrost the rud where I mended my fence after losing old Nell. Just leaning there, guess I was tired. Late afternoon, sky pinking up. You know how the fence cuts acrost the slope to my east wood lot. I've let the bushes grow free – lot of elder, other stuff the birds come for. I was looking down toward that little break between the north woods and my wood lot, where a bit of old growed-up pasture shows through. Pretty spot. Painter fella come by a few years ago and done a picture of it, said the place looked like a coro, dunno what the hell that is, he didn't say.'

I pushed at his brown study. 'You saw it there?'

'No. Off to my right in them elder bushes. Fifty feet from me, I guess. By God I didn't turn my head. I got it with the tail of my eye and turned the other way as if I meant to walk back to the rud. Made like busy with something in the grass, come wandering back to the fence some nearer. He stayed for me, a brownish patch in them bushes by the big yellow birch. Near the height of a man. No gun with me, not even a stick … Big shoulders, couldn't see his goddamn feet. He don't stand more'n five feet tall. His hands, if he's got real ones, hung out of my sight in a tangle of elder branches. He's got brown fur, Ben, reddy-brown fur all over him. His face too, his head, his big thick neck. There's a shine to fur in sunlight, you can't be mistook. So – I did look at him direct. Tried to act like I still didn't see him, but he knowed. He melted back and got the birch between him and me. Not a sound.' And then Harp was listening for Leda upstairs. He went on softly: 'Ayah, I ran back for a gun, and searched the woods, for all the good it did me. You'll want to know about his face. I ain't told Led' all this part. See, she's scared, I don't want to make it no worse, I just said it was some animal that snuck off before I could see it good. A big face, Ben. Head real human except it sticks out too much around the jaw. Not much nose – open spots in the fur. Ben, the – the *teeth!* I seen his mouth drop open and he pulled up one side of his lip to show me them stabbing things. I've seen as big as that on a full-growed bear. That's what I'll hear, I ever try to tell this. They'll say I seen a bear. Now I shot my first bear when I was sixteen and Pa took me over toward Jackman. I've got me one maybe every other year since then. I know 'em, all their ways. But that's what I'll hear if I tell the story.'

I am a frustrated naturalist, loaded with assorted facts. I know there aren't any monkeys or apes that could stand our winters except maybe the harmless Himalayan langur. No such beast as Harp described lived anywhere on the planet. It didn't help. Harp was honest; he was rational; he wanted reasonable explanation as much as I did. Harp wasn't the village atheist for nothing. I said, 'I guess you will, Harp. People mostly won't take the – unusual.'

'Maybe you'll hear him tonight, Ben.'

Leda came downstairs, and heard part of that. 'He's been telling you, Ben. What do you think?'

'I don't know what to think.'

'Led', I thought, if I imitate that noise for him—'

'No!' She had brought some mending and she was about to sit down with it, but froze as if threatened by attack. 'I couldn't stand it, Harp. And – it might bring them.'

'Them?' Harp chuckled uneasily. 'I don't guess I could do it that good he'd come for it.'

'Don't *do* it, Harp!'

'All right, hon.' Her eyes were closed, her head drooping back. 'Don't get nerved up so.'

I started wondering whether a man still seeming sane could dream up such a horror for the unconscious purpose of tormenting a woman too young for him, a woman he could never imagine he owned. If he told her a fox bark wasn't right for a fox, she'd believe him. I said, 'We shouldn't talk about it if it upsets her.'

He glanced at me like a man floating up from under water. Leda said in a small, aching voice: 'I wish to *God* we could move to Boston.'

The granite face closed in defensiveness. 'Led', we been over all that. Nothing is going to drive me off of my land. I got no time for the city at my age. What the Jesus would I do? Night watchman? Sweep out somebody's back room, b' Jesus Christ? Savings'd be gone in no time. We been all over it. We ain't moving nowhere.'

'I could find work.' For Harp of course that was the worst thing she could have said. She probably knew it from his stricken silence. She said clumsily, 'I forgot something upstairs.' She snatched up her mending and she was gone.

We talked no more of it the rest of the day. I followed through the milking and other chores, lending a hand where I could, and we made everything as secure as we could against storm and other enemies. The long-toothed furry thing was the spectral guest at dinner, but we cut him, on Leda's account, or so we pretended. Supper would have been awkward anyway. They weren't in the habit of putting up guests, and Leda was a rather deadly cook because she cared nothing about it. A Darkfield girl, I suppose she had the usual twentieth century mishmash of television dreams until some impulse or maybe false signs of pregnancy tricked her into marrying a man out of the nineteenth. We had venison treated like beef and overdone vegetables. I don't like venison even when it's treated right.

At six Harp turned on his battery radio and sat stone-faced through the day's bad news and the weather forecast – 'a blizzard which may prove the worst in forty-two years. Since 3:00 P.M., eighteen inches have fallen at Bangor, twenty-one at Boston. Precipitation is not expected to end until tomorrow. Winds will increase during the night with gusts up to seventy miles per hour.' Harp shut it off, with finality. On other evenings I had spent there he let Leda play it after supper only kind of soft, so there had been a continuous muted bleat and blatter all evening. Tonight Harp meant to listen for other sounds. Leda washed the dishes, said an early good night, and fled upstairs.

Harp didn't talk, except as politeness obliged him to answer some blah of mine. We sat and listened to the snow and the lunatic wind. A hour of it was enough for me; I said I was beat and wanted to turn in early. Harp saw me to my bed in the parlor and placed a new chunk of rock maple in the pot-bellied stove. He produced a difficult granite smile, maybe using up his allowance for the week, and pulled out a bottle from a cabinet that had stood for many years below a parlor print – George Washington, I think, concluding a treaty with some offbeat sufferer from hepatitis who may have been General Cornwallis if the latter had two left feet. The bottle contained a brand of rye that Harp sincerely believed to be drinkable, having charred his gullet forty-odd years trying to prove it. While my throat healed Harp said, 'Shouldn't've bothered you with all this crap, Ben. Hope it ain't going to spoil your sleep.' He got me his spare flashlight, then let me be, and closed the door.

I heard him drop back into his kitchen armchair. Under too many covers, lamp out, I heard the cruel whisper of the snow. The stove muttered, a friend, making me a cocoon of living heat in a waste of outer cold. Later I heard Leda at the head of the stairs, her voice timid, tired, and sweet with invitation: 'You comin' up to bed, Harp?' The stairs creaked under him. Their door closed; presently she cried out in that desired pain that is brief release from trouble.

I remembered something Adelaide Simmons had told me about this house, where I had not gone upstairs since Harp and I were boys. Adelaide, one of the very few women in Darkfield who never spoke unkindly of Leda, said that the tiny west room across from Harp's and Leda's bedroom was fixed up for a nursery, and Harp wouldn't allow anything in there but baby furniture. Had been so since they were married seven years before.

Another hour dragged on, in my exasperations of sleeplessness.

Then I heard Longtooth.

The noise came from the west side, beyond the snow-hidden vegetable garden. When it snatched me from the edge of sleep, I tried to think it was a fox barking, the ringing, metallic shriek the little red beast can belch dragon-like from his throat. But wide awake, I knew it had been much deeper, chestier. Horned owl? – no. A sound that belonged to ancient times when men relied on chipped stone weapons and had full reason to fear the dark.

The cracks in the stove gave me firelight for groping back into my clothes. The wind had not calmed at all. I stumbled to the west window, buttoning up, and found it a white blank. Snow had drifted above the lower sash. On tiptoe I could just see over it. A light appeared, dimly illuminating the snowfield beyond. That would be coming from a lamp in the Ryders' bedroom, shining through the nursery room and so out, weak and diffused, into the blizzard chaos.

Yaaarrhh!

Now it had drawn horribly near. From the north windows of the parlor I saw black nothing. Harp squeaked down to my door. "Wake, Ben?'

'Yes. Come look at the west window.'

He had left no night light burning in the kitchen, and only a scant glow came down to the landing from the bedroom. He murmured behind me. 'Ayah, snow's up some. Must be over three foot on the level by now.'

Yaaarrhh!

The voice had shouted on the south side, the blinder side of the house, overlooked only by one kitchen window and a small one in the pantry where the hand pump stood. The view from the pantry window was mostly blocked by a great maple that overtopped the house. I heard the wind shrilling across the tree's winter bones.

'Ben, you want to git your boots on? Up to you – can't ask it. I might have to go out.' Harp spoke in an undertone as if the beast might understand him through the tight walls.

'Of course.' I got into my knee boots and caught up my parka as I followed him into the kitchen. A .30-caliber rifle and his heavy shotgun hung on deer-horn over the door to the woodshed. He found them in the dark.

What courage I possessed that night came from being shamed into action, from fearing to show a poor face to an old friend in trouble. I went through the Normandy invasion. I have camped out alone, when I was younger and healthier, in our moose and bear country, and slept nicely. But that noise of Longtooth stole courage. It ached along the channel of the spine.

I had the spare flashlight, but knew Harp didn't want me to use it here. I could make out the furniture, and Harp reaching for the gun rack. He already had on his boots, fur cap, and mackinaw. 'You take this'n,' he said, and put the ten-gauge in my hands. 'Both barrels loaded. Ain't my way to do that, ain't right, but since this thing started—'

Yaaarrhh!

'Where's he got to now?' Harp was by the south window. 'Round this side?'

'I thought so ... Where's Droopy?'

Harp chuckled thinly. 'Poor little shit! She come upstairs at the first sound of him and went under the bed. I told Led' to stay upstairs. She'd want a light down here. Wouldn't make sense.'

Then, apparently from the east side of the hen-loft and high, booming off some resonating surface: *Yaaarrhh!*

'He can't! Jesus, that's twelve foot off the ground!' But Harp plunged out into the shed, and I followed. 'Keep your light on the floor, Ben.' He ran up the narrow stairway. 'Don't shine it on the birds, they'll act up.'

So far the chickens, stupid and virtually blind in the dark, were making only a peevish tut-tutting of alarm. But something was clinging to the outside of the barricaded east window, snarling, chattering teeth, pounding on the two-by-fours. With a fist? – it sounded like nothing else. Harp snapped, 'Get your light on the window!' And he fired through the glass.

We heard no outcry. Any noise outside was covered by the storm and the squawks of the hens scandalized by the shot. The glass was dirty from their continual disturbance of the litter; I couldn't see through it. The bullet had drilled the pane without shattering it, and passed between the two-by-fours, but the beast could have dropped before he fired. 'I got to go out there. You stay, Ben.' Back in the kitchen he exchanged rifle for shotgun. 'Might not have no chance to aim. You remember this piece, don't y'? – eight in the clip.'

'I remember it.'

'Good. Keep your ears open.' Harp ran out through the door that gave on a small paved area by the woodshed. To get around under the east loft window he would have to push through the snow behind the barn, since he had blocked all the rear openings. He could have circled the house instead, but only by bucking the west wind and fighting deeper drifts. I saw his big shadow melt out of sight.

Leda's voice quavered down to me: 'He – get it?'

'Don't know. He's gone to see. Sit tight ...'

I heard that infernal bark once again before Harp returned, and again it sounded high off the ground; it must have come from the big maple. And then moments later – I was still trying to pierce the dark, watching for Harp – a vast smash of broken glass and wood, and the violent bang of the door upstairs. One small wheezing shriek cut short, and one scream such as no human being should ever hear. I can still hear it.

I think I lost some seconds in shock. Then I was groping up the narrow stairway, clumsy with the rifle and flashlight. Wind roared at the opening of the kitchen door, and Harp was crowding past me, thrusting me aside. But I was close behind him when he flung the bedroom door open. The blast from the broken window that had slammed the door had also blown out the lamp. But our flashlights said at once that Leda was not there. Nothing was, nothing living.

Droopy lay in a mess of glass splinters and broken window sash, dead from a crushed neck – something had stamped on her. The bedspread had been pulled almost to the window – maybe Leda's hand had clenched on it. I saw blood on some of the glass fragments, and on the splintered sash, a patch of reddish fur.

Harp ran back downstairs. I lingered a few seconds. The arrow of fear was deep in me, but at the moment it made me numb. My light touched up an ugly photograph on the wall, Harp's mother at fifty or so, petrified and acid-faced before the camera, a puritan deity with shallow, haunted eyes. I remembered her.

Harp had kicked over the traces when his father died, and quit going to church. Mrs Ryder 'disowned' him. The farm was his; she left him with it and went to live with a widowed sister in Lohman, and died soon, unreconciled. Harp lived on as a bachelor, crank, recluse, until his strange marriage in his fifties. Now here was Ma still watchful, pucker-faced, unforgiving. In my dullness of shock I thought: Oh, they probably always made love with the lights out.

But now Leda wasn't there.

I hurried after Harp, who had left the kitchen door to bang in the wind. I got out there with rifle and flashlight, and over across the road I saw his torch. No other light, just his small gleam and mine.

I knew as soon as I had forced myself beyond the corner of the house and into the fantastic embrace of the storm that I could never make it. The west wind ground needles into my face. The snow was up beyond the middle of my thighs. With weak lungs and maybe an imperfect heart, I could do nothing out here except die quickly to no purpose. In a moment Harp would be starting down the slope to the woods. His trail was already disappearing under my beam. I drove myself a little further, and an instant's lull in the storm allowed me to shout: 'Harp! I can't follow!'

He heard. He cupped his mouth and yelled back: 'Don't try! Git back to the house! Telephone!' I waved to acknowledge the message and struggled back.

I only just made it. Inside the kitchen doorway I fell flat, gun and flashlight clattering off somewhere, and there I stayed until I won back enough breath to keep myself living. My face and hands were ice-blocks, then fires. While I worked at the task of getting air into my body, one thought continued, an inner necessity: *There must be a rational cause. I do not abandon the rational cause.* At length I hauled myself up and stumbled to the telephone. The line was dead.

I found the flashlight and reeled upstairs with it. I stepped past poor Droopy's body and over the broken glass to look through the window space. I could see that snow had been pushed off the shed roof near the bedroom window; the house sheltered that area from the full drive of the west wind, so some evidence remained. I guessed that whatever came must have jumped to the house roof from the maple, then down to the shed roof, and then hurled itself through the closed window without regard for it as an obstacle. Losing a little blood and a little fur.

I glanced around and could not find that fur now. Wind must have pushed it out of sight. I forced the door shut. Downstairs, I lit the table lamps in kitchen and parlor. Harp might need those beacons – if he came back. I refreshed the fires, and gave myself a dose of Harp's horrible whisky. It was nearly one in the morning. If he never came back?

It might be days before they could plow out the road. When the storm let up I could use Harp's snowshoes, maybe ...

Harp came back, at 1:20, bent and staggering. He let me support him to the armchair. When he could speak he said, 'No trail. No trail.' He took the bottle from my hands and pulled on it. 'Christ Jesus! What can I do? Ben ...? I got to go to the village, get help. If they got any help to give.'

'Do you have an extra pair of showshoes?'

He stared toward me, battling confusion. 'Hah? No, I ain't. Better you stay anyhow. I'll bring yours from your house if you want, if I can get there.' He drank again and slammed in the cork with the heel of his hand. 'I'll leave you the ten-gauge.'

He got his snowshoes from a closet. I persuaded him to wait for coffee. Haste could accomplish nothing now; we could not say to each other that we knew Leda was dead. When he was ready to go, I stepped outside with him into the mad wind. 'Anything you want me to do before you get back?' He tried to think about it.

'I guess not, Ben ... God, ain't I *lived* right? No, that don't make sense. God? That's a laugh.' He swung away. Two or three great strides and the storm took him.

That was about two o'clock. For four hours I was alone in the house. Warmth returned, with the bedroom door closed and fires working hard. I carried the kitchen lamp into the parlor, and then huddled in the nearly total dark of the kitchen with my back to the wall, watching all the windows, the ten-gauge near my hand, but I did not expect a return of the beast, and there was none.

The night grew quieter, perhaps because the house was so drifted in that snow muted the sounds. I was cut off from the battle, buried alive.

Harp would get back. The seasons would follow their natural way, and somehow we would learn what had happened to Leda. I supposed the beast would have to be something in the human pattern – mad, deformed, gone wild, but still human.

After a time I wondered why we had heard no excitement in the stable. I forced myself to take up gun and flashlight and go look. I groped through the woodshed, big with the jumping shadows of Harp's cordwood, and into the barn. The cows were peacefully drowsing. In the center alley I dared to send my weak beam swooping and glimmering through the ghastly distances of the hayloft. Quiet, just quiet; natural rustling of mice. Then to the stable, where Ned whickered and let me rub his brown cheeks, and Jerry rolled a humorous eye. I suppose no smell had reached them to touch off panic, and perhaps they had heard the barking often enough so that it no longer disturbed them. I went back to my post, and the hours crawled along a ridge between the pits of terror and exhaustion. Maybe I slept.

No color of sunrise that day, but I felt paleness and change; even a blizzard will not hide the fact of day-shine. I breakfasted on bacon and eggs, fed the hens, forked down hay and carried water for the cows and horses. The one cow in milk, a jumpy Ayrshire, refused to concede that I meant to be useful. I'd done no milking since I was a boy, the knack was gone from my hands, and relief seemed less important to her than kicking over the pail; she was getting more amusement than discomfort out of it, so for the moment I let it go. I made myself busywork shoveling a clear space by the kitchen door. The wind was down, the snowfall persistent but almost peaceful. I pushed out beyond the house and learned that the stuff was up over my hips.

Out of that, as I turned back, came Harp in his long, snowshoe stride, and down the road three others. I recognized Sheriff Robart, overfed but powerful; and Bill Hastings, wry and ageless, a cousin of Harp's and one of his few friends; and last, Curt Davidson, perhaps a friend to Sheriff Robart but certainly not to Harp.

I'd known Curt as a thick-witted loudmouth when he was a kid; growing to man's years hadn't done much for him. And when I saw him I thought, irrationally perhaps: Not good for our side. A kind of absurdity, and yet Harp and I were joined against the world simply because we had experienced together what others were going to call impossible, were going to interpret in harsh, even damnable ways; and no help for it.

I saw the white thin blur of the sun, the strength of it growing. Nowhere in all the white expanse had the wind and the new snow allowed us any mark of the visitation in the night.

The men reached my cleared space and shook off snow. I opened the wood-shed. Harp gave me one hopeless glance of inquiry and I shook my head.

'Having a little trouble?' That was Robart, taking off his snowshoes.

Harp ignored him. 'I got to look after the chores.' I told him I'd done it except for that damn cow. 'Oh, Bess, ayah, she's nervy, I'll see to her.' He gave me my snowshoes that he had strapped to his back. 'Adelaide, she wanted to know about your groceries. Said I figured they was in the ca.'

'Good as an icebox,' says Robart, real friendly.

Curt had to have his pleasures too: 'Ben, you sure you got hold of old Bess by the right end, where the tits was?' Curt giggles at his own jokes, so nobody else is obliged to. Bill Hastings spat in the snow.

'Okay if I go in?' Robart asked. It wasn't a simple inquiry: he was present officially and meant to have it known. Harp looked him up and down.

'Nobody stopping you. Didn't bring you here to stand around, I suppose.'

'Harp,' said Robart pleasantly enough, 'don't give me a hard time. You come tell me certain things has happened, I got to look into it is all.' But Harp was already striding down the woodshed to the barn entrance. The others came into the house with me, and I put on water for fresh coffee. 'Must be your ca' down the rud a piece, Ben? Heard you kind of went into a ditch. All's you can see now is a hump in the snow. Deep freeze might be good for her, likely you've tried everything else.' But I wasn't feeling comic, and never had been on those terms with Robart. I grunted, and his face shed mirth as one slips off a sweater. 'Okay, what's the score? Harp's gone and told me a story I couldn't feed to the dogs, so what about it? Where's Mrs Ryder?'

Davidson giggled again. It's a nasty little sound to come out of all that beef. I don't think Robart had much enthusiasm for him either, but it seems he had sworn in the fellow as a deputy before they set out. 'Yes, sir,' said Curt, 'that was *really* a story, that was.'

'Where's Mrs Ryder?'

'Not here,' I told him. 'We think she's dead.'

He glowered, rubbing cold out of his hands. 'Seen that window. Looks like the frame is smashed.'

'Yes, from the outside. When Harp gets back you'd better look. I closed the door on that room and haven't opened it. There'll be more snow, but you'll see about what we saw when we got up there.'

'Let's look right now,' said Curt.

Bill Hastings said, 'Curt, ain't you a mite busy for a dep'ty? Mr Dane said when Harp gets back.' Bill and I are friends; normally he wouldn't mister me. I think he was trying to give me some flavor of authority.

I acknowledged the alliance by asking: 'You a deputy too, Bill?' Giving him an opportunity to spit in the stove, replace the lid gently, and reply: 'Shit no.'

Harp returned and carried the milk pail to the pantry. Then he was looking us over. 'Bill, I got to try the woods again. You want to come along?'

'Sure, Harp. I didn't bring no gun.'

'Take my ten-gauge.'

'Curt here'll go along,' said Robart. 'Real good man on snowshoes. Interested in wildlife.'

Harp said, 'That's funny, Robart. I guess that's the funniest thing I heard since Cutler's little girl fell under the tractor. You joining us too?'

'Fact is, Harp, I kind of pulled a muscle in my back coming up here. Not getting no younger neither. I believe I'll just look around here a little. Trust you got no objection? To me looking around a little?'

'Coffee's dripped,' I said.

'Thing of it is, if I'd've thought you had any objection, I'd've been obliged to get me a warrant.'

'Thanks, Ben.' Harp gulped the coffee scalding. 'Why, if looking around the house is the best you can do, Sher'f, I got no objection. Ben, I shouldn't be keeping you away from your affairs, but would you stay? Kind of keep him company? Not that I got much in the house, but still – you know—'

'I'll stay.' I wished I could tell him to drop that manner; it only got him deeper in the mud.

Robart handed Davidson his gun belt and holster. 'Better have it, Curt, so to be in style.'

Harp and Bill were outside getting on their snowshoes; I half heard some remark of Harp's about the sheriff's aching back. They took off. The snow had almost ceased. They passed out of sight down the slope to the north, and Curt went plowing after them. Behind me Robart said, 'You'd think Harp believed it himself.'

'That's how it's to be? You make us both liars before you've even done any looking?'

'I got to try to make sense of it is all.' I followed him up to the bedroom. It was cruelly cold. He touched Droopy's stiff corpse with his foot. 'Hard to figure a man killing his own dog.'

'We get nowhere with that kind of idea.'

'Ben, you got to see this thing like it looks to other people. And keep out of my hair.'

'That's what scares me, Jack. Something unreasonable did happen, and Harp and I were the only ones to experience it – except Mrs Ryder.'

'You claim you saw this – animal?'

'I didn't say that. I heard her scream. When we got upstairs this room was the way you see it.' I looked around, and again couldn't find that scrap of fur, but I spoke of it, and I give Robart credit for searching. He shook out the bedspread and blankets, examined the floor and the closet. He studied the window space, leaned out for a look at the house wall and the shed roof. His big feet avoided the broken glass, and he squatted for a long gaze at the pieces of window sash. Then he bore down on me, all policemen personified, a massive, rather intelligent, conventionally honest man with no patience for imagination, no time for any fact not already in the books. 'Piece of fur, huh?' He made it sound as if I'd described a Jabberwock with eyes of flame. 'Okay, we're done up here.' He motioned me downstairs – all policemen who'd ever faced a crowd's dangerous stupidity with their own.

As I retreated I said, 'Hope you won't be too busy to have a chemist test the blood on that sash.'

'We'll do that.' He made move-along motions with his slab hands. 'Going to be a pleasure to do that little thing for you and your friend.'

Then he searched the entire house, shed, barn, and stable. I had never before watched anyone on police business; I had to admire his zeal. I got involved in the farce of holding the flashlight for him while he rooted in the cellar. In the shed I suggested that if he wanted to restack twenty-odd cords of wood he'd better wait till Harp could help him; he wasn't amused. He wasn't happy in the barn loft either. Shifting tons of hay to find a hypothetical corpse was not a one-man job. I knew he was capable of returning with a crew and machinery to do exactly that. And by his lights it was what he ought to do. Then we were back in the kitchen, Robart giving himself a manicure with his jackknife, and I down to my last cigarette, almost the last of my endurance.

Robart was not unsubtle. I answered his questions as temperately as I could – even, for instance: 'Wasn't you a mite sweet on Leda yourself?' I didn't answer any of them with flat silence; to do that right you need an accompanying act like spitting in the stove, and I'm not a chewer. From the north window he said: 'Comin' back. It figures.' They had been out a little over an hour.

Harp stood by the stove with me to warm his hands. He spoke as if alone with me: 'No trail, Ben.' What followed came in an undertone: 'Ben, you told me about a friend of yours, scientist or something, professor—'

'Professor Malcolm?' I remembered mentioning him to Harp a long while before; I was astonished at his recalling it. Johnny Malcolm is a professor of biology who has avoided too much specialization. Not a really close friend. Harp was watching me out of a granite despair as if he had asked me to appeal to some higher court. I thought of another acquaintance in Boston too, whom I might consult – Dr Kahn, a psychiatrist who had once seen my wife Helen through a difficult time ...

'Harp,' said Robart, 'I got to ask you a couple, three things. I sent word to Dick Hammond to get that goddamn plow of his into this road as quick as he can. Believe he'll try. Whiles we wait on him, we might 's well talk. You know I don't like to get tough.'

'Talk away,' said Harp, 'only Ben here he's got to get home without waiting on no Dick Hammond.'

'That a fact, Ben?'

'Yes. I'll keep in touch.'

'Do that,' said Robart, dismissing me. As I left he was beginning a fresh manicure, and Harp waited rigidly for the ordeal to continue. I felt morbidly that I was abandoning him.

Still – corpus delicti – nothing much more would happen until Leda Ryder was found. Then if her body were found dead by violence, with no acceptable evidence of Longtooth's existence – well, what then?

I don't think Robart would have let me go if he'd known my first act would be to call Short's brother Mike and ask him to drive me in to Lohman where I could get a bus for Boston.

Johnny Malcolm said, 'I can see this is distressing you, and you wouldn't lie to me. But, Ben, as biology it won't do. Ain't no such animal. You know that.'

He wasn't being stuffy. We were having dinner at a quiet restaurant, and I had of course enjoyed the roast duckling too much. Johnny is a rock-ribbed beanpole who can eat like a walking famine with no regrets. 'Suppose,' I said, 'just for argument and because it's not biologically inconceivable, that there's a basis for the Yeti legend.'

'Not inconceivable. I'll give you that. So long as any poorly known corners of the world are left – the Himalayan uplands, jungles, tropic swamps, the tundra – legends will persist and some of them will have little gleams of truth. You know what I think about moon flights and all that?' He smiled; privately I was hearing Leda scream. 'One of our strongest reasons for them, and for the bigger flights we'll make if we don't kill civilization first, is a hunt for new legends. We've used up our best ones, and that's dangerous.'

'Why don't we look at the countries inside us?' But Johnny wasn't listening much.

'Men can't stand it not to have closed doors and a chance to push at them. Oh, about your Yeti – he might exist. Shaggy anthropoid able to endure severe cold, so rare and clever the explorers haven't tripped over him yet. Wouldn't have to be a carnivore to have big ugly canines – look at the baboons. But if he was active in a Himalayan winter, he'd have to be able to use meat, I think. Mind you, I don't believe any of this, but you can have it as a biological not-impossible. How'd he get to Maine?'

'Strayed? Tibet – Mongolia – Arctic ice.'

'Maybe.' Johnny had begun to enjoy the hypothesis as something to play with during dinner. Soon he was helping along the brute's passage across the continents, and having fun till I grumbled something about alternatives, extraterrestrials. He wouldn't buy that, and got cross. Still hearing Leda scream, I assured him I wasn't watching for little green men.

'Ben, how much do you know about this – Harp?'

'We grew up along different lines, but he's a friend. Dinosaur, if you like, but a friend.'

'Hardshell Maine bachelor picks up dizzy young wife—'

'She's not dizzy. Wasn't. Sexy, but not dizzy.'

'All right. Bachelor stewing in his own juices for years. Sure he didn't get up on that roof himself?'

'Nuts. Unless all my senses were more paralyzed than I think, there wasn't time.'

'Unless they were more paralyzed than you think.'

'Come off it! I'm not senile yet ... What's he supposed to have done with her? Tossed her into the snow?'

'Mph,' said Johnny, and finished his coffee. 'All right. Some human freak with abnormal strength and the endurance to fossick around in a Maine blizzard stealing women. I liked the Yeti better. You say you suggested a madman to Ryder yourself. Pity if you had to come all the way here just so I could repeat your own guesswork. To make amends, want to take in a bawdy movie?'

'Love it.'

The following day Dr Kahn made time to see me at the end of the afternoon, so polite and patient that I felt certain I was keeping him from his dinner. He seemed undecided whether to be concerned with the traumas of Harp Ryder's history or those of mine. Mine were already somewhat known to him. 'I wish you had time to talk all this out to me. You've given me a nice summary of what the physical events appear to have been, but—'

'Doctor,' I said, 'it *happened*. I heard the animal. The window *was* smashed – ask the sheriff. Leda Ryder did scream, and when Harp and I got up there together, the dog had been killed and Leda was gone.'

'And yet, if it was all as clear as that, I wonder why you thought of consulting me at all, Ben. I wasn't there. I'm just a headshrinker.'

'I wanted ... Is there any way a delusion could take hold of Harp *and* me, disturb our senses in the same way? Oh, just saying it makes it ridiculous.'

Dr Kahn smiled. 'Let's say, difficult.'

'Is it possible Harp could have killed her, thrown her out through the window of the *west* bedroom – the snow must have drifted six feet or higher on that side – and then my mind distorted my time sense? So I might've stood there in the dark kitchen all the time it went on, a matter of minutes instead of seconds? Then he jumped down by the shed roof, came back into the house the normal way while I was stumbling upstairs? Oh, hell.'

Dr Kahn had drawn a diagram of the house from my description, and peered at it with placid interest. 'Benign' was a word Helen had used for him. He said, 'Such a distortion of the time sense would be unusual … Are you feeling guilty about anything?'

'About standing there and doing nothing? I can't seriously believe it was more than a few seconds. Anyway that would make Harp a monster out of a detective story. He's not that. How could he count on me to freeze in panic? Absurd. I'd've heard the struggle, steps, the window of the west room going up. Could he have killed her and I known all about it at the time, even witnessed it, and then suffered amnesia for that one event?'

He still looked so patient I wished I hadn't come. 'I won't say any trick of the mind is impossible, but I might call that one highly improbable. Academically, however, considering your emotional involvement—'

'I'm not emotionally involved!' I yelled that. He smiled, looking much more interested. I laughed at myself. That was better than poking him in the eye. 'I'm upset, Doctor, because the whole thing goes against reason. If you start out knowing nobody's going to believe you, it's all messed up before you open your mouth.'

He nodded kindly. He's a good Joe. I think he'd stopped listening for what I didn't say long enough to hear a little of what I did say. 'You're not unstable, Ben. Don't worry about amnesia. The explanation, perhaps some human intruder, will turn out to be within the human norm. The norm of possibility does include such things as lycanthropic delusions, maniacal behavior, and so on. Your police up there will carry on a good search for the poor woman. They won't overlook that snowdrift. Don't underestimate them, and don't worry about your own mind, Ben.'

'Ever seen our Maine woods?'

'No, I go away to the Cape.'

'Try it some time. Take a patch of it, say about fifty miles by fifty, that's twenty-five hundred square miles. Drop some eager policemen into it, tell 'em to hunt for something they never saw before and don't want to see, that doesn't want to be found.'

'But if your beast is human, human beings leave traces. Bodies aren't easy to hide, Ben.'

'In those woods? A body taken by a carnivorous animal? Why not?' Well, our minds didn't touch. I thanked him for his patience and got up. 'The maniac responsible,' I said. 'But whatever we call him, Doctor, he was *there*.'

Mike Short picked me up at the Lohman bus station, and told me something of a ferment in Darkfield. I shouldn't have been surprised. 'They're all scared, Mr Dane. They want to hurt somebody.' Mike is Jim Short's younger brother. He scrapes up a living with his taxi service and occasional odd jobs at the garage. There's a droop in his shaggy ringlets, and I believe thirty is staring him in the face. 'Like old Harp he wants to tell it like it happened and nobody buys. That's sad, man. You been away what, three days? The fuzz was pissed off. You better connect with Mister Sheriff Robart like soon. He climbed all over my ass just for driving you to the bus that day, like I should've known you shouldn't.'

'I'll pacify him. They haven't found Mrs Ryder?'

Mike spat out the car window, which was rolled down for the mild air. 'Old Harp he never got such a job of snow-shoveling done in all his days. By the c'munity, for free. No, they won't find her.' In that there was plenty of I-want-to-be-asked, and something more, a hint of the mythology of Mike's generation.

'So what's your opinion, Mike?'

He maneuvered a fresh cigarette against the stub of the last and drove on through tiresome silence. The road was winding between ridged mountains of plowed, rotting snow. I had the window down on my side too for the genial afternoon sun, and imagined a tang of spring. At last Mike said, 'You prob'ly don't go along ... Jim got your ca' out, by the way. It's at your place ... Well, you'll hear 'em talking it all to pieces. Some claim Harp's telling the truth. Some say he killed her himself. They don't say how he made her disappear. Ain't heard any talk against you, Mr Dane, nothing that counts. The sheriff's peeved, but that's just on account you took off without asking.' His vague, large eyes watched the melting landscape, the ambiguous messages of spring. 'Well, I think, like, a demon took her, Mr Dane. She was one of his own, see? You got to remember, I knew that chick. Okay, you can say it ain't scientific, only there is a science to these things, I read a book about it. You can laugh if you want.'

I wasn't laughing. It wasn't my first glimpse of the contemporary medievalism and won't be my last if I survive another year or two. I wasn't laughing, and I said nothing. Mike sat smoking, expertly driving his twentieth century artifact while I suppose his thoughts were in the seventeenth, sniffing after the wonders of the invisible world, and I recalled what Johnny Malcolm had said about the need for legends. Mike and I had no more talk.

Adelaide Simmons was dourly glad to see me. From her I learned that the sheriff and state police had swarmed all over Harp's place and the surrounding countryside, and were still at it. Result, zero. Harp had repeatedly told our story and was refusing to tell it any more. 'Does the chores and sets there drinking,' she said, 'or staring off. Was up to see him yesterday, Mr Dane – felt I should. Couple days they didn't let him alone a minute, maybe now they've eased off some. He asked me real sharp, was you back yet. Well, I redd up his place, made some bread, least I could do.'

When I told her I was going there, she prepared a basket, while I sat in the kitchen and listened. 'Some say she busted that window herself, jumped down and run off in the snow, out of her mind. Any sense in that?'

'Nope.'

'And some claim she deserted him. Earlier. Which'd make you a liar. And they say whichever way it was, Harp's made up this crazy story because he can't stand the truth.' Her clever hands slapped sandwiches into shape. 'They claim Harp got you to go along with it, they don't say how.'

'Hypnotized me, likely. Adelaide, it all happened the way Harp told it. I heard the thing too. If Harp is ready for the squirrels, so am I.'

She stared hard, and sighed. She likes to talk, but her mill often shuts off suddenly, because of a quality of hers which I find good as well as rare: I mean that when she has no more to say she doesn't go on talking.

I got up to Ryder's Ridge about suppertime. Bill Hastings was there. The road was plowed slick between the snow ridges, and I wondered how much of the litter of tracks and crumpled paper and spent cigarette packages had been left by sightseers. Ground frost had not yet yielded to the mud season, which would soon make normal driving impossible for a few weeks. Bill let me in, with the look people wear for serious illness. But Harp heaved himself out of that armchair, not sick in body at least. 'Ben, I heard him last night. Late.'

'What direction?'

'North.'

'You hear it, Bill?' I set down the basket.

My pint-size friend shook his head. 'Wasn't here.' I couldn't guess how much Bill accepted of the tale.

Harp said, 'What's the basket? – oh. Obliged. Adelaide's a nice woman.' But his mind was remote. 'It was north, Ben, a long way, but I think I know about where it would be. I wouldn't've heard it except the night was so still, like everything had quieted for me. You know, they been a-deviling me night and day. Robart, state cops, mess of smart little buggers from the papers. I couldn't sleep, I stepped outside like I was called. Why, he might've been the other side of the stars, the sky so full of 'em and nothing stirring. Cold ... You went to Boston, Ben?'

'Yes. Waste of time. They want it to be something human, anyhow something that fits the books.'

Whittling, Bill said neutrally, 'Always a man for the books yourself, wasn't you, Ben?'

I had to agree. Harp asked, 'Hadn't no ideas?'

'Just gave me back my own thoughts in their language. We have to find it, Harp. Of course some wouldn't take it for true even if you had photographs.'

Harp said, 'Photographs be goddamned.'

'I guess you got to go,' said Bill Hastings. 'We been talking about it, Ben. Maybe I'd feel the same if it was me ... I better be on my way or supper'll be cold and the old woman raising hellfire.' He tossed his stick back in the woodbox.

'Bill,' said Harp, 'you won't mind feeding the stock couple, three days?'

'I don't mind. Be up tomorrow.'

'Do the same for you some time. I wouldn't want it mentioned anyplace.'

'Harp, you know me better'n that. See you, Ben.'

'Snow's going fast,' said Harp when Bill had driven off. 'Be in the woods a long time yet, though.'

'You wouldn't start this late.'

He was at the window, his lean bulk shutting off much light from the time-seasoned kitchen where most of his indoor life had been passed. 'Morning, early. Tonight I got to listen.'

'Be needing sleep, I'd think.'

'I don't always get what I need,' said Harp.

'I'll bring my snowshoes. About six? And my carbine – I'm best with a gun I know.'

He stared at me a while. 'All right, Ben. You understand, though, you might have to come back alone. I ain't coming back till I get him, Ben. Not this time.'

At sunup I found him with Ned and Jerry in the stable. He had lived eight or ten years with that team. He gave Ned's neck a final pat as he turned to me and took up our conversation as if night had not intervened. 'Not till I get him. Ben, I don't want you drug into this ag'inst your inclination.'

'Did you hear it again last night?'

'I heard it. North.'

The sun was at the point of rising when we left on our snowshoes, like morning ghosts ourselves. Harp strode ahead down the slope to the woods without haste, perhaps with some reluctance. Near the trees he halted, gazing to his right where a red blaze was burning the edge of the sky curtain; I scolded myself for thinking that he was saying goodbye to the sun.

The snow was crusted, sometimes slippery even for our web feet. We entered the woods along a tangle of tracks, including the fat tire marks of a snow scooter. 'Guy from Lohman,' said Harp. 'Hired the goddamn thing out to the state cops and hisself with it. Goes pootin' around all over hell, fit to scare everything inside eight, ten miles.' He cut himself a fresh plug to last the morning. 'I b'lieve the thing is a mite further off than that. They'll be messing around again today.' His fingers dug into my arm. 'See how it is, don't y'? They ain't looking for what we are. Looking for a dead body to hang onto my neck. And if they was to find her the way I found – the way I found—'

'Harp, you needn't borrow trouble.'

'I know how they think,' he said. 'Was I to walk down the road beyond

Darkfield, they'd pick me up. They ain't got me in shackles because they got no – no body, Ben. Nobody needs to tell me about the law. They got to have a body. Only reason they didn't leave a man here overnight, they figure I can't go nowhere. They think a man couldn't travel in three, four foot of snow ... Ben, I mean to find that thing and shoot it down ... We better slant off thisaway.'

He set out at a wide angle from those tracks, and we soon had them out of sight. On the firm crust our snowshoes left no mark. After a while we heard a grumble of motors far back, on the road. Harp chuckled viciously. 'Bright and early like yesterday.' He stared back the way we had come. 'They'll never pick up our trail without dogs. That son of a bitch Robart did talk about borrying a hound somewhere, to sniff Leda's clothes. More likely give 'em a sniff of mine, now.'

We had already come so far that I didn't know the way back. Harp would know it. He could never be lost in any woods, but I have no mental compass such as his. So I followed him blindly, not trying to memorize the route. It was a region of uniform old growth, mostly hemlock, no recent lumbering, few landmarks. The monotony wore down native patience to a numbness, and our snowshoes left no more impression than our thoughts.

An hour passed, or more, after that sound of motors faded. Now and then I heard the wind move peacefully overhead. Few bird calls, for most of our singers had not yet returned. 'Been in this part before, Harp?'

'Not with snow on the ground, not lately.' His voice was hushed and careful. 'Summers. About a mile now, and the trees thin out some. Stretch of slash where they was taking out pine four, five years back and left everything a Christly pile of shit like they always do.'

No, Harp wouldn't get lost here, but I was well lost, tired, sorry I had come. Would he turn back if I collapsed? I didn't think he could, now, for any reason. My pack with blanket roll and provisions had become infernal. He had said we ought to have enough for three or four days. Only a few years earlier I had carried heavier camping loads than this without trouble, but now I was blown, a stitch beginning in my side. My wristwatch said only nine o'clock.

The trees thinned out as he had promised, and here the land rose in a long slope to the north. I looked up across a tract of eight or ten acres where the devastation of stupid lumbering might be healed if the hurt region could be let alone for sixty years. The deep snow, blinding out here where only scrub growth interfered with the sunlight, covered the worst of the wreckage. 'Good place for wild ras'berries,' Harp said quietly. 'Been time for 'em to grow back. Guess it was nearer seven years ago when they cut here and left this mess. Last summer I couldn't hardly find their logging road. Off to the left—'

He stopped, pointing with a slow arm to a blurred gray line that wandered up from the left to disappear over the rise of ground. The nearest part of that gray curve must have been four hundred feet away, and to my eyes it might have been a shadow cast by an irregularity of the snow surface; Harp knew better. Something had passed there, heavy enough to break the crust. 'You want to rest a mite, Ben? Once over that rise I might not want to stop again.'

I let myself down on the butt of an old log that lay tilted toward us, cut because it had happened to be in the way, left to rot because they happened to be taking pine. 'Can you really make anything out of that?'

'Not enough,' said Harp. 'But it could be him.' He did not sit by me but stood relaxed with his load, snowshoes spaced so he could spit between them. 'About half a mile over that rise,' he said, 'there's a kind of gorge. Must've been a good brook, former times, still a stream along the bottom in summer. Tangle of elders and stuff. Couple, three caves in the bank at one spot. I guess it's three summers since I been there. Gloomy goddamn place. There was foxes into one of them caves. Natural caves, I b'lieve. I didn't go too near, not then.'

I sat in the warming light, wondering whether there was any way I could talk to Harp about the beast – if it existed, if we weren't merely a pair of aging men with disordered minds. Any way to tell him the creature was important to the world outside our dim little village? That it ought somehow to be kept alive, not just shot down and shoveled aside? How could I say this to a man without science, who had lost his wife and also the trust of his fellow men?

Take away that trust and you take away the world.

Could I ask him to shoot it in the legs, get it back alive? Why, to my own self, irrationally, that appeared wrong, horrible, as well as beyond our powers. Better if he shot to kill. Or if I did. So in the end I said nothing, but shrugged my pack into place and told him I was ready to go on.

With the crust uncertain under that stronger sunshine, we picked our way slowly up the rise, and when we came at length to that line of tracks, Harp said matter-of-factly, 'Now you've seen his mark. It's him.'

Sun and overnight freezing had worked on the trail. Harp estimated it had been made early the day before. But wherever the weight of Longtooth had broken through, the shape of his foot showed clearly down there in its pocket of snow, a foot the size of a man's but broader, shorter. The prints were spaced for the stride of a short-legged person. The arch of the foot was low, but the beast was not actually flatfooted. Beast or man. I said, 'This is a man's print, Harp. Isn't it?'

He spoke without heat. 'No. You're forgetting, Ben. I seen him.'

'Anyhow there's only one.'

He said slowly, 'Only one set of tracks.'

'What d' you mean?'

Harp shrugged. 'It's heavy. He could've been carrying something. Keep your voice down. That crust yesterday, it would've held me without no web feet, but he went through, and he ain't as big as me.' Harp checked his rifle and released the safety. 'Half a mile to them caves. B'lieve that's where he is, Ben. Don't talk unless you got to, and take it slow.'

I followed him. We topped the rise, encountering more of that lumberman's desolation on the other side. The trail crossed it, directly approaching a wall of undamaged trees that marked the limit of the cutting. Here forest took over once more, and where it began, Longtooth's trail ended. 'Now you seen how it goes,' Harp said. 'Any place where he can travel above ground he does. He don't scramble up the trunks, seems like. Look here – he must've got aholt of that branch and swung hisself up. Knocked off some snow, but the wind knocks off so much too you can't tell nothing. See, Ben, he – he figures it out. He knows about trails. He'll have come down out of these trees far enough from where we are now so there ain't no chance of us seeing the place from here. Could be anywhere in a half-circle, and draw it as big as you please.'

'Thinking like a man.'

'But he ain't a man,' said Harp. 'There's things he don't know. How a man feels, acts. I'm going on to them caves.' From necessity, I followed him ...

I ought to end this quickly. Prematurely I am an old man, incapacitated by the effects of a stroke and a damaged heart. I keep improving a little – sensible diet, no smoking, Adelaide's care. I expect several years of tolerable health on the way downhill. But I find, as Harp did, that it is even more crippling to lose the trust of others. I will write here once more, and not again, that my word is good.

It was noon when we reached the gorge. In that place some melancholy part of night must always remain. Down the center of the ravine between tangles of alder, water murmured under ice and rotting snow, which here and there had fallen in to reveal the dark brilliance. Harp did not enter the gorge itself but moved slowly through tree-cover along the left edge, eyes flickering for danger. I tried to imitate his caution. We went a hundred yards or more in that inching advance, maybe two hundred. I heard only the occasional wind of spring.

He turned to look at me, with a sickly triumph, a grimace of disgust and of justification, too. He touched his nose and then I got it also, a rankness from down ahead of us, a musky foulness with an ammoniacal tang and some smell of decay. Then on the other side of the gorge, off in the woods but not far, I heard Longtooth.

A bark, not loud. Throaty, like talk.

Harp suppressed an answering growl. He moved on until he could point down to a black cave-mouth on the opposite side. The breeze blew the stench across to us. Harp whispered, 'See, he's got like a path. Jumps down to that flat rock, then to the cave. We'll see him in a minute.' Yes, there were sounds in the brush. 'You keep back.' His left palm lightly stroked the underside of his rifle barrel.

So intent was he on the opening where Longtooth would appear, I may have been first to see the other who came then to the cave mouth and stared up at us with animal eyes. Longtooth had called again, a rather gentle sound. The woman wrapped in filthy hides may have been drawn by that call or by the noise of our approach.

Then Harp saw her.

He knew her. In spite of the tangled hair, scratched face, dirt, and the shapeless deer-pelt she clutched around herself against the cold, I am sure he knew her. I don't think she knew him, or me. An inner blindness, a look of a beast wholly centered on its own needs. I think human memories had drained away. She knew Longtooth was coming. I think she wanted his warmth and protection, but there were no words in the whimper she made before Harp's bullet took her between the eyes.

Longtooth shoved through the bushes. He dropped the rabbit he was carrying and jumped down to that flat rock snarling, glancing sidelong at the dead woman who was still twitching. If he understood the fact of death, he had no time for it. I saw the massive overdevelopment of thigh and leg muscles, their springy motions of preparation. The distance from the flat rock to the place where Harp stood must have been fifteen feet. One spear of sunlight touched him in that blue-green shade, touched his thick red fur and his fearful face.

Harp could have shot him. Twenty seconds for it, maybe more. But he flung his rifle aside and drew out his hunting knife, his own long tooth, and had it waiting when the enemy jumped.

So could I have shot him. No one needs to tell me I ought to have done so.

Longtooth launched himself, clawed fingers out, fangs exposed. I felt the meeting as if the impact had struck my own flesh. They tumbled roaring into the gorge, and I was cold, detached, an instrument for watching.

It ended soon. The heavy brownish teeth clenched in at the base of Harp's neck. He made no more motion except the thrust that sent his blade into Longtooth's left side. Then they were quiet in that embrace, quiet all three. I heard the water flowing under the ice.

I remember a roaring in my ears, and I was moving with slow care, one difficult step after another, along the lip of the gorge and through mighty corridors of white and green. With my hard-won detachment I supposed this might be the region where I had recently followed poor Harp Ryder to some destination or other, but not (I thought) one of those we talked about when we were boys. A band of iron had closed around my forehead, and breathing was an enterprise needing great effort and caution, in order not to worsen the indecent pain that clung as another band around my diaphragm. I leaned against a tree for thirty seconds or thirty minutes, I don't know where. I knew I mustn't take off my pack in spite of the pain, because it carried provisions for three days. I said once: 'Ben, you are lost.'

I had my carbine, a golden bough, staff of life, and I recall the shrewd management and planning that enabled me to send three shots into the air. Twice.

It seems I did not want to die, and so hung on the cliff-edge of death with a mad stubbornness. They tell me it could not have been the second day that I fired the second burst, the one that was heard and answered – because, they say, a man can't suffer the kind of attack I was having and then survive a whole night of exposure. They say that when a search party reached me from Wyndham Village (eighteen miles from Darkfield), I made some garbled speech and fell flat on my face.

I woke immobilized, without power of speech or any motion except for a little life in my left hand, and for a long time memory was only a jarring of irrelevancies. When that cleared I still couldn't talk for another long deadly while. I recall someone saying with exasperated admiration that with cerebral hemorrhage on top of coronary infarction, I had no damn right to be alive; this was the first sound that gave me any pleasure. I remember recognizing Adelaide and being unable to thank her for her presence. None of this matters to the story, except the fact that for months I had no bridge of communication with the world; and yet I loved the world and did not want to leave it.

One can always ask: What will happen next?

Some time in what they said was June my memory was (I think) clear. I scrawled a little, with the nurse supporting the deadened part of my arm. But in response to what I wrote, the doctor, the nurses, Sheriff Robart, even Adelaide Simmons and Bill Hastings, looked – sympathetic. I was not believed. I am not believed now, in the most important part of what I wish I might say: that there are things in our world that we do not understand, and that this ignorance ought to generate humility. People find this obvious, bromidic – oh, they always have! – and therefore they do not listen, retaining the pride of their ignorance intact.

Remnants of the three bodies were found in late August, small thanks to my efforts, for I had no notion what compass direction we took after the cutover area, and there are so many such areas of desolation I couldn't tell them where to look. Forest scavengers, including a pack of dogs, had found the bodies first. Water had moved them too, for the last of the big snow melted suddenly, and for a couple of days at least there must have been a small river raging through that gorge. The head of what they are calling the 'lunatic' got rolled downstream, bashed against rocks, partly buried in silt. Dogs had chewed and scattered what they speak of as 'the man's fur coat.'

It will remain a lunatic in a fur coat, for they won't have it any other way. So far as I know, no scientist ever got a look at the wreckage, unless you glorify the coroner by that title. I believe he was a good vet before he got the job. When my speech was more or less regained, I was already through trying to talk about it. A statement of mine was read at the inquest – that was before I could talk or leave the hospital. At this ceremony society officially decided that Harper Harrison Ryder, of this township, shot to death his wife Leda and an individual, male, of unknown identity, while himself temporarily of unsound mind, and died of knife injuries received in a struggle with the said individual of unknown, and so forth.

I don't talk about it because that only makes people more sorry for me, to think a man's mind should fail so, and he not yet sixty.

I cannot even ask them: 'What is truth?' They would only look more saddened, and I suppose shocked, and perhaps find reasons for not coming to see me again.

They are kind. They will do anything for me, except think about it.

MAXWELL'S MONKEY

A shadow maybe. But now and then it went off to do something or get something, and came back into some slightly different position looking like a damn fool.

Maxwell saw it first on waking after a binge. During the evening's riot he had insulted his two dearest friends – the husband saw him home anyhow – and knocked over a baby-carriage. It had no baby in it, but Maxwell reflected it might have had, and wept. Then he was trying to pick a policeman's pocket and lamentably failing. He heard his friend explain: 'Always does that, Officer. It don't mean a thing.' But why would anyone go to the trouble of picking a policeman's pocket unless he meant something by it? And in the hurting morning light, the monkey sat on the foot of his bed.

He threw a pillow.

The pillow went through, unreasonably slowed down. You don't expect an object passing through a ghost to lose momentum. Maxwell said: 'You are a semi-hallucinatory precipitation of gaseous particles, or a thing from outer space. Under either interpretation, your invasion of my domicile constitutes a tort.' Maxwell was the most junior partner in the law firm of Bindle, Bindle, Bindle and Maxwell. 'Get down off my bed.'

The monkey did so, tossed the pillow up on the covers, and resumed its earlier position.

'I see,' said Maxwell. 'You understand speech, you manipulate material objects although they don't necessarily manipulate you, and you prefer the letter to the spirit. Please get me an aspirin.'

The monkey just sat there. It was black, tailless, the size of an Airedale, male. So far as Maxwell could tell it was young and healthy like himself, but probably not hung over.

Maxwell reeled to the bathroom. The monkey paralleled his movements, just out of reach – not that Maxwell felt much desire to grab. Maxwell washed down two aspirins. 'Want one?' The monkey nodded, caught the tablet, and waited for Maxwell to get out of the bathroom and give him room. Maxwell removed the key and stood aside; the monkey entered; Maxwell sighed and locked him in.

The monkey returned through the keyhole and settled back into its normal shape, rumpled, irritated, and larger than before. 'So you *were* hung over,' said Maxwell, getting dressed. The monkey ignored that, imitating

Maxwell's motions with the shirt. Since it had no clothes of its own and showed no inclination to steal Maxwell's, this appeared an empty ritual – shadow work.

For breakfast, Maxwell tossed the monkey some actual burned toast, but wasn't about to pour any extra coffee until the brute got a cup for himself and set it down within Maxwell's reach, looking miserable. Maxwell washed up, the monkey making theoretical motions at a safe distance from the tangible sink. Phony-casual, Maxwell asked: 'By the way, how would you have proceeded if that bathroom door had had no keyhole? Or, say, a Yale lock?'

The monkey replied only by looking grave, which was the way he looked anyhow.

Maxwell could not avoid going to the office. As the most junior partner, he was expected to sweat out a serious quantity of dogwork to justify his existence in what the most senior Bindle described (often) as a situation of substantial trust. He told the monkey: 'I am now about to go downstairs, out, and five stations uptown on the subway. I then walk from Lexington to Third and uptown two more blocks: elevator from main to ninth floor. Any comment? ... No comment.'

He stepped out, quickly closing the apartment door, which had a Yale lock.

A block from the subway entrance the monkey caught up with him.

It had enlarged again, being now as tall as Maxwell, and was rubbing its left hip as if it might be a bit lame, and glowering.

It was one of those lush and tender mornings in May when New Yorkers find it a genuine pleasure to inhale grit. Those who passed Maxwell and his associate paid the monkey no more attention than they would have given to any offbeat shadow. Faint frowns, puzzled glances. One elderly lady opened her mouth but didn't speak. Politeness, Maxwell supposed. Nobody likes to stop a stranger and say: 'Excuse me, sir, you may not have noticed – your shadow is looking more simian than you do this morning.'

Or perhaps the monkey knew some extraterrestrial means of cooperating with Maxwell's wish for obscurity. Decent of him to use it, if so. Descending the subway steps, Maxwell said over his shoulder: 'Sorry about all those doors.'

Understandably, the monkey went unnoticed in the subway crowds. At the moment of Maxwell's apology it had returned to the size of a child, and quit glowering.

At the office Maxwell hung up his hat in his own small room, leaving the door open for his usual early morning contemplation of the back of Sheila Walker's neck.

Miss Walker at twenty-nine was losing hope, but the back of her neck was exquisite.

She did not lack other prettiness of a spaniel-eyed, wistful sort. Though a competent receptionist and secretary to all four partners, she was developing a tendency to flutter and squeak. She recognized it herself with honest dismay. She also found herself clutching her mousy hair at demoralizing sounds, such as the long angry bray of H. K. Bindle clearing his throat for speech. This uproar was no worse than T. J. Bindle's sneeze, and F. W. Bindle, while dictating, scratched his left trouser-leg with dull sonority; so Miss Walker sometimes clutched her hair at all three. Pretty, Sheila at times became beautiful, when nobody was looking at her and she was looking at the back of Maxwell's neck. The back of Maxwell's neck was not exquisite; occasionally not even very clean.

When she noticed Maxwell's monkey following him into the office that morning she felt that to speak of it would be not only tactless but – well, difficult. She said: 'Good morning, Max!' and smiled spaniel-eyed, slamming the typewriter carriage back and savoring the baritone boom of his 'Yo, Sheila!' She too had gone through a bad time since waking – had indeed thought of talking things over with a well-heeled friend of hers who was just about halfway through her third psychoanalyst.

After Maxwell settled in his office, with the door open, she continued tearing away at a brief in the suit of one Jasper Baring against his grand-nephew Judson Baer for defamation of character. The said Judson Baer was alleged to have asserted loudly in a public place, to wit a bar, before six persons bearing witness, that the said Jasper Baring was not fit to carry guts to a bear. Her exquisite neck grew warmer and warmer up over the ears, and she got things all snarled up.

When she could bear it no longer, Sheila flung down her eraser and bravely stepped into Maxwell's office to ask him – flat-out, quickly, before her courage faded – how you spell 'eligible.' 'I keep thinking it's two es, somewhere, but it never comes out looking right!'

'Mm, well, what's the context?' Maxwell asked – not intelligently, mostly in order to keep her in the office while he made up his mind about something.

'Well, it's what this old Jasper said about Jud – no, Judson about Jasper – wait, I'll get it, Max.'

As she fluttered back to her desk, Maxwell was forced to abandon his last doubt. He was not even slightly hung over, and there were two monkeys in the room. His own, and the one standing in the doorway behind Sheila making desperate motions with imaginary papers.

Maxwell's monkey seemed to be more or less off duty, perhaps because Maxwell's desk chair stood close to the wall, which cramps the style of any shadow. Maxwell's monkey was in fact deeply interested in the other one. They were about the same size – quite a nice match, in a way.

'Here it is,' said Sheila, fluttering back. 'You see, H. K. felt we should have like a legal translation of what this old Judson said about – wait – "being then and there at the site known as" – no, it's further on – here: "defendant having then and there uttered expressions including the direct statement that plaintiff was not qualified or eligible to initiate or promote or perform the conveyance or transport of eviscerated material, to wit entrails" – oh, *look* how I spelled evis – oh – oh, damn!'

'You poor kid,' said Maxwell, and made it around his desk fairly fast, heedless of the flying pages of legal size.

The first kiss, intended partly as a consolation job, bounced off her nose. The second, even more complexly motivated, was amateur in execution but far more advanced in concept.

The monkeys too appeared to feel that at least one crisis in their own relations had been met and passed.

During those five or ten minutes – this anyhow was the none too clear impression of both Shelia and Maxwell – three persons passed the office door: F. W. Bindle, who seemed to note the embrace with mixed feelings, some of them green; F. W.'s father, T. J. Bindle, who leered in a manner that could hardly be interpreted to mean anything but 'Nice work Max!' and the most senior H. K. Bindle, who always noted everything that happened, but never said anything unless it could be expressed in sentences of not less than two hundred and fifty words.

A crisis passed usually means another one approached. A week after his monkey's first appearance Maxwell came to see me, not so much distressed as puzzled, not so much puzzled as angry. It took time and bourbon before he could work off those feelings of hostility and resentment which they say we should work off, no kidding.

He told his story coherently. As he talked and drank and brooded, his shadow was more disturbed than he was, but I could not reach any firm conclusion about it.

It has been suggested that they possess some means – possibly a ray, though I don't buy that – of unsettling the observer's vision at its source. I did feel inclined to fault my own visual perception, when Maxwell's shadow strolled off to the bathroom and Maxwell just sat there.

'We've checked out one thing for sure,' he said. 'It won't let you do anything you yourself think is wrong. I mean, it'll *let* you all right, but it gets bigger and meaner and uglier till a man can't stand it. But it goes by what *you* think, not by any other standards. Take cussing. I can't see anything wrong about a bit of normal cussing, so when I do it my monkey doesn't give a damn. But Sheila's got a thing about cussing, her own that is. Last time she let go with a little "hell" or something – and with every provocation, mind you – a couple of other words came along for the ride, and her monkey – my God, I don't care to see that again! Sheila nearly passed out cold.'

'You say there's been this – gradual growth?'

'All week long. If only you damn science-fiction writers would just—'

'Let's stay with the subject. Approximately how large is your shad – your monkey, right this moment?'

'Can't you see?'

'Not clearly, I admit. (Cheers.)'

'That's evident. (What? Oh, cheers.) Why, he's about two gorillas' worth and uglier than dammit.'

'And Sheila's?'

'Size of her maternal grandmother, approximately.'

'Her maternal grandmother was—'

'Is. Stout. About medium-large grizzly size.'

'And you feel that your conduct this week—'

'We've been good as gold. If you confounded science-fiction writers would—'

'Max, now hear this: we didn't invent outer space. It has been there all the time, and bugs me as much as you. Please stick to the subject.'

'Sure, sure, that's how a man talks when he doesn't happen to have a monkey. Oh, well, we drove out across the river the other night and parked, and I admit my feelings ran away with me. Sheila's too I guess. But she said no, and – well, see, the monks had gone outside. No room for 'em on the back seat any more, they've grown so. And they were hulking around out there in the dark, and there's this sudden God-awful pounding on the top of the car as though some lunatic—'

'By which monkey was the pounding?'

'Sheila's. I stuck my head out and saw her. Eyes glow in the dark, damned if they don't. Coming home they rode outside on the roof, and we could see their feet stuck down through the rear windows, I suppose to keep the wind from blowing them away. If only it could!'

'The pounding occurred when Sheila said no?'

'About that time. You see? No pleasing them.'

'In relation to Sheila what did you then do, Counselor?'

'Nothing but nothing, you crumb. She said no. If you damned science—'

'And you claim your own monkey is two gorillas' worth and growing all the time. Max, short of rubbing your two stupid noses in it, how could they make it any plainer?'

He made a show of thinking that over a long while, but the truth is that Maxwell is anything but stupid. He said at last: 'See what you mean of course. But she still says no and she means it.'

I said (and I think well enough of the remark so that I have it in a notebook and may use it again sometime): 'Max, of the many ways of persuading a woman to change her mind, sitting on your butt thinking sad thoughts is not one.'

He left soon after that. I noticed how long it took his shadow to follow him after he slammed the door. He called me four hours later, at two in the morning, sounding peaceful and friendly.

All he had to say was: 'They did too.'

Now that we all have them, things aren't going too badly – maybe even a little better than they used to, as a matter of fact. It probably shows the human race can get along with anything, if it has to. Almost anything.

Mine for instance is occupying the large armchair across the room from my typewriter, finishing up something or other (with *my* ballpoint) and naturally I haven't a God-damn notion what he's produced.

THE PONSONBY CASE

At 5:18 A.M., Tuesday, 18 August 1959, while patrolling that section of Central Park which includes the zoological exhibit, and being then in the area between the south animal building and the pool containing sea lions, I received a call for assistance from Elihu Jackson, who is employed by the city as a night attendant at the said Zoo.

Mr Jackson ran out of the building which houses the elephant, hippopotamuses, and some other fauna, and addressed me as follows: 'Hey, officer! There's a maniac in with the bull, and he's naked as a snake.'

Being aware that in circus and related parlance the term 'bull' is frequently used to refer to an elephant, whether of the male or the female sex, I proceeded immediately to the elephant house, and observed within the enclosure a moderately large male of the Asiatic species, and what appeared to be a human individual approximately 45 years of age, height 5' 2", weight about 180 pounds. Subject individual was seated in, and partly covered by, a pile of hay in a corner of the enclosure. Mr Jackson at this time provided the information that he had heard the elephant mumbling in a way that meant he (the elephant) didn't feel good.

When I entered the building the elephant was located partly inside the enclosure and partly outside in the yard. The head, or front, section of the animal was the section within the enclosure, and he (the animal) was shaking it.

I inquired of subject individual on the hay what he was doing in there. He replied: 'Nothing.' He added, if I correctly understood him, that it was anyway better than the hippopotamus. I then directed Mr Jackson to open the service door and let the man out. Mr Jackson replied: 'He's mean, that bull is.'

Considering Mr Jackson's reply not only unresponsive but lacking in humanity, I pointed out that the door opening on the runway between the enclosure and the central aisle of the building was too small to admit the passage of an elephant and could therefore be opened with impunity.

Mr Jackson replied (verbatim): 'Not on your fanny – soon as I do he'll charge on account he don't feel good. When they shake their head thataway, means he don't feel good.'

I immediately directed Mr Jackson to give me the key to the padlock on the service door and then go outside the building and create a diversion.

He said: 'Do what?'

I said: 'Make a noise.'

He said: 'Oh.'

After some further conversation omitted here as not relevant, Mr Jackson gave the key to me, went outside the building, and made a noise, which as I had hoped induced the animal to retire. In retiring from the enclosure, however, the animal did not back out, but first came all the way in, made a circle of the area, and on his way out, while passing subject individual seated on and within the hay, tapped subject individual's shoulder with his trunk.

Beyond smiling in a manner suggestive of nervousness, subject individual made no response. The animal then, as before indicated, reversed his position in the doorway: that is to say, the head, or front, section was placed outside the building, presumably with reference to the diversion created by Mr Jackson.

I then lowered myself into the runway, opened the service door, and requested subject individual to come out through that. He did so, at which time I observed that he was wearing, in addition to a pair of shell-rim glasses, a pair of bedroom slippers of the color which I understand is known as baby-blue.

Interrogation, by Nussbaum, I. J., Shield No. 28E31416:

Q: Your name, please?

A: Hector Ponsonby.

Q: Middle initial?

A: M. For McWhirter.

Q: Age?

A: Forty-six.

Q: Residence?

A: Worcester, Massachusetts.

Q: And your occupation?

A: I travel in woolen underwear.

Q: But you are not at the moment doing so?

A: No.

Mr Ponsonby then explained, with a command of language which was excellent and coherent, but somewhat too detailed and voluminous for inclusions in this report, that he had intended, by his last answer, to convey the information that he was by occupation a salesman for the firm of Brigham & Bottomley, textile manufacturers of Worcester, Massachusetts, and was in New York in pursuance of his normal commercial activities when the wind blew the door shut. The interrogation continued as follows:

Q: Would you be willing to explain what occasioned your presence in the elephant's hay with no clothes on?

A: Gladly, if someone will lend me a pair of pants. And by the way, is the dog gone?

Interpolation, by Elihu Jackson, who had by then returned: We don't allow no dogs in the Zoo.

Ponsonby: Damn it, you allowed that one.

Second interpolation: There ain't no dogs allowed in this here Zoo.

Interrogation continued, by Nussbaum: Do you feel all right?

A: I feel better.

I then directed Mr Jackson to procure from his locker or from general supply whatever might be available in the way of temporary clothing adaptable to a man of Mr H. McW. Ponsonby's height and weight. I further instructed Mr Jackson that if while thus engaged he should encounter other persons (which I considered unlikely in view of the earliness of the hour) he should make no mention of the incident in the elephant house, out of respect for Mr Ponsonby's status not only as a citizen but as an out-of-town visitor.

I also made it clear to Mr Jackson (wherein perhaps I exceeded by authority) that if any damage to the clothing or inconvenience to himself resulted from his action, adequate compensation would probably be allowed by the city, in consideration of his service to the public peace.

While Mr Jackson was absent, I received from Mr Ponsonby a preliminary account (later verified in every important particular by such investigation as I felt called upon to make) which I enter here, the same being somewhat simplified from Mr Ponsonby's original and to some extent overemotional terms. I would emphasize that this account is not offered in lieu of a formal statement by Hector McW. Ponsonby, the said Ponsonby having stated that he will hold himself available to provide such statement if higher authority so directs.

At approximately 10:55 P.M., 17 August 1959, Hector McW. Ponsonby, being then in occupancy of a suite at the Watkins Hotel, 96A East 68th Street, this city, was in the act of taking a bath. Hearing a knock at the door, he put on the pair of blue slippers previously mentioned in this report, and a bathrobe which he states was of a color matching the slippers, the two items having been purchased together by his wife, Isabel Stuart Ponsonby, of Worcester, Massachusetts, on the occasion of their twentieth wedding anniversary.

He then opened the door of his suite and was requested to sign for and receive a small parcel, by an individual whom I have not been able to trace but who was probably a legitimate employee of one of the metropolitan messenger services. Supposing the parcel had been sent by his wife, Mr Ponsonby did sign for and take possession of same.

Q: You were expecting such a parcel?

A: Not exactly, but she often has to.

Q: Would you enlarge on that?

A: Every damn time I go to New York I *always* forget something.

Shortly after the messenger had departed, Mr Ponsonby, who suffers from myopia, mild, uncomplicated, and who had neglected to put on his glasses before opening the door, discovered that the parcel was addressed, not to him, but to a certain Mr Hercule M. Ponsovic, who (as I ascertained in subsequent investigation) was registered at the same hotel, and still is, being a professional tea-taster of retiring habits.

Immediately upon discovering the error, Mr Ponsonby called after the messenger and ran a short distance down the corridor, around the corner of which the said messenger had by that time disappeared. Having advanced in this direction some twenty feet, Mr Ponsonby distinctly heard the closing of two doors: (1) the door of the elevator; (2) the door of his own suite.

Having verified the closing of his own door – undoubtedly by the wind, then blowing vigorously in advance of a summer thunder-shower – Mr Ponsonby attempted to open it with the only tool in the pocket of his bathrobe – namely, a small comb. This (unsuccessful) exercise is, I suggest, clear evidence of a lack of any criminal background.

Two persons had come up in the elevator that took away the messenger and were now advancing down the corridor on Mr Ponsonby, who at that moment had broken the comb and had thereupon voiced certain expressions verging on the vernacular, which he regrets. He feels they may have been a contributory factor in causing the lady to scream.

These persons (I later ascertained) were Colonel Eustace Bangs, a British visitor late of Her Majesty's Fusilier Guards (it sounded like that), aged 61, and his wife Cordelia, aged 60. Mr Ponsonby's reconstruction of the ensuing conversation is at least in part corroborated by my later interrogation of Colonel Bangs. It appears to have gone approximately as follows:

Mrs Bangs: Eustace, do something!

Colonel Bangs: Well, here now, what's all this, old man? Family hotel, you know, can't run around half naked in a family hotel, you know.

Ponsonby: I got locked out.

Mrs Bangs: Eustace, the man is a sex maniac. Probably has some helpless child in there.

Colonel Bangs: Well now, my dear, mustn't go off half-cocked, you know, might be some explanation, what?

Mrs Bangs: You have only to read one of these dreadful American newspapers. And look at his eye.

Ponsonby: Damn it, lady, there's nothing wrong with my eye!

Colonel Bangs, Now now, my wife's present, you know, can't have cursing and swearing, you know. Now, you—

Mrs Bangs: Be careful, Eustace! He may be armed.

Mr Ponsonby, believing himself in imminent danger of physical contact with a Colonel six feet two inches high, then flung the small parcel, which he had retained throughout his efforts to open the door, in such a manner as to have it impinge on the frontal bone of Colonel Bangs.

This precipitate action caused no damage whatever to Colonel Bangs, but considerable damage to the parcel, which burst and scattered an indeterminate amount of a dry, black substance all over Colonel and Mrs Bangs. I have since determined that the substance was Ceylon tea of a rare type and a very high quality which had been sent to Mr Hercule M. Ponsovic by a friend, as a token of personal esteem. Mr Ponsonby did not do this, he states, for the purpose of proving there was nothing wrong with his eye; he did it, he maintains, because he had to.

From the interrogation of Colonel Eustace Bangs, conducted 19 August 1959:

Q., by Nussbaum: You were aware, Colonel, at the moment of impact, that you had suffered no lasting physical disability of a traumatic nature?

A: Well, yes, you know, dash it, you know, but you can't have people throwing tea all over people.

Mr Ponsonby then ran, discovering too late that the direction in which he ran was a dead end. Turning, he observed Colonel Bangs advancing on him with both arms out, like (he says) a mine sweeper.

(A minor discrepancy in Mr Ponsonby's account should be noted here, but I do not regard it as a reflection on his credibility. For completeness, however: inquiry at the British consulate has established that Colonel Bangs has at no time had any connection whatsoever with Her Majesty's Navy.)

Compelled to run in the other direction, Mr Ponsonby ducked to leeward of the starboard arm, which, as he passed, secured a grip on the blue bathrobe and completely removed it, owing partly to the fact that he (Mr Ponsonby) shot out of the thing (his expression) like a squeezed appleseed. Mr Ponsonby then proceeded down the corridor. He asserts he has no recollection of observing a door marked 'service stairs.' He merely passed through it.

At this point in my interrogation of Mr Ponsonby I noted that the elephant had returned indoors, and instead of shaking his head was now nodding it. I inquired of Mr Ponsonby whether in his opinion this indicated that he (the animal) was feeling good. Mr Ponsonby said he did not know. I inquired also concerning the approximate weight of the parcel he had thrown at the Colonel. Mr Ponsonby estimated it at six ounces.

I then briefly discussed with Mr Ponsonby the experience which the metropolitan police have had with the phenomenon of recidivism in the criminal element, and against this background I inquired whether he, Mr Ponsonby, felt that he would be at all likely, should the circumstances recur, to again throw anything like a six ounce parcel at a retired British Colonel. With every evidence of the utmost sincerity, Mr Ponsonby replied, no, he would not, not if he saw him first. I then requested him to continue his account.

Mr Ponsonby considers that his speed in the descent of the service stairs was between seven and seven and a half miles per hour at the moment when he collided with the slowly moving and lighter bulk of a waiter employed by the Watkins Hotel, whom I have identified as Mr Stanley Moszczenski, age 53. Since the service elevator was in use, Mr Moszczenski had chosen to use the stairs in order to convey to Mr Salvatore Rizzo, on the second floor, a room-service tray containing spaghetti Milanese, Parmesan cheese, hot pepper, and the like. From my later investigation:

Q., by Nussbaum: Mr Rizzo, do you confirm the statement by Mr Moszczenski, so far as you understand it?

A: I don't speak Polish.

Q: But you comprehend the general drift?

A: All I know, I never get the spaghett'. Was midnight supper, very hungry. I never get.

Mr Ponsonby was naturally unaware of Mr Rizzo's position in the matter, during the period he remained seated with Mr Moszczenski at the foot of the service stairs. He does not recollect saying anything to Mr Moszczenski except: 'For God's sake give me your pants!'

The response of Mr Moszczenski, being in Polish, is not a matter of record, but Mr Ponsonby believed at the time that Mr Moszczenski had, as he phrases it, blood in his eye.

As a result of subsequent inquiry I have been able to set Mr Ponsonby's mind partly at rest on this question. It was not blood but tomato sauce. Nevertheless, Mr Ponsonby felt himself somewhat to blame, and since two new doorways were now available, he chose the one nearer to him.

At his impact it opened on a stairway leading to the furnace room, where he noted a number of dark spaces, the most inviting being a large coal bin. Mr Ponsonby gave me to understand that he did not burrow under the coal, since it was summer and the bin was nearly empty. He entered it, he states, simply because it was enclosed on four sides and appeared to offer him a chance to consider his delicate situation. He was, in fact, doing precisely that when a voice over his head remarked: 'Hey, you!'

Mr Ponsonby then observed, hung over the coal bin, a face with pendant gray mustaches. He describes the face as 'bilious,' which I attribute to Mr Ponsonby's troubled state of mind, since this is neither a just nor a tolerant description of Mr Clyde Somerville, boiler-man, unmarried, age 65. Mr Ponsonby reconstructs their conversation as follows:

'What you doing down there?'

'I am not doing anything.'

'Then what's the idea?'

'The wind blew the door shut.'

'What door?'

'My door.'

'Why'n't you open it?'

'Comb wouldn't fit.'

'What comb?'

'The one I blasted, God bust it!'

'You don't want to talk like that if you're going to go messing around in people's coal bins without no clothes on.'

'May I borrow your pants?'

'Matter with your own?'

'I told you, I left them behind.'

'No, you didn't.'

'You can see I did, can't you?'

'Mean you didn't tell me. Had, wouldn't of asked. Why?'

'Why what?'

'Whyja leave 'em behind and go messing around in people's coal bins?'

'The wind blew the door shut.'

'All right, don't get excited. You want some pants I'll get you some pants. All's I want to know is why you got to go messing around in people's coal bins without no clothes on.'

Mr Ponsonby then heard the clamor of a search party coming down the stairs, and he said: 'Please!'

'Huh?'

'Please, if I could have the pants now and explain later?'

'Explain what?'

'Why the wind blew the door shut.'

'Account it's blowing up a storm outside is why.'

The search party, according to Mr Ponsonby's recollection, numbered between eighteen and twenty-four persons, all talking simultaneously. It included Mr Moszczenski, roughly three bellboys, a house detective with a gun, and Colonel Eustace Bangs. Mr Ponsonby asserts that when he emerged from the coal bin fearing immediate encirclement, one bellboy remarked: 'Gawd, I do mean pink!'

(My investigation has established beyond a shadow of doubt that Mr Ponsonby is not and never has been a member of the Communist Party.)

At this phase in my interrogation Mr Elihu Jackson returned to the elephant house with a park attendant's uniform which he said was the best he could do. Mr Ponsonby, apparently under stress of strong emotion, then made some rather incoherent statement to the effect that until now he had never really loved policemen, and while he was putting on the garments the elephant went outside.

Mr Ponsonby resumed his account, explaining that the greater part of his attention had been directed toward the house detective with the gun, which

Mr Ponsonby thought to be of .45 caliber. Mr Jackson interjected the information that if you could believe all you read in them Westerns a .45 can really kill you deader than a dormouse (Mr Jackson's expression). Mr Ponsonby concurred. Nevertheless, it appears that he faced the entire group, including the house detective, long enough to remark either: 'Why don't you all drop dead?' or 'I wish you would all drop dead.'

Although Mr Ponsonby is inclined to think the second version is correct, the first seems to me more likely, because the second is a mere static expression of a wish, while the first embodies the dynamics of a forward-looking proposition appropriate to a man who, through force of circumstances, had become a man of action. It is a difficult point in semantics and perhaps should not be given undue weight.

Then, as a man of action, Mr Ponsonby ran for an iron grille door at the far end of the furnace room and closed it behind him in such a manner as to cause an abrasion to the nose of Mr Clement Gahagan, house detective, age 42.

In the statement (attached) which Mr Gahagan later gave me, he makes it clear that to him the most serious aspect of the episode was the fact that his gun – a .32, not a .45 – went off, owing, he feels, to the unforeseen abrasion and not to any absence of control on his part. In informal conversation Mr Gahagan told me – in good faith, I am sure – that he wouldn't be after shooting the little guy and him naked as a bug.

The bullet, it appears, struck the iron grille, ricocheted, passed through the left branch of Mr Clyde Somerville's mustache, and lodged in a coal bin from which it was later extracted by Jacques LaFourche, age 13, son of the head chef of the Watkins Hotel. My interrogation of Master LaFourche was in part as follows:

Q., by Nussbaum: So you dug her out, Jackie?

A: Well, sure. Can I keep it, Mister? It didn't hit nobody. Can I keep it, huh, can I?

Q: Well, sure.

Since the grille door gave on the outdoors, Mr Ponsonby went there. The short stairway from the grille led to a side alley closed at one end – the inner end. The open end faced 68th Street. Mr Ponsonby is quite clear that at the instant of his emergence from the furnace room, the wind was rising strongly but the rain had not begun to fall. It did fall, however, almost immediately after he heard the grille door reopened and recognized the voice of Colonel Eustace Bangs.

Having checked with the Weather Bureau with reference to the time of commencement of the thunder-shower of 17 August 1959, I am able to pinpoint the time as 11:21, when Mr Ponsonby came out on 68th Street and shot toward Central Park like (he says) a homing dove.

I have experienced some difficulty in securing reliable witnesses for the time between Mr Ponsonby's emergence on 68th Street and his disappearance in the park. The rain was then falling heavily, the entire incident was characterized by extremely rapid motion and observation under those conditions must be somewhat discounted.

It seems to be established, however, that in the course of his passage to the park Mr Ponsonby knocked over one liberal journalist, one Justice of the Court of Common Pleas, and one plumber. The journalist refers to a pink blur, the Justice declined to testify, and the plumber is doubtful, since there is a possibility that he was flattened not by Mr Ponsonby but by the twelve or fourteen persons who, in spite of the rain, were then engaged in hot pursuit.

Mr Ponsonby himself is convinced that at least some policemen were included in that section of the electorate which followed him as he moved rapidly westward. I am doubtful of this; the matter could probably be illuminated by reference to higher authority, but I have not done so. I did, however, make it clear to Mr Ponsonby that the members of the metropolitan police force are not, as he suggested, selected for matched voices, and that when seven or eight of them yell, 'Hey, you!' at the same time, the result is not harmony in the musical sense.

I was able to secure one quite reliable witness to Mr Ponsonby's crossing of Fifth Avenue, namely a taxi driver, Wilkins Krumbhaar, whose vehicle had suffered damage to the right headlight when the same came in contact with a mailbox, because Mr Krumbhaar was obliged to swerve off the Avenue to avoid collision with an unidentified flying object. It was impossible to trace his two passengers, but Mr Krumbhaar distinctly recalls a conversation that took place between them shortly after the abrasion of his right headlight:

'Baby, did you see what I thought I saw?'

'I think so, but if the cabbie saw what you thought I think you saw you could ask him.'

'Driver, did you see what she thinks I thought I saw?'

'Listen, brother. If I hadn't of saw what you wanted to know if I saw what you thought she saw, would I of already clumb the curb?'

Mr Ponsonby remembers leaping over a couple on the grass without attracting their attention, but apart from that his recollection of his passage into the park is not overprecise. He recalls tearing through a tunnel, and up a hill and down a hill, and into a thicket where he crouched, he thinks, about ten minutes, while a distant baying died away in the south. He felt, however, no deep security.

He was then pursued by a Peke.

I have been unable to locate this animal, or to identify it except as to breed. Mr Ponsonby is quite clear that it was a Pekinese, of uncertain age, trailing a leash, having presumably lost contact with its owner and strayed. Mr Ponsonby thinks, but is not certain, that it was a female.

At any rate, upon sighting Mr Ponsonby in the thicket the animal displayed no hesitation, but charged him at once, obliging him to run, he estimates, rather more than a quarter of a mile. The rain having not yet ceased, Mr Ponsonby was uncertain of his direction, but it was firmly fixed in his mind, whether correctly or not, that the animal intended to rob him of his slippers.

It is to Mr Ponsonby's credit, not only as a man of action but as a citizen with a highly developed sense of the decencies, that he retained these slippers, and still had them when he was engaged in climbing some vertical iron bars which, he felt at the time, were unusually high. Having reached the top of them, and observing an elephant on the other side, Mr Ponsonby felt he could go no further.

It must be emphasized that the entry of this Pekinese into the zoo area was not, in any degree whatsoever, the fault of Elihu Jackson, the night attendant referred to earlier. It is my considered opinion that if the owner of a Pekinese is so neglectful as to lose such an animal and allow it to roam at large, the exclusion of it from an unfenced area such as the one under discussion would require the constant activity of so much additional personnel that the city government could not justifiably recommend it in the budget.

The elephant then proceeded to lift Mr Ponsonby with his trunk and set him gently down within the enclosure. Mr Ponsonby recalls saying: 'Nice elephant.'

Mr Ponsonby then walked without undue haste into the indoor section of the elephant's domain, hoping to find some way out of it and into a sanctuary where he might eventually encounter some member of his own species who would not say, 'Hey, you!'

Since the service door was padlocked and Mr Ponsonby was unable to squeeze through the bars, he finally sat down on the hay. The elephant, he says, came inside from time to time, apparently to reassure himself that Mr Ponsonby was making out all right.

Having completed his account to me, Mr Ponsonby was still much troubled with regard to possible charges that might be placed against him, particularly the charge of indecent exposure. So far as my limited authority allowed, I attempted to assure him that any such charge, if raised at all, could probably be dismissed by reference to the commonly accepted legal principle that the law does not concern itself with trifles, or, as I should prefer to state it to my superiors, *de minimis non curat lex.*

(Signed)
Irving J. Nussbaum
Shield No. 28E31416

PICKUP FOR OLYMPUS

This was Ab Thompson – you might have seen him if you were around there in the 1960s: thin nose, scant chin, hair sandy to gray, pop eyes, and a warm depth of passion for anything with wheels. If it had pistons, wheels, some kind of driving shaft, Ab could love it. When the old half-ton bumbled into his filling station, the four cylinders of his lonesome heart pounded to the spark; the best of many voices within him said tenderly: *Listen how she perks!* The bearded driver leaning from the cab had to ask him twice: 'Is this the right road for Olympus?'

A genuine 1937 Chevy, sweet as the day she was hatched. Oh – little things here and there, of course. Ab pulled himself together. 'Never heard of it. You're aimed for N'York – might be beyond there somewheres.' The muddy hood stirred his longing; when this thunder-buggy was made, streamlining wasn't much more than the beginning of a notion. 'Water? Check the oil, sir?'

'Yes, both. Got enough gas, I think.' The driver's voice was fatigued, per-haps from the June heat. Ab Thompson raised the hood and explored. Rugged, rugged ... 'They don't make 'em like this nowadays.'

'I guess not.' In the back of the truck a drowsy-eyed woman in a loose gown of white linen scratched the head of a leopard and kept watch of half a dozen shy little goats.

Ab marveled: it was like the dollar Ingersoll his pop used to brag about – and oh, dear Lord, how long ago was that? Before what they called the Second World War? – Ab couldn't just remember. Naturally this old girl was beat up – beat up bad, and almost thirty years old. But she ticked away. She perked. Needed a new fan belt. Leak in the top of the radiator – dump in some ginger, maybe she'd seal herself up. And the valves ... He showed the driver the spot of dirty oil on the measuring rod. 'She'll take a quart, maybe two.'

'All right,' said the bearded man. The woman murmured reprovingly to the leopard and tied a short rope to the grass collar on his neck. When the oil was in, the driver said apologetically: 'Seems very noisy.'

'That's your valves, Mister. I could tighten 'em some. You got one loose tappet, I dunno – I could tighten 'er some only not too much on account if I make her too tight you don't get the power is all.'

'Well –' the driver scratched the thick curls tumbling over the horns on his forehead. 'Well, suppose you—'

'She ain't had a real valve job in quite some time, am I right, Mister? I ain't equipped for a valve job is the hell of it. But I could look her over, give you an idea, won't cost you nothing, glad to do it. Understand, that there ticking don't hurt nothing, it's just your tappet, but them valves –' Ab spat in embarrassment.

'Yes, look her over. I'd be much obliged.'

'Kind of like a good watch, Mister – got to keep her cleaned up.'

'Yes. Look her over, give me an idea.'

Ab sighed in happiness. 'Okay. Twenty minutes, say ...'

You could pound the daylights out of them, he thought – they'd still perk. Bet she could take a ten-percent grade in high, even now. Actually the valves weren't bad, he saw – sighing over the leaf-gauge, wishing in a brief sorrow like the touch of wings that somehow, somewhere, it might be possible to set up the right kind of shop. Suppose you could stretch the money as far as hiring an assistant – then maybe an addition on the south side, with room for a lift – nuts: no use dreaming ... The valves weren't bad – bit of maladjustment, natural after neglect. She'd perk. They never made them like this nowadays—

The woman in white was exercising the leopard on the rope, in the open space around the gas tanks; a goat bleated peevishly.

Not that there was anything wrong with the new cars, Ab thought – especially the take-off jobs that needed only a twenty-foot clearance to sprout wings and leave the highway: those might be hell-fired cute when they got a few more bugs ironed out. And you couldn't deny the new ground models were slick and pretty: fifty miles to the gallon if you didn't average more than a hundred per. But you take this old baby – 'Mister,' said Ab Thompson, 'you got compression, I do mean. Shouldn't have no trouble on the hills.'

'That's true. I have no trouble in the hills.'

'Starter ain't too good. Might've had some damage, I dunno.'

'I meant to ask about that. The trouble is here in the cab.'

'Huh? Nothin' there but the button you step on.'

'I know. My foot keeps catching on it.' Ab opened the right-hand door; the button looked good enough. 'I thought, if you could build it out a little –?'

The driver showed Ab the cloven bottom of his hoof. 'This slot here – you see, the button catches in it.'

'Oh, hell, instant plastic'll fix that.' Ab trotted to his shack, delighted. Nice to have the right stuff on hand for once. He returned with a gadget like a grease-gun. 'This here is something new in the trade. Hardens on contact with air, I do mean hardens. Stick to anything – got to handle it careful till it's dry. Comes out in a spray, like.' He played the plastic delicately on the starter button, building it out away from the gas pedal. 'Now try that, sir.'

'Oh, fine. Just what I had in mind. Well, the valves—'

'Ain't too bad. But I would recommend you stop some place where they got the equipment. Might go on a long time, or – well, she might kind of start complaining, I dunno. It oughta be done.'

'I'll see to it. Much obliged.' The woman and the leopard climbed back in the truck. 'What do I owe you?'

Ab massaged his neck. 'Three bucks … Thank you, sir. Come again!' The little truck rolled away. 'Jesus, I do mean! Thirty years old and she still perks, just as sweet as you-be-damn.'

DARIUS

According to (Miss) Cassandra Higginson, a housemaid of proven intelligence, the cat Darius was drunk.

Her employer Mrs Follansbee is thought to have dissented from this view. She is alleged to have said to Mr Follansbee: 'Llewellyn, that cat will have to be altered.' Some moments later, since a squirm behind the newspaper indicated that Mrs Follansbee's husband was still alive, she is believed to have added: 'Llewellyn ...'

The later celebrated Mr Follansbee is described by Miss Higginson as a small man with a sort of you-know pushed-around look. Other testimony mentions tufts of ash-colored hair, and pince-nez.

Miss Higginson asserts that the black and white cat Darius had just come singing from the garage. She saw him lurch into Mr Follansbee's lap (the word 'lurch' is taken directly from her deposition) and she claims to have seen Mr Follansbee shelter him with the editorial page of the *New York Times*. She recalls that Mr Follansbee said: 'Now, Darius.' Miss Higginson declares further that she had never considered Mr Follansbee the sort of man who would deliberately allow a cat access to spirituous liquors. It was therefore her view that the cat's manifest alcoholic condition was in some manner the result of his (Darius's) own efforts.

Miss Higginson also states that one hour later Mrs Follansbee again said: 'Llewellyn –' At this point (or juncture) Mr Follansbee put away the newspaper and walked out of the house, in the company of Darius. This took place at or about half past eleven (2330 hours), October 31, 1976. Except for the unsatisfactory evidence of certain persons who were at that time small boys, Mr Follansbee is not known to have been seen since that time.

These boys, seven in number, are thought to have followed Mr Follansbee and the cat Darius for a distance of three-quarters of a mile to the town limits. Their accounts, taken separately, tally in most important particulars. Darius, they assert, was walking beside Mr Follansbee, and both advanced at a rather rapid pace; they do not mention a 'lurch.' The boys were celebrating Halloween. After receiving a nickel apiece from Mr Follansbee (a total expenditure on his part of $0.35) they ceased advising him and Darius to go soak it. They followed him at a wider distance, however, as far as the town line, mainly, they depose, because they believed him to be as nutty as a fruitcake and wished to see what the hell he would do next. What he did (they say) was to climb (with Darius) to the top of a small barren knoll somewhat off the highway beyond the town line, and at that point the boys lost sight of him.

The knoll is not there now. Testimony of Abelard Peabody, builder and contractor, establishes the fact that it was at the time in question.

At 11:59 (2359 hours), October 31, 1976, lightning is known to have struck the top of this knoll, although it was not raining, and a certain quantity of sparks was observed, variously described as green, yellow, purple and 'real queer-looking.' Some object is thought to have floated briefly around the summit, identified by Maisie Schmaltz (profession unlisted) of 60 Maiden Lane as something like a sort of a gray something, only black.

Further research establishes that at 11:59 (2359 hours), October 31, 1976, a secretary at the United States delegation to the United Nations telephoned to an under-secretary of the Soviet delegation to inquire: 'Did you hear anything?' The Soviet under-secretary is thought to have replied: 'Nyet – well, nyet exactly.' The United States secretary may (or may not) have then said: 'Oh, crud!' The conversation is alleged to have proceeded no further.

It is incontrovertible that the cat Darius came home – alone. He was seen returning by two policemen at 1:24 A.M. (0124 hours), 1 November 1976, by a milkman, Konstantin Skourieczenkiewicz, at 2:10 A.M. (0210 hours) of the same night, and by Mr Francis X O'Leary's English bulldog Butch at an hour not precisely determined. Darius was admitted to the Follansbee home by the maid (Miss) Cassandra Higginson at 2:41 A.M. (0241 hours), 1 November 1976. She has testified that he was still singing at this time in a dark and uneducated way, and that he was alone.

Questioned regarding the continued masculinity or sexual integrity of the cat Darius, Miss Higginson deposed that goodness, she didn't look. Questioned further, and the possible importance of this point being made clear to her with great difficulty, Miss Higginson states that he anyway acted as mean as usual.

The disappearance of Mr Follansbee has since been analyzed in the public press with a lack of restraint which has now and then been deplored. The local police department acted at the time with commendable energy and correctness, but found no fingerprints on the knoll. The knoll was removed 26 June 1978, at the insistence of nearby residents, after a photograph of it had appeared in a metropolitan daily (not the *New York Times*) with a large-bosomed lovely in a G-string superimposed, and a caption: *Is this what Follansbee found up there?!!??!*

Mrs Follansbee has repeatedly told representatives of press, radio and television that she does not intend to have her husband declared legally dead when the legally required time has elapsed. She has stated also, in an interview published exclusively by *Film Dreams* and six other magazines of national circulation, that she has forgiven him. In the same interview she also expressed the opinion that no one could understand who had not been through it.

Darius is thought to have remained in the home of Mrs Follansbee, and was seen on several occasions, though not recently. It has proved impossible to determine the precise date of his last public appearance, but it is known to have taken place at some time during the spring of 1980.

The maid (Miss) Cassandra Higginson was dismissed (with a good character) on the morning of October 31, 1979 and entered a nunnery immediately after a very brief newspaper interview which occurred en route. In this interview, her discussion of the period between the return of the cat Darius (1 November 1976) and her own departure from the Follansbee domicile, is condensed to the point of what may be described as uncommunicative brevity. She, in fact, confined herself to the assertion that some people could just as well mind their own dratted business.

Only one additional item has come to light with regard to the Follansbee household – apart, that is, from the commonly known fact that Mrs Follansbee, although ceasing to entertain at home, has continued her activity in several clubs and progressive movements, and is universally conceded to have shown a very brave and sensible attitude. This additional item is based on admittedly unreliable testimony and is included here only for the sake of completeness.

A certain Simeon Stagg, a dealer in hardware, called at the Follansbee home at or about 10:45 P.M. (2245 hours), 27 June 1978, under the unaccountable impression that the house was occupied by some individual (impossible to locate) named Herman Podsnap who owed him (Stagg) twelve bucks for a hunk of soilpipe. On inquiry Stagg freely admitted that he might have had one or two alcoholic beverages. Sworn, Stagg deposed that he looked through the living room window when he was on the point of pushing the buzzer, and saw a lady (presumed to have been Mrs Follansbee) 'knitting sitting on the divan.'

Q: What?

A: Knitting there sitting.

Q: She sat on the divan, and while thus seated was knitting?

A: Ain't that what I said for Christ's sake?

He deposed further that he saw the face of another person reading a newspaper in an armchair, and he says that the face of this person was black and white, about the size of a grapefruit, with a sort of you-know pushed-around look.

WOGGLEBEAST

Molly trotted the two blocks from the supermarket with a roasting chicken for Sunday. Her round blue eyes were tranced with planning. Paper skirts on the drumsticks, toothpick legs for the olives; the raw carrots Danny liked could be cut in funny shapes. Then cold cuts for Sunday supper, and the bones could be boiled up for soup on Sunday evening while they looked at the T.V. or had a game of checkers.

Molly McManus enjoyed the rest of the Friday. She polished the living room floor of the little house and put up two pairs of fresh curtains. Thanks to her planning ahead, she had time for a nice visit with Mrs Perlman next door who was going to have still another baby. She remembered to quit humming when Danny got home because it sometimes got on his nerves – a foreman in an explosive plant cannot have nerves. But she continued humming inside. At dinner she had a pickle-animal. That's easy – you take a pickled onion for the head, slices of gherkin for the body, and the usual legs made out of toothpicks. Danny chuckled and admired it. Molly went to bed happy, folded up in gratitude against his weary bulk, and slept a while in peace.

He was tired, but over the weekend he could rest. Molly worried about his weight. He had no bay window, but there was a hint of it. Bags were showing under his mild gray eyes, and the eyes would redden if he forgot to put on his reading glasses. His step had grown heavy so gradually, one almost forgot how light on his feet he used to be. It seemed to Molly they ought to give him an office job. She woke for an hour or so in the night, thinking about that, watching the rosy reflection of a traffic light glow, die and glow again on the bedroom ceiling. He'd earned an office job. He ought to go straight up there and *tell* them.

And she was oppressed also that night by a special familiar loneliness in her arms. She counted to eight a dozen times or so, synchronizing it with Danny's peaceful snoring, and murmured a prayer which had become little more than a wistful habit. She was forty-one; to have a child at this date would *need* a miracle.

Sunday was good, as planned. Rest had cleared away most of Danny's fatigue – in fact on Saturday he'd taken out his stamp collection and got her to admiring it, which happened only on his best days. Then at Sunday dinnertime, glorious juices rushed out of the chicken at the poke of Danny's carving knife, and the whole apartment wallowed in the golden brown smell. Stuffed and sleepy-faced, Danny let out a hole in his belt, and Molly pretended not to notice – she was not slim herself. The afternoon darkened with February snow that would make driving unpleasant, so instead of taking off for the movies they worked on a crossword puzzle until Danny fell asleep trying to think of a Norse god. By evening they were ready for cold cuts. Molly McManus sat up after Danny got tired of watching T.V. and went to bed, to boil out the chicken bones and mend one of his shirts. In spite of the way everything encouraged you to do it, Molly hated wasting things. It seemed a little wicked as well as silly ...

It crouched on the kitchen table where it had fallen, or jumped, from the strainer full of other bones. Its thin arms reached toward Molly McManus as if in a bow or a supplication, and it looked like a Wogglebeast. 'Why, the poor thing!' said Molly, and as she held out her finger toward its narrow friendly head it seemed to her that the Wogglebeast sat back on its sort-of legs and shook itself slightly – anyway there was a spatter of soup drops on the table top that didn't necessarily come from the strainer.

She hated to disturb it. She dumped the other bones in the garbage and put away the soup, but let the kitchen table alone. She was always up before Danny to get his breakfast, and it wasn't as if they had cockroaches or ants. She slipped into bed thinking some about the Wogglebeast but more about Danny.

In her drowsiness she had left a few other things untidied; her sewing basket, for instance, sitting with its lid off beside the genuine antique rocker in the kitchen. It had come from the old country with her grandmother, a basket of sweet-scented woven grass, the dry gold of it soft with age. When she got up early Monday morning she found the Wogglebeast nestled in this basket, and started to take it out, but although it didn't draw back, it seemed to her that it shook – not its head exactly.

She placed the basket in the back of the silver drawer, leaving the drawer open a crack for air, until Danny had gone to work. Not that he would be unfriendly or unkind at all, but on work-day mornings he could not be quite with her; he never ignored her, but he had to be somehow arranging his thoughts and feelings for the trials and responsibilities of the day. She could see it happening, and help only by letting him alone. And also he was allergic to a number of things, cats and dogs for instance. And if she mentioned the Wogglebeast he might feel he had to do something about it. So – so anyway evening would be time enough.

During the day she made room at the back of the bottom bureau drawer for the Wogglebeast's basket. It was convenient; she could trot up to the bedroom from time to time to see if the little fellow needed anything. She offered it breadcrumbs, cornmeal, a few other things, but evidently it didn't need to eat, which was perhaps only natural. The bureau drawer remained open until she heard Danny drive into the garage, and as she was closing it she resolved to tell him. It really wasn't right or fair not to.

But there had been a near-disaster at the plant. One of Danny's own crew had been careless, inexcusably careless – the man had to be fired. The whole episode was still oppressing Danny McManus like the brushing of black wings, and it was no time to be telling him about anything unusual.

Tuesday night some of the same trouble hung about him. He was grumbling that it was his own fault for not having trained the offender better.

Wednesday he was just tired out, falling asleep in his armchair, face collapsed above the drooped newspaper, defenseless and – well, not young.

By Thursday night Molly was beginning to feel a certain weight of guilt. If she spoke of the Wogglebeast Danny would rightly wonder why she hadn't done so sooner. Besides, it was acting very cooperative, the decent thing, always snug and quiet in the basket a bit before Danny was due home, although that Thursday it had been following her all over the house.

She thought Friday that it would have liked to go with her to the supermarket. But clearly the Wogglebeast itself knew that this couldn't be. It wasn't begging at all, just wistful, and when she got home it was waiting cheerfully in the kitchen and wagging – not its tail, exactly …

That afternoon she felt too lazy for the usual housework, and nearly drowsed off in the antique rocker, thinking a good deal about her grandmother, and how the old soul used to go on and on sometimes about the old country, talking high but soft like a small wind in the chimney, the way her dry laughter now and then would be the sparks of a comfortable burning log. Until – oh, maybe drowsing for sure – Molly heard her own self saying a few foolish things to the Wogglebeast that was resting in her arms: 'It's not as if I ever thought you was a wishing thing exactly, only thinking to myself I am and talking like it might be to myself, but it's best we won't tell Danny at all, you wouldn't know the things he'd do. Too bad we haven't a child, too bad he won't be squaring off and *telling* them to give him office work the way he's earned it and could have it at the drop of a word – but it's only you can't help your mind running on it sometimes, and all …'

That night Danny desired her, like a young man but not heedless, and in the good quiet afterward Molly got up her courage to say a few little things about asking for office work, and though he wouldn't say yes or no he was peaceful and thoughtful about it, not annoyed at all. Once or twice, in the heavy darkness after Danny had fallen asleep, she heard in the bureau drawer a tiny sigh not quite a grunt, very much like the noise a cat will make after turning around three times and settling down in a basket.

It wasn't until Easter Week that Danny found the Wogglebeast. He was already out of sorts, late for work, hunting a missing sock and getting mad instead of putting on another pair, and flinging himself in bull-necked impatience at all the bureau drawers, one foot in an untied shoe and the other bare entirely with all his toes angry. The Wogglebeast had been trying to hide under a brassiere. 'Oh, that,' Molly said – 'oh, that, the little thing looked so much like a something, and wouldn't I be the one to go on playing with dolls at my age, see, the little legs he has and all?' The Wogglebeast never moved while Danny held it up; she was certain of that.

He put it back in the drawer. Not a word. He took another pair of socks. No word, no smile. He could be like that, and often it meant nothing except that he was puzzled. After he had gone Molly just made it to the bathroom, dizzy and sick.

Good and sick, but why? Surely his finding the Wogglebeast hadn't upset her that much. Something wrong with breakfast? – of course not. Unbelieving, merely touching the idea like a dab of cloud that was certain to float away, Molly counted days. How foolish can you get? And yet several times that day she studied her familiar round not-so-pretty face in the mirror, and something in her insisted that it *was* rather pretty. Softer anyhow, and brighter. A different look.

Two days later she walked to the doctor's office, almost furtively, as if she hadn't as good a right as anybody to a rabbit test and all that.

The test said yes.

The doctor said other things beside yes, having known her fifteen years. It puzzled her that behind his professional cheerfulness he was obviously not pleased. When she called it a miracle the best he could offer was a one-sided smile and another string of cautions and good advice. It didn't matter. The choirs sang; her thoughts ran up and down a swaying bridge of rainbows all day long.

It was after the doctor's telephone call saying the test was positive and delivering the first batch of those cautions, that she found the Wogglebeast had emptied her sewing basket, and collected treasures of its own there: an empty spool, a bit of tinfoil, an eraser worked loose from the end of a pencil – nothing of course that anybody else was going to want or that Danny would miss. Molly didn't mind at all, especially when she noticed how it was watching her with the jokesharing gleam in – well, not its eyes exactly …

Danny was not told of the miracle until they were in bed, their faces in darkness. By then Molly was enough used to the idea so that she could quiet his anxiety a little and help him into a precarious but genuine happiness. It occurred to her as she was drifting into sleep, himself holding her as if she were spun glass, that it was going to be simpler now to arrange about Danny's relations with the Wogglebeast. You have to humor a pregnant woman and allow her all sorts of quirks.

She told Dorothy Perlman the next day – on the phone, and casually she thought, but Mrs Perlman came over immediately under full sail, pouring forth advice, suggestions, consolation, sustaining anecdotes, offering a massive shoulder to cry on and restless until it was used. Her first had scared Nathan all to pieces, she said, and even scared her a little, but when the time came it simply popped. Like *that*.

Molly McManus liked people. She was on the silly edge of telling Dorothy about the Wogglebeast, but some hint of a gray disturbance over there in the bureau drawer behind Dorothy's back, like the lifting of a worried – oh, not head exactly – made Molly feel that it might not be just the best idea.

It's not that there's anything *wrong* with a Wogglebeast. Just all that pesky explaining you'd have to do.

It happened that Danny was so obsessed with the miracle he had no mind for anything else. Molly fell into the habit of leaving the bottom drawer more widely open. The Wogglebeast clearly enjoyed that, but took no unreasonable advantages of it. It did sometimes slip out of its basket when Danny was home, but carefully, and only if he happened to be in another room – well, once, on Sunday afternoon when Molly supposed Danny was taking a nap, she did hear the abrupt thump of his feet on the bedroom floor, and the beginning of an exclamation: 'B' Je –' but nothing else happened. Maybe she imagined it.

One evening in August, shortly before their two weeks' vacation in Atlantic City, Danny talked with her more searchingly than he usually did. He wanted a reassurance that she was happy – not in the future with the baby and all, but in the here and now. 'Why, Danny, I am, you know I am. I bet you went to bother the doctor again today.'

'Oh, for the sake of argument I did. Everything is fine, he says, and what else would he say if you went to him running a mortal fever with two busted legs?'

Molly herself knew that nothing could possibly go wrong – miracles don't. But it takes more than aspirin to get a husband through these things; from the bureau drawer came now and then a tiny sigh.

That night she woke in the small hours and noticed the Wogglebeast hesitant and forlorn on the bedroom rug. Danny was sound asleep. She held away a corner of the bedcovers so it could climb up if it wanted to, and as she went back to sleep she felt against her shoulder the dry wiggle of – not its legs, exactly.

And the next day Danny came home announcing that, as he put it himself, he was letting them kick him upstairs from foreman to supervisor. Not office work exactly, he explained to Molly's excited questions, but something like it. 'And so glory be to God you won't be messing around so much with the nasty stuff all day long?'

'It'll be like that,' he said rather carefully. 'I told them, I said, I've been foreman a long time, and now I must be thinking about the heir of The McManus and so forth.'

The Wogglebeast was well-behaved at Atlantic City. Molly had been uneasy about its smothery journey in a suitcase, but it took no harm. She had a little trouble in her mind about the hotel chambermaid, but solved it by admiring a very large handbag in a shop window, which Danny immediately bought for her; it had a compartment where the Wogglebeast was perfectly happy, and even made a sort of game out of covering itself with facial tissues and what not.

They stayed apart from the crowds, and watched the sea and the long changes of the sky. On other vacations they had often gone about with friends, in a round of parties and picnics and nonsense. She had no wish for that this time, and Danny found it natural.

One day on the beach she said, hardly heeding the way her talk was going: 'I wish you'd known my grandmother, Danny. She died when I was twelve, you know, and it was like the milkweed down drying up to a little white-ness and blowing away. O the stories she used to tell, and me with my mouth open and a wind going through my wits if I had any! She told once how they came and carried her away, the Little People she meant, and you had to believe her, the way she had of telling it, how she fell asleep in a meadow on Midsummer's Night, and she eleven years old, and they came for her, and didn't they set her to ride on a milk-white pony and it went straight under-ground with her into their dwelling? The hollow at the foot of an oak it was, and there they fed her cakes and honey and made things out of sticks and leaves that would walk and speak and play the violin. And then I'd ask her, "Grandmother, didn't you bring some of them home, the stick things that walked and made music?" She'd always say, "I did and all, Molly, but you'll remember this was seventy-eighty-ninety years ago, they'd be dust now, and anyhow they couldn't come away with me from the old country ..." '

Snow was falling again when Molly's pains began, rather too soon. In between them, when Danny was telephoning to the hospital, Molly petted the Wogglebeast and tried to explain how it must be quiet a few days in its basket and not worry about anything, anything at all. It was always difficult to decide just how much it understood; but it did seem to be smiling, not with its mouth exactly ...

When Molly came out of the anesthetic, one of the nurses was saying like a litany: 'You're doing just fine, Mrs McManus, just fine.' Well, sure, she knew she was. Daniel was the beginning of a world. She looked with tolerant affec-tion on the busy doctor and nurses, a little sorry for them because they had nothing as wonderful as she did.

So far as the doctor and nurses were aware, the baby was ten yards away in another room, where another doctor had given up trying to make it live. So far as they could see, there was no reason why Mrs McManus should hold her left arm curved like that. No reason why, torn and fading as she was, she should look so extravagantly happy. When the internal hemorrhage passed the point of no return they were still trying.

Danny happened on the sewing basket a while after he came home, and sagged on the bed poking vaguely at it, wondering with some part of his numb mind what had happened to the old dry chicken bone she had fancied so much. It didn't matter. There was nothing in the basket now but some kind of gray powder, and bits of miscellaneous trash – a spool, a scrap of tinfoil, never mind all that. There had always been something about Molly to make you think of a little girl playing with dolls.

The strangest part of it was that you went on living. He sat drooping, considering this, the sewing basket forgotten in his hands, watching the snow gently fall.

ANGEL'S EGG

LETTER OF RECORD, BLAINE TO McCARRAN, DATED 10 AUGUST 1951

Mr Cleveland McCarran
Federal Bureau of Investigation
Washington, D.C.

Dear Sir:

In compliance with your request I enclose herewith a transcript of the pertinent sections of the journal of Dr David Bannerman, deceased. The original document is being held at this office until proper disposition can be determined.

Our investigation has shown no connection between Dr Bannerman and any organization, subversive or otherwise. So far as we can learn, he was exactly what he seemed, an inoffensive summer resident, retired, with a small independent income – a recluse to some extent, but well-spoken of by local tradesmen and other neighbors. A connection between Dr Bannerman and the type of activity that concerns your department would seem most unlikely.

The following information is summarized from the earlier parts of Dr Bannerman's journal, and tallies with the results of our own limited inquiry. He was born in 1898 at Springfield, Massachusetts, attended public school there, and was graduated from Harvard College in 1922, his studies having been interrupted by two years' military service. He was wounded in action in the Argonne, receiving a spinal injury. He earned a doctorate in biology in 1926. Delayed aftereffects of his war injury necessitated hospitalization, 1927-8. From 1929 to 1948 he taught elementary sciences in a private school in Boston. He published two textbooks in introductory biology, 1929 and 1937. In 1948 he retired from teaching: a pension and a modest income from textbook royalties evidently made this possible. Aside from the spinal deformity, which caused him to walk with a stoop, his health is said to have been fair. Autopsy findings suggested that the spinal condition must have given him considerable pain; he is not known to have mentioned this to anyone, not even to his physician, Dr Lester Morse. There is no evidence whatever of drug addiction or alcoholism.

At one point early in his journal Dr Bannerman describes himself as 'a naturalist of the puttering type – I would rather sit on a log than write monographs: it pays off better.' Dr Morse, and others who knew Dr Bannerman personally, tell me that this conveys a hint of his personality.

I am not qualified to comment on the material of this journal, except to say I have no evidence to support (or to contradict) Dr Bannerman's statements. The journal has been studied only by my immediate superiors, by Dr Morse, and by myself. I take it for granted you will hold the matter in strictest confidence.

With the journal I am also enclosing a statement by Dr Morse, written at my request for our records and for your information. You will note that he says, with some qualifications, that 'death was not inconsistent with an embolism.' He has signed a death certificate on that basis. You will recall from my letter of August 5 that it was Dr Morse who discovered Dr Bannerman's body. Because he was a close personal friend of the deceased, Dr Morse did not feel able to perform the autopsy himself. It was done by a Dr Stephen Clyde of this city, and was virtually negative as regards cause of death, neither confirming nor contradicting Dr Morse's original tentative diagnosis. If you wish to read the autopsy report in full I shall be glad to forward a copy.

Dr Morse tells me that so far as he knows, Dr Bannerman had no near relatives. He never married. For the last twelve summers he occupied a small cottage on a back road about twenty-five miles from this city, and had few visitors. The neighbor, Steele, mentioned in the journal, is a farmer, age 68, of good character, who tells me he 'never got really acquainted with Dr Bannerman.'

At this office we feel that unless new information comes to light, further active investigation is hardly justified.

Respectfully yours,
Garrison Blaine
Capt., State Police
Augusta, Me.

Enc: Extract from Journal of David Bannerman, dec'd.
Statement by Lester Morse, M.D.

LIBRARIAN'S NOTE: The following document, originally attached as an unofficial 'rider' to the foregoing letter, was donated to this institution in 1994 through the courtesy of Mrs Helen McCarran, widow of the martyred first President of the World Federation. Other personal and state papers of

President McCarran, many of them dating from the early period when he was employed by the FBI, are accessible to public view at the Institute of World History, Copenhagen.

PERSONAL NOTE, BLAINE TO McCARRAN, DATED 10 AUGUST 1951

Dear Cleve:

Guess I didn't make it clear in my other letter that that bastard Clyde was responsible for my having to drag you into this. He is something to handle with tongs. Happened thusly: when he came in to heave the autopsy report at me, he was already having pups just because it was so completely negative (he does have certain types of honesty) and he caught sight of a page or two of the journal on my desk. Doc Morse was with me at the time. I fear we both got upstage with him (Clyde has that effect, and we were both in a state of mind anyway), so right away the old drip thinks he smells something subversive. Belongs to the atomize-'em-*now-wow-wow* school of thought – nuf sed? He went into a grand whuff-whuff about referring to higher authority, and I knew that meant your hive, so I wanted to get ahead of the letter I knew he'd write. I suppose his literary effort couldn't be just sort of quietly transferred to File 13, otherwise known as the appropriate receptacle?

He can say what he likes about my character, if any, but even I never supposed he'd take a sideswipe at his professional colleague. Doc Morse is the best of the best and would not dream of suppressing any evidence important to us, as you say Clyde's letter hints. What Doc did do was to tell Clyde, pleasantly, in the privacy of my office, to go take a flying this-and-that at the moon. I only wish I'd thought of the expression myself. So Clyde rushes off to tell teacher. See what I mean about the tongs? However (knock on wood) I don't think Clyde saw enough of the journal to get any notion of what it's all about.

As for that journal, damn it, Cleve, I don't know. If you have any ideas I want them, of course. I'm afraid I believe in angels, myself. But when I think of the effect on local opinion if the story ever gets out – brother! Here was this old Bannerman living alone with a female angel and they wuzn't even common-law married. Aw, gee ... And the flood of phone calls from other crackpots anxious to explain it all to me. Experts in the care and feeding of angels. Methods of angel-proofing. Angels right outside the window a minute ago. Make Angels a Profitable Enterprise in Your Spare Time!!!

When do I see you? You said you might have a week clear in October. If we could get together maybe we could make sense where there is none. I hear the cider promises to be good this year. Try and make it. My best to Ginny and the other young fry, and Helen of course.

Respeckfully yourn,

Garry

P.S. If you do see any angels down your way, and they aren't willing to wait for a Republican Administration, by all means have them investigated by the Senate – then we'll *know* we're all nuts.

G.

EXTRACT FROM JOURNAL OF DAVID BANNERMAN, JUNE 1-JULY 29, 1951

June 1

It must have been at least three weeks ago when we had that flying saucer flurry. Observers the other side of Katahdin saw it come down this side; observers this side saw it come down the other. Size anywhere from six inches to sixty feet in diameter (or was it cigar-shaped?) and speed whatever you please. Seem to recall the witnesses agreed on a rosy-pink light. There was the inevitable gobbledegookery of official explanation designed to leave everyone impressed, soothed, and disappointed. I paid scant attention to the excitement and less to the explanations – naturally, I thought it was just a flying saucer. But now Camilla has hatched out an angel.

It would have to be Camilla. Perhaps I haven't mentioned my hens enough. In the last day or two it has dawned on me that this journal may be of importance to other eyes than mine, not merely a lonely man's plaything to blunt the edge of mortality: an angel in the house makes a difference. I had better show consideration for possible readers.

I have eight hens, all yearlings except Camilla: this is her third spring. I boarded her two winters at my neighbor Steele's farm when I closed this shack and shuffled my chilly bones off to Florida, because even as a pullet she had a manner which overbore me. I could never have eaten Camilla: if she had looked at the ax with that same expression of rancid disapproval (and she would), I should have felt I was beheading a favorite aunt. Her only concession to sentiment is the annual rush of maternity to the brain – normal, for a case-hardened White Plymouth Rock.

This year she stole a nest successfully in a tangle of blackberry. By the time I located it, I estimated I was about two weeks too late. I had to outwit her by watching from a window – she is far too acute to be openly trailed from feeding ground to nest. When I had bled and pruned my way to her hideout she was sitting on nine eggs and hating my guts. They could not be fertile, since

I keep no rooster, and I was about to rob her when I saw the ninth egg was nothing of hers. It was a deep blue and transparent, with flecks of inner light that made me think of the first stars in a clear evening. It was the same size as Camilla's own. There was an embryo, but I could make nothing of it. I returned the egg to Camilla's bare and fevered breastbone and went back to the house for a long, cool drink.

That was ten days ago. I know I ought to have kept a record; I examined the blue egg every day, watching how some nameless life grew within it. The angel has been out of the shell three days now. This is the first time I have felt equal to facing pen and ink.

I have been experiencing a sort of mental lassitude unfamiliar to me. Wrong word: not so much lassitude as a preoccupation, with no sure clue to what it is that preoccupies me. By reputation I am a scientist of sorts. Right now I have no impulse to look for data; I want to sit quiet and let truth come to a relaxed mind if it will. Could be merely a part of growing older, but I doubt that. The broken pieces of the wonderful blue shell are on my desk. I have been peering at them – into them – for the last ten minutes or more. Can't call it study: my thought wanders into their blue, learning nothing I can retain in words. It does not convey much to say I have gone into a vision of open sky – and of peace, if such a thing there be.

The angel chipped the shell deftly in two parts. This was evidently done with the aid of small horny outgrowths on her elbows; these growths were sloughed off on the second day. I wish I had seen her break the shell, but when I visited the blackberry tangle three days ago she was already out. She poked her exquisite head through Camilla's neck feathers, smiled sleepily, and snuggled back into darkness to finish drying off. So what could I do, more than save the broken shell and wriggle my clumsy self out of there? I had removed Camilla's own eggs the day before – Camilla was only moderately annoyed. I was nervous about disposing of them, even though they were obviously Camilla's, but no harm was done. I cracked each one to be sure. Very frankly rotten eggs and nothing more.

In the evening of that day I thought of rats and weasels, as I should have done earlier. I prepared a box in the kitchen and brought the two in, the angel quiet in my closed hand. They are there now. I think they are comfortable.

Three days after hatching, the angel is the length of my forefinger, say three inches tall, with about the relative proportions of a six-year-old girl. Except for head, hands, and probably the soles of her feet, she is clothed in down the color of ivory; what can be seen of her skin is a glowing pink – I do mean glowing, like the inside of certain sea shells. Just above the small of her back are two stubs which I take to be infantile wings. They do not suggest an extra pair of specialized forelimbs. I think they are wholly differentiated organs; perhaps they will be like the wings of an insect. Somehow, I never thought of

angels buzzing. Maybe she won't. I know very little about angels. At present
the stubs are covered with some dull tissue, no doubt a protective sheath to
be discarded when the membranes (if they are membranes) are ready to
grow. Between the stubs is a not very prominent ridge – special musculature,
I suppose. Otherwise her shape is quite human, even to a pair of minuscule
mammalian buttons just visible under the down; how that can make sense in
an egg-laying organism is beyond my comprehension. (Just for the record, so
is a Corot landscape; so is Schubert's *Unfinished*; so is the flight of a hummingbird, or the other-world of frost on a window pane.) The down on her
head has grown visibly in three days and is of different quality from the body
down – later it may resemble human hair, as a diamond resembles a chunk of
granite …

A curious thing has happened. I went to Camilla's box after writing that.
Judy[1] was already lying in front of it, unexcited. The angel's head was out
from under the feathers, and I thought – with more verbal distinctness than
such thoughts commonly take, 'So here I am, a naturalist of middle years and
cold sober, observing a three-inch oviparous mammal with down and wings.'
The thing is – she giggled. Now, it might have been only amusement at my
appearance, which to her must be enormously gross and comic. But another
thought formed unspoken: 'I am no longer lonely.' And her face (hardly bigger than a dime) immediately changed from laughter to a brooding and
friendly thoughtfulness.

Judy and Camilla are old friends. Judy seems untroubled by the angel. I
have no worries about leaving them alone together. I must sleep.

June 3

I made no entry last night. The angel was talking to me, and when that was
finished I drowsed off immediately on a cot that I have moved into the kitchen so as to be near them.

I had never been strongly impressed by the evidence for extrasensory perception. It is fortunate my mind was able to accept the novelty, since to the
angel it is clearly a matter of course. Her tiny mouth is most expressive but
moves only for that reason and for eating – not for speech. Probably she
could speak to her own kind if she wished, but I dare say the sound would be
outside the range of my hearing as well as of my understanding.

Last night after I brought the cot in and was about to finish my puttering
bachelor supper, she climbed to the edge of the box and pointed, first at herself and then at the top of the kitchen table. Afraid to let my vast hand take

---

[1] Dr Bannerman's dog, mentioned often earlier in the journal. A nine-year-old English setter.
According to an entry of May 15, 1951, she was then beginning to go blind.

– Blaine.

444

hold of her, I held it out flat and she sat in my palm. Camilla was inclined to fuss, but the angel looked over her shoulder and Camilla subsided, watchful but no longer alarmed.

The table top is porcelain, and the angel shivered. I folded a towel and spread a silk handkerchief on top of that; the angel sat on this arrangement with apparent comfort, near my face. I was not even bewildered. Possibly she had already instructed me to blank out my mind. At any rate, I did so, without conscious effort to that end.

She reached me first with visual imagery. How can I make it plain that this had nothing in common with my sleeping dreams? There was no weight of symbolism from my littered past; no discoverable connection with any of yesterday's commonplace; indeed, no actual involvement of my personality at all. I saw. I was moving vision, though without eyes or other flesh. And while my mind saw, it also knew where my flesh was, slumped at the kitchen table. If anyone had entered the kitchen, if there had been a noise of alarm out in the henhouse, I should have known it.

There was a valley such as I have not seen (and never will) on Earth. I have seen many beautiful places on this planet – some of them were even tranquil. Once I took a slow steamer to New Zealand and had the Pacific as a plaything for many days. I can hardly say how I knew this was not Earth. The grass of the valley was an earthly green; a river below me was a blue and silver thread under familiar-seeming sunlight; there were trees much like pine and maple, and maybe that is what they were. But it was not Earth. I was aware of mountains heaped to strange heights on either side of the valley – snow, rose, amber, gold. Perhaps the amber tint was unlike any mountain color I have noticed in this world at midday.

Or I may have known it was not Earth simply because her mind – dwelling within some unimaginable brain smaller than the tip of my little finger – told me so.

I watched two inhabitants of that world come flying, to rest in the field of sunny grass where my bodiless vision had brought me. Adult forms, such as my angel would surely be when she had her growth, except that both of these were male and one of them was dark-skinned. The latter was also old, with a thousand-wrinkled face, knowing and full of tranquility; the other was flushed and lively with youth; both were beautiful. The down of the brown-skinned old one was reddish-tawny; the other's was ivory with hints of orange. Their wings were true membranes, with more variety of subtle iridescence than I have seen even in the wings of a dragonfly; I could not say that any color was dominant, for each motion brought a ripple of change. These two sat at their ease on the grass. I realized that they were talking to each other, though their lips did not move in speech more than once or twice. They would nod, smile, now and then illustrate something with twinkling hands.

A huge rabbit lolloped past them. I knew (thanks to my own angel's efforts, I supposed) that this animal was of the same size of our common wild ones. Later, a blue-green snake three times the size of the angels came flowing through the grass; the old one reached out to stroke its head carelessly, and I think he did it without interrupting whatever he was saying.

Another creature came, in leisured leaps. He was monstrous, yet I felt no alarm in the angels or in myself. Imagine a being built somewhat like a kangaroo up to the head, about eight feet tall, and katydid-green. Really, the thick balancing tail and enormous legs were the only kangaroo-like features about him: the body above the massive thighs was not dwarfed but thick and square; the arms and hands were quite humanoid: the head was round, man-like except for its face – there was only a single nostril and his mouth was set in the vertical; the eyes were large and mild. I received an impression of high intelligence and natural gentleness. In one of his manlike hands two tools so familiar and ordinary that I knew my body by the kitchen table had laughed in startled recognition. But, after all, a garden spade and rake are basic. Once invented – I expect we did it ourselves in the Neolithic Age – there is little reason why they should change much down the millennia.

This farmer halted by the angels, and the three conversed a while. The big head nodded agreeably. I believe the young angel made a joke; certainly the convulsions in the huge green face made me think of laughter. Then this amiable monster turned up the grass in a patch a few yards square, broke the sod and raked the surface smooth, just as any competent gardener might do – except that he moved with the relaxed smoothness of a being whose strength far exceeds the requirements of his task ...

I was back in my kitchen with everyday eyes. My angel was exploring the table. I had a loaf of bread there and a dish of strawberries and cream. She was trying a breadcrumb; seemed to like it fairly well. I offered the strawberries; she broke off one of the seeds and nibbled it but didn't care so much for the pulp. I held up the great spoon with sugary cream; she steadied it with both hands to try some. I think she liked it. It had been most stupid of me not to realize that she would be hungry. I brought wine from the cupboard; she watched inquiringly, so I put a couple of drops on the handle of a spoon. This really pleased her: she chuckled and patted her tiny stomach, though I'm afraid it wasn't awfully good sherry. I brought some crumbs of cake, but she indicated that she was full, came close to my face, and motioned me to lower my head.

She reached up until she could press both hands against my forehead – I felt it only enough to know her hands were there – and she stood so a long time, trying to tell me something.

It was difficult. Pictures come through with relative ease, but now she was transmitting an abstraction of a complex kind: my clumsy brain really

446

suffered in the effort to receive. Something did come across. I have only the crudest way of passing it on. Imagine an equilateral triangle; place the following words one at each corner – 'recruiting', 'collecting', 'saving'. The meaning she wanted to convey ought to be near the center of the triangle.

I had also the sense that her message provided a partial explanation of her errand in this lovable and damnable world.

She looked weary when she stood away from me. I put out my palm and she climbed into it, to be carried back to the nest.

She did not talk to me tonight, nor eat, but she gave a reason, coming out from Camilla's feathers long enough to turn her back and show me the wing stubs. The protective sheaths have dropped off; the wings are rapidly growing. They are probably damp and weak. She was quite tired and went back into the warm darkness almost at once.

Camilla must be exhausted, too. I don't think she has been off the nest more than twice since I brought them into the house.

June 4

Today she can fly.

I learned it in the afternoon, when I was fiddling about in the garden and Judy was loafing in the sunshine she loves. Something apart from sight and sound called me to hurry back to the house. I saw my angel through the screen door before I opened it. One of her feet had caught in a hideous loop of loose wire at a break in the mesh. Her first tug of alarm must have tightened the loop so that her hands were not strong enough to force it open.

Fortunately I was able to cut the wire with a pair of shears before I lost my head; then she could free her foot without injury. Camilla had been frantic, rushing around fluffed up, but – here's an odd thing – perfectly silent. None of the recognized chicken noises of dismay: if an ordinary chick had been in trouble she would have raised the roof.

The angel flew to me and hovered, pressing her hands on my forehead. The message was clear at once: 'No harm done.' She flew down to tell Camilla the same thing.

Yes, in the same way. I saw Camilla standing near my feet with her neck out and head low, and the angel put a hand on either side of her scraggy comb. Camilla relaxed, clucked in the normal way, and spread her wings for a shelter. The angel went under it, but only to oblige Camilla, I think – at least, she stuck her head through the wing feathers and winked.

She must have seen something else, then, for she came out and flew back to me and touched a finger to my cheek, looked at the finger, saw it was wet, put it in her mouth, made a face, and laughed at me.

We went outdoors into the sun (Camilla too), and the angel gave me an exhibition of what flying ought to be. Not even Schubert can speak of joy as her first free flying did. At one moment she would be hanging in front of my eyes, radiant and delighted; the next instant she would be a dot of color against a cloud. Try to imagine something that would make a hummingbird seem a bit dull and sluggish.

They do hum. Softer than a hummingbird, louder than a dragonfly.

Something like the sound of hawk moths – *Hemaris thisbe*, for instance: the one I used to call hummingbird moth when I was a child.

I was frightened, naturally. Frightened first at what might happen to her, but that was unnecessary; I don't think she would be in danger from any savage animal except possibly man. I saw a Cooper's hawk slant down the invisible toward the swirl of color where she was dancing by herself; presently she was drawing iridescent rings around him; then, while he soared in smaller circles, I could not see her, but (maybe she felt my fright) she was again in front of me, pressing my forehead in the now familiar way. I knew she was amused and caught the idea that the hawk was a 'lazy character.' Not quite the way I'd describe *Accipiter cooperi*, but it's all in the point of view. I believe she had been riding his back, no doubt with her speaking hands on his terrible head.

And later I was frightened by the thought that she might not want to return to me. Can I compete with sunlight and open sky? The passage of that terror through me brought her back swiftly, and her hands said with great clarity: 'Don't ever be afraid of anything – it isn't necessary for you.'

Once this afternoon I was saddened by the realization that old Judy can take little part in what goes on now. I can well remember Judy running like the wind. The angel must have heard this thought in me, for she stood a long time beside Judy's drowsy head, while Judy's tail thumped cheerfully on the warm grass …

In the evening the angel made a heavy meal on two or three cake crumbs and another drop of sherry, and we had what was almost a sustained conversation. I will write it in that form this time, rather than grope for anything more exact. I asked her, 'How far away is your home?'

'My home is here.'

'Thank God! – but I meant, the place your people came from.'

'Ten light-years.'

'The images you showed me – that quiet valley – that is ten light-years away?'

'Yes. But that was my father talking to you, through me. He was grown when the journey began. He is two hundred and forty years old – our years, thirty-two days longer than yours.'

Mainly I was conscious of a flood of relief: I had feared, on the basis of terrestrial biology, that her explosively rapid growth after hatching must foretell a brief life. But it's all right – she can outlive me, and by a few hundred years, at that. 'Your father is here now, on this planet – shall I see him?'

She took her hands away – listening, I believe. The answer was: 'No. He is sorry. He is ill and cannot live long. I am to see him in a few days, when I fly a little better. He taught me for twenty years after I was born.'

'I don't understand. I thought—'

'Later, friend. My father is grateful for your kindness to me.'

I don't know what I thought about that. I felt no faintest trace of conde-scension in the message. 'And he was showing me things he had seen with his own eyes, ten light-years away?'

'Yes.' Then she wanted me to rest a while; I am sure she knows what a huge effort it is for my primitive brain to function in this way. But before she ended the conversation by humming down to her nest she gave me this, and I received it with such clarity that I cannot be mistaken: 'He says that only fifty million years ago it was a jungle there, just as Terra is now.'

June 8

When I woke four days ago the angel was having breakfast, and little Camilla was dead. The angel watched me rub sleep out of my eyes, watched me discover Camilla, and then flew to me. I received this: 'Does it make you unhappy?'

'I don't know exactly.' You can get fond of a hen, especially a cantankerous and homely old one whose personality has a lot in common with your own.

'She was old. She wanted a flock of chicks, and I couldn't stay with her. So I –' Something obscure here: probably my mind was trying too hard to grasp it – '... so I saved her life.' I could make nothing else out of it. She said 'saved.'

Camilla's death looked natural, except that I should have expected the death contractions to muss the straw, and that hadn't happened. Maybe the angel had arranged the old lady's body for decorum, though I don't see how her muscular strength would have been equal to it – Camilla weighed at least seven pounds.

As I was burying her at the edge of the garden and the angel was humming over my head, I recalled a thing which, when it happened, I had dismissed as a dream. Merely a moonlight image of the angel standing in the nest box with her hands on Camilla's head, then pressing her mouth gently on Camilla's throat, just before the hen's head sank down out of my line of vision. Prob-ably I actually woke and saw it happen. I am somehow unconcerned – even, as I think more about it, pleased ...

After the burial the angel's hands said, 'Sit on the grass and we'll talk ... Question me. I'll tell you what I can. My father asks you to write it down.'

So that is what we have been doing for the last four days. I have been going to school, a slow but willing pupil. Rather than enter anything in this journal (for in the evenings I was exhausted), I made notes as best I could. The angel has gone now to see her father and will not return until morning. I shall try to make a readable version of my notes.

449

Since she had invited questions, I began with something which had been bothering me, as a would-be naturalist, exceedingly. I couldn't see how creatures no larger than the adults I had observed could lay eggs as large as Camilla's. Nor could I understand why, if they were hatched in an almost adult condition and able to eat a varied diet, she had any use for that ridiculous, lovely, and apparently functional pair of breasts. When the angel grasped my difficulty she exploded with laughter – her kind, which buzzed her all over the garden and caused her to fluff my hair on the wing and pinch my ear lobe. She lit on a rhubarb leaf and gave a delectably naughty representation of herself as a hen laying an egg, including the cackle. She got me to bumbling helplessly – my kind of laughter – and it was some time before we could quiet down. Then she did her best to explain.

They are true mammals, and the young – not more than two or at most three in a lifetime averaging two hundred and fifty years – are delivered in very much the human way. The baby is nursed – human fashion – until his brain begins to respond a little to their unspoken language; that takes three to four weeks. Then he is placed in an altogether different medium. She could not describe that clearly, because there was very little in my educational storehouse to help me grasp it. It is some gaseous medium that arrests bodily growth for an almost indefinite period, while mental growth continues. It took them, she says, about seven thousand years to perfect this technique after they first hit on the idea: they are never in a hurry. The infant remains under this delicate and precise control for anywhere from fifteen to thirty years, the period depending not only on his mental vigor but also on the type of life-work he tentatively elects as soon as his brain is knowing enough to make a choice. During this period his mind is guided with unwavering patience by teachers who—

It seems those teachers know their business. This was peculiarly difficult for me to assimilate, although the fact came through clearly enough. In their world, the profession of teacher is more highly honored than any other – can such a thing be possible? – and so difficult to enter that only the strongest minds dare attempt it. (I had to rest a while after absorbing that.) An aspirant must spend fifty years (not including the period of infantile education) in merely getting ready to begin, and the acquisition of factual knowledge, while not under-stressed, takes only a small proportion of those fifty years. Then – if he's good enough – he can take a small part in the elementary instruction of a few babies, and if he does well on that basis for another thirty or forty years, he is considered a fair beginner ... Once upon a time I lurched around stuffy classrooms trying to insert a few predigested facts (I wonder how many of them *were* facts?) into the minds of bored and preoccupied adolescents, some of whom may have liked me moderately well. I was even able to shake hands and be nice while their terribly well-meaning parents explained to me how they ought to be educated. So much of our human effort goes down the drain of futility, I sometimes wonder how we ever got as far as the Bronze Age. Somehow we did, though, and a short way beyond.

After that preliminary stage of an angel's education is finished, the baby is transferred to more ordinary surroundings, and his bodily growth completes itself in a very short time. Wings grow abruptly (as I have seen), and he reaches a maximum height of six inches (our measure). Only then does he enter on that lifetime of two hundred and fifty years, for not until then does his body begin to age. My angel has been a living personality for many years but will not celebrate her first birthday for almost a year. I like to think of that.

At about the same time that they learned the principles of interplanetary travel (approximately twelve million years ago) these people also learned how, by use of a slightly different method, growth could be arrested at any point short of full maturity. At first the knowledge served no purpose except in the control of illnesses which still occasionally struck them at that time. But when the long periods of time required for space travel were considered, the advantages became obvious.

So it happens that my angel was born ten light-years away. She was trained by her father and many others in the wisdom of seventy million years (that, she tells me, is the approximate sum of their *recorded* history), and then she was safely sealed and cherished in what my super-amoebic brain regarded as a blue egg. Education did not proceed at that time; her mind went to sleep with the rest of her. When Camilla's temperature made her wake and grow again, she remembered what to do with the little horny bumps provided for her elbows. And came out – into this planet, God help her.

I wondered why her father should have chosen any combination so unreliable as an old hen and a human being. Surely he must have had plenty of excellent ways to bring the shell to the right temperature. Her answer should have satisfied me immensely, but I am still compelled to wonder about it. 'Camilla was a nice hen, and my father studied your mind while you were asleep. It was a bad landing, and much was broken – no such landing was ever made before after so long a journey: forty years. Only four other grown-ups could come with my father. Three of them died en route and he is very ill. And there were nine other children to care for.'

Yes, I knew she'd said that an angel thought I was good enough to be trusted with his daughter. If it upsets me, all I need do is look at her and then in the mirror. As for the explanation, I can only conclude there must be more that I am not ready to understand. I was worried about those nine others, but she assured me they were all well, and I sensed that I ought not to ask more about them at present ...

Their planet, she says, is closely similar to this. A trifle larger, moving in a somewhat longer orbit around a sun like ours. Two gleaming moons, smaller than ours – their orbits are such that two-moon nights come rarely. They are magic, and she will ask her father to show me one, if he can. Their year is thirty-two days longer than ours; because of a slower rotation, their day has twenty-six of our hours. Their atmosphere is mainly nitrogen and oxygen in the proportions familiar to us; slightly richer in some of the rare gases. The climate is now what we should call tropical and subtropical, but they have known glacial rigors like those in our world's past. There are only two great continental land masses, and many thousands of large islands.

Their total population is only five billion ...

Most of the forms of life we know have parallels there – some quite exact parallels: rabbits, deer, mice, cats. The cats have been bred to an even higher intelligence than they possess on our Earth; it is possible, she says, to have a good deal of intellectual intercourse with their cats, who learned several million years ago that when they kill, it must be done with lightning precision and without torture. The cats had some difficulty grasping the possibility of pain in other organisms, but once that educational hurdle was passed, development was easy. Nowadays many of the cats are popular storytellers; about forty million years ago they were still occasionally needed as a special police force, and served the angels with real heroism.

It seems my angel wants to become a student of animal life here on Earth. I, a teacher! – but bless her heart for the notion, anyhow. We sat and traded animals for a couple of hours last night. I found it restful, after the mental struggle to grasp more difficult matters. Judy was something new to her. They have several luscious monsters on that planet but, in her view, so have we. She told me of a blue sea snake fifty feet long (relatively harmless) that bellows cowlike and comes into the tidal marshes to lay black eggs; so I gave her a whale. She offered a bat-winged, day-flying ball of mammalian fluff as big as my head and weighing under an ounce; I matched her with a marmoset. She tried me with a small-sized pink brontosaur (very rare), but I was ready with the duck-billed platypus, and that caused us to exchange some pretty smart remarks about mammalian eggs; she bounced. All trivial in a way; also, the happiest evening in my fifty-three tangled years of life.

She was a trifle hesitant to explain these kangaroo-like people, until she was sure I really wanted to know. It seems they are about the nearest parallel to human life on that planet; not a near parallel, of course, as she was careful to explain. Agreeable and always friendly souls (though they weren't always so, I'm sure) and of a somewhat more alert intelligence than we possess. Manual workers, mainly, because they prefer it nowadays, but some of them are excellent mathematicians. The first practical spaceship was invented by a group of them, with some assistance ...

Names offer difficulties. Because of the nature of the angelic language, they have scant use for them except for the purpose of written record, and writing naturally plays little part in their daily lives – no occasion to write a letter when a thousand miles is no obstacle to the speech of your mind. An angel's formal name is about as important to him, as, say, my Social Security number is to me. She has not told me hers, because the phonetics on which their written language is based have no parallel in my mind. As we would speak a friend's name, an angel will project the friend's image to his friend's receiving mind. More pleasant and more intimate, I think – although it was a shock to me at first to glimpse my own ugly mug in my mind's eye. Stories are occasionally written, if there is something in them that should be preserved precisely as it was in the first telling; but in their world the true storyteller has a more important place than the printer – he offers one of the best of their quieter pleasures: a good one can hold his audience for a week and never tire them.

'What is this "angel" in your mind when you think of me?'

'A being men have imagined for centuries, when they thought of themselves as they might like to be and not as they are.'

I did not try too painfully hard to learn much about the principles of space travel. The most my brain could take in of her explanation was something like: 'Rocket – then phototropism.' Now, that makes scant sense. So far as I know, phototropism – movement toward light – is an organic phenomenon. One thinks of it as a response of protoplasm, in some plants and animal organisms (most of them simple), to the stimulus of light; certainly not as a force capable of moving inorganic matter. I think that whatever may be the principle she was describing, this word 'phototropism' was merely the nearest thing to it in my reservoir of language. Not even the angels can create understanding out of blank ignorance. At least I have learned not to set neat limits to the possible.

(There was a time when I did, though. I can see myself, not so many years back, like a homunculus squatting at the foot of Mt. McKinley, throwing together two handfuls of mud and shouting, 'Look at the big mountain *I* made!')

And if I did know the physical principles which brought them here, and could write them in terms accessible to technicians resembling myself, I would not do it.

Here is a thing I am afraid no reader of this journal will believe: These people, as I have written, learned their method of space travel some twelve million years ago. But this is the first time they have ever used it to convey them to another planet. The heavens are rich in worlds, she tells me; on many of them there is life, often on very primitive levels. No external force prevented her people from going forth, colonizing, conquering, as far as they pleased. They could have populated a Galaxy. They did not, and for this reason: they believed they were not ready. More precisely: *Not good enough.*

Only some fifty million years ago, by her account, did they learn (as we may learn eventually) that intelligence without goodness is worse than high explosives in the hands of a baboon. For beings advanced beyond the level of *Pithecanthropus*, intelligence is a cheap commodity – not too hard to develop, hellishly easy to use for unconsidered ends. Whereas goodness is not to be achieved without unending effort of the hardest kind, within the self, whether the self be man or angel.

It is clear even to me that the conquest of evil is only one step, not the most important. For goodness, so she tried to tell me, is an altogether positive quality; the part of living nature that swarms with such monstrosities as cruelty, meanness, bitterness, greed, is not to be filled by a vacuum when these horrors are eliminated. When you clear away a poisonous gas, you try to fill the whole room with clean air. Kindness, for only one example: one who can define kindness only as the absence of cruelty has surely not begun to understand the nature of either.

They do not aim at perfection, these angels: only at the attainable … That time fifty million years ago was evidently one of great suffering and confusion. War and all its attendant plagues. They passed through many centuries while advances in technology merely worsened their condition and increased the peril of self-annihilation. They came through that, in time. War was at length so far outgrown that its recurrence was impossible, and the development of wholly rational beings could begin. Then they were ready to start growing up, through millennia of self-searching, self-discipline, seeking to derive the simple from the complex, discovering how to use knowledge and not be used by it. Even then, of course, they slipped back often enough. There were what she refers to as 'eras of fatigue.' In their dimmer past, they had had many dark ages, lost civilizations, hopeful beginnings ending in dust. Earlier still, they had come out of the slime, as we did.

But their period of deepest uncertainty and sternest self-appraisal did not come until twelve million years ago, when they knew a universe could be theirs for the taking and knew they were not yet good enough.

They are in no more hurry than the stars.

Of course, they explored. Their little spaceships were roaming the ether before there was anything like man on this earth – roaming and listening, observing, recording; never entering nor taking part in the life of any home but their own: for five million years they even forbade themselves to go beyond their own solar system, though it would have been easy to do so. And in the following seven million years, although they traveled to incredible distances, the same stern restraint was in force. It was altogether unrelated to what we should call fear – that, I think, is as extinct in them as hate. There was so much to do at home! – I wish I could imagine it. They mapped the heavens and played in their own sunlight.

Naturally, I cannot tell you what goodness is. I know only, moderately well, what it seems to mean to us human beings. It appears that the best of us can, with enormous difficulty, achieve a manner of life in which goodness is reasonably dominant, by a not too precarious balance, for the greater part of the time. Often, wise men have indicated they hope for nothing better than that in our present condition. We are, in other words, a fraction alive; the rest is in the dark. Dante was a bitter masochist, Beethoven a frantic and miserable snob, Shakespeare wrote potboilers. And Christ said, 'My Father, if it be possible, let this cup pass from me.'

But give us fifty million years – I am no pessimist. After all, I've watched one-celled organisms on the slide and listened to Brahms' Fourth. Night before last I said to the angel, 'In spite of everything, you and I are kindred.'

She granted me agreement.

June 9

She was lying on my pillow this morning so that I could see her when I waked.

Her father has died, and she was with him when it happened. There was again that thought-impression that I could interpret only to mean that his life had been 'saved.' I was still sleep-bound when my mind asked, 'What will you do?'

'Stay with you, if you wish it, for the rest of your life.' Now, the last part of the message was clouded, but I am familiar with that – it seems to mean there is some further element that eludes me. I could not be mistaken about the part I did receive. It gives me amazing speculations. After all, I am only fifty-three; I might live for another thirty or forty years …

She was preoccupied this morning, but whatever she felt about her father's death that might be paralleled by sadness in a human being was hidden from me. She did say her father was sorry he had not been able to show me a two-moon night.

One adult, then, remains in this world. Except to say that he is two hundred years old and full of knowledge, and that he endured the long journey without serious ill effects, she has told me little about him. And there are ten children, including herself.

Something was sparkling at her throat. When she was aware of my interest in it she took it off, and I fetched a magnifying glass. A necklace; under the glass, much like our finest human workmanship, if your imagination can reduce it to the proper scale. The stones appeared similar to the jewels we know: diamonds, sapphires, rubies, emeralds, the diamonds snapping out every color under heaven; but there were two or three very dark-purple stones unlike anything I know – not amethysts, I am sure. The necklace was strung on something more slender than cobweb, and the design of the joining clasp was too delicate for my glass to help me. The necklace had been her mother's, she told me; as she put it back around her throat I thought I saw the same shy pride that any human girl might feel in displaying a new pretty.

She wanted to show me other things she had brought, and flew to the table where she had left a sort of satchel an inch and a half long – quite a load for her to fly with, but the translucent substance is so light that when she rested the satchel on my finger I scarcely felt it. She arranged a few articles happily for my inspection, and I put the glass to work again. One was a jeweled comb; she ran it through the down on her chest and legs to show me its use. There was a set of tools too small for the glass to interpret; I learned later they were a sewing kit. A book, and some writing instrument much like a metal pencil: imagine a book and pencil that could be used comfortably by hands hardly bigger than the paws of a mouse – that is the best I can do. The book, I understand, is a blank record for her use as needed.

And finally, when I was fully awake and dressed and we had finished breakfast, she reached in the bottom of the satchel for a parcel (heavy for her) and made me understand it was a gift for me. 'My father made it for you, but I put in the stone myself, last night.' She unwrapped it. A ring, precisely the size for my little finger.

I broke down, rather. She understood that, and sat on my shoulder petting my earlobe till I had command of myself.

I have no idea what the jewel is. It shifts with the light from purple to jade-green to amber. The metal resembles platinum in appearance except for a tinge of rose at certain angles of light ... When I stare into the stone, I think I see – never mind that now. I am not ready to write it down, and perhaps never will be; anyway, I must be sure.

We improved our housekeeping later in the morning. I showed her over the house. It isn't much – Cape Codder, two rooms up and two down. Every corner interested her, and when she found a shoe box in the bedroom closet, she asked for it. At her direction, I have arranged it on a chest near my bed and near the window, which will be always open; she says the mosquitos will not bother me, and I don't doubt her. I unearthed a white silk scarf for the bottom of the box; after asking my permission (as if I could want to refuse her anything!) she got her sewing kit and snipped off a piece of the scarf several inches square, folded it on itself several times, and sewed it into a narrow pillow an inch long. So now she had a proper bed and a room of her own. I wish I had something less coarse than silk, but she insists it's nice.

We have not talked very much today. In the afternoon she flew out for an hour's play in the cloud country; when she returned she let me know that she needed a long sleep. She is still sleeping, I think; I am writing this downstairs, fearing the light might disturb her.

Is it possible I can have thirty or forty years in her company? I wonder how teachable my mind still is. I seem to be able to assimilate new facts as well as

I ever could; this ungainly carcass should be durable, with reasonable care. Of course, facts without a synthetic imagination are no better than scattered bricks; but perhaps my imagination—

I don't know.

Judy wants out. I shall turn in when she comes back. I wonder if poor Judy's life could be – the word is certainly 'saved.' I must ask.

June 10

Last night when I stopped writing I did go to bed but I was restless, refusing sleep. At some time in the small hours – there was light from a single moon – she flew over to me. The tension dissolved like an illness, and my mind was able to respond with a certain calm.

I made plain (what I am sure she already knew) that I would never willingly part company with her, and then she gave me to understand that there are two alternatives for the remainder of my life. The choice, she says, is altogether mine, and I must take time to be sure of my decision.

I can live out my natural span, whatever it proves to be, and she will not leave me for long at any time. She will be there to counsel, teach, help me in anything good I care to undertake. She says she would enjoy this; for some reason she is, as we'd say in our language, fond of me. We'd have fun.

Lord, the books I could write! I fumble for words now, in the usual human way: whatever I put on paper is a miserable fraction of the potential; the words themselves are rarely the right ones. But under her guidance—

I could take a fair part in shaking the world. With words alone, I could preach to my own people. Before long, I would be heard.

I could study and explore. What small nibblings we have made at the sum of available knowledge! Suppose I brought in one leaf from outdoors, or one common little bug – in a few hours of studying it with her I'd know more of my own specialty than a flood of the best textbooks could tell me.

She has also let me know that when she and those who came with her have learned a little more about the human picture, it should be possible to improve my health greatly, and probably my life expectancy. I don't imagine my back could ever straighten, but she thinks the pain might be cleared away, possibly without drugs. I could have a clearer mind, in a body that would neither fail nor torment me.

Then there is the other alternative.

It seems they have developed a technique by means of which any unresisting living subject whose brain is capable of memory at all can experience a total recall. It is a by-product, I understand, of their silent speech, and a very recent one. They have practiced it for only a few thousand years, and since their own understanding of the phenomenon is very incomplete, they classify it among their experimental techniques. In a general way, it may

somewhat resemble that reliving of the past that psychoanalysis can sometimes bring about in a limited way for therapeutic purposes; but you must
imagine that sort of thing tremendously magnified and clarified, capable of
including every detail that has ever registered on the subject's brain; and the
end result is very different. The purpose is not therapeutic, as we would
understand it: quite the opposite. The end result is death. Whatever is recalled
by this process is transmitted to the receiving mind, which can retain it and
record any or all of it if such a record is desired; but to the subject who recalls
it, it is a flowing away, without return. Thus it is not a true 'remembering' but
a giving. The mind is swept clear, naked of all its past, and, along with memory, life withdraws also. Very quietly. At the end, I suppose it must be like
standing without resistance in the engulfment of a flood tide, until finally the
waters close over.

That, it seems, is how Camilla's life was 'saved.' Now, when I finally grasped
that, I laughed, and the angel of course caught my joke. I was thinking about
my neighbor Steele, who boarded the old lady for me in his henhouse for a
couple of winters. Somewhere safe in the angelic records there must be a hen's-
eye image of the patch in the seat of Steele's pants. Well – good. And, naturally,
Camilla's view of me, too: not too unkind, I hope – she couldn't help the expression on her rigid little face, and I don't believe it ever meant anything.

At the other end of the scale is the saved life of my angel's father. Recall can
be a long process, she says, depending on the intricacy and richness of the
mind recalling; and in all but the last stages it can be halted at will. Her
father's recall was begun when they were still far out in space and he knew
that he could not long survive the journey. When that journey ended, the
recall had progressed so far that very little factual memory remained to him
on his life on that other planet. He had what must be called a 'deductive
memory'; from the material of the years not yet given away, he could reconstruct what must have been; and I assume the other adult who survived the
passage must have been able to shelter him from errors that loss of memory
might involve. This, I infer, is why he could not show me a two-moon night.
I forgot to ask her whether the images he did send me were from actual or
deductive memory. Deductive, I think, for there was a certain dimness about
them not present when my angel gives me a picture of something seen with
her own eyes.

Jade-green eyes, by the way – were you wondering?

In the same fashion, my own life could be saved. Every aspect of existence
that I ever touched, that ever touched me, could be transmitted to some perfect record. The nature of the written record is beyond me, but I have no
doubt of its relative perfection. Nothing important, good or bad, would be
lost. And they need a knowledge of humanity, if they are to carry out whatever it is they have in mind.

It would be difficult, she tells me, and sometimes painful. Most of the effort would be hers, but some of it would have to be mine. In her period of infantile education, she elected what we should call zoology as her lifework; for that reason she was given intensive theoretical training in this technique. Right now, I guess she knows more than anyone else on this planet not only about what makes a hen tick but about how it feels to be a hen. Though a beginner, she is in all essentials already an expert. She can help me, she thinks (if I choose this alternative) – at any rate, ease me over the toughest spots, soothe away resistance, keep my courage from too much flagging.

For it seems that this process of recall is painful to an advanced intellect (she, without condescension, calls us very advanced) because, while all pretense and self-delusion are stripped away, there remains conscience, still functioning by whatever standards of good and bad the individual has developed in his lifetime. Our present knowledge of our own motives is such a pathetically small beginning! – hardly stronger than an infant's first effort to focus his eyes. I am merely wondering how much of my life (if I choose this way) will seem to me altogether hideous. Certainly plenty of the 'good deeds' that I still cherish in memory like so many well-behaved cherubs will turn up with the leering aspect of greed or petty vanity or worse.

Not that I am a bad man, in any reasonable sense of the term; not a bit of it. I respect myself; no occasion to grovel and beat my chest; I'm not ashamed to stand comparison with any other fair sample of the species. But there you are: I *am* human, and under the aspect of eternity so far, plus this afternoon's newspaper, that is a rather serious thing.

Without real knowledge, I think of this total recall as something like a passage down a corridor of myriad images – now dark, now brilliant; now pleasant, now horrible – guided by no certainty except an awareness of the open blind door at the end of it. It could have its pleasing moments and its consolations. I don't see how it could ever approximate the delight and satisfaction of living a few more years in this world with the angel lighting on my shoulder when she wishes, and talking to me.

I had to ask her of how great value such a record would be to them. Very great. Obvious enough – they can be of little use to us, by their standards, until they understand us; and they came here to be of use to us as well as to themselves. And understanding us, to them, means knowing us inside out with a completeness such as our most dedicated and laborious scholars could never imagine. I remember those twelve million years: they will not touch us until they are certain no harm will come of it. On our tortured planet, however, there is a time factor. They know that well enough, of course … Recall cannot begin unless the subject is willing or unresisting; to them, that has to mean willing, for any being with intellect enough to make a considered choice. Now, I wonder how many they could find who would be honestly willing to make that uneasy journey into death, for no reward except an assurance that they were serving their own kind and the angels?

More to the point, I wonder if I would be able to achieve such willingness myself, even with her help?

When this had been explained to me, she urged me again to make no hasty decision. And she pointed out to me what my thoughts were already groping at – why not both alternatives, within a reasonable limit of time? Why couldn't I have ten or fifteen years or more with her and then undertake the total recall – perhaps not until my physical powers had started toward senility? I thought that over.

This morning I had almost decided to choose that most welcome and comforting solution. Then the mailman brought my daily paper. Not that I needed any such reminder.

In the afternoon I asked her if she knew whether, in the present state of human technology, it would be possible for our folly to actually destroy this planet. She did not know, for certain. Three of the other children have gone away to different parts of the world, to learn what they can about that. But she had to tell me that such a thing has happened before, elsewhere in the heavens. I guess I won't write a letter to the papers advancing an explanation for the occasional appearance of a nova among the stars. Doubtless others have hit on the same hypothesis without the aid of angels.

And that is not all I must consider. I could die by accident or sudden disease before I had begun to give my life.

Only now, at this very late moment, rubbing my sweaty forehead and gazing into the lights of that wonderful ring, have I been able to put together some obvious facts in the required synthesis.

I don't know, of course, what forms their assistance to us will take. I suspect human beings won't see or hear much of the angels for a long time to come. Now and then disastrous decisions may be altered, and those who believe themselves wholly responsible won't quite know why their minds worked that way. Here and there, maybe an influential mind will be rather strangely nudged into a better course. Something like that. There may be sudden new discoveries and inventions of kinds that will tend to neutralize the menace of our nastiest playthings. But whatever the angels decide to do, the record and analysis of my not too atypical life will be an aid: it could even be the small weight deciding the balance between triumph and failure. That is fact one.

Two: my angel and her brothers and sisters, for all their amazing level of advancement, are of perishable protoplasm, even as I am. Therefore, if this ball of earth becomes a ball of flame, they also will be destroyed. Even if they have the means to use their spaceship again or to build another, it might easily happen that they would not learn their danger in time to escape. And for all I know, this could be tomorrow. Or tonight.

So there can no longer be any doubt as to my choice, and I will tell her when she wakes.

July 9

Tonight[2] there is no recall – I am to rest a while. I see it is almost a month since I last wrote in this journal. My total recall began three weeks ago, and I have already been able to give away the first twenty-eight years of my life.

Since I no longer require normal sleep, the recall begins at night, as soon as the lights begin to go out over there in the village and there is little danger of interruption. Daytimes, I putter about in my usual fashion. I have sold Steele my hens, and Judy's life was saved a week ago; that practically winds up my affairs, except that I want to write a codicil to my will. I might as well do that now, right here in this journal, instead of bothering my lawyer. It should be legal.

To Whom It May Concern: I hereby bequeath to my friend Lester Morse, M.D., of Augusta, Maine, the ring which will be found at my death on the fifth finger of my left hand; and I would urge Dr Morse to retain this ring in his private possession at all times, and to make provision for its disposal, in the event of his own death, to some person in whose character he places the utmost faith.

(Signed) David Bannerman[3]

Tonight she has gone away for a while, and I am to rest and do as I please until she returns. I shall spend the time filling in some blanks in this record, but I am afraid it will be a spotty job, unsatisfactory to any readers who are subject to the blessed old itch for facts. Mainly because there is so much I no longer care about. It is troublesome to try to decide what things would be considered important by interested strangers.

Except for the lack of any desire for sleep, and a bodily weariness that is not at all unpleasant, I notice no physical effects thus far. I have no faintest recollection of anything that happened earlier than my twenty-eighth birth-day. My deductive memory seems rather efficient, and I am sure I could reconstruct most of the story if it were worth the bother: this afternoon I grubbed around among some old letters of that period, but they weren't very

---

[2] At this point Dr Bannerman's handwriting alters curiously. From here on he used a soft pencil instead of a pen, and the script shows signs of haste. In spite of this, however, it is actually much clearer, steadier, and easier to read than the earlier entries in his normal hand.

– Blaine.

[3] In spite of superficial changes in the handwriting, this signature has been certified genuine by an expert graphologist.

– Blaine.

interesting. My knowledge of English is unaffected; I can still read scientific German and some French, because I had occasion to use those languages fairly often after I was twenty-eight. The scraps of Latin dating from high school are quite gone. So are algebra and all but the simplest propositions of high-school geometry: I never needed 'em. I can remember thinking of my mother after twenty-eight, but do not know whether the image this provides really resembles her; my father died when I was thirty-one, so I remember him as a sick old man. I believe I had a younger brother, but he must have died in childhood.[4] Judy's passing was tranquil – pleasant for her, I think. It took the better part of a day. We went out to an abandoned field I know, and she lay in the sunshine with the angel sitting by her, while I dug a grave and then rambled off after wild raspberries. Toward evening the angel came and told me it was finished. And most interesting, she said. I don't see how there can have been anything distressing about it for Judy; after all, what hurts us worst is to have our favorite self-deceptions stripped away.

As the angel has explained it to me, her people, their cats, those kangaroo folk, man, and just possibly the cats on our planet (she hasn't met them yet) are the only animals she knows who are introspective enough to develop self-delusion and related pretenses. I suggested she might find something of the sort, at least in rudimentary form, among some of the other primates. She was immensely interested and wanted to learn everything I could tell her about monkeys and apes. It seems that long ago on the other planet there used to be clumsy, winged creatures resembling the angels to about the degree that the large anthropoids resemble us. They became extinct some forty million years ago, in spite of enlightened efforts to keep their kind alive. Their birth rate became insufficient for replacement, as if some necessary spark had simply flickered out; almost as if nature, or whatever name you prefer for the unknown, had with gentle finality written them off ...

I have not found the recall painful, at least not in retrospect. There must have been sharp moments, mercifully forgotten, along with their causes, as if the process had gone on under anesthesia. Certainly there were plenty of incidents in my first twenty-eight years that I should not care to offer to the understanding of any but the angels. Quite often I must have been mean, selfish, base in any number of ways, if only to judge by the record since twenty-eight. Those old letters touch on a few of these things. To me, they now matter only as material for a record which is safely out of my hands.

However, to any persons I may have harmed, I wish to say this: you were hurt by aspects of my humanity which may not, in a few million years, be

---

[4] Dr Bannerman's mother died in 1918 of influenza. His brother (three years older, not younger) died of pneumonia, 1906.

– Blaine.

quite so common among us all. Against these darker elements I struggled, in my human fashion, as you do yourselves. The effort is not wasted.

It was a week after I told the angel my decision before she was prepared to start the recall. During that week she searched my present mind more closely than I should have imagined was possible: she had to be sure. During that week of hard questions I dare say she learned more about my kind than has ever gone on record even in a physician's office; I hope she did. To any psychiatrist who might question that, I offer a naturalist's suggestion: it is easy to imagine, after some laborious time, that we have noticed everything a given patch of ground can show us; but alter the viewpoint only a little – dig down a foot with a spade, say, or climb a tree branch and look downward – it's a whole new world.

When the angel was not exploring me in this fashion, she took pains to make me glimpse the satisfactions and million rewarding experiences I might have if I chose the other way. I see how necessary that was; at the time it seemed almost cruel. She had to do it, for my own sake, and I am glad that I was somehow able to stand fast to my original choice. So was she, in the end; she has even said she loves me for it. What that troubling word means to her is not within my mind: I am satisfied to take it in the human sense.

Some evening during that week – I think it was June 12 – Lester dropped around for sherry and chess. Hadn't seen him in quite a while, and haven't since. There is a moderate polio scare this summer, and it keeps him on the jump. The angel retired behind some books on an upper shelf – I'm afraid it was dusty – and had fun with our chess. She had a fair view of your bald spot, Lester; later she remarked that she liked your looks, and can't you do something about that weight? She suggested an odd expedient, which I believe has occurred to your medical self from time to time – eating less.

Maybe she shouldn't have done what she did with those chess games. Nothing more than my usual blundering happened until after my first ten moves; by that time I suppose she had absorbed the principles and she took over, slightly. I was not fully aware of it until I saw Lester looking like a boiled duck: I had imagined my astonishing moves were the result of my own damn cleverness.

Seriously, Lester, think back to that evening. You've played in stiff amateur tournaments; you know your own abilities and you know mine. Ask yourself whether I could have done anything like that without help. I tell you again, I didn't study the game in the interval when you weren't here. I've never had a chess book in the library, and if I had, no amount of study would take me into your class. Haven't that sort of mentality – just your humble sparring partner, and I've enjoyed it on that basis, as you might enjoy watching a prima donna surgeon pull off some miracle you wouldn't dream of attempting yourself. Even if your game had been away below par that evening (I don't think it was),

I could never have pinned your ears back three times running without help. That evening you were a long way out of *your* class, that's all.

I couldn't tell you anything about it at the time – she was clear on that point – so I could only bumble and preen myself and leave you mystified. But she wants me to write anything I choose in this journal, and somehow, Lester, I think you may find the next few decades pretty interesting. You're still young – some ten years younger than I. I think you'll see many things that I do wish I myself might see come to pass – or I would so wish if I were not convinced that my choice was the right one.

Most of those new events will not be spectacular, I'd guess. Many of the turns to a better way will hardly be recognized at the time for what they are, by you or anyone else. Obviously, our nature being what it is, we shall not jump into heaven overnight. To hope for that would be as absurd as it is to imagine that any formula, ideology, theory of social pattern, can bring us into Utopia. As I see it, Lester – and I think your consulting room would have told you the same even if your own intuition were not enough – there is only one battle of importance: Armageddon. And Armageddon field is within each self, world without end.

At the moment I believe I am the happiest man who ever lived.

July 20

All but the last ten years now given away. The physical fatigue (still pleasant) is quite overwhelming. I am not troubled by the weeds in my garden patch – merely a different sort of flowers where I had planned something else. An hour ago she brought me the seed of a blown dandelion, to show me how lovely it was – I don't suppose I had ever noticed. I hope whoever takes over this place will bring it back to farming: they say the ten acres below the house used to be good potato land – nice early ground.

It is delightful to sit in the sun, as if I were old.

After thumbing over earlier entries in this journal, I see I have often felt quite bitter toward my own kind. I deduce that I must have been a lonely man – much of the loneliness self-imposed. A great part of my bitterness must have been no more than one ugly by-product of a life spent too much apart. Some of it doubtless came from objective causes, yet I don't believe I ever had more cause than any moderately intelligent man who would like to see his world a pleasanter place than it ever has been. My angel tells me that the pain in my back is due to an injury received in some early stage of the world war that still goes on. That could have soured me, perhaps. It's all right – it's all in the record.

She is racing with a hummingbird – holding back, I think, to give the ball of green fluff a break.

Another note for you, Lester. I have already indicated that my ring is to be yours. I don't want to tell you what I have discovered of its properties, for fear it might not give you the same pleasure and interest that it has given me. Of course, like any spot of shifting light and color, it is an aid to self-hypnosis. It is much, much more than that, but – find out for yourself, at some time when you are a little protected from everyday distractions. I know it can't harm you, because I know its source.

By the way, I wish you would convey to my publishers my request that they either discontinue manufacture of my *Introductory Biology* or else bring out a new edition revised in accordance with some notes you will find in the top left drawer of my library desk. I glanced through that book after my angel assured me that I wrote it, and I was amazed. However, I'm afraid my notes are messy (I call them mine by a poetic license), and they may be too advanced for the present day – though the revision is mainly a matter of leaving out certain generalities that ain't so. Use your best judgment: it's a very minor textbook, and the thing isn't too important. A last wiggle of my personal vanity.

July 27

I have seen a two-moon night.

It was given to me by that other grown-up, at the end of a wonderful visit, when he and six of those nine other children came to see me. It was last night, I think – yes, must have been. First there was a murmur of wings above the house; my angel flew in, laughing; then they were here, all about me. Full of gaiety and colored fire, showing off in every way they knew would please me. Each one had something graceful and friendly to say to me. One brought me a moving image of the St Lawrence seen at morning from half a mile up – clouds – eagles; now, how could he know that would delight me so much? And each one thanked me for what I had done.

But it's been so easy!

And at the end the old one – his skin is quite black, and his down is white and gray – gave the remembered image of a two-moon night. He saw it some sixty years ago.

I have not even considered making an effort to describe it – my fingers will not hold this pencil much longer tonight. Oh – soaring buildings of white and amber, untroubled countryside, silver on curling rivers, a glimpse of open sea; a moon rising in clarity, another setting in a wreath of cloud, between them a wide wandering of unfamiliar stars; and here and there the angels, worthy after fifty million years to live in such a night. No, I cannot describe anything like that. But, you human kindred of mine, I can do something better. I can tell you that this two-moon night, glorious as it was, was no more beautiful than a night under a single moon on this ancient and familiar Earth might be – if you will imagine that the rubbish of human evil

465

has been cleared away and that our own people have started at last on the greatest of all explorations.

July 29

Nothing now remains to give away but the memory of the time that has passed since the angel came. I am to rest as long as I wish, write whatever I want to. Then I shall get myself over to the bed and lie down as if for sleep. She tells me that I can keep my eyes open: she will close them for me when I no longer see her.

I remain convinced that our human case is hopeful. I feel sure that in only a few thousand years we may be able to perform some of the simpler preparatory tasks, such as casting out evil and loving our neighbors. And if that should prove to be so, who can doubt that in another fifty million years we might well be only a little lower than the angels?

LIBRARIAN'S NOTE: As is generally known, the original of the Bannerman Journal is said to have been in the possession of Dr Lester Morse at the time of the latter's disappearance in 1964, and that disappearance has remained an unsolved mystery to the present day. McCarran is known to have visited Captain Garrison Blaine in October, 1951, but no record remains of that visit. Captain Blaine appears to have been a bachelor who lived alone. He was killed in line of duty, December, 1951. McCarran is believed not to have written about nor discussed the Bannerman affair with anyone else. It is almost certain that he himself removed the extract and related papers from the files (unofficially, it would seem!) when he severed his connection with the FBI in 1957; at any rate, they were found among his effects after his assassination and were released to the public, considerably later, by Mrs McCarran.

The following memorandum was originally attached to the extract from the Bannerman Journal; it carries the McCarran initialing.

Aug. 11, 1951

The original letter of complaint written by Stephen Clyde, M.D., and mentioned in the accompanying letter of Captain Blaine, has unfortunately been lost, owing perhaps to an error in filing.

Personnel presumed responsible have been instructed not to allow such error to be repeated except if, as, and/or when necessary.

C. McC.

On the margin of this memorandum there was a penciled notation, later erased. The imprint is sufficient to show the unmistakable McCarran script.

The notation read in part as follows: *Far be it from a McC. to lose his job except if, as, and/or* – the rest is undecipherable, except for a terminal word which is regrettably unparliamentary.

STATEMENT BY LESTER MORSE, M.D., DATED 9 AUGUST 1951

On the afternoon of 30 July 1951, acting on what I am obliged to describe as an unexpected impulse, I drove out to the country for the purpose of calling on my friend Dr David Bannerman. I had not seen him nor had word from him since the evening of June 12 of this year.

I entered, as was my custom, without knocking. After calling to him and hearing no response, I went upstairs to his bedroom and found him dead. From superficial indications I judged that death must have taken place during the previous night. He was lying on his bed on his left side, comfortably disposed as if for sleep but fully dressed, with a fresh shirt and clean summer slacks. His eyes and mouth were closed, and there was no trace of the disorder to be expected at even the easiest natural death. Because of these signs I assumed, as soon as I had determined the absence of breath and heartbeat and noted the chill of the body, that some neighbor must have found him already, performed these simple rites out of respect for him, and probably notified a local physician or other responsible person. I therefore waited (Dr Bannerman had no telephone), expecting that someone would soon call.

Dr Bannerman's journal was on a table near his bed, open to that page on which he has written a codicil to his will. I read that part. Later, while I was waiting for others to come, I read the remainder of the journal, as I believe he wished me to do. The ring he mentions was on the fifth finger of his left hand, and it is now in my possession. When writing that codicil Dr Bannerman must have overlooked or forgotten the fact that in his formal will, written some months earlier, he had appointed me executor. If there are legal technicalities involved, I shall be pleased to cooperate fully with the proper authorities.

The ring, however, will remain in my keeping, since that was Dr Bannerman's expressed wish, and I am not prepared to offer it for examination or discussion under any circumstances.

The notes for a revision of one of his textbooks were in his desk, as noted in the journal. They are by no means 'messy'; nor are they particularly revolutionary except insofar as he wished to rephrase, as theory or hypothesis, certain statements that I would have supposed could be regarded as axiomatic. This is not my field, and I am not competent to judge. I shall take up the matter with his publishers at the earliest opportunity.[5]

---

[5] LIBRARIAN'S NOTE: But it seems he never did. No new edition of *Introductory Biology* was ever brought out, and the textbook has been out of print since 1952.

So far as I can determine, and bearing in mind the results of the autopsy performed by Stephen Clyde, M.D., the death of Dr David Bannerman was not inconsistent with the presence of an embolism of some type not distinguishable on postmortem. I have so stated on the certificate of death. It would seem to be not in the public interest to leave such questions in doubt. I am compelled to add one other item of medical opinion for what it may be worth:

I am not a psychiatrist, but, owing to the demands of general practice, I have found it advisable to keep as up to date as possible with current findings and opinion in this branch of medicine. Dr Bannerman possessed, in my opinion, emotional and intellectual stability to a better degree than anyone else of comparable intelligence in the entire field of my acquaintance, personal and professional. If it is suggested that he was suffering from a hallucinatory psychosis, I can only say that it must have been of a type quite outside my experience and not described, so far as I know, anywhere in the literature of psychopathology.

Dr Bannerman's house, on the afternoon of July 30, was in good order. Near the open, unscreened window of his bedroom there was a coverless shoe box with a folded silk scarf in the bottom. I found no pillow such as Dr Bannerman describes in the journal, but observed that a small section had been cut from the scarf. In this box, and near it, there was a peculiar fragrance, faint, aromatic, and very sweet, such as I have never encountered before and therefore cannot describe.

It may or may not have any bearing on the case that, while I remained in his house that afternoon, I felt no sense of grief or personal loss, although Dr Bannerman had been a loved and honored friend for a number of years. I merely had, and have, a conviction that after the completion of some very great undertaking, he had found peace.

THE WRENS IN GRAMPA'S WHISKERS

I called my Grandfather Grandad. His father was the one we called Grampa. Grandad was old as a man needs to be, or I thought so in 1958, when I was ten. As for Grampa, he'd been ten years old himself when the little big guns set up a yattering at Gettysburg. Grampa used to say guns had been growing bigger ever since, but the way he heard it, the ones at Gettysburg killed the soldiers just as dead. It must have been in 1958 when I last heard him make that remark, the summer he was 106 and had decided to sit out on the front porch near-about as long as he pleased.

Grampa had worked hard for his first eighty-odd years, twitching rocks out of the Vermont dirt the way his grandfather had done before him; then he slowed down. He'd always been clean-shaven. At eighty-two he grew a beard, took to reading a lot, on the front porch. 'Built the thing myself,' he said, 'with underpinnings of hornbeam. Believe I can set on it some if I wish, at the commencement of my old age.'

He could. He had three other sons besides Grandad, who was 81 the year I'm talking of, and the others pretty well-grown too. There were seven grand-sons in the direct line, my Pop the youngest, and a flock of granddaughters and great-grands fairly well scattered over the eastern States. Anything the rest of the tribe couldn't fix to run right, my Ma could. No reason Grampa shouldn't subside if he chose.

One June evening in '58 when Grampa was out on the front porch, Ma called to tell him supper was ready. 'Fine,' he says, 'where is it?'

Ma spoke through the window, 'You trying to plague me, Grampa? Right here same as usual, so come and get it!'

Grampa just set. Ma went out to study him. 'You all right?'

'Why wouldn't I be?' says Grampa. 'Never sick a day in my life. Could lick my weight in wildcats, excepting I'm that ornery I'd more likely let 'em live and grieve. Where's my supper?'

Ma was young then as well as handsome. I was surveying the scene through the window because I smelt the unusual. I saw the handsome in Ma pepper up to a sort of glow – after an average fourteen-hour day Ma might have been a mite tired herself. She softened, though. She always did. 'Is it your eyes gone back on you, Grampa, account of all that reading you've been doing? Why'n't you say so?'

'Judy, girl –' Ma's given name was Lyle, but Grampa made no never-minds about that, and would call her Judy, or Millicent, or Beulah, all good family names he'd known at one time or another – 'Judy, long's you got nothing better to do than stand there, will you enlighten me why the good Lord made women with arguing organs? When's there been anything wrong with my eyes? Ain't I setting here on the same porch I built in 1913 with underpinnings of hornbeam, and got Mount Mansfield before my eyes plain as you be, which I don't mean that the way it sounds, for you're a good-looking heifer and no mistake, not to mention two-thirds of Lamoille County and all of it pretty as a picture? Eyes! I'm partial to having supper on time, by the way – always was.'

That was a hazy evening. Mount Mansfield – why, you couldn't see him, not even a rising shadow of him in the mist that was spread all over the far side of yonder. Ma brought Grampa his supper on the porch. When he was done munching, which he did hearty, she carried in the dishes and not a word of complaint.

The mist thinned when it came on dark. Chilly, but I remember the fireflies circulating. Ma fetched a blanket, and Grampa thanked her for it but wouldn't allow her to tuck it around him, because he said that might disturb the wrens that had made a nest in his whiskers.

'Wrens,' said Ma. 'Ayah, there's been a pile of 'em around.'

'Oh, there has you know,' says Grampa. 'I figure these got crowded out of the best places, seeing my eldest boy Joel has been too shiftless lately to put up more houses for 'em.' He meant Grandad, and it was a mite unfair, because Grandad at 81 was entitled to slow down some himself. 'These birds'll be all right though, Judy,' says Grampa, 'if you'll just leave me set, and not bother, and not argue, and while you're about it you might fetch me a couple-three conveniences.'

My room overlooked the roof of the front porch. When I'd gone to bed I heard Ma trying again. No use – Grampa wasn't intending to move. She sat with him a spell, and Pop joined them. While I dozed off I heard the three of them talking about the war. That was 1958, but someway Grampa never got it through his head the war was over. You couldn't always be sure whether he meant the war in the 1940s or the first World War, or maybe even the Spanish War when Grampa might have admired to take a ride up San Juan Hill with Teddy Roosevelt, only they told him at the time that he was a shade too old for such. But that June night, the first one he spent out on the porch, I believe he was talking about the second World War, for while I was dropping off I heard him say you couldn't leave a man like Hitler running loose – Teddy would never have allowed it.

I woke later in the night and heard him snoring – gently for him, which I figured was on account of the wrens. I skun out over the roof and down the porch pillar, careful in case he quit snoring – not that I ever felt scared of Grampa the way some did. I just wanted a look at the wrens.

The mist wasn't quite gone. It was a night of small stars and a high-riding sliver of moon in a milky haze. Being ten and foolish, I was on the porch and beside Grampa's chair before I realized there'd be no seeing the wrens in such a light. He woke and said, 'That you, Saul?'

'Uhha,' I said, 'it's just me.' Peculiar thing – Grampa was forever tangling up the names of Ma, and Pop, and plenty more. As for Pop's brothers and the great-grands, Grampa didn't even try – he called them all Jackson. Someway, though, my name always came out right. Well, I'd been underfoot for ten years in the same house with him, and I guess it helped to know my right name whenever he stumbled over me and needed to say something brisk. 'It's just me, Grampa,' I said. 'I wanted to see the wrens.'

'Why, Saul,' he says, 'the best time for that is real early morning before anyone else is up. Say an hour before sunup, that's when they begin a-twirping and a-fidgeting but don't feel like flying yet, so if you was on hand at exactly that right time, I wouldn't be a one to say you *couldn't* see 'em, understand? Meanwhile I'd admire to learn if you can shinny up that pillar as good as you can shinny down it, and how about doing it near-about as fast as you know how to shinny, before your Ma pops out and gives me an argument about growing boys needing their sleep?'

So I did.

All summer long I kept trying to hit the time exactly right. I didn't have much luck. I'd sneak down too early and he'd send me back, or I'd be late and he'd give me hark-from-the-tomb for being too lazy to get up early the way he used to.

One of the mornings when I was too early he said, 'Oh, by the way, Saul, wasn't you telling me your Great-Aunt Doreen went and lost that amethyst brooch she had from Cousin John Blaine before they was married?'

'Why,' I says, a leg on each side of the pillar and my bare toes working because I was puzzled, 'why, no, I wasn't, Grampa, but it's a fact. She was in a mortal taking about it all last evening, said it was one of the mighty few things she had to remember him by and didn't understand how she could've been that careless.'

'Ayah, well, it come to me the thing likely fell off into the back of her closet, account she forgot to take it off when she hung up her dress and didn't have it pinned on too good. Thought I'd mention it.'

I found it right there, next day, and took off after Aunt Doreen, figuring I'd say the bandits got it and I wrested it away from them single-handed like. Or maybe I'd tease her some and claim she'd stuck it on the back of her dress and folks'd been admiring it. I located her in the kitchen shelling garden peas, red-eyed still and distracted, half the peas going on the floor, and someway none of my projects looked good. Aunt Doreen was shaped like a little Rocky Ford melon and nice all through. I couldn't think, so I said without thinking: 'Know what, Aunt Doreen? I believe you left your window-screen open yesterday morning.'

'My screen, honey?' she says. 'Guess I did. Yes, I washed the glass, likely forgot the screen, I'm that careless,' and she went to crying again, about the brooch. I remember there was a mess of wrens twittering around the kitchen window – appeared to be wrens.

I went on talking without thinking: 'Well, Aunt Doreen, yesterday I happened to see one of them plague-take-it starlings go in your window and fly off with something, didn't pay it no mind, only today I got to thinking and had a look under the tree where he lit, so here she be. You wasn't careless, it was just one of them plague-take-it starlings.'

She grabbed the brooch, and then me, kissed me all to pieces. While I was picking up the peas that were flying around she went into a long story about how the starlings had pestered her and John when they was first married and living over to Lodi, New York – starlings being liable to do anything. So I knew she believed me. Don't know as I ever told a handsomer lie, or got more glory for it and did less harm. Peculiar thing though, how it sprang up full-grown in my empty head while those wrens were busy at the window. Near-about as peculiar as Grampa's knowing where the brooch was, when he hadn't been off the porch in a week and wouldn't've been found dead anywhere near a closet with female clothes in it. I know Grampa expected me to ask about that, but of course, seeing he hadn't let me look at the wrens, I was durned if I would.

But then there was just one morning in late July, when I hit the time so near right I figured I'd give up on it if Grampa still wouldn't let me see them. Pale early light, a few birds starting to talk in the woods, no big chorus yet. Light enough so that Grampa's eyes had begun to shine a natural robin's-egg blue instead of black, and I could make out only about half of the million crinkles around them. The old man had to admit I wasn't more than sixty seconds off, so he showed me a dark spot in the white fluff spreading over his chest, and he said if I'd stand quiet and just look down, not poke around or stir up a commotion, maybe I'd see something, maybe I wouldn't.

All I saw down there was bit of motion. Naturally the nest itself was away inside the beard, for snugness. I couldn't swear they were wrens, although at the time I took his word for it. I'd no more than glimpsed that motion when Grampa said the parent birds were ready to fly, so I'd have to travel back up the pillar and stop bothering. But he suggested that if I was to squat on the porch roof same as if I had good sense, I just might watch them going off. I did that, and I think I caught a faint flicker of them flying west and beyond our lilac hedge. Flying sort of like wrens.

Through August I didn't try, much. It came to me that he thought I was too young, and I was sad about that, but it was the kind of thing where you didn't put up an argument, not with Grampa.

Along in August, Ma and Pop arranged for Dr Wayne to come and see Grampa. Grampa was friendly – called the doctor Jackson and explained how the only reason he'd quit asking for half a dozen sausages along with his lunch was that the smell bothered the wrens, it didn't mean he was off his feed. Soon as Dr Wayne got wound up to saying 'Well, now –' Grampa admitted real polite that lack of exercise had whittled down his appetite, a smidgin. 'But,' says he, 'ain't that natural, Jackson? I'm commencing to get old is the hell of it, and anyway I hate an argument.' After Dr Wayne left, Grampa asked Pop to bring him his shotgun.

Pop says: 'Now look, Grampa—'

'Wheels of the Apocalypse!' says Grampa. 'Am I asking you for shells? Did I say a word about shooting anybody? All I want is the gun, and all I want to do is point it, the next time I see a doctor fussing around my wrens – you think he won't travel? He'll travel. Fetch me my shotgun, Jackson, or I'll commence to believe Judy there has learnt you how to argue, and any man that'll let his wife learn him to argue would suck wrens' eggs.'

So he got his shotgun. Set it by his chair. I remember seeing him pat it and fondle it and shoo away the cat with it now and then. If he was feeling good he'd tell how he bought it in 1913 at Hines' Hardware – damn filling station now where Hines' Hardware used to stand, they call that progress? – and that was the same year he built this porch with underpinnings of hornbeam.

Word got around. If people smell something unusual you just can't make them quit bothering. Not that they didn't have a few fairly smart ideas. There was my Great-Uncle Jonas for instance, Grandad's kid brother, 78 that year, fat, with a gimp leg and a curious disposition. In August he started talking politics to Grampa. Grampa didn't mind – he enjoyed politics, and let Jonas wheeze along on one lungful after another till he got to the point: 'How you going to vote this year, Grampa?'

'How? You parted with your natural senses, boy? When'd you ever know me vote any way except straight Republican? Sooner vote for Coolidge, only I hear he's dead, but it don't matter, this Willkie's a good man, got a lot of sense. Use your head, Jonas.'

'Ayah, well, but that wasn't what I meant. I was wondering—'

'You got any occasion to wonder about a man's politics that would've rid up San Juan Hill with Teddy only they told him he was too old for God's sake?'

'It ain't that, Grampa.' His own father, but even Great-Uncle Jonas called him Grampa – the old man wouldn't answer to anything else. 'Thing of it is, I just wondered—'

'You needn't to wonder. It come to me,' said Grampa, 'that I been paying taxes in this town since the year 1873, and never been in jail so far as I recall – well, there was something about shooting up a street-lamp for rejoicing the day they repealed the Volstead Commandment, and you should've been there yourself only I guess you was still working in the bank that year and kind of surrounded with virtue – I don't hold it against you, Jackson, I mean Jonas. Thing of it is, Jonas, if after all them taxes and never being in jail, this town is so hell-fired puky small and mean they can't wheel one of them new-fangled voting machines onto Joe Durvis' truck and fetch it up here for me—'

'Now just a minute, Grampa,' says Great-Uncle Jonas, 'the Selectmen wouldn't ever hear of it, you know that.'

'Because if they won't,' says Grampa, not listening, 'and far as that goes Joe Durvis'd be perfectly glad to do it for a dollar – if they won't, I'm fixing to stay home and vote socialist, and it won't be ten minutes before the entire county gets to hear about it.'

I don't know what they would've done come November. Long before then, Ma and Pop started worrying about something else – September frost. Grandad helped them worry, stumping around chewing his own short whiskers and remarking how the nights were already sharp and drawing in. Grampa overheard him – was meant to, likely.

'Joel boy,' says Grampa, mild and gentle for him, 'I'd quit a-fretting if I was you. They're fixing to go south any time now.'

'That a fact?' says Grandad. Ma was behind Grandad twisting her fingers in her apron which she seldom did, and I was there, not underfoot, just listening. Aunt Doreen came out too. I couldn't look at Aunt Doreen those days without she'd finger the amethyst brooch and smile half-secret at me and muss my hair on the sly.

'Ayah,' says Grampa, 'or if they don't you can close in the porch – with blankets and thumbtacks, mind, I won't have no hammering around my wrens – and we'll make out with suet and birdseed. But I look for 'em to fly south real soon.'

'It would be a dispensation –' said Ma – 'almost.' She said that soft. I guess Grampa didn't hear, anyhow he paid it no mind.

'We've raised three broods,' Grampa said. 'Three broods, by God. That's unusual, that is. What's the war news?'

Ma told him it was good, and went on to say something about the satellites, which didn't interest Grampa too much. He knew what they were, but claimed it was a waste of time flying the hell all over space when there was still a pile of things down here that could stand fixing if only people weren't too shiftless to notice it.

'Well, bother the war news too,' says Aunt Doreen. 'People could live in peace if they'd mind their own business and learn not to get careless ...'

Pop laid in extra blankets and bought an electric heater on the quiet, but the following week was balmy, no more said about winter. During that week my best friend Will Burke told me something about his kid sister Jenny. Jenny was seven, and she'd had polio the year before, right leg and hip all twisted up and miserable. Dr Wayne couldn't give the Burkes any hope she'd ever walk right or even walk at all. Will told me she was walking.

He'd fetched something to her room and found her out of bed, where she could grab the bedpost if she needed it but standing without it and taking a step or two. She said she'd been as far as the window and back. She made Will swear not to tell the family till she was sure it was real. When Will told me, I had to swear, too, never to mention it – I wouldn't now, only Jenny's been dead some years, anyhow I can't imagine she'd have minded. And she made Will promise to see that her window screen was kept unlocked so the birds could get in.

Will did that – he'd have done anything for Jenny – but he never got to see the birds. I remember he was shook up when he told me. Someway I had sense enough not to suggest Jenny was making it up. She'd said they probably weren't exactly birds, though they looked like it when they folded their arms in under the feathers. Birds, Jenny figured, don't have triangular green eyes on knobby little heads, and they sure enough don't have the sense to bring along a pointed branch and use it for levering up a window screen.

They sang now and then, she told Will, but not quite like birds. More like a kind of talking, if you could only understand it. Which is about the way I felt when the wrens, if you want to call them wrens, were chirping me that twenty-four-carat chunk of mahooha about the brooch and the starling.

Peculiar thing – later on Jenny forgot about the birds, or seemed to. I suppose you're bound to forget a lot of things that happened when you were seven. And of course people forget things that happen when they're older too. Like for instance the time – seems to me it was the following summer – when Joe Durvis and old Martin Smallways who'd been a-snarling and a-feuding over a line fence dispute for twenty-six years appeared to forget all about it. People saw them meet sudden on the green, and supposed it meant trouble, and the small boys and dogs began drifting in so as not to miss anything. But the two of them just look sort of puzzled, and here's old Martin scratching his bald head and saying, 'Hiya, Joe – was you heading for the Ethan Allen?' Off they go to the inn and spend the evening crying into each other's beer happy as two boiled owls. People said there was a lot of wrens around that year too. I don't remember seeing any more than usual. Real wrens, I mean.

It did turn chilly that September of 1958. The morning after the first frost Grampa seemed peart enough. 'They flew south yesterday evening,' he said to Ma, 'same as I foretold, and I got to admit I'm obliged to you for your patience with me and my wrens.'

I wasn't on the porch. Ma told me about it. She didn't give me the whole story till much later, when I was going on sixteen and she figured I might own a little sense in off-hours when I wasn't sparking around with Jenny Burke, who was walking as well as anyone by that time and pretty enough to make you cry. 'He showed me,' Ma said, 'the place where he claimed the wrens nested. Spread out his beard and showed me – well, it's only the truth, Saul, there was a kind of little hollowed-out place, smooth like a bird's nest. Likely he could've made it himself working his fingers around in there, I wouldn't know. He showed me that, and he said to me, "We raised three broods," he says. "Three broods, and that's unusual." Then he asked me what the war news was. I guess I said it was good, and he kind of chuckled, he wasn't paying me much mind, Saul. He was that quiet, a-gazing off at Mount Mansfield, it was a long couple-three minutes before I understood he was gone.'

Yes, that seems long ago, back there in 1958, but this happens to be the same porch with hardly a thing changed, that my great-grandfather built with underpinnings of hornbeam, and I can't think of any reason why I shouldn't sit here myself a while at the commencement of my old age. I'd rather you didn't look now, because the light's wrong and I think they've gone to bed, anyway I can't assert I understand them better than Grampa did, or as well.

I've been around, traveled more than he did. Seen plenty of trouble even though we don't have wars any more – trouble and hating and confusion and this and that, including plenty of people who don't get over things like polio miracle-style, the way my Jenny did.

Peculiar thing, how she forgot about the birds. Maybe at first she just wasn't a-mind to speak of them because of the way people would look at her if she did, but later I think it was a real forgetting, for I don't believe she'd have shied off from speaking to me about them after we'd been married forty-five years. Never brought it up myself of course, being I'd given Will my word I wouldn't mention it.

I've been around, seen a lot. Classmate of mine was one of the first on

Venus. Never did get upstairs myself – just here and there, setting my hand to whatever turned up.

No, I wouldn't be a one to tell you what they look like. If you was going to say I imagine them, I don't mind. I'd want to claim though, that if you mess around for a century or so trying to do things more or less right, you can maybe make a place for some little spark of wisdom with wings on it.

If you've enjoyed these books and would
like to read more, you'll find literally thousands
of classic Science Fiction & Fantasy titles
through the **SF Gateway**

✳

*For the new home of
Science Fiction & Fantasy . . .*

✳

*For the most comprehensive collection
of classic SF on the internet . . .*

✳

Visit the SF Gateway

www.sfgateway.com

Edgar Pangborn (1909–1976)

Edgar Pangborn was born in New York City and pursued music studies at Harvard when just 15 years old. He went on to study at the New England Conservatory but did not graduate from either course. He then turned his back on music, focusing on writing. It was in the early 50s that his writing career flourished, and he produced a string of highly regarded stories for the likes of *Galaxy*, *The Magazine of Fantasy and Science Fiction* and *Ellery Queen's Mystery magazine*.

His work helped establish a new 'humanist' school of science fiction, and he has been cited by Ursula Le Guin as one of the authors who convinced her that it was possible to write worthwhile, humanly emotional stories within science fiction and fantasy. He died in New York in 1976.